TOR BOOKS BY DAVID WEBER

LIKE A MIGHTY ARMY

·◆·

DAVID WEBER

A TOM DOHERTY ASSOCIATES BOOK
NEW YORK

LIKE A MIGHTY ARMY

Maps by Ellisa Mitchell

A Tor Book
Published by Tom Doherty Associates, LLC
175 Fifth Avenue
New York, NY 10010

www.tor-forge.com

Tor® is a registered trademark of Tom Doherty Associates, LLC.

ISBN 978-0-7653-6127-1

Tor books may be purchased for educational, business, or promotional use. For information on bulk purchases, please contact the Macmillan Corporate and Premium Sales Department at 1-800-221-7945, extension 5442, or write to specialmarkets@macmillan.com.

First Edition: February 2014
First Mass Market Edition: January 2015

Printed in the United States of America

0 9 8 7 6 5 4 3 2

For Dot Barnette,
adopted grandmother extraordinaire.
The kids love you . . . and so do we.

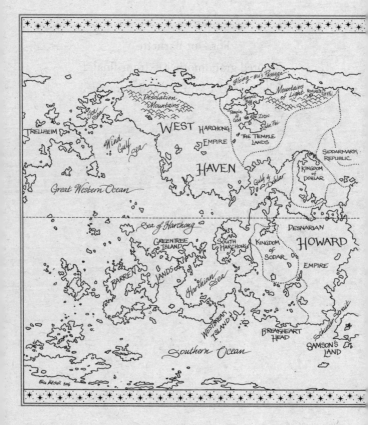

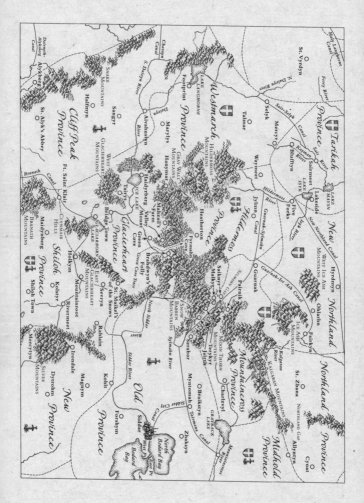

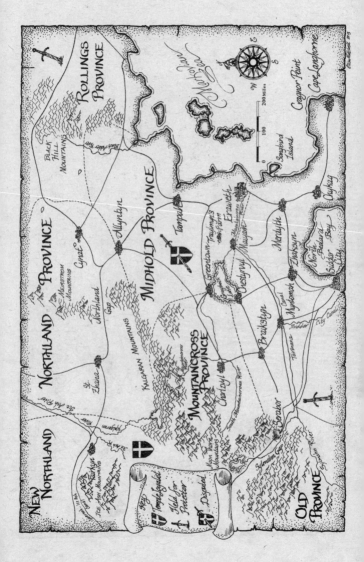

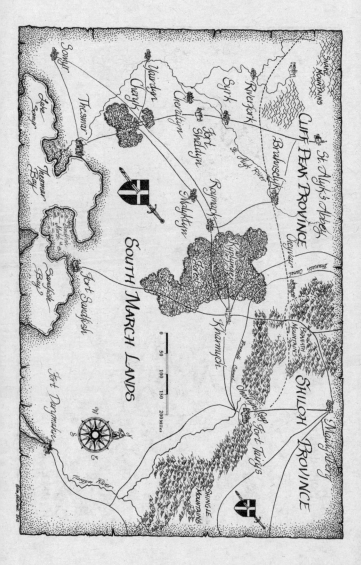

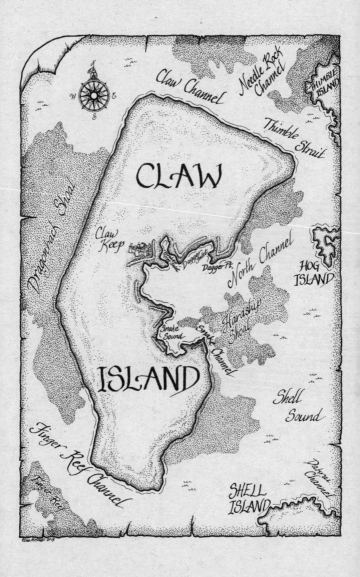

LIKE A
MIGHTY ARMY

. PROLOGUE .

"So that's about it," Nahrmahn Baytz murmured, sitting back in his favorite chair and gazing at the neatly printed pages in his hand.

He no longer required the cumbersome interface of the written word—as a virtual personality residing in his own pocket universe he was quite capable of interfacing directly with the artificial intelligence known as Owl—but he'd found he preferred the comforting homeyness of the way he'd processed information when he was alive.

"Yes," the slender, black-haired, sapphire-eyed individual sitting across the stone table from him agreed. He—or perhaps *she*; the jury was still out on that issue—was Nahrmahn's only regular visitor here on the terrace looking out over the sparkling waters of Eraystor Bay. "I believe I could access the locked files, but my analysis suggests a probability on the order of eighty-three percent that the effort would activate internal security protocols. In that eventuality, the probability that I might extract at least some usable information before complete data dump would approach sixty percent, although the amount of data which might be recovered is impossible to estimate. The probability that the files themselves would be destroyed exceeds ninety-seven percent, however. The probability that security protocols would reconfigure the 'Key's' molecular circuitry, rendering any future examination useless, exceeds ninety-nine percent. Assuming that a civilian Type One AI was used to create the locked files and protective safeguards, the probability that I would myself be overwritten and effectively destroyed would be fifty-nine percent, plus or minus five percent. The probability that my central cortex would survive, albeit with sufficient degradation to preclude self-awareness, would be seventy-two percent, plus or minus the same margin. In that case, the probability of personality reintegration would not exceed thirty-seven percent, although the large number of unknowns precludes refinement of that figure. Assuming that a military Type One AI was used to create the locked files, the probability of my destruction would exceed ninety-nine percent."

Nahrmahn considered the calm face and equally calm tone and shook his head. Owl's self-awareness had achieved full realization and integration only a few months ago, by the standards of the rest of the universe. By Owl's standards—and his own—far longer than that had passed, and the portly little prince had come to regard the AI as a friend and colleague. Yet there were moments, like this one, when Nahrmahn was forcefully reminded that whatever else he might be, Owl was not a flesh-and-blood being. Nahrmahn never doubted that the AI was just as calm as he sounded discussing the virtual certainty of his own destruction should the decision be to continue the investigation into the "Key of Schueler."

He glanced at the polished steel paperweight on the table between them, gleaming with reflected sunlight as it rested on the flattened face which marred the perfection of its spherical shape. It wasn't actually there any more than the table itself was, of course, but if he picked it up, weighed it in his hands, or hit himself on the head with it, it would certainly *feel* real. And there was a part of him which would very much have preferred to throw the actual Key into the deep waters of the real Eraystor Bay as a permanent gift to its fishy inhabitants.

Which, unfortunately, would be as futile as it is impossible, he reflected.

"While the erasure of the Key and its contents would be unfortunate," he said out loud, "I imagine we could survive the loss. I feel fairly confident the rest of the inner circle would agree with me that losing *you* would be ... rather more inconvenient, Owl. On a personal, as well as a professional, basis."

"I confess that I do not find that particular probability projection pleasant," Owl acknowledged.

"I'm relieved to hear it." Nahrmahn's tone was dry, and he laid the report on the table, using the Key to hold the fluttering sheets against the brisk breeze blowing in off the bay. "On the other hand, I would *dearly* love to know what's in those files."

"Aside from the fact that the majority of them are executables and that one of the data files is quite large, I can determine no more without accessing them."

Well, I suppose calling a twelve petabyte data file "quite large" is reasonably accurate. Nahrmahn's thought was as dry as his tone had been as he contemplated how staggeringly huge that number was compared to anything he'd ever imagined might exist when he'd been alive. *And it's the sheer size of the thing that makes me* wish *we could get into it! But not enough to risk losing Owl. Never enough to risk that!*

"I think we can assume the executables have something to do with whatever's under the Temple," he mused, tipping back in his chair again and listening to the rhythmic sound of the surf. "And at least we've managed to confirm that whatever it is requires human activation."

"Assuming that it is activated in response to the Key, that is correct," Owl pointed out. "We have not, however, been able to determine that the detection of proscribed technology by the bombardment system's sensors would not trigger an automatic activation protocol. Nor, for that matter, have we been able to determine whether or not there are additional Keys or even alternative command stations or completely different activation protocols."

"Granted." Nahrmahn nodded. "And there's nothing

in 'Archangel Schueler's' recording to suggest any sort of human agency is going to be required for the 'Archangels'' millennial visit, either. Unfortunately."

"Correct," the AI's avatar agreed, and Nahrmahn's lips quirked. It had taken Owl quite a long time (as AIs measured such things) to grasp the human habit of acknowledging the obvious as a way of indicating one was following someone else's thoughts. Or, for that matter, to grasp the fact that humans could conceivably think he *wasn't* following their thoughts . . . despite the fact that his old, pre-self-awareness persona frequently *hadn't* been following them with anything like true understanding.

The temptation to smile faded as his memory replayed the recordings he'd now viewed over and over. He understood entirely why Paityr Wylsynn and his ancestors had believed they'd been directly touched by God. He would have believed exactly the same thing, had the very image of one of the archangels appeared before him to tell him he and his family had been chosen for a sacred mission. And he also understood why the Wylsynn family had been so fiercely dedicated to its effort to safeguard the soul of the Church of God Awaiting for so long.

So many generations—so many lives!—dedicated to preserving the purity and sanctity of a lie. The familiar, dull anger stirred deep inside once more. *All those Wylsynns, at the very heart of the Church, never knowing or guessing any more than anyone else that she and all her doctrine and all her theology were no more than fabrications deliberately designed to enslave humanity and trap it here on Safehold forever.*

There were times when it was even harder than usual to remind himself that Langhorne, Bédard, and the rest of the Safehold command crew had probably genuinely believed they were doing the right thing. Since his own physical demise, he'd had time to read the copy of Langhorne's original orders which Pei Kau-yung and Pei Shan-wei had stored here in what had become known as Nimue's Cave. He knew now how utterly Eric Langhorne had departed from those orders when he reprogrammed the colonists' memories and created the Church of God Awaiting and its eternal anathematization of advanced technology. And because he knew what those orders had been, even when he truly tried to understand the terror-spawned determination which must've driven Langhorne's decisions, he found it impossible to *forgive* those decisions.

But the Schueler Paityr and the rest of his family met through the Key is nothing like the psychopath who could've written The Book of Schueler, *and that raises yet another maddening question, doesn't it? Who was the* real *Schueler? The author of "his" book? Or the "archangel" charging the Wylsynn family to always remember Mother Church's duty to protect and nurture God's children?*

Unless they somehow, some way, someday physically conquered the Temple and accessed whatever records might be hidden under it without inadvertently awakening their own destruction (or somehow broke into the data so tantalizingly locked inside the "Key"), it was unlikely they'd ever be able to answer that question. And that was a pity, because Nahrmahn Baytz would rather like to have met the man behind that message if *that* was the real Schueler.

He thought about the dark eyes, the high cheekbones, the burr of passionate sincerity in the deep, strangely accented voice.

"We leave you a fallen world," that voice had said, speaking softly and sadly. He'd had to concentrate hard the first two or three times he'd viewed it, because a thousand years of shifting language had changed so many of its sounds so drastically, yet that had detracted nothing from that sincerity or the power of those level eyes. "It's not the world we intended, the one we were charged to create, but even Archangels can be touched by evil and twisted, bent and broken. The war which raged here on Safehold after Shan-wei's Fall is proof enough of that. Yet God has His true plan for all of His work, and especially for all of His children. You who see this message, know that you *are* God's children. I charge you in His name never to forget that. Always to remember that however we Archangels may have failed of our charge, however we may have permitted His world to be marred, it's your task to remember His love and to show a reflection of it in yourselves. It won't be an easy task. It will bring all too many of you to grief and to loss, and there will be far too many times when it seems a thankless, bitter duty. But it is the most *important* task any human being could ever assume. I leave you this message because I leave you as my watchmen, my wardens, the guardsmen upon the wall. The purpose of God's Church is to guide, to cherish, to love, and to *serve* His children. Do not let her stray from that high and holy charge. Do not let her slip into the errors of pride and arrogance, of the pursuit of earthly power or wealth, of forgetting the destiny for which she was created. Be faithful, be vigilant, be *valiant*, and know that the purpose and the task you serve is worth the sacrifice I call upon you to make."

How could the Wylsynns not've been seduced into belief by that message from that *man?* Nahrmahn wondered now. *I know the truth about the "archangels" and the Church, and even* knowing *I feel the compulsion, the hunger—the* need—*to believe every word he said. And no wonder Samyl Wylsynn and his brother rejected Zhaspahr Clyntahn's version of the Inquisition with such loathing! And yet. . . .*

He sighed heavily, for that was the rub. Whatever the recorded Schueler might've *said* could never change the hideous barbarity of the punishments detailed in the book he'd *written*. And it was that book, not his secret recording, which had been read and believed and followed by every living Safeholdian for almost a thousand years. Indeed, it was *The Book of Schueler*'s harsh, uncompromising directions for the fashion in which Mother Church's "purpose" was to be protected and kept pure which accounted for every drop of blood which had been shed, every atrocity which had been committed in God's name.

"Well," he said, "I suppose we've pretty much reached the end of what we can extract from the Key, then. And you're right that we need to remain open to the possibility that some other 'archangel'—or even Schueler himself—could've set up alternate keys or completely separate command stations. In the meantime, though, have you given any more thought to that proposition of mine?"

"Of course I have, Your Highness." Owl smiled faintly, clearly amused by the suggestion that he might *not* have thought about it.

"And would it be practical?"

"Within the specified parameters and limitations, yes. I fail to perceive the purpose for it, however," Owl said. Nahrmahn raised an eyebrow, and Owl tilted his head in a gesture he'd acquired from Nahrmahn himself. "I have, as I am sure you will recall, Your Highness, a less well-developed sense of intuition and imagination than a human. I did not say there *was* no purpose, simply that I failed to perceive one." He shrugged slightly. "Given the contents of my database, it will be decades before it could conceivably be necessary for me to conduct 'experiments' in order to assist humans like Baron Seamount and Ehdwyrd Howsmyn in reacquiring and perfecting lost knowledge and capabilities."

"Granted. On the other hand, there are gaps in your own knowledge base, aren't there? Your records are enormous but finite, and it's entirely possible the two of us might be able to come up with new and useful capabilities which could be produced within the limitations of your industrial module. And from both of those perspectives, your ability to perform virtual experiments could be quite useful, could it not?"

"The possibility exists, yet I trust you will forgive me if I say that I find that the probability that your proposal will serve to divert and entertain you is statistically far greater than that it will lead to an unexpected and decisive new capability, Your Highness. And I trust you will also forgive me if I observe that you are a somewhat unscrupulous—I believe the term 'devious' might actually be more accurate—individual."

"I *am* accustomed to getting my own way," Nahrmahn acknowledged in dignified tones. "At the same time, however, I would point out that getting my way is usually advantageous to those whose purposes I share."

"That is not precisely the way Princess Ohlyvya expressed it during her last com visit," Owl pointed out in return, and Nahrmahn chuckled.

"That's only because she's known me for so long and so well. You, on the other hand, are an electronic personality who has known me for only a brief period of time and who possesses strictly limited imagination and intuition. Therefore, I should find it childishly simple to deceive you into doing it my way. I trust that's clear to you now?"

"Oh, yes," Owl said with a smile. "Perfectly, Your Highness."

JULY, YEAR OF GOD 896

· ✦ ·

. I .
Army of Glacierheart,
Eastmarch Province,
and
First Brigade (Reinforced),
Glacierheart Province,
Republic of Siddarmark

The listening device deployed onto the shoulder of Bishop Militant Cahnyr Kaitswyrth's tunic was far too small for the unaided human eye to see, but it was capable of remarkable sensitivity, and Merlin Athrawes leaned back in his chair in far-off Siddar City, where darkness had already fallen, listening to its take.

"I'm fully aware of the dispatches from Captain General Maigwair," Kaitswyrth snapped, glowering across the chart table at Bishop Gahrmyn Hahlys, Bishop Tymahn Scovayl, and Colonel Wylsynn Maindayl.

Hahlys' and Scovayl's expressions went simultaneously (and almost instantly) blank at the words "captain general," and Colonel Maindayl's lips tightened. The colonel was the equivalent of Kaitswyrth's chief of staff. He looked as if he wanted to object to where his superior was headed, but he glanced from the corner of one eye at the iron-faced upper-priest in the Schuelerite-purple cassock of an Inquisitor standing at Kaitswyrth's right elbow and clamped his jaw.

Kaitswyrth glared at his three subordinates for a long, fulminating moment. He'd never been what someone might call a patient man, yet it was unusual for him to show his frustration this clearly and at the expense of divisional commanders like Scovayl and Hahlys. For that matter, it was unusual—not unheard of, but unusual—for him to vent his ire on Maindayl this way.

Of course, he's under just a bit of stress at the moment, Merlin reflected with a thin smile. *Pity about that.*

"All right," Kaitswyrth continued in a somewhat calmer tone once he'd assured himself that no one was going to venture to argue with him. "I understand your concerns, and I understand the Captain General's concerns, but we're in nowhere near the kind of dire straits Bishop Militant Bahrnabai's dealing with. Of course it's going to turn around and bite all of us on the arse when winter sets in, but at the moment, *we* have a secure supply line clear back to Dohlar through the Charayn Canal; he doesn't. And there's no way the heretics' Shan-wei-damned—" He paused, obviously seeking the word he wanted, then grunted. "No way those smoking, demonspawn, Proctor-inspired, cannon-proof armored ships of theirs are going to get around into *our* rear and knock that canal out. Besides, we've got over two months' worth of supplies backed up between here and Aivahnstyn! I know we're going to have to pick a place and camp there all winter long, once the supply situation really starts to bite. And I know we're going to have to allow time to get the men under roofs, not just canvas, when we do. But it's only the end of July, and Vicar Zhaspahr's right about the need to maintain as much pressure on the heretics as we possibly can *before* the snow stops us."

Interesting that it's "Vicar Zhaspahr" but "Captain General Maigwair," isn't it? Merlin reflected. *Listening to him, you'd never guess they're both members of the Group of Four . . . and that* Maigwair's *Kaitswyrth's commanding officer according to the Army of God's table of organization.*

"I also know Bishop Militant Bahrnabai got hurt badly by the heretics' new weapons." Kaitswyrth's eyes swept his listening subordinates' faces. "On the other hand, they came at him without warning and took him and his people completely by surprise. Not only that, but aside from their new rifle design, *we* sure as Langhorne didn't see any of those 'new weapons' when we overran the heretics' redoubts, did we?"

"No, My Lord," Maindayl said after a moment. "With all due respect, though, I think we do have to remember that the heretics in those redoubts were Siddarmarkian regulars and heretic Marines. The indications are that we're up against the heretics' *army* now, and from the reports about what happened to Bishop Militant Bahrnabai's army, their equipment list isn't the same."

It took courage to argue, even diffidently, with Kaitswyrth, Merlin conceded. Especially with Sedryk Zavyr, Bishop Militant Cahnyr's special intendant, standing there with an expression like a green persimmon fig. Kaitswyrth glowered at his chief of staff for a moment, but then he inhaled and made himself nod.

"You're right about that, Wylsynn," he acknowledged. "And while it may not seem that way to certain people"—he frowned at Scovayl and Hahlys—"I really am aware of that fact. But even if they've got everything Wyrshym told us about, we're not stuck in a damned valley with no flanks and no choice but to go straight at the enemy." He thumped the map on the table between them, showing his army's position in the slice of Eastmarch Province between Glacierheart and Cliff Peak . . . and the very heart of the Ahstynwood Forest. "The Glacierheart Gap's over a hundred and fifty miles wide, for Langhorne's sake! And at absolute worst, the heretics have—what? Ten thousand men? Let's be generous and grant them *fifteen* thousand! That's only a hundred men per mile, and a lot of it—most of it—is covered with trees where their damned long-ranged rifles aren't going to help them very much, now are they?"

Maindayl looked back at him for a moment and Merlin wondered if he was contemplating pointing out how those same trees hampered Kaitswyrth's own mobility. If he was, he thought better of it and nodded, instead.

"Well, there's this to think about, too," Kaitswyrth growled, thumping the map again. "Right now *we're* sitting in the middle of the woods stuck on this damned river like a prong buck sliding down a slash lizard's gullet. I don't know about you, but I sure as Shan-wei don't want to spend the winter sitting out here freezing my arse off. And I especially don't want the heretics to be able to make whatever preparations they want in front of us while we wait for the icicles to melt off our noses. Look."

His finger traced the line of the Daivyn River through the Glacierheart Gap to Ice Lake.

"At the moment, that bastard Eastshare's line of supply is absolutely secure all the way from where he's sitting back to Siddar City. But we're only seventy-two miles from Ice Lake, and we're less than two hundred and eighty from Saithor if we continue straight ahead across the lake and down the Graywater. For that matter, we're less than a hundred and eighty miles from Tairys itself! You think taking out the provincial capital wouldn't knock the heretics back on their heels, whatever they've managed to do to us in the Sylmahn Gap? I'd love to get that far in—or far enough to send a few thousand cavalry to burn the snakes' nest to the ground, anyway!—but I'll settle for punching across Ice Lake. If we can control the point at which the Graywater flows out of the lake, we'll have our hand around Glacierheart's throat at the start of the next campaigning season."

Now that, Merlin thought sourly, *is true enough. I imagine Eastshare would have a little something to say about it, but Kaitswyrth's right about how ugly this could get if he manages to get past the Duke. I wish to hell we had one of the ironclads on Ice Lake right this minute!*

"We've got over a hundred and fifty thousand men, including the Loyalist militia units we've picked up," Kaitswyrth said, tapping the map more gently but even more emphatically. "They can't afford to hold a position too far up the river from the lake for fear we'll get around behind them and cut their line of retreat the same way we did to the first batch of heretics. If we hit them head on and simultaneously hook around to threaten their rear, they'll *have* to retreat, and once we push them back to the lake, they'll be pinned against it, and without all these damned *trees* getting in our way. I'd love to see them trying to load all of their troops onto barges under fire! And if they try to retreat around the shore of the lake without any cavalry, we'll be able to get around them easily and force them to stand and fight in the open. So I don't want to hear any more about all the reasons we should stand fast where we are. At the very worst, we're going to take some casualties and we're going to use up some of those two months' worth of supplies sitting on the river. At best, we're going to drive far enough forward that we'll be clear of the Glacierhearts and into the lowlands when next spring rolls around. And in the meantime, we'll kill a lot more of these heretic bastards. Is that clear?"

His chief of staff and both divisional commanders nodded, and he nodded back—a curt, confident jerk of the head.

"That'll be all, then. I want plans for the movement by tomorrow night. Dismissed."

▼ ▼ ▼

Well, that *isn't exactly what I wanted to hear,* Merlin reflected, climbing out of his chair and crossing to the window to look out across Siddar City's lights. The thunderstorms of the last few days had passed, leaving the air clean and cool, and the lights gleamed clearly against the dark. There weren't very many of them and they weren't very bright by the standards of the Terran Federation in which Nimue Alban had grown up, but they were enough to show the lines of the city's major thoroughfares, at least. He gazed down at them, his expression moody.

Too bad Kaitswyrth couldn't simply go ahead and panic. And he's an idiot for trying to assume Eastshare doesn't have every weapon Kynt used in the Sylmahn Gap. Or maybe it's less a matter of idiocy than the fact that he understands exactly why Clyntahn insisted on redesignating his force as "the Army of Glacierheart" and Wyrshym's as "the Army of the Sylmahn." Sort of underscores what he thinks should be happening, doesn't it? And Kaitswyrth's a lot more likely than Wyrshym to try to give it to him whether it makes sense or not.

Unfortunately he's not that far off on the numbers in front of him, and he's less than a hundred and eighty miles from the Graywater, whether he circles north or south around Ice Lake. He could do that kind of distance in less than two five-days if there wasn't anyone standing around to shoot him when he tried.

And if he managed to cut Eastshare's supply line the way HMS *Delthak* and HMS *Hador* had cut Bishop Militant Bahrnabai Wyrshym's, Eastshare truly would have no option but to retreat. Despite the superiority of his weapons, he couldn't ignore the outflanking potential of a hundred and fifty thousand men.

Time for Seijin *Ahbraim to pay the Duke another visit, I think. Although first I'd better have a word or two with Nahrmahn. And*—he consulted his internal chronometer—*with Cayleb, now that he and Sharleyan are off the com for the evening.*

▼ ▼ ▼

"Your Grace, I apologize for disturbing you, but you have a visitor."

Ruhsyl Thairis, the Duke of Eastshare, looked up as Corporal Slym Chalkyr, his batman of many years, admitted Captain Lywys Braynair to his command post workspace. The CP was a solid log and earth bunker, tough enough to resist a hit even from one of the Imperial Charisian Army's six-inch angle-guns, as befitted the nerve center of Eastshare's position. His engineers had also placed it with careful consideration of fields of fire, though, and the light of the duke's lamps gleamed dully on the rifles racked along one wall.

Now Eastshare raised one eyebrow at his youthful, red-haired aide.

"And what sort of visitor would that be, Lywys," he inquired, and Braynair smiled.

"The sort you told me you always wanted to see, Your Grace. A friend of *Seijin* Merlin's, I believe."

"Ah?" Eastshare stood. "*Seijin* Ahbraim, is it?"

"Yes, it is, Your Grace," another voice—this one a tenor—said, and Ahbraim Zhevons stepped past Captain Braynair. He was as plainly dressed as ever, brown hair pulled back in a short, clubbed braid, and he bowed to the duke.

"It's good to see you," the duke said, extending his right hand to clasp forearms with the newcomer. It wasn't something he would have done with a lot of commoners, but Ahbraim Zhevons wasn't your ordinary run of commoner. Despite the fact that he'd never claimed the title officially, there was no doubt in Eastshare's mind that he was as much a *seijin* as Merlin Athrawes.

"On the other hand," the duke continued as he released the *seijin*'s arm, "you're not in the habit of just dropping by for a casual conversation whenever you're in the vicinity. I thought you'd returned to Siddar City?"

"To be precise, Your Grace, I don't think I ever said I had any intention of returning to the capital," Zhevons pointed out. "Admittedly, I didn't expect to be back here in less than two five-days, but plans change. Unfortunately."

"Unfortunately how?" Eastshare's eyes narrowed.

"I think our friend Kaitswyrth is about to get a bit rowdy. And unless I'm badly mistaken, he's thinking in terms of flanking you out of position. Did you know they've rechristened his command 'the Army of Glacierheart'?"

"Ambitious of them," the duke said dryly.

"I imagine it's Clyntahn's subtle hint about which direction it's supposed to be headed, and I suspect Kaitswyrth's taken it to heart. I think he'd really like to drive you right back into the lake, but he's probably ready to settle for getting *control* of the lake and driving you back on Saithor and Tairys."

"He is, is he?" Eastshare showed his teeth. It wasn't a smile. "My people and I might just have a bit to say about that."

"I don't think he's going to come straight at you, Your Grace."

"And I don't think he'll have any choice *but* to come straight at us, Master Zhevons. This is an excellent position you picked for us. The woods to either side of it are far too thick for him to get formed troops through, and his cavalry's going to be useless here. And you might want to remember that both the river—and the high road—pass right through the middle of our lines. He's not getting around us unless he's prepared to cut entirely new roadways far enough out from the high road that we can't bring them under fire from here with the angle-guns. Which should keep him busy until, oh, sometime around this time *next* summer."

The duke did have a point, Ahbraim Zhevons—who didn't particularly resemble Merlin Athrawes, thanks to the reconfigurable nature of last-generation PICAs—acknowledged. The Ahstynwood Forest clogging the Glacierheart Gap consisted mostly of old-growth Safeholdian species, with very few terrestrial interlopers. Some of those trees were six or even ten feet in diameter—some of the scattering of titan oaks were better than twice that size—and God only knew how deep their roots went. Worse, the old-growth forest was penetrated by broad tributaries of second-growth scrub that interspersed dikes of much smaller, far more densely spaced trees and underbrush, and Safeholdian underbrush was even worse than the Wilderness had been back in the ancient American Civil War. Old Earth had never had wire vine, whose thorns made an excellent substitute for barbed wire, or fire vine, which was just as combustible as its name suggested and poisonous, to boot. Kaitswyrth's Army of Glacierheart wasn't going to be cutting any roadbeds through *that* anytime soon.

"I'm not saying he can't try to work small parties of infantry around us," Eastshare went on, stepping across to the map of his heavily fortified position hanging on the bunker wall. Major Lowayl, his senior engineer, updated that map on a daily basis, and the duke regarded it with the sort of gleaming eye a miser reserved for piles of gold bars. "But he's not going to storm this position without paying cash for every inch of it, and I'll stack my lads up against his in the bushes anytime. I've got two entire battalions of scout snipers out there just waiting for his patrols. If his scouts want to stick their heads into *that* hornets' nest, they won't be taking very many reports home with them again."

Zhevons managed not to wince, although it wasn't easy. The Safeholdian "hornet" was over two inches long, and if its venom was less dangerous to most humans than it was to native Safeholdian lifeforms, somewhere around ten percent of the human race still experienced an extremely violent and potentially deadly allergic reaction to it. Like the terrestrial insect for which it had been named, it was capable of multiple stings . . . and *unlike* the terrestrial insect, it instinctively attacked its victims' eyes first, which made the duke's simile particularly appropriate, given the scout snipers' training.

"I'm glad you approve of the position, Your Grace," he said after a moment, "but I'm beginning to wonder if my own enthusiasm might not've pulled you a little too far forward. You've got sixty miles of river between you and the lake. Can you cover that much distance well enough to be sure he doesn't get batteries into position to close the river against your barges?"

"I can't be certain he won't try it," Eastshare conceded, "but I *can* guarantee he won't enjoy what happens when he does. Colonel Celahk's been working on a little something to keep the spider rats out of the woodwork."

Zhevons cocked his head. Colonel Hynryk Celahk was Eastshare's senior artillerist. A native Old Charisian—and an ex-naval officer, to boot—he had a deep and abiding love for things that went "boom."

"Let's just say that if they want to try to get sixpounders—or even *twelve*-pounders—into position against the Colonel's preparations, they're welcome to make the effort. Even if they force us to retreat downriver, I'm pretty sure Hynryk can convince them to keep a respectful distance from the bank while we do it."

"I see." Zhevons rubbed his chin for a moment, then nodded. "It sounds like I may've been worrying unduly."

"No, not unduly, Master Zhevons," Eastshare said. "We're outnumbered better than ten-to-one. Against those kinds of numbers, there's no such thing as a truly secure position. But I will say friend Kaitswyrth really, really won't enjoy what it would cost him to push us out of these entrenchments. To be honest, though, I didn't expect him to try after what Kynt did to Wyrshym—especially after how badly Brigadier Taisyn already hurt him—so your warning certainly doesn't come amiss. And, while I'm being honest, I might as well admit that he's got at least two months of campaigning season left. If he thinks he has a realistic chance to push us out of the Gap, he'd be a fool not to take it before the snow begins to fly. So I was probably overly optimistic about what he was likely to do. So optimistic he might actually have managed to surprise us without your visit."

"I rather doubt that." Zhevons smiled. "Nice of you to let me down easy, though, Your Grace."

"You *are* a friend of *Seijin* Merlin's," Eastshare pointed out with an answering smile. "I'm *always* polite to friends of *Seijin* Merlin's."

His smile turned into something like a grin, then vanished, and he crossed his arms, contemplating the terrain map beside the diagram of his fortifications.

"Actually," he said after a moment, "it's possible I *have* been a little too overconfident, Lywys."

"Yes, Your Grace?" the young captain responded.

"Go tell Major Lowayl I need to speak to him. I'm afraid he'll have already turned in for the evening, so apologize for waking him."

"At once, Your Grace." Captain Braynair touched his chest in salute, bowed politely to Zhevons, and hurried off, and Eastshare glanced at Chalkyr.

"I think we need some hot chocolate, Slym." He smiled slightly. "It may be a longer evening than anyone except Master Zhevons expected."

"Aye, Your Grace. And might be you'd like a plate of san'wiches to keep it company?"

"That wouldn't be a bad idea at all," Eastshare approved, and the gray-haired corporal braced to a sort of abbreviated attention and withdrew.

"I'm afraid *I* won't be able to stay, Your Grace," Zhevons said apologetically. "I have somewhere else I have to be, and making this detour's put me behind schedule for getting there."

"I understand." Eastshare nodded. "And, again, thank you for the warning. I promise we'll put it to good use."

"All I could ask, Your Grace."

Zhevons bowed and followed Chalkyr out of the duke's workspace, but he'd left another of his microscopic listening posts behind. By the time he'd performed his customary *seijin*'s vanishing act into the surrounding forest—and begun reconfiguring his PICA into Merlin Athrawes while he headed for his stealthed recon skimmer—Major Lowayl had appeared in Eastshare's doorway looking improbably spruce and awake.

"You wanted me, Your Grace?"

"Yes, I did." Eastshare moved back to the wall map and tapped it. "What would you say if I told you I had word Kaitswyrth is planning a frontal attack—with some flanking efforts thrown in for good measure—to force us to retreat?"

"I'd say he needs a good Bédardist to restore him to his senses, Your Grace," the youthful major—he was better than twelve years younger than Eastshare—replied with a smile.

"The sort of confident attitude a general likes to see," Eastshare approved. "But a *prudent* general tries to think about even unlikely things. So, I'm thinking that there are a couple of ways I'd like to tweak our main position. And I want you to pick one of your best engineers and send him back with a suitable workforce—get on the semaphore and talk to Archbishop Zhasyn; if he could scare up a few thousand of these Glacierheart miners and tell them to bring their picks and shovels it couldn't hurt—to Ice Lake. I want a fortified bridgehead where the Daivyn flows into the lake. If we do have to fall back under pressure—or even if I just decide it would be a good idea to shorten our line of communications—I want a *hard* defensive position covering the approaches to the lake."

"Yes, Your Grace." Lowayl pulled out his pocket notebook and began writing.

"All right, once you've taken care of that, I want another fatigue party up here, on the northern end of our position. If I were Kaitswyrth and I was serious about bashing us out of the way, I'd seriously contemplate trying to get around onto the high road to assault Haidyrberg or at least get behind our right flank. And if it should happen he *is* thinking that way, I'd like to be in a position to discourage him. So, I'm thinking—"

Merlin Athrawes listened to the two army officers as he climbed the extended ladder into the recon skimmer, one hand checking the black dagger beard extruding itself to adorn his chin while his facial features resumed their normal configuration, and smiled.

. II .
Ahstynwood Forest,
Southwest of Haidyrberg,
Westmarch Province,
Republic of Siddarmark

"There's something up ahead, Sergeant," Private Pahloahzky announced, and Platoon Sergeant Nycodem Zyworya tried not to grimace.

Shyman Pahloahzky was barely seventeen, with a severe case of acne and blue eyes which had seen far less than he liked to pretend they had. He'd been increasingly nervous since Bishop Militant Cahnyr's army had bloodied itself against the heretic redoubts, and he'd adopted an occasionally irritating swagger in an attempt to disguise it, but he genuinely tried hard to be a good soldier, Zyworya reminded himself.

"And what would that be, Shyman?" he asked after a moment.

"Not sure," Pahloahzky admitted. "I saw something move in one of the trees up there, though. It was too big for a squirrel or a tree lizard."

Zyworya bit his tongue against a caustic recitation of all the things bigger than squirrels or tree lizards which might be found in an unconsecrated forest like this one.

"I see," he said instead. "Well, in that case, I think you'd better tell Lieutenant Byrokyo about it."

"Uh, yes, Sergeant." Pahloahzky swallowed audibly at the thought of facing the lieutenant, and Zyworya hid a smile.

"He's right back there," the noncom offered, pointing back along the trail 2nd Platoon's lead squad had been following, and Pahloahzky went trotting back towards the center of the platoon. Zyworya watched him go, then raised one eyebrow at the private's squad leader.

"You think he actually saw something, Hagoh?" Zyworya asked, and Corporal Raymahndoh Myndaiz shrugged.

"I know damned well he saw *something*, Sarge." The corporal grimaced. "*I* didn't see it, though. Langhorne only knows what it may've been—including the kid's imagination—and he ain't telling me."

Zyworya's lips twitched, but he shook his head reprovingly. "You know how Father Zhorj feels about taking the Archangels' names in vain, Hagoh."

"Who's taking anybody's name in vain?" Myndaiz retorted. "I just said he wasn't telling me what Shyman might—or might not've—seen, and he isn't."

Zyworya shook his head again, then turned to follow Pahloahzky.

Lieutenant Byrokyo, 2nd Platoon's commanding officer, was barely two years older than Pahloahzky, less than half Zyworya's age, and he still carried a hint of adolescent awkwardness around with him, but that was about the end of any similarity between him and the private. Byrokyo was self-confident, educated, and bookish, and he would have made an excellent schoolteacher somewhere.

And he also happened to be one of the Army of Glacierheart's better junior officers, in Zyworya's opinion.

"—big *was* it, Shyman?" Byrokyo was asking as he came into earshot.

"I'm not sure, Sir," Pahloahzky admitted . . . probably more readily than he would've admitted it to one of the platoon's noncoms, Zyworya acknowledged. Young or not, Byrokyo managed to be approachable without ever undercutting his own authority. "I only saw it for a second or two, and the light's really confusing with all those leaves and shadows."

"But it was definitely up in the titan oak?"

"Yes, Sir."

"And it went higher when you saw it?"

"Yes, Sir."

"You can show the Platoon Sergeant which tree and how high up it was?"

"Yes, Sir."

Byrokyo looked at him thoughtfully, then glanced over his shoulder at the waiting Zyworya. The platoon sergeant shrugged and raised one hand in a "beats me" gesture, and the lieutenant smiled slightly.

"All right, Shyman," he said. "Give me a minute with the Platoon Sergeant."

"Yes, Sir!"

Pahloahzky retired to a discreet, out-of-earshot distance in obvious relief and Byrokyo waved Zyworya closer.

"What do you think?" he asked softly.

"Sir, I think Pahloahzky's a good kid who's a little nervous and could be imagining things."

"There's a difference between 'could be imagining things' and '*is* imagining things,'" Byrokyo pointed out, and the platoon sergeant nodded.

"That there is, Sir. Which is why I sent him to talk to you about it."

It was Byrokyo's turn to nod, and he found the fingers of his right hand drumming on the scabbard of his sword. The truth was that serving with the Army of God was nothing like what he'd expected. It was his own fault, he supposed; he'd been so caught up in his books that he'd neglected to consider how shockingly different the reality his sagas recorded might be from the one that actually obtained. And none of those sagas had included the Punishment of Schueler, either. It was one thing when soldiers killed soldiers in battle—uglier and far more brutal than his scholarly imagination had ever suggested, but still different from the far worse things that happened *after* the battle.

His platoon was part of 1st Company of the Zion Division's 1st Regiment, and Zion Division had been savagely hammered leading the assault that finally stormed the heretics' Daivyn River redoubts. The division as a whole had lost over half its original strength in dead and wounded, and even though 2nd Platoon had been more fortunate than that, it had still lost nine of its twenty-four men. Ahtonyo Byrokyo had no intention of losing any more of them, because they were *his* men, men he'd known and led all the way from the Temple Lands. He was responsible for them, and it was better to be overly cautious than not cautious enough.

"All right," he said. "We're not going to jump at any ghosts, Nycodem, but we're not going to take any chances, either. Take Myndaiz' entire squad. Nytzah and I will hold here to watch your backs. Have Pahloahzky point out his titan oak to you, and send a couple of men around to the other side. Give it a good look." He shrugged. "Even if it's entirely his imagination, let's treat it as if it weren't. And make sure he knows we're not just ignoring him. I'd rather have someone with an overactive imagination telling us about things that aren't there than someone who expects to get kicked if he tells us about something he genuinely thought he saw and he just happens to be wrong."

"Yes, Sir." Zyworya sketched Langhorne's scepter in salute, then twitched his head at the waiting private, and the two of them headed back the way they'd come.

▼ ▼ ▼

Corporal Lahzrys Mahntsahlo of 3rd Squad, 1st Platoon, Company B, 1st Battalion, 1st Scout Sniper Regiment, muttered an unpleasant word as the Army of God infantry trotted cautiously down the prong lizard trail. They were in open order—or as close to it as the trail's confines allowed—and they looked damnably alert this time. He'd been afraid one of them had spotted him, but he'd been moving at the moment the fellow came around the bend in the trail. He wasn't moving now, and he held very still, blending into the pattern of sunlight and leaves like a hunting mask lizard, concentrating on being invisible, brown eyes watchful among the lines of his green and black face paint.

The Royal Chisholmian Army had long emphasized the value of skirmisher-trained light infantry, yet Corporal Mahntsahlo wasn't ashamed to admit that, Marines or not, the Old Charisian scout snipers had had quite a lot to teach those skirmishers. For example, the Chisholmians had never worried about actual *camouflage*. He wasn't certain why not, yet there it was; the idea simply hadn't occurred to them. On the other hand, it hadn't occurred to any of the Mainland armies, either . . . and he was pretty sure nobody in the Army of God had figured out yet just how hard to see a scout sniper could make himself, either.

The rest of his team was even better hidden than he was, but it was also down on ground level, where the Church riflemen could get at its members. On the other hand. . . .

The oncoming infantry halted, and two men trotted forward, leaving the trail and forcing a way through the last fringe of the blue leaf thickets, clearly swinging outward to circle around the base of the titan oak. Mahntsahlo's heart beat a little faster, but he reminded himself that just because they were looking didn't mean they'd *find* anything. Then he saw the gawky, skinny kid standing in the middle of the trail next to someone who wore the breastplate of a noncom with the three concentric rings of an AOG platoon sergeant. The kid was pointing to exactly where Mahntsahlo had been when he'd wondered if he'd been spotted. Fortunately, that was at least thirty feet lower than the scout sniper's current position, courtesy of his steel climbing spurs.

He listened to the wind rustling the leaves and waited.

▼ ▼ ▼

"And whatever it was, it was going higher, Sarge," Pahloahzky said, still pointing up into the towering tree. He looked a bit sheepish, Zyworya thought, but he was sticking to his guns.

"I see."

The platoon sergeant scratched his chin for a moment, listening to wind rattle gently in the blue leaf's waxy leaves and the distant voices of birds and wyverns. The narrow, twisting trail they'd been sent to scout actually straightened for the better part of two hundred yards as it passed the titan oak, and the densely growing blue leaf they'd been pushing through for the last half hour thinned out on either side as it entered the footprint of the titan oak's deep shade. A thick carpet of leaves stretched away beyond the massive tree in a sort of green twilight, spangled with patches of sunshine that somehow found chinks in the high canopy. The leaf carpet piled up like silt against an occasional fallen tree trunk and it was still dotted with scattered clumps of the persistent blue leaf, but visibility was far better than it had been. On the ground, at any rate. If there was anything up that titan oak, *he* sure as hell couldn't pick it out of the leaves and branches. But that didn't mean there wasn't something there, and he shrugged.

"Rifles ready," he ordered, and unslung his own rifle.

▼ ▼ ▼

Oh, shit, Mahntsahlo thought as he watched the Army of God infantry raise their rifles. He felt a spurt of panic, until he realized they weren't aimed anywhere near his present position. The relief when he recognized that minor fact was almost painful, but—

▼ ▼ ▼

"All right, Shyman," Zyworya said. "You any good at baseball?"

"What?" The private blinked. "Uh, sorry, Sergeant! I mean, yeah . . . I guess. Played shortstop, usually."

"Really?" Zyworya grinned. He hadn't thought the kid had that kind of reflexes. "In that case, find yourself some rocks and start throwing them up in those branches."

"Yes, Sergeant!"

▼ ▼ ▼

Great. Mahntsahlo suppressed an urge to shake his head as the first rock came arcing up and bounced off the titan oak's bark with a sharp "*thwack*" of impact. The kid had a pretty good arm, and he was only about sixty feet up. The rocks weren't likely to hurt a lot even if they hit him, but they also wouldn't sound like they'd hit wood, either.

Those bastards are just likely to go ahead and fire, whether they actually see anything or not, if that happens, he reflected, *which would be a bad thing. On the other hand, they may not even come close to me, and Captain Gahlvayo wants us to suck in as many of them as we can before they figure out we're here.*

He clenched his jaw, making himself breathe deeply and steadily. In the end, it probably came down to how persistent the damned Temple Boys wanted to be. Lieutenant Makysak would really prefer for him and Corporal Brunohn Sayranoh to give them a little more rope in hopes of getting the column behind them farther forward, but that had to be a judgment call, and the lieutenant trusted them to make the right one. For that matter, Mahntsahlo trusted *Sayranoh* to make the right one, and someone had to make it. If they only tossed a few more rocks and then moved on, everything would be just fine; if it looked like they were settling in for an extended effort, though. . . .

▼ ▼ ▼

Young Pahloahzky must've had a devastating throw to first, Zyworya thought, watching another rock crash up into the foliage. And the kid was obviously enjoying himself, too. It was pretty clear that whatever he thought he'd seen must have moved on by now—there'd been enough rocks up there to cause just about any critter he could think of to break cover! But he might as well let the boy have his fun, and the rest of the squad was grinning as widely as he was.

Another couple of rocks, he decided, *and then we'll*—

The next rock thwacked into the titan oak's bark and Pahloahzky stooped for another. The private was just straightening back up and Zyworya turned to tell him this would be the last one when something else cracked sharply.

That small turn saved Zyworya's life. The half-inch rifle bullet which would otherwise have struck him squarely in the chest slammed into his breastplate at an angle, instead. It was still like being hit with a sledgehammer that drove him back three strides, and Shyman Pahloahzky clutched at his butchered face with both hands as the flattened, ricocheting projectile hit him below his right eye. He went down, hitting the leaves, his hands suddenly crimson while he screamed, and Zyworya's head snapped up and to the right.

A cloud of smoke hung above one of those clumps of blue leaf in the Ahstynwood's sun-and-shade spangled air. It was a good hundred and fifty yards away across the leaf carpet, and he couldn't see a single sign of whoever had fired that rifle. But he didn't have to see the *shooter*.

"Right flank—hundred and fifty yards!" he snapped: "Myndaiz, take first section and find his arse! Second section with me! *Go!*"

The corporal—he should've been a sergeant, but the platoon had received only six replacements, none sergeants, since the bitter fight to take the heretics' redoubts—responded instantly. Five members of his understrength squad took the lead, swinging to the right and moving forward at a half run, bayoneted rifles ready, while the remaining five followed Zyworya, more slowly, prepared to engage with fire. The platoon sergeant heard Lieutenant Byrokyo's voice behind him, snapping orders to Corporal Nytzah's squad. His own brain was too focused on the task at hand to pay much attention to the lieutenant's commands, but after so long together, he knew they were the right ones.

Pahloahzky was still screaming, and Zyworya found a corner of his brain marveling yet again at how slowly seconds could pass at moments like this. He'd never realized how flexible time really was until he'd spent an eternity in howling combat only to discover it had been less than fifteen minutes . . . or seen a score of men killed in the blink of an eye.

Myndaiz' section was halfway to the dissipating smoke cloud when a dozen more rifles fired. They were at least eighty yards south of the first one, stretched in an east-west line almost exactly at right angles to Myndaiz' line of advance. Three of his five men went down instantly, and at least three rounds hit Myndaiz himself. The squad's two survivors wheeled instinctively towards whoever had just massacred the remainder of its men . . . and a half-dozen *more* rifles fired.

The entire section was down, Zyworya realized sickly. Two of them were still moving, crawling painfully back towards him, leaving trails of blood behind them, and he couldn't see a *thing*. The shooters had to be out there—he could see their smoke—but he couldn't see *them*!

"Covering fire!" he barked, and three of the five men with him fired. They had no better target than the drifting smoke clouds, but whoever was behind those rifles had to be reloading—just as Zyworya was—and he wasn't going to go charging further forward with only five men when at least four times that many were waiting in concealment.

He heard Byrokyo and Nytzah's squad coming up behind him, pushing along the narrow trail between the encroaching banks of blue leaf, then flinched as several more rifles fired from a line extending at least fifty yards to either side of the first shooter's position. Another man, this one from Myndaiz' second section, stumbled backwards, ramrod flying from his hands, and collapsed with a bubbling moan, and Zyworya swore viciously. The blue leaf offered partial concealment, but it was about as effective as a sheet of paper when it came to actually stopping bullets, and the tactical situation sucked. Despite the relative openness of the woodland beyond the titan oak, the terrain was too broken for them to form any kind of properly ordered line, and advancing was going to be an ugly business if they couldn't even *see* the heretics! But if they established a firing position here, right around the titan oak, and sent back to Captain Ingrayahn, the rest of the company could come up and—

▼ ▼ ▼

Lahzrys Mahntsahlo bared his teeth.

He really wished the Temple Boys had simply walked on by his tree. Their persistence had knocked that on the head, though. The members of his squad, unable to see exactly how close the thrown rocks had been creeping towards his own position and with no evidence the enemy planned on moving on anytime soon, had opened the ambush quite a bit earlier than he and Corporal Sayranoh had intended. They'd planned to catch as much as possible of the AOG company on the trail; now it looked like they were going to have to settle for a single one of the AOG's small-sized platoons.

On the other hand, the L-shaped "fire sack" had worked just fine. The Temple Boys still hadn't realized there were two full squads of scout snipers hidden out there in what Baron Green Valley had dubbed "ghillie suits." Mahntsahlo had no idea where the name came from, but he'd been astonished by how invisible one of them could make someone. It broke up the wearer's outline in three dimensions, blending him seamlessly into almost any background once it was properly customized. Of course, it couldn't hide the smoke when someone fired, but it was obvious the Temple Boys still hadn't figured out how readily a Mahndrayn could be used from a prone position. Probably because they'd only gone up against them when they assaulted Brigadier Taisyn's Marines in their entrenched position, he thought. Not having encountered them in the open—yet—they couldn't truly begin to imagine all the advantages breech-loading offered. There were dips and hollows in any terrain, and the blind fire from the lead squad's survivors was all going high, obviously looking for the riflemen they assumed must be standing to reload behind trees or one of the scattered clumps of blue leaf. There was, after all, a reason the scout snipers had concealed themselves near exactly those sorts of cover.

Of course, there was also a reason they'd chosen this particular spot for their ambush, and Mahntsahlo peered down, watching the rest of the Temple Boy platoon stacking up in the narrow, slot-like trail where the much denser thickets of blue leaf concealed them from the Charisian riflemen. He could've wished for a bigger bag, but every little bit helped.

The corporal waited another moment, then pulled the preposterously thin strand of braided steel thistle which had been dyed in suitable woodland colors to make it invisible against the thick, rough bark of the titan oak.

▼ ▼ ▼

Nycodem Zyworya never saw the cord move. He had no way of knowing it was connected to the percussion cap–armed lock mechanism spiked to the ground in a concealing drift of leaves at the base of the titan oak. Nor did he know about the length of quick match leading away from that lock mechanism to the devices the Charisian Army had nicknamed "Shan-wei's sweepers," or simply "sweepers," for short, hidden in the blue leaf on either side of the trail where 2nd Platoon's survivors were bunched together.

On a planet called Earth, those sweepers might have been called "claymore mines," instead. They were less efficient than their ancient ancestors because their designers had been limited to black powder rather than more sophisticated explosives, yet they were fully adequate for the task. Spaced twenty yards apart on center, each of the concave directional mines hurled five hundred and seventy-six .50 caliber shrapnel balls in a sixty-degree, cone-shaped blast pattern, and there were five of them on each side of the trail, set back twenty yards into the blue leaf to assure maximum dispersion. On average, each yard of the covered trail received forty-eight balls, traveling horizontally at just over fifteen hundred feet per second.

There were no survivors.

. III .

Charisian Embassy,
Siddar City,
Republic of Siddarmark

"So you think Kaitswyrth's going to go ahead and push it anyway?"

"Well, actually, yes," Merlin Athrawes said, looking across the table at Emperor Cayleb Ahrmahk.

A bottle of Empress Sharleyan's favorite Chisholmian whiskey sat between them, and in his empress's absence, Cayleb had indulged his barbarian Old Charisian habits. The ice clinked as he raised the glass and took another sip, and Merlin sat back, cradling his own glass between his hands. PICAs were not subject to inebriation. Merlin couldn't say he much missed the experience, although there were occasions when he would have liked to be able to "drink to forget," but he still treasured the social experience and a PICA's full sensory capability allowed him to savor the honeyed fire of a truly excellent whiskey.

Without the ice, in his own case.

"And you do, too, Nahrmahn?" Cayleb asked.

"Yes."

Nahrmahn's response was both quicker and more confident than Merlin's as it came over the transparent plug in Cayleb's ear. The emperor raised an eyebrow, and the image of Nahrmahn projected onto his contact lenses shrugged. The Emeraldian prince nursed a glass of his own whiskey and his electronic persona, unlike Merlin, was quite capable of becoming tipsy if he imbibed enough of it. At the moment, however, his expression was serious, even somber.

"I know Colonel Makyn and his scout snipers've been handing his probes their heads," he said. "And left to his own devices, Kaitswyrth's probably smart enough to decide that ramming directly into Duke Eastshare would be a really bad idea. But that zealotry and bigotry of his make him *want* to push forward no matter what, and he's not being left to his own devices. With Clyntahn's not so gentle prods reinforcing his own inclinations, there's a damned good chance he'll ignore good sense and come ahead whatever happens to his patrols."

"If he does, he's going to think what the scout snipers've already done to him was a love tap," Cayleb pointed out.

"Probably. The catch is that he doesn't know that yet, and in a lot of ways, logic is the least important of his problem-solving skills at the moment." Nahrmahn grimaced and sipped whiskey, then shrugged. "I won't go so far as to *guarantee* he won't suffer an attack of common sense, but it's not very likely."

"And he's right about the difference between his supply situation and Wyrshym's." Merlin's grimace was far more sour than Nahrmahn's had been. "In fact, he's more right about that than he realizes, since he doesn't know Ahlverez's going to be redirected from Alyksberg. I don't see the Dohlarans catching up with Sumyrs, but Ahlverez is sure as hell going to try. And with Harless' 'Army of Justice' coming up from Desnair, Thesmar—and Earl Hanth—are likely to find themselves a lot busier than any of us would like."

"All we can do is all we can do," Cayleb said, rather more philosophically than he felt. "At least we've got naval support in Thesmar Bay, and by this time Fyguera has the better part of two hundred thirty-pounders dug in on the city's approaches, with plenty of ammo to keep them fed." The emperor showed his teeth in an evil smile. "I don't know about you, but *I* certainly wouldn't want to launch any assaults into that much firepower!"

"Neither would I," Merlin agreed. "On the other hand, while I'm in a sort of Shan-wei's advocate sort of mood,

I might point out that unlike the Army of God or the Desnairians, Ahlverez has those damned howitzers of Thirsk's."

"And his field howitzers are supposed to smash Fyguera's fortifications exactly how?" Cayleb asked quizzically.

"I did say I was in Shan-wei's advocate mode," Merlin pointed out, and the emperor chuckled.

"That doesn't mean Hanth couldn't still find himself in a world of trouble if he lets himself be surprised by Ahlverez coming down from the north, Rychtyr pushing out of Trevyr from the west, *and* Harless coming up from the south, though," Merlin went on more somberly. "I know. I know! He's too good and too smart to let something like that happen to him, especially with our 'spies'' reports about what's headed his way. But even the best, smartest people can screw up, and that doesn't even consider the sorts of problems things like weather could make for him. So if it's all right with the two of you, I'll just quietly go on worrying about it until we know for sure that it's not going to happen."

"I see your point, but there are other things I'm more inclined to worry about than the possibility of Hauwerd Breygart's brain suddenly turning into bean soup," Cayleb said dryly. "Like how are we going to feed everybody this winter. Especially after General Symkyn gets here with the rest of the first wave."

Merlin nodded, although he was more inclined to look on the bright side of Symkyn's arrival with the nearly sixty thousand troops embarked aboard his transports. Besides, a mere sixty thousand additional mouths wasn't going to matter much against the scale of feeding the entire loyal population of the Republic of Siddarmark after the ravages of the past winter and spring.

"It's not going to be as bad as it was this year, Cayleb," Nahrmahn said. "Of course, I realize 'not as bad as' a nightmare like last winter isn't much of a recommendation, but Owl and I just finished a survey, and the winter wheat crop's actually a bit better than Stohnar and Maidyn've been estimating. A lot smaller than last year's, of course, but remember how much of that got burned in the granaries. The spring wheat's going to be ready to harvest in the southern Republic by early September, too, and there's going to be a lot more of it in the eastern provinces than there was last year. Still not enough to compensate for the loss of all those western farms, especially not with the population shift to the east, but Owl and I calculate that between what's already harvested and what we can expect to see from the fall harvest, the Republic's going to come within about ten percent of being able to meet its own domestic wheat requirements. The corn and potato crops are looking a *lot* better, and soybean production's up by better than sixty percent in the eastern provinces over last year's levels. Livestock levels are still way down—Owl's estimating it'll take at least three years to build back the stocks that were depleted over the winter—but we've managed to import enough cows to at least get dairy production back on its feet. The reduction in meat production's going to help the fodder situation, too; with so many fewer draft and meat animals, the demand for hay and feed grain will be down substantially. The uptick in poultry production's going to cut into that some, but not enough to really notice. And we've got more time to organize food purchases and convoys from Charis, Emerald, and Tarot than we had last year." He shrugged. "The truth is, we ought to be able to feed everyone over this winter. Not with the kind of variety we might wish for, but with enough calories—and enough vitamins—to prevent outright starvation from claiming any more lives. It depends on the weather, of course, but farmers *always* depend on the weather. And I'm pretty sure Baron Ironhill won't be devastated to find our imperial farmers will still have a market for all that additional production they've been cranking out."

"That's probably true," Cayleb acknowledged with a crooked smile. "He's been talking about engineering a 'soft landing' for the agricultural sector ever since Ehdwyrd suggested the term to him."

"Then we're probably in about as good a shape as we're likely to see," Merlin said. The emperor gave him an incredulous look, and he shrugged. "I'm not saying we're in *good* shape, Cayleb—just that the shape we're in is probably as good as it's likely to get . . . and one hell of a lot better than last year. I'm fully aware of how much room for improvement there still is."

"Good. For a moment I was wondering if you'd lost your electronic mind."

"As if you and our pushy, portly little friend were prepared to let that happen!" Merlin snorted.

"I do have two or three other little tidbits to add," Nahrmahn said, recapturing their attention.

"Your idea of 'little tidbits' is enough to make anyone who knows you nervous whenever they hear something like that," Cayleb said. "What is it this time?"

"Well, it happens that I've had Owl doing some research for me. The sorts of things Merlin's never really had time for, given how busy he's been putting out forest fires. And we've turned up some interesting items. For example, do either of you know why Silverlode Island is named Silverlode Island?"

"Because of the color of the sand." Cayleb shrugged. "Every Charisian—I mean, every *Old* Charisian—knows that."

Merlin nodded, but he was looking at Nahrmahn's image with an intent, speculative expression. The enormous island east of Charis was very sparsely populated, thanks in no small part to the ruggedness of its interior and the fact that so little of its territory had yet been "consecrated," or terraformed for human occupation. Personally, Merlin had always thought of it more as "East Charis" than as an island in its own right, and Cayleb's ancestors had always regarded it mainly as a place population could expand to . . . someday, and otherwise pretty much ignored it. Technically, it wasn't even a part of the Charisian Empire, although that was a meaningless distinction, since "Duke of Silverlode" was one of Cayleb's secondary titles and everyone who lived on it owed the House of Ahrmahk personal fealty despite the minor fact that their home island had never been formally integrated into the Kingdom of Charis. In effect, Silverlode belonged outright to Cayleb in his own person rather than to the crown of Charis, and no one had ever been in any hurry to regularize that, since there were less than fifteen thousand people living on an island more than half the size of Old Earth's continent of Australia.

"Every Charisian may know that, but that doesn't make it the real reason," Nahrmahn said with a rather strange smile. "It turns out the *real* reason was one of Shan-wei's little jokes. I wouldn't be at all surprised to discover she'd planted that beach nonsense as part of the cover for it, in fact, and I can't make up my mind whether the real reason for the name's going to make Ironhill happy or drive him to distraction."

"In that case, I think you'd better unravel this little mystery for us," Merlin said repressively, and Nahrmahn chuckled.

"Let's just put it this way," he said. "I'm going to leave at least a part of this as a homework assignment for Cayleb, but did you ever hear of something called the Comstock Lode back on Earth, Merlin?"

Merlin frowned. The term did sound familiar, in a vague, elusive sort of way. He couldn't call it to the front of his memory, however, and he shrugged.

"My, my, I *am* disappointed." Nahrmahn's smile grew even broader. "I think you should consider it a homework assignment for yourself, as well as Cayleb. And once you've done that, we're going to have to figure out how we can go about 'discovering' the truth in a way that makes some kind of sense. Trust me, it'll be worth it if we can."

Merlin's frown deepened. He knew that tone, that smile, and part of him wanted to grab Nahrmahn by the scruff of his immaterial neck and shake him until he disgorged the information he was clearly enjoying *not* disgorging. Unfortunately, the effort would have been futile, and he knew it. From Cayleb's expression, the emperor was thinking very much the same sort of thoughts he was.

"All right, that's all suitably mystifying," Cayleb said after a moment in a moderately martyred tone. "Do you by chance intend to be a bit more forthcoming about those other 'tidbits' of yours?"

"Of course I do, Your Majesty." Nahrmahn blinked guilelessly at the other two. "How could you possibly think I wouldn't be?"

"I don't want you to take this wrongly, Nahrmahn, but have you considered how fortunate you are that you're not simply in Nimue's Cave, instead of here where I can get my hands on you at this very moment, but already dead?"

"The thought had crossed my mind. However," the Emeraldian prince's expression sobered, "in this case I'm not sure exactly what we want to do. I've had Owl scan Commodore Pei's data dump from the original colony records, including all the biometric data, and I've discovered that Paityr and his family really are directly descended from Frederick Schueler." Merlin and Cayleb both stiffened in their chairs, and Nahrmahn shrugged. "For all I know, by this time a third of the population of Siddarmark's descended from Schueler. Without a broader genetic sample there's no way to know that, though. There have to be a lot of collateral descendants simply given how long the Wylsynn family's been around, but I can't even begin to quantify that at this point. So the question is do we tell Paityr? Would he even want to know?"

"Now *that*, Nahrmahn, is a very good question, and one I don't think either of us is even remotely qualified to answer," Merlin said slowly. He looked at Cayleb, who nodded vigorously. "At the same time, I don't know we have any right *not* to tell him. I hope no one will think this is cowardly of me, but I think the person we ought to ask about it is Maikel. He probably knows Paityr better than any of the rest of us. Besides," Merlin smiled briefly, "I think it's the kind of question that comes under the jurisdiction of the Archbishop of Charis, don't you?"

"I certainly do if it gets *me* off the hook," Cayleb said fervently. "This is one 'decision of state' I'm just *delightedly* happy to pass on!"

"Interesting you should put it that way, Your Majesty," Nahrmahn said, and Cayleb looked back at his image with a suddenly suspicious expression.

"Why?"

"Because it turns out Paityr isn't the only member of the inner circle who descends from rarified, one might almost say sanctified, origins."

"Meaning exactly what?" Cayleb's expression was more suspicious than ever, and Nahrmahn shrugged.

"Well, it's just that I've been a bit . . . suspicious about certain elements in the historical record, you might say, ever since you and the Brethren were kind enough to share it with me. Specifically, there's this nagging little question I've had about Jeremiah Knowles and his in-laws."

"What?" Cayleb blinked at the non sequitur. "What does Saint Zherneau have to do with whatever you're talking about? I mean, there wouldn't *be* an inner circle without his journal, but aside from that?"

"Well, it turns out Owl's files have the genetic profiles on him and his wife and also on Kayleb and Jennifer Sarmac. So I had him take a look at them, and it turns out I was right."

"Right about *what*?"

"Well," Nahrmahn said for a third time, "we all know how names've shifted over the last thousand years or so. But did you ever stop to think, Cayleb, how much like 'Sarmac' the name *'Ahrmahk'* sounds?" He smiled beatifically as the emperor gawked at him. "Always nice to be able to track your genealogy back with a degree of assurance, isn't it?" he observed cheerfully.

Outside Treuyr, The South March Lands, Republic of Siddarmark

"Well, that's a lovely bit of news."

Sir Hauwerd Breygart, otherwise known as the Earl of Hanth, was a solid, powerfully built fellow with graying dark hair and brown eyes. He was a calm, purposeful sort under most circumstances—not the kind of officer given to temper tantrums or shouting at subordinates. At the moment, however, those brown eyes were dangerously hard and his expression was not an encouraging one.

"Excuse me, My Lord?" Lieutenant Hairahm Bahskym, Hanth's Marine aide, said with commendable bravery. "Did you say something?"

"No, I *muttered* something," Hanth replied. He glowered at the dispatch which had just been delivered to him, then looked back up at Bahskym. "I imagine you already know what's in this?"

"Ah, I did receipt it and bring it over from the semaphore office, My Lord," the lieutenant pointed out, and Hanth snorted.

"In that case, why are you still standing here? Go get me Major Zhadwail, Major Mhartyn, Commander Karmaikel, and Commander Portyr. I'd tell you to bring me Commander Ashwail and Commander Parkyr, too, if they were available."

"Of course, My Lord." Bahskym touched his chest in salute.

If the lieutenant felt the least surprised at Hanth's decision to call in all of his most senior officers—with the exception of Parkyr and Ashwail, both of whom were in Thesmar at the moment—no one could have told it from his expression. He bowed slightly and disappeared like smoke.

▼ ▼ ▼

"I don't suppose this is confirmed, My Lord?" Major Wyllym Zhadwail asked wryly the better part of an hour later. He was a weathered-looking fellow, four inches shorter than the earl, and the 1st Independent Marine Brigade's senior battalion commander. Given that the entire "Independent Brigade" consisted of just under five thousand men and that two-thirds of its "battalions" consisted of drafted Charisian seamen, it was a possibly grandiloquent title, but no one was inclined to laugh at it, given what it had achieved little more than a month earlier in the Battle of Thesmar.

"You suppose correctly," Hanth replied with a wintry smile. "On the other hand, the numbers are coming from the same people who've been providing all our other numbers, so I'm inclined to accept them for planning purposes."

"Damn," Zhadwail said mildly and shook his head. "I'd sort of hoped they were off this time."

The other officers standing around the map table in Hanth's command tent chuckled, although there wasn't really anything especially humorous about the situation. The earl looked down at the map, and his own inclination to smile fluttered away as he considered the unpromising position and the numbers coming at him.

Sir Rainos Ahlverez alone would be bringing over fifty thousand men south from the capture of Alyksberg. Probably not a *lot* over fifty thousand, given the casualties he'd taken when Alyksberg's defenders mousetrapped him. According to the dispatches Hanth had received, the rearguard General Clyftyn Sumyrs had left to cover his garrison's evacuation had blown up the fortress city's magazines—and themselves—just as Ahlverez' assault columns were swarming over the walls. The best estimate anyone had was that somewhere around four thousand Dohlarans had been killed or seriously wounded in the resultant explosion.

On the other hand, Sir Fahstyr Rychtyr, commanding the force Hanth currently had "besieged" around the city of Trevyr on the Seridahn River, had been reinforced from Dohlar. His roughly forty-thousand-man force was almost back to its original strength, and it had received several thousand additional rifles in the last couple of five-days. Between the two of them, Rychtyr and Ahlverez outnumbered Hanth by roughly eighteen-to-one, but the Royal Dohlaran Army was no longer the only thing he had to worry about. The "Army of Justice," the Desnairian Empire's contribution to the rape of Siddarmark, had crossed the border from the Grand Duchy of Silkiah. It had to come overland, and the going wasn't particularly good around the northern tip of the Salthar Mountains, but something like sixty-five percent of that army was cavalry, which should at least give it pretty fair mobility. More to the point, the Duke of Harless had over a hundred and seventy-five thousand men under his command, not counting his artillerists or civilian supply drovers, which meant that something like a quarter million men were all headed directly for the 1st Independent Marine Brigade's *five thousand* men.

Even for Charisians, those odds might be considered just a *tad* high, Hanth reflected.

"It looks like Sumyrs is going to get here before Ahlverez does," he said finally, looking up from the map again. "That may not sound like much, but it's another seventy-two hundred men. They'll need rest, food, and medical care, but I imagine they'll come in handy for holding Thesmar. And that's what it's going to come to, let's not fool ourselves about that."

"Believe me, My Lord," Major Lairays Mhartyn said feelingly. "The last thing I want to do is be anywhere in the open when that many men come crunching down on us!" He shook his head. "Mind you, if it were only the Dohlarans, I might feel differently about it. Twenty-to-one odds? *Piffle!*" He snapped his fingers. "My boys wouldn't even work up a sweat!"

"Of course they wouldn't, Lairays." Hanth shook his head. "Since those pesky Desnairians *are* going to be coming along, though, I think it's time we started seriously planning to pull back. I'd prefer to do it under cover of darkness so Rychtyr doesn't realize we've gone until we've got the artillery well away. That's going to be up to you and Commander Parkyr, Wahltayr." He looked at Wahltayr Karmaikel, who commanded one of his naval "battalions." "I know Admiral Hywyt's landed a lot more guns to cover Thesmar, but I'd just as soon not lose these, if it's all the same to you."

"Oh, I think we can manage that for you, My Lord," Karmaikel assured him.

"Good." Hanth looked back down at the map for a moment, then up at their waiting faces. "In that case, I don't suppose there's anything more that needs saying. Get back to your commands, and Hairahm here will be bringing around formal movement orders by this evening."

. V .

HMS *Destiny,*
56 Port Royal,
and
Royal Palace,
City of Cherayth,
Kingdom of Chisholm,
Empire of Charis

"A bit different from the last time we sailed, isn't it?" Hektor Aplyn-Ahrmahk, the Duke of Darcos, remarked quietly as HMS *Destiny* and her escorting squadron got under way, accompanied by the explosive wind-ruffling sound of hundreds of wings. The even larger escort of wyverns and seagulls dipped and swirled about the ship in a multi-hued, whistling, calling cloud, and the dark-haired young woman at his side had to lean towards him to hear him. Even listening hard, it was difficult to pull the sound of his voice out of that thrumming aerial thunder and the noise of shouted orders, wind-struck canvas, the song of that same wind singing through the rigging, and the rush and gurgle of water. They stood at *Destiny*'s quarterdeck rail, safely out of the way of the seamen minding the flagship's sails, and the activities of those hurrying, orderly sailors were no longer the mystery to her they once had been.

"And even more different from the *first* time we sailed together," Princess Irys Daykyn agreed. Her left hand stole out to capture his right, and she inhaled the smell of saltwater and tar as if it were some rare elixir, stray strands of hair flying on the wind. "In some ways, I'm a lot more worried about the outcome of this voyage, though."

His hand tightened around hers, and she felt an almost overwhelming need to move closer to him, let her head rest against his shoulder. It would never have done, of course—not in front of all those watching eyes. Although, given the standard Cayleb and Sharleyan Ahrmahk had set. . . .

"I guess I can understand that," Hektor said. "I mean, how could the possibility of going into permanent captivity as a state prisoner of the Charisian Empire possibly compare to the dreadful possibility of going home to face your own fiercely loyal people?" She looked up at him sharply, and he smiled. "With a Charisian fiancé in tow, I mean."

She laughed, but she also shook her head at him, because that was the very crux of the matter, after all.

"You left out the bit about not having to worry about anyone trying to murder Daivyn or me in Charis," she pointed out. "That made any concern about becoming 'state prisoners' rather less pressing than it might've been, given the alternatives."

He nodded in understanding since he'd had more than a little to do with that outcome.

"And it's not just the Charisian fiancé that's making you nervous about going home, either, is it?"

"No, it isn't," she admitted with something rather like

a pensive sigh. "I know I'm simply borrowing trouble worrying about it when none of us know how it's all going to come out," she continued. "Phylyp's certainly told me that often enough! For that matter," her hazel eyes glinted at him, "I believe *you* may've mentioned it a time or three."

"Possibly even as many as four," he said thoughtfully. "Probably not, though. I'm not one of those people in the habit of repeating myself, after all. Still, it *might've* been as many as four."

"More like four *dozen*," she retorted. "'In the habit of repeating' yourself, indeed! I wouldn't want to go around using any words like 'nagging,' but—" She shrugged.

"Well, if you'd just gone ahead and agreed with me the first time, I wouldn't've *had* to keep repeating myself," he pointed out equably.

"I *did* agree with you."

"Oh?" He cocked his head. "Didn't I just hear you say—"

"I agreed *intellectually*. That's not the same thing as being able to actually take your advice. Mind you, I don't think *anyone* could've taken your advice under the circumstances."

"Probably not," he agreed. He looked back at the waterfront and the crowded harbor slipping slowly astern as *Destiny* and her escorts gathered way. "On the other hand, standing on this deck—in almost exactly this spot—as a matter of fact—while discussing weighty political matters seems to be something of a habit of mine. Do you want to talk about it now?"

He looked back down at her and she arched an eyebrow at him.

"I'm serious, Irys, and not just because it's where Earl Hanth helped sort *me* out. It's a good place to talk. I think people spend too much time talking about important things in offices and council chambers. Things . . . focus down too much under those circumstances. I think they'd probably make better decisions if they talked them over in the open air and sunlight more often first."

Her eyes narrowed as she considered the proposition.

He might well be right, she reflected. Of course, the fact that he'd been at sea since his tenth birthday might have a little something to do with his perspective and his aversion to the hushed corridors of power associated with those offices and council chambers. He was far from any typical aristocrat of her acquaintance, and not simply because he'd been born a commoner. She tried to imagine any of the exquisite young sprigs of Corisandian nobility who'd begun vying for her hand before her father sent her to "safety" on a galleon's quarterdeck, oilskins shining in the glare of reflected lightning as he fought a hurricane tooth and nail for his ship's survival.

Her imagination was unequal to the task.

"There's not really that much to talk about, is there?" she said after a moment. "We've made our decisions. All we can do now is carry them out and trust God to get the details straight."

"I don't think He'd object too much if we did a little to kick things along in the right direction ourselves," he observed with another of those smiles she'd come to watch for. "I know I'm just a simple sailor, but one thing a midshipman learns when it comes to getting seamen three or four times his age to do what he wants is that however scared to death he may actually be he needs to *look* confident. I don't imagine it's a lot different for princes and princesses."

"It's no different at all," she agreed. "That's probably one of the things that makes sending princes to sea good training."

"I think that's the way Charis has always seen it," he acknowledged. "Of course, *I* was no prince at the time, but I don't see how the early training's hurt anything now that I've become a duke."

He elevated his nose with a pompous expression, and she laughed and punched his shoulder with her free hand as she recognized the excellent imitation of Emperor Cayleb at his worst. There were those—*many* of those, in fact—who believed Cayleb showed far too little consciousness of the dignity of his crown and far too much readiness to laugh at himself and his many titles.

Irys wasn't one of them. In her opinion, Hektor could've chosen a far less desirable model than his adoptive father, and she treasured his levity even more because of his humble origins. A princess saw far too many nobles take themselves far too seriously. The temptation for someone who'd been catapulted from commoner to the very highest ranks of what was arguably the most powerful empire on all of Safehold to succumb to that sort of self-image must have been great.

Or they must've been great for anyone but Hektor, at least, she told herself, hugging his right arm against her side. He looked down at her quizzically, and she shook her head.

"Just a passing thought," she told him. "Not that you're not right. And when we get to Manchyr I promise I'll carry it all with a bold face! But just between the two of us, I'm not really as brave as Sharleyan. So if it's all right with you, I'll probably go right on sharing the odd moment of anxiety with you. Maybe even leaning—maybe even crying a bit—on your shoulder about it when there aren't quite so many eyes around."

"It's your shoulder, too, now," he pointed out, eyes smiling into hers. "I'll be perfectly happy to make it available whenever it's needed."

▼ ▼ ▼

Sharleyan Ahrmahk smiled slightly.

She sat back in her chair at the head of the council table, watching the imagery projected on her contact lenses as Owl's SNARCs showed her the squadron of galleons making sail for Corisande. She wished Irys and Hektor had Maikel Staynair along to support them, but Cayleb and Pine Hollow had been right about that. Sending Irys and Daivyn home to Corisande with no one "looking over their shoulder" was an essential subtext, and very few people would be able to regard Archbishop Maikel as anything but an official presence. Staynair's pastoral visit to Chisholm gave them a perfectly good reason to keep him there while they sent the exiled prince and his sister on to their homeland as speedily as possible. And if they didn't have Staynair, at least Hektor and Irys had each other. She wished she could take credit for the understanding flowing between them, and she'd certainly done all she could to encourage it, but there were some things not even empresses could command, and the human heart was foremost among them.

They'll do well together, she told herself. *Unless we've misread the situation in Corisande badly, Irys and Daivyn will do well in Manchyr, too, but however that works out, Hektor and Irys will be there for each other. That matters. That matters a lot.*

Her throat tightened as she recalled how much—and how often—that had mattered for her and Cayleb. *The Book of Bédard* said that shared strength made light loads, and for all she'd come to despise the cynical calculation which had created the *Holy Writ* of the Church of God Awaiting, there were countless truths embedded with its lies.

She allowed herself another few seconds to contemplate the young woman and the even younger man on *Destiny*'s quarterdeck, then returned her attention to the council chamber.

"—still not showing anything like common sense, though," Sir Dynzayl Hyntyn, the Earl of Saint Howan, was saying. He shook his head. "I'm beginning to think nothing short of assassinating Rydach's going to change that!"

Sharleyan shook a scolding finger at him.

"We're not going to start down that road, My Lord," she said. "However tempting it may be."

The other three men seated around the table with her and Saint Howan chuckled. It was a rather select gathering—Braisyn Byrns, the Earl of White Crag, Sharleyan's first councilor; Sylvyst Mhardyr, Baron Stoneheart, her lord justice; and Sir Ahlber Zhustyn, her spymaster. If any of the rest of the council had been present, Saint Howan would probably have expressed himself in rather more circumspect tones.

Probably. Given his opinion of the Earl of Swayle and his spiritual adviser Sharleyan was less than certain of that.

"Well, if he's not, he's not," White Crag said rather more philosophically than he obviously felt. "And at least Mountain Heart's starting to show signs of reason."

"*Reason!*" Stoneheart snorted. "More like greed, if you ask me!"

"Not entirely," Sharleyan corrected the lord justice. "Trust me, there's a little fear mixed into that 'reasonableness' of his, too." Her smile was thin. "Not that greed isn't also a perfectly satisfactory motivator where he's concerned."

"And an effective one," Saint Howan agreed a bit sourly. As the Kingdom of Chisholm's Chancellor of the Treasury he was acutely aware of just how many marks the project to improve the Shelakyl River was going to cost. None of which the Grand Duke of Mountain Heart was going to have to come up with.

"Effectiveness is what makes it satisfactory." Sharleyan shrugged. "And he has agreed to drop the level of the tolls he was insisting upon for the rest of the river. In fact," she showed her teeth, "he doesn't quite realize just yet exactly how *far* he's going to end up dropping them before I'm through with him."

"Your Majesty?" Saint Howan tilted his head at her, his eyes questioning. He knew that tone of old.

"One of the reasons I asked Sir Ahlber to sit in with us today concerns the Grand Duke's current political associations," Sharleyan said. She looked at the spymaster. "Sir Ahlber?"

"Of course, Your Majesty." Zhustyn dipped his head to her in a respectful bow, then looked at the other three councilors.

"What Her Majesty is referring to, My Lords, are certain reports I've received concerning Mountain Heart, Duke Rock Coast, Duke Black Horse, and Earl Dragon Hill. It would seem they've been corresponding rather more closely than usual over the last two or three months.

And just recently, Earl Swayle—or more probably the Dowager Countess—has been dispatching quite a few letters and couriers, as well."

White Crag and Saint Howan looked less than happy to hear that. Stoneheart's expression was considerably grimmer than either of the other two's, and he looked sharply at Zhustyn.

"Is there a reason this is the first I'm hearing about all this correspondence, Ahlber?" His tone was crisp, but Sharleyan lifted a hand before Zhustyn could reply and met her lord justice's gaze herself.

"Much of the evidence which has reached Sir Ahlber in this matter has come from . . . irregular sources," she said, and saw the flicker of understanding in the others' eyes. "Irregular sources" were code words for information provided by the network of *seijins* all of the House of Ahrmahk's closest councilors now knew reported to her and Cayleb regularly. "The information was delivered to me first, and I handed it to Sir Ahlber with a specific injunction to keep his inquiries as confidential as possible and to share his investigators' findings solely with me until we'd confirmed enough of that information to feel confident of its reliability. I apologize for instructing him to keep you in the dark, My Lord, but I felt it was essential to make that determination before allowing any hint of my suspicions to spread any further than was absolutely unavoidable. While I trust everyone seated in this council chamber implicitly, there's little point pretending Mountain Heart—and certain other parties—don't have sympathizers and informants scattered more widely than any of us might prefer."

Stoneheart looked at her for a moment longer, then nodded.

"Point taken, Your Majesty," he said a bit heavily. "I apologize for my tone, Ahlber."

"No need, My Lord." Zhustyn smiled wryly. "I imagine I'd've been a little irritated myself if the positions had been reversed."

"Perhaps so," White Crag said. "Now that the matter's

been broached, however, Your Majesty, might we know just what Mountain Heart and the others are up to?"

Cataracts had turned the white-haired first councilor's blue eyes a misty shade of gray, but they could still be disconcertingly sharp, Sharleyan observed.

"Sir Ahlber?" she invited.

"Of course, Your Majesty." Zhustyn squared his shoulders. "At this time, My Lords, we have no definite or admissible evidence of wrongdoing on their parts. Without an official warrant from the Lord Justice, we can't legally intercept any of their letters, and I have reason to believe"—he deliberately avoided Stoneheart's eyes—"that even if we *were* to intercept any of their correspondence they'd probably be expressing themselves in sufficiently circumspect terms to deny us any actionable evidence."

"Oh, I'm quite certain they'd be 'circumspect' in any discussions they might be holding, although I quite understand that all of this is pure speculation at this point." Stoneheart's tone was so dry Sharleyan's lips twitched involuntarily. But the lord justice went on. "If, however, they weren't being circumspect—or if, Langhorne forbid, you *should* find yourself, through no fault of your own, in a position to, ah . . . *examine* the personal correspondence of peers of the realm without having first obtained a warrant from me and Her Majesty—what sorts of things might they be discussing, do you think?"

"The state of the Kingdom and the Empire, My Lord," Zhustyn replied. "And of their responsibility to protect and preserve the Kingdom."

"Not the *Empire*?" White Crag said softly.

"No, My Lord."

"And I feel sure their definition of protecting and preserving the Kingdom would have quite a lot to do with preserving the nobility's role as a check on the overweening ambitions of the Crown," Stoneheart suggested.

"I feel confident they wouldn't allow themselves such disrespectful adjectives as 'overweening,' My Lord, but you've grasped the essential thrust of their discussion, I believe."

"That's . . . worrisome, Your Majesty," Saint Howan said into the silence which followed the spymaster's reply. "Especially after we send almost all the rest of the Army to Siddarmark when the transports get here next month."

"I can't escape the suspicion that the Army's deployment schedule has quite a bit to do with the emergence of this correspondence, My Lord," Sharleyan observed almost whimsically. "So far there's no evidence—or there *wouldn't* be any evidence if we were actually able to examine their correspondence, I mean—that any of them have entered into discussions with the guilds about the impact of importing Charisian manufactory methods, though. Not yet, at any rate. And without being able to count on at least some support from an influential segment of the Commons, they'd be fools to attempt any sort of open action against the Crown. Rock Coast and Black Horse, unfortunately, have demonstrated that they're quite capable of *being* fools, but Mountain Heart's a lot more cautious than they are, and Dragon Hill's too isolated from the others to cherish any illusions about what would happen to him in an open confrontation. I'm afraid Swayle is the real threat at the moment. Countess Swayle's bitterness over what happened to her husband is likely to push her into something . . . intemperate. Especially with Rydach getting behind that bitterness and pushing."

"All the more reason to arrange an accident for him, Your Majesty," Stoneheart growled, and the cold-blooded, pragmatic ruler in Sharleyan agreed wholeheartedly.

Rebkah Rahskail, the Dowager Countess of Swayle, would never forgive Sharleyan for her traitorous husband's execution, and Zhordyn Rydach, her Chihirite confessor, was a past master at playing upon that bitterness. Removing him from the equation would probably simplify things, but she couldn't be sure of that. Rydach was a careful man; even if she'd been prepared to sanction his assassination out of hand—which she wasn't . . . yet—managing it in a way which didn't strike the dowager countess as highly suspicious would be difficult. And if Rebkah decided the Crown had ordered the murder of her beloved and trusted confessor, it was more likely to push her into precipitate action than to cause her to rethink her position.

"I follow your reasoning, Sylvyst," she said, speaking even more informally than was her wont. "I think it might be better to take a page from the way we dealt with Swayle and Zebediah the first time around, though."

"Give them enough rope, you mean, Your Majesty?" White Crag said.

"Essentially." Sharleyan nodded. "Now that Ahlber's actively monitoring the situation, and bearing in mind the input we may yet receive from those irregular sources, they're unlikely to surprise us. And, to be honest, I'd prefer to deal with the situation without giving any of the other great nobles cause to think the Crown may be looking in *their* directions. I'm entirely confident of the loyalty of the East and of the extreme West, and I'd like to keep it that way. So from my perspective, the ideal solution would be to catch only one or two of them actively conspiring against the Crown. Make an example of them— one none of the other great nobles could argue is anything but an open-and-shut case—and then quietly use any damning evidence of . . . tangential involvement with the plotters to convince someone like Mountain Heart to be even more reasonable about something like river tolls."

All four of her councilors sat back in their chairs, their expressions intent, and Sharleyan could almost physically hear the thoughts ticking through the brains behind those narrowed eyes. What she was proposing could be a risky game, especially with virtually the entire Imperial Charisian Army (which just happened to include the entirety of the old Royal Chisholmian Army) off fighting in Siddarmark. But if she could pull it off, pinch out one or two of the most dangerous—and restive—members of the nobility and use the same opportunity to call others to heel. . . .

"It's a bold notion, Your Majesty," White Crag said finally. "One that rather reminds me of your father and Baron Green Mountain, as a matter of fact." The first councilor smiled in memory. "I'm sure you can see the possible downsides even more clearly than I do, but if it works—and especially if it works without becoming general knowledge—the advantages would certainly be considerable."

"I agree," Stoneheart said firmly, and Saint Howan simply nodded.

"In that case, we'll proceed with it until and unless something causes us to reconsider our options," Sharleyan said. "In the meantime, I'd like to take a look at the manufactory site negotiations in Eastshare and Terayth. I know we'd all like to spread those sites as broadly as we can, but I'm still pleased by how well Duke Eastshare's representatives and Earl Terayth have responded. It seems to me—"

AUGUST, YEAR OF GOD 896

✦

Cahnyr Kaitswyrth glared at the map spread across the wall of his river barge office. There were enough red pins in that map to make it look as if it were bleeding, and each of them indicated a spot where the Army of Glacierheart had lost men to one heretic ambush after another.

His jaw tightened at the thought, because the truth was that it was the *Army of Glacierheart* that was bleeding, not the Shan-wei damned map. Every one of those pins represented a half-dozen infantrymen ambushed here, two dozen over there, and a score of cavalry cut down by a storm of fire from riflemen, invisible until the instant they squeezed their triggers as they cantered along the high road in yet another spot, far behind his forward pickets.

And all for nothing. The thought grated its way through his brain. *We don't know any more about that bastard Eastshare's deployments than we knew when we started. And there's no way in Shan-wei's darkest hell I'm going to get artillery around to close the river behind him.*

His teeth ached from the pressure of his jaw muscles as he remembered the one patrol he had gotten clear to the riverbank behind the heretics' position. In retrospect, it was obvious the heretics had known all about the "unguarded ravine" one of his patrols had survived long enough to discover. He reminded himself not to ascribe omniscience to his enemies, but the patrol which had found the gully had gotten far deeper than anyone else and then out again without a shot fired. It was possible the heretics hadn't deliberately let them in . . . but they'd certainly been waiting when he pushed a regiment through that same ravine to secure a lodgment for his guns. That was when he'd found out for certain that Eastshare did, indeed, have the invisible cannon Wyrshym had reported from the Sylmahn Gap. The heretics had moored three barges opposite the point at which the ravine intersected the Daivyn, and those three barges had been packed with field guns and whatever it was they used to launch shells on those steep, arching trajectories to explode overhead and shower their victims with shrapnel balls. Of the four hundred and seventy men he'd sent down the ravine, eighty-six had made it back to the Army of Glacierheart's lines, a quarter of them wounded, and they'd been hunted and harassed by those damned vanishing riflemen every step of the way.

And then there was the probe he'd sent up the high road toward Haidyrberg only to have it ram straight into its own fiendish ambush twenty miles south of the town. He still didn't have any official name for the explosive devices the heretics were using. He'd taken care to avoid officially learning that his men had christened them "Kauyungs" in honor of the most infamous explosion in the history of the universe, since his army's Inquisitors found the name as offensive as it was blasphemous, but it was also more apt than they (or he) liked to admit. It was as if the heretics could put shrapnel shells wherever they wanted and make them explode on cue, but all the shrapnel went in one direction. A handful of his scouts had survived to bring back a half-dozen curved iron plates that seemed to be part of whatever it was, but that brought him no closer to understanding how the things worked. And, unfortunately, whatever those were, they weren't the *only* demonspawn device Shan-wei or Kau-yung had taught the heretics to build.

The column he'd sent to Haidyrberg had paused, understandably enough, when it encountered the entrenchment clear across the high road, bristling with still more of the heretic artillery. It had deployed to either side of the roadbed, sending infantry forward through the thick trees, using the woodland for cover against the enemy guns. That was when they'd discovered that in addition to the explosive man-killers they'd already encountered, the heretics had still more of them which could be buried in the very ground men walked upon. They hadn't been shy about filling the woods beyond the Shan-wei spawned things with more of their accursed riflemen, either. He'd lost upward of three hundred men in that particular misadventure, and when his senior division commander on the spot had thrown a column straight down the road instead, trying to carry the entrenchment at the point of the bayonet, the casualty total had tripled.

I need information, the bishop militant thought almost desperately. *I have to know what we're up against before I go charging forward blindly. But every time I try to get information, all I manage to is to lose more men.*

He forced his jaw to relax, inhaled deeply, and turned his back upon the map. He looked out a porthole, instead, clasping his hands behind him and watching the setting sun turn the Daivyn's waters into a dazzling highway of gold. A highway barred and locked by the heretic duke and his damnable army.

Another beautiful campaigning day spent sitting on my arse, he thought moodily. *There aren't that many days left, and the Grand Inquisitor won't be very pleased if we can't find a way to make use of the ones we still have.*

He thought about his latest conference with Sedryk Zavyr, the Army of Glacierheart's special intendant. The Schuelerite upper-priest was twelve years younger than he himself was and, technically, far junior to him in Mother Church's hierarchy. Every churchman knew not all prelates had been created equal, however, and Zavyr was also Zhaspahr Clyntahn's personal representative, whereas Kaitswyrth had never aspired to a bishop's ring until the Jihad yanked him up from the ranks of the Temple Guard. He had few friends and no allies in the upper ranks of the episcopate, and even someone far better connected than he was would have had ample cause to fear the Grand Inquisitor's ire.

Besides, Vicar Zhaspahr's right, and you know it! he told himself harshly. *There's only one cure for heresy—the same one we gave those bastards of Stahntyn's after Aivahnstyn. Give the leaders to the Punishment, and the others will learn from their example. Langhorne! Even the leaders may repent before it's too late! And if they don't, anyone who raises his hand against God's own Archangels deserves whatever he gets.*

He was beginning to wonder if Captain General Maigwair saw things the same way, though. It was clear from Maigwair's dispatches that he expected Kaitswyrth to stand in place just as he did Wyrshym, but the Army of Glacierheart wasn't nearly as far up the creek as the Army of the Sylmahn. Wyrshym was over nine hundred miles from his last intact canal lock on East Wing Lake; Kaitswyrth had secure, unthreatened communications all the way from the Bay of Bess via the Charayan Canal and the Fairmyn River. Langhorne only knew how long he'd have the sole use of that supply line, but for now it was all his, and whatever Maigwair might think, Vicar Zhaspahr was absolutely right in the point he'd made to Father Sedryk in his private dispatches. If they took the pressure off the heretics—if Stohnar and his allies were able to knock the Army of God back purely onto the defensive—the heretics' morale would rebound disastrously from the shock the Sword of Schueler had inflicted upon it.

We had our boot on their throats! We'd pushed them back everywhere—everywhere! If we let them stop us in our tracks after that, all the momentum shifts to the other side. And Vicar Zhaspahr's right about whose side God's on, too! There comes a time when men who fight for Him have to trust Him to fight for them.

He scowled out at that gleaming, golden expanse of water, his hands clenched behind him. The Dohlarans hadn't expected to be called upon to supply the Army of Glacierheart, and he didn't much trust Dohlaran efficiency under any circumstances. Worse, all the supplies which had been headed up the Holy Langhorne Canal for the Army of Glacierheart would have to be turned around, shipped roundabout to the Gulf of Dohlar before they could travel up the Fairmyn to his present position. That meant he wasn't going to see much in the way of fresh ammunition or replacement soldiers before winter, but his delay here had allowed him to build up ample stocks of powder and shot, and at least the Dohlarans seemed capable of keeping food and fodder moving until the canals starting freezing up in late October. He'd have the mobility to exploit any victory if he could just punch Eastshare out of the way.

He turned away from the porthole, bending his glower upon the map once more, and knew what he had to do.

▼ ▼ ▼

"I don't like it, Father," Bishop Ahdrais Pohstazhian muttered as he stood gazing out into the gray, predawn mist. It wasn't the sort of remark many senior officers of the Army of God would make to their divisional intendants, but Pohstazhian and Father Isydohr Zoay were very much alike. Not physically—Pohstazhian was brown-haired, brown-eyed, and decidedly stocky, whereas Zoay was fair-haired, with gray eyes, thin, and a full head taller— but under the skin. They understood one another, and Pohstazhian knew Zoay wouldn't take him wrongly now.

"I'd prefer having a better idea of what we're about to run into myself, My Lord," the under-priest replied. He was four years older than Pohstazhian, which made him a bit old for his ecclesiastic rank, probably because he was more methodical and organized than brilliant. He was a fiery foe of the heresy, yet like Pohstazhian he preferred a clear plan before committing to battle.

"Unfortunately," he continued now, "Bishop Militant Cahnyr's right. We need to smash this heretic position before they can reinforce it further."

"Agreed. Agreed!" Pohstazhian waved one hand, as if

he could fan away the mist and see clearly. "And God knows we've got numbers enough to do the job, but it's going to cost like Shan-wei." He shook his head. "I don't think a full-fledged assault is what most people would think of as 'fighting for intelligence.'"

"We haven't been able to get it any other way," Zoay pointed out, and Pohstazhian stopped shaking his head and nodded grudgingly.

"I didn't say I see any better way to go about it. That doesn't mean I have to like doing it, though. Especially when I think of all the men who're going to be wounded or dead by afternoon."

"If all goes well the majority of them will be heretics," Zoay said grimly.

"If all goes well," Pohstazhian agreed.

▼ ▼ ▼

"Anytime now, My Lord," Colonel Maindayl said quietly at Cahnyr Kaitswyrth's elbow. Only someone who knew the Army of Glacierheart's chief of staff well would have recognized the anxiety in Maindayl's brown eyes as he peered down at his pocket watch, its hands gleaming golden in the lantern light.

"Assuming they kick off on time, anyway," Kaitswyrth replied sourly.

"Pohstazhian, Scovayl, and Waimyan all know their business, My Lord, and they'd've sent word if they expected to be delayed. They may be off a minute or two either way, but no more than that."

Kaitswyrth only grunted. It wasn't that he disagreed with Maindayl. After Bishop Gahrmyn's Chihiro Division, Khalryn Waimyan's Zion Division, Pohstazhian's Sulyvyn Division, and Tymahn Scovayl's Fyrgyrsyn Division were the three best he had, and Chihiro was still integrating replacements after that fiasco on the Haidyrberg Road, but that didn't make him any happier about what his own orders were about to demand of the men in those units. Plenty of his other divisions could follow where Zion, Sulyvyn, and Fyrgyrsyn led, but it was going to take something special to carry through against the heretics under these conditions. If anyone could do it, they would, whatever the cost, yet. . . .

The bishop militant shook his head. It was too late for second thoughts. They were committed, and in the next few minutes they'd be finding out if it could be done at all.

▼ ▼ ▼

"What was that?"

Platoon Sergeant Ruhfus Hahpkyns raised his head.

"Who asked that?!" he demanded in a harsh whisper. All of his men knew the importance of identifying whoever was speaking at a moment like this. Without that information precious minutes could be lost figuring out who saw what where, but even the most experienced could forget and—

"Me, Sarge," Private Bynzhamyn Makysak replied from his position ten yards farther down the parapet's fighting step. "Sorry."

"So what was what?" Hahpkyns asked, careful to keep his head below the top of the parapet as he moved quietly towards Makysak.

"I dunno." Makysak waved towards the northwest. "I heard *something* out there, but—"

A sudden explosion ripped through the misty, predawn gloom—a flash in the fog and a blast of thunder, followed an instant later by a chorus of screams. A moment later, there was another explosion—then another.

"Stand to!" Hahpkyns shouted. "Runner!"

"Here, Sarge."

"Leg it to the CP. Someone's in the sweepers in Sector Able!"

"Yes, Sarge!"

The runner disappeared up the communications trench, and Hahpkyns cocked and capped his Mahndrayn. He heard metal clicking all around him as the fifty-odd men of 1st Platoon, Company A, 1st Battalion, 5th Regiment, followed suit and then fixed bayonets, as well. There were more explosions—and more screams—out in front of their position, spreading from northwest to southwest like summer lightning, and he felt himself tighten internally.

The Temple Boys wouldn't be setting off that many sweepers across that much frontage unless there were Shan-wei's own lot of them out there!

"What do we have, Ruhfus?" a voice asked, and he turned his head as Lieutenant Styvyn Hylmyn, 1st Platoon's CO, climbed up on the firing step beside him to peer over the parapet. Hylmyn had been sound asleep two minutes earlier, but no one would have guessed it from looking at him.

"Damned if I know, Sir." Hahpkyns shook his head. "From the sound of it, though—"

"Point taken." Like Hahpkyns, Hylmyn was a Chisholmian, although he was barely half the platoon sergeant's age. He was a large, athletic young man, intelligent without being anything someone might mistake for brilliant, but he had determination by the bargeload and an almost frightening level of energy. "Any word back from the CP yet?"

"No, Sir," Hahpkyns replied. "I'd guess Captain Carlsyn's kicking it up the line himself by about now."

"I imagine you're right." Hylmyn nodded, then clapped Hahpkyns on the shoulder. "Hold the fort till I get back."

"Yes, Sir," Hahpkyns said, and watched the lieutenant moving down the line, pausing just long enough to exchange a few words with each of the platoon's squads. From the sound of the explosions, he'd better hurry if he expected to get back before the ball opened.

▼ ▼ ▼

Ahdrais Pohstazhian swore softly and venomously as the "Kau-yungs'" explosions—and the shrieks—came back out of the drifting veils of mist. He and his command group followed in the interval between his second and third regiments, and he had his own suspicion about how the heretics managed their infernal devices. No one in the Army of Glacierheart had yet figured out for certain how the heretics' new rifles worked. Not officially, at least. But one of Pohstazhian's junior officers had suggested that the copper caps they'd captured in the heretics' redoubts might be filled with something like fulminated mercury. Pasquale's injunctions warned about the dangers of such substances, but that was unlikely to deter a pack of Shan-wei worshippers, and according to the lieutenant, a sharp blow would cause something like that to explode, probably more reliably than a flintlock's sparks. But if it could be used to ignite powder charges for *rifles*, there wasn't any reason it couldn't ignite something else, and if Pohstazhian had been the heretics, he would've used some kind of trip wire and a simple striking mechanism to trigger their shrapnel-spewing explosions. He'd shared that suspicion with his company commanders before they started out, but in this kind of light terrain, the only reliable way to find a trip wire was to step on it.

He passed a windrow of bodies. Two were still writhing, and someone in the green armband of a Pasqualate was working on them. His mouth tightened, yet at least there were only six of them. That was a paltry harvest from one of the Kau-yungs, and he felt a little better at the evidence that his advancing troops were staying properly spread out, denying the explosions compact, concentrated targets.

We'll have to close up again once we come up against their main entrenchments, he reflected grimly. *The heretics're likely to shoot hell out of us while we form up, but at least most of the boys ought to still be on their feet when we do.*

▼ ▼ ▼

The senior officers of Cahnyr Kaitswyrth's army had done their best to evolve a workable approach, but their options had been unpalatable, for the Army of God had little of the Royal Chisholmian Army's decades of institutional experience. The Temple Guard from which so many AOG officers sprang had been primarily a peacekeeping force which no one in the world would have dreamed of attacking. As a result, it had been unaccustomed to thinking in the sort of terms in which professional *army* officers might think, which meant it had lacked the sort of baseline assumptions from which the new Imperial Charisian Army had begun. Worse—and even though the AOG's officers were intelligent, for the most part, and had considered as many implications of the new model weapons as carefully as they could—they'd been able to allow only for the threats they knew about. No one had warned them about breech-loading rifles, landmines, claymores, or percussion caps, and no one could plan intelligently to deal with something they didn't know existed.

They'd learned the hard way, storming Brigadier Taisyn's redoubts, just how deadly rifle fire could be to troops crossing a cleared kill zone, and they knew that unlike Taisyn's small, forlorn hope of a force, every one of Eastshare's infantrymen was rifle-armed. They might not yet have fully realized the open field implications of breech-loading, but they'd known they didn't want to advance in line or column in the open through difficult terrain against a heavily fortified position packed with thousands of waiting rifles. They'd tried desperately to find a way to avoid attacking that position at all; unfortunately, their efforts to find a way around 1st Brigade had proved fruitless, thanks in no small part to 1st and 2nd Battalion, 1st Scout Sniper Regiment, and their endlessly inventive ambushes. Almost worse, they had no real doctrine for reconnaissance in the first place, since pre-Jihad engagement ranges had been so short that Mainland armies had never required the sort of scouting Charisian scout snipers were trained to provide. They'd simply marched up to one another, paused outside matchlock or arbalest range, looked the situation over, and then either attacked or marched away again.

That procedure, unfortunately, was no longer applicable, given rifles and the range of new model field artillery.

Engineering officers with spyglasses in titan oaks had been able to construct sketch maps of the terrain between their own positions and the Charisian entrenchments on the far side of the old forest fire scar. In the face of the dense overgrowth of saplings and wire vine which had conquered the blackened clearing in the half dozen or so years since the fire, however, those sketch maps could tell an attacker very little about the actual topography. There was simply no way for the men who'd produced them to actually *see* the hollows and ravines hidden in all that greenery, and the Charisians had made skillful use of the high ground when they planned their entrenchments. Kaitswyrth's engineers had been able to see enough of the Charisian position to find spots where the defensive fire would hopefully be less intense, less concentrated, than in others, and they'd been able to map a depressing number of well-dug-in field pieces, but they'd been completely unable to locate the scores of infernal devices hidden amid that under-growth. Not just the "sweepers" they'd encountered else-where, either. There were also pressure-detonated surface mines—"Shan-wei's footstools," to the Charisians who'd emplaced them—and, even worse, a bounding mine pro-pelled to waist height by an explosive charge before it detonated, spraying shrapnel balls in a three-hundred-sixty-degree pattern. Christened "Shan-wei's fountains," or simply "fountains," they were almost as lethal as the sweepers. The shrapnel patterns were less dense, but they were also omnidirectional; men who'd managed to get past them without triggering one of the trip wires could still be killed when someone behind them was less fortunate.

Kaitswyrth had recognized the risk of sending men forward in visibility so bad it virtually *guaranteed* none of them would see the infernal devices waiting for them, but he had badly underestimated the *density* of the minefields awaiting his columns. Again, that was largely a matter of inexperience, since no one in Safehold's en-tire history had ever encountered a defensive position like this one. Yet even if he'd known exactly how many men he'd lose to the heretics' "Kau-yungs," that only brought him back to those unpalatable alternatives. He could try to get his men close enough to assault the en-emy positions in visibility poor enough to give them at least some protection from the withering rifle and artillery fire he knew would be forthcoming, or he could attack under conditions which gave those men at least a chance of spotting the mines waiting for them. He couldn't accomplish both, and so he'd chosen to take his chances with the mines.

Not that he hadn't tried to have it as *close* to both ways as he could. Dense morning mist was more common than not along the Daivyn at this time of year, and that had offered the possibility of bridging the gap between a night assault and a dawn attack while still giving his infantrymen at least a chance to spot trip wires during their approach.

▼ ▼ ▼

The Duke of Eastshare stood atop his command bunker, gazing into the west as the red and white flowers of exploding landmines ripped holes in the darkness. He knew they were ripping holes in the Church's infantry, too, and he showed his teeth as he watched them inching closer. He and Major Lowayl had far fewer of them than they would have preferred, but the ones they did have had proved even more effective than anyone had hoped. So far, at least. Ruhsyl Thairis wasn't going to make the mistake of underestimating his enemies' adaptability. Once enough of them had survived to realize what the sweepers, footstools, and fountains were and how they worked, they'd begin to evolve techniques to minimize their effectiveness.

Of course, there's only so much adaptability can do about some problems, he reminded himself. *And whatever these bastards may be able to do in the* future, *at the moment they can't do squat.*

The thought pleased him immensely whenever he thought about what had happened to Mahrtyn Taisyn and his men on this very river less than a month before. There wasn't a fire in Shan-wei's Hell hot enough for the men who'd massacred and tortured not only Taisyn's men but General Charlz Stahntyn's entire Aivahnstyn garrison.

We can only hope at least some of Clyntahn's damned inquisitors are close to the front. Not that I wouldn't mind watching a few of them hang as a post-battle celebration. Preferably over a nice plate of fried potato slices and a stein of beer.

A general in the Imperial Charisian Army wasn't supposed to think that way, and the Church of Charis would not have approved of approaching the execution even of inquisitors with such burning anticipation. The policy was set, and those inquisitors *would* be summarily executed, but Cayleb and Sharleyan Ahrmahk weren't Zhaspahr Clyntahn and the ICA wasn't his Inquisition. It would do what it must without exulting in the doing or wallowing in blood vengeance, and that was an end of it.

As a theoretical and philosophical proposition, East-share fully agreed, and he'd made damned sure it was the official policy of his brigade. But he wasn't going to pretend in the privacy of his own thoughts, and so he watched those savage pinpricks of brilliance blaze in the misty dark with a stony lack of expression and rejoiced.

▼ ▼ ▼

"Well, Raymahndoh?" Ahdrais Pohstazhian asked harshly as Colonel Allykzhandro turned back to him from the runner.

"From Colonel Kahlyns, Sir." Allykzhandro's voice was grim. "His men've encountered two new sorts of Kau-yungs." The Sulyvyn Division's executive officer glanced semi-apologetically at Isydohr Zoay as he used the un-sanctioned term, but the Schuelerite only waved for him to continue. "One sounds like the buried ones Bishop Gahrmyn's men encountered near Haidyrberg, but the other sort seems to jump up into the air before it ex-plodes." Allykzhandro shook his head. "Colonel Kahlyns estimates he's lost more than a third of his men already."

Pohstazhian's jaw clenched and he inhaled deeply. Zhandru Kahlyns' 1st Regiment was his leading formation—the men who'd been clearing the heretics' infernal devices with their own bodies and blood.

"We knew we'd take losses," he said. "And the natural thing is to overestimate casualties at a time like this."

Allykzhandro nodded, although Pohstazhian suspected the XO was as unconvinced that Kahlyns was overestimating anything as he was himself. Not that either of them could do anything about it . . . except collect payment in blood from the heretics when they carried those accursed entrenchments.

"Have we heard anything from Fahstyr?" he asked. Bahzwail Fahstyr commanded Sulyvyn Division's 3rd Regiment, following directly behind Kahlyns.

"He's lost some men," Allykzhandro said, "but nowhere near as many as First Regiment."

"Good. Thank Chihiro *something*'s working the way it's supposed to!" Pohstazhian said, then shook his head as he realized what he'd said. "God forgive me," he muttered, and Zoay rested a hand lightly on his shoulder.

"I don't like it any more than you do." The divisional intendant's soft words were punctuated by still more explosions—and screams—out of the gradually brightening mist. "I imagine any war is hard, but the Jihad is hardest of all. You do what you have to do in God's name."

Pohstazhian nodded, but his heart was a stone in his chest. He was using up Kahlyns' men deliberately, sacrificing them simply to clear a path for his other regiments. He had no doubt Zoay was correct . . . and he knew that wouldn't help the guilt he'd see in his own eyes the next time he looked into a mirror.

▼ ▼ ▼

"They're almost into the last belt of fountains, Sir."

Platoon Sergeant Hahpkyns' tone couldn't have been more respectful, Lieutenant Hylmyn reflected, but there was no missing his point.

"No doubt we'll be able to see something sometime soon, Ruhfus," he said soothingly. "I'm sure the Duke would appreciate our waiting until we can actually see what we're using up perfectly good cartridges on, though. Less wasteful that way, don't you think?"

"Yes, Sir."

The noncom turned away to discuss the platoon's readiness with Private Makysak, who happened to be engaged in earnest conversation with one of his squad mates instead of watching his own front at that unfortunate moment, and Hylmyn smiled. He had no intention of ever admitting just how comforting he'd found Ruhfus Hahpkyns' rock-like, experienced steadiness, but it was actually a little reassuring when the platoon sergeant allowed a bit of his own nervousness to show. Not that anyone else was likely to realize that was what he'd just done, of course.

And not that Ahbygayl Hylmyn's little boy Styv wouldn't be far happier himself when Duke Eastshare got around to passing the word.

Of course, he told himself, *as you just reminded Ruhfus, it would help if you had targets you could actually* see. *Suppose it's possible that's what the Duke and Colonel Celahk're waiting for, too?*

Hylmyn never noticed the way the runner standing at his shoulder relaxed as he heard his lieutenant's chuckle through the backdrop of exploding mines.

▼ ▼ ▼

Colonel Stywyrt Sahndhaim, commanding Zion Division's 1st Regiment, swore as the crest of the heretic entrenchments etched itself against the red disk of a rising sun. The parapet rose from the undergrowth like some ominous, mist-shrouded mountain range, made far more ominous by what he and his division had experienced storming the heretic redoubts farther upriver. He knew what waited on the other side of that raw earth—or he thought he did, at least—and he wished fervently that he didn't.

His regiment had advanced side-by-side with Zhandru Kahlyns', losing dozens of men to the heretics' diabolical Kau-yungs, and his mouth was dry at the thought of what was about to happen to the men who'd survived that ordeal.

"Stand ready!" he barked and heard a dozen other

voices rippling away from him, passing on the warning no one in the Army of Glacierheart was actually likely to need.

▼ ▼ ▼

"Open fire!" Hylmyn barked as the mist retreated in golden billows and the advancing waves of men in the Army of God's purple and red stepped out of the thinning tendrils.

"*Open fire!*" Ruhfus Hahpkyns echoed, and fifty Mahndrayns spewed fire as one. The muzzle flashes were blinding, despite the strengthening dawn. They crowned the line of the entrenchments in flame, like the flare of Langhorne's own Rakurai, and the storm front of brilliance rolled away to either hand as the other platoons of Colonel Allayn Hobsyn's 5th Regiment, detached from the 2nd Division's 3rd Brigade to reinforce 1st Brigade, opened fire as well.

▼ ▼ ▼

Unlike the Army of God, the Imperial Charisian Army had abandoned the concept of volley fire. Their breechloading Mahndrayns fired three times as rapidly as muzzleloaders, and they'd been trained to fire as individuals and to pick their own targets. Fifth Regiment had three of its four battalions in the front line. That was just over three thousand rifles, each firing once every five seconds, and 1st Brigade had deployed three regiments to man its fortifications.

A solid sheet of flame from almost ten thousand rifles sleeted over the crest of those entrenchments, so heavy any observer might have been forgiven for thinking it *was* a single volley. But it was far more devastating than any blind-fired volley could ever have been, and the men behind those rifles knew exactly who and what their targets were. The ghosts of Mhartyn Taisyn's slaughtered command stood at their shoulders, and there was no mercy in them.

▼ ▼ ▼

Colonel Sahndhaim cringed as he discovered he'd been wrong. His worst estimate of what awaited his men hadn't come remotely close to the reality. Brigadier Tai-syn had commanded less than four thousand men, half of them pikemen, and they'd been deployed in half a dozen separate redoubts, not concentrated the way *these* riflemen were. They'd savaged the columns sweeping up the hillsides to assault their entrenchments, but they hadn't had the numbers to simply *annihilate* those columns.

First Brigade's regiments did.

Sahndhaim heard the screams, the incredulous curses, of men who'd survived all the way through the heretics' Kau-yungs as that whirlwind of gunpowder and lead crashed over them. His leading companies disintegrated into bodies and blood, and the scattered survivors discovered that not even the deepest faith could survive *some* shocks. It was less fear than sheer astonishment, Sahndhaim thought, yet the result was the same. The toughest-minded raised their rifles and fired back into the face of that tempest, fired at the men who were killing them—men they couldn't even see behind the solid earthen parapets and the rippling wave of fire and the choking cloud of smoke spewing from the heretics' muzzles—but they were the exception. The others—the pitiful handful of others—simply turned and ran.

"Stand!" Sahndhaim heard the command from the surviving officers and noncoms. "*Stand*, Schueler curse you! *Stand!*"

His own voice was shouting the same command. It didn't matter, and he couldn't blame the men bolting away from that holocaust. He knew what they'd already paid in blood and courage to come this far, and they'd grasped what was waiting for them no more clearly than he had himself. Now they knew, and it was simply too much.

His second and third companies advanced into the teeth of their fleeing comrades with fixed bayonets and faces of stone. The refugees parted around them and Sahndhaim heard the bugles sounding as the Holy

Bédard Division advanced on their heels. Major Dahnel Howail, 1st Regiment's executive officer, appeared out of the confusion, face and tunic splashed with someone else's blood, eyes blazing with fury and shame as he watched half the regiment disappear.

"Rally them if you can, Dahnel!" Sahndhaim ordered, pointing to the rear.

"But, Sir—!"

"Don't argue! *Do* it!" Sahndhaim seized the younger man's shoulder and shook him. "I've got something else to do!"

"But, Sir, you can't—!" Howail protested even more vehemently.

"*Go!*" Sahndhaim half threw the major towards the rear, then beckoned to the regimental standardbearer and thrust his way into the pale-faced column of Captain Gahvyn Taylar's 3rd Company. He showed his teeth, fighting to hide his own despair, as he reached his right hand out to the standardbearer. He took the banner from the color sergeant, holding the staff in both hands, waving it over his head, and looked around him.

"Who's with me, boys?!" he shouted. For an instant he thought his men were too shaken to respond, but only for an instant. Then a hard, angry sound—not a cheer, but something an infuriated slash lizard might have produced—came back to him. It lashed him like a powerful wind, foaming in his blood, gilding his despair with a sort of maddened elation.

"All right, then!" He waved the banner again, feeling it stream out, silk snapping in the wind. "*Holy Langhorne and no quarter!*"

"*No quarter!*" his company bellowed, and they charged.

▼ ▼ ▼

"All right, Hynryk." Eastshare glanced at the brown-haired, brown-eyed Old Charisian standing beside him, listening to the roar of rifle fire. "I believe we can assume they're close enough. Open fire anytime you're ready."

"Yes, Your Grace!" Colonel Hynryk Celahk touched his chest in salute, his smile clearly visible as the rising sun turned the rolling waves of smoke to gold in front of them. He'd been waiting literally from the moment 1st Brigade dug in for that order, and he turned to his aide. "You heard the Duke, Wahltayr!"

"Yes, Sir!"

The lieutenant saluted in turn, struck a Shan-wei's candle, and lit the fuse.

▼ ▼ ▼

Ahdrais Pohstazhian's head jerked up as something arced into the sky. He couldn't hear a thing over the cacophony of musketry, and for a moment his mind was blank. Then he realized it had to be another of the "rockets" the heretics used to pass signals, and his stomach tightened. He had no idea what this one was a signal *for,* but he was certain he wasn't going to like it.

He didn't.

▼ ▼ ▼

Each of 1st Brigade's forty-eight companies had its own attached support platoon, each with six three-inch mortars. The brigade as a whole was assigned an organic artillery battalion, with thirty-two twelve-pounders, and two batteries of six-inch angle-guns had been attached to it before it ever sailed for the Mainland. In Siddar City, it had been mated with sixty-four more twelve-pounders and sixteen four-inch muzzle-loading rifles. Ten batteries of field guns—just over two-thirds of 1st Brigade's total—and almost four hundred mortars had been dug in along the line of Eastshare's entrenched position, with carefully planned fields of fire. The Army of God engineers sketching the maps of those positions had spotted most of the eighty field guns; they hadn't even recognized the mortars for what they were. Nor had they been able to see the sixteen angle-guns dug in the next best thing to two miles behind the entrenchments, hidden by belts of untouched forest.

Which meant the Army of Glacierheart had no least

inkling of the fiery hurricane that much artillery could spawn.

When Hynryk Celahk's signal rocket exploded against the morning sky, it found out.

▼ ▼ ▼

Cahnyr Kaitswyrth's eyes went wide as a volcano erupted. The spreading, echoing crash of rifle fire had been bad enough, telling him at least a part of what his columns were advancing into. The runners headed for his position to tell him how much more murderous than even his worst nightmares those rifles were had yet to reach him, but the crushing thunder of the Duke of Eastshare's massed artillery needed no runner. The ground seemed to quiver underfoot as eighty field guns fired in a single long, echoing bellow. It reached out from the center of the heretics' line, that bellow, spreading from the first battery to the last, and the shrapnel of its exploding shells scourged his bleeding regiments mercilessly. Yet for all their fury, all their thunder, the field guns were matched and overmatched by the hell-spawned canopy of mortar shells exploding overhead. It was as if some fiery cloud had spread its wings above his assaulting columns, and the cones of shrapnel shrieking down from it flayed flesh and bone with Shan-wei's own hatred.

▼ ▼ ▼

"I think that's enough, Hynryk," Eastshare said, twenty minutes later.

"Of course, Your Grace." It would have been unfair to call Colonel Celahk's response disappointed, although the duke couldn't think of a better adjective. He cocked his head at his artillery commander, his expression mildly inquiring, and Celahk grimaced. "Sorry, Your Grace."

"That's quite all right." Eastshare patted the artillerist on the shoulder. "And, trust me, my report will describe your guns' effectiveness in the most glowing terms possible. But we don't have an unlimited supply of ammunition and I don't imagine there are very many of them left out there for you to kill. So if you don't mind—?"

"Of course, Your Grace." This time it came out with a chuckle, and Eastshare grinned as Celahk turned back to Lieutenant Sahndyrs.

"Time for another rocket, Wahltayr," the colonel said.

. II .
The Temple,
City of Zion,
The Temple Lands

"And what do *you* think Kaitswyrth thought he was doing?" Rhobair Duchairn asked sourly.

The vicar on the other side of the table glanced around, as if instinctively checking to be certain there were no purple cassocks in earshot. There weren't. The small but comfortable—as all Temple offices were comfortable—chamber was tucked away in Duchairn's territory in the Treasury Wing. Schuelerites found remarkably cool welcome in the Treasury these days, and Duchairn's power remained sufficient to prevent the Office of the Inquisition from insisting on openly stationing spies to look over his assistants' shoulders. Of course, one could never be sure in the Temple. There were those persistent rumors that the Archangel Schueler had left the Inquisition the ability to listen to conversations anywhere in the vast, mystic structure. Duchairn didn't believe it, though. If it were true, Zhaspahr Clyntahn would already have slaughtered far more of his fellow vicars than he had.

Yet, at least.

On the other hand, one needed no *official* agents inquisitor to track possible opponents of the Jihad . . . or the Grand Inquisitor. For all he knew, a dozen of his Chihirites and Langhornites might be eyes and ears of the Inquisition. In fact, he could take it as a given that at least some of them were, so perhaps his guest's paranoia was reasonable, even if the two of them were alone. However—

"I'm not entirely sure," Allayn Maigwair replied after a moment. Duchairn's eyebrows rose, and the Church of God Awaiting's Captain General shrugged. "That Kaitswyrth *was* thinking, I mean," he added acidly.

"Oh."

Duchairn felt his lips twitch, remembering a time not so very long ago when Maigwair would have been far less assertive. A time when he'd run at Clyntahn's heels like a faithful course lizard, too terrified of the Grand Inquisitor to risk anything that might have sounded even remotely critical of him or one of his favorites. And both of them knew Cahnyr Kaitswyrth was one of Clyntahn's favorites.

Or had been, anyway. That might have become subject to change.

"I thought," the Treasurer continued, "that we'd all agreed it was time to stand on the defensive until we could get the canals repaired."

"So did I." Maigwair's expression was sour, but then he shook his head unwillingly. "At the same time, Zhaspahr *was* right about Kaitswyrth's immediate supply situation. I hadn't realized just how much had stacked up along the canal behind him. I'm not saying the fact that he was better supplied than we thought he was justified ramming his head into a hornets' nest that way, but if we were going to take the offensive anywhere, that was probably the best place."

"Really?" The one-word question dripped irony, and Maigwair flushed.

"I didn't say it was a *good* place, Rhobair. I only said that if we were going to do something stupid, it was the *best* place." He shrugged angrily. "Given that we're talking about Kaitswyrth and that Zhaspahr insisted on assigning Zavyr as his intendant, we're probably lucky we didn't get hurt any worse than we did!"

Duchairn was forced to nod. Judging by the preliminary reports, they probably *were* lucky their casualties hadn't been still worse. Or, at least, any worse than they thought they had so far. The jury was still out on how bad their final losses truly had been, and they probably wouldn't know the true toll for a few five-days yet, when something like a final report came in from Aivahnstyn.

That was now the Army of Glacierheart's headquarters, courtesy of the counterattacks the heretical Duke of Eastshare had launched after repulsing Kaitswyrth's catastrophic assault, and that headquarters was apparently finding it difficult to tally its losses at this point. Even if Kaitswyrth was willing to report them honestly, he probably didn't know what they were yet. But the numbers they did have were bad enough. Even before the heretics' counterattacks, the Army of God's blind, headlong assault had cost it the equivalent of seven full divisions—over thirteen thousand in dead, wounded, or prisoners—to the heretics' "Kau-yungs" (and *how* Clyntahn had howled when he'd heard *that* name!), rifles, and—especially—artillery.

It was the sheer weight of the artillery which had broken the assault's back. That much was obvious from the most preliminary reports . . . and it seemed equally clear the sheer shock of encountering that holocaust had broken the Army of Glacierheart's morale, as well. That was the only explanation anyone could come up with, at any rate, and it made sense to Duchairn. Men were still men; even those most willing to die for God's victory must hesitate to die when they knew victory was beyond them despite all valor might do. That was a truth Zhaspahr would do well to remember, however unpalatable he found it. Duchairn was no warrior, yet it seemed obvious to him that the assault's catastrophic losses, combined with the rumors of what had happened along the canals and rivers behind the Army of the Sylmahn—and in the Gap itself—must have had a stunning effect on Kaitswyrth's army.

Something had, at any rate, given the way that army's left flank had crumpled—"dissolved" was probably a better word—before the heretics' attack out of Haidyrberg.

The flank commander hadn't even *tried* to hold his ground, despite an entrenched position and superior numbers, for which Sedryk Zavyr had demanded—and gotten—his head *and* the head of his intendant. And while the rot might have started on the Haidyrberg High Road, it certainly hadn't stopped there.

Kaitswyrth had attempted to shift forces from the center to reinforce his flank, only to have the heretics, whose lookouts had apparently been watching his deployment from their perches high in the titan oaks, drive a wedge of steel and fire into the position he'd weakened. The fire of those terrible, long-ranged cannon—the ones Wyrshym had reported from the Sylmahn Gap—had pounded the entrenchments' depleted garrisons, but far worse had been the lighter, portable cannon the heretics brought forward with them. Their individual shells were far smaller, and they had much less range, but they also fired far more rapidly and detonated reliably in midair, deluging their targets with shrapnel. And they had another advantage, one Duchairn suspected was even more valuable than their rate of fire or the superiority of the heretics' fuses. Their portability meant they could be carried immediately behind the enemy's advancing troops, close enough for them to be directed onto their targets as needed. That let them deliver fire far more flexibly than field guns could, and their arcing trajectories meant they could be deployed out of sight, in hollows in the ground or behind walls or hillsides, to pour in their fire with impunity.

The infantry tactics Wyrshym had described from the Sylmahn Gap had played their part, as well, as soon as the Army of Glacierheart's front began to crumble. The heretics' disregard for normal firing lines appeared to have served them in good stead once Mother Church's forward regiments started giving way. The dense forest behind the hard crust of the Army of God's entrenchments must have been a smoke-shrouded nightmare for officers trying to form line with rifles and pikes, stabbed through by the flash of heretic rifles and illuminated by thunderbolts of shrapnel from above, and the heretics had flowed through the trees to filter remorselessly around their flanks, probing for openings.

They'd found them, too. They'd punched all the way forward to the Haidyrberg High Road to link up with the column advancing into the Army of Glacierheart's rear, and Kaitswyrth had been left no option but to order a general withdrawal before they could reach the river behind his center and cut off any retreat for two-thirds of his army. He'd been forced back along the Daivyn for almost a hundred miles, losing men the entire way, but once he'd finally been clear of the unconsecrated forest, he'd been able to deploy his own infantry and remaining artillery far more effectively. That had slowed the heretics' advance, and he'd used the respite to get labor parties busy farther in his own rear. By the time he'd been pushed back halfway to Aivahnstyn, his new fortifications had been ready, this time with much heavier overhead protection against the rain of shrapnel from those portable infantry cannon, and the heretics had declined to press home a fresh attack upon them. After all, why should they have? They'd driven the Army of Glacierheart clear back into Cliff Peak Province, and along the way they'd probably inflicted casualties greater than their own beginning strength. They'd certainly shattered the *confidence* of Kaitswyrth's army, at any rate. Not even its intendants were going to be able to motivate its battered, tattered divisions to take the offensive again anytime soon. For that matter, Duchairn strongly suspected that Zavyr's confidential reports to Clyntahn told a dismal tale of his *intendants'* morale, given the rather pointed message the heretics had delivered directly to them.

Under the circumstances, it's a not-so-minor miracle Kaitswyrth's men are still capable of defending *themselves*, Duchairn thought bitterly. *And it doesn't bode well for next summer's campaign, either. Assuming there* is *a next summer's campaign.*

Which was rather the point of the present meeting.

"It looks like we're all learning as we go along," he said. "I wish Kaitswyrth had been more willing to learn from Wyrshym's example, but I suppose it's expecting too much for an army commander who's never encountered all these accursed new weapons to really understand what they mean without firsthand experience. And to be fair, Wyrshym never encountered those 'Kau-yungs,' so no matter how carefully he'd read Wyrshym's reports, he couldn't've known anything about them until Eastshare used them against *him*."

"You're probably right," Maigwair sighed. "It would've helped if he'd just followed orders, though. And he *had* encountered the Kau-yungs before he shoved that attack right down the heretics' throats. I *told* him—"

The Captain General waved one hand irritably, and Duchairn nodded. He'd had experience enough of the way in which Zhaspahr Clyntahn could twist and warp a situation until the people caught up in it did things his way. The Treasurer would have liked to tell himself that was how this entire catastrophe had come about, but he couldn't. In the beginning, Clyntahn had been only one member of the Group of Four, unable to simply decree the initial attack on Charis. They'd *agreed* with him, never realizing what they were about to launch or that they were going to effectively hand him the keys to the Temple, because they hadn't bothered to consider the implications of that agreement. Now all the world found itself forced to pay the price for their stupidity, and Kaitswyrth certainly hadn't had the stature to defy Clyntahn and his handpicked intendant if the other three members of the Group of Four didn't!

"Well, one thing's abundantly clear," he said. "With these *newest* new weapons, supply lines and our own weapons production just got even more critical."

"Agreed." Maigwair nodded emphatically. "That's why I had Kaitswyrth send some of the captured rifles to Gorath." Duchairn felt his eyebrow rising again, and the Captain General shrugged. "So far, the Dohlaran foundries have been the most efficient, outside the Temple Lands themselves. For that matter, with all due respect, I think they're actually more efficient even than ours are, and they've got the highest percentage of rifle-armed infantry in the field. If anyone's able to produce this new breech-loading design in large numbers, it's probably them."

"I imagine you're right," Duchairn admitted. "On the other hand, we're a lot more efficient than the Harchongians, and"—he smiled thinly—"we'll be taking over all the Harchongese foundries south of the Gulf of Dohlar by the end of September."

"*All* of them?" Maigwair's eyes widened in surprise. "How are you going to manage *that*?"

What the Captain General really wanted to know, Duchairn reflected, was how he'd managed to pry all those lucrative cash cows out of the hands of the nobles who owned them . . . and of the bureaucrats to whose flow of graft they had contributed so abundantly ever since the Jihad had begun.

"I made it a condition of the new tithe negotiations." Duchairn's smile was thinner than ever. "You'd be amazed how persuasive a Harchongese finds the threat of an additional five percent hike in his personal tithe if he doesn't see reason, especially since each of our assessor's offices now has direct access to the matching Inquisition office. I'd rather not have to impose on Zhaspahr," and let him get his fist into yet another pie, "but knowing his Inquisitors stand behind the Treasury on this one hasn't hurt. And unless I'm seriously mistaken, we'll have control of *all* of Harchong's foundries, north of the Gulf as well as south, by spring. Zhaspahr doesn't like it, even if he has agreed to support my people on this one—you know how attentive he is when it comes to the Harchongians' sensibilities—but I showed him the production figures and finally convinced him we don't have a choice. It won't be as good as having our own workers running them, but we should be able to at least get supervisory personnel into them, backed up by provincial production intendants assigned by Zhaspahr's office to make sure the locals listen to my managers."

"That's good news. In fact, it's *wonderful* news!"

"It's not going to produce instant results, especially in the northern Empire, but it *is* going to help," Duchairn agreed. "And I'm about to provide a sizeable addition to our labor force, too."

"Oh?" Maigwair frowned. "How? I thought we were too strapped for marks to put still more men to work."

"We're too strapped for marks to put more *laymen* to work," Duchairn replied with a smile which was somehow simultaneously wry, pleased, and bitter. "It took Zhaspahr's leaning on the heads of the orders, but we've got Langhorne's own lot of manpower—and *woman*power—busy on the Church's more everyday affairs. As of the first of next month, every major order and all of their affiliates in the minor orders will be required to furnish my office with the names of twenty-five percent of their ordained and lay members—*and* of their lay employees—to be assigned to serve the Jihad where and as required. They howled, of course, but employing those personnel in manufactories or other service positions won't cost the Treasury a half-mark it's not already paying out."

Maigwair whistled softly. It wasn't hard to understand Duchairn's smile now. He'd been after the great orders to support the Jihad more directly for over two years, and they'd refused to budge. They'd come up with excuse after excuse—a few of which had probably even been valid—to avoid his demands. He had to feel intensely satisfied that they'd finally been forced to yield, but the *manner* of their yielding had only reinforced Clyntahn's power yet again.

"That's going to help," he said after a moment. "Probably a lot. But all of this is still going to cost a lot more money than we have."

"True, but your Brother Lynkyn promises me he'll be able to reduce costs by a minimum of ten percent across the board, at least in Mother Church's own foundries and arsenals, and I've come to the conclusion that I have no choice but to turn to an expedient I'd really hoped to avoid. Two of them, in fact."

"What sort of expedients?" Maigwair asked cautiously.

"Our measures in Harchong will improve our cash flow significantly, but it's still going to be a few months before the cash actually starts to flow. In the meantime, my people can account for perhaps fifty percent of the new tithes in advance and begin obligating that amount now. We can't afford to do more than that until we've confirmed that the new revenue stream will be as high as we expect it to be. My new expedients"—Duchairn's lips twisted, as if the word had an actual—and unpleasant—taste—"are a bit more drastic, however. First, Mother Church is going to levy a special tithe across the board. And, second, we're going to require all bankers, manufactory owners, and major landowners, and all of the guilds to buy a new issue of Mother Church's notes at par. The amount of their required investment will be assessed by the Treasury based on the average of their tithes for the last five years, which should provide at least some cushion for those whose income has spiked with the expenditures of the Jihad. And manufactories providing weapons or other direct support to the Jihad will be allowed to pay their required investment in kind, accounting their obligation against their costs in Mother Church's service. The notes themselves will be secured by the value of about one-third of all of Mother Church's remaining secondary properties." He smiled again, at least a bit more naturally. "The assessed value of those properites, of course, will be the ones they held before the Schism. I've managed to keep our core holdings out of the portfolio. And I'm also offering sale of *all* of our holdings in Charis, Chisholm, Emerald, and Tarot at one-quarter of their pre-Jihad value. I don't know how many takers we'll have on that, but at least anyone who does decide to buy will have a doubly strong motive to support our final victory."

Maigwair inhaled sharply. The Treasury's workings had become far less arcane for him as he was forced to deal with the costs of the Jihad, which meant he had some inkling of the long-term future costs to the mainland economies. And he also suspected that even in the teeth of Clyntahn's agents inquisitor, there were going to be people desperate enough to try to evade their unsought financial obligations. For that matter, the combination of the special tithe and the forced loans was going to destroy some of the smaller bankers and manufactory owners outright. He didn't know if the sale of Church properties in the apostate Out Islands would find any takers, even at such attractive prices, but it might. Of course, the suggestion that the Church was simply writing off its holdings there might also strike directly at the Faithful's resolve, since she wouldn't be doing that if she truly expected to put down the heresy at its heart. There were entirely too many double-edged swords in the world already for his taste, and he wasn't at all sure he favored loosing yet another of them. At the same time, the combination of Duchair's onetime measures—and, Chihiro, but he *hoped* they'd prove onetime!—would provide a massive infusion of cash the Church needed desperately.

And when we win, Mother Church will surely redeem her notes at full value, he told himself, resolutely avoiding words like "if" and worries about whether or not Mother Church would be *able* to redeem them at face value, however badly she might want to. Or *not* want to, for that matter.

"I don't have your command of the details," he said after a moment, "but I understand enough to realize how little you could've wanted to do any of those things."

"You're right; I didn't want to do them. Unfortunately, I didn't have much choice. This should at least give us a powerful running start on duplicating the heretics' newest weapons for you. And on funding the supplies you need . . . assuming we can get them to the front *where* you need them, of course."

"I've been thinking the same sorts of things, I promise you," Maigwair said feelingly. "And, speaking of that, where are we on the canal repairs?"

"I still have only the preliminary reports, but I'm sending teams of engineers forward to survey the damage, and I hope they're going to tell me at least some of it's repairable. Unfortunately, it sounds like what we're really talking about here is complete replacement of the wrecked locks, and the pumping stations are probably total losses. In fact, I think the damage to the pumps is even worse than we initially thought it was."

"That's what I was afraid of." Maigwair's expression was grim. "And that doesn't even consider the effect weather's going to have! Will we even be able to pour concrete over the winter?"

"Not north of the Hildermoss Mountains. Not after the winter freeze sets in, anyway. And that's where all the damage is, of course. I had enough engineering supplies deployed forward for us to begin work immediately on the locks between East Wing Lake and the Hildermoss, and the reports I've gotten so far suggest we should be able to get those in before first snowfall. They won't be as good as they were before the heretics destroyed them, but they'll be adequate to our needs. And once we're able to get barges as far forward as the Hildermoss again, we can get as far upriver as Ayaltyn."

"Ayaltyn?" Maigwair shook his head. "Never heard of it."

"That's because it's nothing much more than a shallow spot in the river about forty miles past Cat Lizard Lake." Duchairn leaned over the map on the table between them and tapped the approximate location. "It's a tiny village—or used to be, anyway. According to my reports, there were never more than a couple of hundred people in Ayaltyn even before the Sword of Schueler. By the time the heretics came through, the only people in the vicinity where the ten-man garrison Wyrshym had left to keep an eye on the locks. That's going to get us just under two hundred miles south of East Wing Lake, but it's still over seven hundred and fifty miles as the wyvern flies from Guarnak."

"We should at least be able to move supplies by sled once the canals do freeze over," Maigwair said hopefully, but Duchairn shook his head again.

"That's going to be true to some extent, Allayn, but we've got too many stretches of canal bed—and over seventy miles of aqueduct—which're basically dry now. I'm not sure there's going to be enough standing water in them to provide the kind of ice we usually see in the winter, and without the locks and the pumps, we can't *get* the water into them, either. And even if there is, we're a lot shorter of snow lizards than we are of dragons. Worse, a lot of the dragons we do have are southern hill dragons. We'll have to pull them out of everywhere north of Hildermoss and Westmarch—or, even worse, slaughter them in place for food—by mid-November at the latest. They just don't have the coats to survive a northern winter; we'd lose two-thirds of them before spring. We'll do what we can, but I can't tell you to go ahead and count on sled transport at this point."

The Treasurer paused, thinking about his next words very carefully. Then he cleared his throat.

"One thing we might consider are ways to reduce how many mouths we have to feed," he said, watching Maigwair's expression cautiously. The Captain General's face tightened, but he only nodded, and Duchairn went on with a bit more confidence.

"Half of the Army of the Sylmahn's original infantry were pikemen," he pointed out, "and everything we've seen suggests that pikes are all but useless against the heretics. Perhaps it might not be a bad idea to pull all of them back from the front, into the Border States or even the Temple Lands, where we can feed them without imposing so much strain on the canals. I wouldn't suggest pulling back any of our strength under normal circumstances, you understand." Certainly not anywhere Clyntahn might hear of it, at any rate! "Under these circumstances, and given the relative ineffectiveness of their weapons, though, it seems to me it would only be sensible to consider it."

Maigwair's eyes had gone opaque. He sat for several seconds, then shrugged.

"I see the argument," he agreed. "It might be a bit difficult to do anything of the sort without undermining the Army's morale, of course. And as Zhaspahr's pointed out"—those opaque eyes met Duchairn's across the table unblinkingly—"we need to make every effort to get better weapons into their hands. If we get rifles forward to them, they'd be far more effective."

"That's true." Duchairn nodded. "Unfortunately, the transport problems mean we have a huge logistical log-jam well behind the front. I've got somewhere around thirty thousand rifles stuck short of the Tanshar border at the moment. It's going to be very hard to break them free, with all the emphasis on getting materials to repair the canals forward, and I'm afraid additional new production weapons may be stuck even farther up the line than that."

And I can keep *them jammed where they are for at least another month before I run out of logical excuses for Zhaspahr, Allayn.* He didn't actually say the words, but he thought them loudly, indeed, and Maigwair's eyes flickered.

"The best you can do is the best you can do," he said after a moment. "And you're right; if we can't get rifles into their hands, pikemen are simply going to be useless mouths at the front. Come to that, they're not trained as riflemen in the first place. Might make a lot of sense to pull them back to where we can mate them up with the rifles, ease the strain on your quartermasters, and let us form them into new, properly trained rifle-armed regiments. Then we could move them back to the front for our spring offensive as much more effective units."

"I know the idea has to disappoint you," Duchairn said apologetically. "Looking at all the options and pressures, though, I really do think we may have to bite the bullet and do it."

"As you say," Maigwair agreed with a heavy sigh.

They looked at one another, expressions suitably grave. Then Duchairn shifted in his chair.

"I do have *some* good news," he said. Maigwair cocked his head, and the Treasurer smiled crookedly. "It's not something I'd propose under normal conditions, given *The Book of Langhorne* strictures on the canals, but we're in the middle of a jihad. I expect the Archangels are probably prepared to grant us a few dispensations, under the circumstances."

"What sort of 'dispensations'?"

"Well, it helps that we have the plans for every canal

on file right here in Zion. Since we have the information, I've got crews of carpenters building temporary wooden locks. They'd never stand up to decades of heavy use the way locks are supposed to, but they ought to be serviceable enough to get the canals back on stream at least temporarily. We're also doing a comprehensive analysis of the pumping stations that were destroyed, and I'm having complete duplicate pumps made for each of them. We can barge them forward as far as the canals and the rivers will take us, and we're designing them in components small enough for draft dragons to haul on flatbed wagons from there, so we should be moving the canalhead steadily forward as soon as things begin to thaw next spring. I've put Father Tailahr in charge of it."

"Father Tailahr?" Maigwair repeated.

"Father Tailahr Synzhyn. He's a Hastingite they attached to my staff when we took over the canals to manage your logistics." Duchairn looked up from the map to meet Maigwair's eyes levelly. "He's a Chisholmian."

The Captain General stiffened. The Order of Hastings provided Safehold's geographers and astronomers. It also provided almost half of Mother Church's engineers, with special emphasis on transportation. But however great Synzhyn's expertise. . . .

"Is Zhaspahr aware of that?" Maigwair asked carefully after a moment.

"As a matter of fact, he is." Duchairn's tone was cool. "There are quite a few faithful Chisholmians, you know. There are even some still living in Chisholm, far less people like Father Tailahr who can never go home until we win the Jihad. He's working harder than any other three priests on my staff, as if he feels he has to somehow atone for Sharleyan's sins, and I've personally vouched for him."

Maigwair nodded slowly, obviously hoping Duchairn was right about Synzhyn's reliability. If he wasn't, and if he'd vouched for the man to Clyntahn's face, the consequences for the Treasurer would be severe.

"So what exactly is Father Tailahr doing for you?"

"He's the one who came up with the idea for the wooden locks in the first place. What we're going to do is excavate enough of each destroyed lock to clear the canal bed. Then we'll install one of the prefabricated locks built especially to fit the one we're replacing. The new lock will be somewhat narrower than the old one, and we'll probably lose more water because the wooden panels are going to leak and we'll be filling in between them and the canal wall with earth and gravel ballast, not concrete. They won't last as long, either—we're not sure they'll last through even one normal Siddarmarkian winter—but we'll be able to replace them fairly rapidly if they go down again. And I'll be stockpiling additional timbers and planking as far forward as I can. Father Tailahr and I estimate that if we're able to position them properly and hold reserve work crews in readiness, we ought to be able to replace any three destroyed locks in sequence in no more than three to four five-days. Of course," the Treasurer smiled sourly, "that's assuming the Army can keep the heretics from burning our stockpiles."

"How long to replace the locks we've already lost, at least between here and Guarnak, using this new technique of yours?" Maigwair asked intently.

"That depends on whether or not we'll be able to work through the winter months," Duchairn said frankly. "If we are, and assuming I manage to get the necessary supplies moved forward, we should have the entire canal between East Wing Lake and Guarnak up and running again by the end of March. The problem is that I doubt we *will* be able to work through the coldest months, and Father Tailahr says it's less likely prefabricated locks are going to be as effective in the rivers. Assuming we essentially have to shut down between early November and the end of February, it's going to be mid-April, at least, before we can have all of the canal system you need open again. Once we start getting into warmer weather, we'll be able to work faster; otherwise, I'd be estimating early May."

"March would be wonderful," Maigwair said softly, looking back down at the map and tracing the blue line from East Wing Lake to Guarnak.

"We'll do the best we can, Allayn," Duchairn promised. "No matter what we do, though, keeping Wyrshym supplied through the winter's going to be . . . problematical, even pulling back the pikemen. And that, unfortunately, brings us to the question of Harchong."

Maigwair's face tensed once more, and Duchairn shrugged.

"We certainly aren't going to be able to feed Wyrshym's troops and the loyal population in Hildermoss, New Northland, Northland, and Midhold *and* move the Harchongians to the front, Allayn. I'm sorry, but it simply can't be done without the canals. I'm working on evacuating as many civilians as possible, finding places in the Temple Lands and southern Harchong where we can house and feed them, but there's no way in God's world we can send the better part of a million and a half men forward to the end of a supply line that fragile."

"Zhaspahr's not going to be happy to hear that," Maigwair pointed out.

"Zhaspahr's going to have to deal with quite a few things he won't be happy to hear," Duchairn replied tartly. Maigwair blinked, but Duchairn only shrugged. He was on much surer ground where the Imperial Harchongese Army was concerned, and he'd warned Clyntahn about it from the beginning. "I expect him to pitch another tantrum, but if he insists on sending them forward after I've shown him the figures on the number of troops we can feed, that Harchongese loyalty he counts on so heavily is likely to start getting a little threadbare."

This time Maigwair actually winced, but Duchairn only chuckled.

"Believe me, Allayn, I'm no more eager to trigger one of Zhaspahr's tirades than anyone else, but I've had a fair amount of practice by now. Hopefully I'll be able to divert him by pointing out that I expect to have the canals back up sooner than originally projected if he'll only refrain from forcing every load of construction materials to compete with food for starving troops. But whether that works or not, he simply can't have it both ways. If we start work now, we can throw up barracks for the Harchongians along the Holy Langhorne Canal. They can provide the construction crews themselves, and in most cases, they'll even be able to cut the necessary lumber, too. Langhorne knows Harchongese serfs have enough experience building cabins fit to stand the winter! That'll let us deploy them as far forward as possible while keeping them supplied over the winter, so we should be able to move them up quickly come spring."

"That might work," Maigwair said hopefully. "And—"

He stopped, and Duchairn smiled at him again. This time it was an oddly sympathetic expression.

"And, you were about to say, there's something to be said for taking advantage of the winter to give them better training and weapons," he said.

"Well . . . yes," Maigwair acknowledged. "It's not that I doubt their loyalty or their determination, but. . . ."

Duchairn nodded slowly, wondering how stern a test he dared to give the growing sense of rapport between him and Maigwair.

"Allayn, you and I both know the Harchongians are nowhere near the level of training you've managed for the Army of God," he said after a long, tense moment. "I wonder if you know how bad the weapons picture really is, though?"

He cocked an eyebrow at the other vicar, and Maigwair sighed.

"I know it's bad. Very bad. But it *can't* be as bad as Grand Duke Omar's correspondence is suggesting." Rhobair only looked at him, and his mouth tightened. "Or can it?" he asked.

"Actually, it's worse," Rhobair said flatly, and Maigwair actually paled. "Until the . . . unfortunate timing of the Faithful's spontaneous uprising in Siddarmark took us all by surprise, their manufactories were busy overstating their rifle production in order to justify Church subsidies for rifles—even foundries—that didn't exist. Worse, they hadn't even begun building up the new regiments; they were too busy pocketing the funds that were supposed to be spent on that minor detail. After all, there was plenty of time and they could always follow their usual process and send out press gangs to conscript every serf and peasant in sight when they were actually summoned to the Jihad. So they did."

Maigwair swallowed, and despite his sympathy, Rhobair felt a stab of irritation. The other man was Mother Church's Captain General! Surely he should have been better informed on the state of the Harchongese Army than her *Treasurer* was!

But then he thought better of it. Harchongese corruption was so endemic *they* seldom knew exactly what state they were in, and their aristocracy's one true skill was a legendary ability to hide and obfuscate unfortunate realities. In fact, this time they'd managed to deceive even Clyntahn, although that was probably only because the Grand Inquisitor had wanted so badly to believe them.

"They really do have close to two million infantry and cavalry, as nearly as I can tell," the Treasurer continued. "That's based on reports from my own transportation personnel and the number of rations they're devouring. But I've got my own people looking at their manufactory records now—the *real* records—and I'll be astonished if they've got as many as eighty thousand rifles to arm them . . . and fifteen or twenty thousand of those are in the hands of their Military Police, not combat units. And whether Zhaspahr wants to hear it or not, their officers are barely competent, at best."

Maigwair looked like a man who'd just been shot, and Duchairn shrugged.

"Unless you want to simply use them as human shields to soak up the heretics' fire so our own troops can get close enough to engage the enemy, we've *got* to improve their quality before we commit them to action. And let's be honest here. Given the way Harchongese serfs are treated back home, expecting them to have anything like your regiments' discipline is totally unrealistic. If you add that to the sort of casualties they're likely to take, you've got a guaranteed recipe for troops who're going to be almost as destructive to Mother Church's loyal sons and daughters—especially her *daughters*—as to the heretics."

The two vicars' eyes met across the table, and Duchairn shrugged.

"Since we can't move them up and feed them anyway, this is our one opportunity to give them the training—and the discipline—that might actually make them effective soldiers and not Shan-wei's own scourge upon the Faithful as well as the apostate. I'll come up with the food, the lumber and nails and tools to build their barracks, and *some* way to provide them with at least some rifles instead of arbalests, bows, and pikes. I've got some ideas on that subject, but I guarantee you their senior officers are going to shriek like dying dragons when they hear what I have in mind, and you don't even want to *think* about what the Border States're going to have to say about it! Shan-wei—I think this time I may manage to piss *everybody* off, and I know Zhaspahr's not going to like it. But they lied to *him*, too, this time. I think he's probably going to be . . . determined enough to back me on this if you and I can convince him it'll work. But if I can come up with the weapons for them, *you* have to come up with the officers to train them, because without that, we might as well just drop any rifles we can give them into Hsing-wu's Passage, instead. And, frankly, you need to find a way to put Army of God officers into their battalions when they move up. You've *got* to, Allayn, and you know it."

Their eyes held across the map, and then, slowly, Maigwair nodded.

"You're right," he said softly. "I don't know how I'm going to do it, but I've got to . . . and I will."

Sylmahn Gap,
Republic of Siddarmark

Kynt Clareyk, Baron of Green Valley and commanding officer, 2nd Brigade (reinforced), Imperial Charisian Army, swung up into the saddle of his favorite mount. Wood smoke from cookfires, the sound of distant orders and morning work details, the murmur of hundreds of private conversations, the ringing of a blacksmith's hammer, the whistling of draft dragons roused to labor, and all the other early-morning bustle of an encamped field army swirled about them, and the gelding shifted under him, impatient to be off and doing. He chuckled as he leaned forward and patted the big gray's shoulder.

"Patience, Traveler. I know—I know! *Some* people can be a little slow and grumpy if they don't get their morning chocolate on time."

Lieutenant Slokym looked up with a moderately reproachful expression, then shook his head and climbed into the saddle of a neat, well-coupled bay mare.

"*Some* people," he said, addressing the mare's alert, sharply pricked ears and matching his general's tone almost perfectly, "would've had their morning chocolate on time if they hadn't been required to get someone else *his* morning chocolate first."

The orderly who'd been holding their horses blanched, awaiting the thunderbolt of wrath, but Green Valley only sighed heavily.

"Alas, it is ever my fate to be surrounded by people who seize every possible petty excuse for their tardiness. Besides, the chocolate was cold."

"With all due respect, Sir," Slokym said gravely, a twinkle lurking in his blue eyes, "mine was hot enough to burn my tongue when it came out of the same carafe five minutes *after* yours."

"A mere bagatelle!"

Green Valley waved his hand airily, smiled at his aide,

and touched Traveler with his heels. The gelding stepped off eagerly and Slokym's bay had to move quickly to keep up as the two officers trotted up the high road towards 2nd Brigade's forward positions.

Mountain wyverns swept in lazy circles overhead, white puffball clouds drifted against a polished blue sky, and a brisk breeze blew into their faces. Despite the baron's comments, the time was not many hours past dawn, and the morning was still cool, especially here in the shadows of the Sylmahn Gap. By midday, the sun would be directly overhead and the Gap's depths would be uncomfortably warm by Lieutenant Slokym's Chisholmian standards and still a bit on the chilly side by Green Valley's Old Charisian standards.

The nature of a perfect compromise, the baron reflected dryly. *Neither one of us is going to be completely satisfied.*

"You do have Brigadier Traigair's dispatches and my map case, I trust?" he said in a worried tone.

"Yes, My Lord. I *almost* forgot them, but I remembered in time," Slokym reassured him gravely, and the baron chuckled. The youngster was as commonly born as Green Valley himself, but he was going to make an excellent senior officer someday.

"Good," the general said in a considerably more serious tone. "And have you had any thoughts about his suggestion?"

Bryahn Slokym considered the query. He respected Green Valley more than almost anyone else in the entire world, and he knew the general wasn't asking the question simply to wile away the ride. He had no doubt Green Valley had already made up his own mind about Brigadier Wylsynn Traigair's proposal, but Slokym often thought the general ought to have been a teacher somewhere. Although, to be fair, he *was* a teacher, and a damned good one, the sort who viewed the military education of his aides as one of his primary responsibilities. He didn't use them simply as messengers to be sent galloping off with dispatches or hands to fetch something he'd forgotten. He saw them as future commanders of men who it was his duty to train to command those men well, and his question was entirely serious.

"I understand what the Brigadier's saying, My Lord," the lieutenant said. "I think I understand *why* he's saying it, as well. But I don't think his idea . . . fits neatly into your plans."

"Ah?" Green Valley quirked an eyebrow at him. "I have *plans*, Bryahn?"

"You *always* have plans, My Lord. It's just that sometimes you haven't gotten around to explaining them to anyone else. I'm sure it's just one of those minor matters which occasionally slip your mind. Only because there's so much else going on inside it, of course."

"I see." Green Valley's lips quivered and he returned his attention to the high road before them and the wide stretch of the flooded canal reaching away to their right to lap the feet of the Moon Thorn Mountains. "And why would the good Brigadier's suggestion interfere with my nefarious plans?"

"Because I think you're perfectly happy with the cork you have in the bottle, My Lord." Slokym's fair hair stirred on the breeze blowing down the Gap, and his voice was completely serious. "I think you see our present lines as a perfect opportunity to conserve manpower for, ah, *other* employment."

"Very good, Bryahn." Green Valley gave his aide a look of approval. "And do you have any suggestions as to what that 'other employment' ought to be?"

"No, My Lord." Slokym shook his head with a wry smile. "I can think of several possibilities, but they're all a little too vague for me to trot out for you to decapitate. With your permission, I'd like to think about them a while longer before I make any serious suggestions and risk altering the entire strategic concept of your campaign."

"An officer should always strive to be the soul of tact when pointing out his commander's strategic lapses," Green Valley approved affably, and Slokym chuckled.

The baron gave him another smile and they rode along in silence while Green Valley considered his own thoughts on that very subject.

Young Bryahn was correct that Brigadier Traigair's suggestion was a poor fit for the possibilities taking form within his own mind. Not that he faulted Traigair for a moment. Indeed, under other circumstances, he might have been very tempted to take the brigadier's idea and run with it. But Bryahn was also right that 2nd Brigade's current position on the southern shore of Wyvern Lake was just about perfect from a defensive perspective. Of course, the flipside of that was that Bishop Militant Bahr-nabai Wyrshym's position on the lake's *northern* shore was equally strong. The two of them had rather different options for what they might *do* with that security, however.

Brigadier Wylsynn Traigair commanded the Imperial Charisian Army's 3rd Brigade, whose two regiments had been split up to reinforce 1st Brigade and 2nd Brigade when they were dispatched to the front. Traigair had stayed with Colonel Zhon Tompsyn's 2nd Regiment, which had been assigned to reinforce Green Valley, and functioned as 2nd Brigade (reinforced)'s third-in-command. Like many senior Chisholmian officers, he was of common birth—bald, broad-shouldered, and a bit paunchy, with blue eyes and broad cheekbones—and unshakably loyal to the Crown. He was also a solid, somewhat stolid sort, not given to wild flights of imagination but absolutely reliable. And without the ego involvement which might have made another officer of his seniority resent having his brigade split to reinforce someone else's.

At the moment, 2nd Regiment was responsible for holding 2nd Brigade's forty-eight-mile front. That would have been a daunting task for fewer than forty-five hundred men under normal circumstances, but Wyvern Lake made the task far easier. Admittedly, the lake's shoreline, with its innumerable small inlets and the long peninsula thrusting into it from the southwest, offered a multitude of places where an audacious, offense-minded opponent might use boats to effect a landing. But the Army of the Sylmahn, unfortunately for Mother Church, was neither audacious nor offense-minded at the moment. Wyrshym was a tough-minded and resilient sort, which meant that lack of audacity was subject to change, but for now he was firmly back on his heels, reeling from the catastrophic destruction of his logistic network.

And that doesn't even consider how he's going to react when he gets his latest dispatches from Zion, Green Valley thought with grim satisfaction. *He may've known things weren't going well on the Daivyn, but he doesn't have a clue yet of just how badly Kaitswyrth's been hammered.*

Neither did anyone in 2nd Brigade, officially at least. They had Eastshare's initial dispatches via semaphore, yet the duke himself was still assessing things. He knew he'd won a major victory, but he had yet to realize just how major it actually was. Green Valley, however, *did* know. He'd watched much of the Battle of the Glacierheart Gap through Owl's SNARCs, and he'd tracked every mile of Eastshare's counterattack, as well.

Much of that imagery had been recorded, but he'd watched Kaitswyrth's blind, headlong attack in real time, and he felt a warm glow of pride in Ruhsyl Thairis' performance. Eastshare retained a few blind spots of his own, most stemming from his ingrained sense of aristocratic superiority. Unlike far too many of the nobly born, however, he seldom allowed them to interfere with the clarity of his thinking. Nor, unlike certain other officers Green Valley could have named, did he ever allow contempt for an enemy to distort his thinking. His was a cool, calculating mind, unlikely to erupt in spasms of sudden enthusiasm and completely immune to anything approaching panic.

Even so, I have to admit he surprised me, the baron admitted. *Outnumbered by almost twelve to one and he decides to take the* offensive? *And without any of the SNARC advantages I have, either!*

Eastshare had demonstrated not simply an astonishing ability to calculate odds to a hair but also the sort of instinctive feel for the pulse and flow of battle that no amount of mere training could provide. His sense of the Army of Glacierheart's parlous morale following the catastrophic repulse of its frontal attack had been perfect, and the audacity of his own riposte up the river after Kaitswyrth's left flank crumbled had come within an eyelash of completely cutting off a third of Kaitswyrth's entire army. Of course, if he'd succeeded, he would have "trapped" an opponent who still outnumbered his entire strength by almost four to one, which could have had interesting repercussions—the old tale about the hunting hound who caught the slash lizard came to mind—but it had still forced the whole Army of Glacierheart into headlong retreat. He'd pushed it back a hundred miles; killed, wounded, or captured twenty-nine thousand of its men; and halted his own advance with impeccable timing along the western edge of the Ahstynwood which had become a place of terror for the Army of God. Given what had happened to it under the shadows of those trees, the Army of Glacierheart would be a long time finding the fortitude to venture back into that woodland to test 1st Brigade's positions.

And the bastards don't have as many Inquisitors to help encourage *that fortitude, either.*

Green Valley's thought was harsh with vindictive approval as he reflected upon the Inquisitors who'd been returned—in part, at least—to the Army of Glacierheart. Colonel Makyn's scout snipers had filtered out into what had been dubbed—with no input at all from Merlin ·Athrawes or himself, so far as Green Valley could determine—"no-man's-land" between the two armies in the middle of the night. The rising sun had shown the Army of Glacierheart's sentries the long row of stakes, no more than fifty yards in front of their lines, each bearing an Inquisitor's head.

The sight had not been calculated to improve that army's morale. More particularly, it had delivered an unmistakable message to Zhaspahr Clyntahn's representatives, and it would be interesting to see how they responded.

Those Inquisitors had been spared the sorts of deaths they would have happily meted out to any of Eastshare's men. That wasn't to say all of them had died painlessly or even survived long enough to be taken prisoner and brought before Eastshare for condemnation. The ICA knew Cayleb and Sharleyan's policy where Inquisitors were concerned, and its men were far from immune to the hatred the Inquisition had spawned. Some of them were bound to conclude that if the Inquisitors were to die anyway, they might as well pay a little on Zhaspahr Clyntahn's account first. But by and large, they'd been executed with a minimum of the sort of horror the Army of God had handed out under their orders.

Nor had they been the only ones to pay the price for that horror. There'd been a few instances in which other Army of God personnel had not been allowed to surrender, either, despite the duke's firm orders on that subject. Given what had happened to Mahrtyn Taisyn's Marines and seamen, not to mention General Stahntyn's Aivahnstyn garrison, that had been as inevitable as sunrise. Casualties among surrendering AOG officers had been higher than among their enlisted ranks, but they'd been even higher among the Siddarmarkian Temple Loyalists serving with Kaitswyrth. Although Eastshare was in the process of dealing sternly with the two or three cases of outright massacre of which he'd learned, he obviously realized as well as Green Valley himself that they'd actually been unreasonably fortunate in the restraint 1st Brigade had exercised.

In addition to well over fifteen thousand prisoners (many of them wounded), Eastshare's force had captured twenty-eight twelve-pounder field guns, almost eight thousand perfectly serviceable cavalry mounts (along with over five thousand saddles whose owners no longer required them), almost a hundred first-quality draft dragons, sixty freight wagons, thirty-two canal barges full of supplies the Army of Glacierheart wasn't going to be using, three hundred tons of gunpowder, and almost nineteen thousand rifles. The rifles were muzzle-loading flintlocks, far inferior to the ICA's Mahndrayns, but nineteen thousand rifles were still nineteen thousand rifles. Especially combined with the roughly four thousand Dohlaran rifles the Earl of Hanth had captured at the

Battle of Thesmar and the nine thousand Green Valley's own brigade had captured in the process of pushing Wyrshym's Army of the Sylmahn back from Serabor. All told, those thirty-two thousand rifles would equip fourteen more of the new Siddarmarkian rifle regiments as soon as they could be shipped back to Siddar City or issued to General Fyguera's garrison troops in Thesmar. And between the guns 2nd Brigade had captured in the Sylmahn Gap and those 1st Brigade had captured along the Daivyn, the Republic of Siddarmark Army would also find itself with two full artillery battalions, courtesy of the Army of God. The Royal Dohlaran Army's rather more modest contribution to the Allies' artillery park had been incorporated into the landward defenses of Thesmar.

Not a bad haul, Green Valley reflected. *It would be even better and hurt the bastards on the other side even worse if Duchairn wasn't managing to increase rifle output in both the Temple Lands and Dohlar. And if it didn't look like he was going to manage that in Harchong, too. But still, not bad at all.*

He contemplated that thought for several seconds, then turned back to how best to break the news to Traigair and Colonel Tompsyn.

In addition to 2nd Regiment, Traigair had Major Fumyro Kharyn's 3rd Battalion from Colonel Makyn's 1st Scout Sniper Regiment, and Kharyn's men had found a weak spot in Wyrshym's position at the western edge of Wyvern Lake. There was a narrow tongue of land, little more than two miles wide, between the lake's shore and the foothills of the Snow Barrens. Bishop Militant Bahrnabai clearly knew about it, since he'd posted pickets to watch it and entrenched one of his divisions to hold it, but Kharyn's aggressive patrols had secured control of the mountains which overlooked it. He and Traigair—and Tompsyn—were positive they could get mortars into position to support an assault on the dug-in division. In addition, Tompsyn wanted to use the surprise Green Valley had been working on—the canal barges loaded with additional mortars and field guns—to land troops *behind* Wyrshym's entrenchments.

It was a neat plan, with all the audacity Wyrshym's forces currently lacked, and Green Valley had no doubt that it would work. It might not work quite as well as Traigair thought it would, but it would definitely get them around the western edge of the lake with the opportunity for an overland thrust directly across the Army of the Sylmahn's line of communications. Supply would remain a problem, for while Colonel Brysyn Graingyr, 2nd Brigade's chief quartermaster, and Colonel Mhartyn Mkwartyr, the brigade's senior engineer, had managed to drag the barges Tompsyn was proposing to use up the flooded stretches of the Guarnak-Sylmahn Canal, it had *not* been easy. For that matter, Serabor was still a huge bottleneck. The dams which had been required to flood the Gap in order to slow down the Temple Loyalist rebels and, later, Wyrshym's Army of the Sylmahn made it impossible for barges to pass through the city's locks. Graingyr's teamsters had hauled the barges around the blockage and up the steeply climbing high road on rollers supplied by Mkwartyr's engineers, using teams of up to ten draft dragons for each of them, and then launched them again upstream. With the canal flooded they didn't really have to worry about opening and closing the locks upstream from Serabor, but the plain fact was that the Guarnak-Sylmahn Canal was closed to anything resembling normal operation until the dams were broken—and, equally important, until 2nd Brigade retook Guarnak and repaired the locks upstream from that city. That was one reason the gun barges Tompsyn wanted to use were going to come as such a surprise to Wyrshym, since the bishop militant "knew" they couldn't be there.

Green Valley doubted Tompsyn had thought much beyond the initial breakout into Wyrshym's rear areas. The colonel was a career soldier, but not exactly an experienced quartermaster. An Old Charisian who'd been a Marine, like Green Valley himself, for sixteen years before his transfer to the Imperial Charisian Army, he'd been accustomed to letting the Royal Navy deal with little things like supplies of food and ammunition. Over the past couple of years he'd been far better educated in the centrality of logistics to army operations, but he still had a tendency to think tactically first and logistically second. He saw an opportunity to break the stalemate in a way which promised to bite off several thousand more Army of God prisoners; what happened after that would be up to more senior and better paid heads. Traigair was more accustomed to thinking in terms of supply lines, but he was also a one-thing-at-a-time sort. First get your army around the other side's flank and force them to retreat, *then* think about how you go about keeping yourself in supply to follow the enemy up.

And given what Ruhsyl managed against Kaitswyrth, we might be able to push Wyrshym all the way back from Saiknyr to Guarnak. We might not, too, of course. Wyrshym's men've already encountered our tactical doctrine—and our mortars—and we didn't manage to mousetrap them as thoroughly as Ruhsyl mousetrapped Kaitswyrth in the first place. Worse, their morale's had more time to recover from what we did to them at Serabor. They're a lot less likely to let us "bully" them into giving ground, especially given how hard those pains in the arse Nybar and Bahrkly've been working on modifying their unit structure.

Bishop Gorthyk Nybar, the commander of the badly mauled Langhorne Division, and Bishop Harys Bahrkly, CO of the scarcely more intact Rakurai Division, had been selected by Wyrshym to find answers to the Imperial Charisian Army. Their divisions had been pulled back, leaving fresh formations to hold the front, while Nybar and Bahrkly refitted and considered ways to deal with what 2nd Brigade had done to them. There wasn't a lot they could do when it came to providing things like breech-loading rifles and infantry mortars (neither of which the AOG possessed), but that hadn't prevented them from thinking with a clarity and a lack of panic Green Valley found intensely irritating.

Given how heavily Langhorne Division had lost in the Army of the Sylmahn's drive to Serabor and then as its rearguard during 2nd Brigade's counterattack, it had required heavy drafts of replacements. In fact, it hadn't been restored to full strength even with those drafts, and neither had the other divisions 2nd Brigade had chewed up, despite the large number of replacement personnel Allayn Maigwair had sent forward with each of his invading armies. Without those replacement pools, however, the Army of the Sylmahn would have been in far worse shape, and while he was replacing his losses, Nybar had completely reorganized Langhorne.

Mixed battalions of pikemen and riflemen were a thing of the past in his division. Instead, he had three slightly understrength regiments armed solely with rifles and bayonets while his fourth regiment, more understrength than any of the other three, was armed entirely with pikes. It was clear he had no intention of using those pikemen as anything except a last, desperate reserve—or possibly as the leading edge of an equally desperate assault—and his rifle regiments were experimenting aggressively with open order formations. He was still at a very early stage of feeling his way away from the shoulder-to-shoulder firing lines the Army of God's original tactics had dictated, but he was obviously headed in the right direction, and Bahrkly was following suit with his own division. It was unlikely, in Green Valley's opinion, that the Church would be able to match the ICA's doctrine, with its heavy reliance on the initiative of lieutenants and sergeants at the platoon and squad level. Unfortunately for the AOG, initiative required a certain flexibility and freedom of thought which it would take the AOG years to develop. Worse, it would have to break the Inquisition's unwillingness to *allow* them to develop at that level, and that wasn't happening anytime soon. When those qualities started percolating through Mother Church's junior officers and enlisted personnel, the Group of Four would be well on its way to losing control of its own army, and Zhaspahr Clyntahn, for one, recognized that far more clearly than he had any intention of admitting. Yet that didn't mean the existing Army of God couldn't improve to a point which would make it far more dangerous in the field.

Wyrshym had yet to even consider restructuring his

entire army along the lines of Langhorne and Rakurai, and Green Valley wasn't certain he could have convinced Maigwair to allow such a fundamental reorganization, anyway. In effect, Nybar and Bahrkly were proposing to discard the pike completely, and that would result in a major reduction in the Army of God's field strength. Once upon a time, Green Valley would have assumed Maigwair would never tolerate that sort of reduction, but it had become apparent that the Church's Captain General was substantially more flexible than anyone in Charis had expected. It was entirely possible he would, indeed, recognize how the increased efficiency and lethality of the unit organization Nybar and Bahrkly were suggesting would actually make much smaller armies far more powerful.

Personally, Green Valley would prefer for him to take as long as possible in recognizing anything of the sort, and that was another reason he preferred to shelve Traigair's proposal for the moment. The fact that General Ahlyn Symkyn would be landing in Siddar City with another fifty thousand-plus infantry and cavalry within the next month or so was yet another. He didn't know where those reinforcements would be directed—not yet—but he had a few thoughts of his own about what he might be able to accomplish with some of that manpower.

And I may be able to accomplish some of it even without more manpower, he reflected. *But for any of that to work, I need Wyrshym exactly where he is. Which means the last thing I want to do is to push him into retreating. I want him to hang on to the northern end of the Gap just as long and just as hard—and just as deeply into it—as I can get him to. So I'm afraid poor Kaillee is just going to have to take no for an answer.*

His lips twitched at the thought, but the incipient smile faded into something far colder and his brown eyes hardened as he contemplated the *reason* Brigadier Traigair and his colonel were going to have to wait.

. IV .
Kaihrys Point,
Thesmar Bay,
The South March Lands,
and
The Daiyvn River,
Cliff Peak Province,
Republic of Siddarmark

"I doubt you'll need it in this direction, but at least you've got a good field of fire, Commander."

The Earl of Hanth stood on top of the thick rampart of sandbags, looking out across the bare six-mile width of the Thesmar Narrows, the eighteen-mile-long passage connecting Thesmar Bay to Sandfish Bay. Sun-sparkle danced on the blue sheet of water which had narrowed to little more than four miles between treacherous mudbanks with the receding tide, and the temperature would have been oppressively hot for someone who hadn't been born and raised in Old Charis. Behind him, over the voices of the work parties still laboring on the emplacement, he could hear wind hissing through the tall, stiff grass of North Sandfish Marsh. He could also *smell* the marshes, and he wasn't overjoyed by the scent. The reek of decaying vegetation was almost overpowering at low tide, and he suspected that Grimaldi's own pestilence was waiting patiently for Pasquale to lower his guard even for a minute.

"I could wish the Narrows were a tiny bit *narrower*, My Lord," Lieutenant Commander Bryahn Sympsyn replied. He stood on the firing step, his head several feet lower than the earl's, and raised his spyglass to look across the Narrows at Tymkyn Point, where a matching battery was taking form. "I'd like to be able to interlock fire with Lieutenant Brownyng better than we can from here."

"A man can't have everything, Commander," Hanth said, rather more philosophically than he felt. "From this elevation, you've got a good three miles' range—more, if you use ricochet fire. Besides, the channel's not what anyone would call straight enough for anyone to avoid you, now is it?"

"No, it's not, My Lord," Sympsyn acknowledged. In fact, the deep water channel passed within less than two thousand yards of his battery for a length of almost four miles. Any ship foolish enough to try forcing the Narrows would be within the play of his guns more than long enough for the eighteen thirty-pounders to rip it to pieces.

"And, when you come down to it," the earl continued, "we're less worried about anyone trying to force the channel than we are someone trying to *close* the channel, now aren't we?"

"Yes, My Lord." Sympsyn lowered his spyglass to meet the earl's gaze, and his expression might have been just a little embarrassed.

"Don't worry about it, Commander." Hanth smiled. "I've never known a Navy gunner yet who didn't think in terms of sinking ships rather than fending off soldiers."

Sympsyn smiled back in acknowledgment of his point, and Hanth turned to look inland over the bearded, hissing heads of that marsh grass.

North Sandfish Marsh stretched inland for over eighty miles from the Thesmar Narrows. Most of it was considered impassable, although Hanth knew better. He'd spent hours interviewing marshers who lived in and around the wetlands, supporting themselves off the plentiful bounty they offered if one only knew where to look for it. Unfortunately, they *did* know where to look, and so would any Temple Loyalist marshers, which meant he couldn't rely on Desnairian or Dohlaran columns' inability to find a path through that "impassable" terrain. It would be a muddy, sloppy business, which would probably take days—or even five-days—especially if they tried to drag guns along with them. But if the bastards *did* manage to pull it off, a well-emplaced battery or two would be able to close the Narrows to Charisian galleons, even without exploding shells.

And that was why the Earl of Hanth had ordered the construction of Sympsyn's battery and its sister position across the Narrows. Admiral Sir Paitryk Hywyt, commanding the Inshore Squadron tasked with supporting the defense of the city of Thesmar, would station a couple of galleons and a bombardment ship to support those batteries in the event that some enterprising fellow on the other side decided to try closing Hanth's supply line. Despite that, the earl was less than delighted to be putting two isolated outposts so far from his main position. It was over a hundred and ninety miles from Thesmar to Kaihrys Point, and given the quantity of supplies the Navy had thrown into the city, they had enough food and ammunition to last for months even if someone did manage to close the Narrows. So he supposed some people would say he was worrying unduly, and perhaps he was. Yet he'd long since discovered that while audacity was the handmaiden of success, *overconfidence* was the handmaiden of disaster.

The Emperor summed it up perfectly when he said it seems to be a law of war that he who will not risk cannot win, but that doesn't mean a prudent *gambler doesn't hedge his bets whenever he can. And given the fact that we've got somewhere around a quarter million very unhappy people headed our way, a prudent spider-rat makes sure his hole's going to be ready if he needs it. Not that I have any intention of putting it that way to the lunatics under my command.*

He snorted and shook his head. By this time, his "lunatics" were convinced there weren't enough Dohlarans—or Desnairians—in the entire world to beat *them*. As attitudes went, that beat the Shan-wei out of cowering in terror, but it had its own downsides. If he'd told them to, they would cheerfully have followed him into an attack on the approaching Desnairians, and even with Charisians, that would have been a . . . less than optimal solution to his problems.

His smile faded into grim satisfaction as he watched the twelve-pounders being hauled into position to cover the rear of Sympsyn's battery. Those guns—like the four thousand rifles he'd contributed to General Fyguera's infantry—had been "acquired" from the Royal Dohlaran Army, and while he hoped they wouldn't be needed, he couldn't think of a better use for them if they were.

The wedge of dry land which formed the tip of Kaihrys Point was fifteen feet higher than the low-lying marshlands. Anyone trying to assault out of that sea of mud and reeds would find his columns swept by a hurricane of grape and shrapnel. If he got the battery completed in time—and it would be five-days before any ill-intentioned souls could possibly be in position to attack it overland—he wasn't going to be worried about any mass assaults. The possibility of someone on the other side being smart enough to attempt a surprise attack with smaller, individual storming parties worried him far more, which was why each battery would be protected by a full company of his zealously hoarded Marines, as well.

He drew a deep breath and reminded himself of how far back to Thesmar it was. The trip was a full day's sail even for one of the Imperial Charisian Navy's schooners, and it was time he headed back. Truth be told, he'd had no business coming all the way out here in the first place with the Duke of Harless sweeping steadily around the shore of Lake Somyr. Harless' troops had already occupied the city of Somyr, southwest of Thesmar. In fact, they were a few miles closer to Thesmar at this moment than Hanth himself was. Those were *land* miles, however, and it would take Harless at least another four or five days to cover them even if his logistics train was as good as the Dohlarans' . . . which it wasn't.

Of course, the Dohlarans' *logistics just got a lot more uncomplicated, and that's going to splash on Harless once they join forces, damn it,* he reflected sourly.

Rainos Ahlverez' army had reached Fort Sheldyn on its way south from Cliff Peak after its Alyksberg adventures. With the looming threat of Ahlverez' approach,

Hanth had been forced to let Sir Fahstyr Rychtyr out of his confinement at Trevyr, which meant giving Ahlverez secure communications down the Seridahn River and, via the Sheryl-Seridahn Canal, all the way back to Dohlar. Assuming Desnairians and Dohlarans proved capable of cooperating—which, in Hauwerd Breygart's opinion, was not a foregone conclusion, even with special intendants attached to each army to knock heads together at need—the enormous army about to inundate Thesmar could count on ample supplies to keep it in the field. Thesmar's defenders could be equally well supplied, assuming the batteries kept the Narrows open for Charisian galleons, but those galleons wouldn't be able to do anything about how grossly outnumbered they'd be.

Clyftyn Sumyrs' seventy-two hundred men had come in from Alyksberg, just as exhausted and just as riddled with sickness as Hanth had been afraid they would be, given the rigor of their eight-hundred-mile forced march. General Kydryc Fyguera's four regiments of regulars had been recruited back up to strength out of South March citizens loyal to the Republic, giving them another seventy-eight hundred or so, although the replacements weren't yet as well trained as any of them might've liked. And then there were the five thousand men of his own 1st Independent Marine Brigade and the additional two thousand seamen Admiral Hywyt had managed to scare up by stripping every one of his galleons' companies to the bone. Altogether, it came to twenty-three thousand men, assuming all of Sumyrs' men could be gotten back on their feet by the healers in Thesmar. Which, by his calculations, meant he'd been brought all the way up to eight percent of the combined Desnairian-Dohlaran army headed his way.

That's why you have the entrenchments, Hauwerd, he told himself. *And the guns, and the rifles the Dohlarans were kind enough to provide you.*

He could have wished for a few thousand landmines, too, but that wasn't the sort of weapon Marines usually carried around with them. That was an oversight he planned on rectifying in the very near future, however, and in the meantime, his engineers had improvised by burying thirty-pounder shells rigged to percussion locks or quick match fuses along the approaches to the entrenchments. They had more of them—and quite a few fifty-seven-pounder carronade shells, as well—distributed to the front line positions where their fuses could be lit by hand before they were rolled down into approaching attackers. And one of the reasons Admiral Hywyt had come up with so many seamen to reinforce Hanth's strength was to provide the gunners for the naval thirty-pounders with which those entrenchments bristled.

Hauwerd Breygart wasn't going to make any rash assumptions about the quality of the army about to inundate the southern reaches of the South March Lands, nor was he immune to the sort of anxiety someone facing odds of better than ten-to-one must inevitably feel. Yet as he stood there, taking one last look around before he dutifully reported back aboard the schooner to return to Thesmar, what he felt most strongly of all was confidence.

It's always possible we'll lose it all in the end, he thought grimly. *But if those bastards take Thesmar, they'll do it by stacking their own men's bodies high enough for them to climb over the entrenchments.*

▼ ▼ ▼

"And might one ask where you've sprung from this time, *Seijin* Ahbraim?" the Duke of Eastshare inquired politely.

"From roaming about on the earth and walking around on it, Your Grace," Ahbraim Zhevons responded. Eastshare raised an eyebrow but otherwise only nodded, and Zhevons smothered an inner smile. The duke couldn't possibly have gotten the joke—no one on Safehold had ever heard of the Book of Job—yet the quote had been irresistible, given Merlin Anthrawes' status as Shan-wei's servant. The temptation to smile disappeared quickly, however, as he recalled why he'd come.

"You seem to be rather farther west than the last time you and I spoke, Your Grace," he observed, and it was Eastshare's turn to smile, which he did—broadly.

"You picked an excellent position for us," he replied.

"And that idiot Kaitswyrth was kind enough to assault it. After that, we decided we might as well take advantage of the opportunity he'd been so good as to provide. We're still in the process of prisoner interrogation, but as nearly as we've been able to understand his thinking, he decided he had to have enough manpower to bull his way through us like a rogue dragon, no matter how well dug in we were."

"My sources suggest the same thinking," Zhevons agreed. "And they also suggest his 'Army of Glacierheart' won't be worth very much in offensive terms before winter. Nobody's prepared to guarantee that, of course, but it does seem the inquisitors attached to his divisions have become rather more . . . circumspect than they used to be for some reason."

This time Eastshare's smile was ugly, and Zhevons returned it with equal satisfaction. Despite Cayleb and Sharleyan's proclamation, the Schuelerites in the Army of Glacierheart had remained too deeply imbued with the inviolability of the clergy to truly believe it could possibly apply to *them*. That long, staked line of heads had disabused them of that notion, and quite a few of them had exhibited a pronounced decrease in their eagerness to encourage the units to which they were attached to launch desperate attacks. It was entirely possible they would regain that eagerness—however much he despised and hated them, Zhevons wasn't going to make the mistake of underestimating the strength of their belief—but it was going to take time.

"Unfortunately," he continued, "Ahlverez isn't going to join Kaitswyrth after all. He's headed south—by this time he must be as far as Fort Sheldyn—and Duke Harless has to be closing in on Thesmar by now from Silkiah. Our best information is that Earl Hanth and General Fyguera are even better dug-in around the city than you were on the Daivyn, but if Harless and Ahlverez leave a force to screen Thesmar and simply ignore the garrison, they can probably be as far east as Fort Tairys in another three or four five-days."

Eastshare's face tightened.

"And Fort Tairys is already in rebel hands," he said flatly, and Zhevons grimaced in agreement.

In fact, Fort Tairys wasn't merely "in rebel hands"; General Lairays Walkyr, its commander, had spent months circling it with massive earthworks. They weren't all that well laid out, and they were too extensive for the present garrison of mutineers and rebels to adequately man, but they were certainly powerful, and plenty big enough to hold a *Desnairian* garrison even Charisians would play hell evicting. Which, given its location, would be a very bad thing.

"Once they reach it," the *seijin* said, "they'll be loose in Shiloh with a secure rear. And if they hook back to the north towards your own supply line or head east towards Old Province. . . ."

Eastshare nodded hard.

"The problem is that what we're holding right now is a crust," the duke said. He hauled a map of the Republic out of a drawer and spread it across the table. "They're not getting past us here or in the Sylmahn Gap," he tapped his own position and then Green Valley's for emphasis as he spoke, "but if they get into the heart of the Republic, we simply don't have the manpower to intercept them—or anyplace to put a cork into the bottle the way I've done here and Baron Green Valley's done in the Gap."

"Exactly," Zhevons replied. "There's some good news to go with the bad, though. The Lord Protector's about ready to send a division worth of his new rifle regiments your way. One brigade's ready to move now, and the second will be ready to deploy in a few more five-days."

"Really?"

Eastshare looked up from the map with an interested expression. The Republic of Siddarmark Army fully realized the need to adapt to the new model weapons which had turned all existing military doctrine topsy-turvy. The middle of a war for survival was no time to be creating brand-new unit organizations, however, so Lord Protector Greyghor Stohnar and his seneschal, Daryus Parkair, had decided to stick with the existing

RSA regimental structure, but with five *rifle*-armed companies, each of four hundred and fifty men, per regiment. They'd adopted the Charisian model of combining two regiments into a brigade, yet whereas a Charisian division consisted of two brigades, one of the new Siddarmarkian divisions would consist of three. Given the fact that a Siddarmarkian regiment was barely half the size of its Charisian counterpart, a Siddarmarkian division would remain considerably weaker than an ICA division, but it would still be a big, powerful formation.

At the moment, however, the new rifle regiments which would make up those brigades and divisions were still in the process of coming into existence, and the RSA was undergoing a certain degree of upheaval despite the decision not to change its regimental structure. Some of the upheaval had less to do with weapons and manpower availability than other portions of it. For example, the decision had been made to permanently disband the regiments which had dishonored themselves by mutinying during the Sword of Schueler. Their identities had been extinguished, their regimental numbers expunged from the Army List forever, and their battle honors had been stripped from them. The steadfastness of the units which had remained loyal in the Republic's darkest days would be recognized by continuing to designate them as "infantry regiments," whereas the new regiments being organized to supplement them would not bear the "infantry" designation. The same policy would be followed where cavalry regiments were concerned, although the newly raised regiments would be designated "dragoon regiments."

Those decisions, however, were primarily administrative, a case of what the new and reorganized units were going to be called and how their self-identities would evolve. They had nothing to do with actually getting those units into the field, and the problem there was twofold. First, the men to fill them had to be found and trained, and training cadre was in desperately short supply, given the survival demands of the previous winter.

And, second, the rifles to arm them had to be found somewhere. Eastshare knew the captured weapons he'd sent east would be invaluable in that respect, even if the Church's muzzleloaders were tactically inferior and more poorly made than anything coming out of Charisian manufactories. And he also knew Siddarmarkian rifle production was climbing steadily as the lord protector's number one priority, just as he knew Stohnar and Parkair had been working furiously to get the new regiments stood up. Despite that, he was deeply surprised to hear that four of them—nine thousand men, or seventy percent of his own initial order of battle—were already ready for battle.

"That's welcome news," he said. "And it makes me wonder. . . ."

He stood gazing down at the map, clearly wrapped in thought, and the tip of his index finger moved slowly back down the Daivyn to Ice Lake and from there down the river to its junction with the Snow Water just west of the city of Saithor. From there it traveled down the Graywater River to Glacierborn Lake and tapped twice, thoughtfully.

"I have a strong position here," he said, as if speaking to himself, although he looked up from the map to meet Zhevons' gaze. "I've got the high road and the river to pull back along if I need to, and Kaitswyrth seems to be unwilling to lose any more men trying to probe my positions. I can't count on him staying that flat on his back, but even if he picks himself up and tries a fresh attack, this is perfect terrain for a fighting retreat. And we'd still have that original position in the fire scar you picked out for us if we were to be pushed back that far."

He paused, his eyes focused on something only he could see for several seconds. Then he shook himself.

"I take it, since I haven't heard anything official about those brigades, that they haven't been dispatched yet?"

"I can't say for certain whether they have or not, Your Grace," Zhevons said, not entirely accurately. Or, rather, a bit misleadingly, since the reason he couldn't say for certain had to do with things like SNARCs, recon skimmers, the need to keep track of complicated multiple identities, and coms. "If not, however, I'm sure they will be shortly."

Eastshare eyed him speculatively, obviously thinking over the *seijins'* record of accuracy. No competent general liked to make plans based on unconfirmed information, but it was a much easier thing to do, given Zhevons'— and Merlin Athrawes'—past reliability.

"Colonel Hobsyn's regiment's taken the most casualties," he said, "but with enough artillery and one of Colonel Makyn's scout sniper battalions to keep an eye on the enemy, he ought to be able to hold this position even if Kaitswyrth's army finds its nerve again. Or, at least, to fight a rearguard all the way back to Ice Lake if he has to."

"Yes, Your Grace?" Zhevons said when the duke paused once more.

"I need you to do something for me, *Seijin* Ahbraim."

"And what would that be, Your Grace?"

"I need you and your spies to find out everything you can about Fort Tairys and its garrison. Numbers, who's in command of Walkyr's regiments, how well those regiments are equipped, what sort of artillery it may have, whether or not it's received any rifles, its supply situation, its morale—everything."

"We can do that, Your Grace, although I may not be able to deliver the information to you personally."

"Good. And I'm going to take you at your word about those Siddarmarkian brigades." Eastshare's finger moved once more, tracking south from Glacierborn Lake, past the Clynmair Hills towards Fort St. Klair, at the northern end of the Branath Mountains. "I'm going to send a semaphore message asking to have their movement expedited as much as possible . . . but to hold two of them no farther west than the Glacierheart Border. I'll've had time to think over your reports by the time they get there, and then—"

That fingertip moved once more, tracing the line of the Branath Canal, and Ruhsyl Thairis, the Duke of Eastshare, smiled coldly.

The Delthak Works,
Earldom of High Rock,
Kingdom of Old Charis,
Empire of Charis

"So, overall, you're reasonably satisfied, Ehdwyrd?"

Ehdwyrd Howsmyn tipped back in his office chair as the voice spoke in his ear. It was late, even by his standards, but the new wall-mounted gas lights, powered by the coal gas produced as a by-product of his enormous coking ovens, gave him ample light for paperwork. There was always plenty of that to be dealt with, and he'd sent his secretaries and clerks home hours ago while he grappled with decisions only he could make and waited until he could confer with Cayleb and Sharleyan—and Merlin—without someone wondering why he was talking to thin air.

Now his comfortable chair was turned so he could gaze out at the glowing, gaslit windows of manufactory work floors that were never still. Beyond them were the showers of sparks, the furnace mouths glowing like chinks in the gates of hell, screaming as their incandescent fury rose against the dark with Shan-wei's own ferocity—in more ways than one. It painted the clouds (and the perpetual canopy of smoke) crimson and black above the largest ironworks in the history of Safehold, that furious power and searing energy. Of course, it was actually a *steel*works, but he couldn't blame most of the rest of the world for failing to note the distinction. And spectacular as that vista was, what he was actually watching were the images of his emperor and empress. They were in two completely separate locations, thousands of miles apart, but the com combined their images as if they were seated side by side and projected them onto his contact lenses as they spoke.

"That depends on how you define 'satisfied,' Cayleb,"

he replied. "In some ways, I'm even more pleased than I expected to be; in others, I'm even less pleased." He shrugged. "Sort of par for the course."

Caleb chuckled and leaned back in his own chair in Charis' embassy in Siddar City with a stein of beer in one hand, then took a bite from the salted pretzel in his other hand and chewed appreciatively. Sharleyan—for whom the hour was considerably later than any of the others—sat in her Cherayth bedchamber with a cup of hot tea. Now she sipped delicately from the tissue-thin Harchongese porcelain and shook her head at her husband.

"You Old Charisians really are lowbrow, aren't you?"

"Of course we are," her husband agreed cheerfully. "Also money grubbers perfectly willing to dabble in trade with people like Ehdwyrd, and we all know no proper aristocrat would consider keeping such low company. Just think of, oh, the Earl of Swayle, for example."

"Thank you for reminding me." Sharleyan's tone was frosty, and she grimaced. "When you get your new revolver assembly line running, Ehdwyrd, be sure you send me one. I have a few Chisholmian aristocrats who'd give me the perfect opportunity to field test it for you."

"I'll bear that in mind, Your Majesty."

"Turning from these pleasant fantasies of bloodshed and mayhem," Merlin Athrawes put in, "how does the aforesaid assembly line look, Ehdwyrd?"

The *seijin* was currently perched in the night-struck woods in the foothills of the Branath Mountains overlooking Ohadlyn's Gap and Fort Tairys. There was no real reason he had to carry out his reconnaissance mission for Duke Eastshare in person, given the capabilities of the SNARCs' remotes, but there were times he liked to see things with his own eyes. Besides, the breezy night was pleasantly cool and daylight clear to his enhanced vision.

"In terms of how well it's going to work in the end, it looks very good," Howsmyn replied. "Zosh Huntyr's done even better than I anticipated at adapting our machine tools to pneumatic power, but I'd underestimated some of the tolerance requirements. Working at these sorts of air pressures, even a tiny leak has major implications, and the compressors were more of a pain in the arse than I expected, frankly. It's less a matter of producing the pressure than *regulating* it at so many dispersed locations, and I hadn't considered that side of things properly. I think we're on top of it now, but the whole project only emphasizes the need to step up my inspectors' training programs." He rubbed weary eyes. "It was a lot simpler when I didn't have to worry about things like that."

"I know," Merlin sympathized. "But the fact that we're so far through the process puts us light-years ahead of the Church's manufactories."

"That doesn't make it a lot less exhausting," Howsmyn said wryly, lowering his hands and looking back out the window at the throbbing, clanging, smoking, frenetically busy industrial complex he'd built literally from the ground up.

"Or less satisfying," Cayleb observed softly, and Howsmyn drew a deep breath and nodded.

"Or that," he agreed.

He gazed at his handiwork for several more seconds, then stretched, pushed up out of his chair, and began pacing around his office.

"Styvyn Bruhstair's turned out to be an inspired choice to head the Office of Inspectors. Mind you, I wasn't happy losing my best instrument maker, and I have this unhappy suspicion Paityr's going to take him away from me in the not-too-distant future. I even understand why he's going to—God knows we need someone with Styvyn's qualifications for the Imperial Bureau of Standards—but it'll make a hell of a hole in my own operations. Fortunately, he's just about finished training three deputies. Between the three of them, they ought to be able to almost carry the load he's been carrying by himself for the last year or so."

His listeners nodded in understanding. Styvyn Bruhstair was even younger than Howsmyn himself and a master clockmaker. Safeholdian timepieces had been precision instruments from the very beginning of the human presence on the planet, although each of them had been individually built by master craftsmen like Bruhstair, without a trace of standardization. The Clockmakers Guild was highly respected, and master clockmakers commanded the sorts of incomes one seldom found outside the ranks of Church bureaucrats or star baseball players.

Bruhstair himself was tall for a Charisian, only four inches shorter than Merlin, with a mind like quicksilver and agile fingers capable of incredibly delicate work. A bit nearsighted, he wore wireframe glasses to correct his vision, and he'd become a skilled lens grinder as well as a precision mechanic long before Howsmyn recruited him as his chief instrument maker. Indeed, he'd been fundamental to perfecting the new prismatic binocular "double-glasses" in conjunction with Doctor Zhain Frymyn, the fellow of the Royal College who was busy totally overhauling the Safeholdian understanding of optics. Those double-glasses were yet another item being produced here at the Delthak Works in the Instrument Shop Bruhstair had helped Howsmyn set up.

In addition to his other accomplishments, however, Bruhstair had been put in charge of creating the tools—and skills—required for inspectors on the workshop floor to guarantee uniformity of components. Like so many other aspects of the industrial revolution, Charis style, simply grasping the reason inspection was absolutely essential had required mental flexibility by the dragonload. Figuring out how to accomplish that inspection had required even more, and the Empire of Charis was fortunate Styvyn Bruhstair had that something more. With only very little help from Howsmyn (and, indirectly, from an AI named Owl of whom he'd never heard), he'd reinvented everything from the steel rule—including the end rule, the fillet rule, the hook rule, the depth rule gauge, the key seat rule, and the shrink rule—to spring calipers, firm-joint calipers, transfer calipers, the beam trammel, the combination square, and a dozen varieties of micrometer. Along the way, he and the Royal College had reinvented the vernier scale, as well, and also plug, ring, and snap gauges.

All of which were designed to make sure that, as Caleb was wont to put it, "an inch is an inch is an inch" in every manufactory in Charis.

They were still well short of that goal, although they were closing in on it quickly, and Merlin found it interesting that while the *Holy Writ* stipulated so many things—from the rules for baseball to Pasquale's dictates for public sanitation to how to terraform "unconsecrated ground"—in painstaking detail, the Church of God Awaiting had never attempted to enforce a truly standardized system of weights and measures. Oh, they were *defined* in the *Writ*, but never with the rigor of Pasquale's rules, and Mother Church simply insisted that weight and measure must be "fair," which left an enormous amount of room for variance between strictly local markets and manufactories.

Given "the Archangel Langhorne's" fanaticism, Merlin was pretty sure that hadn't been a simple oversight. No, it was far more likely that—like Langhorne's decision to reimpose Roman numerals on Safehold and revert to pre-metric units of measure—the lack of divinely directed standardization had been deliberately intended to *encourage* variation to further impede any rediscovery of advanced technology. It had taken even Charisians a while to realize how vital truly standardized units were for manufacturing. For that matter, more than a few of the Royal College's scholars had needed time to recognize the importance of reproducible measurements to systematic inquiry and experiments, and Merlin regarded the creation of the Royal (soon to be Imperial) Bureau of Standards and Measurement as one of his more satisfying "stealth" accomplishments.

Howsmyn had been at the heart of that effort from the beginning, and he'd brought Bruhstair into the process years ago. Although it was actually Owl who'd produced the master referents now housed in the BSM's Tellesberg vaults, to which all Charisian measures were to conform, they'd first been applied at Howsmyn's Delthak Works. The Delthak Works had also been commissioned to produce the duplicate referents which had been delivered to Cherayth, Eraystor, and Tranjyr. In fact, the new inch was referred to as "the Delthak inch" far more commonly than as "the Royal inch" or "the Charisian inch." Eventually, Safehold would undoubtedly discover, just as Old Earth had, that "absolute" standards of measurement were chimeras by their very nature, but in the meantime it could get on with the first truly universal system of units in its history . . . and the industrialization it made possible.

Making all the new measuring devices to the exacting standards required was far from easy, and the Instrument Shop remained a distinct bottleneck in Howsmyn's production queue. Making them and ensuring their quality and accuracy was a painstaking process that simply could not be rushed. Bruhstair was busy training still more instrument makers to assist, and output was climbing, but it remained much lower than Howsmyn would have preferred.

"We're fortunate Rahzhyr and the College have had a couple of years to turn out graduates with a sound grasp of the new math," the industrialist continued. "I really hate taking people with that kind of training out of the business of thinking of new and better ways to do things, but we *need* them out on the floor making sure we do the things we already know how to do *right*. And we're using an apprentice program to train more of them on a sort of geometric basis. By the time we have the other works up and running, we ought to have the inspectors they need, and I've been discussing putting some of my inspectors into Parsahn Sylz' manufactories." He grimaced. "Mind you, people like that bastard Showail are going to be a lot farther down my list. I know we need all the production we can get, but since I have to prioritize anyway, I might as well concentrate on the relatively honest members of the business community."

"My goodness," Merlin murmured. "And what has our good friend Stywyrt done to piss you off recently, Ehdwyrd?"

"You mean aside from offering Master Bruhstair a

fifty percent increase in pay to come work for *him*?" Howsmyn inquired acidly. "Or aside from the fact that by my count he's now in violation of fifty-seven of my patents? Or that he's still using underage labor on the side? Or the fact that my inspectors just rejected five hundred tons of his 'first grade wrought iron'? Or the fact that one of his managers who was very careful never to say so in so many words offered those same inspectors a two-hundred-mark bribe to let the pile of crap pass anyway?"

"That bad, is it?" Cayleb's voice was suddenly very cold, and Howsmyn shrugged.

"Look, this is what he's been doing all along. I think he's getting more blatant—probably because both you and Sharley are out of Old Charis for the foreseeable future and he figures the war in Siddarmark's pushing us all so hard he can get substandard materials through in the rush—but it's only a matter of degree, not a matter of kind. I've been letting the patent violations slide because even though my people have to spend twice as much time inspecting anything we buy from him—and Ahlfryd and Dahrail Malkaihy have to do the same thing on the Navy's side—he does produce a lot of iron and a lot of wrought iron, and we need all of that we can get. But if you pressed me on it, I'd admit I'm just about over dealing with him. In fact, Ahlvyno Pawalsyn, Paityr, and I are going to have a little discussion about him when I'm in Tellesberg in a couple of five-days."

"Oh?" Sharleyan's eyes had narrowed intently. Ahlvyno Pawalsyn, Baron Ironhill, was the Charisian Empire's treasurer, and Paityr Wylsynn was both the Empire's intendant and head of the Patent Office.

"I'm going to file suit against the bastard for every single patent he's violated," Howsmyn told his empress grimly. "And then Lord Justice Hyrst will have a few things to say to him."

"Oh, my," Sharleyan said in a rather different tone, the eyes which had narrowed rounding at the implications.

Sir Abshair Hyrst, the Earl of Nearoak, was Old Charis' lord justice, Cayleb's equivalent of her own Baron Stoneheart, and the acknowledged senior magistrate of the entire Empire. He was approaching seventy-two years of age and even better trained than Stoneheart, since he'd been a Langhornite law master and about to be elevated to upper-priest when his older brother and his three children had died in a house fire. Sir Abshair had been forced to leave the Church, relieved of his vows to assume the title of earl, and he'd been Rayjhis Yowance's close friend for decades. He was intelligent, dedicated, stubborn, and increasingly irascible as his rheumatism worsened, and despite—or perhaps because of—his clerical background, he was a fervent (one might almost have said rabid) Charisian patriot and a passionate supporter of the Church of Charis. If Showail was guilty of even half the offenses Howsmyn had just listed, Nearoak would go after him like a dragon through a cornfield.

"Didn't you just say he produces a lot of iron that we need badly?" Cayleb asked, and Howsmyn showed his teeth.

"Yes, I did, Your Majesty. In fact, he has two new open-hearth furnaces about to come online, which'll add appreciably to our *steel* production, as well."

"Then—forgive me if I seem a little slow, Ehdwyrd— but is this really the time to destroy his manufactory's output?"

"Oh, we're not going to do *that*!" Howsmyn shook his head. "No, what's going to happen is that between the restitution and punitive damages he'll owe me for violating my patents, and the additional fines Paityr's going to levy in his persona as Director of the Office of Patents, and the criminal fines Nearoak is virtually certain to levy over the child labor law violations, attempted bribery, and a few other minor irregularities I'm afraid are about to be brought to his notice, our good friend Stywyrt is about to find himself . . . I believe the technical term is 'without a pot to piss in.' In fact, the Crown's almost certain to require him to liquidate his entire ironworks to settle those fines I mentioned, and when that sad state of affairs comes to pass it will just happen that a small cartel in which, by the strangest turn of events, your humble servant just happens to hold a sixty-five percent interest, will offer him a price he can't refuse. At which point, those marvelous new hearths of his will go into production under *my* auspices and with *my* people operating them safely and effectively, with no more *children* getting caught in the damned gears and with somebody at least trying to keep the workers involved free of black lung. I've been waiting months to give him enough rope for this. Now the bastard can by God hang."

Merlin felt his own eyes widen at Ehdwyrd Howsmyn's genuine anger and bitterness. He'd always known how deeply Howsmyn worried about the well-being of his workmen and women and their families. In that regard, he and his mentor Rhaiyan Mychail were quite unlike the majority of manufactory owners, even in Charis. Most Charisian manufacturers had long considered that as long as they paid the going wage, didn't actively abuse their workers, paid their taxes, and made the occasional donation to Pasquale's Basket to care for the indigent and the crippled, they'd done their part. And, to be fair, that had put them far ahead of the vast majority of manufactory owners elsewhere on Safehold. The policy of the House of Ahrmahk had helped to create the attitude that prevented deliberate abuse, but child labor and the toleration of dangerous work conditions had been deeply ingrained into the industrial matrix (such as it was and what there'd been of it before Merlin Athrawes' arrival).

Mychail and Howsmyn had been actively fighting to change that matrix for decades—over forty years, in Mychail's case—and Howsmyn's ferocious campaign to outlaw child labor had won him countless enemies among other manufactory owners. Both of them had believed that paying generous wages, providing medical care and education for their workers' children, and seeing to it those workers were housed as decently as possible were not simply their moral responsibility but good business. Their labor costs had been higher than those of their competitors, but their output per man-hour had been even higher, and their employees had repaid them with a ferocious loyalty and reliability.

By now, six and a half years after their first meeting with Merlin on Helen Island, the model they'd provided to the rest of Charis was so overwhelmingly successful that ever-increasing numbers of their fellow industrialists, like Parsahn Sylz, had adopted it enthusiastically. Even more satisfying, perhaps, most of the rest had been forced to adopt it as well, however reluctantly, if they wanted to retain the workers they required. Yet there would always be at least some like Showail—the sort who would always cut corners any way they could get away with to maximize short-term profits and damn the future.

"Excuse me, Ehdwyrd," Merlin said after a moment, "but would it happen you've decided to make an example out of Showail *pour encourager les autres*?"

"I have no idea what you mean," Howsmyn replied, but the fact that he didn't ask for a translation of the French phrase suggested otherwise to Merlin.

"Of course you don't," the *seijin* said affably. "Ah, would it happen you have similar tallies on other manufactory owners who might conceivably also be violating patents of yours or illegally employing underage workers?"

"Are you suggesting I might've asked Owl and Nahrmahn to use the SNARCs to conduct industrial espionage on my behalf?"

"Perish the thought! I'm merely suggesting the possibility that as a purely fortuitous consequence of the productivity surveys you've had Owl conducting for yourself and Ironhill you may have happened to come into possession of certain information which might lead Ironhill, Paityr, and Nearoak to seek, ah, *sanctions* against certain less savory elements among your competitors."

"You do have a way with words, *Seijin* Merlin," Howsmyn observed.

"But it's an excellent question, Ehdwyrd," Cayleb said, and the ironmaster shrugged. He turned to look back out his windows at the hive of activity.

"I suppose I might as well admit I've been keeping track of those sorts of things. And Paityr already has copies of all of my notes, courtesy of Owl and Nahrmahn. We have to be more careful about how we get them to Pawal, since he's not part of the circle, and neither of us is planning on actively using them to put the other Showails completely out of business unless we absolutely have to. It's more a matter of Paityr quietly suggesting to the survivors after Showail's destruction that they might want to clean up their own acts before he sends his examiners in to investigate certain rumors—remarkably *detailed* rumors, actually—which've come to his attention. I won't pretend I wouldn't love to see some of them smashed as thoroughly as Showail, Cayleb, but I'll settle for having them provide decent working conditions and abide by the labor and worker safety laws you and Sharley've instituted. I can't make them use the minds God gave them to realize how much more they can get out of a healthy, well-fed, educated workforce that believes its employers actually *care* about it, but I'm perfectly willing to drag them kicking and screaming into doing the right thing anyway."

"Remind me not to invite you to Chisholm to explain the virtues of Charisian-style manufactory operation to my House of Lords," Sharleyan said after a moment, her tone dry. "I'm not sure the guild masters would make a properly appreciative audience, either." She shook her head. "By most Chisholmian aristocrats' standards, your Showail would be disgustingly softhearted. *You'd* terrify them . . . and probably rightly so, you crazed utopian!"

"There's nothing utopian about it," Howsmyn said stubbornly. "It's a matter of common sense and pragmatism."

"Of course it is." Cayleb's voice was almost gentle,

and Howsmyn half glared at his image. But the emperor didn't press him.

"So how soon do you think this first production line of yours could actually be up and running?" he asked instead.

"No sooner than the end of September, no later than the beginning of November." Howsmyn shrugged once more, his tone thanking the emperor for the change of subject. "Most probably, somewhere around mid-October. Nowhere soon enough to have any real impact on this year's campaigns, I'm afraid."

"And you're going to go ahead and use the first one to manufacture Mahldyn's revolvers?"

"Probably." Howsmyn dropped back into his chair. "Taigys just about has the bugs worked out of his centerfire cartridge. It's not like we had to invent drawing operations all over again, and we've been producing quality brass for the apothecaries and food preservation for centuries. We've got good availability of zinc—and antimony, when we start casting the bullets—as well, so it was more a matter of figuring out how to seat the primers than anything else. After that, designing the machinery to do the job without oodles of hand labor wasn't all that hard, assuming we get the damned pneumatic power to do its job. Now it's time to start making weapons to use them, and even though revolvers will be less useful than rifles, the pistol shop's a smaller operation. I'm still inclined to think it would make a lot of sense to use it as our pilot assembly line. We can get it up and running faster, and the lessons we'll learn in the process will stand us in good stead when it's time to put in the first rifle lines."

Cayleb frowned—not in disapproval or disagreement but thoughtfullly. Part of him did want to ramp up rifle production as rapidly as possible, but the rest of him recognized that they were already producing rifles faster than anyone else on Safehold. And Howsmyn definitely had a point about the smaller size of the pistol shop . . . and the less critical nature of the demand for sidearms.

Besides, the emperor told himself, *when you have a*

wizard who's in the habit of producing miracles for you, you'd be a right idiot to try to tell him how to tend to his own knitting, wouldn't you, Cayleb?

"What about the heavy industry side?" Merlin asked. Howsmyn cocked an eyebrow, and Merlin shrugged. "I've been a bit busy running around keeping track of armies and things," he pointed out mildly. "And one of the really good things about the existence of the inner circle from my perspective is that I don't have to try to keep tabs on everything myself, anymore."

"Point taken," Howsmyn acknowledged. He thought about the question for a few seconds, then turned his chair so that he could look at the charts on one wall of his office.

"The new ironclad program's playing hell with Dustyn's original plans," he said. "Everybody understands why priorities shifted after the Canal Raid, and Dustyn's people are just ecstatic over Bahrns' after-action report. That doesn't change the fact that we've just completely dislocated things . . . again.

"Engine production for the new river ironclads is going to be a pain in the arse, of course. When isn't it?" He snorted. "Stahlman Praigyr and Nahrmahn Tidewater are pushing it hard, and I've diverted around forty percent of the engines I'd intended for the canal barges to the new ships, which is creating its own problems. Then there's the armor production itself. We're bringing the third rolling mill online here at Delthak early next month, and it'll be able to roll up to ten-inch plate if we need it. On the supply side, Brahd's miners are managing to keep pace—barely—with demand here at Delthak; the Halleck Mountain mines are going into production; and the coke ovens are online at the Lake Lymahn Works. Or at what'll *be* the Lake Lymahn Works when we finally get them up and running, at least. It doesn't make sense to transport the ore to the Delthak Works when the Lake Lymahn blast furnaces will be up in only another month or so, so we're stockpiling the ore and the coke there. The hearths are running several months behind schedule thanks to all the diversions, though, so we'll ship pigs to

Delthak instead of ore until we can get the rest of the foundry operation up there. Even that's going to be a pain, but we can do it if we put enough dragons on it, and Brahd's making good progress with the Windhover River project. He'd really rather be putting down rails, but even if he had the 'automotives' and rolling stock we'd need, getting tracks through the Lizard Range would be a royal pain. Getting dragon wagons through the same route would be almost equally bad, so we're lucky the river's navigable for barge traffic all the way upstream from Fraidys to its junction with the White Tower. We can't get barges as big as the ones we're using *here* that far upriver, but we're building new ones about two-thirds that size which should work fine, and the new docks at Fraidys'll have steam power on the cranes and conveyors from the beginning. Actually, the hardest bit's between Lake Lymahn and Opal Lake, and—"

He stopped himself and grimaced.

"Sorry. Didn't mean to take off on one of my wild-wyvern-chase conversations again. Favorite hobby horses and all that." His grimace turned into a grin. "The real question's whether or not we'd be able to deliver the engines and armor for the new gunboats, and the answer is that I *think* we'll make delivery just about on schedule. We're sure as hell not going to get any of them there *early*, though, and pressing as I know the demand is, there's no way we can divert any more production from the power plants we're going to need here at Delthak, at the other works, at the mine faces, and in at least a half-dozen other places I probably don't even know about yet. I just can't, Merlin."

"As it happens, I agree entirely with your priorities," Merlin said.

"I do, too," Cayleb said, and Sharleyan was nodding firmly. "We're fully aware we're asking the impossible of you, Ehdwyrd. Given the merry hell we've played with your production plans so often already, we have no intention of trying to overrule you or second-guess you."

"I appreciate that," Howsmyn said and drew a deep breath. "Sometimes I feel like a one-armed slash lizard trainer, but, you know, the really remarkable thing is that my people have never let me down once. Not *once*, Cayleb. You think a greedy fool like Showail could say the same thing?"

"No, I don't."

"Should I assume Ahlfryd and Sir Dustyn are redesigning the *King Haarahlds*—again—in light of Captain Bahrns' report?" Sharleyan's smile was wry, and Howsmyn snorted as her eyes twinkled at him.

"Of course they are!" He rolled his own eyes. "When Ahlfryd can tear himself away from the proving ground, anyway. He and Ahldahs Rahzwail have the bugs out of the six-inch and eight-inch breechloaders now. In fact, we're well ahead on barrel and breech production for both of them; it was the recoil system that was the problem, and we're ramping up production on that side now. So now the demonic duo're starting in on the ten-inchers. We've already produced the first proof barrels and breeches and test-fired them successfully from fixed mountings, but the recoil loads for a twenty-two-ton weapon are just a *tad* higher than anything we've dealt with so far. Even the eight-inch only weighs about half that much. So they've got plenty of toys to make loud noises with. And if one of them doesn't blow himself up experimenting with Sahndrah's infernal mixtures, the other one damned well will!"

Sharleyan laughed. Sir Ahlfryd Hyndryk, Baron Seamount, was one of her favorite people, and he did have a veritable passion for things that exploded. Captain Ahldahs Rahzwail was less brilliant, less unorthodox, and less erratic than his superior. Aside from that, however, the two were clearly chips off the same block, and they'd pounced on Doctor Sahndrah Lywys' accidental discovery of nitrocellulose like wyverns on an unwary rabbit. Seamount clearly realized they were at a very early stage, but he was forging ahead with all his formidable energy, and the fact that Rahzhyr Mahklyn had convinced the Brethren of Saint Zherneau to recruit Lywys for the inner circle hadn't hurt a thing.

Of course, that also means poor Sahndrah's discovering

the same thing Ehdwyrd's discovered more than once. Ahlfryd's still figuring out how things go together, which is frustrating enough, but she's *finding out that it's almost more frustrating to know exactly what we need to do and not be able to do it yet,* Sharleyan admitted to herself.

Lywys had taken a sabbatical from the College for a couple of five-days to digest the truth about the Archangels, Mother Church, something called the Terran Federation, and the genocidal Gbaba. She'd spent much of those five-days conversing with Owl. In fact, Merlin had flown her to Nimue's Cave so she could do that conversing "in person," and she'd practically wept as she discovered centuries of the science of chemistry and witnessed the beauty and incredible elegance of processes and principles towards which she'd yearned for so many years. By the time he'd returned her to Tellesberg, she and Owl had worked out exactly what they needed to do to reproduce Poudre B, the original smokeless powder of Old Earth, and also the more stable cordite which had followed it.

Picric acid was also a possibility, especially as a high-explosive shell filling, given the enormous quantities of coal tar being produced by Howsmyn's coking ovens, but its tendency towards long-term instability made Lywys—and the rest of the circle—less than eager to charge full speed in that direction. Producing it would be relatively straightforward, however, and could probably be accomplished on a useful scale more rapidly than Poudre B or cordite.

"More rapidly," however, was a purely relative term. Whichever way they went in the end, the problem would be coming up with the required materials in the quantities they needed, and that would require—among other things—the creation of at least a primitive petrochemical industry. Doctor Zhansyn Wyllys, although not a member of the inner circle, was already headed in that direction, and Lywys and Mahklyn had gotten behind him to push for all they were worth, but they weren't going to have what they needed next month, no matter how hard they pushed.

"In the meantime, Ahldahs has the 'brown powder' ready to go," Howsmyn continued. Back on Old Earth, the same propellant would have been called "cocoa powder," because of the clouds of brown smoke it emitted. "It's even smokier than black powder, but it is giving them better muzzle velocities. And they've converted the Helen Island powder mill to produce prismatic powder, which is providing much more *reliable* velocities from lot to lot. They'll be extending the same processes to all the other mills over the next several months, but they want to be damned sure of their quality control when they do. And despite Ahlfryd's sheer frustration at the fact that he can't have genuine high-explosive shells by sometime next Tuesday, what he already had was better than anything the Group of Four's been able to come up with. What he's producing now is probably a thirty percent improvement on that, and he knows he'll have to settle for that until Sahndrah gets the new powders into production in something like a stable form. In the meantime, she figures she's ready to start providing dynamite—basically Nobel's original formulation, with diatomaceous earth as a stabilizer—for Brahd's miners and work crews. We're building an entire new factory up in the Southern Hanths for her. It'll be close enough to be handy to Delthak but isolated enough to hold down the casualties in case of accidents. It still won't be suitable for firing out of guns, though."

"So we're stuck with black powder small arms for the foreseeable future," Cayleb mused. Then he waved his pretzel hand in a brushing away gesture. "I'm not complaining, Ehdwyrd! Or, maybe I am, but that's only because I'm so well aware of all of the advantages smokeless powder would offer. Trust me, if you and Taigys Mahldyn come up with black powder cartridges with the performance you're talking about, that'll be *plenty* for me for right now!"

"Absolutely," Merlin agreed, and Sharleyan nodded firmly.

"I'm glad you think so," Howsmyn sighed, then glanced at the clock on his desk. "I really need to get home to Zhain," he said. "I know there're dozens of other points we could discuss, but have we covered the major ones?"

"I think so," Cayleb said after a moment. "Or at least we've covered all the ones that're currently on the horizon. I'm sure there'll be plenty of opportunities to worry about more 'major ones' in the fullness of time."

"Oh, you're so right about that!" Howsmyn climbed out of his chair and stretched hugely. "I've got a conference with Brahd about his 'steam automotive' project tomorrow. The day after that, Pahrsahn Sylz and I are supposed to discuss his provision of wrought-iron deck beams for the new ironclads. Then, Thursday, Ahlfryd and I get to talk priorities for breech-loading artillery, Ahldahs wants to discuss a new and improved howitzer with a proper recoil system, and Colonel Hynrykai's going to be in here to discuss how we can increase production of landmines now that we're actually using them in combat. Oh, and Commander Malkaihy's coming up with designs for *naval* mines, which would fill me with greater happiness if they weren't something other people will find a hell of a lot more useful than *we* will. Then there's the conference with Taigys and the pattern makers working on the revolvers, the trip upriver to the mines to inspect the new gallery, the detour home by way of that dynamite plant I mentioned, and no more than five or six more five-days' worth of backed-up paperwork to get cleared away in the next two or *three* five-days."

"Enough!" Cayleb laughed. "Go home. Hug your wife. Get some sleep! The world'll still be here tomorrow, and so will your problems. That's a lesson Merlin taught me. Well, that and that no matter how well you deal with today's problems, you can always count on tomorrow's to be at least equally interesting."

"'*Interesting.*'" Howsmyn snorted. "I suppose that's one word for it!"

"Of course it is," Merlin agreed with a smile. "Which is why some cultures back on Old Earth considered 'May you live in interesting times' to be one of the nastiest curses around."

"I see they knew a thing or two, those Old Earth cultures," Howsmyn murmured with a crooked smile of his own as he turned down the gaslights and opened his office door.

"Yes, they did. But they didn't know *everything*, Ehdwyrd, and one of the things they didn't know about was the way you Safeholdians would grab 'interesting' by the scruff of the neck and shake it till it squeals."

. VI .
Sylmahn Gap,
Old Province,
Republic of Siddarmark

"That semaphore message you've been waiting for is here, My Lord."

Kynt Clareyk looked up from the report he'd been reading with exactly the right mix of anticipation, surprise, and gratification. After his military career was over, he reflected, he obviously had a promising second career on the stage.

He held out his hand and Bryahn Slokym handed him the folded, sealed slip of paper. When he unfolded it, he discovered—not to his surprise—that this dispatch had been sent in his personal code. Because he didn't officially know what was in it, he pulled out his codebook, opened it on his field desk, and began the laborious task of personally deciphering it.

The greatest drawback of semaphore communications was that it was impossible to hide the messages being sent. Anyone with eyes could tell when a tower was sending, and because those towers had to be within visual range of one another, any chain a few hundred miles long was bound to provide an ample number of spots where spies could hide and covertly record any message which passed through. So it was routine practice to send such messages in coded ciphers, but over the centuries, Safeholdians had become rather adept at code cracking. Secular codebreakers trifled with the Church's message traffic at their peril, but it was well known that Mother Church's own semaphore clerks were skilled at breaking even complex ciphers. For that matter, there were rumors (and the more Baron Green Valley learned about the "archangels," the less convinced he became that they were inaccurate) that mystic devices within the Temple could crack any cipher ever used. Whether or not that was so, it *was* true that—for a price, of course— some of those semaphore clerks were willing to decode the system's lay users' messages for their competitors.

That was why critically important messages were routinely sent using what codebreakers on Old Earth had called "onetime pads"—substitution ciphers which would be used only once, for a single message, and then discarded. The fact that this one had been sent in Green Valley's personal cipher indicated just how important it was, and he could almost taste Slokym's burning curiosity. The young lieutenant was outwardly composed, but he radiated the impression of a little boy dancing from one foot to the other.

Green Valley worked slowly and carefully, although Owl (who'd long since scanned every page of Green Valley's codebook) was perfectly capable of simply projecting the message onto his contact lenses without further ado. Lieutenant Slokym might find it a bit difficult to take his general's ability to simply read off the message in stride, however, and it would never do to upset young Bryahn.

He came to the end of the message, tore the used page out of his codebook, carefully ripped the page into small pieces, deposited them in his ashtray, and struck a Shan-wei's candle. He used the stem of the candle to stir the scraps of paper until they were thoroughly reduced to ash, then leaned back and looked up at Slokym . . . whose impatience had risen to near disrespectful levels as he watched his general systematically deal with the housekeeping details.

"Oh, you're still here, Bryahn!" the baron observed in artful surprise.

"Yes, My Lord, I am." Slokym's tone could have been just a tad less . . . overly patient, Green Valley thought, and his lips twitched in amusement.

"Very well," he said, sitting back in his chair. "We have permission."

Slokym's eyes flared like those of a hunting hound who'd just scented the rabbit in the wire vine, and Green Valley allowed himself a matching smile.

"In addition," he continued, "Lord Protector Greyghor informs us that we'll shortly be reinforced by a complete new model division. When they reach us, they'll take over security in the Gap, which will free the rest of the Brigade for . . . use elsewhere. In the meantime, we'll leave Brigadier Traigair to watch the front door while we go sneaking around the back."

"Yes, My Lord!" Slokym's eyes were glowing now, Green Valley noted, and he made a shooing motion with one hand.

"Go tell Brigadier Mylz I need to see him. And get me Colonel Powairs, Colonel Graingyr, and Colonel Mkwartyr, as well."

"Yes, My Lord!"

Slokym slapped his breastplate in salute and disappeared, and as Green Valley pulled out the map on which he'd been sketching out his plans, he wondered how the officers he'd just sent for were going to react to those plans.

Brigadier Zhebydyah Mylz, 2nd Brigade's CO, was a fellow Old Charisian who—like Green Valley—had found himself an Army officer when the Marine brigades raised for the Corisande Campaign transferred en masse to the Imperial Army. He was just under forty years old, with plenty of combat experience from Corisande, and considerably more native aggressiveness than Brigadier Traigair, so the notion was likely to appeal to him . . . within limits, at least. Powairs, Green Valley's chief of staff, would probably see the potential advantages even more clearly than Mylz, although he wouldn't admit it at first. One of his jobs was to serve as Green Valley's sounding board, forcing the baron to consider questions he might have overlooked in his enthusiasm. Mkwartyr wouldn't care one way or the other. A hard-bitten, experienced engineer who looked down his nose at "book learning" (despite carting around a far larger library than he allowed most people to suspect), all he'd want to know was what Green Valley wanted built or blown up. Where they did the building—or the blowing up—didn't really matter to him. Graingyr was likely to approach the idea much the way Powairs did, given that keeping them supplied would fall squarely on his shoulders.

Of course, this may come at them as less of a surprise than I've been fondly anticipating, he acknowledged ruefully. *They've gotten to know me pretty damned well, and if Bryahn could figure out what I have in mind, they could've, too. On the other hand, Bryahn's the one who's in charge of my maps and dispatches, so he's had the opportunity to see my scribblings as I worked on them, which they haven't.*

He smiled at the thought, but the truth was that he'd kept all of this very close to his vest. He trusted his senior officers, and thanks to the SNARCs, he was fairly confident of his ability to identify Temple Loyalist spies elsewhere in his command. "Fairly confident" wasn't exactly the same thing as "absolutely positive," however, as the fate of the Hairatha gunpowder works demonstrated. And whatever the SNARCs might be able to tell *him* about potential spies, none of his other officers had that advantage. The sooner they became privy to what he had in mind and began implementing the detailed planning with *their* subordinates, the sooner there was a risk of his intentions leaking to the enemy.

And given the boot lace on which I'm planning this entire operation, the longer we can keep that from happening, the better.

He looked down at the map, contemplating the terrain, and his smile turned cold and hard.

▼ ▼ ▼

"So that's what we're going to do," Kynt Clareyk told the officers standing around his map table the better part of an hour later. He ran his finger down the line of the Sylmahn River and then east along the Tairmana Canal to its junction with the Mountaincross River at the small city of Maiyam, then northwest to Grayback Lake. "The Seneschal's sending us two regiments of Siddarmarkian cavalry to help out, and they should be here within the five-day. I admit I'd be happier if we had our own dragoons, but the rebel 'cavalry' we're likely to run into's no better than brigands for the most part. I'm confident our infantry columns can deal with anything we're likely to encounter in Mountaincross. The real problem's going to be how quickly we can cover the ground, not what we may run into covering it. Our latest intelligence reports"—which included SNARC reports he was in no position to share—"suggest Chestyrvyl and Greentown are both lightly held, and Maiyam's 'garrison' is supposed to be a single understrength militia regiment. More to the point, we already hold all the locks on the Tairmana Canal between here and Maiyam, and there are no locks on the Mountaincross between there and the lake. That means we'll have secure canal transportation all the way from here to Greentown if we can grab Maiyam before they know we're coming."

"And if we *don't* grab Maiyam before they know we're coming, My Lord?" Allayn Powairs asked respectfully.

"Then we'll be using a lot of dragons, Allayn. Which I'm sure Brysyn will find for us somewhere."

He smiled at Colonel Graingyr, and the quartermaster smiled back. It was not an entirely happy smile, but at least he didn't seem to be panicking.

"And how do you expect Wyrshym to react, My Lord?" Brigadier Mylz asked.

"It'll take him at least a few days to find out about it, unless they've managed to repair a lot more of the semaphore chain the ironclads destroyed than I think they have," Green Valley replied confidently. "And even after he does, there won't be much he *can* do about it. The Moon Thorns, the Ice Ashes, and the Kalgarans are all in his way, and the canals are useless to him after the Canal Raid. He'd have to march around the mountains and haul every pound of supplies overland. That's over two thousand miles by road, and it's only nine hundred sixty miles from Serabor to Greentown by water. Or, for that matter, it's only four hundred and fifty miles from Serabor to Chestyrtyn by road. Either way, we can be there long before he is, unless you think what's left of the rebel militia between here and Grayback Lake is going to stop us."

Mylz snorted.

"That's what I thought, too," Green Valley agreed with a smile. "As a matter of fact, I'd be delighted if Wyrshym *did* try to stop us. I don't see him slicing off a lot of his army and sending it out to the end of a nonexistent supply line, but it would be nice, wouldn't it? Especially if the Lord Protector's in a position to send us additional cavalry. Or if we can get one or two of our own mounted brigades when General Symkyn arrives with the second echelon."

"I agree, My Lord. And I don't disagree with anything you've said. But why do you want to do this *now*? Why not wait until General Symkyn does arrive and we can make the move in strength?"

"Two reasons, Zhebydyah. First, we can't be certain General Symkyn's going to get here on schedule. I think it's likely he will, but one thing an ex-Marine should know is that no one can command wind and wave. It's entirely possible he'll be delayed, and even if he isn't, we can't reasonably expect to see him before the end of the first five-day in September. Now, I realize you and I are both effete Charisian boys, not like these winter-hardy Chisholmians, but if I recall correctly, it *snows* in northern Haven in the winter, doesn't it?"

A rumble of laughter went up, and Green Valley grinned.

"I thought that was what I'd heard," he said. Then his expression sobered. "Seriously, from the records, we can expect snow no later than early to mid-October. If Symkyn doesn't even get here until mid-September, and it takes him six days just to get from Siddar City to Tairmana, we won't have much autumn left. I'd rather be all the way across Mountaincross and into Midhold by the time he disembarks, and I'd really like to get close enough to threaten the Northland Gap before winter shuts the canals down. I don't know if that's practical, but we can push the rebel militia out of Midhold at the very least. That would free up overland communications to Rollings Province and give us the entire northern mountain wall, from the Meirstroms to the Glacierheart Gap."

His subordinates nodded slowly, their expressions thoughtful.

"And the second reason," he went on, "is that Wyrshym's getting too much time to recover. He's dug-in, he's feeling secure—or as secure as he can—and his entire army's probably recouping some of its lost morale. At the same time, he has to've heard about what Duke Eastshare did to Kaitswyrth on the Daivyn. So has the rest of his army, no matter how hard the Inquisition's tried to downplay how bad it was. So if they find out we've launched a flanking move against them, they're going to wonder if we plan on doing the same thing to them. None of them'll *admit* that to anyone, but I want to put it into their brains. I want them thinking about it over the winter. And I especially want them thinking about the fact that we're willing to take the *offensive* when we're outnumbered ten to one. By the time the spring campaign season rolls around, especially this far north, we won't have just General Symkyn's troops. General High Mount will be here with the rest of the Army and there'll be enough new Siddarmarkian brigades in the field to watch our backs while we concentrate on kicking arse . . . or to do a little arse-kicking of their own, for that matter. I don't think the 'Temple Boys' will like that one little bit, and I want to keep them worrying about it."

He paused, letting that sink in, and smiled thinly.

"Until they ran into us here in the Gap, they were riding a wave of success all the way east. Now, between us, the Canal Raid, and the Duke, we've damned well taken the wind out of their sails. I want to keep it that way. I want the *Army* of God to be as nervous about fighting the Imperial Charisian *Army* as the Navy of God is about fighting the Imperial Charisian Navy, and that means 'putting the scare' into them and keeping it there any way we can. We kick their feet out from under them, we stomp on their throats when they go down, we take every opportunity we can find, make, or steal to rip out their hearts, and we show them—we *prove* to them—that their miserable arses are *ours* whenever we decide to put a boot in them. If we can do that, any Temple commander's going to be half defeated before we fire the first shot at him."

He looked around his officers' faces and saw their agreement. There were arguments against what he was proposing, but what he'd said clearly made sense to them. It made sense to him, too, although he also knew several things he couldn't share with them. For example, he knew General Symkyn was actually slightly *ahead* of schedule, and he knew the Earl of High Mount and over two hundred thousand additional Imperial Charisian Army infantry, cavalry, and artillery had cleared Port Royal that very morning, bound for Siddarmark. If they made a fast passage, they could reach the Republic in a little over two months, or by the middle of October. Of course, that was if they made a *fast* passage, and as he'd just pointed out to Zhebydyah Mylz, some things were more likely than others when beating to windward against autumn gales.

And then there was the *third* reason none of them had discussed in so many words. The Temple Loyalists in Midhold knew about the Allies' successes in the Sylmahn Gap and the Canal Raid . . . and that they were now thoroughly isolated from any chance of a rapid link up with the Army of God. One might have expected that to inspire them to dial down the atrocity level, but only if one were not familiar with human nature. Instead, they'd decided to do as much additional damage "in God's name" as they could before they were driven from the province entirely, and any semblance of restraint had vanished over the past several five-days. The calculated and coordinated campaign of terror carried out by Bishop Wylbyr Edwyrds, Zhaspahr Clyntahn's chosen Inquisitor General, was terrible enough; what the native Siddarmarkian Temple Loyalists had degenerated into since the Canal Raid was the stuff of nightmares. At best, Midhold would be decades recovering from what had already been done to it, and the carnage had spread across the border into Rollings Province, as well.

That was going to stop, Green Valley thought grimly. One way or the other, it was going to stop, and he didn't really care how many Temple Loyalist "militia" he had to kill in the process. Not anymore.

On the other hand, unlike any of his officers, he knew exactly what was heading for Thesmar and Shiloh Province. He also knew what Eastshare intended to do about it, and he hoped like hell the duke could pull it off. Unfortunately, there wasn't much Green Valley could do to help with that particular problem, and assuming Shiloh held, they definitely needed to be in the best position they could find to take the war to Wyrshym once again as soon as possible. The combined Desnairian-Dohlaran force swarming into the South March Lands was enormous, but it was also fundamentally less dangerous than the Army of God. And of the two armies the Temple itself had so far put into the field, Wyrshym's was both the more dangerous and the more vulnerable, with no secure river or canal line along which it could retreat in the face of a determined attack.

The Temple still doesn't realize how quickly we can move or how hard we can hit, he thought, gazing down at the map while Graingyr and Mkwartyr started discussing the logistics and engineering train they were going to need. *If I can get close enough, then throw a corps of Charisian cavalry with Charisian artillery across his rear, it's possible we could cut off and destroy his entire army. Even if we can't do that, cleaning out—and hanging—the bastards burning, looting, and raping everything that's left in Midhold will be entirely worthwhile in its own right. But most of all, I want Wyrshym right where he is at Saiknyr and Guarnak while we swing through the Northland Gap and slam the door shut behind him. He's probably smart enough to pull back if he realizes what's coming, but he may not be the one who gets to make the decision, and everything we've seen suggests that Zhaspahr Clyntahn's as fond of "hold to the last man" orders as Adolf Hitler ever was. Who knows? We may just be able to engineer our very own Stalingrad, and that would suit me just fine.*

VII.
Siddar City,
Republic of Siddarmark

"Signal from Admiral White Ford, Sir."

Captain Halcom Bahrns tried not to scowl at the sound of Ahbukyra Matthysahn's respectful voice. The young signalman's shattered elbow was still encased in plaster, and the healers weren't optimistic about how much—if any—use of it he would ever again have. Bahrns had tried to send the youngster to one of the Pasqualate hospitals ashore, or at least to one of the ICN hospital ships, but Matthysahn had proven both stubborn and remarkably adroit at avoiding anything that would remove him from HMS *Delthak*. A lot of Bahrns' crew seemed to feel that way, and despite his injury Matthysahn remained one of the best signalmen in the entire Navy.

None of which made Captain Bahrns any more cheerful about receiving signals from admirals just as he finally sat down for a long overdue lunch.

"Sorry, Sir." Matthysahn shook his head. "It's marked Priority."

"Better and better," Bahrns muttered. Then he gave himself a shake. "Not your fault, Ahbukyra. And I don't suppose I should hold it against Admiral White Ford, either. I'm sure he probably figures I finished lunch hours ago, like any sane captain would've."

"Yes, Sir."

Bahrns unfolded the message, skimmed it, and in a dazzling display of professionalism and self-control did not swear. Instead, he looked up at Trynt Sevyrs, the rather villainous-looking, much-tattooed steward's mate who'd somehow become his personal steward, and shook his head.

"It looks delicious, Trynt, but I've got to go. Put a slab of meat and some cheese between a couple of pieces of bread and I'll eat it in the boat."

"But, Captain—"

"Not negotiable, I'm afraid." Bahrns pushed back from the table, regarding the fried chicken, buttered potatoes, and lima beans with an expression of profound regret. "I have to get changed. So while Trynt's doing his best to keep me from collapsing of hunger on my way to the Admiral, Ahbukyra, I need you to find Brahdlai and tell him to assemble his boat's crew."

"Aye, aye, Sir," Matthysahn acknowledged, and Bahrns allowed himself one last, mournful headshake before hurrying off to his cabin to exchange his worn seagoing uniform for something more suitable for facing a flag officer.

▼ ▼ ▼

North Bedard Bay was a vast, dark blue sheet of water over two hundred and thirty miles across. To the east, it stretched clear to the horizon like a wave-ruffled carpet. To the west, and much closer to hand, the roofs, cathedral spires, and towers of Siddar City rose beyond a broad waterfront which was busier than it had ever been before. That was saying quite a lot, given how much Charisian cargo had passed through the Republic before Zhaspahr Clyntahn had spread death and destruction across two-thirds of Siddarmark. And it was saying even more, given the feverish efforts to ship in enough food to stave off the deliberate starvation he'd inflicted upon the Republic. But that frantic labor was a thing of the past. Food was still being landed in much greater quantities than normal, yet order had been reasserted. That didn't make the docks one bit less busy, however, and the presence of over forty Imperial Charisian Navy galleons, with all their boat and ship-to-shore traffic, not to mention the convoy of military matériel which had just arrived from Old Charis, was enough to make the two-mile pull from *Delthak* to Admiral White Ford's flagship interesting, to say the least.

Brahdlai Mahfyt, Bahrns' personal coxswain, took it in stride. He made it a point to take *everything* in stride, actually, and Bahrns treasured the muscular petty officer's unflappable composure even if he did secretly cherish the hope that someday that composure would crack. Secure in the knowledge that Mahfyt would somehow manage to avoid ramming—or being rammed by—another cutter, launch, whaleboat, or gig on the journey to HMS *Fortune*, Bahrns sat back to enjoy the cool air, brisk breeze, and billowing white cloud. As he watched, a gliding deep-mouth wyvern banked, swooped down, and then beat its wings heavily as it climbed back into the air with the pouch under its beak squirming as some small fish fought to escape. Other wyverns and gulls circled overhead, riding the wind effortlessly, and the incoming tide washed white and green against the seawall.

At times like this, when wind and salt swept over him with their cleansing touch, Halcom Bahrns could almost forget the savagery raging across Siddarmark. Not for very long, of course. The memories of what everyone was calling the "Great Canal Raid" were too fresh and too ugly for that, and he wondered if that would ever change. And yet, for all the ferocity and destruction of the raid, the bulk of the Imperial Charisian Navy found itself with no one to fight. That was . . . wrong. It seemed as if the Navy had been fighting for its life, and for Charis' survival, for as long as anyone could remember, but now it was up to the Army, and Bahrns felt almost left out, as if he were somehow shirking his responsibilities by not being locked in mortal combat with the Temple Loyalists.

You really are around the bend, aren't you, Halcom? he asked himself dryly. *Are you trying to tell me you're bored? And that being bored in the middle of a war is a bad* thing?

He chuckled at the thought, trying to imagine how *Delthak*'s company might respond to that particular proposition. Probably not very well. Still—

"What boat?"

The challenge from *Fortune*'s deck watch plucked Bahrns up out of his ruminations as Mahfyt responded.

"*Delthak!*" he barked through a speaking trumpet, the ship's name warning the galleon that the approaching cutter had the ironclad's captain on board. There was a stir aboard the flagship as Mahfyt brought the cutter alongside and the bowman hooked neatly onto the main chains. The cutter's crew tossed oars in perfect unison, precisely timed, without a single command from Mahfyt, and Bahrns smiled. No one looking at that meticulously drilled crew could possibly have guessed that they'd only come aboard *Delthak* barely a month earlier.

"Smartly done, Brahdlai," he said from the corner of his mouth as he stood in the cutter, looking up, gauging the boat's motion before he made his jump for the battens. Compared to other boat transfers he'd made during his career, this one wouldn't be particularly challenging despite the stiff breeze, since the cutter lay in *Fortune*'s lee.

Of course, the first time you take it for granted's going to be the time you fall into the water, the cutter smashes into you, you get driven under the turn of the bilge, and you drown on a perfectly calm day with no excuse but your own stupidity, he reminded himself.

"Thankee, Sir," Mahfyt replied equally quietly. "And mind that first jump."

Bahrns gave him a moderate glare—which had no effect on the coxswain at all—and then jumped.

As it happened, he timed it perfectly, and climbed nimbly up the ship's tall side to the entry port without mishap. Bosun's pipes shrilled as he came aboard and the side party of Marines snapped to attention and presented arms. He touched his chest to return the salute, turned to salute the colors, and then turned back to find himself facing a towering, massively built captain with enormous shoulders. The man had to be as tall as Merlin Athrawes himself, and probably half again the *seijin*'s weight, and from where Bahrns stood, none of it appeared to be fat. The giant held out a paw-like hand to clasp arms in greeting.

"Captain Zhilbert Kaillee," he rumbled in a strong Tarotisian accent. "Welcome aboard, Captain Bahrns. And please accept my compliments for a job very well done last month."

"Thank you, Sir," Bahrns replied. There wasn't a lot else he could say.

"Admiral White Ford asks you to join us in his day cabin."

"Of course, Sir."

▼ ▼ ▼

Gahvyn Mhartyn, the Baron of White Ford, was dwarfed by his enormous flag captain. A small man, with dark eyes and once-dark hair which had turned mostly silver, he had an alert, thoughtful air about him.

He was also the man who'd commanded the Tarotisian squadron at the Battle of Armageddon Reef and been soundly defeated by then-Crown Prince Cayleb in the first broadside engagement ever fought by galleons. It seemed like an eternity ago, yet less than five years had elapsed since that savage engagement, and Bahrns wondered how it must seem to White Ford and Kaillee. Their navy and kingdom had been utterly defeated and, in the end, their king had been forced to accept Charisian sovereignty. Yet here White Ford was, a *Charisian* admiral and Emperor Cayleb Ahrmahk's port admiral in Bedard Bay. There had to be the odd moment when that rankled, despite the evidence of the high regard in which his onetime enemies held him. Still, Bahrns suspected that the Earl of Thirsk, the other enemy commander off Armageddon Reef, might well have exchanged places with White Ford if he'd had the chance. Besides—

The captain's thought broke off as the man who'd been contemplating the panorama of the harbor through the galleon's stern windows turned to face him.

"Your Majesty!" Bahrns bowed quickly. "Forgive me, I didn't expect—"

"No reason you should've," Cayleb Ahrmahk replied. "In fact, I've been to some lengths to keep anyone from realizing I've come out to talk to you and the Admiral." The emperor smiled, and waved at the tall, blue-eyed man standing quietly in one corner. "I believe you've met Major Athrawes, Captain?"

"Yes, Your Majesty." Bahrns held out his hand to the *seijin* who'd conceived the mad audacity of the Canal Raid. "It's good to see you again, *Seijin*."

"You should never be hasty about these things, Captain," Athrawes replied.

"I beg your pardon?" Bahrns quirked an eyebrow.

"Rushing to judgment about whether or not it's good to see me," Athrawes said with a crooked smile. "I have it on fairly good authority that chaos, confusion, and mayhem follow me about."

"I don't mind a little chaos and confusion as long as the mayhem gets visited on the right people, *Seijin*," Bahrns told him, and the emperor chuckled.

"Well, you did a pretty fair job of visiting mayhem on our foes last month, Captain Bahrns. And as they say, no good deed goes unpunished."

"I've, ah, heard that, Your Majesty." Bahrns regarded his emperor with what he hoped was hidden trepidation, and Cayleb smiled, then waved at the chairs around the polished table under the cabin skylight.

"Since Admiral White Ford's been so kind as to make his day cabin available to us, Captain Bahrns, I think we should all be seated."

"Of course, Your Majesty."

The only person in that cabin junior in rank to Halcom Bahrns was Major Athrawes. However, there were majors and then there were *majors,* and Bahrns couldn't think of anyone Emperor Cayleb was likely to consider senior to this particular major. He waited, watching the *seijin* from the corner of one eye, while Cayleb sat, followed by White Ford, and then by Kaillee. Athrawes only smiled again, as crookedly as before, and took his place behind Cayleb's chair. With the way cleared, Bahrns went ahead and seated himself as a gray-haired, slightly built man appeared, carrying a silver tray laden with crystal decanters and glasses.

"Thank you, Zheevys," White Ford said, nodding towards the emperor, and the valet set the tray on a side table and offered Cayleb his choice of the decanters. The emperor made his selection and Zheevys poured for him, then circled the table. Bahrns was no judge of fine liqueurs and he knew it, so there was no point pretending differently. He simply accepted whatever was poured and sipped politely . . . and almost blinked as golden glory with a smoky aftertaste rolled over his tongue and down his throat.

Maybe I should learn *to judge fine liqueurs,* he told himself, savoring the sunburst explosion. *Not that I could afford this very often, I suspect.*

"I asked you here because His Majesty has an idea that involves you, Captain Bahrns," White Ford said after a moment. "As I discovered once upon a time off the coast of Armageddon Reef, he frequently has ideas that end up making all sorts of difficulties for the ungodly." The small Tarotisian smiled and raised his glass to the emperor. "Now that I'm no longer counted among the *ranks* of the ungodly—except, perhaps, by Zhaspahr Clyntahn—that's just fine with me, you understand. However, I'd like to begin by asking for a report on the condition of your command."

Bahrns stiffened ever so slightly, and Emperor Cayleb shook his head.

"That's not an attempt to 'catch you out,' Captain.

The operation you and Captain Tailahr carried out was bound to overstress your ships, especially when they're so new and we have so little experience operating them. We just need to know how well they stood up to the demands placed on them before we can know whether or not what we have in mind is workable."

"Of course, Your Majesty."

Bahrns suppressed the need for another swallow of that marvelous elixir, set his glass on the table, and faced the emperor squarely.

"To be honest, Your Majesty, the ships stood up far better than I ever expected, but they've still steamed nearly twenty thousand miles. I never would've believed they could steam that far without a major breakdown, and I instructed Lieutenant Blahdysnberg—he's my engineer, Your Majesty—to carry out a complete engine inspection. He's torn them down to do that, and he's turned up some minor problems. The worst is with the starboard engine's condenser, and that one does worry him a bit. Fortunately, the service galleons Sir Dustyn and Captain Saigyl sent along have all the spares he needs, and the mechanics aboard them are doing most of the work under his direction. Despite that, I'm afraid it's going to be some time—probably at least a couple of five-days—before I could honestly report her ready for sea."

"Any problems outside Lieutenant Blahdysnberg's department?"

"Not any significant ones, Your Majesty. We have a few broken armor bolts, the bridge wings had to be rebuilt, it was necessary to replace several of the ventilator intakes, and one of the gundeck blowers broke a fan blade. All of that's already been dealt with, however."

"And *Hador*?"

"I believe Captain Tailahr's repairs are going as well as my own, Your Majesty, but I'd hesitate to speak for him," Bahrns said. He met Cayleb's gaze levelly, and the emperor nodded.

"As you probably know, Captain Bahrns," he said, "*Saygin* and *Tellesberg* are still operating out of Spinefish Bay, and one of the service galleons will be sailing for Salyk in the next day or two. We don't know how much longer they'll be able to go on operating—once Hsing-wu's Passage starts to freeze, it freezes quickly, and we can't afford to get one of the ironclads trapped in the ice. For now, though, they're still operating fifty or sixty miles up the Hildermoss and generally keeping the Army of God around Salyk on edge."

Bahrns nodded, although if truth be told he was a long way from guessing where this was headed. Did the emperor intend to send *Delthak* and *Hador* up to relieve *Saygin* and *Tellesberg*?

"I have something a bit different in mind for you and Captain Tailahr, however," the emperor said, as if he'd read Bahrns' mind, and rumor suggested he might very well be able to do exactly that.

"You do, Your Majesty?" the captain asked when Cayleb paused, and the emperor nodded.

"I do, indeed, Captain. Fortunately, all the pieces for the operation I have in mind won't be available for some five-days yet, so you should have ample time to complete your repairs and maintenance. And I think you'll find it just a bit *warmer* than Spinefish Bay would be, too. Probably in more than one way."

. VIII .

Thesmar,
The South March Lands,
Republic of Siddarmark

"I've never seen so many people in one place," Kydryc Fyguera said softly.

He and Earl Hanth stood on one of the quartet of hundred-and-twenty-foot-tall wooden observation towers Captain Lywys Sympsyn, Hanth's senior engineer, had built at his orders. Fyguera wouldn't have considered the project, himself, for a lot of reasons, including the fact that he wasn't a Marine and didn't have a Marine's instinctive understanding for how much farther someone could see from a masthead. The tower on which they stood at the moment, built using spare spars from Admiral Hywyt's galleons, was in the second line of entrenchments, just behind Redoubt #1 and the bastion known as Tymahn's Angle on the hundred-and-ten-foot crest of Sulyvyn Hill, which extended the visual horizon still farther. With heavy telescopes bracketed firmly to the railing around the tower's square platform, lookouts could see almost twenty miles, sixteen miles beyond their own positions.

The second tower stood roughly in the middle of the position, behind the Island Redoubt and five miles west of Thesmar; the third stood in Redoubt #4 on Mount Yarith; and the fourth stood in the center of the city itself. Equipped with heliographs and signal flags, men in those towers could report every move the enemy made . . . or call down indirect fire from the angle-guns Admiral Hywyt had landed from HMS *Holocaust*, one of his bombardment ships. Fourteen of them were mounted in the forward redoubts and bastions and another ten were positioned in the city itself. Heavier and less mobile than the Imperial Charisian Army's version of the same weapon, the naval angles could fire almost a mile farther, which meant at least one section of them could engage any spot within two or even three miles of the outermost lines of entrenchments. It would have been even nicer if the 1st Independent Marine Brigade had possessed any infantry mortars to add to its weight of fire, but there was plenty—indeed, almost a surfeit—of other artillery available.

As he stood in the warm morning sunlight beside the Siddarmarkian general, Hanth could see the quadruple line of entrenchments spread out about him like some celestial model maker's handiwork. The outermost line ran sixty miles, from Sulyvyn Hill southwest of the city to the thoroughly misnamed Mount Yarith to the northeast; the innermost, just outside the city itself, was barely fifteen miles in length. Open to the east, where the ships of the Imperial Charisian Navy watched Thesmar's back, the position Fyguera had fortified was just under fifteen miles deep at its deepest point, and he'd been working on it for months. It was actually a bit over-large for twenty-four thousand men to hold. If, of course, they'd *had* twenty-four thousand men, which they didn't . . . yet. The healers were guardedly optimistic about the total number of Clyftyn Sumyrs' men who'd be fit for duty over the next few five-days, though, and Fyguera had taken advantage of the Seridahn and the Yarith Rivers when he planned his works.

To be sure, calling the Yarith a "river" was almost as ridiculous as calling the large hill of the same name a "mount." It was more of a wide creek than a river, but its low-lying floodplain ran between Mount Yarith and Shadowline Mountain, to the west. Shadowline really was a mountain, albeit a tiny one compared to the Glacierhearts or Moon Thorns, and the valley between it and Mount Yarith was marshy enough to have made throwing up the entrenchments across it difficult. Fyguera had capitalized on that, excavating deep, wide moats in front of each earthwork barrier. The local water table was high enough to fill them quickly, and his fatigue parties had dammed the stream to create even wider inundations that stretched almost entirely across the valley. The water was over ten feet deep in many places—more than fifteen where the meandering streambed cut through it— and almost five miles across at its widest, and the cover it provided had allowed them to economize significantly on manpower.

The Seridahn, flowing between the southern slopes of Shadowline and Sulyvyn Hill to reach Thesmar Bay, came through a shallower declivity, but it also carried a lot more water than the Yarith did, and Fyguera had made good use of it, as well. Of the outer works' sixty miles of frontage, twenty were protected by flooded ditches and impounded water, and the Siddarmarkian general had incorporated similar inundations to protect the approaches to the inner lines of entrenchments, as well. The position wasn't invulnerable—no position ever truly was—but it was as strong a set of field works as Hanth could have imagined.

Especially with so many guns to cover it, he thought.

As long as Thesmar was in the Allies' hands and could be supplied, it was a dagger at the throat of the Imperial Desnairian Army's overland supply route out of the Grand Duchy of Silkiah. Greyghor Stohnar and Cayleb Ahrmahk might not be in a position to drive that dagger home at the moment, but that would change the instant they could find the reinforcements for the task, and they intended to keep its hilt firmly in their hands until they could. And since they didn't currently have the thousands of infantrymen they would really have preferred to send Hanth, they'd settled for the next best thing: enough artillery to storm Hell.

From the moment his own force had been earmarked for Thesmar, the Imperial Charisian Navy had been throwing guns ashore and digging them in. Quite a few naval galleons were floating higher in the water than they ought to be because their artillery—and artillerists—were now enjoying a delightful vacation in the city the Allies meant to hold at all costs.

All told, there were now two hundred and fifty guns guarding Thesmar. A hundred and thirty-six were naval thirty-pounders, and fifty-four of the rest were stubby fifty-seven-pounder carronades: short-ranged but devastatingly powerful and capable of extraordinarily rapid fire in the close defense role. And there were thirty-six of the handy, maneuverable twelve-pounders, as well, two-thirds of them Charisian and the rest captured from the Dohlarans. The Dohlaran guns couldn't fire Charisian shells or round shot, despite their nominally identical calibers, but they could fire grape and cannister just fine and they'd been positioned primarily as flanking pieces to sweep the fronts of the entrenchments.

The bastions and redoubts of General Fyguera's works had been laid out by Captain Sympsyn and Commander Ahrthyr Parkyr. Neither of them was a trained Army engineer, but unlike the Siddarmarkian Army, the Charisian Navy had ample experience with new model artillery. They'd surveyed the position carefully before they began digging in, and they'd sited their batteries to give as much coverage of the approaches as possible. Most of the few spots of dead ground they couldn't cover with direct fire were flooded by Fyguera's inundations, and they'd already registered the angle-guns on all of them they knew about.

I won't say they can't take the position in the end if they're willing to pay the price, but I can say that they don't have a clue how high that price will be.

The thought touched him with grim satisfaction, and he raised his double-glass, looking through the twin tubes at the ant-like infantry and cavalry swarming about just beyond artillery range. The double-glass wasn't as powerful as the rail-mounted telescopes, but its paired eyepieces presented a three-dimensional image that gave a far greater feel for detail, and he swept it slowly across the panorama before him.

"I've never seen that many people in one place before, either, Kydryc," he said after a moment. "Impressive, isn't it?"

"That's one way to put it," the bald, bull-shouldered Siddarmarkian replied sourly.

Despite the odds marshaled against them, Fyguera seemed far more relaxed than he'd been when Hanth and his Marines and seamen first arrived in Thesmar. Part of that was probably because his garrison and the limited number of civilians who hadn't yet been lifted out were actually well fed for a change. More of it, though, undoubtedly stemmed from the knowledge that he and the men he'd managed to hold together over the terrible winter hadn't been abandoned after all. The sheer quantity of artillery and gunners the ICN had landed was proof enough of that, and the proficiency those men of his had gained with the captured Dohlaran rifles Hanth had handed over had done wonders for their morale and his.

The Siddarmarkian general had also been remarkably unfazed by the lord protector's insistence on putting

Hanth in overall command. It made sense to him, given the fact that most of the defenders' rifles, all of their artillery, and every ton of supplies had been supplied by Charis. Besides, he had even less experience with the new model weapons than their enemies did, and he knew it.

"Well," Hanth pointed out, "cavalry'll be pretty damned useless if it comes to storming entrenchments, and that's half or more of everyone we're seeing out there. And Harless is light on artillery compared to the Dohlarans, according to our spies. Plus there's the little fact that he's a Desnairian noble, and we all know how they feel about 'mere infantry.'" The earl shook his head, his smile reminding Fyguera rather forcibly of a hungry slash lizard. "A general who lets contempt for his adversary govern his planning is a general waiting to get his arse kicked, and I'm of the opinion that our lads have just the boots to do the kicking with."

"Do you really think he'll try an assault?"

"Not if he's got any sense, but that's where the contempt comes in. And to be fair, we should probably add inexperience to the mix." Hanth shrugged. "At least for the next little bit, everybody but us Charisians is operating in the complete unknown, Kydryc. I'm sure Rychtyr and Ahlverez could give Harless some pointers, and Rychtyr at least is smart enough to try. The question is whether or not Harless is smart enough to *listen*. If he isn't, he and his men are going to learn the same way Ahlverez and Rychtyr did—the *hard* way."

▼ ▼ ▼

"Thank you for coming so promptly, Sir Rainos."

Sir Rainos Ahlverez bowed just a bit stiffly to the impeccable sprig of fashion who'd greeted him as he stepped into the huge, brilliantly dyed tent. The young man in front of him couldn't have been more than twenty-five years old, and he was dressed in the height of style for the imperial Desnairian court, which was one hell of a long way from the city of Thesmar. Aside from a light dress sword, he was unarmed, his dark hair was neatly curled, his hands were beautifully manicured, and Ahlverez caught a whiff of expensive cologne when the youngster returned his bow.

"I am Sir Graim Kyr," he said, straightening, "and I have the honor to be aide-de-camp to His Grace, the Duke of Harless."

"Of course. And this is Sir Lynkyn Lattymyr, my own aide," Ahlverez indicated the rather older, more weathered, and much tougher-looking Royal Dohlaran Army captain at his side, "and Father Sulyvn, my intendant."

"Honored, Father," Sir Graim murmured, bending to kiss the Schuelerite's ring. He straightened again and nodded to Lattymyr with the air of someone who'd assayed yet another of his social inferior's position with an expert eye. Then he turned back to Ahlverez.

"If you would accompany me, Sir Rainos, His Grace is waiting."

▼ ▼ ▼

As he followed the young exquisite down the thickly carpeted passage between walls of gently billowing cotton silk, Ahlverez cudgeled his brain, trying to place Kyr in the ranks of the Desnairian nobility. He wasn't having much luck when Lattymyr leaned closer.

"Baron Fyrnach, Sir." The murmur in Ahlverez' ear was so faint even he could scarcely hear it. "Third cousin of Duke Traykhos and Duke Harless' grandnephew."

Ahlverez nodded. Of course he was. And Taylar Gahrmahn, the Duke of Traykhos, happened to be Mahrys IV's first councilor. Sir Rainos understood the necessity of choosing men of good blood for important posts, and clearly family had to be a factor. Still, there was such a thing as attempting to find a *competent* man of good blood instead of one more useless court fop, even if he *was* family. Not that anyone should've expected anything else out of a Desnairian.

They turned a corner and—finally—reached their destination. Ahlverez liked his own camp comforts as much as the next man, but this monster of a tent had to measure eighty yards on a side. It must take hours to erect and strike, and it wasn't exactly something he would've associated with a hard-driving, fast-moving cavalry commander. But since all the world knew that all Desnairian officers were hard-driving, fast-moving cavalry commanders, he must be mistaken about that.

"Sir Rainos Ahlverez, Your Grace," young Fyrnach murmured, bowing to a tallish, balding man with a thin, trimmed mustache and brown eyes. "Father Sulyvyn, his intendant, and Sir Lynkyn Lattymyr, his aide."

He turned back to Ahlverez.

"Sir Ahlvyn Gahrnet, His Grace the Duke of Harless," he said, and went on to indicate the other three men present. "Sir Mahrak Dynnysyn, the Earl of Hankey; Sir Traivyr Bahskym, Earl of Hennet; and Father Tymythy Yairdyn."

Ahlverez and his companions bowed in acknowledgment, and Harless waved for them to seat themselves at the magnificent inlaid table in the center of the spacious compartment. That table had to weigh three or four hundred pounds, Ahlverez estimated, and unlike the folding camp chairs he used in his own tent, the chairs around it were ornately carved and upholstered, obviously a matched set from the same master woodcrafter who'd produced the table.

Whatever Fyrnach's virtues as a military officer might or might not be, he was clearly an asset in a social situation. He managed to get all three of the Dohlarans seated in their assigned chairs and in proper order without as much as a single spoken word. Then he took his own seat beside his granduncle while silent servants poured wine.

Ahlverez studied the others unobtrusively.

Earl Hankey, he knew, was Harless' second-in-command. In his late fifties and very tall, he was fair-haired and brown-eyed, with a badly scarred left cheek. He was broad-shouldered, and despite the fact that he was "only" an earl, he was actually one of the Desnairian Empire's most powerful nobles, with a seat on the Imperial Council.

Earl Hennet commanded the Army of Justice's cavalry wing, and that was enough to make anyone who'd seen new model infantry weapons in action nervous about him. He was long-limbed but not especially tall, and while he wasn't as well connected as Earl Hankey, he wouldn't have held the post he held without a powerful patron. In his case, that patron was Faigyn Makychee, who'd become the new Duke of Kholman after Daivyn Bairaht fled to the Charisians. Makychee had arisen from relative obscurity, but he was a favorite of Bishop Executor Mhartyn Raislair and related by marriage to Duke Traykhos.

Which means he's also related to Fyrnach, Ahlverez thought. *Wonderful.*

"I'm very pleased to see you, Sir Rainos," Harless said after the servants had finished pouring and departed. "The victor of Alyksberg must be a welcome addition to any army."

"Thank you, Your Grace."

Ahlverez didn't—quite—grit his teeth, and he supposed Harless probably genuinely meant it. For that matter, Alyksberg was the first Siddarmarkian fortress to be stormed by a foreign enemy in the last couple of centuries. The fact that it had been blown up in his face and killed so many of his men was just one of those irritating little historical footnotes. Anyway, most of them had been commoners. Not the sort of thing a Desnairian would hold against a fellow.

"And I'm also pleased to see you because your artillery train is so much more powerful than my own." Harless waved one hand at a cotton silk wall, gesturing in the general direction of Thesmar. "We're bringing up our own guns, of course, but yours will be a powerful reinforcement when we attack."

"When we attack," Ahlverez repeated carefully.

"Of course. And as soon as possible." Harless shrugged. "With the heretic navy operating so freely in the Gulf of Jahras, Tabbard Reach, even Silkiah Bay, we—the Empire—can move reinforcements only overland. Oh, our batteries are enough to protect Silk Town and keep the Silk Town-Thesmar Canal open, but"—he grimaced distastefully—"after our Navy's . . . regrettable defeat at Iythria, we can't be certain how long that will be true. I'm assured the situation's currently secure, but even with the canal, we can move no farther north than Lake Somyr by water, and as long as Thesmar remains in heretic hands, the possibility that they'll suddenly reinforce and move against our supply lines can't be ignored. For that matter, it would remain a serious threat to your own supply lines down the Seridahn as we continue our advance towards Shiloh. At the moment, however, our spies and the local Faithful report there are no more than ten to fifteen thousand men in the city." He shrugged again. "The obvious solution is to crush it now, before its garrison can be further strengthened."

Ahlverez sat very still, wishing suddenly that Sir Fahstyr Rychtyr were present. He wasn't especially fond of his own second-in-command, although he was honest enough to admit—at least to himself—that the main reason he wasn't was that he'd ignored Rychtyr's advice when he diverted his own advance to Alyksberg instead of trying to crush Thesmar when it truly *was* weak. Given the many five-days his own . . . unwise diversion had allowed the heretic Fyguera and his garrison to change that state of affairs, he rather doubted the city could be crushed remotely as easily as Harless seemed to assume, not that he had any desire to explain the reasons for that to the Desnairians.

And, he admitted, he found himself wondering if Harless had omitted to invite Rychtyr because he'd wanted to get Ahlverez by himself and overwhelm any resistance to assaulting the heretics before he could discuss it with his own officers. His instructions from King Rahnyld—and Mother Church—were clear. As the commander of seventy percent of the combined Dohlaran and Desnairian field strength in the South March, Harless was the Jihad's senior officer present. Much as it galled Ahlverez, he'd been instructed to accept Harless' "directions"—even the Inquisition hadn't wanted to call them "orders"—for the prosecution of the campaign. On the other hand, it had been made quietly and privately clear to him by the Duke of Salthar, the commander of the Royal Dohlaran Army, that he was *not* supposed to simply hand over command to the Desnairians.

But Father Sulyvyn was remarkably silent on that point, wasn't he? Mother Church is the one behind this sword-point marriage with Desnair, and what do you do if he tells you to shut up and take Harless' orders anyway?

"I agree that Thesmar represents a serious potential threat to your—to *our*—lines of communication, Your Grace," he said after a moment. "And the possibility that the heretics will find the men to turn it into an *actual* threat can't be ignored. Unfortunately, the heretic navy's been landing artillery for five-days now. I've only just arrived myself, so I've had no opportunity to personally reconnoiter the enemy's position, but I'm very much afraid our twelve-pounders are no match for heavy naval artillery. Especially not naval artillery that's been thoroughly dug in behind solid earthworks."

"I realize your guns, like our own, are lighter than naval guns." There might have been just a hint of frost in Harless' courteous tone. "There are, however, some advantages to that, and I understand you also have your own version of the artillery the heretics employed against our fortresses at Iythria."

His expression made the sentence a question, and Ahlverez felt his lips tighten. It was true that his artillery train included several batteries of what the heretics had dubbed "angle-guns." They were much smaller than the heretical version, firing the same shells as his field guns, and he suspected they were also shorter-ranged. What irked him the most about them, however, was the reason he had them, for they'd been the brain children of Lywys Gardynyr, the Earl of Thirsk, and there was no love lost between him and Thirsk.

At the moment, though. . . .

"Yes, Your Grace, we do have some angle-guns. Their shells are no heavier than those of our field pieces, however, and frankly we don't have many of them. I'd have to check to be certain, but I believe we have no more than four or five batteries. A heavier version firing much larger shells is in production and will probably reach us within the next month or two, but for now I seriously doubt the weapons we possess would be enough to breach the heretics' lines."

"I wouldn't expect them to, Sir Rainos," Harless said. "Nor am I suggesting we should attempt to blast a breach through the heretics' earthworks as if they were the stone walls of a castle. No, I have something rather different in mind."

"Different in what way, if I may ask?"

"So far, no heretic's ever been fired upon using the . . . 'angle-guns,' did you call them?" The duke raised an eyebrow, and Ahlverez nodded. "As I say, they've used the weapons against God's loyal sons but they've never been on the receiving end of them. I realize you've had no chance yet to personally observe the heretics' positions, and I'll value your opinion once you've had that opportunity. From my own observation, however, the heretic left appears vulnerable. They've covered the low ground by flooding it, but they can't flood the high ground. I propose—assuming you concur, of course—to assault across Sulyvyn Hill, thus avoiding the flooded ground.

"My scouts report two redoubts atop the hill, each with a half-dozen or so heavy guns. But heavy guns are slow-firing, Sir Rainos. Much slower than our own field guns, at any rate, and I feel sure your 'angle-guns' can fire more rapidly than they, as well. We have many fewer cannon, but their guns are dispersed throughout their defenses while ours can be concentrated in one place, and ours are light enough to be quickly and quietly moved into position. So my intention is to bring them up under cover of darkness and deploy them in a massed battery to sweep the heretics' parapets with shot and shell. We'll open fire just at dawn, when they have no cause to expect it, and use your 'angle-guns' to drop fire directly on their heads at the same time. The surprise of such a sudden bombardment—and of receiving the fire of someone *else's* 'angle-guns'—is bound to dismay them, and their positions can't possibly be heavily manned. Not with the length of their works and the small size of the garrison. Surprised, frightened, and outnumbered, they'll be no match for God's true sons when our assault columns go in with cold steel."

The Desnairian's arrogantly confident expression sent a stab of dismay through Sir Rainos Ahlverez. Worse, Sulyvyn Fyrmyn was nodding, eyes fierce with his burning desire to strike the heresy in the heart, and that was a bad sign. By and large, Ahlverez was of one mind with his intendant, and the only thing he was prepared to waste on a heretic was the powder to blow him to hell. But Fyrmyn's passionate devotion could lead him into . . . enthusiasms which sometimes overlooked practical objections.

And Father Tymythy's another chip off the same block, he thought, glancing at the Desnairian intendant. *As soon as the two of them get their heads together, they'll want us in Thesmar yesterday. And I can't blame them for that, either. It's what they* ought *to* want—*what I* ought *to want—and I do.*

He wondered what really made him hesitate to embrace Harless' plan. Or idea, at least. It would probably be unfair to call it a *plan* at this point, and he had no business rejecting it until he'd actually examined the possibilities. Was what had happened when he rushed in at Alyksberg against another hugely outnumbered garrison affecting him now?

You can't allow the way one batch of heretics tricked you once to deflect you from your duty, he told himself sternly. *And while you're thinking about having been tricked, you might want to remember that the coward who left his men to die to set that trap is inside Thesmar with the rest of the heretics! Don't pretend you don't want to drag* him *out of his burrow!*

"It sounds like an audacious plan, Your Grace," he

said finally. "Until I've actually seen the ground and the heretics' fortifications, I can't form an opinion about its practicality, and I'd like to get some of my own artillerists' views on it, as well. I'd prefer to say neither yes nor no until I've had the opportunity to do those things, but you're quite right about how badly outnumbered they are, and it's true they've never taken fire from angleguns themselves. Perhaps it's time we corrected that minor fact."

. IX .
Gorath,
Kingdom of Dohlar

"So, Lieutenant. What do you have for us today?" the Earl of Thirsk inquired as he walked into Lieutenant Dynnys Zhwaigair's workshop, accompanied by Bishop Staiphan Maik and followed by Commander Ahlvyn Khapahr.

The workshop was well lit, if scarcely luxurious. Thirsk had commandeered the ground floor of a dockside warehouse for Zhwaigair's work, and if its appointments were on the spartan side, it had several other recommendations. For one thing, it was actually inside the Royal Dohlaran Navy's largest dockyard, conveniently placed for Thirsk, as that navy's commander, to visit at need. It was also conveniently placed for Zhwaigair to supervise the six armored "screw-galleys" being hastily built under his direction in that same dockyard. And because it was inside the dockyard's perimeter, it was also easily guarded.

Truth be told, that consideration was the most important of all, Thirsk thought sourly. It was vital to keep any Charisian spies from figuring out what Zhwaigair was up to . . . and equally important to keep any fanatic Temple Loyalists from figuring out the same thing. Zhwaigair's explorations were sanctioned by Mother Church, in the person of Bishop Staiphan and a specific writ of attestation from Father Ahbsahlahn Kharmych, Gorath's intendant. Not, perhaps, happily in Father Ahbsahlahn's case (he was an old-school Schuelerite who'd never been happy with the need to adapt to the heretics' new weapons), but sanctioned, nonetheless. That wouldn't prevent someone among the more ardent against the Reformist heresy and the blasphemous Charisian advances from taking it into his head to murder the lieutenant and burn his workshop to the ground before it could further poison the spiritual health of Dohlar.

Which is also the reason Ahlvyn and I put so much thought into picking the Marines assigned to guard the place, the earl reminded himself more than a little bitterly as Zhwaigair turned from the long worktable and came to attention. *Shan-wei's sides must ache from laughter when I have to worry about whether or not my own Marines will be so "ardent" they decide to kill one of the men the Jihad most needs! And isn't it interesting that Kharmych signed the writ, not Clyntahn? I have to wonder if the Grand Inquisitor's keeping the hem of his cassock clear so no one can accuse him of having been hypocritical when he decides he doesn't need young Dynnys anymore and has him eliminated.*

If not for the fact that Clyntahn clearly didn't worry his head over charges of hypocrisy, Thirsk would've been *certain* that was why the attestation had come from Kharmych. As it was, he couldn't quite decide it wasn't his paranoia speaking.

Of course, even a paranoiac can really have enemies, can't he?

"My Lord," the very tall, fair-haired lieutenant greeted the earl. "My Lord Bishop." He bowed respectfully to Maik before bending to kiss the cleric's ring, then saluted Khapahr.

"Good morning, my son." Maik smiled. The bishop was in his fifties, with a weakness for sweetbreads which accounted for the increased thickening of his midsection. And despite the fact that he was a Schuelerite in the middle of the Jihad, he was also a warmhearted and cheerful man. "I see you've been busy."

"I have, My Lord."

Zhwaigair stepped back, waving at the worktable, and Thirsk realized it was actually four very large tables which had been pushed together to make a single enormous platform. He stepped up to it with the bishop, and his eyebrows rose as he looked at the pieces heaped in neatly segregated stacks on its surface. It looked as if someone had completely disassembled four of the heretics' breech-loading rifles.

"Was it really necessary to take *four* of them apart to figure out how one of them worked, Lieutenant?" he asked a bit whimsically.

"Not to figure out how they *worked*, My Lord, but I did learn quite a few other interesting things about them in the process."

Thirsk nodded. He'd hoped that would be the case, and he'd lobbied hard to have the captured heretical weapons Vicar Allayn had sent to Dohlar handed over to Zhwaigair. Shain Hauwyl, the Duke of Salthar, had been disinclined to grant the request for several reasons. One was the hostility of Thirsk's enemies within the Royal Dohlaran Army, which became only more pronounced every time it turned out he'd been right and they'd been wrong, but the earl suspected that was secondary in this instance. It was more likely that Salthar—a reasonably intelligent fellow, if getting on in years, but still wedded to old-style army tactics—simply hadn't grasped how critical it was for Dohlar to find a way to match the Charisians' capabilities. He'd seen no reason for anyone to fiddle around with dangerous, heretical, potentially proscribed devices when the last thing anyone wanted was to bring the fury of Schueler or Jwo-jeng down on the Kingdom of Dohlar for apostasy. In the end, it had taken a direct order from Father Ahbsahlahn to change his mind, and even that had been issued only after Bishop Staiphan had pestered the intendant for more than a five-day.

"What sort of 'interesting things'?" the earl asked now.

"Allow me to demonstrate, if you will, My Lord?"

"Of course."

"Then if you and Bishop Staiphan will stand to one side—it would never do to get either of *you* oily—I'll ask Ahlvyn to assist me."

"I doubt Paiair would be *too* furious at having to clean a little oil out of my tunic," Thirsk observed, but he also smiled and obeyed the polite command. He found a workbench whose surface was more or less clear and hitched himself up to sit on it. He was short enough his toes didn't quite touch the floor, but he was used to that. The sunlight pouring in through the windows behind him illuminated the piles of rifle parts, and he folded his arms to wait patiently.

"Now, Ahlvyn," Zhwaigair said. "These piles"—he waved at the disassembled rifles—"are arranged in the order I'm going to need. What I want you to do is to pick a piece at random from each pile when I ask for it. Clear?"

"Clear," Khapahr agreed.

"Then let's get started. If you'd hand me a lock plate, please?"

The commander poked around in the indicated stack for a moment, then selected a lock plate and passed it across. Zhwaigair took it, laid it on the tabletop, and pointed at the next stack.

"I need a cock now."

Thirsk and Maik watched as Khapahr selected a part from each pile, handing each in turn to Zhwaigair until the taller lieutenant had all the bits and pieces, including the stock, for one of the Charisian rifles laid out in front of him. Then Zhwaigair opened his toolbox and went to work. His nimble, dexterous fingers moved as confidently as if he'd manufactured all the parts himself, and Thirsk was fascinated as he watched the weapon come together. It took a remarkably brief period for Zhwaigair to complete the task. Then he turned from the tabletop, holding the rifle in his hands.

"And now, My Lord, would you do the honors?"

He passed the weapon to Thirsk, who slid off the

workbench to take it and stood looking quizzically back at him.

"Obviously it's unloaded, My Lord, but would you do me the favor of dry firing it?"

Thirsk gazed at him a moment longer, then shrugged. He'd seen one of the rifles demonstrated the day they were delivered to Zhwaigair, and he turned the lever that dropped the square, massive breechblock down and back through the guides. It moved smoothly, and he raised the rifle high enough to peer into the opened breech and make certain it was truly unloaded. He closed the breech again, giving the lever a small extra pull to be sure it was seated properly, then cocked the hammer. It came back smoothly, clicking as it locked in the fully cocked position, and he raised the rifle to his shoulder, making certain the muzzle was pointed in a safe direction, and squeezed the trigger. There was more slack in the trigger than in any of his hunting weapons, but that was to be expected, since each of those rifles was the work of Hahndyl Metzygyr, a master gunsmith who specialized in sporting weapons for the wealthy. A Metzygyr firearm had been an individual work of art, beautiful to behold, even before the heretics introduced the flintlock to Safehold, and the actions on *his* flintlocks were as much precision instruments as any chronometer. Despite the long pull, the breechloader's trigger broke surprisingly cleanly and crisply, however, and the hammer snapped down on the nipple which should have worn one of the heretics' "priming caps."

He lowered the rifle and turned back to Zhwaigair, both eyebrows raised.

"It functioned properly and smoothly, My Lord," the lieutenant said.

"Of course it did, Lieutenant." Thirsk cocked his head. "I know you well enough by now to realize you really do have a point, but could we get to the part where you make it?"

"Of course, My Lord. My point is that the rifle in your hands was assembled from *randomly chosen* parts. I simply took the ones Ahlvyn picked out and put them together, without a single bit of adjustment or filing to fit."

"And?" Thirsk felt comprehension hovering just beyond his grasp as he handed the rifle to Khapahr.

"And no gunsmith in the world could do that with one of *our* Army's rifles, My Lord," Zhwaigair said flatly. "It's impossible. Our rifles are built in individual shops by journeymen and apprentices overseen by master gunsmiths. It *might* be possible to interchange parts between rifles made in the same shop by the same workers, but even that would be extremely unlikely. The parts in all of these rifles—*all of them*, My Lord—are effectively *identical*. I've measured them very carefully and found some extremely small variations in size, but none of them are significant. And the heretics were kind enough to stamp each of these rifles—and the parts that go into it—with a number code. I'm not certain why they did that, but looking at the sequence of numbers and the proof marks, I can tell you this particular group of rifles didn't just happen to come from the same master gunsmith and his assistants. Not unless they skipped ahead several hundred numbers between individual weapons, at any rate."

"Shan-wei," Ahlvyn Khapahr murmured, and whether it was a curse or an explanation was more than Thirsk could have said.

The earl looked at the bishop and saw the same consternation on Maik's face. Then he returned his attention to Zhwaigair.

"Your family's been involved in the iron trade for a long time, Dynnys," he said, abandoning formality in the face of the lieutenant's revelations. "Do you have any idea how they managed this?"

"Short of direct demonic intervention, you mean, my son?" Maik asked dryly. From another Schuelerite, the question would have been deadly serious, but Thirsk's special intendant smiled crookedly when the earl glanced quickly at him. "I think we can assume this is the product of mortal men," he continued, "although I have no more idea of how it was done than you do, Lywys."

"Neither do I, My Lord," Zhwaigair admitted. "Oh, I can see some ways to approach the problem, but not on the scale the heretics obviously have. My uncle uses jigs—those are devices designed to lock a piece into place in such a fashion that it can be filed or smoothed or cut in only one way—to manufacture small parts, but his jigs are individually designed and built. No one else would have the *same* jigs and fixtures, so parts produced in one manufactory wouldn't fit with parts produced in *another* manufactory, the way the heretics've accomplished here. And judging from the tool marks on some of these pieces, parts that would've been forged and filed in any manufactory I'm familiar with seem to've been *stamped*, instead. That indicates that the heretics are using a lot more powered machinery like trip-hammers and stamp mills than we are. And if I'm right about what they're doing, none of the people actually producing these parts and putting them together are likely to be members of the Gunsmiths Guild, far less master gunsmiths! Given some time to think about it, my uncle could probably set up a shop to do a lot of the same things, but he has no more than a hundred work-men. I can't even begin to estimate what his output might be if he followed the heretics' example with pow-ered machinery, but I can't believe it would be anywhere near what the heretics've actually accomplished. They must have scores of manufactories that size producing these things, and that brings us right back to how that many different manufactories can produce parts which are interchangeable with parts from all the *other* manu-factories. If nothing else, they'd all have to agree to use the same inches and feet . . . and then figure out how to *do* it!"

Thirsk looked at Maik, and the bishop shrugged. Mother Church had already signed off on more innova-tions in the last three years than in the last three *centuries*. It was possible Zhaspahr Clyntahn might go so far as to permit the sort of changes Zhwaigair was describing. It was also possible he wouldn't.

"I understand what you're saying, or I think I do, at

least," the earl said after a moment. "But surely we have far more gunsmiths in all of the realms loyal to Mother Church than the heretics do in Charis. Even granting that our *rate* of production will be lower, isn't it possible our total production could still be higher than theirs?"

"I can't say, My Lord," Zhwaigair replied honestly. "I'm inclined to think it probably could . . . as long as we stick to our existing rifle design rather than try to duplicate this one."

"I beg your pardon?"

"My Lord, many of the parts in this rifle, and especially the breechblock and receiver, are clearly machined using powered tools we don't have. Craftsmen like my uncle could probably create those tools, but first we'd have to design them, then build them, then get them distributed, and in the meantime, we'd be producing none of these weapons. I'd also guess—and it's only a guess at this point, My Lord—that for each rifle of this type we built using our existing system of gunsmiths, we could build as many as ten or even fifteen of our present muzzle-loading rifles. That means each of them would cost ten or fifteen times as much, which I suspect would be a sufficiently serious problem by itself. But it also means we could arm only a tenth or a fifteenth as many of our men with them. And that assumes my off-the-cuff guess is accurate.

"Not only that, but *all* of the metal parts in this rifle are steel, not iron. Our rifles use steel only for high-stress parts like springs, trigger guards, and things like that. We use iron barrels and lock plates, and we use brass in many of the low-stress parts, because steel is so expensive. I don't see any reason why the heretics couldn't've done the same thing, but they didn't. And that suggests to me, My Lord, My Lord Bishop, that their steel production must be far, far in excess of our own. Of anything anyone ever imagined before. And I can also tell you, having worn down a brand-new file testing it, that it's much *better* steel, much harder and tougher, than anything I've ever seen before."

Zhwaigair shook his head, his normally calm expression almost frightened.

"Long before the Jihad, Charis was called 'ironmaster to the world' for good reason, My Lord. Charisian foundries produced more and better iron, wrought iron, and blackheart iron than anyone else. But not in the quantities *this*"—he tapped the steel barrel of the assembled rifle—"seems to imply."

"I see."

Thirsk glanced at Maik again, seeing an echo of his own bitter reflections in the bishop's eyes. Zhwaigair was doing exactly what they needed him to do if Mother Church was to win the Jihad, yet if he expressed himself this frankly, even in a written report, to Zhaspahr Clyntahn and the Inquisition, the consequences for him could well be catastrophic.

But it's not his responsibility to be making those reports, is it? the earl asked himself. *You're his commanding officer.* You're *the one who put him in this workshop to draw those conclusions, the one who's responsible for making someone—anyone—listen to you when you tell them the simple truth. And for dealing with the consequences of what happens when you do.*

He glanced at Khapahr from the corner of his eye, and the man who would have been called his chief of staff back on a planet named Terra returned his gaze calmly. Thirsk had hated involving Khapahr, but he'd discovered he couldn't do it alone, and there were very few men he could trust to help with what had become the most important task in his life.

It would help if I could tell the girls what Ahlvyn's up to, but I can't do that either. I don't think *any of them would balk if I could find a way to get them out of the Inquisition's "protective custody," but I can't be certain of that. And then there are their husbands. And the minor fact that if I breathed a hint of any such thought to anyone and it got back to Kharmych or the Inquisition, we'd all be dead.*

He still didn't know what he'd do if he could get his

daughters out of Gorath to someplace where the Inquisition couldn't make examples out of his family. Surely Mother Church and his kingdom had first claim on his loyalty! How could he even imagine rejecting that claim? But if the only way to win the Jihad, to *preserve* Mother Church and his kingdom, required him to do things for which he would stand condemned in the eyes of the Grand Inquisitor, did he truly have any choice *but* to reject that claim in the name of a greater loyalty?

He had no answer for that question, even now, and he put it aside yet again and looked down at the assembled rifle once more.

"The reports from Sir Rainos and General Rychtyr all emphasized the advantages breech-loading gives the heretics, Dynnys. I hate to say it, but perhaps we have no choice but to accept that we can produce far fewer rifles in order to give the troops we do field the weapons they need to survive in battle. And if iron serves well enough for the barrels of our current muzzle-loading rifles, then it will just have to serve for the breech-loading ones we need, as well."

"I've been thinking about that, too, My Lord," Zhwaigair told him, "and I'm not sure this is the only or even the best way to close a rifle's breech."

"You're not?" Thirsk's question came out sounding more like a statement, and Zhwaigair shook his head.

"I'm not sure my idea's practical. I think it is, and I'd like your permission to discuss it with my uncle and some of his artisans, but it occurs to me that it might be possible to simply drill a vertical hole through the barrel and thread it. If the pitch of the threads was properly planned and cut, we could screw a plug through the holes that would seal the breech even better than the heretics' design does, and without that felt pad they use. The metal-to-metal seal should be gas tight if we get the design right."

Thirsk blinked, then looked quickly back at Maik.

"That sounds like a very interesting idea, my son," the bishop said, and Thirsk heard the additional message buried in Maik's tone. Not only was the idea "interesting," but Thirsk couldn't see a single aspect of it that could possibly rouse the Inquisition's ire against Zhwaigair.

Don't get too optimistic about that, Lywys, he told himself after a moment. *God only knows what could "rouse the Inquisition's ire" these days! As the situation gets worse, the worst of the inquisitors only get more fanatical.*

"This would be faster than simply duplicating the heretics' design?"

"It would certainly be faster unless we could duplicate whatever powered machinery they're using, as well, My Lord." Zhwaigair shrugged. "We could get it into production more quickly because we'd have to change very little about the existing rifles, although I doubt it would be as simple as converting the ones we've already built. And I'd guess that once we do have it into production, we could build a rifle to this design at a rate of, say, one for every four of the existing rifles. It would still represent a huge drop in production rate, but nowhere near as much of a drop as duplicating this design would."

He tapped the barrel of the assembled rifle again, and Thirsk nodded.

"And what about these 'primer caps' of theirs?"

"My Lord, my experience is with iron, steel, and brass, not the mysteries of Bédard and Pasquale, but I'm reasonably certain that what they've done is to take a tiny drop of fulminated mercury and seal it inside the cap, probably with a drop of varnish. When the hammer falls, the fulminated mercury detonates and flashes over to ignite the cartridge."

"I see."

Thirsk's eyes met Maik's once again. From what Zhwaigair was saying, duplicating the heretics' "primer caps" wouldn't be insuperably difficult from a manufactory perspective. From every *other* perspective it would mean a direct confrontation with the teachings of Schueler and Pasquale, however, and it was anyone's guess whether or not Zhaspahr Clyntahn would grant yet another dispensation of such magnitude.

"The advantage these give the heretics is pronounced, My Lord," he said quietly to the bishop. "We have more misfires than they do even in clear weather; in the rain, they fire just as reliably as they do in sunshine . . . and our men can't."

"I understand that, Lywys." Maik's expression was troubled, even worried. "And I agree. But, my son, this is one suggestion you must let come from someone else. I know you're already going to be making quite a few based on the Lieutenant's work. Pick the ones you make carefully. Don't waste your influence on less important ones or ones that someone else can make just as well."

"Influence," indeed, Thirsk thought dryly. *You mean don't use up any more of the limited patience my superiors and Mother Church have where my nagging is concerned!*

"You're probably right about that." His tone acknowledged what the bishop had truly said, and he turned back to Zhwaigair.

"You've done just as well with this task as I've come to expect of you, Lieutenant," he said, the words formal but the tone warm. "Be good enough to write it up for me in a proper report, and I'll see what I can do about getting it into the hands of the people who need to see it."

And we'll just have to hope they read *it after I do*, he added silently.

"Of course, My Lord."

"Good!" Thirsk patted him on the shoulder, then gathered up Khapahr with his eyes. "Ahlvyn, you and I—and the Bishop—are already late for my meeting with Admiral Tyrnyr. I think we'd better be going."

. X .
HMS *Destiny*, 56,
and
Royal Palace,
City of Manchyr,
Princedom of Corisande

The Charisian galleon made her way majestically from the broad waters of White Horse Reach into Manchyr Bay. Despite the lengthy voyage from Chisholm, her black hull with the single white strake of her maindeck gunports was immaculate, and while an admiral's streamer flew at her foremast, another flag flew from her mainmast's lofty head. Its blue field showed a silver crown, and it bore a black canton embroidered with crossed swords in orange. It was not a Charisian flag, for all that it flew in the place of greatest honor, and on this day, flying that banner in this place, the name picked out in gold leaf across that galleon's stern—HMS *Destiny*—seemed somehow more appropriate than ever before.

Her escorting squadron accompanied her watchfully, keeping a wary eye on the blizzard of small craft which had put out to meet her. Manchyr Bay was over a hundred and thirty miles deep, north to south, and almost as wide, and some of those craft were small enough to be perilously far from land. Fortunately, the morning's weather was magnificent, with a tropical sky like a burnished blue dome, a scatter of blinding white clouds, and a stiff topgallant breeze—what would've been called a Force Four wind on the ancient Beaufort Scale—following her into the bay from the southeast. The wind raised waves about four feet tall and pushed her along at a steady seven knots. White water creamed about her bows and her wake trailed behind her, a fading carpet of smoothed green water over which raucous clouds of greedy gulls and wyverns swept and darted. The sun was hot even this early, as it usually was less than seven hundred miles below the equator, for all that it was winter in Safehold's southern hemisphere, and the northeast shore of Manchyr Bay was a dark green blur from the galleon's deck.

Princess Irys Daykyn stood on that deck as she had since shortly after dawn, hazel eyes bright as she gazed at that green blur—the blur of the Duchy of Manchyr, the blur of her homeland, of the coastal hills' coarse, blowing grass and the circling bird wings of the land where she'd been born—for the first time in nearly three years. She was almost three months short of twenty, and that was more than young enough for three years to have seemed an eternity under any circumstances. Under the circumstances which obtained, they *had* been an eternity. There'd been times, more than she could count, when she'd known she would never be allowed to see Corisande again. And there'd been even darker times when she'd known she and her baby brother would not be permitted to live even in exile. Yet here she was, the wind blowing her dark hair in a silken cloud and the heart hunger rising in her throat like an exquisite pain.

A twenty-foot cutter dared the watchful cordon of *Destiny*'s escorts, darting towards the galleon in a flurry of white water and heeling canvas, her lee rails buried as she slid exuberantly across the waves in rainbow clouds of flying spray, a long orange and white streamer blowing starched-stiff at her masthead.

"Princess Irys! *Princess Irys!*" She heard the shout through the sounds of sea and wave, saw someone standing beside the mast. The other woman clung to it for balance, waving the orange and white scarf in her free hand wildly above her head as she recognized the slim, straight figure on the foreign warship's deck. "God bless you, Princess Irys! Welcome home! *Oh, welcome home!*"

Irys' throat closed, and she waved back to the cutter, wondering who that woman was, why she'd come so far out to sea to greet them in so small a craft. HMS *Sea-*

horse, one of the escorts, altered course slightly, bearing down on the cutter. It was obvious her captain had no intention of actually running down the far smaller boat, but her message was clear, and the cutter bore obediently away. Irys heard her name floating back from it one more time, and then *Seahorse* resumed her original course, and she heard someone chuckle softly beside her.

She turned her head, expecting to see her chaperone, the Countess of Hanth. Lady Mairah really should have been with her, given all the commonly born seamen jammed into *Destiny*'s hull and the countless ways in which they might have offended against Irys' birth and lineage. That was the way the no-doubt scandalized nobles of her father's court would have seen it, at any rate. After so long aboard this galleon, though, Irys Daykyn knew there wasn't a man aboard it who would not have died to protect her, and she'd been contaminated enough by her contact with Charis and Charisians to recognize— and treasure—their cheery greetings and nods of welcome.

Lady Mairah might have been born Chisholmian, but she, too, had come to understand Charisian ways, and that was why she'd only nodded and gone right on listening to her stepson Trumyn's reading lesson when Irys announced she was going on deck "for some fresh air." She'd known the real reason Irys wanted to be on that deck, watching that land come closer and closer, of course. Lady Mairah always seemed to know by instinct when what Irys really needed was privacy and time to think, and she'd always tried to let the princess in her charge have that privacy. It wasn't easy on a ship, even one as large as *Destiny*, but she tried.

Irys opened her mouth to thank the countess for her consideration, then paused as she found herself looking into Hektor Aplyn-Ahrmhak's brown eyes, instead. He stood at her shoulder, and she wondered how long he'd been there. In a way, she'd been surprised when he hadn't joined her on deck immediately after breakfast, but then she'd realized he, too, was deliberately giving her space and time. It was like him to realize she'd needed that privacy, but now she was glad he was here, and she reached out to take his hand.

"I understand why the Admiral wants to make sure no one gets too close alongside before we've got you and Daivyn safely ashore," Hektor said. "We've seen what wagonloads of gunpowder can do in city streets; God only knows what a ton or two blowing up close aboard a galleon would do! But I have to say, looking at how many sails are bobbing around out there, that you must be a pretty popular lady." He screwed his face up in a thoughtful expression and nodded wisely. "Of course, I think I'd heard something to that effect before. You don't want to believe everything you hear, though."

"Oh, you don't, don't you?" She punched him on the shoulder with her free hand.

"Well, rumors can be deceptive, you know."

"Yes, I do," she agreed in a softer voice, eyes darkening briefly as she recalled the "rumors" about who'd actually paid for her father's murder. But that was an old pain now, one she'd learned to deal with, and she banished it quickly. "For example," she continued, "I've heard rumors that you're, ah, *emotionally involved* with someone."

"Odd." He looked at her with a puzzled expression. "I've heard the same rumors about *you*."

"Oh, I'm certain you're mistaken, Lieutenant Aplyn-Ahrmahk," she said demurely. "That would scarcely be lady-like."

"No, it wouldn't, would it?" he murmured, and Irys felt a gentle heat across the high cheekbones she'd inherited from her mother as she remembered the handful of moments alone and unsupervised the two of them had managed to seize in Cherayth. Opportunities had been fewer and much further between aboard *Destiny*, given the galleon's crowded state, but they'd been more than enough to banish any fear that theirs would be a bloodless, passionless marriage of state.

"In that case, there couldn't possibly be any truth to

the rumors," she told him just a bit snippily. "For I, Lieutenant, am *always* a lady."

"That's what my stepmother's said upon occasion, too," Hektor observed. "And she sticks her nose up in the air just like that when she does it. I never really believed her, though. About the 'always' bit I mean."

"I believe she and I did discuss something about sailors and reunions after long voyages. Not that I have any personal experience of the matter, of course."

"Oh, of course not."

They smiled at one another, then turned to look back over the galleon's rail at the land slipping slowly past.

"At this rate, we'll make port sometime in the late afternoon," he told her. "Nervous?"

"Oh, no! Why should I *possibly* be nervous?"

"I can't imagine," he said innocently, and moved his elbow as if by instinct to block the jab she aimed at his rib cage.

"What about Daivyn?" he asked in a rather more serious tone, and she sighed.

"Sometimes I think he still doesn't really grasp what's going on at all. Other times, I'm sure he does and he's just pretending—maybe to himself, even more than me—that he doesn't. And still other times, he discusses it with me with this incredibly serious expression. I see a little bit of Father in his eyes when that happens."

"Really?" He looked down at her, and she shook her head.

"Not the ambition, Hektor. It's the . . . *understanding*, I guess. The look Father got when his brain was fully engaged. He really was a very smart man, you know. Not in all ways. Or maybe what I mean is that he was smart without always being *wise*. But he really did care about the well-being of Corisande. Sometimes what he wanted—what he thought would be best for Corisande and what he went about giving it—wasn't really what his people needed or what *they* wanted, but I think he genuinely convinced himself that his ambitions were truly *their* ambitions, as well. I don't think he ever really realized they supported his efforts to expand his power because they supported *him*, not because they wanted anything of the sort themselves. And I've come to think any ruler has to be careful about assuming that the people he actually sees and talks to, the nobles on his council, his diplomats and generals and admirals, really understand—or care about—what's best for his entire realm. It's awfully easy to get trapped inside a bubble like that and ignore anyone outside it, Hektor. I've seen it, and now I recognize the danger, and smart as he was, I don't think he ever did. He played the game by the rules he knew . . . and never bothered to learn another set."

Her tone was somber, her expression sad, and she gazed at that welcoming green blur for several seconds before she looked back up at Hektor again.

"But flawed as he might've been, he truly did care. And if Daivyn does have some of that same concern inside, hiding under the prince learning to be a little boy again, then with a little direction and a little guidance, maybe. . . ."

Her voice trailed off, and Hektor nodded.

"I'll take your word about your father." Irys' heart warmed as she heard the simple sincerity in his voice. How many men whose king had died in their arms could genuinely have believed the prince responsible for that death had sought to be the best ruler he knew how to be, however poorly he'd truly understood the job in the end? "But what I've seen of Daivyn so far is pretty hopeful. He's a *good* kid, Irys, and one of these days—if we can just keep him from being poisoned by toadies and court politics—I think he's going to be a pretty good man, too."

Irys suppressed a chill as she thought about all the ways "toadies and court politics" could poison the mind and the soul of so youthful a prince. Daivyn had celebrated his eleventh birthday only ten days earlier, right here on *Destiny*, and God knew he truly was a baby to be inheriting a throne. That would've been true at any time, far less in times as chaotic as these, and Irys knew

enough about courts and the maneuvering which went
on within them to feel that cold bite of fear. It was so
easy for a child to be shaped for good or ill by the adults
around him, and especially when that child was a prince.
There would always be those who would be prepared to
play the sycophant—or the betrayer—and the cataclysm
of the war wracking Safehold would offer far too many
openings for opportunistic scum.

*Well, we'll just have to keep that from happening,
won't we?* she asked herself tartly. *And he could have
worse influences than Hektor, come to that. But how do
we stand guard against that kind of poison without
making it obvious we're doing it? Without making him
think we don't trust him to protect* himself *against it?
And what happens when a teenage Daivyn starts to fret
about all the people who won't let him do what he wants?
When other people tell him he* can *do what he wants—
whatever* he *wants—start promising him the sun and the
moon and stars?*

She thought about her older brother, wondering—
not for the first time—how much of his petulance and
spoiled refusal to understand the responsibilities which
came with the privileges of birth had been the work of
people just like that. She'd never know about that, for no
one had ever attempted to mold *her* to their purposes.
She liked to think that was because they'd known they'd
fail, but deep inside she had to admit what she'd always
known. There'd been little *point* in any court faction's
attempting to bend her to its purposes, for she'd been
only a daughter. Why waste effort on her when the
future prince himself had been so accessible and ready to
hand? And if Daivyn had been too young to be included
in their plans before their father sent them to Delferahk,
that was no longer the case, was it? What would happen
when—?

She shook herself and inhaled deeply, nostrils flaring
as the salt air filled her lungs, and told herself sternly to
let tomorrow take care of itself. The *Writ* told God's
children to do the best they could each day and trust Him
and the Archangels to look after them when tomorrow

came. Princes and princesses and emperors and empresses were less free to do that than most of His children, for the weight of a crown was heavy, but there were times when even they simply had to stand back and trust Him to get it right.

▼ ▼ ▼

"Well, they've kept their word," Sir Rysel Gahrvai, the Earl of Anvil Rock, said, looking down at the dispatch. The semaphore stations had flashed word of the Charisians' arrival ahead as soon as the first picket boat reached the shore.

"It *looks* like they've kept their word," Sir Taryl Lektor, the Earl of Tartarian, corrected in a finicky sort of tone, and Anvil Rock gave him a glare.

"I don't really think they're very likely to go back on it after *this*." He waved the dispatch at his friend. "That would be just a teeny bit stupid of them, don't you think?"

"Of course it would. And of course I don't think they're going to. I'm simply saying that until we have Irys and Daivyn back on Corisandian soil in one piece, I'm keeping my guard up." Tartarian grimaced. "For that matter, you know damned well—as well as *I* do—that there are people right here in Manchyr who'd prefer to see Daivyn dead at wharf-side rather than seated on a throne as a 'Charisian puppet.' And not all of them would be acting without the Church's blessings. Or *instructions*, for that matter."

"You're right."

Anvil Rock dropped the dispatch on the table and strode to the window. The chamber in which they stood was in one of the palace's taller towers, looking out over the harbor and Manchyr Bay beyond. It was a spectacular view in the midmorning sunlight, despite—or perhaps because of—the scores of windmills which crowned so many of Manchyr's buildings, spinning briskly or slowly, depending upon their size and power, and gilding the city with their own liveliness and flickering motion. Yet the harbor itself looked strangely empty at the moment, despite the miles of orange and white bunting and banners hoisted to dance with the wind from every spire, rooftop, and waterfront crane, because every small vessel which would normally have dotted its waters was absent. The earl knew where they were, and he took the time for a brief, heartfelt prayer that none of them belonged to another of Zhaspahr Clyntahn's "Rakurai" who'd managed to smuggle a few tons of gunpowder aboard.

"You're right," he sighed again. "But the Charisians've made it abundantly clear that they're transporting and treating Daivyn and Irys with all of the respect they deserve. And if that dispatch is right, if they *are* flying the heir's banner, then they're officially underscoring their recognition of him as the rightful Prince of Corisande. That's pretty conclusive evidence that they have no intention of backing off from the terms Phylyp's reported he and Irys accepted."

"And you think members of the Royal Council aren't going to argue that a nineteen-year-old girl had no business 'accepting' any sort of terms in her brother's name?" Tartarian's tone was skeptical, almost scornful. "Shanwei, Rysel! There're members of the *Regency* Council, far less the entire Royal Council, who feel that way! And that doesn't even get us to Parliament or the Temple Loyalists! For someone as smart as we both know Sharleyan Ahrmahk is, she's hanging an awful lot of faith on our ability to convince the entire damned Princedom to ratify a teenager's 'decisions of state.' Especially one like this one!"

"If you think they were bad terms, you should've said so at the time," Anvil Rock pointed out, turning his head to glare over his shoulder once more.

"If I'd thought they were bad terms, I *would*'ve said so at the time. I happen to think they're the best terms we could possibly've hoped for! I'm just pointing out that whether or not the *Charisians* have any intention of 'backing off,' we're going to find Corisandians who think *we* ought to. And some of them—I might mention the late, unlamented Earl of Craggy Hill as an example—may not be shy about trying to do something about that."

"Well, we'll just have to see about that, won't we?" Anvil Rock's expression was grim, his eyes hard as Barcor Mountain granite. "But I've got quite a bit of faith in Koryn and Charlz—and even young Windshare. For that matter, people like Craggy Hill are why we have executioners, and, personally, Taryl, I think we've had just about enough of that kind of crap over the last two or three years. Don't you?"

▼ ▼ ▼

The cheers rolled up from the waterfront as the oared tugs eased *Destiny* against the wharf's thick fenders. They crested and swelled in waves, washing over the galleon and the crowd of dignitaries waiting to greet her like a tempest. Guns rumbled like that tempest's smoky thunder as the fortresses and every warship in the harbor sent up the rolling eighteen-gun salutes due the long-absent heir to Corisande's throne, and her topmen manned her yards while her Marines snapped to attention and presented arms to her royal passengers.

The cheers redoubled as the gangplank ran up to the galleon's side, and the crowd pressing against the cordon of Corisandian troops (there wasn't a single Charisian soldier or Marine in all that raucous shoreside tumult) waved hands, flags, and scarves while others threw clouds of flower petals into the air. The petals swirled like particolored snow in a city which had never seen snow in its life, and Hektor Aplyn-Ahrmhak knew the trumpeters behind the dignitaries were blowing a fanfare only because he could see the raised instruments. No one more than a few feet from the musicians could have hoped to actually hear them in all that wild, unbridled bedlam.

He stood on *Destiny*'s quarterdeck, hands clenched behind him, and watched that crowded wharf through narrow eyes. He was very young for his rank and duties—indeed, he'd celebrated his seventeenth birthday on the same day Prince Daivyn had celebrated his eleventh, since there were only six days between their actual birthdates and Daivyn had insisted that they share. But he'd seen and done a great deal in those seventeen years and been tutored in the duty expected of a naval officer by the finest captain he'd ever known. More, he'd become a son of the House of Ahrmahk. He'd seen the working of politics and policy at the highest level from inside the imperial family, and so he knew why the foreign, common-born duke who'd been betrothed to their princess couldn't possibly be by her side when she and her brother, the rightful Prince of Corisande, returned to their homeland at last. He'd understood how it would be—how it *had* to be—but he hadn't had a clue how *hard* it would be, and his hands gripped even tighter as he thought about how easily a Temple Loyalist fanatic could use that mad confusion to get a pistol close enough to kill the young woman he'd come against all odds to love. It had happened to his stepmother, after all, right here in this same princedom, despite the presence of *Seijin* Merlin and under far less chaotic conditions, and—

Yet there was nothing he could do about it except to trust Koryn Gahrvai to get it right. He was Irys and Daivyn's cousin, and everything Cayleb or Sharleyan—or Merlin Athrawes—had ever said indicated that he and his father were both men of honor . . . and that Koryn was very, very good at his job. If anyone could keep Irys safe, Gahrvai was that anyone, but it was hard—*hard*—to trust a man he'd never met with the most vital task in his universe.

Irys and Daivyn walked between the lines of *Destiny*'s Marines and started down the gangplank, Earl Coris at their backs, and his heart swelled with pride as he watched them. Daivyn was obviously nervous, but he held his head high, and if he simultaneously clutched his sister's hand, who should blame him? Certainly his subjects didn't, for the impossible volume roared still higher as they saw the royal brother and sister. As for Irys, if there was an anxious bone in her body, no one could have guessed it from her graceful, regal carriage. They gained the wharf and the men gathered to greet them stepped forward, and Hektor's proud eyes narrowed as he saw the orange-trimmed white cassock and priest's cap.

The crowd roar diminished suddenly, magically, as the man in that cassock raised one hand. It didn't die away completely, but it faded until a single voice could be heard, and Klairmant Gairlyng, Archbishop of Corisande, spoke.

"Let us pray, my children!"

The crowd noise faded still further, dropping away into a quiet in which the snapping of flags and bunting and the cries of seabirds and sea wyverns disturbed by all the uproar could be heard echoing down from above.

"O most mighty and magnificent God," Gairlyng prayed into that stillness, his voice carrying firm and strong, "we thank You from the bottoms of our hearts for the grace which You have vouchsafed us this day in the return of these our beloved Prince Daivyn and his sister Princess Irys. We thank and praise You for the way in which You have spread Your protecting arm about them, keeping them safe during their long absence, warding them from harm, preserving them from danger. We glorify You for moving so powerfully and mysteriously in the hearts of men and women of goodwill as to bring this moment to pass. We beseech You to remain with them, to guard and guide them, to give them wisdom that they may know and do Your will. We beseech You also to so guide and move the Regency Council, and our Prince's Council Royal, and his Parliament assembled, that we may find that peaceful resolution to the remaining points of contention between Corisande and the Empire of Charis which we know is near and dear to Your heart, as it must also be to the hearts and minds of all good and godly men and women. Be with us in the days to come, strengthen us when we falter, bear us up when we stumble, and bring us in the fullness of time to that place in which You would have us be as Your beloved sons and daughters. We ask this in the name of the love You proclaimed to all men and women in the words and mighty deeds of Your Archangels so many years ago. Amen."

Absolute silence hovered for a long, aching moment, enhanced and not broken by the wash of water around wharf pilings, the sigh of wind in *Destiny*'s rigging, and the crackling pop of that blue flag flying from her masthead, and then the stillness vanished into cheers even louder than before.

▼ ▼ ▼

The last time Irys Daykyn had been in the Grand Council Chamber, her father had occupied the throne behind that long, massive table of gleaming, intricately carved wood. Now that throne sat empty, its cushioned seat occupied only by a simple presence crown, and the dozens of men who'd been seated around the table rose, bowing profoundly, as she and Daivyn stepped through the door, followed by Archbishop Klairmant and Sir Phylyp Ahzgood, Earl of Coris.

"His Highness Prince Daivyn," the door warden announced loudly and unnecessarily. "His Eminence Archbishop Klairmant. Her Highness Princess Irys. The Earl of Coris."

The sound of Irys' heels on the brilliantly polished marble floor was crisp and clear in the silence that followed. She walked beside Daivyn, her hand laid upon his left arm, and her brother's eyes were very bright. Despite his youth, his head was high, his deportment was that of a gentleman escorting a highborn lady with the poise and assurance of someone twice his age, and she saw one or two eyebrows rising among the noblemen waiting for them.

You show them, Daivyn, she thought proudly from behind the calm composure of her own expression. *You remember everything we talked about, and you show them.*

They advanced to exactly the proper spot on the chamber floor, and the Earl of Anvil Rock stepped around the council table. He crossed the black and white squares of marble that glistened in the sunlight pouring down from the high windows set into the chamber's roof and once again went to one knee before them, bending his head.

"Your Highness," he told Daivyn, "in the name of your Regency Council, of the Council Royal, of your Parliament, and all of the subjects of your realm, I welcome you home. Each and all of us have prayed long and hard that we might see this day, and I know I speak for your entire Council when I tell you how deeply my heart rejoices that God and the Archangels have permitted you to return to us safely at last."

"I thank you, My Lord Earl." Daivyn's young voice was clear and admirably grave as he repeated the formal response in which Irys and Coris had drilled him. "The reports of the manner in which you have governed and protected my people and my princedom in my stead and as my regent during my absence have gladdened my heart. And"—he looked directly into Anvil Rock's eyes as the earl raised his head—"I'm very happy to see you again, cousin."

His voice changed subtly with the last sentence, becoming both younger and far less rehearsed, and Anvil Rock had to swallow hard as he looked into those brown young eyes and saw the truth behind them.

"Thank you, Your Highness," he said, and turned his attention to Irys. "We are all equally gladdened and grateful to see you returned safely to us, as well, Your Highness."

"Thank you, My Lord." Irys heard the tiniest waver in her own voice. It surprised her, and she blinked hard, then reached out to Anvil Rock. He took her hand and kissed it, then rose without releasing it and extended his other hand to Daivyn.

"Your places await you," he said.

▼ ▼ ▼

Irys was a little surprised.

Daivyn had been escorted to that empty throne and seated in the smaller, comfortably upholstered chair on the uppermost step of the dais on which it sat (they'd had to put two more cushions in it to make him tall enough, then place a stool so his feet didn't dangle), but she'd expected that. Until he was crowned as Prince of Corisande, he could not be seated in the throne itself, although the position of his chair underscored his right to claim that throne. What surprised her was that she was seated beside him, at his right hand, in the position which would have been granted to Daivyn's consort, had he been old enough to wed. And the reason that surprised her was that she was merely their rightful prince's *sister*, and one who hadn't yet quite attained her own age of majority, to boot. By law, she had no more standing in the Royal Council than she did in the succession. Seating her at Daivyn's right granted her that standing at least temporarily, and she wondered whether it had been Anvil Rock's idea or Tartarian's. Before her exile to Delferahk, she would have wagered that it was Tartarian's. Now, having read the correspondence between Coris and Anvil Rock—and between Anvil Rock and Cayleb and Sharleyan—she was less certain of that. Her cousin had neither sought nor wanted the responsibility which had fallen upon him, and he would have been the first to argue that he was thoroughly unqualified for it, yet he'd discharged his duties well. And along the way, he'd become far more adroit at treading the mazes of power—and shaping those mazes, when necessary—than either of them had ever expected he might.

"Would you honor us by opening our deliberations in prayer, Your Eminence?" Anvil Rock requested, and Klairmant Gairlyng rose from his place at the table, directly to Daivyn and Irys' right as befitted God's direct representative.

"Of course, My Lord," the dark-haired, dark-eyed archbishop replied. He stood, raising his hands in benediction, and bowed his head.

"O God, we pray You to look down upon this Council as it meets to grapple with the many and weighty decisions which await it and all the people of this Realm. We ask You to grant it the wisdom to make those decisions aright, to walk in Your light and to do those things which You would have us do. And we ask You especially to bless Prince Daivyn and his sister and guardian, Princess Irys, that they may shoulder the responsibilities You have placed upon them and lead the people of their Realm in justice, safety, and well-being to bear Your sword under the banner of Your champions against those enemies of Your word and will who have turned even Your Church into a house of corruption, Your Temple into a den of thieves, and Your Inquisition into a pestilence loosed upon the world. Amen."

He never raised his voice. The sonorous words came calm and measured—without any fiery, denunciatory passion but firmly and unhesitatingly and all the weightier for it. They were the words of a priest who knew his own mind . . . and God's, and Irys' eyes went wide in astonishment. The sound of a falling pin would have been deafening as the archbishop calmly seated himself once more. The rustle of his cassock, the whisper of his slippers on the marble floor, were clearly audible in the Grand Council Chamber's petrified stillness, and she managed—somehow—not to look over her shoulder to see Phylyp Ahzgood's expression.

My God, she thought. *I never expected to hear that out of him!*

No one could possibly have quibbled with the first half of the archbishop's prayer, but the *second* half—! In just two sentences, Klairmant Gairlyng had made the position of the Church in Corisande crystal, one might almost have said blindingly, clear. And in the process, he'd overturned centuries of Corisandian precedent with all the subtlety of a sledgehammer and a chisel. Or perhaps a charge of gunpowder.

She drew a deep breath, forcing her brain to work once again. Another archbishop could have gone on ten times as long and said nothing, but Gairlyng had clearly picked that brief prayer's words with deadly forethought.

First, he'd referred to Irys as Daivyn's "sister and guardian," and that gave the Church's formal imprimatur to Sharleyan Ahrmahk's suggestion that Irys should be formally named her brother's guardian and seated on the Regency Council. Second, he'd asked God's blessing on her and Daivyn as they led "the people of *their* realm," a clear indication that he, as God's vicar in Corisande, expected Irys to be directly involved in the governance of the princedom. That she had an acknowledged, *official* standing in Corisande's power and political structures. And, third, and most devastating of all, he'd endorsed Corisande's active engagement in the war against the Group of Four in God's own name . . . and with all the authority of his office.

As she looked around that chamber, saw the expressions of the men seated around that table, she also saw the impact of Archbishop Klairmant's brief, shattering benediction echoing through the minds of the gathered councilors. And if the men behind some of those expressions clearly didn't care for what they'd just heard, that was hardly surprising.

Some wouldn't care for it because of personal ambition, because they'd hoped to shape and drive "Daivyn's" policies to benefit themselves and their families. That, after all, was one reason men acquired power in the first place, and her father had always told her that anyone who expected human beings to think differently had no business on a prince's throne, for his blindness could lead only to ruin.

Others wouldn't care for it because they'd already heard Charis' terms . . . and knew the archbishop had heard them as well. Because in his final sentence, they heard Gairlyng's endorsement of the Princedom of Corisande's inclusion in the Empire of Charis. They resented the thought of Corisande's being subordinated to any other power, the thought of "bending the knee" to a foreign empire which had conquered them by raw military force. Indeed, some of those councilors undoubtedly continued to hold Cayleb Ahrmahk responsible for her father's death, no matter what anyone else might say.

But somewhat to her surprise, the men who were so

clearly angered by Gairlyng's endorsement of those terms appeared to be a distinct minority. She'd hoped for that, prayed it might be so, but she'd never dared to plan upon it, just as she'd never dared even for a moment to think that the archbishop might so unambiguously and unhesitatingly declare in favor of the Church and Empire of Charis. She'd realized in Tellesberg the extent to which Maikel Staynair had moved to withdraw the Church of Charis from secular power and direct, day-to-day involvement in the government of the Empire. She'd been surprised by that, at least until she'd come to know Staynair, but she also knew the process was only beginning even in Old Charis and Chisholm. Here in Corisande, it had scarcely even started, and that meant the archbishop had just put all the avalanche weight of Mother Church's centuries of authority behind the acceptance of Charis' terms. *All* of Charis' terms, including the war against the Group of Four and the Grand Vicar himself.

All in no more than four brief sentences.

"I thank you, Your Eminence," Anvil Rock said at last, and it was obvious from his tone that however much he might agree with Gairlyng, he'd been as astonished as anyone else. Whatever else might be true, there'd been no preplanned coordination between him and the archbishop.

"I thank you for your blessing, your words, and"—the earl allowed his eyes to sweep the chamber, meeting those of every other person in it one by one—"your thoughts. With God's grace, I believe this Council and this Princedom will accomplish all of the tasks to which, as you so rightly say, we've been called in His name."

It had taken two five-days just to get the guns and troops into position, Sir Rainos Ahlverez thought bitterly. Left to his own devices, he could have done it in less than one, but he *hadn't* been left to his own devices.

The formal instructions he'd been certain were on the way had arrived. They'd come from Gorath over Duke Salthar's signature, but he knew they'd actually been written in Zion. He wondered if they'd been delivered to King Rahnyld—officially, at least—by Vicar Zahmsyn's office or by the Inquisition, not that it mattered. And not that he, as a dutiful son of Mother Church, could contest them, however badly he might want to. Worse, he couldn't even argue with the underlying reasoning, since history offered all too many examples of the disastrous consequences of attempting to command an allied army by committee. No, command must speak with a single voice, and it would have flown in the face of logic—and given all manner of offense—to place the commander of the smaller component of that army in command of the entire force. Especially when that commander was a mere knight, whoever he might be related to, and the commander of the larger component was a duke.

Yet the mere fact that they were inevitable, logical, and the decision of God's own Church made it no less maddening to be subordinated to a Desnairian. The Empire had always looked down its collective nose at Dohlar, that feckless little pocket-sized excuse for a kingdom ("Why, it's scarcely more than an overgrown *barony*, you know!"), and Dohlarans had heaped scorn on Desnair's miserable showing against the Republic with retaliatory delight for the better part of two hundred years. The Empire's contempt for Dohlar's obvious desire to ape the mercantilism of Charis had been met by Dohlar's disdain for a realm so backward it continued to practice outright slavery, and the ostentatious lifestyles Desnair's gold mines had bestowed upon its indolent aristocracy evoked as much envy as resentment among Dohlar's less affluent nobility. All of that was true, and more than bad enough, yet to be subordinated to a man who was not merely a Desnairian but might—*might*, on a good day—be able to find his arse as long as he got to use both hands— and someone else helped—made it still worse.

Be fair, Rainos, he told himself, forcing his expression to remain merely thoughtful, as the artillery creaked past him. *You fucked up by the numbers yourself at Alyksberg. Harless probably isn't any more overconfident now than you were then. Well, not a lot more overconfident, anyway. You'd at least bothered to read Rychtyr's reports, and I'm none too sure Harless can read, given how eager he is to "grapple with the apostate Charisians."*

He stepped on that thought hard.

The truth, if he was honest, was that he'd diverted to Alyksberg largely to dodge an open field battle against new model Charisian weapons, but they couldn't avoid them forever, and at least their spies reported that barely a quarter of the Thesmar garrison was made up of Charisian Marines. The rest of the Charisians were mere sailors who were unlikely to relish facing trained soldiers. And the Siddarmarkians were a collection of odds and sods—a skeleton of regulars fleshed out by militiamen and ragged volunteers—half of whom were sick and starving after their forced march from Alyksberg. He understood why Harless might see this as a good opportunity to blood his troops against the heretics. Probably fewer than half the garrison had firearms of any sort, far less rifles, and he had an enormous numerical advantage. And while he clearly hadn't read *all* of the reports, he'd demonstrated at least limited literacy by perusing the ones describing Cahnyr Kaitswyrth's final assault on the Charisian redoubts on the Daivyn River. Ahlverez knew he had, because he'd referred to it at least a dozen times in their last conference.

"I have no intention of disregarding the advantage their entrenchments give them, General Ahlverez," he'd said. "But Bishop Militant Cahnyr proved that when they can't maneuver, when they're pinned in their own redoubts, with their manpower overcommitted covering all of their points of vulnerability, a massive column can overwhelm even Charisian weapons." He'd laid one palm on the report from Kaitswyrth. "Moreover, the fact that they haven't been reinforced, despite their navy, indicates that they don't have any troops to send, and I intend to be in possession of that town before they *do*." The hand on the bishop militant's report had clenched into a fist. "It has been done, it can be done, and it *will* be done, Sir Rainos. And," he'd added blandly, "it will enhearten the army to crush the heretic Marines who dealt your advanced guard such a painful blow."

Ahlverez had felt his own lips tighten, and it had been difficult to keep his expression neutral. Harless had been careful about anything he personally might have said to his allies, but Ahlverez had informants of his own. He knew how Harless had expressed himself to his own senior officers, and there'd been more than one confrontation between some of his own officers and officers from the Army of Justice who'd commented on how a Dohlaran army had allowed itself to be pinned down by a field force barely a quarter its own size.

"Reducing Thesmar and removing the threat to my supply lines is vitally important in its own right," Harless had continued. "And it's almost equally important for Dohlar, since it will eliminate much of the strain supplying the Army of Shiloh will place on your own canals and rivers."

The duke hadn't seemed very enthused by their combined force's new designation Ahlverez had noted. According to his informants, Harless had lobbied hard for simply absorbing Ahlverez's own force into the Army of

Justice. Fortunately, someone back in Gorath had obviously realized how Ahlverez' men and officers would have reacted to that idea, at least.

"I realize there's some risk in our plan of attack," the Desnairian had said. "No one can ever predict the outcome of a battle before it's fought, or there'd be no need to fight it in the first place. And I also realize my own troops have no experience against the heretics' new weapons." The last sentence had seemed a bit perfunctory to Ahlverez. "More than that, a *failed* assault would undoubtedly have an adverse effect on the Army's morale. I doubt the consequences would be much greater than we'd suffer by refusing to even attempt an attack, however. If we appear too timid to try conclusions against a force we outnumber so heavily, it cannot but undermine the men's confidence in us and, ultimately, in themselves. That would be bad enough even among the men of blood and breeding; among the common sort in the ranks, the consequences might well be even worse."

And there, Ahlverez had thought, *you might just have a point. About your men, at least. I'd like to think mine would understand the logic in simply screening and confining the heretics in Thesmar—doing to them what they did to Rychtyr at Trevyr—even if I'm not as sure of that as I wish I were. But you haven't personally reconnoitered the heretics' position the way I have. You've read the reports, looked at sketches, laid it out on the map, but you haven't actually seen those entrenchments and those inundations. And you haven't seen all the fucking artillery in the world looking back across them at us.*

It might not have mattered if Harless *had* personally seen the muzzles of those heretic cannon. He continued to think of artillery as the massive, immobile, slow-firing monsters which had been all but useless in land battles. Indeed, he seemed to think it was a *good* thing the heretics had "been forced" to rely upon naval gunners! He'd apparently grasped the fact that his own field guns fired much more rapidly than *old-style* naval weapons, but he seemed not to have made the mental leap of grasping that new model naval guns did the same thing.

Or that those contemptible, common-born Charisian seamen had more experience in firing them than anyone else in the entire world.

"So we'll attack as planned, as soon as our own artillery is in position," Harless had concluded, and Ahlverez had nodded.

"Of course, Your Grace," he'd said. It wasn't as if he'd had any choice. And perhaps Harless was right. Perhaps they *could* carry Thesmar, even if Ahlverez was grimly certain the casualties would be far higher than the duke believed. There was sometimes something to be said for the courage of ignorance, the confidence to attempt something "older and wiser heads" knew was impossible.

And as the Archangel Chihiro himself had pointed out before one of the battles against the Fallen, when the cause was dire enough, you sometimes had to break however many eggs it took to make the omelette.

But that conversation lay well over a five-day in the past, and Ahlverez' frustration had grown with every passing day while the heretics continued to improve their positions and the Desnairian component of the Army of Shiloh struggled to get into position. It was especially maddening because Harless ought to have known—as Sir Rainos Ahlverez certainly did—that the inefficiency of the Desnairian officer corps had had a great deal to do with the fashion in which the Siddarmarkian Army had kicked its arse up one side and down the other over the centuries. The fact that Desnair hadn't managed to overcome those shortcomings for the Jihad was *not* reassuring, but what was even less reassuring was the fact that Harless' officers obviously thought they *had* overcome them, which said some really horrendous things about how bad the situation had been before the Imperial Army's current reorganization.

The good news was that the worst problems seemed to be at what the Dohlaran Army would have called the divisional level. Even for Dohlar, the regiment remained the primary combat formation and divisions were purely administrative organizations, but division commanders (the most senior regimental commander in each division) were charged with coordinating the movement and supply of all the regiments in their divisions. That at least established a clear chain of command and authority . . . and responsibility. Ahlverez wasn't really certain the Desnairian Army had "divisions" in that sense at all, and it was obvious to him that there was precious little coordination above the regimental level in the Army of Justice. The fact that Desnairian infantry regiments were half the size of Dohlaran regiments only made that worse, as did the obvious contempt for the entire concept of infantry emanating from Harless' senior officers. They clearly continued to regard cavalry as the decisive arm, despite how disastrously they'd fared against Siddarmarkian infantry in the past. Indeed, Ahlverez had heard even Earl Hennet, the official commander of Harless' infantry, quoting the Desnairian aphorism: "Cavalry conquers; infantry occupies."

Odd how poorly that had worked out against the Republic in times past.

At least their better regimental commanders seemed to be figuring out just how screwed up they were, Ahlverez told himself as the last battery moved past him towards its preselected position. Some of them even seemed willing to learn from mere Dohlarans. They'd actually spent the last five-day or so inviting his own company and regimental commanders to dine with them and then picked their brains for the counsel of experience. Even some of their *artillerists* had quietly discussed their trade with his!

Of course, no one's ever going to be able to teach a Desnairian cavalry commander anything about his job, he told himself bitingly, *since no one in the entire world could possibly understand it as well as he does to begin with. They're all naturally born centaurs, after all!*

His mouth twisted at the thought, and he reminded himself—again—that his own dislike for Desnair and Desnairians might well be coloring his evaluation. On the other hand, some things genuinely were so bad that even a tendency to look on the bad side couldn't make them any worse.

We'll just have to see how it all works out, he thought. *And I can't think of a single time I've hoped I'll be proved wrong as much as I hope it this time.*

▼ ▼ ▼

"The listening posts say they're moving up, My Lord," Lieutenant Dyntyn Karmaikel reported.

The brown-haired Marine was very tall for a Charisian—considerably taller than the Earl of Hanth, in fact—with a dour expression that caused some people to miss the quick wit behind it. Hanth, however, knew that dourness reflected the curb bit Karmaikel had set to control his searing anger. He did an excellent job of containing it, truth be told, and he hadn't *needed* to control it before one of the cousins he'd been fostered with died in Zion with Gwylym Manthyr. That was one of the reasons Hanth had chosen Karmaikel as his personal aide. The lieutenant was a good man, despite the anger burning inside him, and Hanth wanted him out of the immediate line of fire until he'd had a chance to lay some of those demons. Far better to give the youngster time before he found himself leading a platoon in combat and had the opportunity to commit the sort of acts that would seal him into bitter vengefulness forever.

Besides, Karmaikel was a very *good* aide.

"They're moving up where we expected them?"

"Yes, My Lord. The listening posts say they can't actually see very much, but from the sounds, they're deploying their guns on Sulyvyn Hill, midway between the Navy Redoubt and Redoubt Number One." The lieutenant grimaced. "Right where they thought we wouldn't realize they'd been digging gun pits."

"Now, now, Dyntyn! At least they *tried* to fool us."

"Yes, My Lord, and they probably *would* have if we'd been deaf and blind."

Lieutenant Karmaikel, the earl observed, seemed disinclined to give the army outside Thesmar the benefit of the doubt. For that matter, Hanth wasn't prepared to give them the benefit of *much* doubt, but as he'd said, the Desnairians and Dohlarans had at least tried. Their fatigue parties had waited until full dark every night, then moved up as quietly as possible to just behind their front line and gone to work on the gun pits. They'd stopped work well before dawn and done their best to conceal the growing line of emplacements behind loads of cut greenery.

They got that one from Taisyn, he thought grimly. *Which at least shows they aren't too proud to learn from someone else. Unfortunately for them, it doesn't work anywhere near as well against someone who can look directly down on it from above.*

The Sulyvyn Hill lookout tower had spotted the enemy's efforts the very first night and carefully plotted them on the engineers' maps. Because a twelve-pounder smoothbore's maximum range was no more than sixteen hundred yards with solid shot—about thirteen hundred for shells—the enemy gun line had to be within twelve hundred yards or so of the entrenchments if it hoped to suppress Hanth's own artillery. They were actually a bit closer than that, and some of the guns they'd brought up close behind their front and hidden behind local terrain obstacles were interesting. They hadn't managed to conceal them anywhere near as well as they clearly thought they had, and Hanth had climbed to the lookout tower to examine them himself through his double-glass. They had shorter, stubbier barrels, like undersized carronades, and he'd come to the conclusion that they were probably the Dohlaran angle-guns the spies had reported.

I could've gone all year without those turning up, he thought now, looking back down at his maps while he considered Karmaikel's report.

He had no reports on their maximum range. They certainly shouldn't be able to match the range of his rifled naval angle-guns, but it was entirely possible they could throw shells farther than their regular field guns, given the angles to which they could probably elevate.

He doubted it could be much over two or three thousand yards, given their barrel length, the fact that they were smoothbores, and the apparent size of their shells, but he didn't like the thought of shrapnel raining down on his own gunners. He'd known of their existence before anyone ever spotted them here at Thesmar, so he'd taken precautions by roofing his riflemen's firing positions with timbers and a two-foot layer of dirt for overhead protection, but he was still in the process of extending that protection to his artillerists. He'd concentrated on the farthest forward batteries, especially here on the Allies' left, where the enemy's preparations were most evident. The work remained far from complete for the batteries in the center and on his right, however, and they *couldn't* provide overhead cover to his own angle-gunners. They had to be out in the open to work their high-trajectory weapons.

We may be going to lose some of them, he admitted to himself. *But not as many as those bastards on the other side are going to lose!*

"All right, Dyntyn," he said calmly. "I assume Major Zhadwail's men have been stood to?"

"Yes, Sir. His battalion's on full alert. And Commander Parkyr's moved up to the Navy Redoubt," Karmaikel added with a careful lack of expression.

"Well, I'm sure that's filled Lieutenant Bukanyn with joy," Hanth observed dryly. "Still, he'll manage to survive, I think."

"As you say, My Lord."

Hanth shook his head without ever looking up from the map. Lieutenant Symyn Bukanyn was officially HMS *Trumpeter*'s third lieutenant. Unfortunately, Admiral Hywyt had completely disarmed *Trumpeter,* distributed her guns to the Thesmar defenses, and turned the galleon herself into a hospital ship. The Navy Redoubt, just behind the first line of earthworks, was armed with six of her thirty-pounders, four of her fifty-seven-pounder carronades, and two rifled six-inch angle-guns. Hanth didn't like having the angle-guns that far forward, since there was no way to withdraw such massive pieces if the enemy managed to break through, but they gave him several miles' reach into the Temple Boys' position. He hadn't used them yet—plenty of time for that after the other side had moved sufficiently juicy targets into their range—and he had no intention of using them tonight, either, although Commander Ahrthyr Parkyr had full authority to bring them into action if he decided it was necessary. That was undoubtedly why Parkyr had taken himself off to the Navy Redoubt, although Bukanyn probably wouldn't see it that way. He was a rather thorny young man, with an irascible personality, but those flaws were accompanied by an extraordinary amount of energy and a painstaking attention to the details of his job.

I imagine Ahrthyr will keep a light hand on the bridle, assuming one's necessary. Of course, I'd prefer for my artillery commander to not get his silly arse killed the very first night, too.

"I think it's probably time we moved outside, Dyntyn," he observed in a resigned tone. He really wasn't looking forward to the climb up the lookout tower in the middle of the night. He wasn't getting any younger. But at least if they got an early enough start he could stop to catch his breath every fifty feet or so.

"Yes, My Lord."

If Lieutenant Karmaikel felt any amusement at his decrepit commanding officer's resignation, he was wise enough to keep it to himself.

▼ ▼ ▼

Colonel Ahlfryd Makyntyr squinted up at the sky. The night was blacker than Shan-wei's riding boots, and he was happy it was so, despite the fact that he was standing in the midst of well over two dozen artillery pieces which were being loaded in complete darkness. His gunners were sufficiently well trained to assuage any worries he might have felt on that score, and the moon would be rising within the hour. Not that it would be much help; they were just past the new moon, and the waxing crescent was little more than a nail paring. The angle-guns had been provided with incendiary rounds, which should do a decent job of illuminating the target, but neither he nor any of his gunners had any desire to be carrying lanterns around with all those powder cartridges just waiting to explode.

Makyntyr grimaced at the thought, but it was secondary. The timing was more important, and Sir Rainos would not be pleased if they got it wrong.

The colonel and Sir Rainos didn't much like each other. Makyntyr had been transferred from the Navy to teach Ahlverez' artillerists their trade. Before that, he'd been *Captain* Makyntyr . . . and a firm supporter of Earl Thirsk's effort to reform the Navy. Given Ahlverez' attitude toward Thirsk, that had created a certain inevitable tension between them. Fortunately, even though Ahlverez was just as bigoted where Thirsk was concerned as Makyntyr had expected him to be, he'd also realized how badly he needed *someone* with Makyntyr's expertise. That had kept him civil long enough for both of them to recognize that they had a job to do, and while they were never going to like one another, they'd settled down into a decent working relationship.

And as long as I don't find some way to screw up, it'll probably stay that way. Probably.

At least Ahlverez was no more enthusiastic about this particular exercise in Desnairian stupidity than Makyntyr was, so he was unlikely to hold its inevitable outcome against his own artillery commander. Whoever got the blame, however, a lot of men were about to get killed, and far too few of them would be heretics.

Now that's a thought you'd best keep to yourself, Ahlfryd, my boy. I believe it's called "defeatism," and I suspect Father Sulyvyn would have a little something to say about it.

No doubt the Schuelerite would, and Makyntyr intended to do everything he could to make the assault succeed, and counting the guns in his own and the Desnairian battery to his right, between him and the Bay, they had four times the artillery they'd observed on the heretics' side. In this particular area of their fortifications, at any rate. But unlike the Desnairians, he knew what "new model" artillery could do, and the guns in those entrenchments were even better protected now than they'd been two five-days ago. He didn't know if the heretics realized the Royal Dohlaran Army had its own angle-guns, but they'd been steadily improving their positions' overhead protection, and the Army of Shiloh's delays had given them entirely too much time in which to work. Worse, all of the Army of Shiloh's guns were lighter than anything on the heretics' side, and at least some of the Desnairian gunners seemed to think that was a *good* thing.

Idiots! I'll guarantee they don't have a clue what Charisian gunners can do.

Ahlfryd Makyntyr did. He'd been a first lieutenant aboard one of the Dohlaran galleons Admiral Gwylym Manthyr had pounded into wreckage before his own ships had been forced to strike at the Battle of the Narrows. Obviously no one in the Desnairian Army had bothered to discuss the implications of that little affair with someone from the Desnairian *Navy*. While it was true that twelve-pounders fired rather more rapidly than thirty-pounders, the difference was far lower than the imperial gunners seemed to be assuming. For that matter, no gun could maintain its maximum rate of fire forever. In fact, once the tubes heated and forced the gunners to slow down, the advantage—if there was one at all at that point—shifted to the thirty-pounder. And he rather doubted that any Desnairian, even in their navy, had any concept of what a charge of canister from a thirty-pounder was like.

Well, they won't be able to say that this time tomorrow, will they? Those who're still alive, at any rate.

Somehow, despite his personal dislike for Desnairians, that thought gave him very little satisfaction.

▼ ▼ ▼

"Stand by," Sir Shailtyn Lywys, the Baron of Climbhaven, said tersely.

The baron crouched in a small lean-to, open to the west but with a solid—*very* solid—wall to the east. He'd made certain of that, since he had no desire for any chink of light from the bull's-eye lantern to warn the heretics what was coming. He needed that lantern to keep an eye on his watch, however, and for one of the few times since the Army of Justice had headed north, he felt a sense of profound satisfaction.

Climbhaven was sixty-five years old, and the riding accident which had crippled his right leg thirty years ago had left him with continual low-grade pain which tended to flare up into something far more acute upon occasion, especially in cold or rainy weather, and had ended his cavalry career forever. The bitterness of his forced retirement had added an even sharper edge to a naturally crotchety personality over the ensuing decades, but while Climbhaven was a tiny barony, so small it appeared only on the largest scale maps, it was also an ancient one, and the current baron was related to many of the Empire's most powerful families. He was even a connection by marriage to Duke Traykhos, and he'd traded shamelessly upon those connections when Mother Church decreed the massive enlargement of the Imperial Army for service in the Jihad.

All the connections in the world couldn't put him back in command of a cavalry regiment, however, and so he'd ended up as the Army of Justice's senior artillerist . . . despite the fact that he'd never even seen an artillery piece two years ago. Most of the Imperial Desnairian Army's officer corps could have made that statement, however, and he'd done his best to master his new responsibilities since. Along the way, he'd been amazed by the "new model" artillery's lethality, and he was looking forward to unleashing that lethality upon the heretics.

And that accounted for his current satisfaction. Denied regimental command or not, the entire Army of Shiloh was awaiting *his* signal. His gunners would open the attack, and he was determined they'd do it precisely on time.

He watched the second hand sweep around the watch's

face. No one would fault him if he was off a minute or so either way, but he wasn't going to be. Not tonight.

He raised his left hand, aware of the lieutenant standing to one side, where he could see into the lean-to's illuminated interior and simultaneously be seen by the crews of the nearest guns. Climbhaven never looked away from his watch. He simply waited, and as the second hand reached thirteen, his hand slashed down.

▼ ▼ ▼

It was certainly impressive, Hauwerd Breygart acknowledged.

He stood atop the lookout tower with Karmaikel and a signalman, and the darkness to the west exploded as scores of muzzle flashes ripped the night apart. The fiery streaks of the shells' fuses burned their way through the dark, and his eyes narrowed as some of those streaks rose in high arcs before they came plunging towards earth once more.

So those were angle-guns. Not a surprise, but still good to know. We'll have to get the sketches circulated so everyone else knows what they look like, too.

The thought moved through the back of his brain; its front was busy watching to see how effective that hurricane of light and thunder truly was.

One of the problems the enemy had created for himself by moving his guns up in darkness was that none of the gunners had been able to register their fire. They knew the entrenchments' general direction, but that wasn't the same thing as being able to aim properly, and most of the initial salvos had very little effect. Shells that actually hit the earthworks—and didn't just bounce off—were simply absorbed, and black powder was a fairly anemic explosive, when it came down to it. The quantities packed into a Temple Loyalist twelve-pound shell, especially one with most of its internal volume taken up by shrapnel balls, did minimal damage to the solidity of an earthen berm twenty feet deep at its base.

Only a minority of them did hit the entrenchments, however. The majority landed short, and while some of the short rounds managed to ricochet into the earth-works' face before they detonated, at least a third of the rounds fired went high, instead. Most of the overs whistled well beyond the waiting Allied infantry and artillery, and only a handful exploded in midair at a point which might actually have thrown shrapnel into the defenders.

Hanth doubted that came as a total surprise to the enemy gunners, and it certainly wasn't a surprise to him or Commander Parkyr. While he was pretty sure the Army of Shiloh had expected the sudden, completely unanticipated eruption of artillery to have a severely demoralizing effect on its enemies, it probably hadn't hoped to inflict much actual damage with its first few salvos. What it *had* achieved, however, was to put at least a dozen incendiary rounds behind the Allies' parapet. Packed with saltpeter, sulfur, and meal powder, they gushed light and flame through the holes bored through the shell walls for that very purpose as they bounced and rolled. Fortunately, most of them landed in the empty space between the first and second lines of entrenchment, with nothing much to set on fire, but they accomplished their primary purpose.

▼ ▼ ▼

Baron Climbhaven leaned heavily on his cane, watching as the heretics' parapets were suddenly etched against the Shan-wei glow and smoke of his incendiary shells. He was breathing hard, his heart racing with the exertion of dragging his bad leg to his present position, but it was worth it when he heard the nearest gun captains shouting to their crews.

They can see what they're shooting at now, *by Chihiro!* he thought exultantly. *Now lay it to the bastards!*

▼ ▼ ▼

"*Open fire!*" Lieutenant Symyn Bukanyn barked as the first enemy rounds thudded to the ground around and behind the heavily dug-in battery of the Navy Redoubt.

There'd been some argument over exactly what to call that battery. Originally, it had been labeled simply

"Redoubt #2" on the engineers' plat, but Bukanyn had been unwilling to settle for that. He'd wanted to christen it the "Trumpeter Redoubt," given where its guns—and commander—came from. Unfortunately, that name had been pinched by that insufferable sprout Dairyn Sahndyrsyn, HMS *Trumpeter*'s fourth lieutenant, before Bukanyn got his bid in, and Earl Hanth had decided it was a case of first-come, first-served. So Bukanyn had been forced to settle for the Navy Redoubt, although at the moment he at least had the satisfaction of knowing Sahndyrsyn's battery was over eleven miles away on the slopes of Shadowline Mountain. He might have gotten the name Bukanyn wanted, but Bukanyn and Lieutenant Fraydyk Hylsdail in Redoubt #1 were going to fire the Navy's first rounds in the defense of Thesmar.

And if the Navy Redoubt didn't get its first shots off before Redoubt #1, Symyn Bukanyn would know the reason why.

Fortunately for Bukanyn's gunners, they did.

▼ ▼ ▼

Baron Climbhaven winced as the enemy fired. They were enormously quicker off the mark than anyone had expected. Clearly the heretics must have gotten some hint of what was coming! And the shells smashing back at his artillerists were far heavier than he'd anticipated. He remembered a discussion with Ahlfryd Makyntyr in which the Dohlaran had suggested his Desnairian allies might be underestimating the destructiveness of naval artillery. At the time, he'd put the warning down to Dohlaran timorousness. After all, the Dohlarans had allowed themselves to be penned up in their defenses around Tairys by a mere handful of those fearful "naval guns." Of course they'd emphasize how deadly dangerous they were!

Perhaps he owed them an apology, he reflected, although he'd see himself damned and in hell before he offered one.

He ducked, losing his cane (and his footing) and going flat on his face as a heretic shell slammed into the ground in front of him, bounced high into the air, and then detonated. He heard the splattering impact of shrapnel balls driving into earth—or flesh—and a sudden chorus of screams. Only his fall had taken him out of the path of those projectiles, and his aide had been less fortunate.

He groped for his cane, found it, levered himself upright, and wondered if he'd have the opportunity to issue any apologies whether he wanted to or not.

"Hit them! *Hit the bastards!*" he shouted, stumping forward into the nearest gun emplacement on his cane.

▼ ▼ ▼

"What do you think, Sir?" Sir Lynkyn Lattymyr asked quietly.

Ahlverez glanced at his aide, then back at the blazing line of the Army of Shiloh's artillery, and shrugged.

"It's too early to say, but it's just possible Duke Harless and Baron Climbhaven are in the process of changing their opinions about the ineffectiveness of those slow-firing naval guns."

▼ ▼ ▼

The Earl of Hanth remembered a conversation with Kydryc Fyguera what seemed like decades ago. He'd assured the Siddarmarkian general that no one in the Royal Dohlaran Army was going to be able to match the skill of Imperial Charisian Navy gunners. He supposed that had been arrogant of him, but the ICN had earned its expertise the hard way. Accustomed to firing from moving decks at moving targets, it was child's play to fire from fixed platforms of heavy timbers at targets that *didn't* move. And that didn't even consider Charis' other advantages, like the dispart and tangent sights mounted on its pieces. The dispart sight was a simple post on the muzzle swell to allow for quick, accurate alignment of the weapon's point of aim. That alone would have been a significant advantage, but the tangent ring sight on the weapon's breech was mounted on a steel bar that was fixed perpendicular to the axis of the bore in a bronze case. The bar was graduated in yards and moved up and down in the case guides, with a thumbscrew to fix it in place. Raised to the proper height, it automatically adjusted elevation for range when aligned with the front sight and the target. It wasn't perfect, given the differences in ballistic performance between different lots of powder, but it was far better than anything on the other side and it allowed all the guns in a battery to be fired at the same elevation.

As Lieutenant Bukanyn's battery fired now.

▼ ▼ ▼

Symyn Bukanyn watched the strike of his battery's first shells. They landed short, which was better than landing long, and he watched several hit the ground and skip. At least two of the ricochets exploded above the enemy gun line, where their shrapnel balls had to have inflicted casualties, but that was an unacceptably low percentage. Obviously they'd underestimated the range to the gun pits the Temple Boys had been so sneakily building for the last five-day or so.

"Make your range twelve hundred! Cut your fuses for two seconds!"

Acknowledgments came back and he saw gun captains bending over their tangent sights, sliding the bars up, squinting to make sure the gradations were properly aligned, while the number two on each gun set the fuses. They worked quickly, urgently, apparently oblivious to the enemy shells slamming into their protective earthworks or whistling overhead, and he felt a rush of pride in them.

▼ ▼ ▼

Earl Hanth winced as the first Dohlaran angle-gun shells exploded above the Navy Redoubt. They were as light as he'd hoped, but that didn't mean they weren't dangerous. Cones of shrapnel streaked down from each white and red explosion, smashing into his men's positions like leaden rain. He couldn't hear the screams from here, but he knew they were there.

▼ ▼ ▼

Symyn Bukanyn *could* hear the screams, yet there weren't many of them. Firing a thirty-pounder under a protective roof was a . . . noisy proposition, but nothing gunners trained to fire from a galleon's gundeck were unaccustomed to, and Earl Hanth's insistence on providing overhead cover—and Commander Parkyr's decision against manning the angle-guns until they were needed—paid a handsome dividend as the shrapnel slashed downward. Looking out through the broad firing slits that served as his battery's gunports, Bukanyn saw the earth ripple in a heave of dust and dirt as shrapnel impacted all around the position.

He couldn't even hear the balls that hit the overhead.

One of the Temple Loyalist shells hit the ground, rolled, and skittered to a wobbling halt directly in front of the number five thirty-pounder. The shell's fuse had been cut too long or else it had burned too slowly, but in the event, that worked for the gunners who'd fired it. Instead of detonating overhead as they'd planned, the evil thing simply sat there, rocking, spouting sparks, hissing, and then detonated like Shan-wei herself. Three of his men went down as some of its shrapnel ripped in through the firing slit. One of the wounded was screaming, the sound high and shrill as he clawed at the bloody ruin of his face, and it was only a matter of time before the enemy twelve-pounders found the range, as well. That could be more dangerous than the angle-guns. If the Temple Boys got themselves sorted out, started throwing accurately fused shells at those firing slits in *horizontal* salvos, casualties were likely to soar.

Assuming someone gave them the *time* for that, of course.

Bukanyn's eyes were like flint as the battery's attached corpsmen pulled the casualties clear, but he never looked away from his target.

The guns were reloaded and relaid, and his smile was as cold as those stony eyes.

"*Fire!*"

▼ ▼ ▼

Colonel Makyntyr staggered as the heretics found the range.

There were no more than six shells in the salvo, but the greater height of the heretics' position atop the hill gave them a direct line of fire down into Makyntyr's gun pits. It wasn't the vertically plunging fire of his own angle-guns, praise Chihiro, but it was bad enough. The massive thirty-pounder shells exploded no more than twenty or thirty yards short of his positions and the spreading patterns of shrapnel arrived like Langhorne's own Rakurai. The guns had been skillfully dug-in, their muzzles just clearing the low earthen walls where the spoil of the gun pits had been thrown up to protect them, but the heretics' height advantage negated much of that protection. Screams went up as the shrapnel claimed its harvest of blood, torn flesh, and shattered bone, and his gun crews' faces were stone as they reloaded with desperate haste.

▼ ▼ ▼

Both the Navy Redoubt and Redoubt #1 were in action now. The Army of Shiloh's gunners fired as quickly as they could reload, pouring shells into the Allies' lines, but Hanth's gunners fired back much more slowly. Not because they couldn't have fired faster, but because they were shooting with cold deliberation. Protected by overhead layers of timber and earth, they returned that tornado of fire with the icy professionalism of the Imperial Charisian Navy, delivering concentrated thunderbolts to their foes.

As he watched the volume of fire going back and forth, as he saw the explosions hammering the enemy's guns, Hauwerd Breygart knew how it was going to end. The only question was how long the enemy would endure his gunners' fire before they started trying to extract their surviving artillery from the death trap they'd thrust it into.

▼ ▼ ▼

Well, Sir Rainos Ahlverez thought bitterly, *so much for that brilliant inspiration.*

The steady flashes of the heretic guns were like coals blazing up to the steady rhythm of a blacksmith's bellows. If there was any diminution of their fire, *he* couldn't see it. And whatever Harless might think, they weren't firing so slowly because of their weapons' clumsiness. No, they were firing that slowly because they were taking careful aim and slaughtering the Army of Shiloh's artillery.

It might be a different story in open terrain, where the greater number of their lighter weapons could be brought into play against guns that weren't dug-in behind walls of solid earth. But they weren't in open terrain, and matching their guns against the heretics in a duel like this one was a losing proposition.

Sir Rainos Ahlverez didn't intend to lose any more of his guns—or his *men*—than he had to, and he turned to Captain Lattymyr.

"Go to Colonel Makyntyr. Tell him that on my authority he's to begin pulling—"

His head snapped up in disbelief and he wheeled back around as the golden voice of bugles cut through the bedlam. It was only a single bugle, at first, but it was taken up by others—by dozens, and then by scores, and Sir Rainos Ahlverez swore vilely, betrayed by his own incredulity, as he recognized the call.

They were sounding the charge.

▼ ▼ ▼

"Dear God," Hanth muttered in disbelief.

Visibility was so poor in the gunsmoke-smothered dark that he couldn't convince himself he'd actually seen it. Not at first. But then the lightning glare of muzzle flashes reflected from the standards at the heads of the bayonet and pike-bristling columns.

Not even a Desnairian could believe he's managed to suppress our guns! What in the name of heaven are the idiots—?

"What in God's name do they think they're doing, My Lord?"

Lieutenant Karmaikel had obviously seen the same

thing, and Hanth looked at his aide for a moment while his brain grappled with it. Then his nostrils flared and he shook his head sharply.

"I doubt they *are* thinking," he grated, eyes straining as that vaguely seen movement was veiled by smoke and darkness once more. His jaw clenched, and he shook his head again, like a man trying to shake off a hard punch. "If there's anything remotely like an actual *thought* behind this, though, they have to be hoping a massive enough assault can carry the outer works by sheer weight of numbers despite our batteries."

"That's . . . insane, My Lord," Karmaikel said slowly, and there might have been an edge of horror in his voice, despite his bitter hatred for all things Dohlaran.

"That or the act of a man who hasn't figured out how badly the rules've changed. Or maybe both." Hanth snorted harshly, and his voice was hammered iron. "There's a term *Seijin* Merlin and Emperor Cayleb've taken to using—a 'learning curve,' they call it, from the charts Baron Green Valley uses to measure units' level of training. The 'learning curve' of whoever the hell is in command over there is about to get one hell of a lot steeper."

Wind pushed aside a wall of smoke, reflected gunfire flashed off those standards once more, and he turned to the signalman at his elbow.

"Signal Captain Sympsyn. Enemy infantry is advancing. Illuminate in three minutes."

"At once, My Lord!"

The signalman turned to the bulky, swivel-mounted contraption on the lookout tower's rail. It was almost three feet tall and equally wide, with a lever on its side, and the signalman approached it cautiously, despite the thick glove on his left hand. The smell of heated metal rose from it, for it was searingly hot thanks to the lanterns blazing inside it, and his gloved hand gripped the steel-loop handle on its side so he could peer through the ring sight at the command post at the lookout tower's base.

He aligned it carefully, then began flipping the lever on its side in a practiced, staccato rhythm.

▼ ▼ ▼

"Signal from Earl Hanth, Sir!"

Captain Lywys Sympsyn turned as the shout wrenched his attention from the volcano smoke and fury. He couldn't see the actual muzzle flashes from here—there were too many earthen walls in the way—but he could see their reflections lighting that smoke with flame as the guns belched thunder.

Now he looked in a different direction, up at the lookout tower—a blacker shape rearing against a night-black sky. The fury of the artillery exchange picked out the latticework of its supporting spars in a lightning glare like Shan-wei's own crown, but what mattered to Lywys Sympsyn at that moment was the light blinking from its lofty platform. Its oil-lamp flames would have been all but invisible in daylight, despite the brilliantly polished reflector and the lens which the Royal College had designed to concentrate its light, but against the night it burned with bright, fierce clarity. Daylight was the province of the heliograph or the signal flag; darkness called for other means, and he waited as patiently as he could while the signalman read off the flashing message.

"'Enemy infantry is advancing,' Sir. 'Illuminate in three minutes.'"

▼ ▼ ▼

"That *idiot*! That Shan-wei-damned, *witless*, mother-loving, *dog-fucking*, Desnairian piece of *shit*! That—!"

Ahlverez dragged himself to a white-hot, shuddering halt. Much though Harless deserved every word, it wasn't going to do any good . . . or make any difference.

Maybe not. But maybe if I get at least some of it out of my system now, I'll be able to face him later without cutting his throat the instant I get into range!

He knew what Harless was doing, although until this

moment he wouldn't have believed anyone could be stupid enough to try it. The Desnairian had realized there was no way his guns were going to silence those "slow-firing, ineffective" naval guns after all, so he was throwing in the infantry columns, instead. The Army of Shiloh's guns would be forced to stop firing when their own infantry blocked their line of fire; until then, they'd continue to pour shells at the heretics, hoping to knock back the defensive fire. That was part of the plan Harless had discussed with his senior officers when planning this night's debacle. But the infantry wasn't supposed to be committed until after the bulk of the heretics' artillery had been silenced by his own guns. Now, like a gambler unwilling to acknowledge that Andropov's luck had turned against him, he was casting the dice in one last grand gesture, to win or lose it all.

But it was a wager which would be paid in lives, not marks, and in that moment, unwillingly, Ahlverez realized what the Earl of Thirsk must have felt when Ahlverez' own cousin ignored *his* advice off Armageddon Reef.

At least they've got the cover of darkness and all that smoke, he told himself, trying to pretend he wasn't grasping at straws. *The heretics may not even realize they're coming until our guns go silent. Even then, they won't be able to see well enough to aim. It'll be blind fire on their part, and maybe—just maybe—the infantry can get close enough to rush the parapets.*

▼ ▼ ▼

Lywys Sympsyn checked his watch under his command post's lantern and pulled the fire striker from its belt holster. It was an absurdly simple device which someone should have thought of years ago: just a cylindrical steel tube about three inches tall and an inch in diameter with a screw set into its bottom and a hinged, tightly fitting cap at the top.

He flipped up the top with his thumb to expose the toothed steel wheel and wick. The body of the striker was filled with cotton saturated in distilled fire vine oil which could be replenished by removing the bottom screw. Personally, Sympsyn would've preferred something less smoky (and less poisonous), but few things in all the world were more flammable or harder to extinguish than fire vine oil, and when his thumb spun the wheel against the spring-loaded flint in a shower of sparks, the wick from the oil reservoir burst into instant flame.

And smoky or not, a corner of his brain reflected, *it still smells a hell of a lot better than a Shan-wei's candle!*

His mouth quirked at the incongruity of the thought at a moment like this one and he touched the flame to the first fuse.

▼ ▼ ▼

Sir Rainos Ahlverez wondered why his teeth didn't crumble into powder under the pressure of his clenched jaw muscles as the first heretic rocket streaked into the night. The Desnairian guns had already gone silent as the three columns on the right of the assault swept past them. His own artillery would have time for no more than a single additional salvo before it had to cease fire, and he knew—somehow he *knew*, even before it happened— what that rocket foretold. Oh, yes, he knew, and he wondered in that moment, in a strange, still corner of his brain, who he hated more, the Duke of Harless or the heretics?

He watched the rocket climb, riding its own fiery breath like a curse, trailing a banner of smoke. It rose higher than he would have believed possible, and then, suddenly, it exploded. But not in the colored bursts of light he'd been warned the heretics used as battlefield signals. No, it birthed something else entirely: a single brilliant, artificial star blazing above the Army of Shiloh's advancing infantry like some bizarre midnight sun.

He stared up, slitted eyes glittering in its light, and he could just make out something above it. Something that held it up, drifting on the wind like some fire-breathing wyvern come straight from Shan-wei's hell. And then a second rocket streaked up to join it. And a third.

The pitiless light streamed down across the infantry columns, exposing them in all their naked vulnerability, and the heretics' artillery retargeted.

. XII .
Charisian Embassy,
Siddar City,
Republic of Siddarmark

"Anything more I should know before our meeting with Greyghor and Daryus?" Cayleb Ahrmahk inquired as the gentle breeze flapped the awning.

Merlin had given up on convincing him not to perch on rooftops, especially since he was developing an increasingly severe case of "cabin fever." Cayleb had always hated sending men into battle while he stayed out of the line of fire, and that was getting worse as Charisian troops found themselves in direct combat with the Army of God and its allies. The fact that he could actually see what was happening to those troops through Owl's SNARCs was simply icing on the cake. It wasn't as if Cayleb were deliberately seeking to attract the attention of a potential rifle-armed assassin so much as the fact that he was spending far too much time in one office or conference or another. Besides, the emperor was never happy indoors when he could be outdoors . . . at least when his empress was somewhere else.

The *seijin* had at least prevailed upon his nominal liege lord to allow carpenters to create a proper deck atop the embassy, set far enough back to make lines of fire from street level difficult to come by. In fact, they'd set something of a fashion, with rooftop decks appearing on increasing numbers of townhouses here in the Republic's capital. Siddar City had been larger than Tellesberg before the Sword of Schueler; now the city was more packed than ever with the influx of refugees. There'd never been a lot of room for the sorts of landscaped gardens the wealthier inhabitants of Tellesberg favored, so perhaps it wasn't too surprising that the city should have begun sprouting additional rooftop decks. They made pleasant vantage spots, especially with the colorful awnings most of their owners had added, although Merlin wondered how well they'd weather the upcoming winter. Siddar City's buildings and rooftops tended to be well coated with grime and soot from coal fires, and he had his doubts about what all of those splendidly varnished or painted decks were going to look like come spring.

At the moment, however, the breeze was pleasant and the view was soothing as Merlin stood behind Cayleb's rattan chair and watched the capital's early-morning bustle.

A bustle which, he knew, only deepened Cayleb's awareness of the difference between his own "sheltered" existence and what was happening in places with names like the Glacierheart Gap and Thesmar.

Under the circumstances, the fact that the emperor's question had come out in a merely interrogative tone was actually fairly remarkable.

"Not really," the *seijin* replied. "I've talked to Nahrmahn, and he says there're no surprises in last night's take from the SNARCs. Ahlverez is being a bit more restrained in conversations with his officers than he was during the attack, though."

"He could hardly be *less* restrained," Cayleb pointed out with a smile. "I've known people with an excellent command of invective, but he rose to heights I wouldn't've imagined he was capable of."

"Are you surprised?"

"No." The smile in Cayleb's normally warm brown eyes vanished as they went suddenly cold and bleak. And satisfied. "No, I'm not surprised at all."

The Earl of Hanth's timing had been impeccable, and the quantity of canister a thirty-pounder could spew out was staggering. A twelve-pounder field gun fired thirty of the golfball-sized shot to an effective range of three or four hundred yards; a thirty-pounder fired eighty of them, with an effective range of *six* hundred yards. And at that range, it dispersed that torrent of shot in a pattern sixty yards across, like the devil's own shotgun.

The Duke of Harless' leading infantry had been seven hundred yards from Hanth's entrenchments when the first flare blossomed above them. None had gotten within a hundred yards, and casualties had been horrendous. Of the almost eight thousand Desnairian and Dohlaran infantry committed to the attack, a third had been killed outright—at least half by artillery fire alone, before they ever entered effective range of the Marines' rifles—and another three thousand had been wounded. Half those wounded had been taken prisoner, and almost three hundred *un*wounded men had allowed themselves to be taken prisoner, as well, even with those prisoners knowing exactly what the Inquisition was likely to do with such craven traitors if they ever fell back into its hands again. Less than twenty-three hundred had made it back to their own lines unscathed. A casualty rate of over seventy percent was enough to destroy any unit ever raised, and it would be a long, long time before the devastated regiments could be reconstituted as effective fighting formations.

If they could ever be restored as *effective* formations at all.

"You know, Harless actually reacted a lot faster than Ahlverez gives him credit for," Merlin said after a moment.

"He got his men *massacred,* Merlin!"

"I didn't say it was a remotely smart thing for him to do in the first place; I just said he reacted faster than Ahlverez thinks he did." Merlin shook his head. "He didn't know about the new parachute flares, either, so he had a better excuse than Ahlverez wants to admit for thinking he could get close enough to rush the parapet under cover of darkness and all that smoke. Not a *good* excuse, but at least *an* excuse. And whatever else, he'd realized what was happening and called off the second wave even before the first-wave units broke."

Cayleb looked over his shoulder at the *seijin,* then grimaced.

"All right, I'll give you that much. But he should've damned well known better before he sent them in at all!"

"I agree, and Ahlverez certainly thinks the same thing, but much as it pains me, we need to be fair to Harless. Oh," Merlin waved a hand as Cayleb's eyebrows flew up, "I'm not suggesting he's a military genius! But we can't afford to underestimate the other side, and even if he's not in the same league as somebody like Gorthyk Nybar or Bishop Militant Bahrnabai, he may not be as completely feckless as Ahlverez thinks he is. He screwed up because of his own prejudices and inexperience—*personal* inexperience—and it cost him a hell of a lot of men. But he had the excuse that he *was* inexperienced, which is a hell of a lot more than Kaitswyrth had when he launched that assault on Eastshare. And he *learned* from it, Cayleb. I'm not saying he won't find fresh mistakes to make, but I'll be surprised if he makes this one again, and we need to remember the difference between incompetence born of ignorance and incompetence born of outright stupidity."

"You're probably right," Cayleb said after a moment, looking back out over Siddar City's roofs. "I'm not prepared to rule out outright stupidity in his case just yet, though."

"I admit the jury's still out," Merlin agreed. "Let's not forget *Ahlverez'* performance, though. That man, at least, is a *lot* smarter than I thought he was. He's still a stiff-necked, bigoted fanatic who prefers to substitute aristocratic rank for ability and who's likely to allow his thinking to be swayed as much by fervor as logic. He's as ambitious as the next noble, too, and it's obvious he really can hold a grudge until it dies of old age. Earl Thirsk shouldn't be trusting him behind him with a dagger anytime soon, for example. But *Desnairian* noblemen make his bigotry look like the ravings of a utopian anarchist! Worse, he's demonstrated he can learn from experience, and I really wish he hadn't."

"I believe you're the one who pointed out that we

can't expect the villains to have a monopoly on stupidity. I suppose it follows that we can't expect our side to have a monopoly on *competence,* either."

"I'm afraid not. And at the moment, given the opportunity, Ahlverez would have a hard time deciding who he'd sooner put a bullet into: Harless or a heretic. The longer that goes on, the happier I'll be. In the meantime, Nahrmahn and Owl're keeping an eye on them. They'll let us know if anything unanticipated—like a sudden lovefest between them—happens. And unless it does, I don't think anyone has to worry about whether or not Hauwerd and Fyguera will manage to hold Thesmar." The *seijin* shrugged. "For now, I don't know anything new about the situation there that we could share with the Lord Protector or Parkair. Not without getting into those interesting questions we need to avoid, anyway."

Cayleb's lips quirked at Merlin's dry tone. Greyghor Stohnar and his ministers had been deeply impressed—actually, "astonished" might have been a better word—by the depth and efficacy of the Charisian spy network in the Republic. Delighted, of course, but also a bit miffed by the fact that the Charisians had been able to emplace such an extensive intelligence system without ever being noticed by Henrai Maidyn's counterintelligence agents. Under the circumstances, they were disinclined to complain, and they were also disinclined to joggle the Charisians' elbow by demanding any details about who their spies were and how they were organized. The Siddarmarkians understood the need to maintain operational security; they'd had conclusive proof of the impressive accuracy of their ally's reports; and the ancient aphorism—"if it isn't broken, don't fix it"—had survived among Safeholdian humanity.

They would have been even more impressed by the Charisian's intelligence reports if they'd realized those reports were deliberately providing occasionally *inaccurate* information. Of course, had they analyzed those inaccuracies and "errors," they would have discovered the mistakes always had relatively minor implications, although Merlin sincerely hoped they never guessed that they'd been included to prevent them from realizing that Charis' spies were simply *too* good.

And then there was Aivah Pahrsahn, who'd come to function as a sort of general clearinghouse for the Allies' intelligence reports. Her own net of agents in the Temple Lands provided quite a few of those reports (including information from Zion, where Merlin and Nahrmahn remained very hesitant about operating sensor remotes aggressively), and while she held no official standing with the Republic or the Empire, no one in either of those realms doubted her complete and total dedication to the downfall of the Group of Four. Of course, no one in either of those realms thought for a moment that she was putting all of her cards on the table any more than they were, either. For example, Merlin found it very interesting that none of Madam Pahrsahn's agents (to judge from her reports to Cayleb and Lord Protector Greyghor, which, according to Owl's remotes, weren't always precisely identical to reports from her agents to *her*) had apparently noticed that half a dozen or so vicars had died recently under mysterious circumstances.

And more power to her, he thought now.

She was just as good as Nahrmahn Baytz when it came to putting together bits and pieces, however, and given that Bynzhamyn Raice, Charis' official spymaster, was in far distant Tellesberg and that Henrai Maidyn's crushing responsibilities as the Republic's finance minister left him very little time to spend running spy networks, at the moment turning her into the Allies' effective intelligence minister had struck both Cayleb and Stohnar as perfectly logical.

After the fact, at least. It rather amused Merlin that neither of them had even considered making that decision until they woke up one morning and realized they'd already made it.

They sure did find all kinds of "logical reasons" in the end, though, didn't they? he thought.

"What about Eastshare and Kynt?" Cayleb asked,

and Merlin blinked as the question pulled him back up out of his thoughts.

"I think Stohnar and Parkair are about as up-to-date on both of them as we could want," he said. "Stohnar, at least, is a little more nervous about Eastshare's strategy than he wants to admit, but he's onboard with it. Which isn't to say he won't be happier when that brigade of his reaches Glacierheart to reinforce Hobsyn. But Kaitswyrth isn't going to be trying anything aggressive for five-days yet, at the least, after the way he got his ass kicked up between his ears. And even if he did, Eastshare left enough artillery—and enough scout snipers—to give him nightmares in that kind of terrain.

"As for Kynt, the turnaround on our semaphore messages to him is barely an hour. That keeps us about as up-to-date as it gets, and so far there's no sign Wyrshym even realizes he's moved back from Wyvern Lake. He'll be finding out in the next couple of days, when Kynt starts sweeping up the Temple Loyalist militia in Mountaincross. I'm rather looking forward to that." The *seijin* bared his teeth briefly. "Those bastards've run up a damned steep tab, and it's past time they got a chance to start paying it back down."

Sapphire eyes met equally cold eyes of brown for a moment, and then Merlin shrugged.

"As I say, everyone's up-to-date on Glacierheart and Mountaincross. Certainly up-to-date enough there's no point risking someone like Mahldyn or Aivah wondering how we get information back and forth at superhuman speed. I think we could reasonably expect another report about Thesmar from *Seijin* Ahbraim in about another five-day, though. That should give us enough time for my mysterious network of *seijins* and their sympathizers to get us a message from him." He smiled crookedly. "For that matter, if *Seijin* Merlin can find a reason to be somewhere else, *Seijin* Ahbraim could brief us in person."

"Don't you ever find that a bit confusing?"

"Frequently, actually." Merlin's smile grew even more

crooked. "Frankly, the hardest bit's remembering what conversations each of my various personalities have had with whom."

Cayleb chuckled, but then his expression turned rather more serious.

"Are we burning that candle from too many ends, Merlin? I know it's useful, and I know you were at least half joking just now, but it was a valid point. How many people can you be—how many balls can you keep in the air—before you finally drop one and we wind up with something we can't explain away?"

Merlin grimaced, because Cayleb had a point.

So far as they were aware, none of the Group of Four had discovered that *Seijin* Merlin had "visions." They'd been careful to restrict that particular cover story to a very small group of Charisians, despite how useful it had proven. The members of the inner circle knew the truth about the network of SNARCs upon which those "visions" depended, but they still provided a handy explanation for people like Ahlfryd Hyndryk and others who'd been cleared for that story and needed access to the information but hadn't been included in the inner circle.

Unfortunately, "visions" could be almost as unhappy an explanation as the truth if they came to the Inquisition's attention, and Merlin Athrawes had become increasingly visible. Or, rather, the fact that he was more than simply Cayleb Ahrmahk's most lethal bodyguard had become increasingly evident to the Group of Four. That had been inevitable, really, although Merlin's prominent part in rescuing Irys and Daivyn from Delferahk had made it even worse.

The Church of God's propagandists had labeled Merlin as Cayleb's "demon familiar" even before that particular adventure, given the *seijin*'s uncanny ability to prevent assassinations, yet the *Inquisition* had carefully not made the accusation openly for years. There'd been several reasons for that—including the fact that Zhaspahr Clyntahn would have faced the rather pressing problem that while Mother Church taught that demons existed, she also taught that their appearance in the mortal world would be answered with a divine response . . . which, unhappily for the Inquisition, hadn't happened.

But that reluctance to label him as a demonic presence had changed after the escape from Delferahk provided too much evidence of Merlin Athrawes' "superhuman" abilities for even the Inquisition to quash. Worse, the increasing evidence of his "*seijin* spy network" clearly proved he wasn't the only *seijin* in the woodwork, and that threatened to turn into a serious problem. Both *The Testimonies* and *The Commentaries* made it clear that the original *seijins* had fought on the side of the Light during the War Against the Fallen. Since those same sources made it crystal clear that no *seijin* would ever raise his hand against the authority Langhorne himself had bestowed upon Mother Church, he must manifestly be something else.

Unless the Group of Four weren't God's champions after all, of course.

Given the alternatives, the Inquisition had made the label official. He could not be a true *seijin*; therefore, he must be the spawn of evil against whom the true *seijins* had always fought, and the Grand Inquisitor had solemnly proclaimed that the "Demon Athrawes" was to be slain by any means possible by any faithful child of Mother Church. Assuming, that was, that anyone was willing to get close enough to him to make the attempt.

That was undoubtedly the best explanation available to them, although it still left the problem of where his divine opposition was. Merlin expected Clyntahn and Rayno to use any Charisian reverse as proof that God and the Archangels were taking a stand against Shanwei's servants, but that was exactly what they'd been doing as the Sword of Schueler drove the Republic towards collapse, and the argument was rather less convincing after the last couple of months. And, of course, remarkably few Reformists—and *no* member of the Church of Charis—paid much attention to Clyntahn's proclamations these days.

Yet a sort of bred-in-the-bone respect for *Mother Church*'s decrees lingered. Merlin suspected that respect gave even Clyntahn's pronouncements at least a subliminal toehold even with many who consciously rejected them. That was inevitable after so many centuries of the Church's unquestioned authority, and thereby hung the problem. The many extraordinary abilities tradition assigned to *seijins* could cover quite a bit, but there were limits in all things. They really couldn't afford to have people, especially people in critical positions, starting to wonder if perhaps in this particular case Clyntahn knew what he was talking about. If they did, the damage to the Church of Charis' credibility could be disastrous, for if Merlin *was* a demon, all the accusations of blasphemy, corruption, perversion, child-sacrifice, demon summoning, and Shan-wei worship became damnably more believable.

"The possibility of one of my personae dropping a ball is one reason I'm glad we're filtering so much of our 'spy network's reports' through Aivah these days," he admitted. "And thank God Owl's such an accomplished forger!"

Despite his concern, Cayleb chuckled. Over a score of Merlin's "informants" were now reporting directly to Aivah Pahrsahn. Every one of them had completely different handwriting, and with Nahrmahn looking over Owl's shoulder, the AI had incorporated personal quirks and turns of phrase into each of those agents' writing styles, as well.

"The truth is," Merlin continued, "that we're in a better position than ever to feed information from the SNARCs to people who need to have it. And it doesn't hurt anything for Aivah to be able to share Nahrmahn's original 'written reports' with other people, either."

"Which doesn't say a thing about whether or not *Seijin* Merlin, *Seijin* Ahbraim, and *Seijin* Whoever're going to keep their various personalities straight," Cayleb pointed out. "Not to mention the fact that at least some people are starting to wonder why no one ever realized there were dozens of *seijins* running around before you turned up in Old Charis. For that matter, they're wondering where all the rest of those *seijins* are, and there's a real limit on the number of them you can give faces to, Merlin."

"I know." Merlin gave Cayleb another of his crooked smiles. "Overall, I think the advantages outweigh the disadvantages, though."

"So do I, but that doesn't mean we don't need to be aware of what those disadvantages are and disaster proof ourselves against them as well as we can."

"Agreed."

There were times, Merlin reflected, when he had trouble remembering Cayleb Ahrmahk had turned twenty-six barely four months earlier. That youthfulness helped explain Cayleb's impatience and resentment when he couldn't personally lead his navy or army in the field, but Merlin was more than prepared to put up with that as a minor price for the rest of the emperor's personality. As a general rule, one didn't normally associate the sort of careful analysis and forethought Cayleb habitually produced with someone as young as he was. Especially since a Safeholdian twenty-six-year-old was barely twenty-four and a half *standard* years old. For that matter, Sharleyan was only twenty-eight Safeholdian years old, which was a long way short of ancient and decrepit, now that he thought about it. Perhaps it didn't strike him that way more often because Merlin himself was only thirty-three T-years old. Subjectively, at least; the PICA in which he resided was the next best thing to a *thousand* years old.

People grow up fast on this planet, he thought. *Especially people like Cayleb and Sharleyan, who don't have much choice about it. Maybe that's one reason I feel so comfortable with them, because God knows Nimue had to grow up pretty damned fast, too.*

He snorted suddenly as he realized what he'd just thought. Maybe he really was becoming too many different people? He seemed to be finding partitions between his various personalities in the damnedest places!

Lord. I hate to think what a good Bédardist would

*think if he figured out how many people're running
around inside what passes for my brain!*

"What?" Cayleb asked, and Merlin shook his head.

"Just thinking about some of the differences between
Safehold and the Federation," he said, mostly honestly.
"You do realize you and Sharleyan scarcely qualify as
gray-haired elder statesmen by the Federation's standards, don't you?"

"The thought has crossed my mind," Cayleb said
dryly. "We tend to do a lot of things younger than the
Federation did, though."

"That's exactly what had occurred to me." Merlin
grinned. "I imagine it's going to occur to Hektor and
Irys before very much longer, too."

"No, it's not." Cayleb chuckled. "They never heard of
the Federation, remember? Not that I expect any objections from them—especially Hektor! That would require
him to be able to think rationally about the subject, and
I don't really think 'thinking' is what he's doing at the
moment. Mostly, I mean."

"You're a fine one to talk!"

"I know," Cayleb agreed cheerfully, and Merlin
laughed.

The emperor had a point, though, he reflected.
Eighteen—sixteen and a half T-years—was the age of
majority in most Safeholdian realms. It was nineteen in
Siddarmark and twenty in the Temple Lands and Corisande, but eighteen was more common. Nor was it unusual to marry even earlier than that, at least among the
upper classes.

Merlin had been a bit surprised to discover that marrying age among the middle class actually averaged several years higher than among its social superiors, but it
made sense when he looked at it. Mother Church discouraged marriages between couples who would be unable to support themselves or their families. That was
one reason betrothals lasted as long as they often did;
Mother Church was making sure the prospective groom
would be sufficiently well established to provide for his
bride and the brood of children they were supposed to

produce as part of their responsibility to fruitfully multiply. That held as true for yeoman farmers as it did for artisans, merchants, fishermen, and sailors, too. As a consequence, middle-class and lower-class couples tended not to marry until their mid to late twenties. It was only among the very poor, where unions tended to be more . . . informal, and among the relatively wealthy, where the wherewithal to support a family was readily available, that younger marriages were common. And they were commonest of all among the aristocracy, where the provision of heirs—the sooner the better—was one of the overriding reasons to wed in the first place, as the birth of one Princess Alahnah Ahrmahk demonstrated.

"I have to admit Gairlyng's reaction to your and Sharleyan's terms took me by surprise," Merlin said thoughtfully. "He really knocked the opposition to them on the head, didn't he?"

"It *looks* like he did, anyway." Cayleb's tone was cautious. "It's only been seven days, Merlin; there's plenty of time for it to come apart. I agree the Council's not going to balk, but don't forget Parliament has to sign off on it, too."

"And whose fault is that?" Merlin demanded.

"Ours," Cayleb acknowledged. "Although, if I recall correctly, you agreed with us."

"Who am I to argue with experienced, devious, Safeholdian Machiavellians? Besides, Nahrmahn thought it was a good idea, too."

"Which only demonstrates that, dead or not, he can still read politics and diplomacy better than ninety-nine percent of the human race," Cayleb pointed out, and Merlin nodded.

The truth was that he'd had his own doubts about Cayleb and Sharleyan's insistence that Charis' terms had to be ratified by Prince Daivyn's Parliament, not simply by his Regency Council and the Royal Council. After Klairmant Gairlyng's head-on attack there was little doubt the Royal Council would endorse the Regency Council's decision to accept Charis' conditions, but there'd been no way to predict that ahead of time. That was one reason Sharleyan had specifically required Daivyn and his guardians to submit her proposed conditions directly to Parliament, where a small collection of powerful individuals would find it far more difficult to block their acceptance.

But that was *only* one of the reasons, and not the most important one. And despite his own fears about the political and religious hand grenade a parliamentary debate could turn into, Merlin had ultimately decided she was right. Cayleb had agreed with her from the outset, which would have made any of Merlin's objections moot, anyway, of course. Merlin was perfectly prepared to advise the Empire's corulers when they asked him to, but the ultimate decisions were theirs. In this case, though, the more he'd thought about it, the more he'd come to agree that placing the decision before the entire Parliament—the closest thing Corisande had to a genuine national forum—for an open, public vote would cut the legs out from under any charge that a corrupt cabal of ambitious and apostate aristocrats had sold Corisande to Charis in return for the bribes of personal power and wealth. No one doubted Clyntahn and the Group of Four would insist that was exactly what had happened, anyway, but the *people of Corisande* would know better.

Merlin had never disagreed with the desirability of establishing that, but he'd been more than a little worried over how close he'd expected the vote to be. If the margin of approval was razor thin, it would emphasize the shakiness of the new arrangement. Worse, it might inspire those who'd opposed acceptance to resort to extra-legal means of reversing the decision. God knew they'd already seen enough of *that* in Corisande! And even if they avoided that, the Group of Four could be counted upon to argue that despite all the corruption and all the pressure brought to bear upon the people of Corisande's representatives, the vicious heretics and servants of evil had been able to muster only a tiny majority to vote in favor of the heretics' blasphemous demands . . .

assuming, of course, that any true child of God could believe for a moment that the vote count had been honest in the first place!

Of course, if Parliament comes through with a strong majority in favor of the terms, it'll provide every single advantage Sharleyan and Cayleb—and Nahrmahn—argued that it would, he thought. *And it looks like Gairlyng's provided just that sort of majority to accept all of them, including Hektor and Irys' marriage. I was really afraid that might be the sticking point for a lot of them, but Gairlyng's last sermon seems to've put that fear to rest, too! When the Archbishop of Corisande spontaneously announces from his own pulpit that he's prepared to solemnize the wedding the instant Parliament approves it—that he's not simply willing to but positively* looking forward *to it because he's convinced it will be* "a true marriage of heart and soul"—*it's just a tad difficult for anyone to argue that Sharleyan held a dagger to Irys' throat.*

"You do realize Hektor didn't expect to be getting married for at least another year or so?" he asked.

"Of course he didn't, but I guarantee he's not going to *argue* about it!" Cayleb retorted with a laugh. "Didn't you just love his expression when he heard Gairlyng's sermon?"

"I'll admit the phrase 'poleaxed' came to mind."

"And didn't Irys look like a cat-lizard with a fresh bowl of milk?" Cayleb shook his head. "If I hadn't known better from the SNARCs, I'd've sworn she'd put Gairlyng up to it!"

"Actually, what made me happiest was how few other people in the Cathedral looked *un*happy over that sermon," Merlin said more seriously. "Admittedly, there weren't many Temple Loyalists in the congregation, and anyone who *was* there was probably already inclined to go along with whatever Gairlyng had to say, but it still struck me as a good omen."

"It's certainly not a *bad* one, anyway," Cayleb agreed, then cocked his head as the clock tower in Protector's Palace began to chime the hour.

"We need to get over there," he said, climbing out of his chair. "Is there anything else you can think of that we should be bringing up?"

"Not really." Merlin shook his head. "That old phrase about 'sufficient unto the day' comes to mind at the moment. Besides, I don't want to suggest anything that could turn this into one of those all-hours meetings you and the Lord Protector seem to be so fond of."

"I am *not* 'fond' of them!" Cayleb said severely. "Although," he conceded in a magisterial tone, "the quality of Greyghor's beer does go a fair way to reconciling me to the arduous demands of my weighty—my *many* weighty—responsibilities."

"Is *that* what they are?" Merlin rounded his eyes, then nodded with an air of sudden understanding. "Weighty, are they? That probably explains why you seem so heavy when I end up carrying your semi-conscious imperial carcass back to the embassy afterward."

"You do not!" Cayleb said with a laugh, and Merlin sighed.

"So *sad* that you're so far gone in drink you can't even remember it."

"I think we'd better leave this particular topic right where it is, *Seijin* Merlin," Cayleb announced as they started down the stairs.

"I bow to your tyrannical authority," the *seijin* murmured.

"And so you should. But why are you so concerned about how late I'm planning to stay out carousing—I mean, *consulting*—with Greyghor and Daryus?"

"Because I have an errand to run." Merlin's voice was much more serious, and Cayleb paused and looked back at him, one eyebrow arched.

"Today is Nahrmahn and Ohlyvya's anniversary," Merlin said softly. "I promised Nahrmahn I'd deliver his anniversary present to her in person."

Cayleb stood gazing at him for several seconds, then reached out and touched him very gently on the arm.

"In that case, I promise to be home in time for supper," the Emperor of Charis told his personal armsman.

"You know you really didn't have to deliver this in person, Merlin. Owl's remotes could've brought it to me just fine."

"I promised a certain somewhat overweight virtual personality I'd put it into your hands my very own self." The tall, blue-eyed *seijin* smiled down at Ohlyvya Baytz on the real world original of Nahrmahn Baytz' favorite balcony. "He was fairly insistent. Besides," the smile softened, "I'm sort of fond of you myself, you know."

"Yes." The Dowager Princess of Emerald was no taller than her husband had been; she had to stand on tiptoe to kiss Merlin on the cheek. "Yes, I know."

She turned to gaze out over the moonlit waters and Merlin stood beside her, drinking in the quiet city-murmur of Eraystor and the patient, unceasing voice of the breeze blowing out to sea. He understood exactly why Nahrmahn had always loved this particular vantage point, and the combination of location and design gave anyone standing on it an oasis of near perfect privacy.

Not a minor consideration when everyone knows Seijin *Merlin's thousands of miles away in Siddar City*, he reflected.

"It's still a bit strange," Ohlyvya mused. "Having him back, I mean. There are times when all my faith in this newfangled 'technology' reverts back to believing in old-fashioned magic around you, Merlin. Oh," she waved as if brushing away something only she could see, "I understand the difference between them now. Not the way you do, since you grew up with it, but well enough that I seldom find myself walking around waiting for the Rakurai to come sizzling in the window! But that's not remotely the same as being able to take it for granted, and being able to talk to him, to 'see' him over the com link, even if I really know it's only Owl generating the image for me . . . that's *magic*."

"I hope it's good magic."

"It's *wonderful* magic," she said, looking up at him. "To be able to talk to him after I lost him forever? I can't think of a greater gift you could've given us, Merlin."

"But talking to him isn't quite the same thing, is it?" he asked gently. Her head cocked, and he shrugged. "As you say, I grew up with technology and computer-generated imagery. I take—or Nimue Alban *took*, anyway—that kind of communications for granted. But electronic meetings, com conversations, were never quite the same as sitting in the same room, talking across the same table. Or the same as being able to reach out and touch the person you're talking to."

"Of course it's not," Ohlyvya agreed. "It's just more than anyone else in the world's ever been given." She patted the blackened breastplate of an Imperial Guardsman, and her eyes were warm in the lamplight spilling through the glass doors onto the balcony. "Am I human enough to want still more? To wish I *could* touch him again? Of course I am! But that doesn't keep me from recognizing a magnificent gift when I see it."

"I'm glad you feel that way." He put one large, sinewy hand over the far smaller one on his cuirass. "Too many things I've had to do, or been able to do, here on Safehold've had double edges, Ohlyvya. I'm glad this isn't one of them."

She smiled up at him again, and he reached into the canvas shoulder bag, bearing the emblem of an imperial courier, which he'd brought with him when the recon skimmer's tractor beam set him soundlessly on the balcony. The package that came out of it was wrapped in brightly colored paper, and Ohlyvya laughed. That paper was the red and gold of Emerald, blazoned with the silver flying wyvern of the House of Baytz on its dark blue shield. The wyvern was edged in red, making it the personal crest of the dowager princess, but the repeating design had been flipped so that images of the wyvern confronted one another, mirror-imaging each other in an endless procession, and the wyverns' wings beat steadily whenever the package was moved. No printer on Safehold could have produced that paper, and she shook her head with a huge smile.

"You'll have to take the paper with you when you leave, but the crest is a nice touch." She ran a fingertip over the flying wyverns, and her expression softened. "I wish Nahrmahn Gareyt knew his father was still alive, too. And Mahrya. They miss him."

"And he misses them. But one day, after we've kicked the Church's butt. . . ."

"As you say—one day," Ohlyvya agreed.

She hefted the package and raised one eyebrow as she realized how light it was. And how yielding.

"He made me promise not to tell you what's in it," Merlin told her. "But I will tell you that this is something he had Owl whip up especially for you. And Owl had to do quite a bit of research to pull it off, too."

"Really?" Ohlyvya's eyes sparkled, and she set the package on one of the balcony's stone tables to open. "Nahrmahn always has loved thinking up presents no one sees coming. I think it's part of the little boy in him. I remember once he spent five-days meeting with Hahl Shandyr. I thought they had to be working on some kind of deep, dark international plot. Then, on my birthday, I found out he'd had Hahl's agents interview my parents' stable master to find out which had been my favorite horse as a girl, and then sent an order to the same breeding farm—this was thirteen or fourteen years later, you understand—to get—"

She stopped in midsentence as the package came open. It contained two items, and her fingers were very gentle as she picked up the first one and tilted it to catch the lamplight through the glass door.

Golden glory glittered on her palm. The locket was an inch across, the golden links of the chain which would support it around her neck were set with small, perfectly cut rubies, and the pendant's face bore her and Nahrmahn's interlocked initials.

"It's beautiful," she half whispered.

"Open it," Merlin said. She looked up at him, then obeyed his invitation, and her lips trembled as she saw Nahrmahn looking out of it at her. It was a much younger Nahrmahn, standing arm in arm with a much younger Ohlyvya.

"How—?"

"He had Owl make it from the state portraits the two of you sat for on the first anniversary of your coronation," Merlin replied. "He said he thinks they got the colors right."

"Oh, they did—they did!" Ohlyvya shook her head. "This is so much better than the portraits, though. They're so stiff and formal! We should've commissioned one just like this at the time."

"Then I'm glad Owl was able to help repair the oversight. And if anyone asks where it came from, just tell them he had it made for you and left it for me to deliver as a surprise." Merlin smiled. "It'll even be the truth."

"Thank you," she said softly. She gazed at the portrait for several more seconds, then closed the locket, slipped the chain over her head, and turned to the second item in the package.

Her eyebrows rose as she lifted the gossamer fabric and held it up against the light. It felt insubstantial as air, yet it was totally opaque. Or it appeared to be, at any rate. Not the slightest gleam of lamplight leaked through it, yet it was curiously hard to determine where its edges ended. Indeed, she could scarcely see it—even its color seemed oddly elusive and hard to pin down—but it was clearly a garment of some sort, even though she'd never seen anything like it.

"What in the world is *this*?" She shook her head with something suspiciously like a giggle. "I'd have a pretty fair idea of what he had in mind if he were here to give it to me himself! Of course, in that case it would've been a lot more transparent. Besides"—she looked up at Merlin with a wicked smile—"he always preferred fluttery, floaty négligées."

"Somehow I'm not incredibly surprised," Merlin said dryly, and for just a moment Nimue Alban looked out of those sapphire eyes at Ohlyvya in shared, fond amusement. But then he shook his head and his expression turned more serious. "Actually, what you have there is a VR suit."

"A 'VR suit'?" Ohlyvya repeated carefully, and he nodded.

"As I said, Nahrmahn and Owl had to do quite a bit of research before they could build it. No one'd used them in the Federation for a good seventy years before the Gbaba turned up—not since we developed direct neural interfacing—so Nahrmahn had to reinvent the wheel to figure out how to make it work. And, to be honest, the technology available before we shifted over to the neural interface wasn't nearly as good as what he and Owl put together for this one, even if Owl did have to figure out about a third of it from scratch."

"*This* is a piece of technology?" Her tone was dubious, and he chuckled.

"Oh, yes! We all know Nahrmahn's always been an ingenious fellow when it comes to getting something he really wants. The minor bagatelle of being dead hasn't changed him one bit in that regard."

"But what's it for?"

"Well, as you may've noticed it has neat little footies and gloves. It opens up the back so you can climb into it—I'll show you how that works—and once you've sealed it again, it'll extrude a hood that covers your head, as well."

"That sounds . . . ominous." She held it up and looked at its opacity again. "I don't know if I want to wear a blindfold and fall over the furniture, Merlin!"

"Oh, that's not going to happen. What this is, Ohlyvya, is your own virtual reality unit." Her eyes darted from the fabric to his face, and he smiled. "I know it makes steel thistle silk feel like lead, but don't let that fool you. It's riddled with molycirc sensors and biofeedback contacts, and the inside of the 'hood' provides complete audio and visual—and olfactory—input. And it's tied directly into Owl's CPU, Ohlyvya. As long as you're wearing it, you *can* visit Nahrmahn. And you *will* be able to touch him again when you do."

Her eyes glowed, and his smile segued into a grin.

"Obviously, you can't just wander around in public with a hood over your head. And, as I'm sure you've figured out, this is something that needs to be next to your skin. On the other hand, as you and I have both observed upon occasion, Nahrmahn's a devious sort who tends to think ahead, and according to him, the suit's smart fabric will mold to your skin once it's on, and it's programmed to externally duplicate skin coloration and texture.

"Owl loaded the entire operator's manual into the suit's memory, and you're not going to want to leave it on for any extended periods until you've had the opportunity to read that fully and get used to how it works, if only because of the disorientation that can cause. In fact, the software's governors will kick you back out into the 'real world' if you try to stay in VR for more than a couple of hours at a time. They can be adjusted later, or even turned completely off, but it'd probably be a good idea to leave them until you've got a lot more experience with it. Once you've gotten used to it, you should be able to wear it—and use it—a lot more freely. Of course, you're going to want privacy while you're working on building that experience! In fact, Nahrmahn suggested to me that I might want to get it to you as early in the evening as possible so you could begin practicing with it this very night."

Ohlyvya snorted and rolled her eyes, and he chuckled.

"On the other hand, he also asked me to tell you that when the suit's deactivated, the hood and the gloves reabsorb into the rest of the suit, which means you can wear it under your regular clothing and 'turn it off' if something comes up that requires your attention while you're using it. The entire shutdown cycle takes less than three seconds. And, obviously, when you're able to guarantee you *won't* have to deal with someone else. . . ."

"I understand entirely, Merlin Athrawes," she told him firmly. "And, bearing in mind that I do, would you mind very much helping me figure out how to climb into this thing—*Nimue*—and then taking yourself off?"

"Oh, I think that could probably be arranged, Your Highness."

▼ ▼ ▼

He stood on the balcony, looking out across the moonlit water, listening to the wind while he nursed a glass of wine. It was very quiet, aside from the ceaseless voice of that wind, and he took another sip, thinking about his life, the decisions he'd made, the things he'd done . . . or not. The compressibility of his transformed existence gave him plenty of time to think, and—

"Nahrmahn?"

The soft, beloved voice came from behind him, and for just a moment he froze. Despite all he'd done so that he might hear it once again without the interface of a communicator, despite how desperately he'd longed for this moment, he froze. Unable to breathe—although, to be fair, he really didn't *need* to breathe, any longer—he stood very still, prolonging the moment, the exquisite pain of anticipation. And then, slowly, he turned.

She stood on the balcony, just outside the glass door to the suite they'd shared for so many, many years. Her dark hair, lightly streaked with silver, stirred on the breeze, a golden locket gleamed on its ruby-set chain about her neck, and her heart was in her eyes.

"Ohlyvya," he breathed softly, her name almost but not quite inaudible against the background wind song. "Oh, Ohlyvya."

He heard the tremble in his own voice, and he couldn't see her very clearly for some reason. He blinked hard, feeling the tear trickle down his cheek, feeling the thunderous beat of the racing heart death had stilled so many months before, and raised one hand, holding it out to her.

"Ohlyvya," he said, one more time, and then she was in his arms, her lips soft and warm upon his own, and the wall between their realities came crashing down.

SEPTEMBER, YEAR OF GOD 896

· ✦ ·

I

Siddar City,
Republic of Siddarmark

The weather-battered galleons made their stately way towards the docks and quays lined with silently watching Siddarmarkians. The frenetic cheers which had greeted the first wave of Charisian soldiers were muted, and the crowd seemed poised, waiting, without the jagged edge of desperation which had spurred those earlier cheers. The sense of anticipation, of relief, was no less, but the wave of fire and destruction sweeping across the Republic had been halted, or at least stayed, by these men's predecessors. It would have been too much to say that the people of Siddar City felt *confident* of the war's outcome, but the despair which had hung above the city like smoke had been replaced by determination and something which bade fair to *become* confidence.

Merlin Athrawes stood with Lord Daryus Parkair and the bevy of senior Siddarmarkian officers waiting at quayside. Emperor Cayleb had intended to be there, but he and the lord protector had been delayed in a meeting with the Council of Manufactories Stohnar had created to rationalize the Republic's contribution to the Allied war effort. From what Merlin could see courtesy of the SNARCs, that meeting was probably going to continue well into the evening.

He watched canvas vanishing from yards, saw the spurts of white as anchors plunged into North Bedard Bay's deep blue water. Spacious as Siddar City's waterfront was, it could berth only a tithe of the transports, far less their escorting warships, and large, oared lighters were already heading out to meet the others. The oar-powered tugs fussed around the closest galleons, nudging them towards the quays, and the Republic's seneschal stirred beside him as Parkair recognized the standard of a Charisian general officer flying from the lead ship's mizzen peak.

Fenders squeaked and groaned as the galleon nuzzled ponderously against them. Mooring cables went aboard, tension was taken, and the gangplank ran out from dockside. There was silence for a moment, broken only by the waterfront sounds which never completely stopped—the cries of birds and wyverns, the endless, patient slapping of waves and water, the background of workmen's voices, the crackling pop of flags and command streamers. Then a stocky, gray-haired man in the still bizarre-looking camouflage-patterned field uniform of the Imperial Charisian Army with the golden sword of a general on his collar came down the gangplank, followed by a very young golden-haired army captain and a grizzled-looking colonel.

The quiet held until the general's boot touched the stone of the quay, and then the regimental band at the seneschal's back burst into music. The music was high, fierce, and wild, rising on the skirling voice of the war pipes, founded on the percussion of the Republic of Siddarmark Army's deep-voiced drums, and the name of that song was "The Stand at Kharmych Crossing," the march written by Fhrancys Kaisi a hundred and ten years before to commemorate the 37th Pikes epic stand in the Battle of Kharmych. The cheers which had hovered unvoiced burst free as the gathered civilians and officers recognized the defiance of that music, for the 37th Infantry Regiment, heir to the 37th Pikes' battle honors, had stood just as valiantly in the Sylmahn Gap this very year—stood in the teeth of rebellion, mutiny, and treason; stood in the face of atrocity and massacre; stood amid the bodies of its fallen; stood until it was no more than a colonel, a captain, and a single under-strength company . . . stood until the Republic's Allies had stormed to its rescue and driven the Army of God back up the Gap like a hurricane from the sea. No one on that waterfront could miss the meaning of that music, and they rolled up upon its wings, those cheers, waves of sound beating at the heavens, as Daryus Parkair stepped forward under the bright September sun to exchange salutes and then clasp Ahlyn Symkyn's forearm firmly.

▼ ▼ ▼

The lamps burned in weary eyes as efficient servants refilled the various glasses, tankards, and steins. The Republic of Siddarmark, Merlin Athrawes reflected, was the only Mainland realm where an emperor, the elected ruler of almost a hundred and thirty million people, half a dozen generals (all but one of them of common birth), a lowly major, the wealthiest banker in the entire Republic, two foundry owners, the grand master of the Gunmakers Guild of Siddarmark, and an industrial expert who'd never known his father's name could sit around a table littered with maps, charts, dispatches, the ruins of sandwiches and salads, fried potato slices, overflowing ashtrays, and their choice of beer, wine, or whiskey. The mere thought of the highest of the high rubbing elbows with such plebeians in a rolled-up-sleeves conference would have sent any Mainlander aristocrat storming out of the room. And that fact was one of the many reasons Siddarmarkians and Charisians got along so well . . . and why those other Mainland realms should tremble in fear.

"I don't know about you, Your Majesty," Greyghor Stohnar said, pinching the bridge of his nose and leaning back in his chair, "but I'm exhausted. Of course," he lowered his hand and smiled at Cayleb, "I'm also a rather older man than you are. No doubt my endurance isn't what it was once."

"Your endurance seems to be doing just fine, My Lord." Cayleb grinned. "Not that I'm above pretending I'm only deferring to your advanced decrepitude when I graciously agree to stagger home to bed, you understand. I believe it's called 'diplomacy.'"

Stohnar snorted, and laughter muttered its way around the table.

"With your permission, Your Majesty, I'll admit I'm looking forward to a bed that doesn't move tonight, myself. Sailing beats the Shan-wei out of marching, but it wasn't the very smoothest passage in the history of the world," Ahlyn Symkyn said, with generous understatement, considering the stormy weather the troop convoy had encountered. Then he laid one palm flat on the marked up map in front of him. "And at the moment, my brain's fair bursting with all that's been crammed into it, come to that."

"Yours isn't the only worn-out brain at this table, General," Daryus Parkair said wryly. "Mind you, I think it's been worth it."

"Yes, it has." Stohnar's tone was much more serious. "It's been very much worth it . . . assuming it all works."

"With all due respect, My Lord," Henrai Maidyn corrected gently, "if even *half* of it works, it's been *entirely* worth it."

Stohnar looked at him for a moment, then nodded.

"A valid point, Henrai. And I agree entirely. I suppose it's a bit greedy of me to want all of it to work."

"After last winter, My Lord?" Cayleb snorted harshly. "I don't think it's unreasonable to expect things to even out. Your people've stood up to attack on a scale the world's never seen, never imagined. There's not another Mainland realm that could've survived something like the Sword of Schueler, and everyone around this table knows it. I think we owe your citizens a little something for that kind of fortitude—and we *damn* well owe Clyntahn's butchers a little something on their behalf. I'm looking forward to making a rather large downpayment."

The sound that went around the table this time was much colder, Merlin thought. Colder . . . and hungry.

And well it should be. I suppose the Canal Raid could be considered a downpayment, and so could what's happened in the Sylmahn Gap and the Glacierheart Gap. But much as we may've hurt them there, we still haven't hurt them anywhere nearly as badly as they hurt Siddarmark over the winter and spring. Despite what Eastshare did on the Daivyn, we're still playing defense. It's past time we found a way to make them dance to our tune for a while, and these are just the people to make that happen.

He looked around the chamber, under the canopy of pipe smoke drifting about the age-blackened rafters, and considered all that had been "crammed into" the minds of the men in it.

Another thing that set Siddarmark apart from the rest of the Mainland—and underscored its kinship with Charis—was the fact that the generals seated around the table hadn't turned a hair when they found civilians seated with them. And not *simply* civilians. Even the most senior of officers occasionally had to accept that civilians would have a voice in their deliberations if the civilians in question happened to be their political masters. But these civilians were merchants, bankers, and even mere artisans who worked with their hands. Those were the civilians who got their orders after the great and the powerful had decided what was to be done, and their function was to obey those orders, do as they were told, and otherwise keep their mouths shut. It certainly wasn't to argue or make excuses about why it *couldn't* be done.

Even in Siddarmark the degree of input the lord protector's Council of Manufactories enjoyed was a distinct departure from previous practice, but the Siddarmarkian social matrix had made it easier for him to create it. And the fact that, in yet another similarity with both Old Charis and Chisholm, the Republic of Siddarmark Army had traditionally drawn the majority of its officer corps from the middle class helped enormously.

Stohnar had selected Tymahn Qwentyn, head of the House of Qwentyn, Siddarmark's great banking dynasty, to head his council. The Qwentyn banking empire had been brutally wounded by the Sword of Schueler and the collapse of traditional trade patterns. Tymahn had to be even better aware of that than Merlin was, yet he'd unhesitatingly placed his contacts, his connections, and his personal wealth at the Republic's service. It was quite possible he'd ruined himself and his family in the process, although no one would have guessed it from his expression or manner.

On the other hand, he didn't know—yet—that Ehdwyrd Howsmyn was about to make a major investment in the House of Qwentyn. That investment made good, hard business sense, and Qwentyn's contacts would open countless doors in the Republic for Howsmyn both during and after the present war. But it was more than that, as well—a way for the Charisian Empire to repay a portion of its debt to the one Mainland realm with the courage and fortitude to stand beside it in the teeth of the Inquisition itself.

The other senior members of the Council of Manufactories present were Zhak Hahraimahn, Erayk Ahdyms, Bahrtalam Edwyrds . . . and Aivah Pahrsahn.

The white-haired, rather frail-looking Hahraimahn was an old friend of Henrai Maidyn's. He was also the ironmaster to whom the chancellor and the lord protector had turned for the limited number of rifles they'd dared to order before the Sword of Schueler. He'd also been equally clandestinely experimenting with the new model artillery, in the process of which he'd acquired a new business partner in the form of Aivah Pahrsahn. The combination of her investments in Hahraimahn's foundry, in Siddarmarkian mining properties in Glacierheart and Mountaincross, and in two of Siddar City's four major shipyards went far towards explaining her membership on the council, although her role as the Allies' spymistress had a little something to do with it, as well.

Erayk Ahdyms was a junior partner of Hahraimahn's. At fifty-six, he was sixteen years younger than his widowed associate, with sandy brown hair, gray eyes, and broad shoulders. A fervent Reformist, he was quick-witted and quick moving. In many ways, he reminded Merlin of a somewhat older Ehdwyrd Howsmyn, and he showed a fierce interest in acquiring the latest Charisian industrial techniques. Not just because he recognized how badly the Republic's Army needed those capabilities, either. No, he was looking forward to the end of the war, as well, and he clearly wanted to build a robust Siddarmarkian industrial base to compete with Charisian supremacy. He was being rather discreet about it, and Merlin wondered how he would react if he discovered Cayleb and Sharleyan Ahrmahk were simply delighted by the notion of Mainland competition.

Within reason, of course.

A man as smart as Ahdyms would almost certainly figure that out in the end, although it was unlikely he'd realize what actually motivated his Charisian allies' attitude. Despite the way in which Safehold's economy had grown in size and sophistication over the last century and a half, many of its thinkers remained firmly mired in the concepts of what had been called "mercantilism" on Old Earth. It wasn't exactly the same *sort* of mercantilism, given the huge differences in the population patterns and the fact that every enclave on Safehold had begun with exactly the same technology base. The basic ideas of protectionism and the creation of fixed trading relationships closed to outside competition had been part of the Safeholdian matrix for a very long time, however. That was, in fact, the basis for a great deal of the pre-Jihad resentment of Charis' industrial and maritime power. The notion that an empire whose dominance in those areas bade fair to become absolute might actually favor free trade and competitive commerce from an economic perspective would take some getting used to. The fact that the entire purpose of the present war was to subvert the technological stasis created by the Church of God Awaiting and that spreading the new technologies as widely as possible was the best way to do that would remain Charis' little secret for as long as possible . . . hopefully even from a smart cookie like Ahdyms.

For the moment, any such suspicion was the furthest thing from Ahdyms' mind as he and Hahraimahn sat on either side of Brygham Cartyr, Ehdwyrd Howsmyn's envoy to the Council of Manufactories. Cartyr and his support staff had arrived only last five-day, bringing with them crate loads of technical drawings, manuals, and working models. Cartyr himself was a stocky, powerfully built man in his early forties, with typical Charisian coloring and the scarred hands of a fatherless boy who'd begun as a sweeper in one of Rhaiyan Mychail's manufactories when he was barely ten years old. In many ways, he and Howsmyn had both been mentored by Mychail, and it was no accident he'd been chosen for his present position, although the thought of how a Desnairian—or even a Dohlaran—might have reacted to taking instruction from a mongrel whose speech still bore an echo of his guttersnipe origins beggared the imagination. In *Siddarmark*, however, the reaction had been quite different, and Qwentyn, Ahdyms, and Hahraimahn couldn't've cared less how he spoke.

And then there was Bahrtalam Edwyrds, possibly the most interesting member of the council. About midway between Ahdyms and Hahraimahn in age, Edwyrds was the head of the Gunmakers Guild in Old Province. That made him, effectively, the senior member of the guild in the entire Republic, and he was the man Hahraimahn had tapped to assemble the gunmakers who'd constructed the rifles Stohnar (and Aivah Pahrsahn) had ordered from him.

He was also the one man at that table whose entire professional life was about to be destroyed by the changes the Council of Manufactories was busy midwifing.

The innovations Charis had already introduced into its own industrial sector, much less the ones Howsmyn was even now putting into effect, made that as inevitable as the rising of the sun. The days of highly paid, skilled artisans assembling firearms—or anything else—one handmade piece at a time were numbered and dwindling quickly, and Edwyrds knew it. Yet even though his Reformism was less fervent than Ahdyms', Bahrtalam Edwyrds was a fierce Siddarmarkian patriot, loyal to his lord protector and his constitution, with boundless contempt for the traitors who'd betrayed both. And on top of that, he was smart—smart enough to see the changes coming and recognize that the guilds would have no choice but to adapt. Indeed, to disappear. Trying to fight those changes would be as fatal as trying to swim across North Bedard Bay. So like a skilled seaman in the face of the tempest, Bahrtalam Edwyrds would ride the winds of revolution and innovation and encourage his fellow guildsmen to do the same. The new manufactories would require large numbers of experienced supervisors, and that was exactly the role into which Edwyrds meant to slot as many members of his guild as could see the writing on the wall.

Some of them—too many, really, for Merlin's peace of mind—were apparently blind to that writing, and he didn't like to think about what was going to happen to them and to their families when the future came calling. Nor did he like to think about what might happen if they and others of like mind dug in their heels and tried to resist that future. At least some of them were going to, and when that was coupled with the inevitable disruptions of a truly industrialized economy, the consequences would be ugly.

And maybe not just here in the Republic, either, he thought grimly. *There's always those idiots in Chisholm to worry about, too!*

But no one at this meeting questioned the necessity of embracing the new techniques as rapidly as possible, just as every one of them understood how dependent the Republic's military options—and fate—were on the efforts of the Council of Manufactories and their Charisian allies. The total prewar output of every gunsmith in Siddarmark would have sufficed to build just over four thousand rifles per month. Hahraimahn and Edwyrds had found ways to significantly improve production rates in Old Province, but even there, in the Republic's most populous single province—and even with the influx of refugees, which had included many of the surviving gunsmiths from provinces which had gone over to the Temple Loyalists—production was barely a thousand per month. They could probably increase that to as much as fifteen hundred, but it wasn't going much higher as long as the Republic retained the Gunmakers Guild's traditional processes. Worse, the numbers were far lower for the other loyal provinces, not simply on an absolute basis but in proportion to their population, because Hahraimahn and Edwyrds' arrangements had yet to be duplicated outside Old Province. At the moment, the entire Republic was doing well to produce forty-eight hundred rifles per month. That meant the eighty thousand Charisian muzzle-loading rifles handed over to Daryus Parkair's regiments as the Charisian Expeditionary Force re-equipped with Mahndrayns represented seventeen months—almost two Safeholdian years—of the Republic's current production . . . and eighteen of the new Siddarmarkian rifle brigades.

So, yes, Greyghor Stohnar and his generals knew exactly how important the Council of Manufactories' input into military decisions had become.

"I'm thinking we'll be in a fair way to making that downpayment for you, Your Majesty," Symkyn said. The general took a long pull from his beer and thumped the stein back down on the tabletop. "Mind you, I'd be a mite happier if His Grace had waited until we were actually here before setting off for Fort Tairys, but he's like a cat-lizard. Fling him any which way you like, he's a way of landing on his feet. Truth to tell, he and Baron Green Valley are a lot alike that way. And I *do* like what His Grace has in mind for those bastards in the South March."

"I can't argue with you there, General," Maidyn said, but his expression was troubled, and he snorted when Stohnar quirked an eyebrow at him.

"I agree that Duke Eastshare has his eye on the prize, My Lord. And if he can actually pull it off, those motherless Desnairians are going to think they're back in the middle of our *last* war! I just find it difficult to convince myself that even *Desnairians* are going to let us get away with it."

"That's because you've been watching the Army of God and the Dohlarans, not the Desnairians, My Lord,"

Merlin said. "For all their other flaws, the Dohlarans have at least some appreciation for the potential of amphibious operations, and Kaitswyrth tried hard to scout Duke Eastshare's position on the Daivyn before he ultimately attacked. He didn't manage it, but he tried, and everything we've seen out of Wyrshym indicates he understands the need for aggressive scouting. And, even more important, both of them actually try to *confirm* the reports they get from Temple Loyalist sources.

"Desnair really doesn't have any concept of amphibious operations, and we all know how poor Desnairian logistics have traditionally been. The fact that the Church is helping manage their supply arrangements this time doesn't seem to have changed their *internal* grasp of the problem's realities, and I think they persist in viewing galleons and blue water transport as simply barges which may be a bit larger than most of the ones they're used to. And as far as figuring out what Duke Eastshare is up to, Duke Harless doesn't have any idea how good our spies and scouts are. Or, rather, of how *bad* his are in comparison to ours."

"The *seijin's* right, Henrai," Parkair put in. "For all the Desnairians' love affair with horses, they've never understood the function of scouts the way we have, and there's no indication they've fixed *that* problem this time around, either." He shook his head. "They've got a fair grasp of how to use cavalry screens to hide what *they're* doing, but they've never made proper use of their light horse to figure out what *we're* doing. They ought to have regiments out on sweeps—preferably as much as a hundred miles in every direction—and according to our reports, they're barely *twenty* miles out. Beyond that, they seem to be relying on reports from Temple Loyalists, and as Aivah's demonstrated"—he nodded courteously in Madam Pahrsahn's direction—"they don't seem to grasp that not all of those Temple Loyalists are quite as loyal to the Temple as they profess."

"And unlike Wyrshym, at least," Aivah put in, "Harless puts very little effort into confirming or disproving those 'Temple Loyalists'' veracity." She smiled whimsically. "As nearly as we can tell, his measure of reliability is very simple. If the reports confirm what he already thinks, they must obviously be accurate, whereas if they don't—"

She shrugged eloquently, and several of the others chuckled appreciatively.

"Even better," Cayleb's smile was far more wicked than Aivah's, "where the southern jaw's concerned, the best cavalry screen in the world won't help them."

"All very well for you, Your Majesty," Symkyn said. "You're not going to have to explain to my lads why so many of them are turning around, cat-lizard-in-pan, to go straight back aboard those ships!"

"I would, of course, General," Cayleb assured him, "except for the need to maintain operational secrecy. Given that paramount consideration, I don't see how we could possibly allow anyone but you yourself to break that—I mean, to *give* them that news."

His general gave him a somewhat skeptical look, and Stohnar hastily raised a wineglass to conceal something closer to a grin than a smile.

"Given the number of Temple Loyalists here in the capital, there's no way to prevent Kaitswyrth and Wyrshym, at least, from learning that General Symkyn's arrived," Aivah said. "I'm sure there are messenger wyverns headed for their headquarters right this minute. I think it may be possible to prevent them from realizing that 4th Brigade's reembarked, though."

Merlin gazed at her thoughtfully. Thanks to Owl's SNARCs, he knew she was correct about those messenger wyverns, and a part of him was tempted yet again to steer her counterintelligence teams to the people sending them. In fact, he and Nahrmahn had done precisely that where the more effective and efficient spies were concerned. The ones who were left provided too much information to the Army of God's field commanders for his peace of mind, but much of their information was wrong or, even better, grossly exaggerated. Not only that, but duplicating the iron curtain he and Bynzhamyn Raice had drawn around Old Charis for King Haarahld would have been impossible in Siddarmark. There were simply too many ways for spies and their messengers to slip in and out of cities when they didn't need boats to report back to their masters.

Given that it wasn't feasible to shut them down completely, he agreed wholeheartedly with Aivah's ploys to manipulate the information available to them. Dummy encampments, wooden cannon, false shipping orders, covered "ammunition barges" loaded with rock ballast, and infantry regiments which marched west in the morning, then circled around to their starting points to march past again the next day, all helped to convince Kaitswyrth and Wyrshym that the forces facing them in Westmarch and the Sylmahn Gap were being heavily reinforced when, in fact, the reverse was true.

Meanwhile, she and Parkair had established a tight security cordon around the major encampment on East Point on the far side of Unity Strait—the channel connecting Bedard Bay to North Bedard Bay—from the city. Anything they really wanted to keep out of the Temple Loyalist spies' sight was normally tucked away at East Point, and the Charisian 4th Infantry Brigade could easily be shifted there as part of the capital's garrison.

"You're thinking about lightering them back out aboard ship from East Point in the middle of the night, aren't you?"

"That's exactly what I'm thinking, *Seijin* Merlin." She smiled. "And I'm also thinking it would be very helpful if Brigadier Mathysyn could leave a few of his men behind. Just enough to be visible here in the city in their uniforms on a semi-regular basis, you understand."

"I've always admired a cunning mind, Madam Pahrsahn," Symkyn said with an answering smile. "And there's always a few sick or injured in a force this size. I imagine the Brigadier and I shouldn't find it so very difficult to come up with a score or so of warm bodies." His smile grew a bit broader. "For that matter, we've quite a few spare uniforms, and they do say it's the clothes that make the man, don't they?"

"I do believe I've heard that, General," she agreed, and raised her glass to him.

Merlin joined the chuckle that answered the exchange. He doubted Aivah's subterfuge would hold up indefinitely, but it was likely to work long enough to at least thoroughly confuse anyone on the other side.

He turned his head to gaze at the huge map hanging on one of the conference chamber's walls. The flag-headed pins showed the latest information on all of their own forces and most of the enemy's. At the moment, there was one very large Charisian flag stuck into the dot representing Siddar City, but that was going to be changing.

The first echelon of the Expeditionary Force had consisted of the 1st Infantry Division and half of the 2nd Infantry Division, which had been split into two reinforced brigades under Eastshare and Green Valley. Symkyn's second echelon was considerably larger—three more infantry brigades (the rest of the 2nd Division and the entire 3rd Division) plus the 1st, 2nd, and 3rd Mounted Brigades—plus the remainder of the entire Expeditionary Force's artillery, engineering, and medical trains.

The 3rd Mounted would be on its way to reinforce Green Valley within the five-day, as soon as its horses had regained their land legs after the voyage from Raven's Land. Symkyn, with the 3rd Infantry Division and the 1st and 2nd Mounted, would be dispatched to reinforce Eastshare just as rapidly, but the 4th Infantry Brigade would be headed somewhere else entirely.

His eyes moved down the East Haven coast and through the Tarot Channel to where another Siddarmarkian flag stood out of the map's surface at a small dot labeled "Thesmar," and he smiled.

▼ ▼ ▼

"A moment, please, Merlin."

Merlin turned to look down as Aivah Pahrsahn laid a hand on his elbow. The meeting had finally broken up, although Cayleb and Stohnar were still discussing something with Maidyn, and he cocked an eyebrow.

"And how may I serve you, My Lady?"

She shook her head at his gently teasing tone. It was something of a joke between them, although he doubted she'd recognized the sincerity with which he used it.

Unlike any of the Siddarmarkians in this room, he knew she'd been more than entitled to that form of address by birth. Or would have been, if her father had ever acknowledged his daughter. Nor did any of those Siddarmarkians realize she'd been reared as the adopted daughter of one of the Church of God Awaiting's powerful dynasties even without that acknowledgment. They had no idea of the personal sacrifices she'd made, the world of privilege upon which she'd turned her back in the name of a greater responsibility and her own fierce beliefs.

"I've been reading the most recent reports from some of your agents in the Temple Lands," she said. "I know you and His Majesty see copies of most of them, and there's a point in one of the most recent which probably needs . . . clearing up."

"Ah?"

He raised an eyebrow, and she grimaced. It was a very graceful grimace, no doubt the well-trained product of her avocation, and very attractive it looked on her beautiful face. At the same time, he suspected there might be a trace of . . . embarrassment, perhaps, behind it.

"Yes, well, it's the one from *Seijin* Zhozuah."

"Oh. *That* report," he murmured.

Zhozuah Murphai was another Ahbraim Zhevons, although Merlin had physically impersonated the fair-haired, gray-eyed Murphai only a time or two. That was because "*Seijin* Zhozuah" was officially stationed in Zion. Despite how cautious Merlin and Nahrmahn remained about utilizing SNARCs in the vicinity of the Temple itself, much of the city could be safely covered by the remotes, and Murphai picked up quite a lot of information simply by listening to conversations outside the danger zone. Including. . . .

"I assume you're referring to those rumors he's reported?" he continued after a moment.

"Yes," she acknowledged.

"And would it happen that you're bringing this up because there's a kernel of truth behind those rumors?"

"Yes," she sighed. "In fact, there's quite a *substantial* kernel of truth behind them."

"I see." He regarded her for a few more heartbeats, his head cocked. "How many?" he asked.

"Nine," she said, and shrugged. "It was almost ten, but Vicar Nicodaim changed his plans at the last moment."

"Nine," he repeated carefully, and felt both eyebrows rise when she nodded. That was more than he'd estimated. Clyntahn and Rayno must be doing a better job of suppressing the news than he'd expected.

"May one inquire as to exactly how you've managed that?" he asked politely. "I assume it *was* you, since no one else with the reach and . . . audacity to assassinate members of the Council of Vicars comes readily to mind."

"Yes, it was me. Or my people, at any rate."

"And the reason you've never mentioned this little endeavor would be—?"

"Because I wasn't certain how some of our allies would feel about murdering vicars, no matter what sort of diseased excrescences on the human race the vicars in question might be," she said flatly.

"You mean—?"

He waved his hand, unobtrusively indicating the other men in the conference chamber, and she shook her head.

"Some of them might have a few qualms about it, but most of them?" She snorted. "They know who the enemy is, Merlin. I'm not worried about anyone in this room shedding any tears of remorse over a few discreet assassinations in Zion. But the only way to keep a secret really secret is to not tell anyone else about it, and this is one 'endeavor' I don't want leaking prematurely. So far, the only one who's *officially* killed any members of the vicarate is Zhaspahr Clyntahn, and he justified it by trumping up that travesty of an investigation and waving around a handful of tortured confessions."

Her lovely face turned grim for a moment, hard as Glacierheart granite.

"As soon as word gets out that someone's assassinating vicars, Clyntahn and Rayno will use it to whip up outrage among the Temple Loyalists. They might even be able to convince some Reformists that actually killing men consecrated to the orange is going a step too far, so as long as he's willing to suppress the news rather than admit the vicarate's vulnerability, I'm perfectly prepared to go along from our side, as well. And even leaving that aside, there are operational considerations. My people in Zion are living on a knife's edge, Merlin. I'm the only one who knows how to contact them, and I do that as infrequently as possible. I intend to keep it that way, and if more people learned they exist, I'm afraid there'd be pressure to use them for more general spying or 'micromanage' "—she smiled briefly as she used the word Merlin and Cayleb had introduced into the Allies' lexicon—"their targeting. I'm not saying the pressure would be irrational, given the situation, but it would place them at far greater risk. Every time *I* send *them* a message, I put them in danger, and trying to coordinate or control their operations from here would require me to do that far more often." She regarded him levelly. "I'm not prepared to do that. I *won't* do that."

"I see."

Merlin considered what she'd said . . . and what she hadn't. He didn't doubt she contacted them as infrequently as she could, especially since he still hadn't caught her at it, even with the benefit of his SNARCs. But clearly there was at least some communications flow in the opposite direction, given her ability to keep track of "her people's" accomplishments, and he found himself wondering how that flow was managed. He started to ask, but didn't.

"May I ask if you have a specific targeting criterion, other than the ability to get to them?" he asked instead.

"The priority list was drawn up based on some of that information Adorai delivered to Archbishop Maikel and on some more . . . personal considerations of my own. But each operation has to be carefully evaluated and planned, and access is a critical part of that planning. That and escape routes afterward." Her voice dropped and she looked away. "We've lost some people since they began active operations, anyway, but none of them have been taken alive."

Merlin's face tightened, remembering a locket Ahnzhelyk Phonda had worn around her neck, even in her own bed, and laid a hand on her shoulder.

"Why, Aivah?" he asked quietly.

"Because someone has to," she said flatly. "The vermin on that list represent everything that's wrong with the Church—every perversion, every degradation, every self-serving debasement. They use the power of the Church, the mantle of God Himself, to steal and corrupt and victimize, and Clyntahn and Rayno use what they know about them to buy their acquiescence in murder and atrocities." Her dark eyes were cold, bottomless— the eyes of a slash lizard or a kraken. "My people don't have the power of the Temple Guard or the reach of the Inquisition. They can't move openly, just as no one dares to openly criticize Clyntahn's butchery, but every one of his creatures we kill weakens his and Rayno's grip on the rest of the vicarate, be it ever so slightly. Who knows? The Archangels promise us miracles; maybe even some of the pigs swilling at Clyntahn's trough will mend their ways if we kill enough of the others. And if they don't?"

She looked up at him, and her smile was even colder than her eyes.

"If they don't, at least the world will be a little better place—and Hell will have a few new tenants. That has to count for something, Merlin."

II

Tellesberg Palace,
City of Tellesberg,
Kingdom of Old Charis,
Empire of Charis

"You're late." Baron Ironhill skewered Ehdwyrd Howsmyn with a stern eye as the ironmaster entered the airy council chamber. The warm breeze sweeping through the open windows plucked playfully at the edges of sheets of paper, and the Empire of Charis' treasurer shook a finger. "This sort of persistent tardiness will *not* be tolerated, Master Howsmyn!"

Howsmyn made a rude gesture with his right hand and sauntered—positively sauntered—to his own chair.

"I'm devastated by your displeasure, My Lord," he told his old friend, and Ironhill chuckled. He'd been doing more of that in the last few five-days.

"I'm sure you are. Nonetheless, you are"—the baron pulled out his watch and examined it—"no less than six *minutes* late! I trust there's an explanation?"

"I stopped by The Broken Pot," Howsmyn replied serenely. "I've got a hangover, too, so if you could moderate your volume, I'd appreciate it deeply."

Ironhill shook his head and restored his watch to his pocket, then glanced around the table at the other two men present.

"Don't look at me," Sir Domynyk Staynair told him. "If I had my druthers, *I'd* be in The Broken Pot right now, too!" The high admiral, who looked more like his brother every day as his hair grew progressively more silver, shifted the wooden peg which had replaced his lower right leg on its footstool. "Nothing *I* like better than endless shoreside meetings!"

"You're a sad, sad influence, Admiral Rock Point," Trahvys Ohlsyn observed. Ohlsyn—the Earl of Pine Hollow and the Empire's first councilor—was Nahrmahn

Baytz' cousin, although he was as wiry as Nahrmahn had been plump, and his brain was very nearly as sharp. He was also—like Howsmyn and Rock Point but not Ironhill—a member in good standing of the inner circle. "And I never suspected you Old Charisians were such hedonists."

"We're not," Ironhill growled. "Some of us *are* sots, though."

"Really?" Pine Hollow cocked his head in a gesture which reminded all of them of his cousin. "Odd that I'd never noticed. However, now that we have all of that out of our systems, what say we do a little work for a change?"

The others chuckled, although there was more than a trace of sourness in the amusement, given the schedules the four of them maintained.

"Ahlvyno," the first councilor went on, "since everything we're going to be talking about has to do with money, one way or the other, why don't you take the chair?"

"Fair enough." Ironhill nodded to the earl and then leaned back in his well-cushioned armchair, regarding Howsmyn rather more seriously. "I know Domynyk's scheduled for more meetings down at the dockyard this afternoon, Ehdwyrd. And I understand"—his smile turned suddenly cold and satisfied—"that you and Earl Nearoak have an appointment to discuss the terms for winding up Stywyrt Showail's liquidation. I'm looking forward to the Treasury's share of that, and not just because I can always use the marks. Since we all have so much on our plates, though, I thought we'd start with the two of you; Trahvys and I can discuss the business that doesn't involve you after you've left."

"Sounds good to me," Howsmyn agreed. "I stopped by King's Harbor on my way down from Delthak to get the latest update from Ahlfryd and Captain Rahzwail, but first, I brought this."

He placed a heavy, varnished box on the table before him and opened it.

"Ah." Rock Point's eyes lit, and Howsmyn smiled at him.

"No, you don't get this one," he told his friend. "*This* one is the third one ever made. It's intended for the Emperor and it'll be leaving for Siddar City with the next packet boat. The *first* ever made—and the second one just like it—will go along to keep it company, but not to His Majesty."

"*Seijin* Merlin?" Ironhill's eyes were bright and interested as Howsmyn lifted the pistol from its velvet-lined nest.

"It seems appropriate, since the original was his," Howsmyn pointed out, and the baron nodded.

"Of course, we've made some improvements. Master Mahldyn and I have three new patents just on the pistol. That doesn't begin to count the ones on the cartridges, the bullet-making equipment, *or* the new rifles. He's going to be a wealthy man before this is all over."

"And deservedly so," Pine Hollow murmured.

"Absolutely," Howsmyn agreed with total sincerity. He'd steered Taigys Mahldyn subtly, but all the major features of the new weapon—and its ammunition—had been devised by the head of the Delthak Works pistol shop, and the final result was even better than he'd hoped.

The new revolver had a solid frame with a swing out cylinder, rather than the removable cylinder of Merlin's original cap-and-ball design. It was beautifully made, with polished checkered grips of dark, satiny Safeholdian teak inlaid with golden medallions bearing the arms of the House of Ahrmahk.

"This is the extractor rod," Howsmyn said as he swung the cylinder wide and touched the rod protruding from its front. When the cylinder was locked in place, the rod fitted into a protective shroud under the weapon's six-inch barrel. "When you press it like this"—he demonstrated—"it moves through the center of the cylinder and this star-shaped extractor catches under the cartridges' rims and clears all six empty chambers in a single stroke."

He laid the pistol aside and reached into his briefcase for a pair of bright, hollow brass cylinders. The shorter was a bit over an inch long while the longer measured almost exactly two inches, but both seemed to be the same diameter, and he stood them on end beside each other.

"These are handmade, and you don't want to know how long it would take to produce worthwhile amounts of ammunition that way. Fortunately, we won't have to, and these work fine for testing purposes and to provide the *seijin* enough rounds to play with. They're both forty-five caliber, and this"—he picked up the shorter of the two—"pushes a three-hundred-fifty-grain bullet out of a six-inch barrel at approximately one thousand feet per second. That's actually about fifty feet per second faster than the standard infantry Mahndrayn, the Mark IIa, and only about thirty feet per second lower than the Mark IIb, the sniper version. As nearly as we can calculate it, this round's initial muzzle *energy* is virtually identical with the Mark IIa's, though, because of the rifle's heavier bullet."

Ironhill's eyebrows rose in surprise, and Howsmyn smiled. Then he picked up the second, longer cartridge.

"*This* is the round for what we're calling the Model 96 Mahndrayn from its year of introduction. That's the official name; most of us at Delthak just call it the M96 for short. The extra case length is necessary because the powder charge is better than twice as heavy as the revolver's. It's a smaller diameter than the fifty caliber round of the existing rifles, but it fires a longer bullet that's actually thirty percent heavier. Well, it's lighter than the sniper rifle's, actually, but we're using the same round and rifling in all the versions of the Model 96, and using the same caliber in the revolvers and the new rifles will simplify case production. For that matter, it'll give us some advantages in bullet production, despite the differences between the bullets' weights and ballistic profiles.

"We're going to have to set up two separate ammunition production lines when we convert the existing Mark II rifles, because it turns out the new round's properties are incompatible with the older weapons. In fact, they're different enough that the M96 needs a completely different—and deeper—pattern of rifling. We've also decided against providing the conversions with magazines. Taigys came up with a design for them—he calls it a 'trapdoor' design, because it uses a hinged block that swings up—that still constitutes a huge improvement and shortens the conversion process to less than a quarter of the time to build them from scratch. Settling for a single-shot will make them tactically inferior to the M96, but it would take three times as long to convert them to magazines. And while I know this may upset Domynyk, what I'm thinking is that as we convert the existing Mahndrayns, we withdraw them for service with the Marines, where pitched combat is less likely, and supply the new M96s to the Army. If we get production up to the levels I'm anticipating, we should be in a position to retire them entirely within a year or two. In fact, we might be able to pass them directly to Siddarmark rather than to the Marines as soon as they're converted."

"I'm always happy to hear about ways to not spend money, so your conversion idea sounds great to me," Ironhill said. "By the same token, though, if we pass the conversions to Siddarmark, will you be able to produce enough ammunition to supply the Republic as well as our own troops?" He shook his head. "And while I understand there are huge tactical advantages in the new weapons, won't adopting these metallic cartridges of yours mean we can't use paper cartridges anymore . . . or captured Temple gunpowder?"

"That's already true with the Mahndrayns, Ahlvyno," Staynair pointed out. "They rely on primer caps." He shrugged. "If we run out of caps, we're SOL, to use His Majesty's charming term."

"Domynyk's right," Howsmyn agreed. "And the new machinery will produce ammunition more rapidly than our existing arrangements, since it's going to combine the old paper cartridge and the primer cap in a single package. The ammunition'll be safer to handle, too. And while using brass cases will push up *material* costs, compared to the paper, the man-hours per round will go down considerably. Overall, the metallic rounds will actually cost the Treasury less."

Ironhill considered that for a moment, then nodded in acknowledgment, and Howsmyn went on.

"This round may be the same caliber as the revolver's, but the bullet's much heavier—five hundred grains, not three hundred—and the M96's muzzle velocity will be almost six hundred feet per second higher than the revolver's. That's why the case is so long; getting that kind of performance out of black powder requires a heavy charge, and we're using what Taigys calls 'pelletized' powder—the same thing Alfryd's calling prismatic powder for the artillery, on a smaller scale—as well. As you can see, the bullet itself is the same basic shape as the Mark IIb's." He touched the tip of the bullet, which would have been called a "spitzer point" back on Old Earth. "It has the same 'boat tail' design, too, and Taigys"—and Owl, he carefully did not add aloud—"came up with something he calls a 'gas check.' It's basically a copper disk at the base of the bullet to prevent the propellant charge from melting the lead. Our test firings indicate that with that and a lubricant to protect the sides of the bullet from melting, as well, we get higher muzzle velocities and better accuracy without the kind of lead fouling we experienced when we pushed the velocity on the Mark IIb this high. We're using the same water quenching process we came up with for the sniper weapons, and after trying several alloys, we've found that adding false silver seems to give us the best combination of hardness and workability.

"At any rate, according to the ballistic pendulum, this round generates three and a half times the muzzle energy of the revolver round. And because of its shape and greater weight, it maintains that velocity to a much greater range. According to Doctor Mahklyn's calculations, this round will have roughly the same striking power at nine hundred and fifty yards that the standard revolver has at two hundred and fifty. Of course," the industrialist grinned suddenly, "I don't imagine anyone besides *Seijin* Merlin's going to score any hits with revolvers at that kind of range!"

"Oh, I don't know," Rock Point said with a slow

smile of his own. "I imagine *Seijin* Ahbraim might pull it off, as well."

"All right, I'll grant you *Seijin* Ahbraim. Most mere mortals won't, though."

"Probably not," the admiral conceded.

"That sounds really impressive," Ironhill said. "I thought you and Ahlfryd wanted to wait for this new guncotton Doctor Lywys is working on, though. I hate to sound like a mark-pincher, and I know we're one hell of a lot better off than we were three months ago, but that's my job. And unless we're very lucky, I'm going to be looking at Shan-wei's own inflation in prices once the new mines actually start producing!" He shook his head. "I don't think even Desnair's ever had a situation quite like this one."

The others nodded, although Howsmyn wondered if Pine Hollow and Rock Point found it as hard to suppress their smiles as *he* did. The fact that Ironhill knew about *Seijin* Merlin's "visions" had made things surprisingly simple after Prince Nahrmahn dropped his little Silverlode Island surprise. Merlin had simply sent a letter to Pine Hollow giving him the location of the deposit—the *first* deposit, that was—with an estimate of its extent Ironhill had been willing to accept because everything else Merlin had ever told him had been accurate.

And in this case, he'd been very happy—one might even have said delighted—to take Merlin's word, since Nahrmahn's comparison to Old Earth's Comstock Lode actually understated the case. In fact, Merlin had understated the real numbers to Ironhill, in turn, lest even the baron's faith in the *seijin*'s visions prove insufficient this time around.

The Mohryah Mountains which formed the huge island's mountainous spine covered an area seventy percent greater than the ancient North American state of Texas and were home to at least *four* major ore lodes which Shan-wei had somehow failed to mention to Langhorne and his command crew. The most accessible—which was *not* the richest—was between eighty and ninety percent as large as the Comstock and, like that strike, consisted of both gold and silver "bonanza ore," layers of ore in discrete masses, up to hundreds of feet in depth in spots, and soft enough it could be cut out with a shovel. The Comstock Lode had produced almost seven million tons of silver and gold ore in a twenty-year span; this one would produce less, but a higher percentage of it would be gold. Shan-wei's data included a highly accurate estimate of the ore body's extent, and the total production from what had already been labeled the Mohryah Lode was likely to top four million tons of silver and almost two and a half million of gold. Given the richness of the ore, that would come to a tidy total of just over ten *trillion* 896 Charisian marks. It wouldn't all be coming in at once—indeed, it would take months for the first shaft to be sunk, even knowing exactly where to begin—but it promised to provide a handy little nest egg.

And, as Ironhill had said, it also promised to inflate prices badly if Charis was careless about how it was dumped into the economy, which made it fortunate the entire island was effectively the House of Ahrmahk's private property. Cayleb and Sharleyan could determine exactly how much of that gold and silver came out of the ground at any one time, and in the meantime, Ironhill had begun issuing interest-bearing promissory notes at six percent compound interest with ten-year expiration dates. That meant each of them would be worth a hundred and eighty percent of face value when they were redeemed, which, coupled with Charis' reputation, was good enough for most people to take the notes even before the new ore strike was made public.

"I do have to keep reminding myself not to run wild with all that promised wealth," Ironhill continued. "And I'm still robbing Paityr to pay Pawal in too many cases while we wait for it to start pouring in, too. So I have to ask if it's really worthwhile to introduce an entirely new round loaded with black powder if we're just going to turn around and change everything as soon as the new propellants become available?"

"That's really a two-part question, Ahlvyno." Howsmyn picked up the rifle round, cupping it in the palm of his hand. "The first is how quickly the new propellants will become available, and the answer there is that it won't be as soon as we'd hoped." He grimaced and closed his hand on the cartridge. "They seem to have a pretty good handle on what they need to do; the problem is figuring out *how* to do it, especially in quantity, and that's going to take several more months. We should have the first revolver production line up in the next few five-days, though, and we'll be ready to start conversion on the Mark IIs about the same time. Since we're using the revolver to prototype my new assembly processes, it's going to be the end of October or so before we start up the first M96 line, but Doctor Lywys' current estimate is that it'll be sometime late next spring or even early summer before we can produce guncotton-loaded cartridges. I don't think we can justify not putting the black powder rounds into production in the interim.

"At the same time, there's no question that when they do become available they'll be a significant improvement over this round." He opened his hand to show the shiny brass cartridge again. "Our best estimate from the numbers Doctor Lywys and Doctor Mahklyn can give us is that with guncotton, the M96's muzzle velocity will be close to a thousand feet per second higher than with black powder . . . and without the huge volumes of smoke. We can't take full advantage of the longer ranged accuracy and hitting power this cartridge theoretically makes available because black powder produces so much smoke visibility's obscured; that won't happen with the new propellants."

Ironhill was nodding slowly, expression thoughtful, and Howsmyn shrugged.

"We're taking the new powder into consideration in these designs," he said, setting the rifle cartridge back on the table beside the pistol round. "For example, one reason to go to a completely new design is that while the steel in the Mark II's much better than anyone had a few years ago, the steel we can produce now is even better, and that's a significant factor when we start talking about the sort of muzzle velocities guncotton's going to make possible. We could go on using alloyed bullets at those velocities, but it'll probably make more sense to gild them with something with a higher melting point, like copper. We'd considered that for these rounds, but copper's one of our bottlenecks, and demand is already going to increase when we go to the metallic cartridges. In fact, we actually looked at steel cartridges, instead, but brass has superior expansion and elasticity. At any rate, once the guncotton propellant becomes available, we should be able to convert using the same cartridges and weapons; we'll just use lighter charges in the same cases. We'll probably go to guncotton for the 'Trapdoor Mahndrayns,' as well, if only because of the smoke issue, but I wouldn't feel comfortable loading their cartridges to the same pressures and velocities as the M96's designed to handle."

"All right, that answers my questions." Ironhill grimaced. "Now all I have to do is figure out how to pay you for them. I don't suppose you'd care to provide the first, oh, ten or twenty thousand of them as samples, would you?"

"I'm afraid not," Howsmyn said politely. "Because you're a friend and a valued customer, I will offer you a nice discount, though. Say, two percent?"

Ironhill laughed.

"Actually, given the number of these things we're going to be buying, a two percent discount would probably save me a fortune in the end! I guess you're worth it, though. His Majesty seems to think so, anyway."

"He's not done costing you money yet, Ahlvyno," Rock Point said.

"Of course not. Aside from what the Treasury stands to recoup from that bastard Showail, I *never* see him unless it's going to cost me money!"

"But, as you say, His Majesty thinks he's worth it," Pine Hollow pointed out with a smile. "And so"—the smile faded—"do the men we've deployed in the Republic."

"True," Ironhill acknowledged a bit more soberly and

turned back to Howsmyn. "So what does Domynyk have in mind this time?"

"As I said, I stopped off to talk with Ahlfryd and Captain Rahzwail—and Sir Dustyn. The second flight of the new ironclads is a couple of five-days behind schedule at the moment, although Commander Malkaihy and Commander Hainai expect to make that up. Part of the problem was that last load of wrought iron from Showail, frankly."

The industrialist grimaced, then gave himself a shake.

"Anyway, we're in decent shape where they're concerned, but production of the new guns is running *ahead* of schedule. We already had quite a few gun tubes; now mount production's catching up, and the weapons for the improved *River*-class ships will be ready well before the ships themselves are. Half the new hulls are already afloat or ready for launch, but it's going to be at least a month before the first one commissions, and I already have enough of the new guns to arm the first flight of the new ships *and* replace the thirty-pounders aboard the original ironclads. I'd really like to go ahead and send the extras off to Siddarmark in the next convoy."

"Domynyk?" Pine Hollow looked at the high admiral.

"Suits me." Rock Point snorted. "Worst case, the last half dozen of the improved *Rivers* are delayed a month or two waiting for their guns and we get the four originals into service instead. And Shan-wei knows they aren't doing anyone any good sitting in an ordnance warehouse here in Old Charis!"

"Do you have enough of the new shells?" Ironhill asked.

"That's why Domynyk said I was going to cost you more money," Howsmyn replied with a smile. "The new copper driving bands work even better than Ahlfryd and Captain Rahzwail expected, and they've finally gotten their 'brown powder' into production at Hairatha. When you add up the tighter, more efficient bore seal, the smoother shell body, and the ballistic qualities of the 'prismatic powder,' the new six-inch is probably as effective as—maybe even more effective than—the existing eight-inch. We've got enough of the new shells in inventory to provide each existing ironclad with about ninety rounds per gun, and the line's in place for volume production, but we won't have any additional ships mounting the new gun until the improved *Rivers* begin commissioning. If we re-arm the existing ships, they won't be able to fire the six-inch round the existing angle-guns do, but do we want to commit the money and the resources to starting up production when they're the only units that can use it?"

"Domynyk?" Pine Hollow asked again, and the high admiral nodded sharply.

"Definitely." His voice was flat, positive. "One thing Ehdwyrd didn't mention is that he's ready to begin production on the new *angle-guns*, as well, and they'll fire the same shell. We'll start by converting the existing tubes to the new mounts, but there's no point continuing to build stud-rifled barrels if a better design's available. We're going to need lots of angle-gun shells down the road, and not all that *far* down the road. That's reason enough from the logistic perspective to get that line of his fired up, and even if it weren't, the tactical consequences of getting the new guns to Bahrns and the other ships in the Republic would more than justify it. I know funding's always an issue, Ahlvyno, but this is one spider-rat hole that definitely needs money poured down it."

"All right," Ironhill sighed. "Consider your point made."

He jotted a note on the pad at his elbow, then looked up again.

"And the *King Haarahlds*?"

"Dustyn's finished playing with the redesign in light of Captain Bahrns' after-action report and he's laying down the first three this five-day," Rock Point said. "He says eight months to commission—his crews learned a *lot* working on the ironclads—which means they should be ready for service next July. Personally, I think he'll do better than his estimate, the way he always does, but that may only be my optimism talking."

"I think he probably will have the hulls finished earlier than he's estimating," Howsmyn agreed. "And I'm *pretty* sure the guns will be ready early, too. The armor's going to be a closer run thing, though."

"The engines are good?" Rock Point asked. "They're not going to cause Pawal here any more anxiety?"

"I don't believe so," Howsmyn said with admirable gravity.

The new engines were fiendishly expensive, and the treasurer had expressed some concern over committing funds in such quantity to yet another untried bit of technology. That had been before he knew about the Mohryah Lode, and it had been hard to blame him for his worry. The *King Haarahld*s would be the first ships powered by triple-expansion machinery rather than the double-expansion engines used in the smaller ironclads, and each of those engines would produce six hundred shaft dragonpower—which would have been fifteen thousand *horse*power back on Old Earth. More than that, the redesigned *King Haarahld*s would displace over eleven thousand tons . . . and be built without masts or sails. The notion of relying solely on steam for the ships' propulsion had more people than Ironhill a bit worried, so Olyvyr had provided wells and footings to mount three masts as a purely emergency measure. And it had *better* be something used only in emergencies. By Olyvyr's (and Owl's) estimate, they would be capable of no more than two knots in average conditions under sail, thanks to the drag their twin screws would impose.

"Stahlmhan's had the test engine up and operating continuously at two-thirds power for over a month now," he continued. "Given Dustyn's speed estimates, that's long enough for one of these ships to steam from here to Cherayth two and a half times. Of course, they'd have to stop to re-coal in Zebediah if they steamed the whole way that fast, but I think the machinery's been about as well proved as it can be before it's installed in an actual ship."

"Good," Rock Point said, and then grinned almost

impishly. "And now that that's settled, I think we can let you go for that meeting with Nearoak and Showail. And don't forget this." He picked up the revolver, returned it to its case, and handed it back to the ironmaster. "Maybe you'll get a chance to try it out."

. III .
Branath Canal,
Glacierheart Province,
Republic of Siddarmark

"Well, it beats walking, Sir," Sailys Trahskhat said, standing at the rope-and-stanchion arrangement which served as a railing. "Not so sure 'bout the direction, though."

Byrk Raimahn—*Colonel* Byrk Raimahn, of the 1st Glacierheart Volunteers—stepped up beside him, gazing over the side at the muddy brown water of the Branath Canal's southbound lane. The northbound lane was occupied by an identical barge, also headed south, its deck and low superstructure covered by seated Charisian infantry busily cleaning weapons and sharpening bayonets.

How, he wondered, *did a good Charisian boy end up a* colonel *in the Republic of Siddarmark Army in command of a regiment of bloody-minded Glacierheart miners and mountain clansmen? Talk about herding cat-lizards!*

The hardheaded, independent, self-sufficient citizens of Glacierheart would have been a handful under any circumstances. Their sense of almost implacable self-reliance and stubborn integrity went a long way towards explaining why—and how—the reformist-minded folk of Glacierheart had crushed the rebellious Temple Loyalist militia which had attempted to seize the province as part of the Sword of Schueler. The bitterness and atrocities of the winter mountain warfare against the Temple Loyalists of Hildermoss had only honed that iron-ribbed determination and burnished it with an edge of ferocity . . . and a deep, burning hatred which was rare among the mountaineers. A third of the men who'd enlisted in the 1st Glacierheart Volunteers were mountain trappers and hunters like Captain Wahlys Mahkhom; the rest were miners, farmers, and small-town artisans, and all of them tended to be very tough customers. Mining was always a dangerous, brutal occupation, and farming in Glacierheart was no picnic, while most of the artisans in question had themselves come out of the mines or off the farm before they were apprenticed in their current trades. His mountaineers, Raimahn often thought, might possess the closest thing Siddarmark had ever produced to the legendary toughness of Harchongese serfs, but there was a vast difference between them and the stolid, almost animal-like endurance of the Harchongians.

They didn't take well to military discipline, his Glacierhearters. When it came to orders, especially in combat, they were fine; they showed a bit less interest in maintaining smart formations, salutes, proper military courtesy, or any of the other hundred and one things that differentiated a professional soldier from a civilian *off* the battlefield. On the other hand, miners were accustomed to working conditions where their lives often depended on discipline—both their own and that of their fellow miners—and they had a short way with anyone whose *lack* of discipline threatened the unit's actual functionality. In fact, the punishment they handed out was almost always more severe even than the famed discipline of the Republic of Siddarmark Army's regulars. Tough or not, it was a very rare Glacierhearter who committed the same infraction twice once his mates had . . . reasoned with him. And once he got back out of the infirmary, of course.

The regulars—even the Charisian regulars—had been inclined to look down upon the 1st Glacierhearts at first. The handful of Brigadier Taisyn's surviving Marines had been quick to set the record straight, however, and the high percentage of hunters and trappers in Raimahn's regiment made it particularly well suited to the sort of light infantry tasks at which the Army of God was least adroit. In fact, Duke Eastshare had started using the

Volunteers for jobs he would normally have assigned to his scout snipers.

The fact that my miners and canal builders are more accustomed to working with explosives than most people doesn't hurt any, either, Raimahn thought with grim amusement. *Wahlys, especially, took to planting sweepers and fountains with genuine artistry. I only wish there weren't so many times I worried about what's going on inside him.*

He sighed, mouth tightening as he thought about Wahlys Mahkhom's slaughtered family. Too many of his Volunteers could have told the same story, and he knew he was going to have trouble preventing the kind of counter-atrocities Eastshare was trying to avoid. He only hoped the duke would remember what Glacierheart had endured.

And he also hoped the duke knew what he was doing pulling so much combat power out of Glacierheart. At the moment, the 1st Glacierheart Volunteers and the rest of Eastshare's column were halfway between Glacierborn Lake and Fort St. Klair, skirting the western face of the Clynmair Hills. That was a long way from the Glacierheart Gap, and he hoped like hell the forces Eastshare had left behind were up to keeping the Army of Glacierheart out of the province for which it had been named. They *probably* were, but "probably" wasn't a word Byrk Raimahn was fond of when it came to the safety of the people he'd spent the last half year of his life defending. They were important to him, and he would rip the throat out of anyone who threatened them with his bare hands.

Calmly, Byrk, he told himself. *Calmly! The Duke knows what he's doing, and even if he hasn't actually told you what he has in mind, you've got a pretty good idea, don't you? After all, there's a reason he told you to make sure you had plenty of picks and shovels.*

And explosives, of course.

St. Kylmahn's Foundry,
City of Zion,
The Temple Lands

Brother Lynkyn Fultyn looked up from his pad of notes as Vicar Allayn Maigwair strode into his office. Nights were already unpleasantly chill in the northern Temple Lands, there'd been ice in some of the fountains come dawn, and the day remained distinctly cool. In short, it was a typical early September morning in Zion . . . despite which, Fultyn, who'd been born in the high foothills of the Mountains of Light, had his office windows open. Fortunately, the breeze through them wasn't strong enough to be a problem for Maigwair's more temperate sensibilities, but it carried the whiff of coal smoke and hot iron, the clangor of hammers on anvils, and the louder, slower, rhythmic thud of water-driven drop hammers.

St. Kylmahn's Foundry wasn't actually in the precincts of Zion, but it was close enough to come under the city's direct jurisdiction, and it had been growing rapidly for the past several years. By now, it was the largest single industrial operation in the Temple Lands, although the Inquisition's reports all suggested that its output remained dismally short of the heretic Howsmyn's accursed Delthak Works. Maigwair was grateful for the estimated production figures, depressing though they might be, although he could wish Clyntahn's agents inquisitor might have provided a little more insight into *how* Howsmyn was accomplishing such feats.

That would undoubtedly have been asking too much, of course. The heretics clearly understood the necessity of maintaining security about their capabilities, so it was understandable if the Inquisition found it difficult to obtain that information, especially from someplace as distant—and which had demonstrated such fiendishly good counterintelligence—as the Kingdom of Charis. He would have felt happier, however, if he'd been able to convince himself that was the only reason so little of that information was available.

Zhaspahr's tendency to pick and choose what he decides to tell the rest of us about is going to get all of us killed, he thought grimly. *It was bad enough when I only thought* that *was what he was doing. Now that I've got proof—*

He chopped that thought off with the efficiency of long practice. He had a suspicion this conference was going to come close enough to the fringes of what Clyntahn would consider allowable—or even tolerable— without adding *that* to the fire, and while no ears except his and Fultyn should be privy to their conversation, it was far safer to assume otherwise. If the Grand Inquisitor was keeping a king wyvern's eye on what the heretics were up to, he was keeping an even closer one on what Mother Church's loyal sons were doing. It would never do to allow Shan-wei's corruption to sneak past him, after all.

Even if it does risk losing the Jihad. And even if Zhaspahr knows as well as I do—or damned well should, anyway!—that Shan-wei's had precious little to do with anything that's happened since—

Another thought it was best to strangle at birth, he reminded himself, and nodded to Fultyn.

"Brother Lynkyn."

"Your Grace." Fultyn stood, bowing, and then bent to kiss the ring Maigwair extended across the desk to him.

That desk was awash in a sea of paper, with an island of bare wood in its center to make space for Fultyn's notepad, a silver tray bearing a bottle of increasingly rare Chisholmian whiskey, and a pair of cut crystal glasses. Its top was scarred with old burn marks where Fultyn had set an overheated pipe bowl to cool while he puzzled over the latest cryptic hints of the heretics' capabilities, and there were rings to mark where glasses had been set and left. The edge of one stack of paperwork was stained brown where he'd spilled a cup of tea, and the scent of his tobacco, a bit stale but fragrant, permeated the very fabric of the paper and clung to walls and upholstery—even the window curtains—despite the breeze and the tang of burning coal. It was a comfortable workspace, untidy as a dragon's cave but with the aura of a place where someone with an active, agile mind exercised it regularly.

And a damned good thing, too, Maigwair thought, watching Fultyn uncap the whiskey and pour for both of them. He hadn't asked if the vicar wanted the whiskey; by now it was an established ritual, and Maigwair sipped appreciatively.

"That's good," he said with a sigh, and Fultyn nodded. Neither commented on just how rare Chisholmian whiskey—and Charisian manufactured goods—had become in the Temple Lands. Even the Charisian-built farm equipment was breaking down, and more and more precious capacity and craftsmen had to be diverted to repairing it and away from the Jihad.

Well, that particular problem's going to ease a bit when the snow begins to fly, isn't it, Allayn? the vicar thought sourly. *Of course, it'll be back to bite us on the arse even harder come spring.*

"So!" He set his glass on the desk before him, laying his hands on either side and trapping it in the diamond of his touching thumbs and index fingers. "Your message said you've reached some conclusions, Brother."

"Some, Your Grace," Fultyn acknowledged. "To be honest, quite a few of 'my' conclusions are a matter of agreeing with young Zhwaigair in Gorath. The boy has an excellent mind. I could use him here."

Their eyes met, and Maigwair's nostrils flared.

"I agree with you about Lieutenant Zhwaigair," he said after a moment. "I think he's doing excellent work where he is, though, and we need someone like him in Dohlar, as well as here. I'd rather not put all our assets in one basket."

Fultyn looked back at him for a moment, then nodded. Everything Maigwair had just said was true, but both of them understood his last sentence was the real reason for leaving Dynnys Zhwaigair where he was . . . far away from the Grand Inquisitor and with Bishop Staiphan to keep a protective eye on him.

"Well, at any rate, the Lieutenant's done his usual excellent job of writing up his observations and conclusions," Fultyn said after a moment, looking down at the top sheet of his pad. "His comments about the interchangeability of the parts of the heretics' new rifles match my own observations. I think he's also correct to argue that it depends on a truly universal set of measurements. Unfortunately, establishing something like that would be far more difficult than might first appear. I think it's likely the heretics have spent years in the effort, and my own observations suggest it isn't yet completed. At the same time, it also appears that just as their Delthak Works have been exporting their new practices and techniques, they've been spreading their standardized measurements with them. Unless the Lieutenant and I are both badly mistaken," he glanced up to meet Maigwair's eyes, "they're now far enough along to establish interchangeability between parts from even widely separated manufactories. That's going to increase their production rates still more and it's also going to significantly improve serviceability levels in the field for them. As just one example of that, their armorers won't have to individually make replacement parts when some component of a rifle breaks. They can carry stocks of the parts most likely to fail and simply replace them when they do."

He paused until Maigwair nodded in glum understanding, then continued.

"As I say, I'm certain that process has taken them years and, frankly, we can't duplicate it soon enough to affect the Army of God's situation in Siddarmark. Nor is that the only problem we face. To be honest, Your Grace, I hadn't followed the implications of the heretics' extensive use of steel where we use iron—or, for that matter, of the *quality* of their iron—and the extent to which they've clearly refined their forging and machining processes as completely as Zhwaigair did. The simple truth of the matter is that as deceptively simple as the heretics' rifle design is, we can't duplicate it in the quantities we would require, and we certainly can't approach the parts interchangeability that they've achieved. I'm sorry, Your Grace, but we just can't do it."

"I was afraid of that," Maigwair sighed.

"I'm not saying the situation's hopeless, Your Grace. In fact, I think very highly of young Zhwaigair's proposed rifle design. We can readily incorporate it into new-build weapons, and we can convert existing weapons fairly easily if we withdraw them to our central facilities. For that matter, it may be possible to equip the armorer's wagons to perform at least some conversions in the field."

"Really?" Maigwair straightened.

"Conversion will weaken the rifles' stocks somewhat," Fultyn cautioned, "so they'll be a bit more fragile. While I hesitate to underestimate soldiers' ability to break things, however, I don't believe it will constitute a significant drawback. And Zhwaigair's estimates of how much more labor and time will be required to produce his design may be overly pessimistic. He doesn't know about Tahlbaht and the improvements he's come up with for us, and—possibly even more to the point—I'm fairly sure he's underestimated the rate at which we can produce the necessary screws. I think he's thinking like an ironmaster's nephew, but iron may not be the best metal for them and I suspect he hasn't properly considered all the possible sources for the workmen to make them. I won't be certain until I've had the chance to make a few inquiries, but I estimate that once Tahlbaht and I have had the opportunity to discuss it, we could probably produce one of young Zhwaigair's rifles—slightly modified from his original design, perhaps—in no more than twice the time required for the existing rifle. We may even be able to improve on that number, although at this point we'd clearly be wiser to err on the side of caution. It certainly won't require more than three times the man-hours, however, and even that rate is twenty-five percent better than he's estimated."

Maigwair nodded slowly, his eyes thoughtful, as he

considered the implications of what the other man had just said . . . and how fortunate it was that he was in a position to say it. The truth was that Lynkyn Fultyn and Tahlbaht Bryairs were the crown jewels of the Army of God's weapons manufacturing capability, and it was only by the Archangels' grace he had the two of them.

The black-haired, bearded Fultyn was a Chihirite, like Maigwair himself, although he was only a lay brother. There were several reasons for that, including the fact that he'd never felt a vocation for the priesthood. More ominously, however, he'd been disciplined several times in his youth for his curiosity and willingness to question received wisdom where the accepted practices of craft and manufactory were concerned. He'd survived mainly because the "received wisdom" he'd been most apt to question had simply been dogmatic, unthinking responses by superiors who, irritated by his willingness to think for himself, hadn't bothered to check the actual doctrinal authorities before they quashed him. Of course, he'd only made things worse when he'd persisted in appealing to higher authority and it turned out those dogmatic superiors were wrong. Indeed, more than one of them had creatively misconstrued the *Writ* (or even knowingly miscited it) simply to shut him up, and they hadn't appreciated it when he went over their heads . . . and won. None of the questions he'd raised had actually transgressed the Proscriptions, but he'd managed to exasperate enough senior churchmen—"infuriate" might really have been a better verb—to preclude any possibility of a career in the priesthood, even if he'd wanted one.

That same willingness to challenge what he saw as needlessly inefficient practices had gotten him interested in metallurgy and the development of manufactories for Mother Church. His belief that the Church ought to be directly engaged in the promotion of manufactories in the Temple Lands had received virtually no support from the vicarate prior to the Jihad, however. Maigwair was aware of that. In fact, he'd been part of it, although he'd since realized that the Church's natural aversion to dangerous and unrestrained innovation had been taken entirely too far. Of course, the fact that it had been cheaper to buy the manufactured goods Mother Church—and the vicarate—required from Charis, via Siddarmark, without the risk of introducing that contaminating innovation into the Temple Lands themselves had been a factor, as well.

But the Jihad had changed things completely. At least, it had in Allayn Maigwair's opinion, and in Rhobair Duchairn's, and the two of them had seen in Fultyn the man they needed to coordinate their own manufacturing programs. It had taken them almost two years to convince Clyntahn, thanks to those youthful disciplinary hearings, but Fultyn had been put in charge of St. Kylmahn's three years ago, and output had increased dramatically under his leadership.

In no small part, that was as much due to the efforts of Tahlbaht Bryairs as to Fultyn's leadership. Bryairs was thirteen years younger than Fultyn and as red-haired, blue-eyed, and fair as Fultyn was dark. He was also taller than Fultyn and clean-shaven, but his brain was just as sharp, although it worked in rather different ways. That was what made them so effective. Fultyn was constantly looking at processes, concepts, new ideas, while Bryairs was focused on the most efficient way to accomplish any given task. The proliferation of water-powered machinery, the emulation of the "hydro-reservoirs" the heretics had devised, and an unceasing effort to find more efficient ways to combine the labor of St. Kylmahn's workforce were all passions of his.

Which is why I have to worry about protecting him *from the Inquisition, as well*, Maigwair reflected glumly, unaware of how his thoughts matched the Earl of Thirsk's. Not that Thirsk's worries would have surprised him.

It was a particularly frustrating thought because there was actually nothing inherently revolutionary in Bryairs' "circles of production," as he called them. They were simply an expansion of the traditional workshop environment, but whereas the typical pre-Jihad workshop might have consisted of two or three master gunsmiths, supported by half a dozen journeymen and another half-dozen apprentices, Bryairs' "circles" used a single master gunsmith to supervise up to twenty-five or, in some cases, even thirty workmen . . . and women.

The guilds, needless to say, had screamed like gelded dragons at the very thought. Bad enough to dilute the supply (and earnings) of masters and journeymen, but Bryairs' circles brought in workmen from completely outside the Gunmakers Guild, as well. Worse, he'd insisted they be given tasks which would have been restricted to apprentice-level guild members . . . and paid them less than half of what the Gunmakers Guild had previously extorted from Mother Church. And as if determined to make bad worse where the guilds were concerned, he'd brought in *women* and employed them on tasks which had always previously been the monopoly of accredited guildsmen.

Obviously, the relatively unskilled workers he'd brought in couldn't build entire rifles and pistols the way traditionally trained gunsmiths had done it, but Bryairs hadn't even tried to teach them to do that. Instead, he'd trained each of them to perform a specific task—to make a specific part or to assemble the parts made by others. He had yet to approach the interchangeability the heretics had attained, but within each of his circles the workers quickly became a smoothly functioning team. The parts they produced weren't interchangeable with those of any other circle, but they required only minor adjusting and fitting within their own group.

And production had soared. Mother Church's manufactories were far from matching the output of something like the heretic Howsmyn's huge facility, but St. Kylmahn's Foundry's production rate was double that of any other Mainland manufactory, and there were a great *many* of those Mainland manufactories.

Maigwair and Duchairn were aggressively exporting Bryairs' methods to every other Church facility. The guilds' opposition was a given, but it had become a muted opposition of late. Not that the guildsmen had suddenly discovered that their faith required them to subordinate their own interests to Mother Church's survival. It appeared, though, that however suspect the Grand Inquisitor might find the heretics' new inventions and processes, he saw nothing demonic in simple improvements in the organization of workers using traditional techniques. Not since the tide of victory in the war he'd instigated against Siddarmark had been halted, at least.

"St. Greyghor's and St. Marytha's have both instituted their own circles, now," Fultyn continued, "although Tahlbaht estimates they'll take another month or so getting to the production levels we've attained here. At the same time, he's still tweaking our own circles, and we'll export anything he comes up with to enhance our productivity to the other foundries as quickly as possible. We should have all of Mother Church's manufactories reorganized by spring, and I understand we're assuming control of the Harchongese foundries as well?"

"Yes, we are," Maigwair said. "I don't know how well his circles are going to work for Harchongians, but we can always hope. And I think it would be a good idea to explain them to the Dohlarans and Desnairians, as well."

"The Dohlarans are already over thirty percent more productive than we were before Tahlbaht's changes, Your Grace," Fultyn said—without, Maigwair noted, mentioning his own contributions to St. Kylmahn's improved efficiency. "I'm not certain we want to disrupt their production until we've got our own reorganized fully, not just here but in all our manufactories. It might be better to leave them where they are for now, since their production would actually drop, initially at least, while they shifted to an entirely new organization."

"And the Desnairians?"

"Your Grace, with all due respect, not even Tahlbaht's circles are going to make a huge difference there. For that matter, I'm not certain it would even be possible to implement them effectively. I'm in favor of anything that will improve matters, of course, but their guilds are even more . . . resistant than ours."

Maigwair grunted in unhappy agreement. With a

population almost seventy percent greater than that of the Temple Lands, the Empire actually produced fewer rifles every month, which was ridiculous. Except that it wasn't ridiculous, given the Desnairian attitude toward anything smacking of "trade." The epithet "nation of shopkeepers" had been merely scornful when most Mainlanders applied it to Charis; from the Empire's slave-owning aristocrats, it had been more in the nature of a scathing denunciation, and the Church's natural wariness of Charisian innovation had confirmed their attitude towards manufactories. Far better to purchase what they required from someone else than to sully their own hands and contaminate their own lands with practices any God-fearing child of Mother Church must find suspect. Especially when those practices upset the traditional social balance. Tolerating the rise of a tide of common-born manufactory owners could only undermine the sense of honor, integrity, and moral ardor which were both the hallmarks and the responsibility of the nobly born. One had only to glance at Charis' mongrelization to realize *that*!

And just to make bad worse, the Desnairian guilds liked things that way. Charisian goods might be cheaper, affordable by far more Desnairians than domestically produced goods, but what did that matter? If they produced less, they could simply charge more, and they'd forged an alliance with the aristocracy to keep an iron lock on the Empire's internal markets, systematically excluding foreign competition.

Not even the requirements of the Jihad were going to overcome that situation anytime soon. Desnairian nobles were almost as stiff-necked and prone to nepotism as Harchongians (although they were thankfully somewhat less addicted to outright graft), the Empire was a long way from the Temple Lands, and its aristocrats were less moribund than their Harchongese counterparts. They possessed a greater sense of national identity, and however inefficient they might be, they were deeply involved in the management of their realm, rather than relying on the monolithic bureaucracy which truly governed Harchong. If those aristocrats and powerful, disgruntled guilds decided to drag their feet in introducing Bryairs' new techniques, Desnair's already anemic output of small arms and artillery would drop still further.

And the bastards will claim it's all because of our insistence on "imposing techniques foreign to our own experience and practices." They may work just fine in the Temple Lands, and among those barbarian Harchongians, but they're clearly totally unsuited to Desnairians.

"Assuming we leave Dohlar where it is for now and write Desnair off entirely, what sort of production numbers are you looking at?" he asked.

"Any figure I give you's going to be based on guesstimates, Your Grace," Fultyn said. "They'll be the *best* guesstimates I can give you, but I'm not in a position to guarantee them at this point."

"I understand, Brother Lynkyn. And any estimate you give me will be used only internally and treated *only* as an estimate," Maigwair assured the monk. *Don't worry*, he added silently. *I'm not going to throw any numbers out where Zhaspahr's likely to hear them and decide to make you an example to encourage our other manufactory managers if we don't meet them.*

"Well, with that proviso, Your Grace," Fultyn said, turning to a page of his notepad. "At the moment, we're producing approximately twenty-four thousand rifles per month in the Temple Lands, Dohlar, Desnair, Harchong, and the Border States combined. We're also acquiring about five hundred per month from Silkiah now that the Grand Inquisitor's ruled the demilitarization provisions no longer apply to the Grand Duchy, and we can expect those numbers to climb quite a bit, although all that production's going directly to Desnair. Assuming we bring Silkiah into full production and we're able to apply Tahlbaht's methods across the board with the same proportionate increase in productivity we've seen here, production would be about fifty-two thousand per month. I'd love to see the Harchongese numbers climb higher than that, and I think they probably would, but it's far too early to even suggest we could accomplish it. For that matter, it's entirely possible we'll be able to tweak our own production still further, but I can't promise anything of the sort at this time. Too much depends on factors I can't begin to evaluate meaningfully."

"Those numbers are for our present muzzle-loading design?"

"They are, Your Grace. What I'd really like to do would be to concentrate production of the breech-loading design here in the Temple Lands, at least initially. We'll have the circles in operation sooner than anyone else, and if my projections are remotely accurate, we could produce on the order of twelve thousand per month of the new weapon."

"Even at fifty-two thousand, it would take close to a month's production just to replace the rifles we lost in July and August," Maigwair pointed out.

"True, Your Grace. But we'll have as many as five or even six months' production between now and next spring. Well, between now and the northern thaw, anyway, and if my estimates are anywhere near accurate, we should be very close to that level—outside Harchong, at least, and they represent no more than twelve percent of the total—by February."

Maigwair nodded, but his expression was unhappy. Every pikeman in the Army of God needed to be re-armed with a rifle if he was going to be much more than a target for the heretics, and even at Fultyn's fifty-two thousand a month, it would take over two months just to rearm the AOG's remaining pikemen.

Except, of course, he thought grimly, *that there's no way that's going to happen if Rhobair's little brainstorm works.*

He suppressed a grimace there was no point letting Fultyn see, but Duchairn had certainly been right about how much screaming his—no, *their*, now—proposal was going to evoke. In fact, the commanders of the army their plans would help most were doing the loudest screaming of all . . . which probably proved they were on the right track!

The thought made him chuckle suddenly, and Fultyn looked at him very strangely. He started to explain, then shook his head and brushed the thought away. There'd be time to tell Fultyn about it if—when—everyone finally bowed to the inevitable and allowed Duchairn to have his way.

"What if we completely halted production of pikes and concentrated that part of our workforce on making additional rifles?" he asked instead.

"We're not talking about the same sets of skills, Your Grace. As I say, the critical factor for the *new* rifle is going to be the speed at which we can turn out the necessary screws for the breech plugs. We might see another ten percent increase, at least here in the Temple Lands and in Dohlar. The increase would be smaller in Desnair and Harchong, although it might be worthwhile."

"And if we cut back on artillery production?" Maigwair inquired, fully aware that his question was a counsel of desperation.

"Again, it's a completely different set of workmen," Fultyn replied. "And, frankly, Your Grace, we're going to need to answer the heretics' artillery as badly as we need to answer their infantry weapons."

Maigwair grimaced, wishing he could dispute the point.

"I have reached some tentative conclusions about the heretics' artillery," Fultyn continued, flipping to another page. "The unexploded shells and shell fragments Bishop Militant Bahrnabai sent back were most informative. Unfortunately, we don't have any examples of whatever the heretics are using to cause shells to detonate on impact, and their conventional fuses function exactly the same way our own do, although the powder in them burns more consistently, which is what makes them so much more reliable. Oh, there are some detail improvements we can incorporate—in particular, their screw-in metallic fuses are highly ingenious—but even if we adopt their new design, it's unlikely to make much difference unless we can also improve the powder in them.

"I haven't been able to determine how those man-portable angle-guns of theirs work, but I've come to suspect it has as much to do with metallurgy as with anything else. Given Lieutenant Zhwaigair's observations about the quantity and quality of steel they're using in their small arms, I'm fairly certain the portable angle-guns use high-quality steel tubes, not iron. At present, I question whether or not we could produce similar weapons in quantity, given how much heavier and thicker an iron tube would have to be, but we're looking at the possibility of designing a spring-powered launcher to fire similar shells. The range would be much shorter, but the launcher might actually weigh *less*, not more, which ought to make it even more portable, and they'd be even simpler and cheaper—and faster—to manufacture. Assuming it's possible to produce them at all, of course. That's something else I have Tahlbaht and his staff looking into.

"As for the shells themselves," he flipped another page, "they're definitely using studs to engage in the cannon's rifling. We could duplicate that, but I'm inclined to wonder if it might not actually be faster and cheaper to enclose the shells in a lead . . . call it a slipper, I suppose. I'm thinking in terms of something that would form a sort of skirt—offer a hollow base, like a rifle bullet—that would expand into shallower rifling grooves than the heretics appear to be using with their stud arrangement. If it worked, it would probably mean we wouldn't need those copper things they fit to the bases of their shells. 'Gas seals' we should call them, I suppose. Whatever we *call* them, though, that's what they do; seal the barrel behind the shell to prevent the force of the powder from escaping around it. I'm not at all certain a lead coating would work as well as I hope, but I think it should be tried. If nothing else, lead's a lot cheaper than copper and we wouldn't have to machine the shell base the way they do to make their gas checks stay put.

"Whatever we do in terms of acquiring rifled artillery, though, we obviously can't cast it in bronze, Your Grace.

The rifling would quickly erode into uselessness. It might last longer if it turns out we *can* use something softer than the heretic's studs to engage it, but I can't believe it would last long enough to be practical. It might be possible to produce a harder liner that could be inserted into a bronze tube, but it would almost certainly have to be made from wrought iron, which would cost far more time and money."

"Why not iron?" Maigwair's tone was curious, not accusatory, and Fultyn shrugged.

"Cast iron's too brittle, Your Grace. We'd have to expand the liner to lock it in place, probably by firing a charge, and cast iron would crack when we did. We might try black iron, instead. It would have most of the properties we need, and it's less expensive than wrought iron, but it still requires a five-day or more of heat treatment and it's trickier to ensure quality and consistency."

Maigwair grimaced in understanding. Neither he nor Fultyn could have explained the physics and chemistry of the process the way Ehdwyrd Howsmyn could have, but the vicar had received a much more extensive practical education in foundry work than he'd ever wanted over the past few years.

"Black iron" was a relatively new improvement on the cast iron which had been part of Safehold since the Creation itself. It had first been developed less than seventy-five years ago in Dohlar, where the secret of its manufacture had been zealously guarded until the Charisians—who else?—discovered how to duplicate it. It took its name from the outstanding visual difference between it and regular cast iron. When a cast-iron bar was broken, the exposed metal was gray in color, with white or silvery streaks throughout; when a bar of black iron broke, the fractured surface was far darker and streaked with black. Ehdwyrd Howsmyn could have told them that was because the carbon—anywhere from one and a half to five percent—which produced cast iron's brittleness and accounted for its gray coloration had been converted into nodes of graphite, instead. The annealing process which converted the carbon produced a far more malleable metal, suitable for the kind of hammering and forging processes which quickly fractured cast iron and with a much higher tensile strength. Indeed, in many ways it was a better material than wrought iron, and cheaper to produce, to boot. Unfortunately, as Fultyn said, the annealing process took time. It also required a highly experienced ironmaster, and they simply didn't have enough of those to go around.

"The heretics could probably do it with a steel tube," Fultyn continued in the tone of someone making an admission he wished he didn't have to. "We can't produce steel in those quantities. Yet, at least. There are some hints in the most recent reports from the Inquisition that suggest the heretics've come up with an entirely new process that we might—*might*, Your Grace—be able to duplicate with more information and a little time. For now though, I'm afraid I just don't see an affordable way to liner bronze artillery."

"I'm afraid we're going to have to make it work, however expensive it is," Maigwair said unhappily. "It's clear that the heretics' advantage in range and accuracy is . . . significant."

"Agreed, Your Grace. I think, though, that we're going to have to go with cast-iron tubes. We're getting much better and much more consistent results out of our iron guns than we were—so much better that I'm confident we could switch completely to iron for our smoothbore artillery. And I don't think we'd have any problems—not any insurmountable ones, at any rate—cutting rifling grooves into iron guns. On the other hand, bore pressures are bound to go up with the increased weight of shells like the ones the heretics are using, and we've already had far too much experience with burst iron cannon compared to bronze simply because bronze is more elastic. That can only get worse as bore pressure increases, but I've been discussing that problem with some of my senior artificers, and we *may* have come up with a solution."

"What sort of solution?" Maigwair asked intently.

"Well, a lot will depend on trying it out experimentally, but the bore pressure's going to peak heavily at the moment the powder charge detonates, then drop rapidly as the shell moves up the barrel. That means the greatest pressures will be at the breech, where they've always been, but even higher. What we've done with the current guns is simply to increase the thickness of the barrel walls, but that would be self-defeating in terms of weight and mobility if pressures go as high as I'm afraid they will. For that matter, the thicker a barrel wall gets, the more proportionately brittle it becomes. Given that, our thought is that we might cast and rifle the iron barrel using the techniques we've largely perfected for the smoothbore guns, then fit a band of wrought iron around the breech. If we heat the band red hot to expand it, then force it over the breech and cool it with a spray of cold water, it will effectively weld itself to the gun as the hot metal shrinks. That would reinforce the most vulnerable portion of the gun with the more . . . flexible strength of the wrought iron."

"It'll still be more expensive—and take more time—than to simply rely on cast iron by itself?"

"Yes, Your Grace, it will. Quite a bit, in fact, although it would cost far less than to try producing the entire gun out of wrought iron, which would be our other option. But iron guns strong enough to fire rifled shells to the ranges we clearly need would be massive, very heavy weapons. Far heavier than our current field guns. If the banded approach works, the pieces would be much lighter—not as light as our present guns, but far, far lighter than if they were made solely out of iron."

"I see." Maigwair inhaled deeply. "In that case, by all means, proceed with your experiments as quickly as possible."

"Of course, Your Grace."

Fultyn made a note on his pad and flipped to the next page. He gazed at his own handwriting for a moment, then cleared his throat.

"And that, Your Grace, brings us to the heretics' 'priming caps,' I'm afraid."

Maigwair smiled thinly at the other man's suddenly

more tentative tone. Production circles, shell design, banded artillery—none of those things required any innovations treading too closely upon the Proscriptions. The heretics' priming caps were another matter.

"Yes?" he responded as encouragingly as he could.

"I believe Lieutenant Zhwaigair's correct about that, too," Fultyn said. "My examination of the caps Bishop Militant Cahnyr captured on the Daivyn confirms that the heretics are using fulminated mercury. What they appear to have done is form the cap, insert a bit of fulminated mercury into the cup, then seal it with simple varnish. I'm not a Pasqualate or a Schuelerite, so I can't say whether or not this constitutes an actual violation of Pasquale's Law or the Proscriptions, but I imagine it must at least . . . press closely on Pasquale's Law, Your Grace. Its tactical advantages are obvious, but without a special dispensation. . . ."

"I see." Maigwair leaned back in his chair as Fultyn let his voice trail off. He'd been afraid he was going to hear exactly that.

"There are some countervailing considerations, Your Grace," Fultyn continued after a moment. "For one thing, I don't have any reliable estimates for the man-hours involved in producing them. And, of course, a rifle fitted to use them couldn't be primed with loose powder if the supply of caps ran out."

Maigwair nodded, although he strongly suspected Fultyn was presenting arguments which would take the onus for pushing the introduction of similar caps off his shoulders. Making it clear he'd considered the arguments against just as carefully as he had the arguments for and that, as a dutiful son of Mother Church, he would defer to the final judgment of his ecclesiastic superiors.

Well, you knew he was a smart fellow, Allayn, didn't you?

"We need to find out how to make them and determine what would be required to produce them in quantity," he said after a moment. "The apparent increase in reliability's simply too great for us not to at least consider acquiring. At the same time, I suspect the Grand Inquisitor may be . . . hesitant about extending any dispensations in this regard beyond the manufactories under Mother Church's direct control." *Assuming he's willing to grant one even there, of course!* he thought, meeting Fultyn's eyes levelly until the other man nodded ever so slightly. "So I think what we need to consider is modifying this new breech-loading design to use primer caps and building it here and in the other Temple Lands manufactories. Assuming the Inquisition determines that the new caps don't violate the Proscriptions—or that a *general* dispensation can be granted in view of the necessities of the Jihad—I'd like to convert all our rifles to that system in the fullness of time. For right now, it seems to me, we ought to concentrate on producing enough breechloaders to equip a company or two in each infantry regiment. That would provide our divisional commanders with a force capable of skirmishing toe-to-toe with the heretics, backed up by the conventional muzzleloaders."

"Of course, Your Grace," Fultyn agreed, and Maigwair nodded yet again.

I know how much Zhaspahr hates granting "dispensations" that weren't his idea to begin with, he reflected grimly. *But if he wants to win this Jihad—and survive—he'd damned well better find it in his heart to let Lynkyn and me give our men the weapons they need to survive.*

▼ ▼ ▼

"Well *that's* irritating," Nahrmahn Baytz murmured balefully.

The portly little prince sat in the electronic analogue of his Eraystor palace library, rather than on his balcony, and his expression was less than delighted. St. Kylmahn's was far enough from the Temple itself for the SNARCs to observe with impunity, and he'd been keeping an eye on Brother Lynkyn for quite some time. He'd realized long ago that Fultyn had a dangerously capable brain. Back in the days when he'd been an independent prince involved in the Great Game the decision to have him—and his assistant, Bryairs—assassinated would have made itself. But, like Lieutenant Zhwaigair in Dohlar, they were doing exactly what Nimue Alban needed them to do. *Merlin Athrawes'* priorities might have become a bit more complicated, but there wasn't much question about Nimue's, and from her perspective, Fultyn, Bryairs, and Zhwaigair were pearls beyond price. They were stretching their minds, learning to think critically and innovatively, and pushing the envelope of allowable technology. And the very qualities which made them so dangerous to the Empire of Charis also made them weapons which must ultimately turn in Zhaspahr Clyntahn's hand.

I could wish they were just a little less capable while they were about it, though, Nahrmahn thought dourly. *For that matter, I wish* Duchairn *were a little less capable! If he and Maigwair get away with it—and I think they will—they're actually going to turn the Harchongese Army into an effective fighting force, and that's the* last *thing we need. Aside from* this *damned thing, anyway.*

He scowled at the neat technical drawing Owl had provided. It really was an ingenious design, he thought— one that virtually duplicated what had once been called a "Ferguson Rifle" back on Old Earth. Actually, Zhwaigair's design, especially as modified by Fultyn, was superior to Ferguson's in some ways. It was heavier and longer, but it also avoided the weakness in the wrist of the stock which had been part of Ferguson's original design and the longer barrel and conical bullet would improve its ballistics. The breech screw was a multi-start thread design, like Ferguson's, but with ten threads per inch instead of Ferguson's twelve, and Fultyn's decision to make it from brass instead of iron or steel would make good use of the bronze smelting capacity which would be useless for the production of rifled artillery. And Fultyn had put his finger unerringly on an advantage Ferguson hadn't had. When the British officer had developed his weapon, the breech plug's design—essential to the rifle's effectiveness—had precluded any chance of putting it into general service, despite its enormous tactical advantages. The combined gunsmiths of eighteenth-century England would have been hard put to manufacture as many as a thousand multi-start screws to acceptable tolerances in an entire year, which made it impossible to build the weapon in sufficient numbers.

Safehold, unfortunately, had certain advantages England had lacked. It couldn't produce the screws to standardized dimensions in widely separated locations, but with the addition of a few specialists in plumbing to Bryairs' circles, they could produce them in much higher numbers than Zhwaigair had estimated. No single manufactory's screws would be interchangeable with any other's, but that was already true for the parts of their muzzle-loading rifles. The manufacture of the screws would drive up expense, but Nahrmahn and Owl had even better figures on the Church's production numbers than the Church did, and even Fultyn's man-hour estimates were overly pessimistic.

If he had to be this inventive, why couldn't he at least have gone with a single-*start screw?* Nahrmahn groused. *Surely he could've justified it on the basis that it would be simpler and cheaper to manufacture!*

And it would also have required ten complete revolutions to disengage a plug with uninterrupted threads. The multi-start screw required only a single partial turn of the trigger guard to which it was attached, which would speed the rate of fire considerably. And the breaks in the threads would actually help clear them of fouling; the built-up powder would be scraped off and fall through the openings each time the plug was locked up to fire. Without that, the fouling from the black powder would quickly "varnish" the screw to an extent which would make it difficult or even impossible to operate without a thorough cleaning.

It remained to be seen how well the weapon would work in action, but according to Owl's research, the original Ferguson had been capable of six to ten aimed shots per minute . . . with a flintlock. It had also been capable of up to sixty shots between cleanings, which compared favorably with any existing Safeholdian muzzle-loader. If Clyntahn was willing to allow the Army of God to use primer caps, it ought to be able to reach the higher end of that rate of fire. And, of course, since the innovative bastard had specified a *top*-opening breech, it would be almost as easy to load from a prone position as a Mahndrayn.

The more he thought about it, the more attractive assassins seemed, but he pushed the temptation firmly aside. It *was* what they needed if they truly meant to break the Proscriptions' grip on Safehold, after all.

Besides, the pains-in-the-arse have already spread drawings all over the damned Temple Lands. We'd need an army of assassins to deal with everyone who's seen it, and I doubt even Aivah has that many available!

He sighed and shook his head, then grinned suddenly.

It's not really funny, I guess, but it's comforting to know even Merlin can make mistakes. He and Ehdwyrd were so pleased when Mahndrayn came up with a design that would be just outside the Mainland's capabilities. One it would take them at least a year and a half to put into production because first they'd have to develop the machine tools and processes. Now the clever little protégé he wouldn't let me assassinate's come up with a design that's at least as effective and they can start producing the damned thing inside a month!

He sat back and tossed the technical drawing onto the tabletop with a chuckle.

It was almost worth finding out what Zhwaigair and Fultyn had come up with if only because of how he was looking forward to Merlin's expression when he and Owl told *him* about it.

"Well, it only took three five-days longer than it should have," Sir Rainos Ahlverez growled. He made it a habit to be careful about the audience to whom he displayed his disgust. At the moment, that audience consisted solely of Captain Lattymyr and Colonel Makyntyr, however. He trusted their discretion. Besides, they were probably even more disgusted with their "allies" than he was.

No, he told himself. *They can't possibly be* more *disgusted with those arseholes than I am. They're probably as disgusted, though*.

That might not be the best attitude for an army commander marching off to war shoulder-to-shoulder with his allies in the sacred cause of Mother Church and God Himself. It was, unfortunately, the one with which he was stuck.

"Three five-days might be a little severe, Sir." Makyntyr frowned judiciously. "I don't think it took them much more than *two* five-days more than it would've taken us from the time the order was given."

"Probably not," Ahlverez growled back. "But the bastard *ought* to've given the order at least one damned five-day earlier than he did instead of getting almost six thousand men killed or wounded for nothing."

"Now there, Sir, you have a point," the artillerist, whose relationship with his own general had improved considerably since the assault, acknowledged.

The three of them sat their horses on the crest of a low hill watching the enormous column get under way. Solid regiments of Desnairian cavalry led the way, of course. How could it have been otherwise? Certainly no reasonable person would suggest *Dohlaran* cavalry might be as well suited to that duty! The very thought was preposterous. And, equally of course, it only made sense to keep the components of each portion of the Army of Shiloh brigaded together, given the differences in their supply systems and organization. It was purely a coincidence that that happened to put virtually all of what had been the Army of Justice on the road in front of Ahlverez' troops.

Just as it was purely coincidental that Harless had chosen Sir Fahstyr Rychtyr to command the detachment being left behind to keep Thesmar invested. The Desnairian duke had been careful to allude to Rychtyr's greater experience against the heretics, but there was no doubt in Ahlverez' mind—or of the rest of his army, for that matter—that the duke's real reasoning was somewhat different. Obviously, anyone who'd allowed himself to be besieged by an inferior force was sadly lacking in aggressiveness and determination. Best to leave him behind where he could sit in the sort of fortified position he apparently preferred. Apparently not even the casualties *he'd* taken trying to storm a fortified heretic position were enough to change Harless' opinion in that regard.

Well, at least Harless' prejudices mean we've got somebody competent covering the canalhead at Trevyr, Ahlverez reflected grimly. *That means our supply line back to Dohlar should be intact. And that we get an extra day in camp while we wait for him to get the Shanwei out of our way.*

"I wish to Chihiro *we* were leading the march, Sir." Captain Lattymyr kept his voice low, as if he were afraid they might be overheard even on their isolated hilltop.

"Come now, Lynkyn!" Makyntyr said. "Surely you must acknowledge that the sheer striking power and splendid martial ardor of our vanguard must sweep all opposition aside!"

Ahlverez' lips twitched, although he knew he should step on his subordinates' scorn for their allies. Fortunately, both Makyntyr and Lattymyr were smart enough not to show it—openly, at least—in front of anyone else.

"Actually, Sir, I wasn't thinking in terms of combat

power," Lattymyr replied. "I was thinking in terms of speed."

Makyntyr's sardonic expression turned sober, and Ahlverez nodded.

"I was thinking the same thing. Their quartermasters ought to be shot, assuming the court-martial didn't decide on something more lingering." He grimaced. "For an army so in love with cavalry, they seem awfully short on wagons and draft animals."

"That's because they are." Makyntyr shrugged disgustedly. "To be honest, I think they expected all along to forage on the countryside, whatever they may say now. Mind you, I would've thought the reports about what was happening in the Republic might have suggested even to them that forage would be hard to come by. That's what they suggested to *us*, anyway. On the other hand, they did start later than we did, and the South March climate means there should be grass, at least, pretty much year-round. And to be fair—much as the thought of being fair pains me just at the moment, you understand—they've got a lot more cavalry than we do, and horses eat a lot. They would've needed a lot more wagons to haul enough fodder."

"Then they should've brought them," Ahlverez said flatly.

"I think Duke Harless has begun to figure that out, Sir." Lattymyr managed, Ahlverez noted, to leave out the word "even" immediately before Harless' title, and he hadn't tacked "at last" onto the end, either, but his audience heard both of them anyway. "Sir Borys certainly has, at any rate. According to Lieutenant Kahsimahr, there's not a lot he can do about it at this point, though."

Ahlverez looked at the captain and raised one eyebrow. Sir Laimyn Kahsimahr, the youngest son of the Duke of Sherach, was assigned to the staff of Sir Borys Cahstnyr, the Army of Justice's quartermaster. In fact, as nearly as Ahlverez could determine, Kahsimahr *was* Cahstnyr's staff. Although the youngster—he was only in his middle twenties—seemed both energetic and intelligent, he was rather in the position of a man trying to bail out Gorath Bay with a teaspoon.

Cahstnyr was over seventy, and owed his position to the fact that he was the brother of the Duke of Sherkal, who'd been prevented from lending his own talents to the Army of Justice because he was even older than Sir Borys. Cahstnyr seemed a decent enough type who took his duties seriously. Unfortunately, he clearly had very little idea of how to *discharge* those duties. The size (or absence) of his staff and the appointment of someone as manifestly unequal to the task as he was himself only underscored the Desnairians' casual attitude toward the task of keeping an army in the field supplied. Logistic incompetence had contributed more than a little to how roughly the Siddarmarkian Army had handled them in the past, and it was a pity they hadn't taken that lesson to heart.

What made it even more infuriating was that Mother Church had taken over responsibility for moving supplies in the Desnairians' rear areas. Traffic moved almost as smoothly and efficiently along the canals and high roads from Desnair to the Army of Shiloh's position before Thesmar as it did from Dohlar. And that, unfortunately, simply meant that a veritable mountain of Desnairian supplies was accumulating at that point, since the Duke of Traykhos had graciously declined Vicar Rhobair's offer to assist the Imperial Desnairian Army's efforts to keep itself fed in the field. Why he'd done that was more than Sir Rainos Ahlverez could divine, although he was willing to grant the possibility that Traykhos actually believed the Army of Justice was equal to the task. He couldn't imagine what might have convinced Traykhos of that, however.

Be fair. Their supply arrangements could be still worse. Just think about the Harchongians! For that matter, our quartermaster corps was a disaster waiting to happen before we reorganized it, and you damned well know it. Just like you know you're damned lucky you have Tymplahr himself running it for you. Especially after you tried so hard to avoid him!

He frowned. That wasn't one of his happier memories, but it was one he made himself reflect upon every so often, just as he made himself revisit his original attitude towards Makyntyr. Sir Shulmyn Rahdgyrz, the Baron of Tymplahr, had been intimately involved in building up the pre-Jihad Navy as part of King Rahnyld's effort to control the Gulf of Dohlar. In fact, he'd been both knighted and raised to the nobility for his services to the Crown . . . and to the Navy. He was able, unusually honest, and a fervent son of Mother Church, and those three qualities explained why the Duke of Fern had chosen him to organize the Army's supply system in cooperation with Vicar Rhobair's advisers. The fact that he'd worked so closely and enthusiastically with Earl Thirsk in his efforts to rebuild the Navy—and that he and Thirsk were close friends—explained why Ahlverez had tried to decline his services.

He'd done a remarkably good job, and when the Army had been ordered into the field, he'd volunteered (successfully, despite Ahlverez' quiet opposition) to command the quartermasters he'd trained. The fact that he'd been made a general, with two full colonels as his immediate subordinates, said volumes about the differences between Desnairian and Dohlaran attitudes when it came to keeping their men fed and supplied. Ahlverez had come to realize, even before uniting with the Army of Justice, that the failure of his effort to decline Tymplahr's services had been one of the more fortunate things ever to happen to him. Since coming under Harless' command and seeing the Desnairian arrangements, he'd spent more than one night in prayerful thanks to the Archangels for proving how much wiser than him they were.

"And just what did young Kahsimahr have to say about it?" he asked Lattymyr after a moment.

"Well, he didn't want to be openly critical of Duke Harless or Sir Borys, of course, Sir. But from the questions he was asking, what he'd really like would be to overhaul their existing arrangements into something more like ours. There aren't enough dragons or wagons for them to do that, though, and even if there were, they don't have the drovers or the organizational structure to support it. From a couple of the things he said—and even more from things he *didn't* say, to be honest—Sir Borys is already tearing his hair out over the situation, and he's given Laimyn—I mean Lieutenant Kahsimahr—a lot of extra authority to try to straighten out the situation."

"Authority?" Makyntyr snorted. "How much 'authority' can a lieutenant have, Lynkyn?"

"A bit less than a captain, Sir," Lattymyr replied with a smile, and Ahlverez chuckled. "Seriously," his aide went on, smile fading, "I happened to overhear him ripping a strip off a colonel day before yesterday."

"A colonel?" Makyntyr repeated, eyebrows rising.

"Yes, Sir. One of Earl Hennet's regimental commanders." The captain shrugged. "Laimyn chewed him up one side and down the other—respectfully, of course—over something to do with transporting the officers' personal baggage in the quartermaster's wagons. I don't think he was in favor of the idea."

His superiors laughed, despite themselves, and Lattymyr shrugged.

"What may be even more important, the colonel *took* it, Sir Rainos, and I doubt he would've if he hadn't expected Hennet or Harless to support Laimyn if he pushed it. That's one of the reasons I think they're genuinely doing their best. It's just that the hole's so deep they can barely see daylight looking straight up at midday."

Ahlverez found it remarkably easy to stop laughing as he contemplated the accuracy of his aide's last comment.

Where the Royal Dohlaran Army assigned individual dragon-drawn wagons to each of its regiments, the Imperial Desnairian Army relied upon a centralized transport pool. Each Dohlaran regiment's wagon moved with its regiment, whether on the road or in the field. As it was depleted, it returned to the main transport column moving down the canals or along the roads behind the rest of the army. If there was time, it was reloaded and sent back to rejoin its assigned regiment. If there was insufficient time for that, its drovers simply exchanged it for a fully loaded wagon and hurried back.

The size and weight of the articulated wagon a dragon could draw—twenty or thirty tons, in anything like reasonable going—allowed the army to move smoothly, confident its supplies would keep up with it. That wasn't to say that even a Dohlaran army moved at anything much above a walk once it was forced to abandon the speed and efficiency of the canals, but it did move at a *steady* walk, with a ten-minute rest stop each hour. And if a unit was forced to halt for some reason, it simply moved off the road to be bypassed by the rest of the army without anyone finding himself suddenly out of supply and starving.

The Desnairians had nowhere near that flexibility. They had sufficient carrying capacity for their army's ammunition and food, but there was no way they could possibly transport sufficient fodder for over a hundred thousand cavalry mounts, half that many again remounts, meat animals, *and* their draft animals. They simply didn't have enough wagons for that, and the ones they did have formed a column of their own, moving at the rear of their entire vast force. The cavalry could at least find grass to graze their horses and the quartermaster could graze the accompanying cattle, and it was late enough in the year that any volunteer crops which had sprung up untended by the vanished farmers at the scores of abandoned farms could be scooped up, as well . . . assuming they hadn't yet rotted in the fields, at least. That meant they probably *could* forage for the fodder and grazing they required, but sending out foraging parties— and stopping to graze—could only slow their rate of advance. And then there was the problem that the South March Lands had been so sparsely populated. It was over eight hundred miles from Thesmar to Fort Tairys, their objective, the last two hundred on little better than country lanes and farm tracks. The high road, built to the *Writ*'s standards, offered good, hard going as far as the town of Kharmych, but without the network of secondary roads found in more populous provinces. That meant the entire Army of Shiloh had to move along the same highway like some huge, lurching serpent.

Left to its own devices, with its well-organized supply train and wagonloads of fodder, Ahlverez' army could have made fifty miles a day along that high road and over twenty miles per day even cross-country. Unfortunately, his army was trapped behind the *Duke of Harless'* army, which would do extraordinarily well to make twenty miles a day even with the high road, given the need to send out those foraging parties and stop to graze its horses. Its cavalry and infantry regiments alone would have formed a seventeen-mile column. By the time artillery, supply wagons, remounts, livestock, the inevitable camp followers, and the personal servants required by all those aristocratic officers were added, it was the next best thing to *twenty*-seven, even with the herds of meat animals and remounts spread off the road as much as possible.

Which means, given how damned slow we're going to move, that Harless' rearguard units will end up every night seven miles west of where his vanguard bivouacked the night before. And that we might as well sit on our arses here at Thesmar for a solid five-day before we set out to overtake them.

They weren't going to do that, of course. It would have underscored their allies' sluggishness, which might've been taken as a deliberate insult. So, instead, they'd set out around midday tomorrow, by which time the rear of Harless' army might actually be out of sight from the heretics' entrenchments.

"You're probably right, Lynkyn," he said finally. "I'm sure they *are* doing the best they can. And the truth is, we ought to be helping them any way we can. I tried to suggest that to Duke Harless, but—"

He chopped himself off before he suggested that Harless seemed more focused on protecting the honor of the Imperial Desnairian Army by insisting it could meet its own needs than on finding the help he clearly needed. And that young snot Fyrnach hadn't helped one bit. Whatever Harless might think about Desnairian honor, his grandnephew's attitude was perfectly clear, and despite his relatively junior rank he was in a position to do plenty of damage simply by manipulating the duke's schedule or selectively choosing which reports to draw to his attention.

"We'll just have to do the best we can," he said instead, eyes back on that enormous column as it lurched away from Thesmar. "And if the time comes that the Duke calls on us to assist Sir Borys and young Kahsimahr, we need to be ready to do what we can. Remind me to discuss that with Sir Shulmyn this afternoon, Lynkyn."

"Of course, Sir."

.UI.
St. Bahzlyr Canal,
Tarikah River,
Tarikah Province,
Republic of Siddarmark

"Well, *this* is a Shan-wei-damned mess." Sygmahn Dahglys glowered out over the racing water, then gave himself a shake and looked over his shoulder at Father Avry Pygain. "Sorry about that, Father."

"I've heard worse, Master Dahglys."

The brown-haired, brown-eyed Chihirite upper-priest had extraordinarily long arms and legs for his height. He looked rather like a stork when he walked, Dahglys thought, and he had a fussy clerk's way about him. That was reasonable enough for someone who belonged to the Order of the Quill, though—they *were* clerks and scribes—and however fussy he might be, he was sharp and efficient when it came to discharging his duties as Archbishop Arthyn Zagyrsk's secretary.

"As a matter of fact, I've heard a *lot* worse over the last year or so," Father Avry sighed. "And for a lot less cause than this."

"It'll be a right bastard setting this right, begging your pardon, Father," Sairahs Mahkgrudyr agreed. The fair-haired Canal Service pilot spat into the water in obvious disgust, ice-blue eyes bleak and hard with the hatred of a man who'd spent thirty-five years piloting barges along the thousands of miles of canal the *Holy Writ* required men to maintain and *preserve*, not wantonly destroy.

"They knew what they were doing, right enough," Wyllym Bohlyr put in through the teeth clenched on the stem of his pipe. "Saw that clear enough in Fairkyn, and now this." He shook his head. "Knew exactly where to put the charges, didn't they just?"

The silver-haired Fairkyn lockmaster—who no longer had any locks to run, thanks to the same batch of heretics—had a point, Dahglys reflected, studying the damage with the eye of a trained engineer.

The broad, brown water-filled ditch running in front of them, its surface lashed with yellow ribbons of foam, had once been the St. Bahzlyr Canal, a four-mile stretch of the Tarikah River canal system. It had cut across a meandering eleven-mile loop of the river, reducing any barge's journey by over six miles and simultaneously avoiding three sets of shallows, each of which would have required their own locks for anything much larger than a rowboat. Unlike most of the canals in the Temple Lands, where the walls and floor were poured concrete, or the newer canals farther south here in Siddarmark, where kiln-fired brick was often used, the St. Bahzlyr's walls were native stone, shaped by hand, squared, and laid up with mortar. Because the river level dropped almost forty feet between the St. Bahzlyr's upper and lower ends, it required a set of locks at each of those ends, and the heretics had blown both of them into kindling. The splintered remnants of the upper lock's stout nearoak timbers still hung from the gate frame, tracing lines of foam in the water racing through the broken lock chamber. Charges had also been set in the walls of the chamber itself, ripping them apart and spilling shattered stone and mortar into the water. And, not content with that, the heretics had planted additional charges at three separate spots along the St. Bahzlyr's length, caving in the walls at each of them.

The water roaring unfettered through the canal cut had done the rest.

"It's the scour that makes most of the problem," he said. "With the gates gone and the stonework blown to Shan-wei's hell the current just ripped everything apart. And the head of water behind the weir only made it worse. I'm half afraid we'll have to open a breach in the weir to relieve the pressure before we can get the canal properly cofferdammed."

He looked away from the ruined lock chamber at the sturdy stone weir stretching across the Tarikah. Before the heretics destroyed the St. Bahzlyr, the crest of the weir had been a smother of white and brown water, pouring over the top of the ten-foot structure. Its primary function had been to raise the water level behind it, impounding what amounted to a lake almost five miles long, to ensure sufficient water to supply the heavily used canal, especially during periods of low water. Admittedly, the outflow from East Wing Lake meant low water was a rare occurrence along this stretch, but it did happen. Even if that hadn't been true, the drop between this point and the canal's lower locks required the extra water, particularly during harvest season when barges passed through it virtually end-to-end, each carrying its own charge of water down the canal. In addition, the weir supplied sluices on the south bank of the river which had powered the waterwheels of more than half a dozen grist mills and manufactories.

The grist mills and manufactories were charred wreckage now, courtesy of the heretics, and the water flow across the weir's crest was a shadow of what it ought to have been. Even with the spillways wide open, though, enough water had been forced through the St. Bahzlyr to shred its walls once the stonework's integrity had been violated. Worse, it was *still* shredding them. The current was like a monster prybar, levering the individual stones out of the mortar and then gouging at the ballast and earth behind them.

"Whether we break the weir or not, the first step's closing off the upper end," Dahglys said, planting his hands on his hips and glowering at the river some more. "And it's going to take time, and it's going to take manpower, and we don't have enough of either of them to get it done before snowfall."

His companions looked at one another silently as someone finally said what they'd all known from the instant they set eyes on the problem. Unfortunately, their orders were to repair the canal before winter closed down operations, and those orders carried the Grand Inquisitor's own imprimatur.

"Father Tailahr will be shipping us the prefabricated timbers for the lock chambers within the next five-day or so," Dahglys continued. "The chamber's—both sets of chambers have—been so thoroughly washed out, though, that it'll take at least three or four five-days just to clear the wreckage, square the walls, and set footings for the timbers. We'll still have to hang the new gates, replace the windlasses and the valves, install the planking, and ballast it all right and tight. And that doesn't even consider the fact that we've got to rebuild at least three miles of canal wall between here and the lower locks." He shook his head and looked at Pygain. "I can get the materials we need, I think, Father, but I just don't have the manpower."

"There's never been enough local manpower to maintain the canals in Tarikah and Icewind," Mahkgrudyr said with a sigh. "We've had to ship in work crews from the east every spring."

"Not an option this year, Sairahs, I'm afraid," Bohlyr replied around his pipe, his expression grim, and Dahglys nodded.

"I can bring in some labor from the Border States," the engineer said, "but not enough. And not quickly enough to get this done on schedule."

He and his companions looked at one another again.

None of them cared to suggest that disappointing the Grand Inquisitor would be a very bad idea.

"Is there any way you and Archbishop Arthyn can help us out, Father?" the engineer asked finally, and Pygain's face tightened.

"I'd be surprised if Tarikah's present population is even thirty percent of what it was last fall," he said very carefully and precisely. "We've consolidated as many as possible of the surviving people into the bigger towns and villages, and we managed to get seed into the ground. We've been blessed by the weather this summer, and it looks as if the harvest will be good where we were able to plant, but we need the men and women in the fields to gather it. If we don't, they'll starve this winter the way so many did *last* winter."

"I'm afraid that's part of the problem everywhere," Dahglys sighed. "Not to the same extent it is here, of course." His nostrils flared as he recalled the deserted farms, the empty villages, the unplanted fields and empty pastures—too often dotted with the bleached bones of livestock—he'd passed on his journey from the Temple Lands. "Our labor needs are in competition with the mines and the manufactories arming the Army of God, and all of it's happening just at the moment we're coming up on the farmers' busiest season. But the fact remains. Without enough manpower from *somewhere*, there's no point even starting before spring. And if we can't get it finished before the spring floods, it'll be the end of April or even May before we get done."

The silence turned harder and colder. Every one of them knew the Army of the Sylmahn's very existence depended on repairing the damage. Winter would close the canals down by early November, whatever happened, and no one liked to think about the privations Bishop Militant Bahrnabai's men would endure once the snow began to fly. At the moment, long lines of dragon-drawn wagons were managing to keep the Army of the Sylmahn supplied, but it was a near thing even in summer and early fall. When the high roads were covered in ice and snow, when the southern hill dragons had to be withdrawn to a climate they could survive, the bishop militant's supply line would turn into a thin, badly frayed supply *thread*, and it was virtually inevitable that the heretics would do everything they could to make his situation still worse.

"There *might* be a way," Pygain said finally.

His normally warm eyes had darkened, and his expression was grim. His companions looked at him warily, and he grimaced.

"I could speak to Father Zherohm," he said, his tone manifestly unhappy, and Dahglys' jaw tightened.

Father Zherohm Clymyns was a Schuelerite upperpriest attached to Bishop Wylbyr Edwyrds' staff, and Edwyrds was the Inquisitor General for Icewind, New Northland, Mountaincross, Hildermoss, and Westmarch. That made him the man charged with sifting those accused of heresy and apostasy . . . and sending them to the Punishment of Schueler if they were adjudged guilty.

And so far, very, very few of them had been adjudged anything else.

Clymyns was one of Edwyrds' special Inquisitors, responsible for ferreting out those who'd managed—so far, at least—to conceal their heretical leanings. Judging by the number of "secret heretics" he'd hauled before the Inquisition, he was very good at his job, too. And, Dahglys knew, he was also one of the Schuelerites who believed a heretic should make recompense in this world before he was sent to the hellfire and torment he'd earned in the next. He'd been arguing for some time that those confined in the Inquisition's concentration camps might be profitably used as forced labor. It wasn't as if someone who'd turned his or her face against God and the Archangels had any legal rights, and there'd be time enough to put them to the Punishment after Mother Church had required them to help repair and rebuild all that had been destroyed in the Jihad their heresy had loosed upon the world.

Dahglys understood the argument, but nausea rippled at the thought of employing what amounted to slave laborers already condemned to death. He had a strong suspicion the Inquisition would insist on providing overseers, and the methods they were likely to employ would be brutal and pitiless. Indeed, Clymyns had scarcely even attempted to veil his belief that they might as well be worked to death, for what did it matter what happened to the bodies of those already condemned to burn in hell for all eternity? Surely there was no need to waste food or warm clothing, medical care or weather-tight housing, on those who had willfully made themselves the enemies of God Himself?

Sygmahn Dahglys was a loyal son of Mother Church. He loved God and the Archangels, he revered their teachings, and he was dedicated heart and soul to the defeat of the heresy. But the thought of being part of what someone like Clymyns would make of those laborers' lives was enough to sicken anyone.

The Book of Schueler required they be put to the Punishment. That was harsh, even cruel, but it was clearly God's command, and the Inquisition taught that its purpose was not simply to punish sin but to attempt to reclaim the sinner even from the lip of the grave. Dahglys was horrified that anyone should set his own will against God's and condemn himself to such a penalty, yet the *Writ* was clear and unflinching. No loyal son of the Church could deny that it must be done.

But if that was true, then let it be done swiftly. Let Mother Church and the Inquisition show the condemned at least that much mercy. There was no need to turn the time they had left into a thing of horror. No need for men who served God to lower themselves to the level of Shanwei and those who served *her*.

And who's going to be the first to tell Clymyns or Archbishop Wyllym that, Sygmahn? Are you? Are you going to set your will in opposition to the Inquisitor General and the Grand Inquisitor himself? Are you going to question the measures required, however terrible they may seem, if the Jihad's going to be won? And will you let your own queasiness prevent you from putting this canal back into operation when it must *be put back*

*into operation if the Army of the Sylmahn's going to
hold against the legions of hell?*

"How many men could Father Zherohm provide?"
he heard his own voice ask.

"I'm not certain," Pygain admitted. "At the moment,
there are somewhere around twenty thousand in the
camp at Traymos. That's the closest one."

Dahglys nodded slowly. Traymos was on the southern
shore of Cat Lizard Lake, a hundred miles from the St.
Bahzlyr, but the . . . workers could be transported almost all of that distance by water. Of course, a third of
those twenty thousand were almost certainly children,
or too young—or too old—to stand up to the demands
of the task, at any rate. But even so. . . .

"We'd have to feed and house them."

"I'll speak to His Eminence." Pygain's expression
turned even tighter, if that were possible. "I'm sure he'll
insist on providing the best living conditions he can for
those assigned to the task."

*So Archbishop Arthyn isn't an admirer of Father
Zherohm?* Dahglys kept his own expression as neutral
as possible. *I suppose that's good to know. At least it's a
way to salve your conscience, isn't it, Sygmahn? You can
tell yourself they'll actually be better off working for you
than in one of the Inquisition's camps. Shan-wei! It'll
probably even be* true, *and isn't that a hell of a thing?*

"All right, Father," he sighed. "You'd better go ahead
and inquire into the possibilities. And while you're doing that, I'll send a semaphore message back to Zion
and ask Father Tailahr to expedite those materials."

. VII .
Greentown,
Traylmyn's Farm,
and Maiyam,
Midhold Province,
and Guarnak,
Mountaincross Province,
Republic of Siddarmark

"Slow down. Slow down, man!" Colonel Walkyr Tyrnyr snapped. "You're not making any sense. Or if you are, you're going so damned fast *I* can't tell it!"

Tyrnyr, the commanding officer of the Army of God's 16th Cavalry Regiment, wasn't a naturally choleric man, but he sounded undeniably testy at the moment, and who should blame him? Between the so-called militiaman's accent and how rapidly he was gabbling out his report he was practically incoherent—or incomprehensible, at least—and what he seemed to be saying was preposterous, anyway.

"They've taken Chestyrvyl." The militiaman drew a deep breath and forced himself to slow down, although Tyrnyr still found his rustic Siddarmarkian accent difficult. "I don't think more'n a dozen men got away, and they're sendin' a column from Chestyrvyl cross-country t' Charlzvyl. They're less'n thirty miles from Maiyam on th' canal, too, and they're Charisian regulars—you c'n tell from the uniforms! Must be forty or fifty thousand of 'em, Colonel!"

Tyrnyr glanced across the field desk at Major Ahrthyr Wyllyms, his second-in-command. Wyllyms looked as astonished as Tyrnyr felt. Which wasn't a great deal of help at the moment.

"They don't *have* forty thousand men," the colonel said, turning back to the militiaman. "The heretics never had more than thirty thousand Charisians in the Gap to begin with, and they're still in contact with our lines south of Wyvern Lake."

Unless, a small voice in the back of his brain said, *they've landed reinforcements at Siddar City and our spies just haven't told me yet. But speaking of telling us yet—*

"Why haven't we heard about this before they got so damned far along the canal? That's almost eight hundred miles from Wyvern Lake as the wyvern flies, and the heretics are no frigging wyverns! *Somebody* should've seen them and reported them before they got that far east of the Gap!"

"How should I know?" The militiaman sounded a little testy himself, the colonel noted. "Major Bryskoh got word from Colonel Tahlyvyr at Maiyam by boat up th' river and 'cross the lake. Colonel Cahstnyr's come in by semaphore. There's no semaphore line from Greentown t' here, so the Major sent me."

Tyrnyr grunted and raised one hand in a semi-placating gesture. He should have thought of that for himself. The fact that his brain was still trying to cope with the preposterousness of the fellow's news was no excuse. And the fact that the message was from Haimltahn Bryskoh suggested he ought to pay attention to it however preposterous it sounded, he thought.

Bryskoh, who commanded the 1st Greentown Militia, had no formal military training, but he wasn't a fool by any stretch of the imagination. A prosperous farmer and miller before the Rising, he'd become the leader of the Faithful in and around the small city of Greentown, where the Mountaincross River flowed into Grayback Lake from the north. His "militia" consisted almost entirely of civilian volunteers, like the fellow in front of him, but they'd had the better part of a year to acquire discipline, and unlike some of the bands fighting in Mother Church's name, they'd done just that. And they'd shown themselves ready to do their duty, however grim, without letting that discipline break down.

Lyndahr Tahlyvyr, commanding the Maiyam Militia,

was one of the rare Midhold Faithful's officers who could claim pre-Rising military experience, which was the main reason he'd been given the strategically important post he held. Unlike Bryskoh, he'd been a lieutenant in the Siddarmarkian regulars, and a relatively good one, as far as Tyrnyr could discover. That was the good news. The bad news was that he'd been in command of his understrength "regiment" for less than a month. It was composed of the same sort of volunteers as the 1st Greentown, but they were more poorly armed than Bryskoh's men and Tahlyvyr had been given little time to instill the sort of discipline that provided unit cohesion.

And then there was "Colonel" Brysyn Cahstnyr, commanding the 3rd Mountaincross Rangers at Charlzvyl and self-appointed to his present rank. Cahstnyr and his men—like too many of the "ranger" companies operating against the heretics in Midhold and Mountaincross, in Tyrnyr's private opinion—were no better than brigands themselves. He couldn't fault their fervor or their faith, or even their determination to drive out heresy and apostasy with fire and the sword, but they'd spent their time swooping down on isolated farms and small villages, identifying the heretics to be burned out and seeing to the necessary burning, rather than organizing or drilling as *military* units.

Walkyr Tyrnyr would shed no tears for heretics or their get. And if the victims of excesses by Cahstnyr's men or the other "ranger" companies weren't heretics, they ought to have made sure the Inquisition knew it before Cahstnyr and his ilk came calling. For that matter, the whole Republic had been one huge nest of heresy just waiting to happen, or the Grand Inquisitor would never have launched the Sword of Schueler. It was past time the entire source of corruption was burned out once and for all. But there was nothing in *The Book of Schueler* about raping and pillaging, and the brutal tactics of men like Cahstnyr contributed to the breakdown of discipline and military effectiveness. He wanted people like Cahstnyr as far away from his own command as possible, where their possibly . . . excessive enthusiasm for punishing the servants of Shan-wei was less likely to infect his cavalrymen.

Of course, the report also raised the question of what had happened to Major Kahlvyn Rydnauyr. His 5th Mountaincross Rangers—such as they were and what there was of them—were (or had been, at any rate) responsible for garrisoning what had once been Chestyrvyl at the extreme southern end of the lake. He and Cahstnyr were very much of a likeness. Tyrnyr would miss neither of them if something nasty truly had happened to them, and it sounded as if something had in Rydnauyr's case, at least. Still, the rangers knew the geography and terrain of eastern Mountaincross and southern Midhold better than anyone else, so just how had these Charisians, or whoever they were, managed to surprise even Rydnauyr so completely?

He frowned as he considered that, but what really mattered at the moment was that neither Bryskoh nor Tahlyvyr was likely to send off hysterical messages without first trying to be sure they knew what they were talking about. Cahstnyr was another matter, of course, and Bryskoh was simply relaying reports from him and Tahlyvyr. That was a pity, since of all three Faithful commanders, Bryskoh was the most levelheaded and possessed the best judgment. Tyrnyr would've been much more willing to believe the reports if they'd come from Bryskoh and one of the others had been the fellow simply passing them along.

Still, what Bryskoh's runner had said made sense. The main semaphore line followed the high road from Allyntyn to Charlzvyl, in the fork where the North Mountaincross and South Mountaincross Rivers met two hundred and thirty miles west of Grayback Lake. From there it went south to Braikstyn and then on to Siddar City, skirting around the lake, and Greentown was served by a secondary connection to the main line. The line south of Braikstyn had been burned by the Faithful in the early days of the Rising and not repaired, which had turned Charlzvyl into a stub at the far end of the semaphore chain and probably didn't do much for Cahstnyr's panicky sense of isolation at the moment.

Tyrnyr's own regiment was stationed southeast of Greentown, however, covering a line between that city and Maiyam, in the middle of farming country which had never been connected to the semaphore at all, which left him floating in space as far as the rapid transmission of information was concerned. Colonel Bairystyr, the CO of the 73rd Cavalry Regiment and the senior officer of the screen Bishop Militant Bahrnabai had thrown out southeast of the Kalgaran Mountains, had his headquarters almost directly on the semaphore line north of Greentown, so he was undoubtedly already in possession of Bryskoh's message. It was a pity that Tahlyvyr's boat to Greentown hadn't bothered to pass the message to Tyrnyr as it went past, but at least he had it now. And it was probable that Tahlyvyr *had* sent a courier overland to Colonel Bryntyn Pahlmair's 53rd Cavalry, northeast of Maiyam itself. It wouldn't do to make any assumptions in that regard, however.

"Find a courier," he told Major Wyllyms, still gazing down at the map. "Send him off to the Fifty-Third with all the information we currently have."

"Yes, Sir."

Well, that part was easy enough, Walkyr, the colonel told himself. *And what do you propose for your second move?*

He ran a fingertip along the line of cavalry pickets Bairystyr had established as per the bishop militant's orders. That line was almost three hundred miles long, which was a lot of ground to cover with less than a thousand men. Their function was to locate and identify any effort by the heretics' regular forces to move into Midhold and to assist Faithful units like the 1st Greentown and Maiyam Militia—and even Cahstnyr's rangers—as needed against the threat of heresy and Shan-wei worship. Bishop Militant Bahrnabai had never intended them to stop the advance of "forty or fifty thousand" Charisian regulars, but he did expect them to stop or to at least slow down and harry any smaller, lighter forces.

And he'd placed Bishop Zhaksyn Mahkhal's Port Harbor Division and Bishop Qwentyn Preskyt's St. Fraidyr Division at Allyntyn to deal with anything Bairystyr's cavalry couldn't. But Allyntyn, unfortunately, was three hundred and fifty miles as a wyvern might fly northeast of Greentown, scarcely in a position to support Tyrnyr and his cavalrymen at the moment.

He and his fellow cavalry commanders had been forced to split up their regiments into quick reaction forces. His headquarters were forty miles northwest—more north than west, really—of Maiyam, and he had two of his four companies with him. Captain Adym Zhadwail, commanding his first company, had the other two thirty miles farther to his own west, so that between them they could cover the ninety miles of the screening line which was the 16th Cavalry's responsibility. Bairystyr's 73rd had the ninety miles between his own position and the Kalgaran foothills, and Pahlmair's 53rd had the last ninety miles, beyond Maiyam. If he'd been Bairystyr, Tyrnyr would've put his own regiment in the center of the line, but considering how long it had taken Bryskoh's message to reach him here, perhaps Bairystyr had known what he was doing when he stationed himself so close to the main semaphore line.

None of which helped a great deal when it came to deciding what to do if the heretics were moving on Maiyam in force. Especially if they were already that close to the town. They could easily have already reached Maiyam—and destroyed Colonel Tahlyvyr's garrison—by the time the message reached him.

Well, assuming there really is a column advancing towards Charlzvyl, it's way too far away for me to do anything about it. Cahstnyr's just going to have to be Bairystyr's problem, and welcome to it. Greentown is my responsibility, according to orders, but Bryskoh ought to be safe enough for now. Even if they've actually taken Maiyam already, they'll have almost two hundred miles of river and lake to cross before they can threaten him directly, and that assumes Tahlyvyr didn't destroy the Maiyam Locks before they pushed him out of town. So the first move is obviously to concentrate my forces and find out what has—or hasn't—actually happened at Maiyam.

"All right, Ahrthyr." He looked back up at his executive officer. "When you send the message to Colonel Pahlmair, tell him we'll be taking Third and Fourth Companies to Maiyam. I suggest he concentrate his own regiment and join us at Traylmyn's Farm so we can proceed together."

Traylmyn's Farm had once been a small, relatively prosperous farming village. These days it was a clutter of charred ruins, but it made a convenient rendezvous point forty miles northeast of Maiyam on a farm road between the town and the Greentown High Road.

"After that, send a messenger to Zhadwail. Tell him to bring First and Second Companies to join us at Traylmyn's Farm as quickly as possible. Also send a courier to Major Bryskoh with a copy of our message to Pahlmair and my orders to Zhadwail. Instruct the Major to forward both of them to Colonel Bairystyr by semaphore. Also inform him that he needs to maintain a high alert against the possibility of heretics crossing the lake in canal barges in case they really have taken Maiyam and got the locks intact."

"At once, Sir!" Major Wyllyms slapped his breastplate in salute, then turned and left the tent quickly when Tyrnyr nodded to him. The colonel watched him go, before he turned back to Bryskoh's messenger.

"I suspect you know the tracks and trails around here better than I do. We'll find you a horse, and then I'd like you to guide my courier to Major Bryskoh and make sure the message gets there as quickly as possible."

"I c'n do that," the Siddarmarkian replied.

"Good." The colonel shook his head, looking back down at the map, trying to think of anyone else he should be sure was informed of his proposed movements. "I doubt this is going to turn out to be as bad as the initial messages suggest, but I'm not going to take any chances either. We'll find out what's really going on, then do a little something about it."

▼ ▼ ▼

"Do you think they've started to scurry around yet, Sir?" Lieutenant Slokym asked, gazing up the river towards Grayback Lake.

"Oh, I imagine they have," Baron Green Valley replied with a thin smile. In fact, he was watching the AOG's cavalry screen "scurry around" at that very moment, courtesy of the SNARCs. And very satisfying scurrying it was.

He stood on the docks reaching out into the broad, deep-flowing Mountaincross River above Maiyam. They'd managed to take the town remarkably intact, largely because Colonel Lyndahr Tahlyvyr's garrison had consisted of a single understrength "regiment" supported by the majority of Maiyam's adult—and semi-adult, unfortunately—male population. Casualties among the civilian defenders had been even heavier than among the militamen, and there was little Green Valley's healers could do for all too many of them. The screams of wounded, barely adolescent boys—and the torn, lifeless bodies of their brothers—were enough to turn anyone's stomach. On the other hand, Kynt Clarek had seen a lot of things fit to turn his stomach here in the Republic, and there was only one way anyone could bring those things to an end.

He'd like to blame Tahlyvyr for those broken, too-young bodies, but the decision hadn't been the colonel's. The orders had come from Father Bryntyn Ahdymsyn, the Schuelerite under-priest who'd been Maiyam's schoolmaster before the rebellion. It had been his demand that had sent those boys—many of them his own students—into battle, and the one point Green Valley could see in his favor was that at least he'd died leading them, fighting at their head with no better weapon than a sword he'd never been trained to use. Tahlyvyr had tried to argue with the priest, and he'd done his best to put the boys in the positions of least danger, however little good it had done in the end. He'd also realized Green Valley was coming before his men actually arrived. Not all of the Temple Loyalist commanders between Maiyam and the Sylmahn Gap had been equally alert.

Company A of the 1st Scout Sniper Regiment's 4th Battalion, mounted for the occasion on horses borrowed from the Siddarmarkian cavalry regiment attached to Green Valley's Charisians, had seized Chestyrvyl, at the southern terminus of the lake from the single company of Temple Loyalist guerrillas—the so-called 5th Mountaincross Rangers—squatting in the ruins of its burned buildings. The "rangers" had outnumbered Captain Rehgnyld Ahzbyrn's men by barely two to one and they'd never had a clue Ahzbyrn was coming until his men hit them. It had gone against the grain to let any of the scum who'd wreaked such havoc in Mountaincross and Midhold escape, but the scout sniper captain had obeyed orders, and almost a dozen of the four hundred rangers had gotten away.

Major Kahlvyn Rydnauyr, Chestyrvyl's commanding officer, had not been among them. Under the circumstances, and given Rydnauyr's practice of burning suspected heretics' houses with their owners still inside while his men used anyone who escaped through the boarded-up windows or doors for target practice, Green Valley had already decided not to ask exactly how it was that the major had ended up with a pistol ball behind his left ear. He did regret that Father Zefrym Shyllyr had escaped before he could receive the same treatment, however. Shyllyr had lacked even the excuse of being an Inquisitor, but the Langhornite under-priest had attached himself to Rydnauyr's command as its "chaplain," and whatever he'd lacked in formal ecclesiastic authority he'd more than made up in pure, vicious fanaticism. He'd actively encouraged Rydnauyr's atrocities, and Green Valley—acting upon unspecified "spy reports"—had formally designated him an "acting Inquisitor," subject to imperial policy where Inquisitors were concerned, before sending Company A off to Chestyrvyl. He'd really hoped Ahzbyrn would be able to enforce the policy in his case.

Well, you may catch up with him yet. For that matter, there's a better than even chance the son-of-a-bitch will manage to drown himself for you.

The thought gave the baron a certain satisfaction. Shyllyr was too terrified of the retribution he'd earned to even think about coming back ashore anywhere where the "heretic hordes" might get their hands on him, so he'd set out on the ninety-four-mile voyage from Chestyrvyl to Greentown across the longest portion of lake by himself in a rowboat.

Colonel Tahlyvyr was also dead, a fact which Green Valley came much closer to regretting. He'd been a Temple Loyalist, an extremist, a mutineer, and a traitor, but he'd at least tried to keep his militia regiment under discipline and under control. It was possible he might have attempted to surrender, but he hadn't had time for that. The Maiyam Locks connecting the Tairmana Canal to the Mountaincross River were a critical part of Green Valley's planning, and Zhaspahr Clyntahn had granted a blanket dispensation allowing the destruction of locks and canals when the Jihad's military necessity required it, despite the *Writ*'s prohibition of such actions. It still wasn't anything someone was going to undertake lightly, or when he wasn't pretty damned certain the Inquisition would agree it truly had been necessary, but thanks to the SNARCs, Green Valley had known Tahlyvyr planned to do exactly that. As a consequence, he'd ordered Brigadier Mylz to take the town—and especially the waterfront area—as quickly as possible, and Colonel Preskyt Tahnaiyr's 3rd Regiment had discharged the assignment with dispatch.

Tahnaiyr's 1st and 3rd Battalions had circled around to the river east of Maiyam under cover of darkness, then stormed the waterfront at the point of the bayonet. They'd lost sixty men in the attack, but their assault had been preceded by a brief, violent mortar bombardment, and they'd made liberal use of the newly improved hand grenades provided by the Delthak Works.

Black powder grenades were fairly anemic, and iron casings tended to fragment into a very few large, fairly low velocity pieces, which inflicted relatively few casualties and gave them a short radius of lethality. They'd proved a disappointment in the Corisande Campaign, but Ehdwyrd Howsmyn's artisans had taken up the challenge, and the new grenades used cylindrical, stick-mounted *tin* casings instead of iron. Each of them was actually a double-walled cylinder, two inches wide and four and a half inches tall, reinforced longitudinally with three thin, equally spaced iron strips. The flat top was closed by an iron plate, attached to the reinforcing strips with screws, and the central cavity was packed with two pounds of pelletized gunpowder through a threaded opening in the bottom before the throwing stick was screwed into it. The one-inch gap between the inner and outer walls was packed with lead balls, with molten sulfur poured in around them to prevent them from shifting, before the top plate was secured, and a lanyard through the hole drilled lengthwise through the stick connected to a friction primer. It was a hefty weight, but the throwing stick helped considerably, and the cloud of musket balls which punched through the tin walls when it detonated was devastating. It had also turned out to be quite effective at starting fires, although the Delthak Works promised specialized incendiary and smoke grenades sometime soon.

This was the first time they'd been used in combat, and coming on the heels of the mortar bombardment—which none of Tahlyvyr's men had ever encountered before, either—they'd been even more devastating to the Temple Loyalists' morale than to their bodies. The men detailed to fire the charges intended to blow the locks had fled with their companions, and Tahlyvyr had been killed leading a hopeless charge to retake the waterfront long enough to destroy them.

Whatever else he may've been, the man had guts, Green Valley reflected. *I'm not going to shed any tears for him, but if I'd had the chance I would've preferred to take him alive.*

What mattered at the moment, though, was that he had Maiyam and none of the garrison had escaped across the deep, swift-flowing river. There were a handful of fugitives dodging through the fields and forests *south* of the river, but none of them were on the Army of God's bank and none had escaped upriver by boat, which meant Wyrshym's screening cavalry regiments were operating blind.

"Find Major Dyasaiyl, Bryahn," he said, still gazing up the river towards the lake. "Tell him I want his scout snipers to get across on the ferry and push out a couple of miles towards the Greentown High Road. Warn him to keep a special eye on the road to Traylmyn's Farm, too. I'm sure he would anyway, but if there are any Temple Boys in the vicinity, that's where they're most likely to be, I think. And if I were Wyrshym, they'd be cavalry, not infantry. Tell Dyasaiyl I want observers and couriers who can get back to the river before any Temple Boy cavalry comes calling. Hopefully without being spotted themselves. Then ask Colonel Tahnaiyr if I can borrow Major Naismyth."

▼ ▼ ▼

"Heretic regulars? At Chestyrvyl and Maiyam? That's ridiculous!"

Bishop Militant Bahrnabai Wyrshym glared at the brown-haired young lieutenant who'd had the misfortune to bring him the semaphore dispatch. Lieutenant Ghordyn Fainstyn was the bishop militant's junior aide, an efficient young man who normally enjoyed his superior's favor. At the moment, that favor seemed somewhat less pronounced than usual.

Wisely, the young man said nothing, and after a moment, Wyrshym's glare abated. He dropped the dispatch on his desk and sat back in his chair, transferring his gaze from Fainstyn to Colonel Clairdon Mahkswail, his *senior* aide. Mahkswail, who would have been called chief of staff in the Charisian Army, looked back at him rather more calmly than he actually felt.

"How in Chihiro's name could they possibly have Charisian *regulars* that far east of the Gap?" Wyrshym demanded in what both aides recognized was a rhetorical question. "Did they manage to pull them away from our front without anyone even *noticing*?"

That was a rather less rhetorical inquiry. Indeed, it was a distinctly *pointed* one, and Mahkswail grimaced.

"I don't think so, My Lord, but it's possible they might've pulled at least some strength away." The colonel's expression was as unhappy as his tone. "I hate to say it, but the truth is that those damned 'scout snipers' of theirs are better than any light infantry we've got. Even with local guides, trying to get our patrols around their flanks to see what's going on behind their front is a losing proposition. We're still trying, but we're taking a lot of casualties for very little return."

"And the upshot is that we don't really *know* what they may be doing in their rear areas," Wyrshym said sourly.

"Essentially, yes," Mahkswail admitted. "The reports we're seeing are the best ones anyone can give us, My Lord. I'd be less than honest if I suggested that they were anything remotely like definitive and complete."

"Wonderful."

Wyrshym closed his eyes, raised his hand, and pinched the bridge of his nose. He was confident Allayn Maigwair understood the situation on his front and why he was stuck here, holding the cork in the Sylmahn Gap against the heretics just as they'd held the cork at Serabor against him, despite his numerical advantage. From conversations with Auxiliary Bishop Ernyst Abernethy, the Army of the Sylmahn's special intendant, he was rather less confident Zhaspahr Clyntahn shared Vicar Allayn's views.

Frankly, the bishop militant was astounded Clyntahn had been willing to even consider, far less agree to, Vicar Allayn's decision to pull his pikemen back to the Border States, on the far side of his sundered supply lines. There were less of them than there had been—Wyrshym had been turning them into riflemen as rapidly as he could, given the relatively low number of new rifles which had managed to make their way to the front—but there'd still been over thirty thousand. That made thirty thousand less mouths for him to feed, which would be a godsend over the winter, but it also left him with little more than sixty-five thousand men, a quarter of them cavalry. Once fighting spread beyond the Sylmahn Gap, he was going to be far too thin on the ground to pursue the sorts of adventures Clyntahn wanted him to undertake, and that could prove . . . unfortunate.

Wyrsym got along well with his own special intendant on a personal level. He liked Bishop Ernyst, and he knew he was fortunate to have the young Schuelerite instead of one of the narrow-minded, intolerant zealots like Cahnyr Kaitswyrth's Sedryk Zavyr or even some of the other Inquisitors assigned to the Army of the Sylmahn's regiments. Nonetheless, Abernethy had no choice but to pass along the reports from the Grand Inquisitor and deliver the directed homilies to the troops every Wednesday, and their tone suggested Clyntahn's patience was limited, to say the least.

And he won't take kindly to any suggestion that the heretics are even thinking *about retaking southern Midhold and eastern Mountaincross, either. That's the farthest east the "Rising" succeeded—Allyntyn's less than three hundred miles from the coast. Shan-wei, it's less than* nine *hundred miles from Siddar City! He won't take kindly to coughing up the crown jewel of his Sword of Schueler, whatever the reason. That means he's going to insist I do something to prevent it when I don't even know where the heretics found the men to make the effort!*

The bishop militant suppressed a temptation to use language which would have been far more suitable for simple Colonel Wyrshym of the Temple Guard, because if Clyntahn did insist on that, he was very probably going to be right—or much closer to it than usual—if only for all the wrong reasons.

He lowered his hand and opened his eyes again, looking at the huge map on his office wall. A large red pushpin represented his own headquarters at Guarnak, which remained the Army of the Sylmahn's primary supply head, despite the heretics' canal raid. Other, smaller pins represented other forces, including the one at Allyntyn in Midhold, representing Bishop Qwentyn Preskyt and Bishop Zhaksyn Mahkhal. Their four thousand men were there ostensibly to support the Faithful throughout Midhold, but their true purpose—as Vicar Allayn, at least, understood perfectly well—was to protect the Northland Gap.

It was unlikely the heretics could drive him out of his present position with frontal attacks up the Sylmahn Gap. His defenses were too strong for that. Even if they'd been willing to take the casualties, any assault could only have failed, so they had to be considering other approaches to removing him. There weren't a lot of those "other approaches" available, however, and there'd be even fewer once they evacuated their enclave at Salyk on Spinefish Bay. That had to happen in the next month or so—certainly by early November—because of the ice, and while they might—*might*—land troops at Ranshair to come at his rear that way, instead, he rather thought it was too late in the year for that, as well. Ranshair Bay usually froze, as well, and the heretics wouldn't want to put a significant force into the field when winter might be all it took to cut its supply lines.

Wyrshym's lips twitched with bitter amusement at that thought. He'd had more experience of his own with cut supply lines than he'd ever wanted.

But with Salyk and Ranshair struck from the list, that left an overland attack through Midhold, Northland, and the Northland Gap as the most likely threat. There were ports and fishing villages along the Midhold coast where supplies could be landed even in winter if they had to be. Not that it was likely such measures would be necessary. The road and canal net to Grayback Lake and then to Allyntyn was well developed and seldom seriously hampered by winter weather. Yet while he'd been aware of the possible threat for quite some time, Wyrshym hadn't considered it an immediate probability simply because he'd known the only available Charisian forces were still bogged down in the Sylmahn Gap, thirteen hundred miles from the *Northland* Gap. But if there truly were Charisians at Chestyrtyn, they were already more than halfway there . . . and less than five hundred straight-line miles from Allyntyn.

All of which suddenly made that four-thousand-man garrison look a lot less secure than it had appeared five minutes ago.

"All right," he said finally, turning back to Mahkswail. "Until we hear something more from Bairystyr, we have to assume the Charisians truly have taken Chestyrtyn and are advancing on Maiyam and, probably, Greentown. I'm inclined to think the column attack on Charlz-vyl's a diversion. If I were the heretics, I wouldn't waste effort on the place; I'd want the Maiyam Locks and the line of the Mountaincross to Greentown a lot worse than a mostly destroyed town in the fork of two rivers I wasn't planning on using anyway." He shook his head. "No. Maiyam would give me the best supply line for an advance on Allyntyn, and as soon as I had Braikstyn and Greentown, I could pacify everything between there and the mountains with secondary forces. Considering the opposition, I could even do it with militiamen without rifles."

Mahkswail nodded, and Wyrshym continued.

"Send a dispatch to Bishop Qwentyn. Tell him . . . tell him he's to deploy his cavalry to most effectively protect the Faithful in Midhold, coordinating with the Faithful's forces in the field to the best of its ability, while maintaining a sufficient screen between Allyntyn and Greentown to locate, identify, and harry any advance in his direction."

"Yes, My Lord." Mahkswail's tone indicated that he understood why the mealymouthed arse-covering first half of Bishop Qwentyn's orders was necessary. And that the *second* half was the critical one.

"After you do that, instruct Bishop Gorthyk, Bishop Adulfo, and Bishop Harys to prepare their divisions for movement. I want them fully supplied with food, ammunition, winter clothing, and artillery support. Find the wagons and dragons wherever you have to, and make their rifle regiments up to full strength even if that means drafting men from other divisions. If anyone complains, tell them they can discuss it with me personally. Bishop Gorthyk will be the officer in command. Tell him to plan on moving to Allyntyn on very short notice and that he'll assume command of all of our forces in Midhold from Bishop Qwentyn if it proves necessary to send him there. And after you've done all that, I want a hard look at any additional cavalry we can squeeze out to send with him. Horsemen aren't doing us any good in the Gap, and if the heretics truly are pushing into Midhold, we need as much mobility as possible to deal with them."

"Yes, My Lord."

"And while the colonel's doing that, Ghordyn," Wyrshym continued, turning to Lieutenant Fainstyn with a wintry smile, "I want you to request Bishop Ernyst to join me here at his earliest convenience. Please inform him that it's very important I have the latest available information on possible additional heretic troop landings. If they really have moved significant forces into Midhold, they have to've come from somewhere, and we need to know where—and in what sort of strength—as quickly as we can."

▼ ▼ ▼

Walkyr Tyrnyr felt an uncomfortable itch between his shoulder blades. There was no reason for it that he could see, and he told himself it was simply nerves. He'd united his regiment with Bryntyn Pahlmair's as planned last night and, as the senior colonel, taken command of the combined force. No regiment was ever fully up to strength, but he still had over six hundred troopers moving down the farm track towards Maiyam, which was certainly a sufficiently powerful striking force to look after itself. And if he could get them across the Maiyam ferry to reinforce Tahlyvyr. . . .

Of course, that assumed Tahlyvyr was still in possession of Maiyam, but he'd become cautiously more optimistic about that as the 16th and the 53rd trotted steadily south without encountering any refugees from the town. He wouldn't have cared to try swimming the Mountaincross himself, but there were enough boats in the town that *someone* should've gotten across before any heretic raiders could seize the place. By his calculations, they were within three or four miles of the river by now, though, riding across the desolate, largely abandoned fields, and they'd met absolutely no one.

At least the weather was clear and dry. Tyrnyr was from the Duchy of Malansath, near the coast of the Gulf of Dohlar, and September nights this far north were overly chilly for his taste. There'd been frost this morning, and it had taken him the better part of an hour to get the blood circulating properly. Still, it had warmed up nicely since. The sky was clear, with only a handful of puffy white clouds, the sun was bright, and the breeze out of the north was merely brisk, without the bite it had carried right after dawn. It had turned into a pleasant day for a ride, in fact, and at this rate they'd reach the river in—

His thoughts paused as a horseman came cantering towards the 16th's standard. He recognized one of his scouts, and those itching shoulders of his tightened as he observed the trooper's rapid pace. He threw up his hand and his bugler sounded the halt as he drew rein.

"Well, Sergeant?" he said as the scout reached him.

"Begging your pardon, Sir, but there's what does look t' be heretic regulars—Charisians, at that—up ahead."

"There are?"

The noncom nodded and a hollow sensation in the vicinity of his stomach joined the tension in Tyrnyr's shoulders.

"Yes, Sir. Hard t' mistake those uniforms."

"How many?"

"Don't have a hard count, Sir, but I don't see how it could be more'n a couple of hundred."

"You're confident of that?" Tyrnyr asked, deliberately keeping his tone calm, refusing to pressure the sergeant, even if it did sound suspiciously short of the "forty or fifty thousand" he'd been warned to expect.

"Like I say, we couldn't get a hard count, but it can't

be much more'n that, Sir. I think they spotted our patrol, because they were just forming up on a little hill off in the fields t' one side of the road when we saw them. Don't think they wanted t' play catch-as-catch-can with cavalry in the open, and can't say I blame 'em, given how flat and open it is between here and the river. I circled round the far side of the hill myself, though, just t' make sure they weren't hiding something nasty on t'other side of it, but it's not that much of a hill, when all's said. Barely big enough for the lot of them, and nothing behind it 'cept more weeds and empty pastures."

"No guns?"

"None I could see, Sir. Might be they've got a few of those portable angle-guns, but they can't have many if they do. No place t' put 'em."

"I see." Tyrnyr inhaled deeply. "Thank you, Sergeant. You've done well. Get back to your patrol and keep an eye on them."

"Yes, Sir!"

The noncom saluted, turned, and trotted back to the south, and Tyrnyr turned to Major Wyllyms.

"Thoughts?"

"Beats the Shan-wei out of me, Sir," Wyllyms said frankly. "It's not good news they're north of the river, though. That's for sure. Do you think they've taken Maiyam?"

"I don't know what I think." Tyrnyr drummed the fingers of his right hand on the pommel of his saddle while he considered. "There shouldn't be *any* Charisians north of the river. On the other hand, the Sergeant seems pretty confident there are only two or three hundred of them. Somehow I doubt the heretics would have the equivalent of a couple of our companies swanning around up here on their own! Oh," he stopped drumming to wave his hand, "if they've got the manpower to take back Midhold, it'd make sense for them to do it. That's why the Bishop Militant has us out here in the first place. But no matter how hard I try, I can't quite convince myself they'd be stupid enough to stick a force that small out on its own to get the chop."

He removed his helmet and ran his fingers through his hair, frowning thoughtfully for most of a minute. Then he squared his shoulders and nodded.

"The only one way to find out what's going on is to go look. The Sergeant's right about how flat the terrain is, so it's not like they could hide another couple of thousand men to jump on us. And if they don't have artillery, they've got to be feeling a little nervous. I'm going to assume they do have some of those small angle-guns of theirs, whether the Sergeant saw them or not, but as far as I know their gunners have never tried to use them with five or six hundred cavalry coming straight at them. I imagine that might shake their aim a bit."

"So you're planning an attack, Sir?"

"I'm not attacking anything unless I think I can kick its arse," Tyrnyr said frankly. "It's not my job to get a lot of our lads killed gloriously—it's my job to find out what's going on and report it to Bishop Qwentyn at Allyntyn. That doesn't mean I'll pass up the opportunity to run over these bastards if it offers itself, though." His smile was bleak. "We all want some of our own back after Serabor. More to the point, any prisoners we take will tell the Bishop everything he wants to know by the time the Question's through with them."

"Yes, Sir." Wyllyms' smile was even colder than Tyrnyr's.

"We're also not going to do anything without making sure Bishop Qwentyn'll be fully informed if it should happen something goes wrong," Tyrnyr continued. "Go inform Colonel Pahlmair that I intend to advance, observe the situation, and—assuming conditions appear favorable—attack. And while you're doing that, send couriers to Colonel Bairystyr and also directly to Allyntyn. Inform them that we've confirmed the presence of Charisian regulars in Midhold, north of the Mountaincross River, and that I'll be sending additional reports as more information becomes available."

▼ ▼ ▼

"I sure do hope the Major isn't being overly clever about this," Lieutenant Ahbraim Mahzyngail murmured as he watched the Army of God cavalry.

"It wasn't the Major's brainstorm," Lieutenant Trumyn Dunstyn replied from the corner of his mouth.

The youthful lieutenants stood just below the crest of the small hill (although in their opinion calling such a miserable elevation a "hill" maligned a perfectly respectable noun). The standard of Company A, 2nd Battalion, 3rd Regiment, Imperial Charisian Army, had been planted atop that hill by Major Cahrtair Naismyth, Company A's commanding officer. Mahzyngail commanded the company's 2nd Platoon, while Dunstyn commanded 1st Platoon, and their men happened to be deployed along the eastern face of their hill, waiting to find out what the Temple Boys had in mind.

"It was Baron Green Valley himself, _I_ heard," Dunstyn continued.

"Really?"

Mahzyngail perked up, and Dunstyn smiled crookedly. The men of 2nd Brigade—for that matter, the men of the entire Imperial Charisian Army—had enormous faith in Green Valley's judgment. His ability to read a tactical situation was almost as legendary as Emperor Cayleb's ability to do the same thing at sea, and he constantly pounded home the need to husband manpower carefully when he critiqued training maneuvers. Both those qualities tended to reassure people he sent to do risky things that he planned on getting as few as possible of them killed and probably knew what he was doing when he sent them out.

Probably. Even Emperor Cayleb had made mistakes upon occasion, after all. Still, some things were less likely than others.

And the baron had better have it right this time, Dustyn reflected. Company A had been deliberately parked in its exposed position, with only half its organic mortar platoon in support, when the mounted scout snipers came galloping back to Maiyam with word that enemy cavalry was headed that way. There could be several reasons for that, but the one that struck Dustyn as most likely was that Baron Green Valley wanted to tempt the Temple Boys into attacking them and figured even they'd be smart enough to leave a full battalion supported by field guns alone. Dustyn had no objection to engaging the Army of God. Any awe he might have felt for the Temple Boys had been pretty thoroughly laid to rest during the advance from Serabor to Wyvern Lake. And Duke Eastshare had kicked arse and taken names along the Daivyn, too. The lieutenant *would* prefer, however, to have something like at least equal odds, and at the moment the odds looked distinctly *un*equal.

▼ ▼ ▼

"Be damned, Sir," Major Wyllyms observed. "They *are* standing there with their bare arses blowing in the wind, aren't they?"

"So it would appear," Tyrnyr replied, peering through his spyglass.

The sergeant's numerical estimate seemed to be pretty much spot on. The reports he'd read suggested that an Imperial Charisian Army company was about twice the size of an Army of God infantry company, and he saw a single standard atop the hill. So call it between two hundred and two hundred and thirty men. And there were no field guns anywhere around. The sergeant had also been correct in his estimate that the heretics couldn't possibly've crammed more than a half dozen of their small angle-guns into the available space. And the patrol which had been left to keep an eye on them while the sergeant reported back had seen no evidence the heretics were trying to reinforce this isolated detachment.

On the other hand, they weren't trying to *withdraw* it, either, which Tyrnyr damned well would've been doing in their place.

Assuming he could, that was.

Somehow they must've gotten across the river and then been stuck on this side, he decided, lowering the spyglass and pursing his lips pensively. *But how? The scouts've swept all the way to the riverbank now without seeing any boats on this side. Maybe they got across on the ferry and sent it back to Maiyam for reinforcements? But if they did, why hasn't anyone joined them? Unless. . . .*

"I think they did attack Maiyam," he said slowly. "I never did put much faith in that 'forty or fifty thousand' business, but the heretics might've sent a force smaller than that after the Maiyam Locks. If they did they were probably hoping for surprise, but Tahlyvyr obviously knew they were coming, since he got his messengers off to Bryskoh and Colonel Pahlmair. It's possible—maybe even probable—they managed to push him out of the town, anyway. He didn't have that many men, unfortunately. And if the heretics did take the town, they probably took the ferry, too, which would explain how these fellows wound up on our side of the river."

"And why didn't they fall back on Maiyam when they spotted us, Sir?"

"I've been wondering that myself, and I think it's possible Tahlyvyr may've managed a counterattack. I don't think he was able to retake the town, though. In fact, if my suspicions are accurate, any counterattack's been beaten off by now. There's certainly no fighting going on over there at this point, anyway. I know the river's too broad for anyone to make out much in the way of details on the other side, but I'm pretty sure our scouts would be able to see powder smoke and hear gunfire if anyone was still engaged. It's possible he did manage to retake it and that's why the fighting's over, but I think it's more likely he only managed to burn the ferry and strand these bastards over here. If so, that's pretty good news."

"*Good* news, Sir?"

"Well, the best we could expect, anyway." Tyrnyr grimaced. "If they came up the canal, they brought barges with them, Ahrthyr. And if they had barges on the river, they could've used them to pull these people back. Or, assuming they weren't going to pull back, to *reinforce* them. So obviously they don't have barges on the *river*, and the only reason that would be true is that Tahlyvyr managed to blow the locks."

"I see."

The major nodded slowly, his expression thoughtful, and Tyrnyr methodically hung the spyglass back across his shoulder. He gazed at the infantry on the hill for a moment longer, then inhaled sharply.

"What matters at the moment, though," he said more briskly, "is that they *are* stuck on our side of the river, and we've got them outnumbered three-to-one. I think we ought to see about making them properly welcome, don't you?"

▼ ▼ ▼

"All right, boys." Captain Dustyn Baikyr's voice was level, almost soft, like that of a man soothing a skittish thoroughbred. "It looks like they're forming up. You'd think they'd know better than to charge formed infantry, but their cavalry's used the fire wing against the Siddarmarkians, so they might try that here, too, instead."

"I wish they *would* be stupid enough to try that against Mahndrayns, Sir," Lieutenant Mahzyngail said almost wistfully, and Baikyr chuckled.

"Well, they wouldn't head this way if they didn't intend to try *something*, Ahbraim. And if it's just the same to you, I don't think we'll let them tempt *us* into charging *them*."

All four of the captain's platoon commanders chuckled and he nodded.

"Looks like they're about ready. Get back to your men and tell them I want these people's arses kicked up between their sorry ears!"

▼ ▼ ▼

Walkyr Tyrnyr rode forward, trotting out in front of his regiment to consider its alignment. His men were no longer the spotlessly attired cavalrymen with gleaming accoutrements who'd set out from Zion so many months before. Their uniforms were shabby, their armor scuffed, the leather of saddles and tack worn, but their originally natty appearance had been replaced by a certain scruffy toughness. They were veterans, leaned down and hardened,

although they'd had precious little opportunity to execute the sort of tactics in which they'd originally trained.
Tyrnyr was proud of them, and as he gazed at them he
was conscious of his own eagerness to employ them
the way they'd been meant to be employed.

Here and there he saw troopers checking the priming
on the pairs of double-barreled saddle pistols they'd
been trained to use for the fire wing, which would have
called a caracole on a planet called Old Earth. The tactic
had become possible only since the invention of the flintlock pistol, but it had been used effectively several times
against Siddarmarkian heretics by Bishop Militant Cahnyr's cavalry during his advance out of Westmarch into
Cliff Peak. Dohlaran cavalry had used it successfully in
the South March, as well, but no one had yet attempted
it against *Charisian* heretics, and Tyrnyr had his doubts
about how well it would work in their case.

The fire wing called for cavalry to ride directly towards the enemy at a half gallop, several ranks deep. As
each rank entered pistol range, it turned sharply to the
left or right so its riders could each discharge one pistol
into the enemy, then turned sharply in the other direction so that he could fire a second pistol before swinging
away to clear the range for the next oncoming rank. The
idea was to deluge the enemy with a close range, rolling
hail of pistol fire which would, in theory, disorder his
formation, at which point the solid block of lancers
coming on behind the pistoleers would smash straight
through the wavering line.

Experience had shown it worked—as at Aivahnstyn—
under the right conditions. But the Siddarmarkian regiments against which the fire wing had succeeded had
been *pike* regiments, their missile troops equipped only
with arbalests or smoothbore matchlocks. These were
Charisian regulars, which meant they were equipped
with rifles. Pistol fire would be a poor match for rifle
fire, even if he did have twice as many men and each of
his pistols did have two barrels. On the other hand, unlike the Siddarmarkians, they *didn't* have pikes . . . and
if they actually fired their rifles, they'd take even their

bayonets out of play while they reloaded. Besides, that formation lacked the dense, deep ranks to present the forest of pikeheads that had made the Siddarmarkian Army so deadly against cavalry. It had to be far more fragile than the pike blocks which had bested Desnair so often, and that made this a time to take a lesson from the past and use his armored lancers to deliver the classic, decisive shock attack that broke infantry and then rode down the survivors.

He considered the distance between his regiments and the heretics. Eight hundred yards, he estimated; the Charisians were visible only as elongated forms, the details of uniform and body shape blurred by distance, although he could make out an occasional extended arm as an officer or a noncom gestured in his direction.

That was plenty of distance to build speed, and the flat cropland was ideal terrain. Call it fifty yards at a walk, another fifty at a slow trot, a hundred at a maneuvering trot, two hundred at a maneuvering gallop, and the last four hundred at the charge. Two and a half minutes, total, and barely fifty seconds to cross the final four hundred yards where rifle fire was likely to be effective. A muzzle-loading rifle would do well to get off two shots in that interval, especially one encumbered by the fixed bayonet which always slowed reloading, and any infantryman who *didn't* fix his bayonet in the face of a cavalry charge was a dead man. The heretics' breech-loading rifles were almost certain to do better than that, but they had to maintain an all-round facing if they didn't want him to curl around an exposed flank. That meant there were scarcely seventy rifles actually facing his men. Even if each of them got off three rounds, not two, that was only two hundred, and he didn't care if they *were* Charisians, a lot of them were going to miss, rifles or not, with six hundred cavalry coming right down their throats. And when they realized their rifle fire wasn't going to stop the charge after all. . . .

He nodded once, crisply, then trotted back to the 16th's standard, and looked at the bugler.

"Sound Advance."

▼ ▼ ▼

The notes of the AOG's bugles rose high, golden, and sweet, and more than one of the waiting Charisians swallowed hard as that mass of horsemen stirred, shifted . . . and started forward.

The sixteen companies of cavalry were formed into eight lines, each seventy-five yards across and three yards deep. Combined with the two-yard interval between lines, the formation stretched the next best thing to forty yards from front to back, and its frontage was twice Company A's. It began to move slowly, but it gathered speed with a sort of stately majesty, churning dust into the warm September air.

Early-afternoon sunlight flickered as six hundred lances came down, and a fresh bugle call sent the cavalry from a slow trot to something just short of a gallop. The sound of hooves was an approaching thunder, and then the bugles sounded once more and the thunder accelerated yet again.

"Steady boys—steady," Company A's platoon sergeants said. "Wait for the word. *Wait* for it. We'll tell you when it's time."

Aside from that, there was silence on the Charisians' hill, and the same sun that gleamed on Army of God lanceheads glittered on Charisian bayonets.

The bugles sounded yet again as the range fell to four hundred yards and the horses stretched into a full gallop across the table-flat cropland. That was still long range for aimed rifle fire, even for Charisian infantry with tangent sights, and so they waited, letting the range fall still further, obeying their sergeants and waiting . . . waiting. . . .

"*Fire!*"

The range was two hundred yards, and the half-inch bullets hit their targets like Shan-wei's sledgehammers. Horses screamed and went down, here and there men flew out of their saddles, their plate cuirasses woefully insufficient to turn those massive bullets, yet the charge never hesitated. A few horses stumbled over fallen fellows, crashing to the ground, rolling over their riders, leaving gaps in the lines. But most of them avoided the obstacles, the gaps closed up, and the survivors were galloping at over four hundred yards per minute.

"*Fire!*"

A second volley crashed home with even more accuracy, creating bigger holes in the tight formation, and the bugles were sounding, sounding, driving the 16th and 53rd Cavalry towards the enemies of God and the Archangels on the wings of the Jihad.

"*Holy Langhorne and no quarter!*" Both regiments took up the cry, riding with it in their ears, eyes hard and hating as the enemies of God came into their reach.

"*Fire!*"

A third volley roared, and thirty percent of the 16th Cavalry was down, dead or wounded, but the survivors leaned forward, lances at the thrust, screaming their war cries, with the 53rd right behind them.

"*Present bayonets!*"

Those glittering bayonets steadied, presenting a thicket of steel . . . and Colonel Tyrnyr's battle plan came apart.

The great romantic fallacy of cavalry warfare was that cavalry charged. That its effectiveness lay in mounted men's ability to ride down infantry, ramming home an attack with cold steel, driven by all the weight and momentum of horse and rider alike. That heavy horse shattered infantry by the sheer, ferocious impact of its charge.

But cavalry *didn't* charge. Not the way the bards described it, because horses were not fools. Nor were they predators. They were herbivores, herd animals, the natural *prey* of predators, and their primary defense against threats was to run *away* from them, not towards them. They could be trained to carry men they trusted towards a threat, but that changed none of their basic instincts, nor did it change physics. A seven- or eight-hundred-pound horse, moving at fifteen or sixteen miles per hour, would suffer significant, even catastrophic damage if it collided with a solid obstacle a quarter of its own weight. Horses' legs were fragile, designed to withstand the vertical shock of trotting or galloping but not the lateral shearing stresses when they collided at speed with another body, human or equine, and cavalry mounts knew it. Galloping horses didn't attempt to avoid fallen humans out of the goodness of their hearts; they did it because they knew how badly *they* could be injured if they tripped over those humans. And as anyone who'd ever attempted to train a horse for the steeplechase quickly learned, they would refuse to jump even light wooden rails or hay bales if they thought the barricade was too tall. In point of fact, the highest obstacle allowed in steeplechase events was only five feet, and the obstacle in front of these horses—who were *not* steeplechasers, and had not the slightest interest in *becoming* steeplechasers— averaged over five and a *half* feet tall.

It was also fringed with nasty, sharp bayonets.

At the Battle of Waterloo, on distant, long-dead Old Earth, Marshal Ney's French cuirassiers launched charge after charge upon the British infantry squares . . . uselessly. Because the truth was that throughout history, "shock" cavalry depended not upon physical shock, but on the *moral* shock of a man on foot facing several tons of mounted, usually armored horsemen charging straight at him in a drumroll of hoof-pounding thunder. While it was true that a charging horse would be badly injured if it slammed headlong into a human being, it was a given that the much smaller human would fare at least as badly, and that didn't even count the (usually) better armored lunatic on the horse's back, who was bound to be waving around a sword or—even worse—a long, pointy lance. The natural reaction when faced by such an obvious threat was the same sensible response horses favored when faced by predators: *run away!* But infantry that *didn't* run away— infantry that held its ground—discovered those same horses' disinclination to ram headlong into a dangerous obstacle.

Horses would cheerfully pursue a fleeing enemy. They were even willing to charge other horses and let the maniacs on their backs hack and hew at one another to their hearts' content, as long as both formations were open enough they might hope to find a way through.

But bayonet-armed infantrymen standing shoulder-to-shoulder, with no nice horse-wide gaps between them? Never.

In conjunction with artillery or the musketry of supporting infantry, cavalry could be devastating against that sort of target. A formation solid enough to repel a cavalry charge was an ideal target for small arms, round shot, grapeshot, or canister. If the infantry stood in solid ranks, it suffered massive casualties; if it adopted a more open formation to minimize its fire casualties, it became easy meat for the horsemen.

Unfortunately for the Army of God, it had no artillery or supporting infantry, and its horses, their ears already full of the screams of other wounded and dying horses, refused to break their legs—or their necks—against that solid, unshaken, bayonet-bristling wall of infantry.

▼ ▼ ▼

"Second rank, independent targets! Third rank, *grenades*!"

The second line of infantry opened fire once more. Using their weapons' breech-loading capability to maintain the threat of their bayonets even as they reloaded, they chose their targets and fired. And the line behind them pulled the lanyards and heaved smoking showers of hand grenades over the heads of their fellows and into the cavalry beyond.

Explosions thundered, spewing hundreds of round lead bullets, and the shrieks of wounded horses rose like hideous music. The bugle was still sounding across the bedlam of shots, shrieks, screams, and explosions, but then a grenade or a bullet found the bugler, and the martial melody died with the player.

"*Mortar platoon, engage!*"

The six three-inch mortars in the pits at the very apex of the hill began to cough, sending ten-pound projectiles into the farthest portions of the AOG formation. They were impact-fused, exploding as they hit the ground, throwing their own sheets of shrapnel balls to join the hand grenades.

It lasted eleven minutes from the moment the two cavalry regiments accelerated to a full gallop. One minute to reach the Charisian front line, three minutes of shrieking madness in a cauldron of devastation, and seven minutes for the terrified survivors to get out of range of the vengefully pursuing mortar bombs—time-fused now, to shower the deadly cones of shrapnel from above.

Of the six hundred and nineteen cavalrymen who began that charge, two hundred and fifty-three—an astonishingly high number, really, and almost half of them still with horses—survived to fall back in its wreckage.

Colonel Walkyr Tyrnyr and Major Ahrthyr Wyllyms were not among them.

. VIII .

HMS *Powerful*, 58,
Jahras Island,
Gulf of Jahras,
Desnairian Empire

"Be seated, gentlemen."

The dozen senior captains and commanders in Admiral Payter Shain's day cabin settled into chairs around the round, polished table. Zhak Haukyns; Shain's flag captain and HMS *Powerful*'s commanding officer, sat directly across from his admiral and laid a folder on the tabletop in front of him.

Sunlight through the cabin's windows sent patterns dancing across the low overhead as it reflected off the waves while the ship lay to her anchors off Jahras Island. The Imperial Charisian Navy had seized the island—little more than a vast sheep farm, five miles across—as an advanced base in the gulf of the same name. The shepherds who lived on it had been too wise to offer any resistance, and they'd been astonished to learn that the invaders actually intended to *pay* for the sheep they carried off. The island offered a source of water and good holding ground for anchors, but precious little more. Still, it *was* a place where men could go ashore, stretch their legs, and get a little exercise, and the mutton made a worthwhile addition to their normal rations.

The skylight was open, as were the quarter windows, admitting what breeze there was. There wasn't a great deal of it, which was unfortunate, since the day was blisteringly hot, as might be expected less than seventy miles above the equator. Shain's servant bustled about, making certain each of his guests had a filled glass, then bowed his way out with smooth efficiency.

"I don't expect the subject of today's meeting to come as a vast surprise to any of you," Shain said with a slight smile as he picked up his own wineglass. He sipped appreciatively and leaned back in his chair. "Our orders have arrived. We'll commence active operations throughout the Gulf the day after tomorrow, with instructions to take, burn, or sink everything we find, with special emphasis on privateers and the shipyards building them."

His smile grew broader—and colder—as he let their stir of reaction circle the table before he continued.

"The delay," he said then, "was occasioned by our wait for our latest arrivals." He gestured gracefully to where Captain Symyn Mastyrsyn, the commanding officer of HMS *Rottweiler*, sat side-by-side with Captain Bryxtyn Abernethy, HMS *Earthquake*'s CO. "I expect they'll make themselves useful."

Abernethy was one of the increasing number of ICN officers who'd grown to adulthood as the subjects of someone other than King Haarahld of Charis. In fact, he was a Tarotisian, which still inclined some Old Charisian officers to be prejudiced against him, given King Gorjah III's betrayal in the Group of Four's initial attack on the Kingdom of Charis. Shain wasn't one of them, partly because he realized Abernethy—who'd served as a lieutenant aboard one of the few galleys to escape the battles off Armageddon Reef—had had no choice but to obey the orders of his lawful superiors. And, if Shain was going to be completely honest, partly because his emperor and empress had made it very, very clear that not just Chisholmians, but Emeraldians, Tarotisians, and even Zebediahans were all *Charisians* now. Their officers and enlisted personnel were to be treated accordingly, and Payter Shain, who had a closer acquaintance with both his monarchs than many a serving officer, was far too wise to argue with them.

There were still relatively few non-Charisians or Chisholmians in command of major warships, but that was primarily because there'd been fewer senior officers in any of the Charisian Empire's other member states when they *became* member states. Numbers were growing, however, and non–Old Charisians were becoming more and more thoroughly integrated into the junior officer corps. Within another few years, there'd be plenty of Tarotisian and Emeraldian accents in a meeting like this one.

For now, however, Abernethy's arrival had been particularly opportune, since *Earthquake* was one of the angle-gun-armed bombardment ships. Her high-trajectory firepower would be a welcome addition when it came time to engage the batteries the Desnairians had erected to protect the bays and inlets where their ship-yards were busily building the privateers which came swarming out of the Gulf of Jahras despite all Commodore Ruhsail Tyrnyr's overworked blockaders could do. Tyrnyr was intercepting at least fifty percent of them from his base on Howard Island, but once a privateer got to sea there were countless ports along the Desnairian, Delferahkan, Harchongese, and Dohlaran coasts where she and her sisters could find safe harbor and continue the increasingly intense pressure on Charisian maritime commerce. The majority of the Desnairians' shipbuilding capacity remained concentrated in the Gulf of Jahras, however. Burning out the privateers at the source would be far more economical than trying to hunt them down once they'd gotten to sea, and *Earthquake* was just the sledgehammer for the task.

Mastyrsyn's command was quite a different breed of kraken. His ship had been the brainchild of High Admiral Lock Island, whose sense of humor had led him to name her in honor of Keelhaul, the huge rottweiler who'd been his constant companion. And, like Keelhaul, this *Rottweiler* was big, tough, and dangerous, despite the fact that she mounted only thirty guns.

She'd been designed to carry no less than eighty-eight guns, as a unit of the *Thunderer* class. New developments—like the shell-firing cannon—had supervened, however, and Lock Island had ordered *Rottweiler* and her first five sisters cut down to a single gundeck. The result was a tremendous, flush-decked galleon—at a hundred and ninety-five feet she was the longest galleon ever built, twenty feet longer and eight feet broader than even the *Sword of Charis* class—with only fifteen gunports on a side. She retained her original sail plan, which made her extremely fast, and the weight saved by removing two entire gundecks' worth of height had allowed the shipyards to armor her with three-inch steel plates backed by almost three feet of solid Charisian teak. Her armor covered her sides from weather deck to three feet below the waterline, where its thickness tapered to one and a half inches, yet with the reduction in topweight, she was still able to show fifteen feet of freeboard, which meant she could work her guns in even the roughest weather.

Only the fact that Sir Dustyn Olyvyr had adopted diagonal planking and used iron bolts between frames to increase their longitudinal strength let the converted ships carry the weight of their armor without catastrophic hogging, and even so it was probably thinner than Olyvyr and his designers would have preferred. Nor did it do anything to protect her masts and rigging. Despite that, she and her sisters—two more had already joined the fleet and a third would commission within the next month or so—were the best protected blue-water warships ever to sail the seas of Safehold. They were, in fact, the *only* blue-water warships protected against the shellfire.

That would have been enough to make her a much

appreciated addition to any squadron likely to encounter well-dug-in shore batteries, but protection was far from the only thing she brought to the fight. She might mount only thirty guns, but unlike the standard thirty-pounders most Charisian galleons carried they were six-inch rifled angle-guns, mounted on two-wheeled Mahndrayn broadside carriages. There'd been some concern that using studded shells would slow the rate of fire unacceptably in a broadside gun, but tests had reassured the worriers. Using the new carriages, her gunners were able to more than match the rate of fire from ships armed with the old-style carriages and hold their own even against other galleons with Mahndrayns. The greater accuracy of a rifled shell was of less value to naval gunners, whose firing platforms and targets tended to move in several dimensions at once in anything other than a dead calm, but the elongated shells' greater range, weight, penetration capability, and much more powerful bursting charges gave her guns enormous hitting power.

"I can see where waiting for *Rottweiler* and *Earthquake* made sense, Sir," Captain Tymythy Tyrnyr said, "but there's still one thing that worries me just a bit, and that's the little matter of finding people to shoot at."

Several people chuckled. Tyrnyr, the commander of HMS *Valiant* and one of Shain's senior captains, was a direct, hardheaded officer. He was also an Emeraldian, with a stocky build, slightly less than average height, and a dry sense of humor. Despite his tone's ironic whimsy, however, the question was serious . . . and well taken. With over two thousand miles of coastline, the Gulf of Jahras offered hundreds of places shipyards capable of building schooners or brigs could be quietly established. Shain commanded a squadron of twelve galleons, twenty naval brigs and schooners, *Rottweiler, Earthquake*, and a handful of store ships. If all of his warships had been stationed in a line in clear weather, their lookouts could have covered roughly fourteen thousand square miles of seawater, which sounded like a lot. But it would have amounted to little more than a rectangle six hundred and thirty miles long and twenty miles wide. Even if he'd been prepared to operate his ships as singletons, he could have kept less than a third of the Gulf of Jahras' coastline under observation at any given moment.

"I take your point, Tymythy," he said. "I do, however, have something a bit more subtle in mind than simply sailing around in the middle of the Gulf in hopes the privateers will be sufficiently angered by our presence to sail out to the attack."

The chuckles were louder this time, and Tyrnyr smiled. Shain smiled back, then allowed his expression to sober.

"The other thing we've been waiting for," he went on, "was a report from our spies. Actually, I suspect it's from *Seijin* Merlin and *his* spies."

The amusement of a moment before was suddenly muted. The officers in his day cabin were senior enough to have been exposed to the detailed reliability of reports from Merlin Athrawes' astounding network of agents. Most of them, Shain knew, suspected—as he did, himself—that many of those agents were also *seijins*.

"We have a list of building and fitting-out locations which, as of approximately two five-days ago, was as complete and accurate as our spies could make it," he told them. "Obviously, we can't rely on it as *Holy Writ*, but I think we'll be able to find someone for you to shoot at, Tymythy."

"That suits me right down to the ground, Sir," Tyrnyr told him.

"Even with that information in hand, we're going to have quite a lot of work for fellows like you, Commander Slohvyk," Shain continued, turning to one of the more junior officers present. His HMS *Termagant* was an eighteen-gun schooner—fleet, fast, maneuverable, and easily as powerful as any of the privateers being built around the Gulf. The young man sat a bit straighter, and Shain smiled. "In addition to burning out this modest nest of privateers, His Majesty's instructions to take, burn, or sink apply to any Desnairian shipping foolish enough to attempt to cross the Gulf, Paidrho. I'm sending *Termagant, King Wyvern*, and *Falcon* to keep an eye on Mahrosa Bay. You'll be the senior officer in command, and I don't want you entering the bay itself without heavier support. I also don't want any coasters making it *out* of the bay until we get around to bringing you that support, however."

"Yes, Sir!"

The youngster's eyes gleamed, and Shain considered adding another word or two of caution. Paidrho Slohvyk was only twenty-seven and possessed of a naturally aggressive nature. That could be a potentially dicey combination, but he also had almost fifteen years of experience at sea, despite his youth. Besides, aggressiveness was a precious commodity in a naval officer.

"Eventually," the admiral said instead, looking around the table once more, "we'll move the blockade inside Mahrosa Bay itself. With any luck, we'll be able to shut down the east end of the Mahrosa Canal completely. I'd like to land raiding parties to blow up the locks, but Mahrosa's a major town with a garrison to match, so I'll settle for putting them out of action with Captain Abernethy's angle-guns. Even if we do, we won't be able to keep them from offloading the barges farther west and sending them up the coast by wagon, but according to our best information, the high road between Mahrosa and Handryl's more of a pious hope than a reality, whatever the maps show. And, for that matter, Handryl's a lot smaller than Mahrosa and it isn't supposed to be heavily fortified or garrisoned. That may change once we start burning things down around the entire coast of the Gulf, of course. If it doesn't, though, I'm going to think very seriously about seizing Handryl outright."

One or two of his officers looked . . . thoughtful in response to his last sentence, he noticed.

"I know our Marine contingents've been pared to the bone to support operations in the Republic," he told them. "And I don't propose to get excessively adventurous. As His Majesty's said on occasion, an adventure is someone *else* being cold, wet, hungry, frightened, and miserable far, far away from you, and I'm no fonder of getting *personally* involved with them than the next man."

This time, several people laughed outright, and he allowed himself a grin.

"Nonetheless, if we *can* take Handryl, we cut the only so-called high road east of the Mersayr Mountains . . . and *that* effectively cuts overland communication from Mahrosa all the way to Silkiah. With our squadron in control of the Gulf, *all* their supplies would have to go overland west of the mountains, through North Watch, or down the Hankey and Altan Rivers and then across Hankey Sound. At the very least, I imagine they'd find our presence there just a *bit* of a distraction, and we might be able to turn it into a sort of vest-pocket Thesmar when they try to do something about it. If nothing else, we could make them divert the resources to do something about us in Handryl . . . and then just sail away, laughing down our sleeves, after they do."

This time the thoughtful expressions seemed less concerned with their flag officer's sanity than with the merits of his proposal, he observed.

"That's for the future, however. At the moment, Captain Haukyns and I have been giving some thought to more immediately pressing objectives. I'll let him lay out the fruits of our labor and then we'll see what sort of insightful improvements you lot can come up with. Zhak?"

"Of course, Admiral." Captain Haukyns smiled. "Not that this bunch of idle layabouts is really likely to improve upon our own brilliant analysis. Still, I suppose it would be only polite to give them the opportunity."

"That was my own thought," Shain agreed gravely, "although I was far too tactful to say it."

Laughter rumbled again, and Haukyns opened the folder in front of him.

"Given the information we've received, Kalais is probably the best place to begin. We already knew they were building privateers there, but according to our spies, we were wrong in at least one regard. Kalais' artillery hasn't been upgraded. It's all still old model guns, most without even welded trunnions, and there's no indication the Desnairians will be able to change that situation with so much of their foundry capacity diverted to their army. Hitting Kalais first will give us an opportunity to get the Squadron accustomed to working together and test our tactics before we go up against a tougher target. After that, we thought—"

. IX .
Siddar City,
Republic of Siddarmark

It was noisy inside the converted waterfront warehouse. Things tended to be that way when hammers were sounding on anvils, dozens of men were trying to communicate with one another, hand-powered bellows were fanning forges, rain pounded on the roof, and every so often someone dumped what sounded like a ton or so of scrap metal on a stone floor.

Klymynt Abykrahmbi was used to the noise. In fact, he was used to considerably worse noise. What he wasn't used to was the trio of Marine guards walking behind him, each armed with one of the new cap-and-ball "revolvers" *Seijin* Merlin had introduced in addition to his slung rifle.

He paused just inside the door, looking for the man he'd come here to find. It was sufficiently smoky—and crowded—to complicate what ought to have been a relatively simple task, and he sighed and slicked rainwater off the bald spot about which his wife and both of his sisters had teased him unmercifully for the last three years. His father still had a full head of distinguished-looking silver hair at sixty-three, and it seemed particularly unjust that Klymynt should be going bald before he reached half that age.

Of course, there was a lot of injustice going around these days.

Abykrahmbi's jaw tightened, and he rubbed the knuckle of his left index finger over what would have been called his walrus mustache back on Old Earth as the memory rolled through him.

Siddarmarkians had always gotten along better with Charisians than the majority of Mainlanders. Indeed, that was one reason Zhaspahr Clyntahn's suspicion of Siddarmark's orthodoxy had been so compulsive, and Charisians and Siddarmarkians had been intermarrying for generations, despite the weary miles of seawater between them. In fact, Abykrahmbi had relatives right here in Siddar City. Unfortunately, he had two less than he'd had before the Sword of Schueler. His twelve-year-old cousin Fraydrykha had been raped and murdered when the Temple Loyalist mob attacked the Charisian Quarter, and his Uncle Zhustyn had died attempting to protect his daughter from her killers. He'd been unarmed—that was how great the surprise had been—and by all accounts there'd been at least seven attackers, but he'd managed to kill at least one of them while his daughter's screams rang in his ears. Afterward, they'd mutilated both bodies, flung them into a smashed and looted shop, and set fire to the place, whether to hide the evidence of their crimes or to deface their victims still further was more than Abykrahmbi could say.

His Aunt Lyzbet was still trying to understand how her own countrymen could have done such things, and Abykrahmbi often thought that only the need to somehow keep her other two children alive through the winter of privation which had followed had kept Lyzbet Sygayl sane.

Or as sane as anyone could be, under the circumstances.

Unlike his aunt, however, Abykrahmbi understood how it had happened. He understood that the darkness that lived inside most human beings was stronger and darker in some. And he understood that things like his cousin's horrible death were inevitable when the corrupt, lying piece of kraken shit in the Grand Inquisitor's chair gave that darkness the stamp of God's own approval. And just as he understood that, he understood how someone like Clyntahn and the actions he endorsed could lead other men to embrace the sin of hatred and the hot thirst for vengeance. That was why he'd jumped at the chance when Ehdwyrd Howsmyn needed volunteers for the technical mission to the Republic.

Klymynt Abykrahmbi had never thought of himself as the godliest of men even before the Sword of Schueler. He did his best, but he'd also been aware his best fell short of what God and the Archangels truly desired from their children. On the other hand, Mother Church had always taught there was absolution for any sin, as long as the penitence was genuine, the contrition was real, and the sinner truly sought to amend his life in the future.

He fully intended to seek that absolution . . . as soon as the last Temple Loyalist in the Republic of Siddarmark had choked out his last maggot-ridden breath at the end of a rope.

He inhaled deeply and forced himself to put that thought aside as he finally spotted the person he'd been seeking.

"This way, Corporal," he said, and the senior member of his escort nodded, then twitched his head at the pair of privates, and the three of them followed him across that crowded, noisy floor.

Abykrahmbi nodded to those he knew, stopping to speak to several of them. He wasn't in that big a hurry, and it was a major part of his responsibilities as Brygham Cartyr's assistant to keep his finger on the pulse of workshops like this one. There were several processes under way on the busy floor, but the biggest single activity was the conversion of Siddarmark-made muzzle-loading flintlocks to take percussion caps. A third of the conversion work was being done by the trained armorers who'd arrived with the second echelon of the Charisian Expeditionary Force to set up the CEF's rear area repair shops. For the most part, though, they were serving in the instructor's role, teaching Siddarmarkians, not all of them gunsmiths—a fact, Abykrahmbi knew, that irritated the Gunmakers Guild to no end—to perform the same task.

Similar instruction was going on all across the workshop. Abykrahmbi wasn't sure it was the most effective way to improve the Republic's manufacturing efficiency, but it was the policy which had been adopted, and he grasped the underlying logic. Charisian manufactories held a huge margin of superiority when it came to speed and quality of production, and it must have been extremely tempting to Emperor Cayleb and Empress Sharleyan to export that same capability to Siddarmark. Unfortunately, they couldn't do that—not overnight, at any rate. It was difficult enough to create the same sorts of manufactories in Chisholm, and the unvarnished truth was that it was more important to continue building that capability throughout the Empire than it was to create it here on the Mainland. If Siddarmark fell after all, Charis would have to fight on alone, and she'd require every scrap of capacity she could find for that.

So the decision had been taken to send advisers—"technical missions," as the emperor and empress called them—to assist the Siddarmarkians in building their own manufactories but not to divert thousands of trained workers to get those Siddarmarkian manufactories up and running. And the Republic understood the logic, too. Chancellor Maidyn and Lord Protector Greyghor were concentrating on building up the ability to *repair* first and to manufacture second in a division of labor that made the best use of Charis' steadily growing capabilities. Rifle and bayonet manufacture was a glaring exception to that rule, and the lord protector was pushing ahead with the construction of a major iron and steelworks of his own just outside Siddar City, using plans provided by the Delthak Works.

Makes a lot of sense, really, Abykrahmbi thought. *This way he trains scads of workers, gets them accustomed to the new techniques and new ways of thinking, before he puts up the manufactories he's going to need them to work in. It's just a damned pity we can't do everything at once!*

He smiled wryly at the thought. He'd gotten so accustomed to watching Ehdwyrd Howsmyn that it was sometimes hard to remember that other people *couldn't* do everything at once.

He paused again, laying one hand on the shoulder of a Siddarmarkian supervisor and exchanging a few words with the man, then—finally—found himself close enough to the man he'd been looking for to call his name.

"Zhak! Yo, Zhak!"

The wiry, dark, and very young ICN lieutenant turned and smiled as he recognized Abykrahmbi. Zhak Bairystyr held out one of his large, strong hands, with its calluses and ingrained oil and coal dust, and clasped forearms with his friend.

"Klymynt! I didn't expect to see you down here today."

"I didn't expect to *be* down here today," Abykrahmbi replied with a grin. "But then I dropped by *Delthak* looking for you, and they told me you were over here. So I trudged the entire three hundred yards from the dockyard to find you."

"I am smitten—*smitten*, I tell you—by your staunch devotion to duty."

"And well you should be. Especially since I was forced to subject not merely myself but also Corporal Brownyng and his men to the arduous privation of our forced march."

"My apologies, Corporal," Bairystyr said dryly, looking over Abykrahmbi's shoulder at the slightly taller Marine.

"No problem, Sir," Brownyng replied. He was a typical Old Charisian—brown-haired and brown-eyed with a tanned complexion—and he had the solid, weathered look of a long-term, professional soldier. Looking at the sleeve of his tunic, Bairystyr could just make out where a sergeant's stripes had been removed, and he wondered what Brownyng had done. Whatever it was, it clearly hadn't reflected any doubt about his capabilities if he'd been assigned to bodyguard Abykrahmbi. Of course, that raised another interesting question.

"Is there a *reason* the Corporal has to go everywhere with you?"

"I'm afraid so," Abykrahmbi sighed. "Do you remember Zhorj Trumyn?"

"I don't think so." Bairystyr searched his memory. "Name doesn't ring any bells, anyway. Why?"

"He was another member of Master Cartyr's staff."

"*Was* another member of Master Cartyr's staff?" Bairystyr pounced on the verb tense, and Abykrahmbi nodded.

"He was on his way to a conference with Master Ahdyms last five-day. There was a riot." Abykrahmbi's nostrils flared. "Zhorj was killed."

"I'm sorry to hear that." Bairystyr rubbed his right eyebrow thoughtfully. "I *did* hear about the riot, though. Over in Tanner's Way, wasn't it?"

"Yes. We thought that was a relatively safe part of town, but it was too close to the docks, apparently. Or to the sailmakers' lofts, anyway." Abykrahmbi grimaced. "You know how those bastards blame *us* for all their problems!"

Bairystyr nodded. It would have been foolish to expect skilled workers whose trades had been disordered by the new Charisian approach to producing goods not to resent Charis. Not that their resentment was going to change anything. They'd be far better employed, in Zhak Bairystyr's opinion, learning new trades or adapting to the ways in which their existing trades had changed, but that was probably expecting too much of human nature.

"Somebody realized Zhorj was a Charisian," Abykrahmbi said. "Or—and I think this is more likely, actually—they recognized the three men he was with as supervisors from Master Ahdyms' foundry and figured out who Zhorj was from who he was keeping company with. Anyway, somebody started screaming about Charisian heretics snatching food out of the mouths of starving babes and before anyone knew it, it was a full-bore riot. It spread across two or three square blocks before the City Guard got on top of it, and at least three shops burned. At the end of it, the Guard took up a right young bastard named Naigail—Samyl Naigail. Found his knife still in Zhorj's back, but he swears he didn't do it, of course. Nobody believes him, and I'll be surprised if he doesn't hang within the five-day."

One of Bairystyr's eyebrows rose at the bitterness of his tone. Anyone could be excused for taking a friend's death personally, but Abykrahmbi wasn't going to be surprised if this Naigail stayed unhanged for another five-day; he was going to be *disappointed*.

Abykrahmbi recognized his expression and shrugged.

"Sorry. It's not just that the rancid little son-of-a-bitch murdered Zhorj, Zhak. Once the Guard grabbed him, witnesses started coming out of the woodwork. It seems Naigail spent the attack on the Charisian Quarter torching shops and homes . . . when he wasn't doing something worse. If there's anyone in this entire frigging city who's overdue for a date with the hangman, it's him."

Bairystyr nodded. He couldn't disagree with the sentiment, assuming the testimony against Naigail was truthful. And however *he* might feel about it, he understood exactly why Abykrahmbi would feel nothing but vengeful satisfaction when the executioner sprang the trap.

"Anyway, they've decided all of us heretical Charisian masterminds need bodyguards when we wander around the city." Abykrahmbi snorted. "And if I have to have someone following me around, I could do worse than Ahldahs here."

"I see." Bairystyr looked at the corporal again. "Master Abykrahmbi's a civilian, Corporal," he said. "Mind you, he's always struck me as a fairly *smart* civilian, but he's still a civilian who happens to be both a friend of mine and an asset to the Empire. Don't take any crap off of him when it all falls in the shitter. In fact, you have my direct order to hit him over the head and drag his unconscious arse out of the line of fire if that's what it takes."

"Aye, aye, Sir!"

Brownyng jerked to attention and touched his chest in salute, and Abykrahmbi smiled. But then his smile faded as he realized both Bairystyr and Brownyng were absolutely serious.

"Zhak—"

"Klymynt, it isn't a game." Bairystyr met his friend's eyes levelly. "I know you're not stupid enough to think it *is* a game, but it'd only take a heartbeat for someone to plant a dagger in *your* back. I'm perfectly willing to believe the riot that killed your friend was spontaneous. I'm equally prepared to believe it *wasn't*, and the fact that they've assigned you a permanent bodyguard suggests someone considerably senior to both of us has his own doubts about that spontaneity. If it wasn't spontaneous, if someone does try to add you to the bag, an instant of hesitation on your part or on Corporal Brownyng's could get you killed, too, and I'm not going home to that pretty wife you've described to me to tell her it happened on my watch. Do you understand me?"

"Yes, of course I do."

"Good. And now"—Bairystyr inhaled deeply—"just what brought you down to the waterfront seeking me out?"

"Well, actually, I was looking for Lieutenant Blahdysnberg, first, but they told me he and Captain Bahrns were off at some sort of conference, so that left you and Lieutenant Cahnyrs. And since I know you, you're the lucky one."

"Lucky exactly how?" Bairystyr asked cautiously.

"We're expecting a convoy in from Tellesberg, and when it gets here, we're going to have to open *Delthak*'s casemate like a cracker box. Somebody'll have to help the dockyard figure out how to do that, and guess who just got elected?"

"I beg your pardon?" Bairystyr stared at him, and Abykrahmbi chuckled a bit sourly.

"We're going to need a rather . . . large opening," he explained. "It seems Master Howsmyn and Admiral Seamount—oh, and Captain Rahskail—have completed work on the new six-inch breechloader, and enough of the new guns and carriages are on their way to Siddar

City to rearm your ship. And given all the other things we're rushing around doing, we're going to have Shanwei's own time getting them mounted on schedule. So, since you're *Delthak*'s engineer, in charge of all those stokers and seeing to all of those repairs and things, and since I'm sure you're going to be up to your elbows in grease getting these newfangled recoil systems to work the way they're supposed to, I thought it would be best if I just went ahead and warned you now that they were coming. You can expect them sometime early next five-day."

. X .
Imperial Palace,
City of Cherayth,
Kingdom of Chisholm,
Empire of Charis,
and
Charisian Embassy,
Siddar City,
Republic of Siddarmark

The late afternoon was sunny and surprisingly mild, almost balmy, for late September in the Kingdom of Chisholm. The evening chill waited patiently behind that sunlight, but on such a golden day some of the fifty thousand or so Imperial Charisian Army troops aboard the vast convoy sailing out of Port Royal actually felt cheerful at the prospect of their voyage to Siddarmark. Others—wiser or simply more experienced—were less cheery about the whole business. It was over nine thousand miles for a wyvern to Siddar City, and they were no wyverns. Worse, they'd be fighting headwinds the entire voyage. And, worse still, they'd be crossing the body of water mariners had christened "The Anvil," and not because it offered such pleasant opportunities for yachting.

However glum some might be, however, the mood aboard those crowded transport vessels was primarily one of anticipation. The semaphore chain across Raven's Land was carrying messages from the Mainland once again, which reflected a sea change among the Raven Lords. And because it was, Chisholm knew how decisively the Imperial Army had halted the Army of God which had swept to within six hundred miles of Siddar City itself. The troops departing Port Royal on that sunny afternoon tide, under those clouds of sea wyverns and seabirds, sent on their way by the fortresses' saluting guns, felt a fierce pride in their fellows and an equally fierce satisfaction at the vindication of the radical new style of warfare in which they'd been trained.

There was as much hatred as pride and determination aboard some of those transports, for the same semaphore messages had reported what had happened to Brigadier Taisyn's men, just as they'd reported the atrocities, the concentration camps, the burned farms and villages, the dead civilians lying by the high road's verge, where starvation or disease had pulled them down.

Temple Loyalist sentiment in Chisholm had been stronger than in Old Charis. Hard-core Temple Loyalists had been a minority, yet Reformists and pro-Reformists had constituted a bare majority of the Chisholmian population before Queen Sharleyan married King Cayleb. It was the depth of Chisholm's devotion to the child-queen it had watched grow into a powerful monarch without ever losing her own devotion to the people of her realm which had carried the Kingdom into support of the Church of Charis. That had been enough, especially after they met Emperor Cayleb, decided he truly loved the queen *they* loved, and concluded that he was worthy of her. And yet even though the Chisholmian Reformists embraced the need to reform Mother Church's abuses,

Chisholm as a whole had possessed far less of the fiery ardor which gripped Old Charis.

Perhaps that was inevitable, since Chisholm had never been the object of an unprovoked assault engineered by the Church of God Awaiting. Chisholm had lost heavily in lives and ships when it was forced to participate in that assault, however, and the more astute among Queen Sharleyan's subjects had realized that if Zhaspahr Clyntahn could destroy Charis merely because he *suspected* its orthodoxy, it was almost inevitable that he would break Chisholm to his bridle as well in the fullness of time. The murder of Gwylym Manthyr and his men had underscored the threat, and so, Chisholm had given itself to the war against the Group of Four, prepared to play its part, to make the sacrifices demanded of it, but still without that spark of true fury, that sense of having met the monster face-to-face, stared into its maw, smelled the stench of its carrion breath.

But the massacre of Brigadier Taisyn's command, the torture and murder of entire armies, the starvation and death of millions, all at the orders of Zhaspahr Clyntahn, had hit the Kingdom like a handful of gunpowder cast across dimly glowing coals. Those who'd been ambivalent saw suddenly the true difference between the two sides. Even many Temple Loyalists—especially among those who'd clung to their old faith out of habit and a natural suspicion of the forces of reform and change— had been shaken to the core, and quite a few of them had become Reformists over the past few months.

Inevitably, the Temple Loyalists who remained had become even more fiercely dedicated to the "legitimate" Church. Even though the Crown specifically protected their right to worship in the manner of their choice, the savage denunciations of Zhaspahr Clyntahn and the Inquisition they heard daily forced them into a defensive posture that hunkered down, hunched its shoulders against the storm, and clung passionately to its faith. In fact, many of them flatly denied the reports from the Republic. They were—must be—lies created to vilify

Mother Church's loyal sons! The keeper of men's souls must occasionally be stern, as *The Book of Schueler* commanded, but she would *never* murder children or condone rape, arson, and massacre on such a scale!

Those who believed that were losing ground steadily, however. And the men of the Imperial Charisian Army, which had grown out of the Royal Chisholmian Army, had been staunchly devoted to the Crown and to the Empire long before the first Charisian boot stepped onto a Siddarmarkian wharf.

There were very few qualms aboard those ships, standing out from Port Royal into Kraken Bay.

▼ ▼ ▼

"Well, there they go," Cayleb Ahrmahk said.

It was four hours earlier in Siddar City, but sunset was coming sooner every day. It was already dark outside the windows of his embassy study, because unlike Port Royal's sky, the Siddarmarkian capital's was anything but cloudless. Rain drummed on the embassy's roof, gurgling through downspouts and splashing on the paving, and the coal fire on his hearth was welcome.

"Yes, they do," his wife agreed from her own palace apartment in Cherayth.

She leaned back in a comfortable chair, holding a drowsy Princess Alahnah in her lap while Sairaih Hahlmyn guarded her privacy like a restless dragon. The empress had been involved in one meeting after another since shortly after dawn before she'd finally announced that she was spending the evening with her daughter. With Sergeant Seahamper outside her door and her personal maid poised to annihilate any member of the palace staff who even *looked* like intruding upon Her Majesty, she could be reasonably confident of her ability to converse with Cayleb and their allies without interruption.

And after a day like today, she needed that conversation.

"You do realize White Crag and Sir Ahlber are a lot more worried about sending the entire Army to the

Republic than they want to admit, don't you?" Cayleb asked now, and she snorted.

"Is there some reason you think I arrived in Cherayth aboard this morning's turnip wagon? Of course they're worried! They're my First Councilor and my spymaster. It's their *jobs* to worry, Cayleb."

"And they're not entirely wrong to, either, Sharley," Merlin Athrawes put in.

He was in his own room, arranged in the lotus position with his eyes closed. He'd taken to parking himself in that posture whenever he was officially meditating, and his ability to remain inhumanly still for hours on end—motionless, scarcely even breathing—had polished his official persona as mystic warrior quite nicely. No one looking at him could have guessed from his serene expression what was passing through his mind, but his voice over the com carried an edge of concern he would have allowed very few people to hear.

"The more fervent they get and the more isolated they feel, the more likely someone like Countess Swayle or Duke Rock Coast is to do something stupid," he went on. "And this is the first time since your father took the throne that virtually the entire Army's been out of the Kingdom."

"I realize that." Sharleyan's voice was far more serene than Merlin's. "And before you or Cayleb hit me over the head with it, I also know what the SNARCs are picking up from Rock Coast and that snake Rydach. We're keeping an eye on them, though, and it's not as if the 'entire Army's' really out of the Kingdom. We've got the training cadre here in Cherayth, and the new recruits are shaping up nicely. There's not much question about *their* loyalty, and I think the Zebediahans coming in from Hauwyl may be even more rabidly loyal than my Chisholmians!"

There was some truth to that, Merlin reflected. In fact, there was quite a lot of truth to it. Although the Imperial Charisian Army had now deployed virtually all of its combat formations to Siddarmark, its training battalions remained behind. That represented a good twenty thousand men, many combat veterans, two-thirds of them stationed in or just outside Cherayth or in Maikelberg, the Royal Chisholmian Army's traditional headquarters, less than three hundred miles to the north. And she was right about the recruits those training battalions were taking on. It might be too much to say Chisholmians were "flocking to the colors" at this late date, but the influx of new volunteers was enough to make any thought of conscription unnecessary. Still more were coming in from Emerald, Tarot, and Zebediah, and the Zebediahans' enthusiasim burned bright.

I guess it shouldn't be that surprising, he thought. *Hauwyl Chermyn's the first honest grand duke Zebediah's had, and he's sudden death on abuses of power. Doesn't have much patience with corrupt judges, either, and didn't that come as an unhappy surprise to the previous grand duke's cronies?*

Zebediah had been no paradise even before Corisande conquered it. Now, after decades of Hektor Daykyn and Tohmys Symmyns, Hektor's choice as grand duke, the people of Zebediah had been given a taste of honest, efficient governance, and it had come as a profound shock to the grand duchy's system. Not all Zebediahans, especially among the nobly born, were pleased with the new arrangements, but Chermyn's reputation as a highly competent general—and the thirty thousand well-officered and equipped men at his command—were more than enough to convince anyone who might contemplate rebellion to rethink his position. The Baron of Green Valley had systematically dismantled the Zebediahan Army which had been the last grand duke's creature, and Chermyn had built well upon Green Valley's foundation. In addition, the last of the aristocracy's armies of personal retainers had been disbanded by imperial edict, Grand Duke Hauwyl had embraced that edict enthusiastically, and his troops had seen to its enforcement with speed and efficiency. For the first time in Zebediahan memory, the Army was actually seen as protector, not predator.

The Reformist clergy Maikel Staynair and Archbishop Ulys had sent to Zebediah to support the Church of Charis were even more effective shock troops than Chermyn's army. The Church of God Awaiting in Zebediah had made the mistake of assuming Zebediah was another Harchong, or perhaps Desnair, and aligning itself firmly with the aristocracy. Mother Church had also become more and more openly supportive of the Corisandian conquest as Hektor of Corisande emerged as the Group of Four's counterweight against Haarahld Ahrmahk, which represented an equally serious error. It wasn't that the long-suffering Zebediahan serfs and commoners had turned against the Church so much as that they'd turned against the Church's *policy* . . . and the clergy sent to enforce it. The parish priests who'd spoken up for their parishioners, the abbots who'd done their best to mitigate the nobility's excesses and, too often, those of their ecclesiastic superiors, the Pasqualate nuns who'd served in the hospitals, the Bédardist Sisters of Charity who'd ministered to the growing poor in Zebediah's towns and cities had become even more beloved, but they'd also been separated from the powerful and mighty of Mother Church in the popular mind.

And as in every other realm where the opportunity had offered, *those* clergy—those priests, those abbots, those nuns—had responded to the Reformist message. Indeed, they'd responded passionately, and they'd brought the Zebediahans who saw them as Mother Church's true face into the arms of the Church of Charis.

So, yes, it shouldn't be a bit surprising that Zebediahans—especially the freed serfs—were enlisting by hundreds and thousands. And Sharleyan was right about their loyalty.

"If Rock Coast and his cronies should be foolish enough to see the Army's absence as an opportunity, it will . . . end badly for them," Sharleyan said now. Her thin, cold smile went a bit oddly with the baby napping in her arms, Merlin thought, and yet it seemed completely appropriate. "In fact, part of me almost wishes they *would* try something. If they're willing to give me the opportunity for a little surgery where they're concerned, I'm perfectly willing to do the cutting."

"In a theoretical sort of way, I agree with you," Cayleb said. "Can't even argue that I haven't set up the same sort of surgery myself upon occasion. But I'd just as soon not see you and Alahnah in the middle of that sort of mess. And however beneficial it might be in the long term, the short-term consequences for any of our people—*your* people—who got caught up in it could be ugly."

"I know. I know!" Sharleyan grimaced. "That's why I'm not going out of my way to draw them into doing exactly that. But if the opportunity *does* come along, it'll be the *last* time any of them are stupid enough to try it. It's remarkable how detaching a traitor's brain from his circulatory system prevents recidivism."

"I can live with that," Cayleb replied. "Just . . . be careful. There're enough things going wrong in the world that I'd just as soon not have to worry about you and Alahnah—and your mother, and Green Mountain—while I'm stuck in this damned embassy!"

"Cayleb, you *have* to be there, love." Sharleyan's voice was much gentler.

"No, I don't," he disagreed sourly. "I'm sitting here while Kynt and Eastshare and Hauwerd Breygart and God only knows who else're out doing something worthwhile in the field. I ought to be out there, too, damn it!"

"I understand your feelings, and I know it's frustrating, but—"

"It's not just 'frustrating,'" Cayleb interrupted. "It's *wrong*. I've got no business sending other men out to be killed while I sit on my arse!"

Behind his serene, meditating expression, Merlin grimaced in dismay. He'd known Cayleb's "inactivity" was eating at him, but the speed with which the conversation had segued was unusual, to say the least. To be honest, Merlin agreed with Sharleyan . . . but *sympathized* with Cayleb. For all the impressive maturity Cayleb and Sharleyan had both shown, the emperor was a very young man. Too young to have developed the calluses which accepted that a head which wore a crown was not expendable, especially when an empire was so new that its ultimate stability still depended upon its charismatic rulers.

It's not as if he were Alexander of Macedon, though, Merlin thought. *He knows it, too, and that's part of the problem. He's built better than that, he and Sharley, and he knows that if anything happens to him she'll still be here to carry on, and so will Maikel, and the rest of the inner circle. The Empire won't disintegrate into warring factions. But even if that's true, he and Sharley are the face of the opposition to the Group of Four, even more than Maikel, and he's smart enough to know that, too. That's why Clyntahn and his Rakurai tried so hard to kill both of them. The reason he's still trying. Losing either one of them would be a catastrophic blow. He knows that, but he doesn't feel it. And even if that weren't true, he knows he's good, that leading men in battle is something for which he has a natural gift . . . that isn't being used.*

"It's not 'wrong,' Cayleb," he said quietly. "It just hurts."

Cayleb started to reply quickly, hotly. But then he stopped himself and his jaw tightened.

"It's like the times I have to kill people I don't want to kill," Merlin continued. "People whose only real offense is believing what they were taught from childhood and being in the wrong place when I come along. You know how . . . difficult I find that, but Nahrmahn was right. Sometimes there truly isn't another option, and I'm the only person who can do it.

"Right now, you're the only person who can do what *you're* doing. In another few months that may change, but for right now, you need to be here in the capital where you and Stohnar can discuss everything from strategy to industrial allocations face-to-face. And you and I *both* have to be here to control and manage the information flow to Aivah and Maidyn from the SNARCs."

Cayleb glowered for several moments, his shoulder muscles as tight as his face. Then, finally, he relaxed and shook his head.

"Point taken," he half growled. "I don't like it, I'm

not *going* to like it, and I'm not going to do it one minute longer than I have to. But you did sort of put my . . . pettiness into perspective, Merlin."

"That wasn't my intention, and it's not 'pettiness.' "

"I know it wasn't your intention. That's what made it so effective." Cayleb's lips twitched into a sour smile. "I'll try to be good. Or *better,* anyway. Let's not be asking for any miracles."

"Heaven forbid." Sharleyan made no effort to keep her amusement—and relief—out of her tone, and Cayleb smiled more broadly.

"Turning to more cheerful matters," he said with deliberate briskness, "it looks like you did an even better job with Irys and Coris than we thought, Sharley."

"I'd like to be able to take credit," his wife replied, "but you and Maikel had a little input into the terms yourselves. And I have to admit I never counted on Gairlyng's contribution!"

"It goes back to what you and Cayleb've been saying from the beginning, Sharleyan," Merlin said. "What's conquered by the sword depends on the sword to *stay* conquered. I hate to say it, given the amount of damage he's doing, but we're damned lucky Clyntahn doesn't understand that mercy and justice are deadlier than any rifle or bayonet."

"It wouldn't help him if he did," Cayleb said grimly. "He can't rely on mercy and justice because what he wants—what he *needs*—is intrinsically at odds with both of them. He might be able to rely on them in some places, far enough away from the actual conflict, but for him they'd always be no more than a façade, a mask, and sooner or later people would realize it."

That's true, Merlin thought. *And so's the corollary— that sooner or later people realize that when you and Sharley offer mercy and justice it's who you really are, not a ploy.*

"All the same," he said out loud, "I really didn't expect it to sail through Parliament the way it did. I think the fact that it wasn't a unanimous vote—that so many of the Lords voted openly against accepting the terms . . . and lost—may even work in our favor. No one's going to be able to claim it was a put-up job, with the Lords forced to vote in favor at bayonet point. At the same time, the overwhelming majority in the Commons has to serve as pretty firm notice to the dissenters that the rest of the Princedom isn't putting up with any foolishness."

"And the fact that there won't be any retaliation against the Lords who voted against it should demonstrate we meant what we said about the rule of law," Sharleyan agreed. "Even if we do know some of them would jump at the chance to rebel if they thought they could make it work."

"But they can't make it work, and with Coris, Anvil Rock, and Tartarian to advise Irys and Daivyn, they won't get a *chance* to make it work," her husband observed in satisfied tones, then laughed suddenly. "And on top of that, there'll be Daivyn's brother-in-law and *his* advice. I'm sure it'll have a . . . profoundly moving effect on Irys, at least."

"You're a bad man, Cayleb Ahrmahk," Sharleyan told him with a grin. "Not that Hektor won't give her perfectly good advice, if she asks. I think he's smart enough not to cram it at her, though. He'd darned well better be, at any rate!"

"After the bee you put in his ear before he sailed for Corisande?" Cayleb rolled his eyes. "I really expected to hear him saying 'Yessssssss, Mom. I under*staaaaannnnd!*'"

"I was not that bad, Cayleb, and you know it!"

"No, you weren't," Cayleb conceded. "And fortunately he's not only smart enough to understand why you raised the point but smart enough to've refrained from doing it on his own even if you hadn't warned him."

"I was surprised Parliament went along with Gairlyng's suggestion to schedule the wedding so soon," Merlin put in. "I think it's a good idea—especially coming from the Corisandian side, not ours—but I expected a little more hesitation out of Parliament. A little push-back from the Lords, at least."

"Unless and until Parliament gets around to changing the law, the Crown would pass through Anvil Rock's nephew before it passed through Irys, anyway," Sharleyan pointed out. "Mind you, we happen to know courtesy of the SNARCs that Anvil Rock and Tartarian—and Gairlyng—intend to quietly change that as soon as they can get away with it. It's going to be at least a few years, though. In fact, my own feeling is that it would be best to wait until Daivyn's assumed the Crown in his own right and pushes for the change himself.

"For Parliament at large, however, it's more a case of cementing *us*—Cayleb and me—to the Daykyn Dynasty rather than the other way around. They've decided that if they're going to be part of the Empire, they want to be included on the best possible terms and with the best possible representation at the very highest level. And how better to accomplish that than to marry their prince's sister to the Emperor and Empress' son?"

"Put that way, it makes a lot of sense," Merlin acknowledged. "I guess I really still don't think like a dynast."

"It's going to be a while yet before Safeholdian rulers *stop* thinking like dynasts," Cayleb said. "The only place with a real tradition of elective rulers is here in the Republic, and even Siddarmark's more like that place you and I were talking about back on Old Earth than the Terran Federation ever was, Merlin."

"Venice?"

"That's the place. It may be an elective system with a constitution to keep it that way, but elections and political decisions are in the hands of—what? Fifteen percent of the total population?"

"About that," Merlin agreed. "But only because those are the acknowledged 'great families.' And even if the Constitution's property qualifications give them a lock on actually holding office, the *franchise* is a lot broader than that. More and more of the middle class was leaking over into the great families even before the Sword of Schueler, and the pressure to lower the property threshold for office holders has been building for forty years now. Given how many members of the great families went over to the Church—and how big a chunk of the middle class stayed loyal—I'm pretty confident there'll be some significant changes in the political equation after the smoke clears. And unless I'm badly mistaken, Stohnar and Maidyn see that as clearly as *I* do. I'd say they have at least half an eye on engineering a soft landing when the Siddarmarkian establishment has to bow to the new realities. Their example could make for some interesting challenges for you absolutist Charisian monarchists, too."

"Smile when you say that, *seijin*!" Cayleb retorted. "If you think *we're* going to have challenges, just imagine what it's going to be like in Harchong!"

"I prefer not to, if it's all the same to you. I'm not particularly fond of the Harchongese aristocracy, but it's going to be ugly when the wheels start coming off—especially in *northern* Harchong."

"Personally, I'll be surprised if the southern provinces don't secede," Sharleyan said. "That's where all the merchants and industry are already, and the rate of industrialization south of the Gulf's only going to make the southerners' even more restless. Especially when the aristocrats try to turn back the clock as soon as the war's over, and you *know* they're stupid enough to try just that."

"That's certainly possible," Merlin agreed, "but I'm betting it'll be even worse in the north. That's where most of the 'Mighty Host of God and the Archangels'' conscripts are from, and if Maigwair succeeds in turning them into an effective fighting force, there's likely to be hell to pay. At least some of those serfs aren't going to be very happy about being sent home to their owners again, and that could turn *really* ugly."

"Uglier than we've already seen in the Republic?" Sharleyan asked grimly. "Because I've got to tell you, Merlin, I can live with a little 'ugly' for the people behind what's happened there. Some 'sauce for the wyvern' seems in order."

"I can't say I disagree, Sharley." Merlin grimaced.

"The problem's that a lot of people who didn't have any choice about what happened will get ground up in the gears. And as I mentioned to Domynyk once upon a time, peasant wars—slave rebellions, really, because that is what it would be—may be the only things even more ghastly than religious wars . . . for *both* sides."

There was silence for a long moment, then he inhaled deeply.

"We seem to be wandering a bit from the topic of Corisande," he observed.

"That's because Corisande's pretty well sewed up," Cayleb replied. "When Gairlyng pushed Parliament to set October twenty-second for Daivyn's coronation and the twenty-fourth for the wedding, I knew it was all over except sweeping up the flower petals. I believe it's called 'a done deal,' Merlin."

"And the fact that Maikel's going to be arriving in Manchyr in time for both of them won't hurt one bit," Sharleyan agreed in tones of profound satisfaction. "There's a reason Koryn Gahrvai's already discussing how best to integrate his Corisandian Guard into the Imperial Army, Merlin."

"Don't sprain your elbow patting yourself on the back, dear," Cayleb suggested with a grin. "Mind you, I agree you deserve the dragon's—or perhaps the dragoness', in this case—share of the credit, but modesty is a pleasing characteristic in a ruler."

"You are *so* lucky I don't have a recon skimmer I could use to fly to Siddar City and kick you somewhere painful, Cayleb Ahrmahk!"

"I know where you could borrow one," Merlin put in helpfully.

"Off with his head!" Cayleb said.

"Nonsense. I'll write you a pardon in my own hand, Merlin! Pick me up on the palace roof at midnight."

"Tempting," Merlin said with more than a trace of wistfulness. "Very tempting. But"—he opened his eyes and rose smoothly from the lotus—"since I can't do that for the two of you, I'll do the next best thing. I think we've finished all the business that needs to be discussed, and you two haven't seen each other face-to-face in way too long. You go ahead and talk. I'll find something else to do."

OCTOBER, YEAR OF GOD 896

· ✦ ·

. I .
Spinefish Bay,
Icewind Province,
Republic of Siddarmark

The pall of smoke above what had once been the town of Salyk was thicker than it had been, despite the rain. There was ice in that rain, tiny bits of sleet rattling off HMS *Tellesberg*'s armor. They slid slowly down the rain-slick steel and Captain Lainyr Dahglys shivered in the raw, wet chill despite his gloves and the warm watch coat under his oilskins.

It was a thoroughly miserable day, with low clouds and no hint of sunlight. Spinefish Bay was a gray, wrinkled wilderness, the waves barely two feet tall as they washed onto the stony shingle. In a lot of ways, he'd be far from sorry to be shut of this place, yet a bitter reluctance washed through him with the same persistent rhythm as those listless waves.

The bastards're just waiting, he thought, raising his double-glass to peer shoreward once again. *I wonder how they'll phrase their reports? I'll damned well bet one thing they* won't *do is admit they're sitting there with their thumbs up their arses while we pull out in our own good time. Whatever they tell him, though, that bastard Clyntahn will turn it into another glorious triumph for the defenders of Mother Church!*

His mouth twisted at the mental image his own words provoked. If it had been up to him, they'd've stayed here, holding Salyk till Hell froze over, but it wasn't up to him, and they *couldn't* stay. Not because Hell might freeze over, but because Spinefish Bay most certainly would.

Most of the galleons had already left, carrying every single civilian—and also every cow, every pig, every chicken and rabbit—from Salyk. Only the warships and the last troop transports remained, and *Tellesberg* and her sister *Saygin* were anchored close inshore, smoke pluming from their funnels to merge with the cloud cover as they lay between the land and the bombardment ships *Whirlwind* and *Tornado*. The ironclads' thirty-pounders were run out, covering the flanks of the innermost entrenchments while the bombardment ships angle-guns waited to punish any Temple Loyalist foolish enough to press too closely upon the rearguard. Most of the artillery had been withdrawn along with the bulk of the garrison. The last two batteries of twelve-pounders were falling back to the docks even now, and the Temple Loyalists had learned enough about Shan-wei's fountains and footstools to keep a respectful distance.

It was a picture-perfect example of a planned withdrawal, Dahglys thought. They were leaving at the time of their choosing, evacuating their men and material on their own schedule, unmolested by the Army of God which had "besieged" Salyk for so long. It had been a peculiar "siege," since the port's seaward approaches had never been seriously threatened. The Temple Boys' one attempt to push guns far enough forward to reach the waterfront had turned into a costly catastrophe. They'd tried to move the guns under cover of darkness, but rocket-launched flares had illuminated them and *Tellesberg* and *Saygin* had moved in close and devastated the guns, their gunners, and the fatigue parties which had been supposed to emplace them before dawn. Instead of the guns, over four hundred Temple Boys had been permanently emplaced by the defenders' burial parties.

The troops and civilians in Salyk had actually been far better fed and healthier at the height of the "siege" than they'd been since the preceding autumn. Dahglys hadn't seen the gaunt faces and emaciated bodies which had greeted the original ICN relief force when the ice melted in the spring. The ironclads had arrived too late for that. But he'd been ashore to see the cemeteries, the long lines of wooden grave markers, the painted dates which all too often told the tale of a *child's* life cut short by starvation. He knew what the citizens of Icewind and especially of Salyk had endured, and he hated—he absolutely *hated*—abandoning all they'd fought and starved and suffered to hold.

But there's already ice forming on the bay. We're lucky it's been a relatively mild autumn, but it's only a matter of time, and the Emperor and Lord Protector Greyghor are right. Best we pull out now instead of being forced to improvise a withdrawal or find ourselves caught by a surprise cold snap that freezes the bay—or even Hsingwu's Passage—solid.

There was no question in his mind that they were doing the right thing . . . and as he looked around at the dreary, rainy sky, felt the snow loitering on the far side of that raw, wet breeze, knowing that made him feel not one bit better.

"Signal from the shore, Sir. The artillery's lighters are pulling for the transports now. The last infantry's falling back to the boats. And—"

A sudden, earthshaking bellow made the rest of the signalman's report superfluous. They'd landed plenty of gunpowder in Salyk over the preceding months, and the garrison had seen no reason to pull it all back out again.

He raised the double-glass again, looking past the dark columns of smoke from the torched warehouses and barracks, and saw the fresh wings of smoke—white and gray, this time, shot through with a fierce red glare—as the first charges blew apart the gun emplacements and magazines in the outer ring of entrenchments. Almost exactly one minute later, the next ring of earthworks erupted like a man-made volcano. One minute after that, the third ring exploded, and then it was the innermost line of entrenchments.

He lowered the double-glass as longboats and cutters lifted the last of the rearguard from the docks. As the oarsmen pulled strongly, white water curling at the boats' stems, the town itself exploded. The blasts leveled every structure, leaving nothing to shelter any garrison the Army of God might choose to leave over the coming winter. And then, when the boats were clear, the waterfront—the broad expanse of docks and wharves and warehouses the Imperial Charisian Navy had improved and expanded during the months of the siege—disintegrated into splinters and flying timbers. The fragments soared upward, many of them trailing smoke or drawing lines of fire against the sullen gray clouds, and then they hit the rain-dimpled water in feathers and fountains of foam.

Dahglys looked at the rolling billows of smoke obliterating what had once been a community of brightly painted homes and red-tiled roofs. He let the image sink fully into his memory, then drew a deep breath and stepped from the exposed bridge wing into the conning tower's warmth. He looked across the polished voice pipes and the handles of the engine room telegraph at Lieutenant Brahd Solayran, *Tellesberg*'s first lieutenant.

"Show's over, Brahd," he said. "Time to be going."

. II .

The Temple,
City of Zion,
The Temple Lands

"I suppose whoever it is is still running rings around you, Wyllym?"

When Zhaspahr Clyntahn decided to use an unpleasant tone, it was very unpleasant indeed. Now he sat behind his desk, hands folded on the blotter, beefy face showing an expression which probably would have been called "petulant" on a man who did not command the power of life and death whenever he chose to exercise it, and glowered at Archbishop Wyllym Rayno.

"Unfortunately, Your Grace, that would be an accurate way to describe it," Rayno replied, hands tucked into the sleeves of his cassock, as he met his superior's angry eyes with the levelness of long practice. "I've shared my reports with you on a five-day basis," he continued. "As those reports have indicated, our sole real success was the interception of the assassins dispatched against Vicar Malikai. That cost them five of their number. Unfortunately, we took none of them alive—two of them poisoned themselves—and as many as three others escaped in the end."

Clyntahn snorted. Vicar Malikai Bordyn was not one of the vicarate's brighter lights. His loss would have been no more than a minor inconvenience, if not for the intended manner of his demise and the impact it might have had. Despite Rayno's best efforts, word that someone was assassinating vicars was circulating more and more freely. So far, they'd at least apparently managed to prevent anyone from realizing the vicars who were being killed weren't merely targets of opportunity—that they were being skillfully and methodically stalked. They'd also managed to downplay the fact that they'd been among Clyntahn's closest supporters . . . for reasons which all too often had more to do with the power of blackmail than the fervor of conviction. The knowledge that Clyntahn's allies were at special risk might not have done a great deal for those allies' loyalty.

"I trust you won't take this personally, Wyllym," the Grand Inquisitor said nastily, "but *dead* assassins strike me as a piss-poor source of information."

"I agree," Rayno acknowledged. "We did learn a few things from them, however, although most of those things merely confirm that these people are very well trained, well organized, and understand the essentials of operating covertly better than anyone Mother Church has encountered since the War Against the Fallen itself. For example, all of the dead were completely devoid of anything which might have suggested their origin, identities, or the location of their headquarters. In many ways, one might almost think of them as counter-Rakurai, except that they're operating as an organized group rather than the individuals we've dispatched against the heretics."

As the archbishop had hoped, Clyntahn's ire seemed to settle a bit at the reminder of his own brainchild and its successes. Rayno wasn't about to breathe any sighs of relief just yet, but every little bit helped. He also chose not to mention that however spectacular some of the Rakurai's successes might have been, the heretics had done a far better job of intercepting or preventing their attacks than the Inquisition had achieved against the organization his agents inquisitor had nicknamed the Hand of Kau-yung. They were careful to avoid using the name where Rayno might hear it, but there were very few things of which Wyllym Rayno did not hear eventually.

"Three of our agents inquisitor have disappeared over the last month, however, Your Grace," he continued in a graver tone. "This suggests that each of them got too close to *someone* operating against Mother Church. Given these assassins' effectiveness, it's very tempting to conclude that the someone—or someones—in question was those for whom we're searching. I'm not prepared to assume that's necessarily the case, but I'm having all of their reports for the last year analyzed and compared to one another. It may be that we'll find some common element that might give us a lead to these murderers."

Better not to mention his own fear that not all the vanished agents inquisitor had gone missing as the result of hostile action. It was unfortunately possible that at least one of them might actually have been an agent of the Hand of Kau-yung planted upon the Inquisition, instead.

"Humph." Clyntahn frowned, then shrugged. "I suppose if that's the best you can do, that's the best you can do."

He sounded as if he begrudged every word—which he no doubt did—and let silence linger for a moment before he changed the subject.

"You said you had something you wanted to discuss

with me. Since I rather doubt that it was your continuing lack of progress against these murderers, why don't you go ahead and tell me what it was?"

"Of course, Your Grace." Rayno bowed slightly. "First, Vicar Allayn's clearly pleased by your decision to grant the dispensation regarding the new primer caps. Also, my agents inquisitor suggest that Vicar Rhobair's analysis of the increased production rate—and lowered costs—achieved by the St. Kylmahn Foundry's new methods is essentially correct. Indeed, some evidence suggests he's actually underestimating the improvement."

Clyntahn's expression was an interesting mix of satisfaction and disgruntlement. Rhobair Duchairn's incessant harping upon the cost of the Jihad and the fragile state of their finances had passed well beyond the irritating stage, and the notion that there might actually be some *positive* news was a relief. At the same time, he'd almost hoped Duchairn had exaggerated the projections from St. Kylmahn, instead, because it would have provided the pretext to eliminate Brother Lynkyn Fultyn, whose pernicious influence was pushing Maigwair further and further in the direction of simply ignoring the Proscriptions. After all, Fultyn would clearly have lied to Duchairn, and if Duchairn had attempted to shield him or protect him from the Inquisition, it could only have weakened Duchairn's position.

That position needed weakening, too. The unfortunate downturn in the Army of God's fortunes in Siddarmark—due, whatever anyone else might say, to Maigwair's failure to predict the heretics' canal raid and, even more, to the stupidity of Duchairn's transport managers, who'd failed to destroy the locks in their path—had actually *strengthened* Duchairn. It was bitterly unfair—and inconvenient—but the repair of the crippled canals and the need to replace and upgrade the Army of God's weapons had forced Clyntahn to make concessions to the united front of Duchairn and Maigwair. Worse, all indications were that the working relationship between the treasurer and captain general was growing steadily closer. Had Clyntahn been foolish enough to allow any substantial army garrison to be posted in Zion itself, that relationship could have been ominous, but he'd ensured that all the armed power in and around Zion, Port Harbor, and the Temple was under the *Inquisition's* control. He meant to keep it that way, and in the end, of course, the problem was only temporary. Eventually, Duchairn's lily-livered bleating over the stern necessities of the Jihad must inevitably bring him back into conflict with Maigwair as the military commander responsible for waging that Jihad.

"In addition, Your Grace, some new information has come into our possession from Siddar City."

"Ah?" Clyntahn straightened in his chair, eyes narrowing intently.

"Indeed, Your Grace." Rayno bowed once more. "One of our Sword Rakurai returned it to us."

The archbishop noted the pleased flicker in Clyntahn's gaze. Unlike the Rakurai dispatched for the purpose of striking the heretics in the hearts of their own realms, the Sword Rakurai held a much broader commission. Forbidden to associate themselves with any of the Faithful in the realms to which they had been assigned—an unhappy and infuriating concession to the efficiency of the heretics' counterintelligence capabilities—they were intended primarily as gatherers of information. The lack of any support structure reduced their reach, but they were highly trained and chosen for demonstrated initiative. And, privately and without mentioning it to Clyntahn, Rayno had taken care to select Sword Rakurai who *weren't* eager to die for God. Men who would recognize the value of surviving for future service to Him and His Church, instead.

"What might this information be, and how did he obtain it?"

Clyntan didn't ask for the man's identity. Security for all the Rakurai, and especially the Sword Rakurai, was almost insanely tight. By his own direction, not even Clyntahn knew which had been assigned where, even though he continued to make a point of personally vetting each of the Sword Rakurai. From that point on, however, their identities and assignments were solely in Rayno's hands. Given what had happened to every *other* effort to penetrate the heretics' defenses, that paranoia had proved itself very much worthwhile.

"He obtained it, Your Grace, as the result of an operation which struck down four of Shan-wei's servants in the heart of Stohnar's capital." Rayno allowed himself his first smile of the interview. "There remain many Faithful in Siddarmark, even in Siddar City itself, Your Grace. Many of them have more than one reason to hate Charis, and our Sword Rakurai had made it his business to seek out several groups of Faithful who were . . . most vocal in their opposition to the Charisians' presence. In accordance with his instructions, he was careful not to attach himself to any of those groups, yet he'd identified them and marked them down for potential use.

"Last month, he recognized one of the Charisian 'advisers' in the employ of the heretic Howsmyn, deep in conversation with several of the Siddarmarkian heretics laboring to copy Charisian methods as they passed through the streets en route to a meeting of Stohnar's 'Council of Manufactories.' Our Sword Rakurai got ahead of them, entered one of the taverns he knew a particularly fervent group of Faithful favored, and as soon as the heretics came close enough, he pointed them out."

Clyntahn produced his first smile of the meeting, as well—a cold, predatory thing which would have looked very much at home on a kraken.

"It turned very quickly into a riot," Rayno continued. "A riot our Sword Rakurai used to get close enough to the Charisian to personally strike him down. All three of the Siddarmarkians were killed, as well, and the Faithful went on to burn the businesses of several heretics and heretic sympathizers before the City Guard managed to disperse them.

"It was only afterward that our Sword Rakurai realized the potential value of the briefcase he'd seized from the Charisian."

The archbishop paused, and Clyntahn leaned towards him.

"What sort of 'value'?" he demanded.

"Why, a complete description of the heretics' new steel-making process, Your Grace," Rayno said, and nodded at the sudden change in Clyntahn's expression. "I'm no mechanic myself, so my ability to assess the information is limited. I believe there are some gaps, and I could wish there were more technical drawings to accompany the text. In addition, it deals only with blast furnaces and something called 'open hearth' furnaces, not with all the other devices our agents suggest the heretics have employed to increase their productivity so markedly. However, as part of the description of the furnaces, there's also a discussion of something called a 'steam engine.' I've found no directions for building one of them, but there's a lengthy description of the principles upon which they work. I suspect our own mechanics and artificers might be able to create 'steam engines' of their own if those principles were shared with them."

"Schueler," Clyntahn said very softly. Then he shook himself, hard.

"Tell me more about this 'steam engine,'" he said.

. III .

Allyntyn,
Midhold Province,
Republic of Siddarmark

Baron Green Valley shivered despite the fire crackling on the grate of the more or less intact house he'd commandeered as his headquarters. It stood on what had been the better side of town, and houses in northern Siddarmark were strongly built, with thick walls to hold heat in winter and shed it in summer. Unfortunately, like most of Allyntyn, this one's condition was less than pristine. There were holes in the roof, the second-floor windows had been boarded over, there were drafts in the damnedest places, and most of the legal owner's furniture had been used for firewood by the previous occupants.

Despite which, it was in better shape than the majority of the town. And the fact that the fire on his grate was coal-fed, whereas the Temple Loyalists had been reduced to burning the furniture before their hasty withdrawal from Allyntyn, said a great deal about the difference in the state of their supplies.

He stepped closer to the fire, rubbing his palms briskly. Technically, the northern hemisphere's autumnal equinox was less than a month past, but he remembered how one of the Siddarmarkian cavalry officers attached to his command had described Midhold's climate. "One month of summer, five months of winter, and four months of damned poor sledding," he'd said, and nothing Green Valley had seen yet contradicted him. Technically winter or not, there'd been a heavy frost overnight before the fog came up shortly after dawn, and this raw, dreary morning was quite cold enough for Green Valley's Charisian-born sentiments. Winter in Chisholm had been a miserable experience, but Allyntyn was well north of Alyksberg. In fact, it was at almost the same latitude as Ramsgate Bay, and without the moderating influence of the Chisholm Current.

He grimaced and turned to the map on the table in the center of what had been someone's formal sitting room. That table was one of the few items of furniture to have survived, and he found himself wondering if its owner would ever return to claim it. For that matter, was that owner even still alive? He liked to think so. He liked to think *someone* in the riven and harrowed wasteland which had once been Midhold Province would survive and someday take up the task of putting his and his family's lives back together again.

That was harder to believe on some days than on others.

He frowned at the map's penciled-in positions of his own and known enemy units. He was actually rather better informed about those enemy units than young Slokym had been when he updated the map, and Owl was quite capable of showing him detailed topographical maps with real-time imagery. He preferred that in a tactical situation, but somehow he still found it easier to think and plan looking at the sorts of maps he'd grown up with.

So far, his march around Bahrnabai Wyrshym's flank had gone well, and the Temple Loyalist cavalry had lost heavily learning to leave Charisian infantry well enough alone. Wyrshym had reacted to the threat by shoring up his left with his better infantry divisions, however, and the lessons Nybar and his fellows had learned were obvious. They were paying far more attention to scouting—and to denying his own patrols freedom of movement—and there were *no* pikemen in their order of battle. They'd also developed a love affair with the shovel. Bitter experience had taught them the difference in vulnerability between riflemen who had to stand upright to load their weapons and riflemen who could lie on their bellies behind fallen logs or farmers' rock piles. There wasn't much they could do about the fact that they were stuck with muzzleloaders—yet, at least—but they'd discovered the beauty of entrenchments and breastworks.

I really wish they were Desnairians, he thought, his finger resting on the position of Gorthyk Nybar's Langhorne Division in the middle of the Northland Gap. *These troops aren't just better disciplined and motivated, they're better led, and that's a pain in the arse. Their cavalry took it in the ear the first few times we ran into them, mostly because of how well they'd done against the Siddarmarkians in the western provinces. But the survivors did learn, and they did it fast. Worse, they made sure they passed the lessons on to their people who hadn't run into us yet. So they're smart, they're not afraid to learn, and they're willing to admit it to their superiors—in the Army, at least—when they screw up. That's a bad combination, and if Nahrmahn's right about this new rifle of theirs, things're going to get worse.*

Still, taking one thing with another, he was far happier to be in his shoes rather than theirs.

At the moment, his two Charisian infantry regiments were both understrength by five or six hundred men, although the majority of those troops would be returning from the healers over the next few five-days, and Major Dyasaiyl's battalion of scout snipers was down to just over a thousand men. But Brigadier Mohrtyn Braisyn's 3rd Mounted Brigade had joined him last five-day, and the 1st Brigade of General Fhranklyn Pruait's rifle-equipped 2nd Siddarmarkian Division had also joined. Counting his roughly twenty-four hundred Siddarmarkian cavalry, he had twenty-three thousand men, not counting his artillerists, and that was two-thirds of Wyrshym's total field strength, now that he'd sent the pikemen to the rear. Then there were the twenty thousand or so Siddarmarkian militiamen not under his command but productively occupied in rooting out the last nests of Temple Loyalist "rangers" in Midhold and western Mountaincross.

They were being no gentler about it than they had to be, those militiamen, and the exodus was headed in the opposite direction this fall. Green Valley took no pleasure in the thought of exposing anyone's noncombatants, especially children, to cold and hunger, but it was also hard to work up as much sympathy for them as he supposed he ought to feel. At least they weren't being ambushed by their own neighbors as they struggled through the Kalgaran Mountains' steep, stony paths. And while the Republic's militia was grimly determined to punish any "ranger" rearguard it could overtake, it didn't go out of its way to harry their women and children. As for Green Valley's men, they'd been ordered to push fleeing Temple Loyalists through the Northland Gap as firmly but gently as possible.

And not just out of the goodness of my heart, either, he reflected grimly. *Every mouth that "flees the heresy" is another one Wyrshym'll have to feed and house over the winter. And in another few five-days, we're going to start making his situation even worse.*

At the moment, his own supply lines were in good shape, despite the fact that the weather was turning steadily nastier. The first few five-days of autumn had been unseasonably mild, but the local weather prophets predicted a hard winter, and Owl agreed with them. By mid-November, at the latest, rivers and canals were going to freeze hard in the northern reaches of East Haven. In some ways, however, that would actually improve his logistics, given how successfully Cayleb's semaphore negotiations with the Raven Lords had turned out.

The Raven Lords had few export commodities, but they did have two: snow lizards and caribou. Raven's Land snow lizards were actually smaller than the Mainland species, especially the ones bred in North Harchong and on the vast Temple Lands farms up near Hsing-wu's Passage, but the caribou—genetically modified by Shan-wei's terraforming teams like so many of the Old Earth species introduced to Safehold—were much larger than their ancestors. Raven's Land bull caribou *averaged* over seven hundred pounds, and bulls as big as eight hundred and even nine hundred had been recorded. One legendary specimen, Goliath of Tymythtyn, had actually been weighed at just over eleven hundred pounds, although rumor had it the scales had been . . . adjusted for the occasion.

Neither snow lizards nor caribou were as efficient as dragons for sheer draft power, but they were better suited to the northern climate than even Mainland mountain dragons. That was a good thing, because once one got north of Grayback Lake, there were no canals and virtually no navigable rivers in Midhold—a big part of the reason Midhold, despite its proximity to Old Province, had boasted barely a third of Old Province's pre-rebellion population. True, the Black Adder River flowed out of the Black Hill Mountains, but only its lower reaches were navigable and it didn't go anywhere particularly helpful to Green Valley, anyway. That meant his supplies would have to be hauled overland, just like Wyrshym's. But he had less men to feed and thanks to the Raven Lords' evolving attitude towards the Charisian Empire—and its gold—he was confident he'd have all the caribou and snow lizards he needed when the time came.

But that time isn't here yet, he reminded himself. *Right now we need to consolidate, build up a forward supply point here at Allyntyn while the militia finishes cleaning out the "rangers," and make sure the troops are properly winterized. Let Wyrshym sweat while he worries about what we plan to do next.*

It was likely, or at least possible, Wyrshym would decide Green Valley was going into permanent winter quarters, since Safeholdian armies seldom campaigned in winter very far north of thirty-five degrees latitude. But no law said an army *couldn't* conduct active operations during the winter months, and the ICA had given quite a bit of thought as to how one might do exactly that. Green Valley's troops would shortly be equipped with proper winter uniforms, and his mounted infantry's horses were all High Hallows.

The High Hallow breed was the result of several centuries of selective breeding by the Dukes of High Hallow in Chisholm, starting from Old Earth Morgan horses who'd already profited from the attentions of Pei Shan-wei's geneticists. They were smaller and lighter—and far more stubborn—than the powerful, spirited chargers Mainlander armies favored, not to mention being shaggy and far from dashing in their heavy winter coats. In fact, Brigadier Braisyn's men had already heard a few comments about undersized, runty ponies, but they didn't much care. Shaggy and less flamboyant a High Hallow might be, but they could get by on less feed, keep going when those dashing chargers collapsed and died, and thrive in temperatures which would kill most other breeds in short order. More, they had the sheer, stubborn determination to keep them on their feet when even *their* stamina should be at an end. They would have fared much less well in a climate like that of Old Charis or Corisande, but they weren't *in* Old Charis or Corisande. And if they looked less impressive thundering across a field of battle behind streaming banners and the blare of bugles, that was just fine, because Charisian mounted troops had no intention of launching the sort of glorious charge which had gotten

Colonel Tyrnyr's troopers massacred at Maiyam. If they absolutely had to engage in mounted combat, they would, but as a general rule they preferred to leave that sort of foolishness for Desnairian or Harchongese aristocrats. *Charisian* cavalry were dragoons—mounted infantry who depended on their horses for mobility but fought on foot with rifles, bayonets, hand grenades, and (increasingly) revolvers. That was the reason their formations were described as "mounted regiments" rather than "cavalry regiments." And for that kind of combat, especially in ice and snow, the High Hallow was the perfect mount.

A point Baron Green Valley intended to demonstrate to Bishop Militant Bahrnabai sometime in the next few months.

He smiled down at the map again for a moment longer, then turned back to the fire, rubbing his hands and offering them to the warmth.

. IU .
Sarkyn,
Tairohn Hills,
and
Archbishop's Palace,
City of St. Uyrdyn,
Princedom of Sarkyn

The breeze was decidedly on the nippy side this morning, Mahlyk Pottyr thought grumpily.

And well it should be! It wouldn't be so very many more five-days before the Holy Langhorne froze solid. Under most circumstances, Pottyr would have been looking forward to that. He'd been born and grown up in Mhartynsberg, just across the Sardahn border into Charlz, and he'd seen sixty-five northern winters. All the signs indicated this one was going to be as cold, hard, and early as the last one, but the lockmaster's cottage here in Sarkyn had thick walls, a snug roof, and a well-filled coal cellar. Once the canal froze, Pottyr should have been able to look forward to spending the short winter days and long winter evenings in his favorite armchair in front of the fire, listening comfortably to the icy cold moaning as it prowled the Tairohn Hills on paws of snow-clawed winter wind.

Circumstances were rather different this year, however. Pottyr wasn't sure he really believed all the tales of bloodshed, murder, and starvation coming out of the Republic. He'd seen too many refugees, often emaciated or missing ears or fingers—or both—to frostbite straggling westward along the canal to doubt there was a horrifying amount of truth to them, but still. . . .

He gave himself a shake, hands deep in his coat pockets, and wished he'd been smart enough to grab his gloves before venturing out. The sunlight pouring down on Sarkyn and touching the canal water with reflections like laughing mirrors had no body, no strength. It lay across the town like an in-law's smile, feigning a warmth it didn't truly feel. He'd be glad to get back indoors, out of the sharp-edged breeze, but this was one of the special barge trains.

They're all *special, Mahlyk,* he scolded himself. *The Army needs every ton of cargo we can get forward, even if it is piling up at Lake City. Damned heretics!*

Pottyr couldn't remember ever seeing so many barges, even on the Langhorne, but the semaphore kept him in touch with the other lockmasters between Sarkyn and Lake City. The Canal Service had never much cared about political borders; its job was to keep the canals open, come what might, and its senior members stayed in close touch with one another. He'd been horrified—and enraged—when the Charisian Shan-wei worshippers shattered the entire northeastern arc of the system, and the messages about the mountains of cargo stacking up at Lake City and Traymos were grim proof of the damage. Vicar Rhobair's crews were accomplishing near miracles, even if Pottyr couldn't really like the slapdash nature of their repairs, but they'd never set all that right before spring. And in the meantime, the endless chain of draft dragons being shipped back west for the winter suggested that logjam of cargo wouldn't be moving very fast overland, either. He was a dutiful son of Mother Church, but even so, there were times he wondered how much sense there was in continuing to rush supplies eastward if no one could get them to the Army of God at the end of it all.

Plenty of snow lizards going up with 'em, Mahlyk! More to come, 'cording to the manifests. Saw the runners for them sleds, too, didn't you? You just worry 'bout gettin' 'em east of Sarkyn. Reckon Vicar Rhobair can take it from there! Prob'ly manage just fine 'thout your advice while he's at it, too.

He snorted at the thought, then moved a little closer to the edge of the lock chamber's solid, centuries-old stonework as the draft dragons whistled and the first of the special barges nudged obediently into it.

It didn't look particularly dangerous, despite the bright red, black-barred streamers all the specials flew at bow and stern. Appearances could be deceiving, however, and it was Mahlyk Pottyr's job to get it and its companions safely through his locks and back on their way to Bishop Militant Bahrnabai.

The Holy Langhorne was one of the world's most ancient canals, and the oldest canals had the fewest locks. The same chapters of the *Writ* which detailed the construction practices to be followed by mere mortals made the reason for that scarcity of locks abundantly clear. Where men were forced to detour around mountains, build steep stair steps of locks to carry the canal barges forward, the Archangels hadn't cared what might have lain in the way. Anyone who doubted that was the case only had to look at the canal cuts right here in the Tairohns. Why, the sides of the Ambyltyn Hill Cut, no more than four miles east of Sarkyn, towered over four hundred feet above canal level at the cut's deepest point! And smooth, like polished marble!

He shook his head, once more wondering how anyone could possibly be as insane as these Charisian heretics, mad enough to flout the word and spit upon the wisdom of the agents of God who'd simply commanded the Ambyltyn Cut into existence. Did the fools think they were mightier than the hills and mountains? That *they* could somehow defy the immortal, omnipotent will before which the very bedrock of the world had bowed its head in meek obedience?!

Fortunately, that wasn't something he had to worry about. His business was with the Sarkyn Locks, and that was enough for him. Even the Archangels had found it necessary to provide the occasional lock to maintain the water levels in those endless, arrow-straight stretches of canal, and that was the reason Sarkyn existed. It was a small town, really, with no more than a few hundred houses, a sparse necklace of hardscrabble hill farms beyond them, and the town church, but its locks were a critical step in the Holy Langhorne's progress, and that was why someone with Pottyr's experience had been put in charge of them.

It was also why he made it a point to personally supervise the transition of the specials.

There were six of them in this barge train, and the shiver he felt as he looked west along the canal towards the widely spaced, still waiting barges had little to do with the morning's sharpness. Lock dimensions meant barges on the older canals had to be smaller than those on some of the newer canals. The Holy Langhorne had been built to accept barges a hundred and thirty feet long, with beams of up to thirty-five feet, but when mortal hands had taken over the task of canal building from divine will, they'd been forced to accept more modest dimensions, at least until the invention of gunpowder. Those canals' barges were limited to no more than a hundred and ten feet in length, with beams which could not exceed twenty feet, and Pottyr's present charges were twenty percent shorter than the Holy Langhorne could have handled, far less the even bigger eastern barges. The ones hauling grain out of Tarikah Province or coal from the Ice Ashes had almost four times the capacity of today's specials, and the lockmaster was just as happy that was true.

It meant each of them could transport "only" four hundred and fifty tons of gunpowder.

Vicar Rhobair had imposed stringent, ruthlessly enforced restrictions on the powder barges' movements. They traveled in special barge trains, preceded by cavalry patrols, each barge guarded by its own platoon of infantry, accompanied by the bloodthirsty prohibition of anything remotely like an open flame anywhere along their route. No other barges were permitted to travel with them—*especially* not the passenger barges. And no one but official Canal Service personnel were permitted within fifty yards of the locks themselves as the barges passed through, given that human beings always provided ample fodder for accidents, however carefully the catastrophic consequences might be explained to them. The barges in each train were required to maintain a four-hundred-yard separation during transit, and none were ever allowed to lock through simultaneously with any other barge.

He watched water begin to flood into the lower lock chamber, lifting the first barge for the next stage of its journey. The barge nudged against the fenders as the water level rose, and the lock tenders adjusted the tension on the tow lines.

The contact between the barge's hull and the fenders was slightly harder than usual. Only *very* slightly; even pushed by a combination of the incoming water and the sharp breeze, the impact was little more than a caress.

But it was enough.

A shiver ran through the carefully stowed cargo. The powder was sealed in casks, stacked on their sides and carefully chocked to prevent them from shifting, with each layer of casks cushioned from the ones above and below by a padding of woven straw. It was no one's fault, really, that one cask in the bottommost tier had a cracked barrel stave. It had been damaged in loading, but the crack was so small no one had noticed at the time . . . just as no one knew about the dusting of gunpowder which had sifted through the crack to gather between the damaged cask and its neighbor over the course of the thirty-five-hundred-mile journey from Lake Pei.

And not one of the alert, watchful humans carefully following every one of Rhobair Duchairn's meticulously thought-out safety regulations ever saw the harmless little motion that generated just enough friction.

The explosion killed seventy-eight people outright, including Mahlyk Pottyr, who wouldn't be sitting in front of his fireplace this winter, after all. Another sixty-one were injured.

▼ ▼ ▼

"Excuse me?" Lawrync Zhaikybs, Archbishop of Sardahn, frowned at the upper-priest in the Schuelerite-purple cassock. "*What* did you say?"

"I said this sort of sabotage will not be tolerated, Your Eminence," Father Hahskyll Seegairs replied flatly from the other side of Zhaikybs' desk.

Seegairs was thirty years younger than the white-haired, rather frail archbishop. He was a swarthy, chunky man with a shaved head and brown eyes as hard as his face. He was also a senior member of Inspector General Wylbyr Edwyrds' staff, and his expression was unyielding as he stood in Zhaikybs' office in St. Vyrdyn Archbishop's Palace. It was a rather small archbishop's palace, but the Princedom of Sardahn wasn't a particularly wealthy archbishopric.

"*Sabotage?* What evidence of sabotage do you have, Father?"

"The fact and location of the explosion."

Seegairs' voice was flatter than ever, his eyes like polished flint in the lamplight.

"That's *all*?" Zhaikybs tried to keep the disbelief out of his own tone, but those flinty eyes flickered.

"Don't think for a moment that I don't take this incident very seriously, Father," the archbishop said after a moment. "But I've read Mayor Thompkyn's semaphore report to Prince Styvyn, and I've personally interviewed

Father Mahkzwail, Vicar Rhobair's deputy here in the capital. There's no mention in the Mayor's report or in Father Mahkzwail's preliminary findings of *sabotage*."

"The precautions which are routinely taken in the transport of the Army of God's gunpowder are extraordinary, Your Eminence," Seegairs replied. "I've personally reviewed them, and so has the Inquisitor General and the Grand Inquisitor himself. There's no reasonable 'natural' explanation for how and why a barge loaded with gunpowder in accordance with those regulations, and which had already traveled almost four thousand miles, should simply spontaneously explode. Not simply explode, but to do so at the very moment it was passing through a critical canal lock—the *first* lock in almost sixty miles of canal!"

Zhaikybs stared at him. Then he shook his head.

"Father, no one other than the guard detail, all of whom were on deck at that moment, as per Vicar Rhobair's regulations—and all of whom had been with the powder from the day it was first loaded aboard—had any contact with the barge. How could anyone possibly have caused it to explode at that particular time and place?"

"Obviously, someone else *did* have contact with it." Seegairs returned Zhaikybs' incredulous gaze with something far more like contempt than an upper-priest should normally show an archbishop. "The saboteur *had* to have contact to cause the explosion."

Zhaikybs bit his lip against a quick, angry suggestion for exactly where Father Hahskyll could put his circular logic.

"I appreciate that it's the Inquisition's responsibility to investigate a disaster like this as thoroughly as possible," he said instead, after a moment. "And I also appreciate that the possibility that it *wasn't* an accident has to be carefully considered. But not one of the surviving witnesses saw anyone anywhere near the lock who shouldn't've been there. The barge train's cavalry had cleared the vicinity of everyone except the lockmaster, his two assistants, the lock tenders, and the barge guards, as per Vicar Rhobair's standard procedures. I obviously can't speak for the guards, but Lockmaster Pottyr and his personnel have passed hundreds of barges and thousands of tons of powder through Sarkyn without any previous problem or difficulty. Are you suggesting that with that record one of them suddenly decided to blow up *this* particular barge, instead of any of the earlier ones, and kill himself in the process?"

"If not one of them, then someone else from Sarkyn." Seegairs' eyes were stonier than ever. "The timing, the placement, the fact that the barge had already come so far without a single hint of trouble, all underscore the fact that it had to be sabotage. And it would have taken someone thoroughly familiar with the procedures you've just described to *thwart* them, which strongly suggests that whoever it was must've been from Sarkyn or the immediate area. Assuming, of course, that it wasn't Pottyr or one of his regular work crew. As for why someone who'd always appeared to be a faithful son of Mother Church should lend himself to so heinous an act, even at the cost of his own life, Shan-wei is the mother of lies, deceit, and deception. How can we know what blandishments, what false promises, she could offer someone who'd already secretly sold her his soul?"

"But no one saw any *sign* of that! Not a hint, not a suggestion—*nothing*!"

"No?" Seegairs tilted his shaven head and his lip curled. "No one saw anything? Or did they simply fail to *mention* it to my agents inquisitor?"

A sudden icicle went through Lawrync Zhaikybs. Agents inquisitor? Seegairs already had his own agents inquisitor in Sarkyn?

"I'm afraid, Your Eminence," the upper-priest continued, "that there isn't a great deal of point in continuing this discussion. My investigators have already established that only a deliberate act of sabotage could have detonated that load of gunpowder at that specific, disastrous point in time and in that specific position. There is no question," the words came slow, measured, hewn from granite and ribbed with steel, "and I've so reported to the Inquisitor General."

"But—"

"I've also received the Inquisitor General's response," Seegairs went on, overriding Zhaikybs' attempted response, "and his instructions have been transmitted to the security detachment escorting the gunpowder and to my agents inquisitor on the ground in Sarkyn."

"Instructions?" For the first time, anger glittered in Zhaikybs' voice. "What sort of '*instructions*,' Father?"

"Heresy and treachery against God must—*and will be*—punished." Seegairs met the white-haired bishop's eyes with the flat stare of a serpent. "We *will* discover which heretics made this possible, Your Eminence. And we *will* determine why not a single soul in that entire town ever caught so much of a hint of what was planned or brought it to Mother Church's attention. And when we've sifted the witnesses, when we've discovered the full depth of this betrayal, those responsible for it *will* be given to the Punishment."

"The people of Sarkyn belong to *my* flock, Father!" Zhaikybs' voice crackled as he met that flat-eyed glare. "I repeat that I see no sign, no evidence, of deliberate sabotage—*none at all*—and that you proceed further with this at your peril! I will see the evidence of your agents inquisitor myself before I permit you to take these extraordinary actions in my archbishopric!"

"That decision, unfortunately, doesn't lie with you, Your Eminence. Under the Grand Inquisitor's personal instructions, the Inquisitor General has the authority— and the responsibility—to protect the canals and transportation system supporting the Army of God against additional attacks by the enemies of God. Bishop Wylbyr will make such determinations and issue such instructions as may be necessary to discharge that responsibility. In this regard, his decisions supersede those of any local authority, secular or temporal."

"*I forbid it!*" Zhaikybs' fist slammed his blotter, but Seegairs only inclined his head coldly.

"Your Eminence, I very much fear that in this instance you have no power to forbid any decision by the Inquisitor General. His instructions have already been passed to Sarkyn. You are, of course, free to contact the Grand Inquisitor directly and ask him to overrule Bishop Wylbyr. Until and unless he does so, however, I and my fellow Inquisitors will obey our own superiors. I can see that you're distressed, quite reasonably, but no good purpose can be served by continuing this discussion. I called to explain the Inquisitor General's decision and directives as a matter of courtesy. Having done so, I must now take my leave. I regret that you find yourself unable to accept the Inquisitor General's position, and I will of course transmit your concerns to him. For now, however, good night."

He bowed ever so slightly to the archbishop, turned, and walked out of Zhaikybs' office without another word.

. V .
HMS *Rottweiler*, 30,
Dahltyn,
Gulf of Jahras,
Desnairian Empire

"We'll bring her a quarter point to larboard, if you please, Master Mahkbyth!"

Symyn Mastyrsyn's was a powerful voice, trained to carry through the tumult of battle, but the cacophony raging around HMS *Rottweiler* threatened to drown it out anyway. Ahmbrohs Mahkbyth, *Rottweiler*'s first lieutenant, had been expecting the order, however.

"Aye, aye, Sir!" he shouted back from where he stood beside the armored galleon's wheel, and Captain Mastyrsyn turned back to more pressing concerns.

Unfortunately, when Sir Dustyn Olyvyr and Baron Seamount had planned *Rottweiler*'s conversion from ship-of-the-line to ironclad, they'd altered the ship's rails and bulwarks. The hammock rail in which the crew's tightly rolled hammocks had been stowed as a lightweight bulletproof breastwork had been transformed into a rack on the inside of a solid armored bulwark six and a half feet tall. The idea was to protect the men working the guns from enemy fire, and Mastyrsyn couldn't argue with that necessity. But raising the bulwark had a distinctly limiting effect on visibility even before clouds of gunsmoke were added to the equation. There was only so much a man could see through a gunport . . . even when the gunport in question wasn't full of a cannon that insisted on firing at the most inconvenient moment.

Sir Dustyn had called on the Royal College's Doctor Frymyn to help solve the problem, however, and she'd come up with an answer. She called it an angle-glass—an ingenious device consisting of a hollow metal tube mounted vertically in brackets on the inside of the armored bulwark. Its lower end had what looked like the eyepieces of a standard double-glass, and the tube itself was fitted with mirrors that bounced light and images down to them.

Given the ironclad's length, there was rather more space than usual between *Rottweiler*'s gunports, and Sir Dustyn Olyvyr had used some of that space to fit four angle-glasses on either side of the ship, bracketed to the inner face of the armored bulwarks. Now Mastyrsyn used the side-mounted crank to raise the aftermost starboard angle-glass to a comfortable height and bent to the eyepieces, peering through the smoke as *Rottweiler* drove past the flaming, slowly foundering wreck of the Imperial Desnairian Navy galleon which had moved in to engage her. The galleon's captain had been brave enough, Mastyrsyn supposed, but it was hard to admire a man who'd gotten his ship and two-thirds of his crew killed when he ought to have known better. Dahltyn was the third town—although calling it a "town" was probably a bit excessive—Admiral Shain's squadron had attacked in the last four days, and *Rottweiler* had led each of those attacks. By now, even Desnairians should have figured out there was *some* reason cannonballs kept bouncing off of her.

You could be being a little hard on him, Symyn, he told himself. *Maybe he knew* exactly *what was going to happen. Given how Clyntahn went after Duke Kholman and Baron Jahras' families after Iythria, he may've figured it was better to get himself blown to hell than be accused of cowardice.*

Whatever his thinking, he'd accomplished exactly nothing, for *Rottweiler*'s armor had done all Sir Dustyn had promised. It was dimpled here and there where shot had bounced off, and they'd had to replace two of the securing bolts, but nothing had come even close to penetrating it. Several of the shells which had hit her had simply disintegrated; for that matter, quite a few solid shot had broken up on impact. In fact, her armor had performed so well Mastyrsyn had to make a conscientious effort to remind himself she wasn't really invulnerable. An unlucky shell through a gunport, for example, would be no laughing matter, and while they'd been fortunate so far in avoiding serious damage aloft, only a fool would count on that continuing indefinitely.

For right now, though. . . .

He rotated the angle-glass, watching the fire raft drift towards *Rottweiler*. It wasn't really a raft—it looked like an old cargo lighter—but it had no crew, no masts, and no oars, so Mastyrsyn wasn't about to dignify it with the term "fire *ship*." It was the first time the Desnairians had tried that tactic, and he wondered what had taken them so long. But at least they'd caught the tide properly to send it drifting down on *Rottweiler* and the line of conventional galleons passing her to larboard while she interposed herself between the shore batteries and their unarmored sides. Smoke and flame belched suddenly upward from a second fire raft, coming along behind the first, and Mastyrsyn turned from the angle-glass and raised his speaking trumpet.

"Master Fynlaityr!"

Lynx Fynlaityr, *Rottweiler*'s gunner, looked up and cupped one hand behind his right ear to indicate he was listening.

"I'd take it kindly if you disposed of this little bonfire

to starboard, Master Fynlaityr! I'm sure the shore batteries will keep!"

"Aye, aye, Sir! We'll do that thing!"

Fynlaityr started passing orders and Mastyrsyn turned back to the enemy.

The fortifications *Rottweiler* had closed to engage were in a sad way, he noted with cold satisfaction. The ancient masonry wall of the original fort was badly damaged, but that was to be expected. The battery of new model twenty-five-pounders at its foot, on the other hand, had been properly mounted behind an earthen berm which would have absorbed round shot without damage all day long. It would have been equally effective against thirty-pounder shells, but *Rottweiler*'s shells were more than twice as heavy and filled with ten times the bursting charge. The battery's magazine protection had proved . . . inadequate against that weight of fire. At least five of its twenty twenty-five-pounders had been destroyed outright by the explosion, and it was unlikely any gunners who'd been fortunate enough to survive would be going anywhere near its remaining pieces while his gunners dealt with the fire rafts.

Rottweiler's guns were grouped in three-gun divisions, five per broadside, each under the control of a lieutenant or a midshipman, and Mastyrsyn saw Fynlaityr standing beside Lieutenant Graisyn, commanding the forward starboard division. The gunner's arms were crossed as he watched the youthful lieutenant with an almost fatherly expression. Graisyn fussed for a moment over the division's number two gun, then stood back and raised his sword.

Mastyrsyn couldn't hear the command through the general bedlam, but he saw the sword come down. All three guns fired as one, and all three of them scored direct hits. Explosions roared, the target's side disintegrated into splinters and fresh gouts of smoke.

Fynlaityr was already pointing out the second raft to Graisyn, and Mastyrsyn nodded in satisfaction. The only disappointing aspect of the attack was that just as their spy reports had indicated, the Dahltyn yards had completed four new schooners which were waiting only for their crews before putting to sea. They'd hoped to surprise those schooners and add them to Admiral Shain's squadron, but shifting, fluky winds had delayed the attack until well after dawn, and a lot of the smoke billowing above the harbor came from the schooners in question, set ablaze to prevent their capture. From the looks of things, the landing parties would be able to add the yards themselves to the bonfire shortly, along with the half-built hulls of two more schooners and a brig, the piles of timbers, the waiting sails, paint, turpentine, and pitch, and all the other components that went into building a ship.

The seaman in Symyn Mastyrsyn grieved for the ships which would never sail, never have the opportunity to pit their strength and speed against the sea and its power. The naval captain in him rejoiced at those towers of smoke and showers of sparks and that, after all, was what mattered.

Next time I'll have to remember to bring the marshmallows, he thought as the nearer fire raft rolled up on its shattered side in a cloud of mingled smoke and steam. *But for right now, I'll settle for sinking that bitch right where she is.*

. VI .
Guarnak,
Mountaincross Province,
Republic of Siddarmark

Bishop Militant Bahrnabai Wyrshym was not in a pleasant mood as he gazed out his window at the Guarnak canalfront.

There were several reasons for that, including how little water there was in that canal. Then there were the beached—and burned out—barges and warehouses serving as reminders of the Charisian raid which had left such ruin in its wake. Too many of the supplies which had been salvaged or shipped in since were under canvas rather than the weather-tight roofs which would soon be needed, thanks to that arson, despite all his work crews had been able to accomplish.

Depressing as that was, what he *couldn't* see from his office was even more depressing. The road net which now constituted his army's only line of supply was already feeling the effect of sleet and snow, especially in the higher elevations. His quartermasters couldn't keep the dragons on their feet much longer in the increasingly inclement weather, and the Harchongians were being their usual Harchongese selves, charging exorbitant prices for the snow lizards which were going to be a far less efficient substitute for the dragons. The Temple Lands had sent more than two thousand of them forward, but less than six hundred had yet arrived. Worse, the Temple Lands couldn't send many more without seriously crippling their own transport system over the winter months.

The fact that the heretics had driven the Faithful completely out of Midhold and out of all of Mountaincross east of the Moon Thorns and Kalgarans, inflicting heavy casualties in the process, made him no happier. There was at least one brighter side to that particular situation, however. The Mountaincross rangers had suffered badly in the process, and try as he might, Wyrshym couldn't convince himself that was a bad thing. Aside from their knowledge of local terrain, they had virtually no military value and, frankly, he didn't want them corroding the discipline of the Faithful militia he'd incorporated into the Army of the Sylmahn. *Those* militia had been transformed into soldiers worthy of the name, and he refused to see all that good work undone by brigands, rapists, and thieves.

The influx of thousands of additional hungry civilians—the best current estimate put it at in excess of two hundred thousand of them, with more to come—was something else entirely. He was moving them farther west in one enormous convoy after another, as rapidly as he could, but until they got at least as far as Tarikah *he* had to feed them somehow, and this was a bad time to be dipping into the supply magazine he'd managed to build up here at Guarnak. The only good news on that front was that Archbishop Arthyn had managed to plant more cropland than anyone had anticipated, and the mild weather—up until the last few five-days, anyway—had given the crops time to ripen. Labor to harvest them had been in critically short supply, but Wyrshym had diverted as many of his rear area personnel to help as he could. Several of his pike regiments had paused on their way west to assist, as well, but even that would have been too few hands if not for Inquisitor General Wylbyr and Father Zherohm. Wyrshym knew he should feel no qualms over conscripting the labor of heretics and suspected heretics, and he couldn't pretend he wasn't vastly relieved that labor had been available. But neither could he pretend that when food came up short this winter, as it inevitably must, the miserable inhabitants of Wylbyr Edwyrds' concentration camps, including the very ones who'd labored to make the harvest possible, would starve first.

There was probably enough abandoned housing in Tarikah for the refugees, and that was good news, too. Yet while they might have roofs over their heads, they'd still need fuel, and there was precious little of that, since the sources which should have delivered the winter's supply of coal during the warmer months had been . . . unavailable.

Tarikah's coal traditionally came from Glacierheart and the Ice Ash Mountains via the New Northland Canal and the Guarnak-Ice Ash Canal, both of which had suffered significant damage from the Sword of Schueler during the Rising. When they'd been put back into operation, they'd been needed to supply Wyrshym's own advance; and then the heretics had smashed the entire Guarnak-Ice Ash and the critical western locks of the New Northland. Not only had no fuel been shipped from the east before they were put out of action, but even the Holy Langhorne Canal, the only remaining route to Tarikah, could send it no farther east than East Wing Lake. Nor had they been able to ship it via Hsing-wu's Passage and the Hildermoss River. Even if the accursed Charisian Navy hadn't been patrolling the Passage, sudden death on any shipping on the broad waterway which had always been Mother Church's own, the heretic garrison at Salyk had sealed the mouth of the Hildermoss like a spiked cork. Besides, the Temple Lands, from which the fuel must now come, had always been a net *importer* of coal, and the ever increasing demand of the foundries and manufactories supporting the Jihad only made that worse.

There were rich coalfields in North Harchong, but with so few canals and navigable rivers, shipping it anywhere had always been prohibitively costly, so there'd been little incentive to mine it. Harchongese production had increased over the last two years, despite the expense, but the loss of Glacierheart and Mountaincross coal had been a near catastrophic blow to Mother Church's coking ovens. Indeed, one reason for Cahnyr Kaitswyrth's advance into Glacierheart had been to secure control of the Glacierheart mines.

And that didn't work out, either, did it? Wyrshym reflected sardonically. *By now, all those mines must be back into full operation, and I'm sure they've spent the last few months shipping coal east to Stohnar and his friends, instead.*

And then there were those "exhortations" from the Grand Inquisitor.

Allayn Maigwair's dispatches showed a grasp of the military realities; Zhaspahr Clyntahn didn't seem to care very much about them. He was incensed by the manner in which the Faithful had been "driven from their homes by the bloodstained bayonets of heretics, blasphemers, and murderers." Not content with hurling anathemas at the aforesaid heretics, he wanted to hurl the Army of the Sylmahn at them, as well, although precisely how he expected that to happen was a bit less clear.

It wasn't as if Wyrshym didn't *want* to counterattack.

Indeed, he'd been contemplating just that long before Clyntahn started fulminating. It had been *so* tempting to leave a portion of his own force to confront the heretics south of Wyvern Lake and pull the rest of it around to the northeast, through the Ohlarn Gap and Northland Province, to hit Green Valley head on. Granted, with the pikemen's departure his numerical advantage was less than it had been, but his actual combat power had increased and he still outnumbered the heretics substantially. The loss ratio would undoubtedly have favored Green Valley, but he ought to have been able to make his superiority in numbers effective outside the straitjacket of the Sylmahn Gap. If the Charisian general had been so considerate as to move far enough west, it was even possible Wyrshym might have gotten his far more numerous cavalry into Green Valley's rear and done to the heretics' supply lines what those accursed armored ships had done to his own.

But desperately as he'd wanted to do that, Green Valley had amply demonstrated that he was no fool. It was unlikely he would allow his army to be so badly outmaneuvered as to be encircled or destroyed. At best, he might have been forced back south of Grayback Lake, which would have accomplished exactly nothing for the Army of the Sylmahn. And to manage even that would have required Wyrshym to draw heavily on the supplies he'd accumulated so laboriously at Guarnak. He'd dared not do anything of the sort when Green Valley's displacement of the Faithful had already inflicted such a dangerous strain on those same supplies. He could all too easily have found his army literally starving to death, and he strongly suspected that was precisely what Green Valley had hoped he'd do.

So far, Clyntahn had restricted himself to dictating blistering homilies to the Army of God's chaplains; launching salvo after salvo of anathemas at the heretics, cursing them root and branch unto the hundredth generation; and "strongly urging" Wyrshym to be as aggressive and proactive as possible. The bishop militant was more grateful for Ernyst Abernethy—and the way he'd been corrupted by exposure to the realities the Army of God faced—with every passing day. The auxiliary bishop couldn't argue openly with the Grand Inquisitor's views or ignore Clyntahn's correspondence, but he could—and did—craft his own reports and correspondence very carefully.

And it wasn't as if there wasn't *any* good news, Wyrshym reminded himself. Rhobair Duchairn's most recent estimate was that his repair crews ought to have completed repairs to the locks between Cat Lizard Lake and Five Forks, where the New Northland Canal joined the Hildermoss River, by mid-April, and the campaigning season in northern East Haven never started before May. That was better than Wyrshym had dared hope . . . and that accomplishment, too, would owe a great deal to the slave labor from Edwyrds' concentration camps. Wyrshym wondered, in his darker moments, if Father Zherohm's efficiency would extend to slaking the canals' mortar with the ground skeletons of the camp inmates who would undoubtedly die laboring on them in the subzero temperatures of a Siddarmarkian winter.

In his even darker moments, he knew how relieved he was that those inmates were there to do the dying if it would reopen the canals he needed so desperately.

In addition to the more optimistic estimates about the repairs, Duchairn and Maigwair were promising him new and improved artillery by spring. Even allowing for the state of his supply line, Maigwair believed they might actually get the first few rifled field pieces to him by the end of November, and apparently one of his foundry masters had come up with at least a partial answer to the heretics' portable angle-guns. In the meantime, he'd received an entire artillery regiment—four six-gun batteries—of full-sized angle-guns of his own. The concept had been copied from the Royal Dohlaran Army's, but they were longer barreled and, unlike the Dohlarans' twelve-pounders, the Army of God's had been designed to fire the Navy of God's standard *twenty-five-*pounder shells. They'd have far less range than the heretics' angle-guns, but that still represented a vast improvement on anything the Army of the Sylmahn had previously possessed. More had been promised, and according to his latest messages from Maigwair the reliability of the artillery's fuses had also been improved.

But most enheartening of all was the new breech-loading rifle—the "St. Kylmahn Rifle," they were going to call it. They'd actually sent a half dozen to Guarnak, accompanied by the caution that they were still experimental models, and he'd experienced the first true optimism he'd felt since the canal raid as he examined one of them and personally fired it. The name was apt, he thought, both because the rifles had been manufactured at St. Kylmahn's Foundry and because Saint Kylmahn was one of the most revered of Mother Church's warrior saints. He'd suffered martyrdom in the War Against the Fallen fighting under the command of the Archangel Chihiro himself, and no name could have been more fitting for such a magnificent weapon.

Wyrshym had achieved an aimed rate of fire of six rounds per minute with the unfamiliar rifle, fifty percent higher than a trained, experienced rifleman could manage with a muzzleloader. He was confident that someone properly trained with a St. Kylmahn would be able to do even better. And if the hope in Maigwair's private, wyvern-delivered letter turned out to be accurate—if he and Duchairn *were* able to convince Clyntahn to allow duplication of the heretics' "priming caps"—his infantry would finally have a weapon which could meet the accursed Charisian infantry on their own ground.

The bishop militant's nostrils flared as he considered that possibility. Then he shook himself and turned away from the window. Hopeful as all that sounded, he was unlikely to receive the new rifles in useful numbers before February or even March. The Army of the Sylmahn would have to survive the winter without them, and that promised to be an unpleasant experience. But he'd experienced unpleasant things before. With a little luck, he'd live long enough to experience them again. And in the meantime, he had all of those reports and plans and conferences to work his way through if he intended to hold his army together long enough to kick the heretics' arse.

As motivators went, he thought, his eyes hardening, that one would take some beating.

. VII .
City of Cherayth,
Kingdom of Chisholm,
Empire of Charis

"My God it's brisk out there!"

Tahvys Sahndfyrd shivered dramatically and made a beeline towards the iron stove. The cavernous fireplace which had once heated (more or less) the large, luxuriously furnished office had been closed with brickwork through which the Delthak Works stove had been ducted to the old flue, and a great improvement it was, too. Now he parked himself directly by the stove, holding his hands out over it, and Byndfyrd Raimahnd chuckled.

"You only *think* it's 'brisk out there,' Master Sahndfyrd." The slightly built, silver-haired banker shook his head. "Spoiled by the climate in Tellesberg, that's what you Old Charisians are!"

"It's brisk enough to do for me," Sahndfyrd replied tartly. He was twenty years younger than Raimahnd, with brown hair and brown eyes which always looked a bit owlish behind their wire-rimmed spectacles. Of course, owls were predators, and they were quite sharp, those eyes.

Raimahnd only smiled, although it was still at least ten degrees above freezing. Which, he supposed, probably *was* on the frigid side for someone who'd been born and raised in Tellesberg. He remembered his own single trip to the Charisian capital, with its brilliant flowers, exotic birds, and overpowering sunlight and wondered how well Sahndfyrd would survive a Chisholmian winter.

Or *if* he was going to, for that matter.

"Have a seat," he invited. "If you want, you can pull that armchair over by the stove."

"Don't think I won't," Sahndfyrd said with a twinkle.

The Old Charisian wasn't the most tactful individual Raimahnd had ever met, which might be something of a handicap in his mission to Chisholm, but he had a sense of humor, he was smart, and he knew the new manufacturing processes inside and out.

"That was a nice touch, with Her Majesty," the Chisholmian said now, sitting behind his desk as Sahndfyrd did, indeed, pull one of the armchairs to within a couple of feet of the stove.

"I wish I could claim credit for it, but she and His Majesty started the practice in Old Charis two years ago. It does rather make the point that the Crown's behind our efforts, though, doesn't it?"

"It certainly does," Raimahnd agreed, although the truth was that he was a bit in two minds about it.

Having Empress Sharleyan herself turn the first spadeful of dirt for the new manufactory with a silverplated shovel had definitely underscored the Crown's commitment. The fact that the Chisholmian treasury was a ten percent partner in the endeavor should have made that clear enough for anyone, but not everyone had realized that, despite his best efforts to make it public knowledge. Besides, the visual impact of Sharleyan stamping on the shovel to drive its blade into the earth of Chisholm was far more immediate.

It had also drawn quite a crowd, which was the reason Raimahnd's feelings were ambiguous. Her appearance had communicated Sharleyan's support for the industrialization of Chisholm to the common folk in a way the esoteric details of investments and capitalization never could. And, as always, she'd been greeted by wildly enthusiastic cheers. Unfortunately, not everyone in the crowd had been equally enthused. In fact, the guilds were beginning to recognize the implications of Charisian-style manufactories in Chisholm. They weren't entirely in favor of the notion, to say the very least, and those same enthusiastic crowds could all too easily provide cover for some lunatic with a pistol.

It wasn't as if that very thing hadn't happened to Sharleyan before.

"How long do you think it'll take—the construction phase, I mean?" Sahndfyrd asked. "Like you say, I'm a Charisian—beg pardon, an *Old* Charisian—and I don't have a very good feel for how winter weather's likely to slow things down here in Chisholm."

"The foundations will be in by the end of the month, unless we get really bad weather between now and then." Raimahnd turned a silver letter opener in his hands while he considered the question. "Once they are, we'll run up the framing timbers and roof it over, then hang canvas for windbreaks. After that, we should be able to go right on working whatever the weather does. My best guess is that the building itself will be structurally complete by . . . the middle or end of March. After that, it's a matter of installing the machinery, and that depends on your Master Howsmyn."

"And on how well the war's going," Sahndfyrd pointed out a bit sourly. "Still, that's better than I expected. And unless something does come along that completely reorders Master Howsmyn's priorities—which, I'm afraid, has happened more than once—we should make delivery no later than April fifteenth."

"Then I imagine we'll be in operation by the end of July. Unless we have trouble with the workforce, of course."

"How likely is that?" Sahndfyrd cocked his head, those owl's eyes sharper than ever, and Raimahnd shrugged.

"To be honest, I don't know. There's a lot of enthusiasm among the people who're *investing* in the manufactories and among the unskilled workers. The workers, especially, have heard stories—wildly exaggerated, some of them—about how well paid Charisian manufactory workers are and how the owners take people without trades and train them to do what's needed. I imagine there'll be some disappointment when they find out the workshop floors aren't really paved in gold, but we're still talking about an opportunity to triple or quadruple their earnings, and some of them will do even better than that. I'm sure you've seen how some of the aristocracy feels about the whole idea, though, and the guilds're going to be less and less happy as the damage to their prestige and economic power sinks in. I don't expect to see a lot of open, public opposition, but I *am* afraid we'll see some acts of sabotage and vandalism."

Sahndfyrd nodded, his expression thoughtful. Byndfyrd Raimahnd was one of the wealthiest bankers in Chisholm, and a close associate of the House of Tayt. In fact, he'd enjoyed a warm, personal friendship with Sharleyan's maternal uncle Byrtrym Waistyn, the Duke of Halbrook Hollow, for over thirty-five years. Halbrook Hollow's treason had hit Raimahnd hard, but he was scarcely alone in that, and his own loyalty to Sharleyan—and Cayleb—had never wavered.

That wasn't to say the banker was a wildly enthusiastic Reformist, because he wasn't. Like Halbrook Hollow, he'd been horrified by the thought of mortal rulers defying the majesty of the Church of God Awaiting. At the same time, he'd been well aware of how corrupt the men governing Mother Church had become, and that had been enough, coupled with his loyalty to the House of Tayt, to pull him into resolute if not eager support of the war against the Group of Four.

He'd poured quite a bit of his personal fortune into that support. Assuming the Empire of Charis won, those investments would make him a fabulously wealthy man. Perhaps not on the level of an Ehdwyrd Howsmyn, but staggeringly so by anyone else's standards. Of course, if the Empire of Charis *lost*, he wouldn't have to worry about returns on investments, because he was one of the people who would most certainly be dead.

"I wish I understood how anybody could pass up the chance to get in on something like this," Sahndfyrd said after a moment. "I know it's happening, and I can see where Temple Loyalists would resist anything that could help us win the war, but that's not what's driving most of them. Or not as nearly as I can tell, anyway."

"The reason you can't understand is that you're a Charisian—an *Old* Charisian." Raimahnd smiled as he repeated Sahndfyrd's earlier emphasis, then snorted and tossed the letter opener onto his blotter. "You people are all shopkeepers, remember? You worship the almighty mark, not what *really* matters! All those smoky, messy, smelly manufactories of yours, disrupting the social order the Archangels themselves clearly ordained when they were wise enough to make *their* forefathers noblemen and filling the purses of men of no blood—no lineage! Offering *commoners* a chance to dominate the economy?! What can Their Majesties possibly be *thinking*?" He shook his head with a grimace. "Of course no proper noble wants to sully his lily-white hands with anything reeking of trade and manufacturing!"

"I know that's what they think, Byndfyrd. I just don't understand *how* they can think it, especially at a time like this."

"Tahvys, some of them still resent the hell out of the way King Sailys kicked their sorry arses. Anything that strengthens the Crown's reach and power—and God knows building a manufacturing sector like the one in Old Charis can't do anything *but* strengthen the Crown—is anathema to them, because they still dream of the day when the House of Lords reclaims its rightful place as the dominant power in Chisholm. Mind you, *I* think it's more likely the Archangels will return in glory tomorrow, but some of them are still invested in doing just that. Then there're the ones who're genuinely disdainful of this whole newfangled notion—nothing more than a fad, probably—of manufactories. Their family fortunes are founded on the ownership of *land*—on wheat fields and vineyards and sheep and cattle. That's what they understand, and they don't want anything to change an arrangement that suits them so well. And, finally, it's *new*. It's not traditional, not familiar, and the *Writ* itself warns against the dangers of too much innovation."

His expression tightened with the last sentence, and Sahndfyrd looked at him thoughtfully.

"You're not entirely comfortable with all of this your-self, are you?" he asked softly, and Raimahnd stiffened. It was the first time the Old Charisian had asked him that question, and he started to answer quickly, then paused and made himself give it the consideration it deserved.

"No," he acknowledged finally. "Not entirely. But I'm even less comfortable with a lot of other things that are happening right now. I wish we didn't have to change. That the world could continue the way God and the Archangels intended without all this dangerous tinker-ing with God's plan. But the world's already stopped be-ing what I'd like it to be, and the more I hear about what the Inquisition's doing in Siddarmark, the more I read Zhaspahr Clyntahn's denunciations, and the more I listen to men like Maikel Staynair and Archbishop Ulys, the more I realize I have to choose a side. *I* have to choose, whether I want to or not—I don't agree with Archbishop Maikel in all ways, but he's right about that—and I can't choose to leave Mother Church in the grasp of someone like Clyntahn."

He shook his head slowly, eyes looking beyond Sahnd-fyrd to something only he could see, and his voice was low-pitched and sad.

"I can't begin to tell you how much I hate realizing that when this struggle is over it's going to be impossible for the Church of Charis to ever return to its obedience to the Grand Vicar and the Temple, Tahvys. I know some of the Reformists still believe—or hope, at least—that the unity of Mother Church can be restored once Zion's been purged of corruption. It's not going to hap-pen, though. It can't. There's been too much bloodshed, especially in Siddarmark, and too many people will never forgive Mother Church for allowing that to hap-pen. And much though it grieves me, I don't think they ought to. So here I am, a man who always wanted to be a loyal son of Mother Church—a man who's spent sev-enty years of his life trying to be just that—dedicating the rest of my life to making the Schism permanent."

"Why?" Sahndfyrd asked gently.

"I could say it's because I'm loyal to my Queen. I could say it's because I'm appalled by Clyntahn's atrocities, by the realization that he sees no distinction between his will and God's. I could say it's because that even as much as this tide of innovation and change distresses me, I see how much better they'll make life for so many Chisholmians. I could say all of those things, and they'd all be true, but the biggest reason I've betrayed Mother Church? It's the only way to save her. She can't—she won't—reform herself, so someone has to *make* her—the Reformists are right about that—and who else can possibly do that?"

Silence fell, hovering between them for several minutes until Raimahnd inhaled sharply.

"Listen to me nattering like an old woman! I believe you had something else you wanted to discuss?"

Sahndfyrd looked back at him, thinking about all the other "somethings" he wanted to discuss. Like how they were going to encourage manufactories in central and western Chisholm, away from the canals serving Lake Megan and Lake Morgan. The coal in Eastshare, the iron deposits in the Sharon Mountains, the fact that small barges could use the Paul River to haul that iron ore downriver to the lakes—all of those made eastern Chisholm a natural initial foothold. That was, after all, one of the reasons Ehdwyrd Howsmyn had established his Maikelberg Works on Lake Morgan. Another, of course, was that it just happened to put the Imperial Charisian Army's primary arsenal and heavy weapons facility right outside the ICA's front door, handy for deliveries . . . and easy to protect. The Maikelberg Works had delivered its first locally produced Mahndrayns and rifled field artillery just last five-day, and there were ample arguments in favor of concentrating as much as possible of Chisholm's industry around that well-guarded center and the transportation advantages of the twin lakes and the Edymynd and King Sailys Canals. But the Crown remained determined to foster the same sorts of development throughout as much of the Kingdom as possible, and Tahvys Sahndfyrd and Byndfyrd

Raimahnd were supposed to be figuring out how to make that happen. But somehow, at the moment. . . .

"I'm sure we both have a lot we need to discuss," he said, "but for just now, I'm a poor half-frozen Charisian lad, lost and forlorn in this barren northern wasteland. I need a guide to a hot meal, a good bottle of whiskey, and an evening of quiet conversation about something that has nothing at all to do with wars and manufactories."

Those owl's eyes gazed very levelly at the banker sitting behind the desk, and the lips under them smiled.

"You wouldn't know where I might find such a fellow, would you?"

. VIII .
Holy Langhorne Canal,
Earldom of Usher,
The Border States

Rain dripped endlessly from the branches of native Safeholdian waffle bark and nearoak and imported Terran chestnut, ash, and yew as the winter evening limped toward night. It was cold, that rain, even colder than the patient, biting wind, and the well-rugged horse sighed deeply, grateful for his heavy blanket. Grain crunched in his feed bag, and tendrils of wood smoke rose white as the horse's steaming breath from the small, carefully hidden campfire.

That fire burned in a stone-faced fire pit in a well-sheltered hollow three hundred yards north of the Holy Langhorne Canal. Had trackers or woodsmen examined the fire pit, measured the depth of its ash, explored the carefully hidden campsite, they would quickly conclude it had been there for more than a five-day at the very least. That, after all, was the conclusion they were supposed to reach, and the remotes of an AI named Owl had gone to considerable effort to be sure they would.

In fact, it was less than *two* days old, and the single individual sitting between it and the water, perched in the shooter's blind on the lip of the canal cut, had arrived barely three hours ago.

His hair was brown, but his eyes . . . those were dark as sapphire, and harder than any stone, and *his* breath made no plume.

This particular iteration of him didn't have a name. It had never needed one, since it had never existed prior to today, and he'd used at least some of his waiting time considering what he might call himself. Something that spoke to the darkness of the purpose that brought him here, he thought. Something the Inquisition would find easy to remember, whether it understood it or not.

He'd gone to some pains to equip this particular persona properly and set the stage for its work this night. It was entirely possible he'd need it again, and he couldn't afford to leave any questions about who'd been responsible.

Not after Sarkyn.

I suppose we're lucky they didn't just burn the place down and plow the ruins with salt while they were at it, he thought harshly. *They probably* would *have, if they hadn't wanted to leave enough witnesses to get the message out.*

Those sapphire eyes went even harder, the face in which they lived still colder and bleaker. By Owl and Nahrmahn's best estimate, the population of Sarkyn was now thirty percent of what it had been. Thirty-six of the town's citizens—twenty-three men and thirteen women—had suffered the full rigor of the Punishment of Schueler after the denunciations began. And they *had* begun. When the "impartial investigators" had already decided witnesses were going to come forward and *were* going to name names—and when the interrogators had been ordered by the Inspector General to use whatever means were necessary to produce those witnesses— names would, indeed, be named. At least three of the executed men had deliberately implicated themselves, even knowing what awaited them, in order to spare others, and one of the women the Inquisition had murdered had been a harmless forty-year-old with the intellect of a ten-year-old. But the Inquisitors had, by God, found the hidden heretics, the betrayers of Holy Langhorne and Mother Church, who'd somehow detonated four hundred tons of gunpowder in the middle of their own town.

Of course none of the executed culprits had *personally* set off the explosion. Not even the Inquisition could explain how they might have managed that and still been around for execution. But they'd *known* about the plot, and they'd conspired afterward to conceal what had actually happened. That made their guilt just as great as that of whoever had set the actual fuse, and so they'd paid the penalty for their crimes.

And purely as a precaution, to prevent any repetition of Mahlyk Pottyr's and Mayor Wylyt Thompkyn's heinous crimes, over nine hundred of the town's citizens, a quarter of them children, had been taken into "preventative custody" and transported to Camp Fyrmahn, the Inquisition's concentration camp in Westmarch Province.

Some of them might even survive the winter.

I guess just butchering Siddarmarkians gets boring. Plenty of those to go around—they've got whole concentration camps full of them! How much challenge is there in catching more of them? *Better to try some different quarry, see how Sardahnan screams compare to Siddarmarkian ones. I imagine a fellow gets bored just listening to the same old sounds day after day.*

His mouth twisted and he closed his eyes for a moment.

I'm probably being unfair. They didn't do it just for the personal satisfaction. Oh, it did satisfy *them. Proved how virtuous they were, punishing the guilty. But that wasn't the only reason they did it. They wanted to make sure anybody who might be tempted to really* try *something like blowing up one of their powder barges would damned well know better. I wouldn't be surprised if Clyntahn had been primed for months, waiting for an opportunity just like this. He might've preferred for it to happen in the Republic, but maybe not. Maybe having it happen outside Siddarmark worked out better for him. It sure as hell reinforces his claim that heretics are everywhere, just waiting to betray the Church if not for the ever vigilant Inquisition! And the example's not going to be lost on anyone who might even think about actually trying to sabotage the Jihad.*

He closed his eyes, wishing he could close the eyes of his memory as easily. But he'd watched the imagery. Not all of it—in fact, he'd been able to handle only a very small amount of it—but enough. Enough to know he'd never forget it . . . and enough to take measures.

▼ ▼ ▼

Hahskyll Seegairs' pen scratched busily across the page.

It was chilly in his cubbyhole cabin, despite the tightly closed windows and small coal-fired stove, but Father Hahskyll was a man of austerity. His fingers were cold, but he ignored the discomfort, warmed by the satisfaction of knowing he'd accomplished a distasteful task without flinching, as his duty had required.

He would have preferred to return to the Inquisitor General's headquarters in Tarikah, but he'd been ordered to Zion by the fastest route. That was why his barge flew the golden scepter banner which gave it priority over all other traffic. When darkness fell, the red lanterns already blazing at bow and stern would assure the same precedence, although the mere fact that they were moving after nightfall should make that superfluous. Normal traffic was already mooring for the night, as the Canal Service regulations required, leaving only Vicar Rhobair's "specials" on the water, and they hadn't seen another barge in hours.

Seegairs hated this diversion from his responsibilities in Siddarmark. He wasn't so consumed by pride as to believe his was the only nose capable of sniffing out heresy, yet the proof was there to see. Hahskyll Seegairs had uncovered more hidden heretics in the Republic than any two of Wylbyr Edwyrds' other personal aides.

And now there was the horror of Sarkyn. However badly he might be needed in the field, someone had to report personally to the Grand Inquisitor about the blasphemous treason they'd uncovered, and who better than the Inquisitor who'd ferreted it out to begin with? Especially if that weak-spined old woman Zhaikybs truly had protested to Vicar Zhaspahr. It was important to place the evidence proving Seegairs' suspicions—and Bishop Wylbyr's, of course—had, sadly, been well founded before the Grand Inquisitor. Who would have believed such an extensive network of heretics could have concealed itself so tracelessly? Yet there they'd been, hidden until the Question stripped away their mask. Surely their mere existence only reemphasized how wise the Office of Inquisition had been to organize the Sword of Schueler before the cancer in Siddarmark could spread still further into the healthy tissue of the Mainland!

He regretted the necessity of such stern measures, yet the need to win through to the truth had been too great to allow false mercy to stay his hand. And it would have been no kindness to the heretics themselves. Perhaps at least a few had repented at the very end, shown the eternal torment waiting for them by the foretaste of the Punishment's rigor. It was never too late to return to the Faith and find the cleansing mercy of God. And if they *hadn't* repented, by now they'd learned that anything they'd suffered at Mother Church's loving hands had been but a shadow of the eternal price awaiting those who freely gave themselves into Shan-wei's service.

Someone knocked on his cabin door, although calling this undersized closet a "cabin" seemed a gross exaggeration. The knock came again, quietly, and he laid his pen in the inkstand and sat back.

"Enter!"

The door opened to admit another Schuelerite upper-priest of about Seegairs' age. Unlike Seegairs, the newcomer had a full head of dark hair and a close-cropped beard, and Seegairs knew him well. They'd been at seminary together, and trained as Inquisitors under Archbishop

Wyllym's own tutelage. Of course, he'd been only Father Wyllym at the time, but they'd known even then that he was destined to do great things in God's service. So he had, and he'd remembered his students when the time came.

"What can I do for you, Vyktyr?" Seegairs asked, waving the newcomer into the only other chair.

"I have that report you asked for." Father Vyktyr Tahrlsahn sat, leaned forward, and laid a folder on Seegairs' desk. "I can't say there're any surprises."

"I didn't really expect any." Seegairs shrugged. "On the other hand, given that our friend Father Mahkzwail appeared less than eager to cooperate with us, it seemed like a good idea to double-check what he told me in St. Vyrdyn against the supervisor's estimates."

"Do you really think he'd've dared lie to the Inquisition?"

"I don't know." Seegairs ran a hand over his shaved scalp, eyes dark. "Shan-wei hides in so many places—sometimes even in the hearts of men who have no idea she's taken them for her own. Archbishop Lawrync, for example." He lowered his hand and shook his head. "There's a man on the very lip of hell, willing to give the Holy Inquisition itself orders that would have stayed our hand, left all those heretics and demon worshippers in Sarkyn undiscovered! But was it because he sympathized with them, or simply because of squeamishness, a desire to turn aside from the severity the Archangels demand in times like these? Did Shan-wei seduce him into active evil, or did she simply present herself in the guise of gentleness and mercy?"

"Schueler knows we've both seen enough of that," Tahrlsahn agreed. "Like Father Myrtan. You know him, don't you? Myrtan Byrk?"

"Fair-haired fellow, a little younger than you or me?"

"That's him. He was with me when Vicar Zhaspahr sent me down to Gorath after those heretics Earl Thirsk tried to withhold. I'd always thought he had the true iron in him, but he kept urging me to go easy on them on the way back to Zion, kept whining about how sickly they were, how many of her own Shan-wei was claiming along the journey. He *said* it was because he wanted them to reach Zion alive to be properly sifted, but I've never really been sure."

"It's hard sometimes." Seegairs sighed. "Hard for people who *don't* have enough of Schueler's iron in their souls, like Zhaikybs and Byrk, I mean. And maybe for Father Mahkzwail, too. That was why I wanted you to check."

"The work crew supervisor says basically the same thing he did," Tahrlsahn replied. "Despite everything Pottyr and the others did, the explosion really only destroyed the eastbound locks. In fact, three of the lock chambers are still intact even in the eastbound flight, and the westbound locks are already back in service. The explosion knocked out some of the pumps and fractured a couple of the main pipes, but the work crews could get to the damage fairly easily. The transfer lock's still working, too, so they can shunt barges from one lane to the other. Traffic will be slowed, but they can take both directions' barges through the westbound side until the other one's fixed."

"And the supervisor's estimate on that?"

"Agrees with Father Mahkzwail's." Tahrlsahn shrugged. "The Sarkyn Locks aren't on Vicar Rhobair's list for prefabricated repair sections because they're so far behind the front there seemed no way the heretics could get to them. The supervisor's managed to short-stop timbers and other materials that were being sent forward to the Lake City stockpiles, though. It won't be pretty, but he says he's fairly confident they can have the replacement chambers framed in before the freeze. Whether or not he'll be able to carry out all the other necessary repairs before spring is more than he'll say at this point."

"A lot better than it could've been," Seegairs observed. "And if that snake nest had been left intact to try *again*. . . ."

His voice trailed off and they looked at one another in grim satisfaction.

Silence lingered for several seconds, then Seegairs gave himself a shake.

"Well, now that we've got that out of the—"

He broke off and froze, head cocked, listening hard. "What the Shan-wei was *that*?"

▼ ▼ ▼

The drover in the howdah never heard the shot that killed him.

The five-hundred-grain bullet struck him a half inch above and in front of his right ear at sixteen hundred feet per second, well above the speed of sound, and his head disintegrated as kinetic energy threw his corpse from his seat. It sprawled over the edge of the howdah, out from under the rain shelter, and blood steamed in the drizzle.

The dragon didn't like the explosive crack of the rifle, but it was well trained. It stopped instantly when its drover released the guide rein, and the PICA who'd decided he would call this version of himself Dialydd Mab was glad. The dragon had never hurt anyone, after all.

The dead drover's assistant popped his head out of the barge deckhouse. From his expression, clearly visible to Mab's enhanced vision despite the gathering darkness and drizzle, he hadn't heard—or recognized, at least—the sound of the shot. He was trying to figure out why the dragon had stopped, not what had happened to the drover to cause *him* to stop, and his observations on what was about to happen to the towline as momentum carried the barge over its slack length were pungent.

Mab's right hand rose from the trigger of the rifle Owl had manufactured from the Delthak Works' plans. This was the first time an M96 Mahndrayn had ever been used in action, and he couldn't think of a more fitting time or place. His rising thumb flipped up the bolt handle and moved it smoothly to the rear. The spent case flew clear and his hand rotated, pushing the handle forward once more, chambering a new round and cocking the rear-locking bolt on the return stroke, then dropped straight back down. His index finger found the trigger.

Another shot exploded, echoing along the canal cut, and the assistant drover's head disappeared back into the deckhouse in its own eruption of blood.

The other passengers must have figured out what was happening when the corpse hit the deck at their feet. Half a dozen Army of God infantry swarmed onto the deck, checking the priming of their rifles as they looked for the shooters who'd fired those two shots, and Mab's thin smile was far colder than the raw, wet twilight.

He worked the bolt of Taigys Mahldyn's brainchild a second time, found a target, squeezed.

▼ ▼ ▼

"Gunfire?!"

Seegairs stared at Tahrlsahn, his expression startled. There wasn't any fear in that expression, but there was confusion in plenty, and Tahrlsahn shook his head. He opened his mouth, then snapped it back shut as a deafening volley of rifle fire exploded from the barge's deck.

The cabin door flew open and another Schuelerite, one of Seegairs' assistants, shoved his head through it, his eyes wild.

"Both drovers're dead!" he blurted, and Seegairs' expression hardened as he saw the huge bloodstain splattered across the other priest's cassock. "And the helmsman, too!"

"What's happening? Who's doing all that damned shooting?" Seegairs demanded while gunfire continued to hammer the air.

"I don't know! Somebody's up on the west side of the embankment."

"Some*body*? You mean *one* 'somebody'?"

"I don't know!" the other Schuelerite repeated. "*I'm* not a soldier! The sergeant was shouting something about 'get the bastard.' It *sounded* like he meant one person! I started to ask him and then—"

He broke off with a shudder and Seegairs' eyes narrowed.

"The sergeant's dead, too?" he demanded, and the other priest nodded, his face white with fear.

▼ ▼ ▼

Dialydd Mab pressed the release and the empty ten-round magazine fell out of the rifle. He inserted a fresh one, chambered a round, and looked for another target.

It was difficult to find one. The scene before him was daylight clear to his light-gathering optics, but there was no one left alive among the bodies sprawled across the barge. Four of the vessel's passengers—three Inquisitors and one soldier—had attempted to escape by plunging over the side. Unfortunately for them, his high perch had given him a clear field of fire. Two of the Inquisitors floated lifelessly in the canal; the third Schuelerite and the soldier had gone to the bottom already.

The remaining handful of AOG riflemen had scrambled back inside the deckhouse as soon as they realized the devastatingly accurate fire ripping through them didn't care how dark it was. He'd placed every one of his bullets within less than an inch of his point of aim in conditions under which all they could see of *him* were muzzle flashes. Worse, they'd realized all that death and destruction was coming from a *single* marksman. There was only a single rifle—only *one* of them—on top of the embankment, yet whoever was behind it had already killed a dozen of them, and done it with terrifying speed. Many of the Church's soldiers had heard rumors about the new heretic pistols that could fire for hours without reloading. Most hadn't really believed the whispered accounts, and even if they had, no one had warned them *rifles* could do the same thing. Yet that was obviously what they faced, and so they'd gone to ground, found cover wherever they could.

Return fire crackled sporadically back in Mab's direction. It was more scattered than it had been, slower even than the usual restrictions of muzzle-loading might have imposed. Partly that was because they were reloading full-length rifles in the cramped confines of the barge's deckhouse, but it was also because they were firing through loopholes hastily cut through window shutters or even hacked through the planking of the hull. Anywhere they could find some protection against that impossible rifle blazing away out of the gloom.

Out of the darkness, actually. Full night had arrived, and the barge's defenders fired blindly, their only hope that enough unaimed fire might actually hit whoever had slaughtered so many of their fellows.

Mab located one of the loopholed shutters, settled his sights, and waited until a reloaded rifle poked back through the opening. His own rifle cracked before the muzzleloader could, and someone shrieked as his bullet punched through the flimsy cover.

He smiled with cold satisfaction and went patiently searching for his next victim.

He didn't really have to be here in person. He could have simply provided Owl's remotes with similar weapons and sent them to do the deed, yet he'd never seriously considered doing this any other way.

A corner of his mind felt a detached sort of pity for the soldiers on that barge. Probably at least half of them were conscripts, who hadn't volunteered even for the Army of God, far less to serve the Inquisition. Yet whatever had brought them into the Church's service, they were part of what had happened at Sarkyn. Seegairs and Tahrlsahn and the other Inquisitors had been the brain and the malice behind that barbarism, but these soldiers had been the hands that carried it out, and at least some had lent themselves to it as willingly as any Schuelerite.

Besides, they were between him and his prey.

He killed five more of them before the survivors refused to shoot back even from hidden positions. They huddled there, terrified, and he set the rifle's safety and laid it aside.

He'd chosen his position because it was forty miles from the nearest town. Even the Inquisition would find it difficult to accuse innocent townsfolk of complicity this far from their own homes, and the campsite Owl had built, like the tracks of the horse on which Mab had ridden to the ambush site, would offer additional evidence that the attack had been launched by an outsider. That might not prevent someone like Seegairs—or Clyntahn—from launching reprisals against the locals anyway, but it was the best protection he could give them.

And now it was time to finish this and give them a little more protection in the process.

The dead helmsman had fallen across the tiller, nosing the vessel into the bank. It waited for him, motionless, and he strode down the steep embankment as if the rain-slick grass and mud were a broad staircase and it was full daylight instead of night. He crossed the tow road and stepped into the spill of illumination from the running lights with a revolver in each hand, then leapt lightly to the barge's deck.

▼ ▼ ▼

Hahskyll Seegairs gripped his pectoral scepter in his left hand and a double-barreled pistol in his right as he heard someone land cat-lizard-footed among the bodies topside. A babble of half-hysterical prayer spilled from someone behind him—it sounded like Tahrlsahn—and he heard the harsh breathing of the four soldiers crouched in the darkness between the remaining Inquisitors and the barred deckhouse door. The lamps had been extinguished, plunging the interior into darkness to provide concealment for its occupants while any attacker was silhouetted against the running lights. He smelled gun oil, powder smoke, the stink of blood, and the sweat of fear, and his stomach was a singing void. His nostrils flared as he tried to beat down his own terror, but that terror refused to be subdued. He didn't want to believe the panicky soldiers' insistence that all this death and carnage had been wreaked by a single rifleman, yet his own hearing told him it had. He'd heard the shots coming with incredible rapidity yet clearly from the same weapon, and an icy fist gripped his heart as he tried to imagine how that could have been made possible.

Whoever had jumped onto the barge's deck was as still and silent as the death he'd visited upon the bodies strewn across it. The stillness twisted already tormented nerves still tighter, and Seegairs heard his own voice muttering a childhood prayer for protection against evil.

▼ ▼ ▼

Dialydd Mab waited while the SNARC's remotes swarmed into the barge's interior and located his targets. There were only thirteen left; four soldiers, five priests, and two Schuelerite lay brothers crouched in the deckhouse while the last two crewmen huddled in the bottom of the hold.

Fine. He knew where they were, and he raised his booted right foot.

▼ ▼ ▼

The deckhouse door flew open.

Wood screamed as the locking bar's bulkhead brackets ripped free, and Hahskyll Seegairs had a moment to see a towering, broad-shouldered shape etched against the forward running light. It was barely a flicker in the eye of eternity, and then the shape's hands vomited fire.

Seegairs realized he was screaming, although he couldn't hear the sound of his own voice through the thunder of gunfire in a confined space, and the pistol in his hand jerked up. Yet even as it moved, he seemed trapped in quicksand, the air resisting movement like thick syrup. The pistol rose slowly, *so* slowly, and the deckhouse was Shan-wei's own cauldron of crisscrossing thunderbolts.

No one could fire as rapidly as that nightmare shape. *No one!* It simply wasn't possible!

The first two soldiers were dead before the door's panels smashed back against the bulkhead. One of them discharged his rifle, but it was a dead man's shot, burying itself in the deck; the second simply tumbled sideways . . . into one of the remaining soldiers.

Jostled by his falling companion, the AOG private shoved back, trying desperately to free himself of the spasming corpse and bring his bayoneted rifle into play. The second round from the revolver in Dialydd Mab's right hand hit him squarely in the throat.

The fourth soldier did manage to fire his weapon. He was less than four feet from his target, but that shape of darkness and muzzle flash never paused. It fired again, and the last of the soldiers was down.

"Demon!" Seegairs shrieked and discharged both pistol barrels.

He hit the attacker—he *knew* he'd hit him!—but his target didn't even stagger, and then he screamed again, this time in agony, as a revolver bullet shattered his right knee. He went down, both hands clutching at the pain, and heard the drumbeat thunder of those impossible pistols go on and on and on. . . .

▼ ▼ ▼

The last Schuelerite went down.

Dialydd Mab stood in the choking fog of gunsmoke, listening to the shrieks, and the thing that troubled him was that those sounds of anguish *didn't* trouble him. He holstered the revolver in his left hand, cleared the other's cylinder, and began reloading.

▼ ▼ ▼

Seegairs sobbed, curled into a twisted knot, hands hot and slick with the blood pumping from his ruptured flesh. Agony was his entire world, yet even through the pulsing waves of pain he felt a deeper, crawling horror as the man who'd turned the deckhouse into a slaughter pen calmly reloaded his monstrous weapons. It was impossible to hear anything after so much gunfire in so small a space. Yet there was enough light through the broken doorway to touch the falling cartridge cases with glitter as they fell to the deck, and his terrified eyes crawled up to the long-fingered hands methodically replacing them in the revolver's cylinder.

They finished with the first pistol and holstered it, then started on the second.

▼ ▼ ▼

Mab took his time.

He could have reloaded far more quickly, but he chose not to. He chose to stand there in the darkness, in the smell of smoke and blood, in the sobs of the wounded, and replenish each chamber individually. One at a time.

The barge's defenders had hit him three times. That was better than he'd actually expected, but small arms fire was no threat to a last-generation PICA. Even if it had been, the antiballistic smart fabric of the shirt under his coat would have prevented any damage. He wondered if Father Hahskyll realized both rounds from his pistol had hit their target without any effect at all and hoped the Schuelerite had.

He slid the second revolver back into its holster, then stepped across Seegairs, ignoring the Inquisitor's sobs of pain. He never doubted the depth of the man's anguish, but it was little enough compared to the agony he'd inflicted upon others . . . and it would be over soon.

He bent, and bloody hands flailed frantically at his wrist as he twisted his left fist in the front of Vyktyr Tahrlsahn's cassock. Tahrlsahn screamed as Mab plucked him from the floor one-handed, as easily as he might have picked up a kitten. Mostly it was born of pain, that scream, as shattered bone and cartilage shifted in his left knee, but panicky terror fluttered at its heart. Mab wondered if the upper-priest had begun to realize he and Seegairs had been deliberately immobilized rather than killed outright.

"Please! *Please!*" the Inquisitor whispered. "Oh, *please!*"

"It's a little late for that, Father Vyktyr," a deep, deep voice said, and Tahrlsahn whimpered as the monster thrust him backward.

His toes, he realized, were at least an inch above the deck, yet the impossibly strong arm holding him didn't even quiver.

"I wonder how many people have said the same thing to *you*?" that rumbling voice continued.

"I didn't—I don't—"

Tahrlsahn couldn't have explained even to himself what he was trying to say, and it didn't matter anyway.

"I've been looking forward to this moment," his captor overrode him, and his whimper became a high whine as something cold touched his throat in a dull gleam of steel.

"This is a Charisian midshipman's dirk." The level calm of the other man's voice was the most dreadful thing Tahrlsahn had ever heard. "I brought it along for the occasion. I don't know if you remember the names, but

Gwylym Manthyr and Lainsair Svairsmahn were friends of mine."

Breath sobbed in Vyktyr Tahrlsahn's nostrils and his eyes were huge, for he did recognize the first of those names.

"Understand me, Priest," that executioner voice said, "because for the first time in your life, you're about to hear the truth. Your Langhorne was no 'Archangel,' just a lunatic, a liar, and a mass murderer. Your Schueler was a psychotic, your Church is nothing but an obscene lie, and you've helped torture and murder thousands in the name of a religion whatever God there truly is would spit upon."

Tahrlsahn's brain whirled, whiplashed by terror and anguish. No. No! It was a lie. It *had* to be a lie—*all* of it!

"Look at me, Priest." Despite himself, Tahrlsahn obeyed, and squealed in horror as his captor's sapphire eyes began to *glow* with hellish brightness. "I'm older than your Church," the abomination behind those eyes told him. "I'm older than your *Holy Writ*. I was born, lived, and *died* before your first ancestor opened his eyes on this world, and I will personally destroy your Church. I will eradicate it from the face of the universe. Men and women will remember it only as what it truly was—a monstrous, perverted lie concocted by madmen who only *thought* they were gods. They'll be known for what they truly were . . . and so will the butchers who served them. Think about that, *Priest*. Take that thought to Hell with you. Langhorne and Schueler are waiting for you there."

Tahrlsahn stared into those blazing blue eyes, then grunted in fresh, explosive agony as the dirk split his heart. The hilt's cross guard slammed against his breastbone and fourteen inches of steel drove straight through his body. Five inches of that bloody blade protruded from the far side of the deckhouse wall, pinning him with his feet still off the deck, and that dreadful promise followed him into the darkness.

▼ ▼ ▼

Dialydd Mab stepped back, watching the life and horrified knowledge fade from Vyktyr Tahrlsahn's eyes. Then he reached into his coat's inner pocket, withdrew the letter, and tucked it into the neck of Tahrlsahn's cassock, where no one could fail to find it. No doubt the Grand Inquisitor would dismiss it, brush aside its promise just as he'd brushed aside Cayleb and Sharleyan's promise that Inquisitors taken on the field of battle would find no quarter from Charis. After all, Clyntahn was in Zion, secure from any hand of vengeance.

Yet even as he dismissed it, a small, poisonous worm of doubt would gnaw its way into the secret places of his heart. And whatever he might say—or even truly think—the letter's content would leak. Other Inquisitors would hear of it, just as they'd heard of rows of heads on stakes along the Daivyn River, and unlike their master, they were *not* secure in Zion.

He turned from Tahrlsahn's corpse. He'd brought only a single dirk, but the Army of God had been kind enough to provide plenty of bayonets. He bent to detach one from a dead man's rifle and heard Hahskyll Seegairs' high, piercing squeal of panic as he, too, saw the glowing eyes Tahrlsahn had taken to Hell with him.

"I haven't forgotten *you*, either, Father," he promised.

. IX .
Cheryk-Kahrmaik High Road,
The South March Lands,
Republic of Siddarmark

The rain turned what would have been a miserable night into a wretched one. It was cold, heavy, and persistent, and it showed no sign of abating anytime soon. Nor did Sir Rainos Ahlverez expect it to. He'd grown up in the Duchy of Thorast. In fact, the estate on which he'd been born lay at almost precisely the same latitude as his present soggy position. Unlike the Army of Shiloh's Desnairian commander, he was thoroughly familiar with the seasonal weather patterns, and this pounding rain had come out of the west which, at this time of year, strongly suggested more rain would follow close upon its heels.

He stood in his tent's open fly, listening to water beat on its canvas, and tried not to think about how miserable his men must be. Each of his infantrymen had been issued a smallish tarpaulin which could be laced together with the ones issued to the other members of his sixteen-man section. In theory, if all sixteen were combined, they formed a tent large enough for the entire squad, and smaller numbers of men could combine their tarpaulins to provide nominally adequate cover.

In fact, it was often difficult to find something to use as tent poles, and even when that problem failed to present itself, the junction points had a nasty tendency to let wind—or rain—slip through. There were similar arrangements for the cavalry, and each man had also been issued an oilskin poncho, although quite a few had managed to "lose" their ponchos early on in the campaign. Before they realized just how miserable a good, drenching rain could be. Others had arranged to lash them to the sides of their attached supply wagons, usually after presenting a suitable bribe to the drovers. That was a better arrangement, although it still left the minor problem that unless the poncho's owner realized it was going to rain before the army broke camp in the morning, the wagon—and his poncho—would be out of reach when the rain actually began falling.

Ahlverez knew all of that, and while he possessed in full an aristocrat's ability to quash any softhearted feelings he might cherish for the men in the ranks—he was a general, not a Pasqualate!—he also knew their present misery would make them less efficient on the march, less effective in combat, and far more susceptible to coughs, colds, and all the other ills to which flesh was heir.

Yet for all their misery, his troops were far better off than the majority of the Duke of Harless' men. Not all of them, of course. His cavalry regiments and the majority of his officers had both better tentage and an abundance of orderlies, batmen, and servants to tend to their needs. Ahlverez fully realized that he himself was provided with servants whose sole function was to see to his own comfort. He had very few of them, however, and there was a difference between the commander of an entire army and a captain in a cavalry regiment. There was a reason the Royal Dohlaran Army had imposed draconian limits on the number of servants and camp followers its units might take into the field with them.

And we were damned smart to do it, Ahlverez reflected glumly, looking out into the silvery shimmer of the rain, lit by the lanterns of his headquarters group. *If I'd ever doubted that, watching Harless trying to move his army through this slop would've cured me!*

Unfortunately, Ahlverez' army was stuck behind Harless', and there wasn't a damned thing he could do about it. What had looked like a march of three five-days when they left Thesmar was well on its way to taking twice that long, and Ahlverez couldn't quite convince himself the heretics wouldn't find something unpleasant to do with the extra time. The dearth of any inhabitants in the vicinity—even Faithful Siddarmarkians made themselves scarce when Desnairian foragers swept through like locusts—had dried up what had been the Dohlaran Army's best information sources, and he felt as if the entire Army of Shiloh was advancing blindly into some black, bottomless void.

He'd strongly considered asking for—or even demanding—permission to pass his troops through the Desnairians, knowing that they could have reached Fort Tairys and relieved General Walkyr long before Harless' troops could. Unfortunately, he'd known permission would be denied and that asking for it could only have intensified the building tension between him and the Desnairian commander. Despite that, he'd sent home private dispatches, pleading, almost *begging* Duke Salthar and Duke Fern to grant him the discretion to operate independently. Not that he expected it to do any good . . . especially when Father Sulyvyn declined to endorse his request. Ahlverez' intendant remained focused on combining with the much larger Desnairian component of the Army of Shiloh in order to provide Mother Church's mailed fist with the greatest possible weight.

"Weight" is it? Ahlverez' lips tightened. *They'll be lucky if they haven't lost a quarter of their men to sickness or desertion by the time we get to Fort Tairys! Just how much "weight" are they going to be able to add to an attack after that?*

The answer, he suspected, would be "not very much."

▼ ▼ ▼

Merlin Athrawes was unable to read Ahlverez' mind as he considered the imagery, but if he *had* been able to, he would have found himself in agreement with the Dohlaran.

The "Army of Shiloh" lay sprawled along the high road like a vast, sluggish, untidy serpent. A very wet and muddy serpent. And, like any marching formation, its fastest speed was that of its slowest element . . . which happened to be what had originally been called the Army of Justice.

By the standards of medieval armies, the Desnairians weren't doing all that badly; by the standards of which they ought to have been capable, they were a shambling disaster. The fall and winter rains of southern Siddarmark were setting in with a vengeance, which, given the effect it had already exerted on the invaders, was the one good aspect of what promised to be a nasty winter. The provisions of *The Book of Pasquale* and the efforts of the Order of Pasquale kept Safeholdian armies' sickness rates enormously lower than for any preindustrial army in Old Earth's history, but they were certain to rise in this sort of weather. Even better from the Allies' perspective, the miserable travel conditions slowed Harless' foraging parties, which in turn further slowed his army's rate of march. It also gave the handful of farmers who hadn't already refugeed out of the South March time to get themselves and their families out of the Army of Shiloh's path, taking as much as possible of their livestock with them and making the foragers' task that much harder.

But what was killing their mobility even more effectively than the weather, he thought with profound satisfaction, was the fact that no one but the Imperial Charisian Army had ever thought about adopting a corps organization.

Safeholdian armies moved in one solid mass because until very recently no single element of an army could fend for itself without the support of its other elements. Before the introduction of the rifled flintlock and the socket bayonet, light infantry—missile troops armed with bows, matchlocks, or arbalests—had required heavy infantry—pikemen—to hold off cavalry. The same had held true for the mounted arms; horse archers could shower heavy cavalry with arrows or arbalest bolts from well beyond the reach of sword or lance, but missile-armed cavalry was unable to withstand the charge of heavy horse which managed to force combat upon it and shorter-ranged than missile-armed infantry. And so, all the elements had to be kept together. Not only that, but it was difficult to deploy quickly for combat. If a commander knew the enemy was in the vicinity, he tried to arrange the units in his marching column so that they could form for battle as rapidly as possible, but "rapidly" in this case meant "somewhat faster than an arthritic snail." It had always taken the better part of a day for a traditional Safeholdian army to simply align itself to engage an opponent . . . under good conditions. Under *bad* conditions, it could take far longer. Fortunately, any foe it had been likely to run into had faced the same problems.

The Army of God was in the process—thanks in no small part to Bishop Militant Bahrnabai and Bishop Gorthyk—of recognizing how much the situation had changed, but they were only starting to grasp the implications. Mostly that was because until the last month or so they'd still been hampered by hordes of pikemen. That had imposed the same need to combine light and heavy infantry, and it would take a while for Maigwair's withdrawal of the pikes from his order of battle to change his own thinking. For that matter, so far he'd been able to withdraw them only from the Army of the Sylmahn; Kaitswyrth was still lumbered with them, and would be for some time to come.

The Imperial Charisian Army had never had—and the reorganizing Republic of Siddarmark Army no *longer* had—pikemen. All Charisian infantry were equipped with rifles and bayonets, and that meant they could not only look after themselves against opposing infantry, but as Major Naismyth's company had demonstrated to Colonel Tyrnyr's cavalry, they could kick the butt of opposing horsemen, as well. There was no need to combine specialized elements in an era in which the rifleman reigned supreme. For that matter, the same thing was true of Charisian *cavalry*. The mounted infantry of the ICA's dragoon regiments had no interest in fighting opposing cavalry from horseback as long as they could find a convenient spot to dismount and shoot them from behind rocks, trees, and rail fences, instead.

That meant Charisian formations were far better articulated, far more flexible, than anyone they were likely to face. And the Charisian army had capitalized upon that articulation by developing a corps organization. So far, the relatively small size of the field formations Charis had been able to deploy had prevented the Empire's commanders from making use of that organization's full advantages, but as more and more of the ICA's strength arrived in Siddarmark, that would change.

A senior Charisian field commander was trained to divide his force into separate corps, each of around thirty-six thousand—ideally, two infantry divisions and a single mounted brigade—plus artillery. Corps commanders were chosen for ability and initiative, then provided with their own corps staffs, which took a great deal of strain off an army commander and *his* staff. Even more important, however, each of those corps was eminently capable of looking after itself in combat, and by dividing his strength, a commander could maneuver on a far broader front. He could advance on separate but parallel routes, decreasing the sort of congestion which was slowing the Army of Shiloh's pace so disastrously and giving him a far better chance of finding the enemy. Each of his corps was well suited to holding its ground against the attack of even a much larger force—especially one which was handicapped by a traditional mix of pikes and missile troops—while his other corps closed in to envelop the enemy or massed to crush one flank. By the same token, any one of his corps could attack an enemy force and pin it in place until the rest of his corps came up in support. Even divisional commanders were trained to divide their divisions into brigade-sized "corps" as part of Charis' unabashedly offensive tactical and operational doctrines.

The time was coming, Merlin thought, and sooner than anyone on the other side could possibly suspect, when commanders like Eastshare, Green Valley, and Symkyn would demonstrate just what that meant. Nahrmahn Baytz was entirely correct about the implications of the Church of God Awaiting's new rifle design, and both the Army of the Sylmahn and the Royal Dohlaran Army were getting better much more rapidly than Merlin liked, but painful as the lessons they'd already learned had been, there were more—and worse—to come.

. X .
Fort Raimyr,
North of Siddar City,
Republic of Siddarmark

"I could wish we had better confirmation of the bastards' position," Greyghor Stohnar said. "*And* of just how bad their supply situation really is."

The lord protector's expression was sober, with more than an edge of worry, despite the afternoon sunlight as he and Emperor Cayleb rode towards the rifle range.

Neither he nor Cayleb was able to get away from council chambers, meetings, discussions, and maps nearly so often as they wished. The lord protector was more than twice Cayleb's age, but it had been his habit, before the Sword of Schueler, to ride at least two afternoons a five-day, and he'd been an accomplished polo player since boyhood. For the last year or so, however, his bodyguards had been adamant about the need to restrict his exposure to those who wished him ill, and Cayleb—the heretical foreign potentate who'd propped up Stohnar's apostate regime— was probably the one human being in the entire Republic more hated by the Siddarmarkian Temple Loyalists than he was.

They'd put their joint foot down this morning, however, and the unified front of the heads of state of the two most powerful realms in all of Safehold had sufficed— narrowly, but sufficed—to overrule those bodyguards. Which explained how the two of them, accompanied by Daryus Parkair and surrounded by a horde of Charisian Imperial Guardsmen and troopers of the Siddarmarkian Protector's Guard, found themselves riding across the grounds of Fort Raimyr, the huge military base just north of Siddar City. The Protector's Guard had lobbied hard for requiring the lord protector and his guest to use a closed carriage for the trip, preferably with two other carriages dispatched to alternate destinations as decoys to divert the packs of assassins loitering just outside the Protector's Palace's gates—probably with field artillery concealed under their coats—but Merlin and the rest of Cayleb's Guardsmen had known there was no hope of that. And so he and Stohnar had been permitted to enjoy the lengthy ride through a surprisingly warm and sunny day.

Enjoy it they had, yet even on a day like this, on what amounted to a pleasure excursion, the reports and maps they spent so much time poring over were their constant companions. Now Cayleb shrugged in response to Stohnar's remark.

"Aivah has a remarkable record for getting it right where the Temple's involved," he pointed out, his own tone almost placid. "And we have Duke Eastshare's and General Wyllys' dispatches about their own progress. I agree it would be . . . comforting to have proof our current information on the other side's correct, but I'm afraid there's only one way to find out for certain. And in another couple of days, we will." He smiled crookedly. "One way or the other."

Stohnar snorted.

"Tactful of you to give *Aivah* credit. But you're right, of course. Between her sources and your own rather remarkable spy network"—he glanced at the tall, sapphire-eyed Guardsman riding to the left of Cayleb's chestnut—"we've been given remarkably solid analyses of the Group of Four's intentions and actions. And remarkably ugly they've been."

His mouth tightened and his eyes went bleak and hard. The report Aivah Pahrsahn had shared with them the day before had dealt with the conditions in Inquisitor General Wylbyr's concentration camps and their grinding, ongoing death tolls. No one on Safehold, outside the inner circle of Merlin Athrawes' allies, had ever heard of men named Adolf Hitler, Joseph Stalin, or Pol Pot, but Wylbyr Edwyrds seemed determined to emulate their accomplishments. It was going to get worse before it got better—all of them knew that—and that was one reason Stohnar and Cayleb had agreed to back Green Valley's plans, despite the lateness of the year and the severity of winter in northern Siddarmark. The camps were concentrated in the Republic's northwestern provinces, and the shortest route to their liberation lay directly through Bahrnabai Wyrshym's Army of the Sylmahn.

Yet passionately though both of them longed to break through to the camps, they knew they couldn't do it *now*. And the primary reason they couldn't was the vast sprawl of the Army of Shiloh grinding its way across the South March towards Fort Tairys. Duke Harless' costly failure against Thesmar was reassuring evidence of the quality of that army, but its sheer size made it a threat which simply had to be countered. More than that, the evidence that the *Dohlaran* component of the Army of Shiloh had grown steadily more experienced and dangerous couldn't be overlooked. Nor could the wreckage Shiloh Province had already become. The loyal Shiloh militia and the SRA regulars sent to reinforce them had found themselves hard-pressed to retain control of the province north of Kolstyr and east of the Blackbern River. Three-quarters of it was in rebel hands or reduced to a burned wasteland *no one* held. If an army the size of the Army of Shiloh was added to *that* situation. . . .

The liberation of the Inquisition's concentration camps at the earliest possible moment was a moral imperative; stopping the Army of Shiloh short of the province for which it had been named was a *survival* imperative. And that was what had led to the current conversation.

"The problem," Stohnar continued, "is that even Aivah's current estimate of Harless' position is only an educated guess. Granted, I think it's a good one. Based on what we've seen out of the Desnairians so far, I'd be shocked if they were actually closer to Fort Tairys than we're estimating. But I've been shocked before—the 'Sword of Schueler' comes to mind as a recent example of how that works—and as good as your army is, and as skillful as the Duke's proved himself, the thought of his being caught between the Army of Shiloh and Fort Tairys with barely fourteen thousand men is enough to keep me awake at night."

"I can't disagree with any of that," Cayleb replied, which was an interesting choice of words, Merlin reflected. Cayleb *could* have set the lord protector's mind at rest, but not without bringing up little things like SNARCs and satellite reconnaissance. "On the other hand, Duke Eastshare won't exactly be all alone by the time he reaches Fort Tairys. I don't think nine thousand new model Siddarmarkian riflemen will hurt his chances one bit, especially under General Wyllys' command."

"His Majesty's right about that, My Lord," Parkair said. "And Wyllys is actually bringing along more artillery than the Duke. *That's* not going to hurt any, either."

Stohnar nodded, and his expression relaxed remarkably. Stahn Wyllys was one of only two Republic of Siddarmark Army colonels to have survived the bitter fighting in the Sylmahn Gap. In the process, his 37th Infantry Regiment had been reduced to a single badly understrength company, commanded by the regiment's youngest—and only surviving—captain. He'd been promoted to general following Green Valley's relief of the Gap's defenders, and his 37th Infantry had been reconstituted and assigned to the 1st Rifle Division, RSA. Which was fitting, since General Wyllys had been named to command that division. General Fhranklyn Pruait, the only other regimental commander to survive the Sylmahn Gap, had been given command of the 2nd Rifle Division.

Those divisions had had no time yet to fully assimilate Charisian doctrine. Their muzzle-loading weapons weren't as well suited to Charisian tactics, anyway, but the officers responsible for raising and training their regiments had spent long hours discussing such matters with the Charisian training cadre assigned to assist. Too many of their men were new recruits, volunteers who'd flocked to the Army to defend the Republic and their families . . . or to seek revenge. They were motivated, well trained, but largely inexperienced, and the question of how well they would perform once battle was actually joined loomed large in many minds, not least their own. Yet Cayleb Ahrmahk's confidence in Stahn Wyllys and his men was completely genuine, and it showed.

Two of the 1st Rifle Division's three brigades had been earmarked for the advance on Fort Tairys. Sent up the Siddarmark River by barge as far as Holkyr, on the Glacierheart border, and then overland into Shiloh, they and the ICN thirty-pounders on field carriages accompanying them were currently well south of Maidynberg on the Maidynberg-Raisor High Road. Screened by an attached regiment of cavalry, their advance had reached the point at which the miserable excuse for a road net branched off from the high road toward Ohadlyn's Gap and Fort Tairys, little more than a hundred miles from its objective. Despite the fact that Wyllys had marched over four hundred miles through territory still swarming with Temple Loyalist partisans—the Shiloh equivalent of the Mountaincross "rangers"—and killed over a thousand of them along the way, Lairays Walkyr, the commander of the Fort Tairys garrison, had learned of his approach only two days earlier. Partly, that was because the ill-disciplined survivors had, understandably, been more focused on taking to their heels than on warning Fort Tairys. But it was also because Walkyr had never made any effort to enlist them as a screen for his position, and that said some truly unflattering and reassuring—to his enemies at least—things about the aggressiveness of his reconnaissance efforts.

The fact that he continued to remain blissfully unaware of the *Charisian* force advancing rapidly towards him along the Branath Canal said even more.

Despite that, Fort Tairys was a formidable position. Built over a century earlier, during the wars between Desnair and the Republic, its thick walls were kiln-fired brick with a rubble fill and its position commanded the roadway through Ohadlyn's Gap between Shiloh and the South March. Up until two five-days ago, it had been garrisoned by only five infantry regiments and a single cavalry regiment, with a nominal strength of around thirteen thousand. Whatever Walkyr's preparedness might have been like, however, there was little doubt in the minds of Shiloh's Temple Loyalists of what would happen if Fort Tairys fell. Although Walkyr hadn't called for them and was deeply concerned about his ability to feed them now that he had them, they'd scraped up four additional regiments of militia and volunteers and sent them to Fort Tairys' support. The 9th Cavalry was badly understrength, but most of the infantry regiments were at full strength or very close to it, which meant Walkyr now had better than nineteen thousand men under his command. Those numbers would have been more impressive if the quality of his regiments had been less suspect. Unfortunately for Walkyr, they consisted of mutineers and ill-trained volunteers who were even less

experienced, no matter how many towns and farmsteads they might have burned, than Stahn Wyllys' men.
Still worse, from his perspective, he had no new model
artillery, no rifles, and only a relative handful of matchlocks.

The defenders expected the fort's walls and the earthworks Walkyr had thrown up to make up for a lot, but
he might have been wiser not to attempt to cover the
entire gap. The outer circumference of his entrenchments ran for over sixty-eight miles, which meant that
even with the infantry reinforcements he hadn't asked
for, he had less than one man for every six yards of parapet. In fairness, he'd anticipated having to defend
against an attack from only one side of the mountains at
a time, which would have reduced his frontage by fifty
percent, and he'd been building his fortifications not
simply for his own command but for the much larger
garrison he expected the Army of Shiloh to install there
to protect its rear as it advanced farther east. And if he
had no new model artillery, at least the fort had been
equipped with fifty old-style guns. Despite the guns, the
reinforcements, and the entrenchments, however, the
question wasn't whether or not Eastshare and Wyllys
could take Fort Tairys; it was whether or not they could
do it before the Army of Shiloh arrived. And despite the
Army of Shiloh's sluggardly pace, that might prove a
near run thing.

"I'd feel better if Wyllys had all three of his brigades
with him," Stohnar confessed after a moment.

"General Wyllys has all the manpower he needs,"
Cayleb said dryly, "and Duke Eastshare was right—we
need his third brigade on the Daivyn just in case
Kaitswyrth recovers his nerve. I know any commander
prefers to have more men than he believes he needs
rather than find out he doesn't have quite enough after
all, but I'm not very concerned about that in this case.
Timing, yes; whether or not he and the Duke have the
strength to do the job, no."

"You're right, of course," Stohnar sighed. "I suppose

it's just an example of needing to find something to worry about."

"I wouldn't go quite that far." Cayleb's tone was even dryer, and he smiled. "I think it's more a case of waiting for the other shoe, and God knows *that's* not unreasonable after the last year or so."

"Agreed." Stohnar inhaled deeply as their party reached the rifle range. He and Cayleb had spent several hours inspecting the troops, watching training regiments pass in review, and generally encouraging the Republic of Siddarmark Army's new formations. Now, however, the lord protector looked at Major Athrawes and smiled with the air of a man looking forward to a special treat.

"So, are you prepared to dazzle us all, *Seijin* Merlin?"

"'Dazzle' might be putting it a little strongly, My Lord," Merlin replied mildly. "I think 'impress' might come closer to the intended effect."

"I think you mean '*reassure*,'" Parkair observed with a snort and cocked his head at Cayleb. "I've found the *seijin's* existing revolvers quite impressive enough, Your Majesty. I can't quite escape the suspicion that a large part of today's objective is to reassure us by demonstrating fresh evidence of the superiority of Charisian weapons. Or I suppose what I really should've said is the *steadily increasing* superiority of Charisian weapons."

"I wouldn't put it quite that way myself," Cayleb said placidly. "Of course, I'm an instinctively tactful and diplomatic soul."

"I've noticed that," Stohnar agreed and looked back at Merlin as the *seijin* dismounted. "And I'm quite prepared for all the reassurance I can get."

"One tries, My Lord," Merlin murmured and advanced towards the targets prepared for his demonstration.

Five stout wooden posts had been set into the ground side-by-side to form a line about forty feet long. A nested pair of RSA breastplates had been hung on each of them, forming a double thickness of steel, and a helmet perched on top of each post. Merlin stopped twenty-five yards from the line of targets, facing them, and drew the revolver from his right side holster.

It wasn't identical to the one Ehdwyrd Howsmyn had displayed to Ironhill, Pine Hollow, and Rock Point in Tellesberg and which now rode at Cayleb's side. The cylinder on the emperor's pistol was two inches long and had six chambers; the one on *Seijin* Merlin's was *three* inches long and had only five. The pistol also weighed twice as much and had over an inch more barrel length, and there was a reason for all of that. While Merlin's weapon would happily fire the standard forty-five caliber pistol round, it was *designed* to fire the all-up rifle round, instead. Even the Delthak Works' best steel required thicker chamber walls to withstand those sorts of pressures. That was why there were only five of them, spaced rather farther apart. But the trade-off was that it produced a muzzle velocity of twelve hundred feet per second and, coupled with the rifle cartridge's heavier bullet, generated substantially better than twice the muzzle energy of the standard round.

It was undoubtedly a case of overkill for any merely mortal opponent, but Merlin could live with that. In fact, he was all in favor of overkill. After all, he never knew when Cayleb was going to be stupid enough to go slash lizard hunting with a spear again.

Taigys Mahldyn had produced a double-action design and this revolver's action was silky smooth, its parts individually fitted and polished in a way the production pistols would never be. The trigger had a much longer pull when fired double-action, however, and Merlin suspected that most of his fellow Guardsmen would fire the production weapons in single-action mode, thumb-cocking the hammer before each shot, whenever accuracy was more critical than rate of fire.

A PICA had certain advantages when it came to things like that.

The pistol rose smoothly, sweetly balanced in his hand, and thunder rolled. Flame stabbed from the muzzle as rapidly as he could squeeze the trigger, and holes appeared magically in the doubled breastplates, blasting not simply through the steel but punching through the supporting posts in sprays of splinters, as well. He emptied the cylinder, then he raised the muzzle to the vertical, his thumb found the release, and he swung the cylinder out and hit the ejector rod. The expended cartridges kicked free, gleaming in the sun, and he dropped the muzzle once more, pointing it at the ground, while his left hand flashed to the leather case on his belt.

The new revolvers were overwhelmingly the children of Mahldyn's mind and imagination, but Ehdwyrd Howsmyn had personally sketched out one important accessory. It was a remarkably simple concept, really: rather like another, truncated revolver cylinder only a half-inch deep with a knob on the end. Back on Old Earth, similar devices had been called "speedloaders," and five fresh cartridges nosed into the pistol's empty chambers in a single, smooth movement before Merlin twisted the knob to release their bases. The cylinder clicked closed, the pistol rose again, and aimed shots blew the helmet off the top of each post in succession before the echoes of the first five shots had completely faded.

He cleared the cylinder a second time and reloaded in rather more leisurely fashion, blue eyes dark with memories of a barge on the Holy Langhorne Canal. Then he holstered the weapon, gathered up his expended brass, and turned back to his audience. The cloud of powder smoke had rolled away like a small, lonely fog bank, and Cayleb grinned hugely as Merlin raised one eyebrow. Half the Protector's Guard's horses were still kicking and shying, although Stohnar and Daryus Parkair had their own mounts firmly under control. Even the lord protector and the seneschal wore stunned expressions, however.

"Langhorne!" Parkair shook his head. "That *was* impressive, Merlin!"

He touched his skittish horse with a heel and moved closer to the targets, leaning from the saddle to insert the tip of his little finger into the hole punched through one of the paired breastplates, then straightened once more and shook his head.

"The sheer hitting power's astonishing, although I do understand that most mere mortals won't be able to handle those portable twelve-pounders of yours!"

"Actually, My Lord, the recoil's not all that bad," Merlin said. Parkair's expression bordered on the incredulous, and Merlin shrugged. "These are heavy pistols—a lot heavier than the standard version—and that soaks up a lot of the recoil. They're still more lively than the standard revolvers, but most people could handle the recoil without too much trouble. The weight of the weapon itself would bother most of them more, I suspect."

"I think we'll just take your word for that for the moment, *Seijin*," Stohnar put in dryly. "I'm sure the normal version will be quite powerful enough for most of us. And, frankly, what impressed *me* most was the combination of how quickly you could fire and *reload*." It was his turn to shake his head. "Until this moment, I truly didn't understand how much firepower one man holds in his hand with one of those things. Now I'm beginning to, I think, but I'm still having trouble extending it to the 'magazine rifles' your Master Howsmyn's promising us."

"They won't be able to fire that rapidly, My Lord," Merlin replied. "They're what Master Mahldyn calls a 'bolt-action' design. The rifleman will have to manually operate a cocking handle for each shot. On the other hand, I believe they finally settled on a ten-round magazine. Not only will each magazine hold more cartridges than a revolver, but a rifleman will be able to change magazines even more rapidly than someone can reload a pistol with one of Master Howsmyn's speedloaders."

He smiled very, very coldly.

"I don't think the Temple Boys are going to like that one little bit," he said.

"Don't much like the looks of this, Sir!"

Lieutenant Zherald Cahnyrs had to shout over the wind and the wash and thunder of water as Captain Halcom Bahrns stepped onto the bridge wing and fought to close the armored conning tower door behind him. It was, the lieutenant admitted, probably the most unnecessary understatement of his entire life, and he ducked as another burst of icy white spray exploded across the bridge.

He straightened once more, glistening oilskins pasted against his body by the steadily strengthening wind, and wiped his eyes. There was no point trying to actually dry his face; the best he could hope for under these conditions was to keep his vision reasonably clear.

Not that what he could see was particularly enheartening.

Captain Bahrns managed to get the door shut and dogged, then fought his way across the staggering bridge, clinging to the lifelines he'd ordered rigged three hours before, to Cahnyrs' side.

"I can't say I much care for it myself." He managed, Cahnyrs noted, to raise his voice enough to be heard without sounding as if he were bellowing. It must be a trick someone learned after he became a captain.

"The glass is still falling, too," the captain continued, clipping his canvas storm harness to one of the ring bolts set into the bridge's stout timbers. He turned, shading his eyes against the flying spray, scanning the wave-torn horizon, and Cahnyrs thought his shoulders seemed to tighten for a moment. The lieutenant looked in the same direction and his stomach clenched with dismay.

"When did we lose sight of *Kahrla Bordyn*?" Captain Bahrns' voice was flat.

"She was there less than ten minutes ago, Sir." Cahnyrs raised his arm and pointed, feeling his own storm harness jerk at his body. "There, about two points off the quarter. She was lagging badly, though." He glanced at the starboard lookout, who nodded in confirmation, then looked back to his captain. "The visibility's closed in since the last time I saw her, but I don't know if it's closed in enough for us to lose sight of her. Bryxtyn?"

"Second Lieutenant's right, Cap'n." The seaman was an experienced man, and he met Captain Bahrns' gaze levelly. "More like five'r six minutes since I seen her, I'm thinking. Might be it's closed in enough, but truth to tell, I don't think it has."

The captain nodded. His expression was neutral, but his eyes were grim, and Cahnyrs understood entirely. *Kahrla Bordyn* had two infantry companies—better than five hundred men, with their support platoons— embarked. But surely it was simply a case of worsening visibility! *Kahrla Bordyn* was a well-found ship, a stout galleon with an experienced captain, far better equipped to survive in heavy weather than a ship like HMS *Delthak*. She *had* to be back there somewhere.

"Was there any sign she was in distress?"

"None, Sir," Cahnyrs replied, and Bryxtyn shook his head, agreeing with him. "She'd reduced to double-reefed topsails, but she seemed well enough. I didn't see any rockets or distress signals, but at that distance in these conditions, I might not've seen signal flags even if she was showing them."

The captain nodded. One of the things Cahnyrs most admired about Captain Bahrns was that he never chewed a man out for admitting something like that. God help anyone who tried to excuse a failure to do his utmost, but the captain preferred subordinates who offered the information he needed to fully understand what they were saying rather than keeping silent for fear of provoking their commander's ire. Langhorne knew Cahnyrs had seen enough other captains who would have torn a strip off of him, if only to vent their own anger and fear.

Captain Bahrns simply turned his back on the horizon where *Kahrla Bordyn* ought to have been and peered ahead into the tumbled white and green wilderness as the steadily growing waves heaped up and pounded the ironclad's low, bluff bow. Actually, they were pounding *over* the bow, burying the short foredeck and slamming into the curved casemate's triply secured port shutters. He stood there for several minutes, then gave himself a shake and reached up to slap Cahnyrs on the shoulder.

"The First Lieutenant or I'll be in the conning tower if you need us, Zherald."

"Aye, Sir."

The hand on Cahnyrs' shoulder tightened for a moment. Then the captain unclipped his storm harness and made his way back to the armored door.

▼ ▼ ▼

It was much quieter inside the conning tower, although "quieter" was a purely relative term aboard a twelve-hundred-ton ship battering her way into the teeth of what would have been called a Force Seven wind back on Old Earth. That wind came brawling out of the southwest, directly up the Tarot Channel, at almost forty miles per hour, piling fourteen- or fifteen-foot waves before it. The waves' white crests blew horizontally upon its breath . . . and *Delthak*'s freeboard was only eleven and a half feet.

Bahrns nodded to the helmsman and to the signalman and telegraphsman of the watch, then crossed to the conning tower's tiny chart room and peered down at *Delthak*'s current estimated position. According to it, they were a hundred and forty miles east-northeast of Seahorse Island, and there were any number of other places he would rather have been. Especially since the weather promised to continue getting worse before it ever got better.

His jaw tightened as he thought about *Kahrla Bordyn*. By any standard he could think of, the galleon was more seaworthy than his own command. *Delthak*'s shallow draft showed in the violence of her motion, but at least she showed less tendency to drive to leeward, since she offered the wind a smaller target without the masts and complex rigging of a galleon. And she'd actually proven rather more buoyant than Bahrns had anticipated when he first took command. But that was very little comfort when he listened to the water roaring along her sides, ripping at the port shutters. There was some leakage around any gunport lid, even *Delthak*'s heavily armored ones, no matter how tightly closed they were. That was only to be expected. He didn't much care for the way water spurted in around the edges of the forward shutters, though. And if any one of those port shutters carried away, seawater would roar exuberantly into the ship with probably fatal consequences.

Of course it would, he told himself. *And that's why you took so much extra care in* securing *the damned things, isn't it?*

True. That was true enough. It didn't make him feel a great deal better, but it was certainly true.

He gave himself a mental shake, spreading his feet for balance as the deck heaved underfoot. His ship had advantages of her own, he reminded himself firmly. As long as his stokers stayed on their feet and managed to feed the boilers, *Delthak*'s propulsion—unlike that of the transport and war galleons clawing their way southwest—was independent of the wind howling around her hull. And her pumps were steam-powered and highly efficient; despite the leakage around her port shutters and the additional water inevitably finding its way aboard as her timbers worked in the seaway, they'd so far stayed ahead of the influx with almost ridiculous ease. He did feel some concern over the safety of Lieutenant Bairystyr's stokers and oilers in the confines of *Delthak*'s boiler rooms and engine spaces, but the truth was that they were far safer even there than topmen sent aloft to reef and hand sail in this kind of weather.

As long as her hull holds together and none of the port shutters get stove in, she'll do fine, he told himself. *Just fine.*

Of course, some might have wondered just how well a converted river barge *could* hold together in conditions like these, especially with its hull burdened by so many tons of armor plate. Fortunately, Sir Dustyn Olyvyr had wondered the same thing when he turned Howsmyn's rough calculations into a finished product. The barges in question had been designed to carry heavy cargoes and be suitable for coastal traffic, but not even a lunatic would have considered sending them all the way from Tellesberg to Siddarmark in their original conformation. Their frames had been heavy and closer set than in the majority of canal barges, however, and Olyvyr had strengthened them and reinforced her longitudinal strength by running steel bars with threaded ends between each pair of ribs and securing them with heavy washers and massive nuts. That reinforcement—along with the extra freeboard he'd insisted upon adding at sides and bow and the breakwaters he'd added to the foredeck—had increased *Delthak*'s final displacement by a few inches, which was not a minor consideration in river or canalwater, but along with the six solid inches of teak backing the armor they'd also turned her hull into an immensely strong box.

Which, given the vicious power of the fall and winter southwesters that came howling up the Tarot Channel from the Sea of Justice, might prove to be a very good thing indeed.

▼ ▼ ▼

"Captain! Captain, Sir!"

Halcom Bahrns' eyes opened instantly as the hand touched his shoulder. Even before the lids were fully raised, he sensed the ship's more violent motion.

"Yes?" He sat up, raking the fingers of his right hand through tousled brown hair. "What?"

"Sorry to disturb you, Sir." Midshipman Tairaince Sutyls stood back, gray eyes worried in his fourteen-year-old face. "Lieutenant Blahdysnberg's respects, and you're needed in the conning tower."

The young Chisholmian was obviously clinging to the comfort of the message's formality, Bahrns noted, and produced as reassuring a smile as he could manage.

"My compliments to the Lieutenant and inform him I'll be there as quickly as possible, Master Sutyls."

"Aye, aye, Sir. Your compliments to Lieutenant Blahdysnberg and you'll be there as quickly as possible."

The boy saluted and disappeared, and Bahrns swung his legs over the edge of his wildly swaying cot and shoved his feet into his sea boots. He'd turned in fully dressed, and he reached for his oilskins as he stamped his feet fully into the boots.

He was through his sea cabin's door no more than fifteen seconds behind Sutyls.

"Captain on deck!"

"As you were," Bahrns said briskly, crossing the conning tower to Pawal Blahdysnberg. The first lieutenant had just stepped back into the conning tower from the bridge wing, judging by the water running down his oilskins, and he straightened at the sound of Bahrns' voice, turning from where he'd been peering aft through one of the conning tower's view slits.

"Sorry to disturb you, Sir." His voice was taut, his expression worried.

"I don't imagine you would've if you'd had a choice. What is it?"

"It's *Tellesberg Queen*, Sir. She's firing distress rockets."

Bahrns felt his stomach muscles tighten. *Tellesberg Queen* was another of the transports. Substantially larger than *Kahrla Bordyn*, she carried an entire artillery battalion, minus its draft animals, and two companies of scout snipers. That was over a thousand Charisian soldiers and thirty-two field guns in addition to the galleon's own crew.

"Where is she?"

"About five miles dead astern," Blahdysnberg said grimly. "It's getting on towards night, and it's already dark as Shan-wei's heart, but I'm pretty sure she's lost her fore topmast and topgallant. She may've lost her entire foremast. I didn't see any sign of her course or her headsails, anyway."

The lump of stone in Bahrns' stomach became an iron round shot. The foremast was critical to a ship's maneuverability, not least because it supported the all important headsails. Without their leverage forward, her ability to hold anything remotely like a steady course in these conditions would be seriously impaired. And a ship that *couldn't* hold a steady course in these conditions. . . .

He turned and stepped into the chart house, beckoning for Blahdysnberg to follow. The lieutenant obeyed the gesture, and Bahrns looked down at the chart.

"We're here?" He tapped the last penciled-in location.

"About here, Sir," Blahdysnberg corrected, tapping a point fifteen or twenty miles to the southwest. "Chief Kuhlbyrtsyn updated it at two bells."

Bahrns nodded, frowning ferociously at the unpromising chart. If Blahdysnberg's estimate was correct, they'd come over seventy miles since he and Cahnyrs had spoken on the bridge wing that morning. They were off the southernmost tip of Seahorse Island and perhaps fifteen miles from a nameless hunk of tideswept rock and sand forty miles southeast of the island. In theory, if they turned sharply to starboard and headed due west they could get into the lee of Star Island to Seahorse's southwest, but the passage between Star and Seahorse was barely thirty miles wide and perilous at the best of times, which these sure as hell weren't. Besides, where would they go after that? Into Malitar Sound? That was a ships' graveyard—shallow, treacherous, and littered with shifting sandbanks. In this weather, given the seas the wind must whip up along its length, the Sound would be Shan-wei's own parlor; no one who set foot inside it would ever come out alive. No, they were a good six or seven hundred miles from the nearest safe harbor: Sekyr Island in Clanhyr Bay.

From the feel of things, the weather wasn't finished getting worse, either. If *Tellesberg Queen* was out there in that howling murk without a foremast it was unlikely she'd live to see the dawn, far less Clanhyr Bay, and there was no power on Safehold which could help her.

Unless. . . .

Are you certain you even want to think about this? a preposterously calm voice asked in the recesses of his mind. *It's completely insane—you do realize that, don't you? Do you really want to hazard your own ship— your own* men—*on such a harebrained, lunatic notion?*

In point of fact, he couldn't think of anything he wanted to do less, but that wasn't really the point. He was an officer of the Imperial Charisian Navy.

"Master Blahdysnberg," he said with unaccustomed formality, one hand still resting on the chart. "Be good enough to call all hands, if you please."

▼ ▼ ▼

This is insane, Zherald Cahnyrs thought.

He was back on the bridge wing, eyes gritty with fatigue after having been rousted out of his cot. He wasn't officer of the watch this time, however. Instead, he stood braced in the conning tower doorway, his eyes on Captain Bahrns while showers of spray burst over the bridge like crazed waterfalls. There was rain in that spray, now, although no one could taste its freshness through the torrents of salt. The waves breaking across the foredeck swept down the sides of the casemate no more than three feet below his feet, boiling white around the bridge's supporting stanchions. They'd been substantially strengthened after the Canal Raid, but all it would take would be one rogue wave, a little higher than the others, to reach the bridge wing and sweep over it. In fact, that had already happened twice, and Cahnyrs was none too optimistic about just how adequately the support structure had been strengthened in the face of this sort of abuse.

Even more frighteningly, those same waves threatened to sweep over the *top* of the casemate, as well as down its sides, and if that *happened*—if those crashing walls of water found a way down the ventilator intakes or carried away one of the funnels. . . .

He forced himself not to think about that. It wasn't easy, but if he concentrated solely on the captain it helped.

▼ ▼ ▼

Halcom Bahrns glanced over his shoulder at Lieutenant Cahnyrs. Like young Sutyls, the lieutenant was a Chisholmian, and he stood barely one inch under six feet, which made him a giant by Old Charisian standards. At the moment, however, he looked at least as young and frail as Sutyls.

Bahrns sympathized, and he turned back, peering over the bow—or the crashing, surging water where the bow was supposed to be, at any rate—and drove his own mind back over his preparations.

So far as he knew, no one had ever attempted what he proposed to do. That meant he was making it all up as he went along, and it was entirely possible no one would ever know he had because he'd managed to kill his entire crew in the process.

That's enough of that, *Halcom!* he told himself sternly, and closed his eyes as a fresh surge of green water roared past just below the gratings under his feet.

The messenger line had been seized to the three-inch hawser which had been secured in turn to *Delthak*'s stern anchor chain. Managing that under the current conditions had been not simply incredibly difficult but extraordinarily dangerous. Technically, Blahdysnberg had been in charge of the operation, and he'd certainly been *responsible* for it, but he'd also been wise enough to allow Chestyr Dyllahn, *Delthak*'s boatswain, and Brahdlai Mahfyt, Bahrns' coxswain, free rein to deal with it.

The first step had been to get rid of the anchor itself, which meant someone had to go out onto the miniscule quarterdeck to unshackle it. The good news was that the quarterdeck was in the lee of the casemate, which meant the worst force of the waves sweeping over it was broken by the superstructure. The bad news was that even so, the quarterdeck was at least two feet underwater *be-*

tween waves and under up to six feet of water whenever a wave swept the length of the ship. And the water could easily be twice that deep with very little warning.

It would have been difficult to decide whether Dyllahn or Mahfyt was the more powerfully built, and Bahrns had no idea how they'd decided who got to go out to drown himself, but Mahfyt had ended up in a double storm harness triple-lashed to the ladder rungs set into the casemate's after face. That was enough to keep him from being washed overboard, although it certainly wasn't enough to prevent cracked or broken ribs and atrocious bruising.

They'd let him out the after hatch between the funnels on top of the casing and he'd climbed down the ladder, snaphooking one of his two safety harnesses to each rung as he descended it. Then, standing thigh-deep in ice cold water, he'd ducked under, found the securely lashed anchor, and—using the wrench lashed to his right wrist—unfastened the shackle's massive lugs one by one.

Dyllahn had followed him through the casemate hatch, standing in it with two seamen hanging on to his legs and his own safety harness locked into place, and fed the end of the three-inch hawser, a shackle already spliced into it, through the hatch and down to where Mahfyt stood in that surging cauldron of water and wind shriek. Then the boatswain had climbed down to join the coxswain, and the two of them had somehow managed to secure the hawser to the end of the anchor chain. In the process, Dyllahn had broken three fingers and according to the ship's healer, Mahfyt had at least six broken ribs. They'd both been half dead by the time they finished, and two members of Mahfyt's boat crew had been forced to clamber down into that maelstrom to carry their coxswain back to safety, but somehow they'd done it, and now it was up to Halcom Bahrns to make sure their efforts weren't in vain.

" 'Nother rocket, Sir!" the lookout sang out, and Bahrns nodded.

Tellesberg Queen was still there, then . . . unless yet another galleon was in distress. It seemed incredible to him that even one of the new, improved rockets could fight its way through a wind like this one, and he wondered how badly and how far off course it had been blown before the lookout saw it. Not too far, he hoped. It was the only guide he had to the ship's position.

He watched the sea, as much of it as he could see, and gripped the railing, feeling the shuddering vibrations as *Delthak* slammed through the waves. It was going to be far more a matter of timing, instinct, and the pattern of those vibrations than of vision, and he knew it.

All right, My Lady, he thought. *We've gotten to know each other better these past months. Now let's see if we can truly do this.*

He closed his eyes, concentrating on the fusion of his hand with the bridge railing, emptying his mind, waiting. . . .

"*Now*, Master Cahnyrs! Hard a starboard! Stop starboard engine, full ahead larboard!"

▼ ▼ ▼

Zherald Cahnyrs had no idea what had prompted the captain's timing. He could see absolutely no difference in the incoming waves or howling wind, but he never hesitated. His head whipped around.

"Hard a starboard! Stop starboard engine! Full ahead larboard!" he barked into the conning tower.

"Helm hard a starboard, aye, aye, Sir!" PO Crahmynd Fyrgyrsyn acknowledged, spinning the wheel.

"Stop starboard, aye, aye!" the telegraphsman sang out, yanking the brass handle to the full stop position. "Full ahead larboard, aye, aye, Sir!" He rocked the other handle all the way forward, and HMS *Delthak* lurched to starboard.

The big rudder bit hard, yet the suddenly unbalanced thrust of her screws drove her still harder. She swept round, heaving, rolling madly as she took those heavy seas broadside. She went up on her starboard side, tipping as if she meant to roll completely over. But she didn't. Somehow, she didn't, and she was two-thirds of the way around when the far larger and heavier wave, the one Halcom Bahrns had known was coming even though no eye could have seen it, hit her. It drove her the rest of the way around, pushing her head to the northeast.

"*Wheel amidships!*" Bahrns shouted. "Ahead two-thirds both engines! Steady on north-nor'east!"

Cahnyrs had been thrown from his feet by the violent motion. White pain ripped through his left arm, and a corner of his mind decided he must have broken it. He was sprawled across the raised lip of the conning tower door, water washing around him, but he heard the captain's commands and repeated them hoarsely.

HMS *Delthak*, obedient to the madmen who crewed her, settled down on her new heading and another rocket pierced the spray and rain to burst in glory below the clouds ahead of her.

▼ ▼ ▼

Halcom Bahrns rubbed sore, salt-burning eyes as *Tellesberg Queen* loomed out of the storm-lashed night. The galleon had lost not simply her foremast but her jib boom, as well. She retained only a stump of her bowsprit, and she lay hove-to under triple-reefed main and mizzen topsails. There was other damage aloft, and the loss of the foremast and the dynamic tension of all the rigging associated with it had weakened everything still standing. It looked as if they were pumping hard, as well, and just to make bad worse, they were closer to Seahorse Island than he'd thought and the wind had backed from the southwest to the south-southeast. Lightning had been added to the mix, on top of everything else, but at least it gave them bursts of better visibility, although he could have done without the sight of surf breaking in white fury on the southern tip of Seahorse Island and—

A jagged burst of lightning glare showed him the two signal flags streaming from her mainyard, stiff as shredded boards on the howling wind. Number 21: "I am in distress," and Number 23: "I am taking on water."

"All right," he said, though no one could possibly hear him unless he shouted. "One more time, My Lady."

Even from the extreme end of the bridge wing, visibility astern was much more limited than ahead at the best of times. On the other hand, the lightning let him see farther . . . when he could see at all. The serried ranks of waves had to have reached more than twenty feet in height, their crests toppling and tumbling, rolling over in wind-torn spray that baffled and confused the eye. If it wasn't a strong gale already, it would be shortly, for it was *still* building strength, and he felt the breath of necessity hot on his neck.

Maybe so, he told himself, *but rushing will only get you killed. Patience, Halcom. Patience. . . .*

He stood there, gauging the moment, then nodded to himself.

"Hard to larboard!"

Delthak staggered and rolled as she answered her helm, but this time she was bringing her bow to wind and wave. She climbed up the flank of a mountain of water, lurched to larboard, and went sledding down the wave's back. Her screws came completely out of the water for a moment, racing, shaking her like a cat-lizard with a spider-rat. Then they bit into the sea again, driving her down into the trough between waves. Another massive wall of water crashed into her larboard bow, white and green exploding vertically upward with the sound of a cannon shot. The shock of the impact slammed the soles of Bahrns' feet as if someone had hit the grating under them with a sledgehammer, but then she was around, sweeping astern of *Tellesberg Queen* to come up on the galleon's larboard side barely sixty feet clear.

Bahrns clung to the bridge railing, fumbling for his speaking trumpet, watching men stagger and lurch towards the galleon's rail. Clearly they thought he was insane to bring his ship so close under these conditions. Two signals streamed from his own mast's yardarms—Number 73: "Stand by to receive a line" and Number 75: "I am preparing to take you in tow"—but he had no idea if anyone over there had seen them in these conditions.

"*Stand by!*" he screamed through the speaking trumpet. "*Stand by to receive a line!*"

No one seemed to hear him, and he repeated himself, lungs burning, throat feeling ripped and raw. They had to hear him quickly. He couldn't allow *Delthak* to lose way, so the line had to go across while she steamed past *Tellesberg Queen*, but if no one realized it was coming. . . .

Lightning ripped at the night and he waved his trumpet wildly up at *Delthak*'s signals, *willing* someone aboard *Tellesberg Queen* to see and recognize them. Surely *someone*—

Then he saw an arm waving back from the galleon's deck. He couldn't be sure if that meant he'd been understood. On the other hand, he was already parallel with the other ship as she drifted to leeward. He looked aft to where one of Dyllahn's seamen stood clinging to a guy wire on the starboard funnel, watching him. He swung the hand with the speaking trumpet again, pointing it at the galleon like a sword, and the seaman waved in reply and turned away.

An instant later the weighted end of the light messenger line went whipping through the stormy tumult. It carried to *Tellesberg Queen*'s deck and a dozen hands pounced on it quickly and began hauling it aboard.

"Slow to one quarter!" he shouted, and *Delthak*'s motion became heavier and wilder as her speed through the water slowed. She rolled with tooth-snapping force, protesting, but *Tellesberg Queen* needed more time.

The three-inch hawser went across, and someone in an officer's uniform, staggered to the galleon's rail opposite Bahrns' bridge wing.

"We're passing our anchor chain!" Bahrns bawled. "It's the only line we've got that will stand the strain!"

The other man stared at him for a moment, then nodded sharply and turned away, shouting to his own crew. There was a flurry of purposeful motion as the end of the hawser came aboard and someone knocked the stopper out of the larboard hawsepipe so the line could be fed below to the forward capstan.

Bahrns heaved a huge sigh of relief as the capstan began to turn, taking the heavy hawser aboard. He saw water exploding out of it as the tension came on and the kinks straightened, and he turned back to Lieutenant Cahnyrs, still at his post in the conning tower door with his splinted arm in a sling.

"Tell Lieutenant Bairystyr to begin veering the anchor chain—slowly. Slowly!"

. XII .
The Temple,
City of Zion,
The Temple Lands

"Rage" was far too weak a word.

"Anger" or "wrath" didn't even come close. The only possible description as Wyllym Rayno stood absolutely motionless in one corner of the luxurious apartment was "mad, frothing frenzy."

It wasn't the first time Zhaspahr Clyntahn had reduced this chamber's furnishings to a shambles, but this time it was as if the room had been devastated by an earthquake and then threshed by a tornado. Furniture had been upended, glassware smashed, paintings ripped off the wall, books torn apart, sculptures crushed. . . .

Clyntahn's fury had rampaged through his suite for over an hour. Rayno didn't know how much longer; the beautiful grandfather's clock which had cost enough to feed and house a Zion family for at least two years had been turned into wreckage thirty-six minutes into the Grand Inquisitor's screaming eruption, and the archbishop hadn't dared to check his watch since. The prudent rabbit did not draw attention to itself while a blood-mad wyvern circled overhead, and this was a time to be *very* prudent. Indeed, for all of Rayno's considerable intestinal fortitude, all he truly wanted to do was run for his life. In all the years he'd served Zhaspahr Clyntahn, he'd never—*never*—seen the vicar in such a pure, unadulterated fury. It was remarkable, he thought now, that Clyntahn's howling apoplexy hadn't brought on a genuine stroke or heart attack.

He'd thought once or twice that the Grand Inquisitor was beginning to calm, but each time Clyntahn's glare had returned to the shredded copy of the letter which had so enraged him. And each time, his hurricane passion had roared up afresh. Now, though, he stood almost motionless, shoulders heaving as he panted, amid the broken bits of priceless artwork, the shards of splintered crystalware, and the snowdrift litter of pages ripped from books. Some of those books dated back almost to the Creation itself, and gems gleamed in the corners of the room where they'd been ripped from embellished covers . . . or gone skittering when Clyntahn hurled the irreplaceable books against the wall with all the rage-fueled fury of his shoulders and back.

The archbishop watched silently, his face clear of any expression, and tried not to breathe as his superior slowly, slowly, lifted his hands and ran his fingers through his sweatsoaked, disordered hair. He paused with those hands at the back of his head, fingers interlocked, and Rayno heard air hiss as he inhaled deeply.

Silence hovered, fragile and afraid of itself—or of Zhaspahr Clyntahn—for what seemed an eternity but was probably only seconds. Then Clyntahn turned, darted one bloodshot glare in Rayno's direction, jerked his head for the archbishop to follow, and stalked out of the wreckage and ruin he'd wrought.

The next to last thing in the world Wyllym Rayno wanted at that moment was to find himself alone with Clyntahn in the Grand Inquisitor's office. The *last* thing he wanted was to reawaken that shrieking fury and direct it at himself, and so he followed silently, calmly, at Clyntahn's heels.

Behind them, terrified servants crept out of hiding, surveyed the rubble, and began sifting through it for anything which might actually have survived.

▼ ▼ ▼

"All right," Clyntahn grated.

He sat behind his desk, hands clenched on his blotter as if to choke his own anger into submission. His knuckles were bruised, two of them scabbed with blood, and he was going to have to ice his hand to get his ring of office off before it did damage to his swollen ring finger. He seemed unaware of that at the moment, and Wyllym Rayno had no intention of pointing it out to him.

"What do we know about this miserable son-of-a-bitch, this . . . Mab, that isn't in his goddamned letter?" he continued.

"Nothing, Your Grace," Rayno replied in his most neutral tone. "The Inquisition's never heard of him, and I'm inclined to think the name is an alias."

"Why?" Clyntahn demanded flatly, and Rayno met his still fiery eyes.

"Because his *true* name is in Mother Church's records somewhere, Your Grace. If nothing else, his birth record's on file in some parish church. He knows we're going to search those records as they've never been searched before, and if we find *him*, we find his family, the village he grew up in, the teacher he knew at school. I find it difficult to believe anyone who would—and could—do what this man has would leave such . . . hostages to fortune where we might find them."

Clyntahn's jaw muscles bunched. Then they relaxed once more, and he nodded slowly.

"Makes sense," he acknowledged. "And it probably explains the name's outlandishness, too. It's made-up nonsense."

"Almost certainly, Your Grace."

"I don't care whether or not he's in our records, though." Clyntahn's voice sounded as if he were chewing granite boulders. "I want him found. I want him identified. And I want him dead. Here—right here in Zion, that's where I want him, Wyllym!"

"I've already issued instructions to accomplish just that, Your Grace. The task will be . . . difficult, however.

We have no idea what he looks like or where to find him, and you know the handicaps under which we operate in lands controlled by the heretics. We've begun the hunt, yet I'd be less than truthful if I told Your Grace I anticipate bringing our quarry to bay anytime soon."

The archbishop braced for a fresh outburst, but Clyntahn only jerked a short, choppy nod. His unhappiness was evident, but his brain seemed to be once more functioning well enough to recognize the inescapable truth.

Or, at least, to recognize *an* inescapable truth, Rayno amended silently. The Grand Inquisitor was quite capable of ignoring *other* inescapable truths, and the archbishop devoutly prayed he wasn't going to ignore sanity when the time came to hear it.

"In the meantime, we have to decide how to respond," Clyntahn growled. "I don't have any doubt the son-of-a-bitch's letter will start turning up on walls all over both Havens soon enough."

"I fear you're correct, Your Grace."

Rayno had considered pointing out that they had no evidence that whoever continued to post those mysterious broadsheets had ever heard of a man named Dialydd Mab. Experience, however, had taught him it was always safer to anticipate the worst. And "the worst" in this case was going to be very bad indeed.

The archbishop closed his eyes briefly, recalling his own feelings when the bloodsoaked envelope addressed in a clear strong hand to "Zhaspahr Clyntahn, Grand Fornicator" had been delivered to his office. He'd stared at it, listening to the report of where and how it had been found. About the only thing he'd wanted less than to open it was to deliver it to Clyntahn, yet he'd realized as the report rolled over him that withholding information he knew would enrage the Grand Inquisitor wasn't an option this time. Whoever this Mab was, he intended to make his point brutally and completely clear. The information would reach Clyntahn one way or another, and if the Grand Inquisitor learned about it some other way and then discovered Rayno had attempted to keep him in the dark. . . .

So he'd gone ahead and opened it, and his face had gone white as he read it.

To Zhaspahr Clyntahn, greetings.

I have no intention of wasting invective upon you. First, because no invective could be adequate. Second, because others might equate it to the same baseless vituperation you spew forth daily.

The entire world has learned how fearless you are when you need not face your foes. There is no realm where the truth of your butcheries, your tortures, is unknown. Yet you have never once ventured out from behind the protection of the Inquisition and the Temple Guard. You lack the courage even to walk the streets of Mother Church's own city, be you ever so surrounded by bodyguards, far less to risk your own precious blood in what you claim to be "the service of God." Others may die in their millions in the Jihad you proclaimed; you have no intention of doing so yourself.

Yet you and I both know—as the rest of the world is coming to learn—that what you do, what you are, has nothing to do with "the service of God." You worship not Him but the pleasures of the flesh, wealth, luxury, the power of life and death. You glory not in God, but in the terror you have made of your office and the Inquisition as you and your servants torture, maim, and kill anyone who dares to defy not God, but you.

You have made it abundantly clear that no amount of innocent blood, no amount of agony, will sway you from your vile ambition to turn the Church herself into no more than a shadow of your own corruption. And in the filth you recruit to serve the Office of Inquisition, you have found apt tools. Tools such as Vyktyr Tahrlsahn and Hahskyll Seegairs.

The time has come to deprive you of those tools.

There were those warriors in the War Against the Fallen who did what others could not. Mortal men called them seijins, *and many thought their powers were supernatural, gifts bestowed upon them by God. Whatever the men who thought that might have believed, however, the* seijins *were not angels, nor were they demons.*

Nor are they extinct.

You have proclaimed Merlin Athrawes a demon. As in so many other things, you have lied. Yet this much, at least, is truth—he is but one of many, and you do not know where the others of us may be or what we may accomplish. We claim no special divinity, but we are determined that you and the corruption you spawn will not succeed, and so we have given our service to Charis and the Church of Charis and sworn that the day will come when you answer for your crimes and render your account to God.

As Emperor Cayleb and Empress Sharleyan have proclaimed, your Inquisitors stand condemned wherever they may be taken. Know, now, that they stand condemned wherever they may be found, *as well. We will not be able to reach all of them; but we will be able to slay any of them we can reach, and those who lend themselves to special foulness, like Tahrlsahn and Seegairs, will be sought out. We will find them, and they will die. We do not torture for the sake of torture as they—and you—delight in doing, but they will find no more mercy at our hands than their victims have found at theirs.*

You—and they—may choose to ignore this letter. You may continue to butcher prisoners of war, to send thousands of innocent men, women, and children to concentration camps and to the Punishment. You may continue to torture and terrify. In the fullness of time, all of you will face the penalty appointed by God for your crimes. We are not Him, but be aware—all of you, from this moment on—that whatever He may hold in store for your souls, your lives are already forfeit and we will claim them where, as, how, and when we choose.

Dialydd Mab

"This can't go unanswered," Clyntahn grated. "Bad enough when that bastard Eastshare massacres consecrated priests on the field of battle. We *cannot* allow the murder of our special Inquisitors so far from the battlefront to pass without consequences."

"What . . . consequences do you have in mind, Your Grace?"

The Grand Inquisitor scowled at the diffident question, and Rayno folded his hands in the sleeves of his cassock, bracing himself to deliver another of those inescapable truths.

"We start by returning to this Sarkyn place and completing its cleansing. Let's see how this bastard Mab feels about *that*!"

"Forgive me, Your Grace, but that might be . . . ill-advised."

"*What?!*"

Despite decades of experience, Rayno flinched as Clyntahn exploded out of his chair, hands braced on his desktop, leaning across it with fiery eyes. The archbishop made himself sit motionless, looking back at his superior. Silence crackled and then, ever so slowly, Clyntahn sank back into his chair.

"Explain yourself."

The two words came out like Zion icicles, and Rayno inhaled as unobtrusively as possible. He spent one precious moment praying that what he was about to say could somehow reach through Clyntahn's fury. Frankly, he wasn't prepared to offer odds that it would, yet he had to try.

"Your Grace," he said, "I anticipated your likely reaction. Indeed, my own initial response was exactly the same. But before I brought this letter to you, I thought it best to send inquiries back up the canal as far as Sarkyn to determine what else might have transpired along the barge's route. I have the responses to those inquiries in my office, but to summarize what I discovered, the commander of the Sarkyn garrison is dead. His second-in-command is dead. His *third*-in-command is dead. The commanders of the infantry companies assigned to cleanse Sarkyn at Father Hahskyll's direction are dead—all of them—picked off by marksmen at extreme range. The commander of the detail which escorted the suspected heretics from Sarkyn to Camp Fyrmahn is dead, picked off by a marksman as he exercised his horse. All of the lay brothers assigned to assist Father Hahskyll were aboard the barge with him and are also dead, as is their entire Army escort . . . who'd also assisted at Sarkyn. And I've discovered that four *additional* noncommissioned officers and eleven privates who particularly distinguished themselves in cleansing Sarkyn are now dead, as well. Most of them were killed when a single patrol was ambushed; two of the noncommissioned officers, including a company first sergeant, were found in their own quarters—in their own beds—with their throats cut, however. No one has been able to explain how their assassins penetrated their barracks without a single sentry noticing a single thing."

Clyntahn's expression had gone very still as he listened. Now Rayno paused, letting silence refill the office.

"Your Grace," he said at last, "I agree that these murders represent a very dangerous challenge. Yet whoever this 'Seijin Dialydd' may actually be, it seems clear that he does represent a major organization with frightening capabilities. He denies demonhood, and perhaps he's telling the truth—certainly, we found where the assassins who murdered Father Vyktyr and Father Hahskyll had camped waiting for their opportunity, and one doubts demons would require campfires or lean-tos. But however that may be, he and his . . . allies have demonstrated a very long reach. Whatever we do, news of what happened to Father Vyktyr and Father Hahskyll—and to the soldiers who assisted them at Sarkyn—*will* spread. My agents inquisitor will do all we can to at least slow the telling and retelling, but it would be folly for us to pretend we could actually *stop* it. No doubt we would be able to complete the cleansing of Sarkyn as you desire, yet if we do that, and if this so-called *seijin* and his allies then succeed in killing only one or two of the Inquisitors and soldiers who carry out that task, what happens when *that* story begins to spread, as well?"

It was very, very quiet in Zhaspahr Clyntahn's office for a very, very long time.

. XIII .
Fort Tairys,
Shiloh Province,
Republic of Siddarmark

"Charisians? *Charisians?!*" General Lairays Walkyr stared at Colonel Syngyltyn's messenger in horror. "They're *Charisians?*"

"Yes, Sir," the lieutenant, who'd been a corporal before the Rising, seemed a bit taken aback by Walkyr's reaction.

"I see." The general made himself inhale deeply and nodded. "I see," he repeated. "Tell Colonel Syngyltyn I'd like to see him here as soon as possible."

"Yes, Sir." The lieutenant touched his breastplate and withdrew, and Walkyr shoved up out of his chair, walked to the window, and stared blindly out across the fortifications he'd spent the last ten months building.

He'd been anxious enough when forces loyal to the apostate Stohnar were reported within a single day's march of Fort Tairys from the east, but that hadn't been totally unexpected. Obviously it would have been better if the Faithful had managed to seize control of all of Shiloh, but they hadn't, so it was only reasonable for Stohnar and his heretical allies to seek to reclaim the western portion of the province as soon as they thought they could. The fact that they clearly felt that time had come said things Walkyr didn't really want to consider about how the Jihad was going elsewhere, yet his best estimate indicated that they couldn't have much over seven or eight thousand men. He'd made provision to hold Fort Tairys indefinitely against an attack from the interior of the Republic in far greater strength than that. And even more to the point, the messages he'd received from Duke Harless before saboteurs destroyed the semaphore somewhere between the fort and the town of Kharmych had reassured him that the duke's huge army would arrive to relieve him shortly.

No one had warned him to expect enemy forces—and especially not *Charisian* forces—from the *west*, however. Worse, he hadn't had even a whisper of warning until yesterday evening, when he'd ordered Syngyltyn to send out scouts to identify the unknown interlopers reported at Kharmych. He'd hoped—or *allowed* himself to hope—that it might be Duke Harless' vanguard, although the timing had been against it. His next preferred outcome would have been for the report to prove an unfounded rumor. His *least* preferred outcome was for it to turn out to be the enemy, instead.

He wasn't any too happy that they'd gotten this far south before anyone even noticed them, either. Still, the territory west of Fort Tairys had been virtually depopulated in the Rising, so it probably shouldn't be *too* surprising that the heretics hadn't been spotted sooner. But Charisians? Reliable news had been hard to come by from the beginning, yet nothing he'd heard had suggested the heretics might dare to withdraw troops from the outnumbered blocking force facing Bishop Militant Cahnyr along the Daivyn.

But where else could they have come from, assuming Syngyltyn's cavalry had identified them properly? The only way they could have gotten here was down the Branath Canal, and Walkyr drummed nervously on the windowsill as he considered that. Father Naiklos Vahnhain, the Schuelerite under-priest who'd joined Walkyr in his seizure of Fort Tairys, had been confirmed as his special intendant as soon as they'd been able to communicate with Mother Church. And they'd received the Inquisitor General's authorization to destroy canal locks if the Jihad required it three months ago. In fact,

Colonel Mhartyn, commanding the 6th Infantry Regiment, had urged Walkyr to destroy or disable the Branath Canal locks at least as far as the point at which it crossed the Kharmych-Fort St. Klair High Road. He'd wanted to go further than that, in fact, and put the entire southernmost three or four hundred miles of the canal completely out of service.

Colonel Zahmsyn, commanding the 15th Infantry Regiment, had agreed with Mhartyn, and Walkyr had been torn between agreeing with them and preserving a vital resource.

His decision has been complicated by the need to assert his authority. Mhartyn and Zahmsyn were both regulars, just as Walkyr had been. But whereas Zahmsyn and Walkyr had been captains before the Rising, Mhartyn had been a major. Walkyr's present rank had been self-granted, with Father Naiklos' strong backing, on the basis that the man who'd successfully seized Fort Tairys from its garrison was the logical officer to command its defense. His promotion had been confirmed by the Office of the Inquisition, and Mhartyn and Zahmsyn had accepted it, however grudgingly.

Despite that, Mhartyn—as the officer who'd brought sixty percent of his regiment over to the Faithful intact—clearly resented his subordination. Zahmsyn might, as well, but if so, he concealed it better. However obediently Mhartyn accepted Walkyr's orders, it was obvious he felt he ought to have been placed in command. That created certain problems where it came to taking Mhartyn's advice, since it was vital to avoid the appearance that Walkyr was dancing to the colonel's direction. Despite that, Walkyr had been inclined to go along with him, at least as far as disabling the locks between Kharmych and the fort. His earlier orders from Mother Church, however, had stressed the importance of preserving the canal so that the forces advancing out of Desnair would be able to move rapidly into the rear of the heretics facing the Army of Glacierheart if that proved necessary. No one had changed those orders, and Father Naiklos had argued vehemently that destroying locks when there weren't even any enemy troops in the vicinity would run directly counter to Mother Church's overall strategy.

And he was right, Walkyr thought now, glumly. *But I thought we'd know when the heretics headed this way— that there'd be time to do something about the canal before they actually got here!*

Unfortunately, he'd been wrong.

Maybe it's going to turn out to be a good thing all those damned militia turned up, after all. Walkyr's lips twitched humorlessly. *If Syngyltyn's right, figuring out how to feed them over the winter's likely to be the least of my problems.*

He inhaled again, deeply, then returned to his desk and rang the handbell. The office door popped open almost instantly.

"Yes, Sir?"

"Meeting here in my office in twenty minutes," Walkyr said, rather more crisply than he actually felt. "All regimental commanders."

"Yes, Sir!"

The orderly saluted and disappeared once more, and Walkyr seated himself back behind his desk and put his head in his hands as the door closed.

▼ ▼ ▼

"Don't we have *any* better idea of the numbers?" Major Bryahn Kyrbysh asked.

Kyrbysh commanded the 3rd Maidynberg Militia, the most recently formed of Walkyr's original regiments. He was also the youngest of the general's regimental commanders—a black-haired, brown-eyed, intensely focused young man with a manner which fringed on the abrupt as often as not.

"No," Colonel Clareyk Syngyltyn replied a bit repressively. Kyrbysh looked at him, and Syngyltyn shrugged. "Their cavalry screen's too strong to penetrate. All I can tell you for certain is that there's infantry—and presumably guns—coming at us from both sides."

Kyrbysh looked less than delighted, but then he and

Syngyltyn didn't much like each other. Kyrbysh was perfectly prepared to burn out heretic farms or towns, but he disapproved of disorganized, disorderly, freelance activities, whereas Syngyltyn's cavalrymen had spent a lot of time doing just that. In fact, Syngyltyn had been busier setting fires than recruiting additional troopers. During the time Kyrbysh, Colonel Maikel Zahmsyn, and Colonel Nathalan Hahpkynsyn had created their Maidynberg Militia regiments virtually from scratch, Syngyltyn's strength had actually declined. Admittedly, it took longer to train cavalry than infantry, but Syngyltyn had used up men and worn out—and broken down—far too many irreplaceable horses on raids to burn already abandoned farms, and however satisfying his men might have found their efforts, arson didn't seem to have produced the information on enemy movements cavalry was *supposed* to provide.

"Without more information, I don't see how any of us can contribute any useful advice, Sir," Kyrbysh said after a moment, turning back to Walkyr. "We all understand the importance of holding the fort until Duke Harless reaches us. At the same time, this is obviously a coordinated pincer movement. They intend to come at us from both sides at once, and I doubt they'd do it at all unless they figured they had the numbers to get the job done before the Duke gets here."

"That assumes they know the Duke is coming." Father Naiklos gave Kyrbysh a hard look. "If they're unaware he's marching to our relief, they're the ones who'll find themselves trapped between us and the Army of Shiloh!"

"That's true, Father," Dahglys Mhartyn acknowledged. "I suspect they *do* know, though. They certainly know about the attack on Thesmar, and whether we like it or not, their navy has free run of the sea. I'm no sailor, and I don't know how long it would take a ship from Thesmar to reach Trokhanos, say. As soon as one did, though, the semaphore would tell the heretics the Duke's broken camp. It wouldn't take a genius to guess where he has to be headed. They may not know how many men he has, but I think we have to assume they do know he's on his way."

"And so what do you recommend, Colonel?" The under-priest's voice was unyielding. "That we simply abandon our position?"

"I never said that, Father." Mhartyn's Southguard accent was a bit more pronounced than it had been, but he faced Vahnhain without flinching. "I'm simply pointing out that whatever plans we make should be based on the most realistic assumptions about the enemy's strength and preparedness available to us. Assumptions which are too pessimistic will leave us half defeated before we even begin, but overly *optimistic* assumptions may prove even more dangerous."

"Schueler knows we've seen more'n enough 'optimists' get bit on the arse," Colonel Helfryd Vahlverday growled. "Nobody 'spected the heretic bastards to get in an' burn Raisor to the ground, now did they?"

He glowered around the table. Half of Walkyr's militia consisted of the three regiments of "Raisor Volunteers," which had been raised by the Shiloh Faithful after the heretic raid on the town of the same name. Major Olyvyr Bekyt and Colonel Tobys Shraydyr, who commanded the first two regiments of Volunteers, had at least some pre-Rising militia experience; Vahlverday did not. He'd distinguished himself by his zeal in stamping out pockets of heresy around Raisor, however, and a senior Inquisitor had nominated him to command one of the new regiments. He was short on training in movement and tactics and Walkyr was certain he'd be a disaster in an open field battle, but he was a ferocious disciplinarian, his men trusted him, and his lack of training would be a much less serious disadvantage defending a fortified position.

"I'm forced to agree with Colonel Mhartyn and Colonel Vahlverday," Syngyltyn said into the brief silence which followed. "At the same time, I'm afraid I have to point out that the enemy's cavalry strength appears to be at least five times our own, and their lead elements are already on the road between here and Kharmych.

Even if we wanted to abandon the fort, we'd have to fight our way through Charisian horse and foot and they'd have the advantage in numbers."

A shiver ran down Walkyr's spine at that thought. He was inclined to think Syngyltyn was overestimating the numbers of the enemy's horsemen, and he was overlooking the fact that the heretics' cavalry was split, with half of it trapped east of the Branath and Shingle Mountains. Yet if half the whispered tales about Charisian weapons capabilities were accurate, the thought of facing them in the open and probably outnumbered was one to chill the boldest heart.

He looked around his office, seeing his own worry reflected in every other face, and realized where the conversation was going to end. It would take a while, yet the final decision was about as inevitable as decisions came.

It's too bad the semaphore's down, he reflected unhappily. *I really would like to be able to tell Duke Harless how much we'd appreciate his getting here as quickly as possible.*

. XIV .
Kharmych,
The South March Lands,
Republic of Siddarmark

"You do have a habit of turning up at opportune moments, don't you?" Duke Eastshare asked, looking up from the map on his folding desk with a smile as Captain Braynair escorted Ahbraim Zhevons into his tent. The *seijin* looked as wet, muddy, and cold as anyone in Eastshare's column, but if it worried him, he hid it well.

"As Major Athrawes would say, one tries, Your Grace," he replied with a slight bow.

"May I assume you and your colleagues have fresh information about Fort Tairys for me?"

"At least some." Zhevons accepted a mug of hot apple cider from Corporal Chalkyr. "Not as much as I'm sure you'd like, I'm afraid."

"Show me a general with all the information he wants, and I'll show you an idiot," Eastshare said tartly, and Zhevons chuckled.

"It's a little better than that, Your Grace." The *seijin* sipped appreciatively, then lowered the mug. "Our best estimate is that they have somewhere over nineteen thousand men inside their perimeter now that those 'Raisor Volunteers' have come in. Kyrbysh's made his regiment almost up to full strength, too, but Syngyltyn's managed to lose a couple of hundred more cavalry, mostly by doing stupid things in this kind of weather."

Eastshare grimaced. Thanks to Zhevons' associates, he had far better information on the opposing commanders than he'd had any right to expect. Colonel Clareyk Syngyltyn was young for his rank and responsibilities, little more than thirty. On the other hand, Major Rhobair Tymyns, who commanded the 2nd Provisional Cavalry Regiment which had been attached to Eastshare's brigade, was even younger, probably no older than Emperor Cayleb himself. And whereas Syngyltyn had started out with eighteen hundred men and was down to no more than a thousand after operational losses, Tymyns had started out with barely five hundred and was now up to over *two* thousand *despite* operational losses. Part of that was courtesy of the cavalry mounts Eastshare's men had captured from Kaitswyrth, but more important, Tymyns understood horses were actually fragile creatures. Properly cared for, they were capable of amazing endurance; casually or poorly cared for, they broke down—and died—with appalling speed.

"Well, Major Tymyns *has* reported the rebel cavalry isn't pressing his men very hard," the duke observed dryly. "If Syngyltyn's managed to turn that many of his troopers into infantry, we know why, don't we?"

"Yes, we do," Zhevons agreed and sipped more cider. "On the other hand, cavalry probably won't be very useful once you and General Wyllys get down to business."

"True." Eastshare nodded, then frowned as he listened to the galloping patter of raindrops on the canvas overhead. "It's going to be muckier and muddier than I'd anticipated, though, and I'm sure the fatigue parties will curse my name more inventively than Clyntahn. But if we've got a couple of five-days to work with. . . ."

"I can't make any guarantees," Zhevons said, "but I will say I'd be absolutely astonished if Harless was able to get his vanguard here anytime within the next three five-days."

"And if he hears about an attack on Fort Tairys and he's smart enough to strip off Ahlverez and send him ahead?"

"The Dohlarans could cut that by a good five-day," Zhevons acknowledged. "From his record to date, though, the thought won't even occur to him."

"I'd like to think you're right about that, but is even he really *that* stupid?"

"It's not actually stupidity, Your Grace." Zhevons cradled his mug in both hands and frowned down into it, like a man seeking exactly the words he wanted. "It's more . . . blindness and blinkers than outright stupidity," he said finally. "Harless isn't an imaginative man; there's no doubt about that. Worse, he knows what he knows that he knows, as Master Howsmyn might put it, and he's not about to chase any wild wyverns into the unknown as long as the methods he knows are working. And the problem he has right now is that they *are* working."

Eastshare looked at him in disbelief, and the *seijin* snorted.

"Oh, they aren't working by *your* standards, Your Grace. Or by the Republic's. Or by the Army of God's for that matter. But they're working as well as the Imperial Desnairian Army's methods have traditionally worked, and *that's* the yardstick he's using. That's where his lack of imagination comes in. He hasn't had Ahlverez' experience, and because he's insisted on leading the entire march from Thesmar with his own troops, he truly doesn't realize how much faster Ahlverez could be moving, even in this weather, without the rest of the Army of Shiloh in the way. He'd like to get to Fort Tairys sooner, and he's frustrated by how long it's taking, but he genuinely thinks he's getting there as quickly as he can, and the truth is that he's pushing his own baggage train and men hard enough to take significant losses from straggling."

Eastshare's expression shifted slowly from disbelief to thoughtfulness. Then he nodded.

"You may have a point. In fact, now that you've explained it, I think you do. But even if you do, I'm not making any comfortable assumptions about his—what was it you called them? 'Blindness and blinkers,' was it?" The duke's forefinger tapped his map, tracing the line of the high road through the Kyplyngyr Forest, the broad swath of "unconsecrated" native Safeholdian forest between Kharmych and Roymark. "I think we'll just put some *good* cavalry scouts out this way, and maybe a company or two of scout snipers in among the trees. If His Grace of Harless' imagination is underdeveloped, I think the least we can do is *stretch* it for him, don't you?"

. XV .
Fort Tairys,
Shiloh Province,
Republic of Siddarmark

"Well, *that's* confirmed," Colonel Kyrbysh said sourly.

He and Maikel Zahmsyn stood on the muddy summit of an earthen embankment watching scattered horsemen drift towards them. All of Clareyk Syngyltyn's remaining cavalry were safely within Fort Tairys' defenses. That didn't leave much doubt about who the newcomers had to be, and the rain had actually stopped . . . at least briefly. The better visibility made it obvious the oncoming cavalry was Siddarmarkian, but Kyrbysh's prized spyglass had verified that the infantry columns slogging up the muddy track on its heels wore the mottled uniforms which could only belong to Charisian regulars.

"Could be worse." Zahmsyn's tone was equally sour. "It could be Charisians on *both* sides of the damned mountains!"

Kyrbysh grunted and wondered once again if Walkyr was truly fool enough to attempt to hold the entire area he'd fortified. To be fair, throwing up the earthworks had given his regiments something to do besides sit around and worry. And he *had* laid out his outer perimeter in the assumption that when the Army of Shiloh arrived to relieve him, it would want a large, well-fortified position here in Ohadlyn's Gap. But *surely* he had to realize the position was far too large for the forces under *his* command to man adequately!

Oh, the entrenchments were certainly impressive, with each parapet fronted by a deep ditch and covered by a thick abatis. Most of the ditches were knee-deep, or even waist-deep in water, thanks to the rain, and they'd done their best to provide overhead cover for the firing steps. If they'd just had the men to man them, they would have been a formidable obstacle. Unfortunately, they *didn't* have the men, and the heretics' simultaneous arrival at the eastern and western ends of the gap made a bad situation even worse.

I'll bet you we're actually close to even in manpower, Kyrbysh thought bitterly. *And according to what they always told me in the Militia, that means the defenders should have the advantage. Yeah—sure!*

He glowered some more. It seemed to be a given that they'd have to mount at least a token defense of the outer works, although he hoped to Langhorne Walkyr would settle for holding the second line of defenses rather than the first. Even the second line was fifty-two miles long, but a twenty-five percent reduction was nothing to sneer at. For that matter, the road—and the only way through the Gap for anything larger than a cliff lizard—ran directly through Fort Tairys, and the line of works protecting the fort itself was only *ten* miles long.

Of course, we used up all those nice abatises on the

first and second lines, didn't we? Still, getting the front-age down to three feet per man would be Schueler's own improvement on damned near twenty *feet per man!*

It struck him as a bad sign that Walkyr still hadn't decided—or bothered to tell his commanders, at any rate—which of the several defensive plans they'd discussed he intended to follow. Those Charisian heretics weren't wasting any time, judging by the speed of their marching columns, and if they guessed how thinly stretched Fort Tairys' garrison was, they might just throw an assault straight at the entrenchments.

And it shouldn't take a military genius to figure out *how thinly we're stretched, now should it?*

"We can't hold the outer lines, Maikel," he said flatly. "If we try, we'll get reamed. We may actually outnumber the bastards, but if we spread out to cover everything, they'll hit us at nine- or ten-to-one odds at a point of their own choosing and smash right through us."

"Wish I could disagree," Colonel Zahmsyn growled after a moment. "Happen you're right, though." He showed his teeth. "For a Militia officer, you've your head screwed on better'n quite a few Reg'lars I could mention."

"The question is whether we ask for orders or use our initiative," Kyrbysh pointed out, glancing at the heliograph fifty feet east of their current position.

Under the plan for defending the entire position, he and Zahmsyn were responsible for the thirty miles of entrenchment directly threatened by the Charisians' arrival. Since they had roughly four thousand men between them, that meant each of their men had to cover "only" fifteen yards or so of frontage. Unless, of course, they wanted to retain a useful reserve for some silly reason. Somehow that struck him as a losing proposition. Unfortunately, he wasn't at all certain how quickly General Walkyr would respond to a militarily correct request for permission to fall back. If Father Naiklos happened to be standing at the general's shoulder when the request arrived, the decision time would probably double, however. Much as Kyrbysh respected the priest's bright, searing faith, there was no point pretending

Vahnhain was anything like flexible. Indeed, that faith of his made him even *less* flexible when it came to anything that resembled giving ground before the heretical, apostate foes of Mother Church.

No doubt that helped account for all Father Naiklos had managed to accomplish, but it wasn't always a useful character trait.

Zahmsyn was clearly uncomfortable at the notion of withdrawing without authorization. His regiment was built out of the remnants of three regiments which had suffered massive casualties during the Rising, and he'd done well hammering them into a cohesive unit. Despite that, there was a reason he'd been old for his rank before the Rising. No one could ever accuse him of doing an inch less than his very best, yet he'd always been more of a stolid, slogging, stubborn fighter than a thinker.

He wasn't stupid, however, and he, too, glanced at the heliograph, then inhaled deeply.

"Something your very first sergeant teaches you is that there's times it's easier to beg forgiveness than ask permission, Bryahn. I'm thinkin' this here's one of those very times." His unhappiness was obvious, but there was no hesitation in his brown eyes. "If we're minded to pull back 'thout disordering our companies, we'd best get started soon."

"Pull back to our secondary positions, you think?" Kyrbysh asked, suddenly aware of how grateful he was for Zahmsyn's bluff, unimaginative presence.

"At least." Zahmsyn's voice was flat. "I'm thinkin' it'd be best to fall back all the way to the third line, truth to tell."

"We'd be giving up the hills on either side to the heretics' artillery. That might not be a very good idea if half the stories about those 'new model' guns of theirs're true," Kyrbysh pointed out, and Zahmsyn made a sound somewhere between a laugh, a grunt, and a curse.

"If they can get guns up there, happen they can get 'em up on the flanks of the outer works, too. And if they get eyes up there and see how thin the outer works're held, happen we're screwed come what may, as I'm thinkin' *you* just pointed out."

"Actually, I believe I did." Kyrbysh considered for a moment. "I think we should fall back to the second line, send a runner to General Walkyr to tell him what we're doing, and ask if he wants to consider shortening our lines still farther. If we get started now, we can probably pull the guns back without too much trouble."

And, he very carefully did not say out loud, considering the six miles or so between their present position and Walkyr's office, *if we've already started the guns moving before our runner gets to Walkyr and he can get a message back to us, it'll be far too dangerous to turn them back around and risk getting our artillery caught by a sudden heretic rush while we're trying to re-emplace it.*

"I'm thinkin' that's a very good point, Colonel Kyrbysh," Zahmsyn said dryly, an unusual gleam of amusement lighting his eye. "In fact, I'm thinking we'd best get right on that. Immediately."

"So do I, Colonel Zahmsyn." Kyrbysh smiled. "So do I."

▼ ▼ ▼

"Too bad they were smart enough to pull back after all, Your Grace." Brigadier Zhorj Maiksyn grimaced.

"Now, now, Zhorj." Duke Eastshare's tone was gently reproving. "You know these people really aren't Kaitswyrth." They stood atop what had been the outermost parapet of the Fort Tairys position in the foothills southwest of the fortress. It was just under three miles to the next earthen berm, which said quite a lot about how ambitious Walkyr's plans had been, and he studied the inner works through his double-glass while they spoke. "And fair's fair. They never expected to get hit from both sides simultaneously."

"Well, with all due respect, Your Grace, they damned well *should*'ve considered it when they laid out this abortion." Maiksyn shook his head in disgust. "It's not just too damned big to hold with the troops they've got, most of it's in the wrong damned place, and half—hell, two-thirds!—of the outer works can be dominated by artillery in the hills."

"True." Eastshare lowered his double-glass to smile at his senior field commander. "On the other hand, you've been thinking about modern artillery for years now; these people've never even *seen* a new model piece. Hard to blame them for thinking in terms of obsolete monsters like the ones in their own positions."

Maiksyn glowered some more. He'd started as an engineer himself, and he was clearly disinclined to make any concessions where the stupidity of the *rebels'* engineers were concerned.

"At any rate," the duke continued in a grimmer tone, "the outer works don't matter and never did. But that innermost ring around the fort itself could be a pain. I think they'll at least try to hold the third line, but that won't last for long. Then we'll be up against entrenchments they've got almost enough men to man. And once we get past *them*, we're up against the original fortifications, because there's no way around them. Unlike the rest of this—'abortion,' you called it, wasn't it?—the *fort's* actually in the right spot to defend what needs to be defended. Worse, whoever designed it knew what he was doing and we'll be pushing them back into it. If they had any sense, that's where they'd be already!"

"Can't, Your Grace," Maiksyn countered respectfully. Eastshare cocked an eyebrow at him, and the brigadier shrugged. "Caught betwixt and between is what they are. Too many men to squeeze into the original fort; too few to hold the entrenchments outside it. They try to pull everybody back inside, they'll be like sardines in a jar, and us putting angle-gun shells and mortar rounds right in amongst 'em. Don't think they'd like that above half."

Eastshare nodded slowly. Maiksyn might well be right, although he still anticipated a nasty tussle. If there was time, Colonel Raimahn's Glacierheart miners would undoubtedly prove their worth, but if it took that long, even Harless might get here in time to raise the siege.

"Well, in that case I suppose we'd best get the artillery

up. We'll start by seeing how serious they are about holding the second line. And I think, if we can convince them not to, we might be able to get the four-inchers up on those hills east of the fort." The duke smiled thinly. "The men who designed that fort didn't know new model artillery was coming, either. They never imagined that someone might actually be able to get guns up there . . . or that they'd have the range to reach the walls if somebody did manage it. I think we should see about taking advantage of that, don't you?"

"Aye, Your Grace. That I do."

"I think we'll use the Sixth for security on the guns. One battalion should be more than enough against anything this lot might get up to. We'll use the Fifth to man the front line, and Lutaylo's other three battalions will form our reserve."

"Sounds reasonable," Maiksyn said. "Might want a company or two of young Tymyns' cavalry in reserve, too." He hawked and spat on the ground. "Don't think much of this Syngyltyn, but I suppose even he might get up to mischief if the crack he's in is deep enough."

"So he might," Eastshare agreed. "All right, I'll leave all of that in your hands, Zhorj. But please tell Colonel Makyn I'll be sending Lywys to make contact with General Wyllys and I want a squad of his scout snipers to make sure he gets there safely. It'll probably be another hour or two before he's ready to go, but since they've pulled back and left us these lovely, mucky hillsides and lizard paths, we might as well make use of them. Which is why I also want Lywys and his keepers to keep an eye out for likely semaphore positions along the way."

"Aye, Your Grace," the brigadier repeated, and Eastshare nodded in satisfaction. First Brigade was Makyn's command, and the duke had never been inclined to snatch the reins out of a perfectly competent subordinate's hands.

"In that case," he started down the muddy face of the abandoned earthwork towards his horse, "it's all yours. I'll expect a progress report in a few hours."

"Aye, you'll have it."

"I know I will, Zhorj." Eastshare paused to smile. "It just eases my mind to hear my own voice saying it."

▼ ▼ ▼

"They shouldn't've pulled back so quickly," Father Naiklos Vahnhain growled. "We shouldn't've given up the outer works without at least *some* fight—not after spending so much effort *building* them!"

He and Lairays Walkyr sat in the general's office as darkness closed down, sharing a pot of something the cooks called tea. They'd run out of hot chocolate months ago, and the last of the real tea had gone the same way shortly before word of the heretics' impending arrival reached Fort Tairys. The beverage Walkyr's cook had provided as a substitute was hot, but that was about all anyone could say in its favor. Vahnhain suspected it had been made using either burnt breadcrumbs or ground acorns, and he'd firmly resolved not to ask which.

Walkyr took a long, slow sip of "tea" while he weighed his intendant's complaint. Part of him agreed with Vahnhain; another part—which he suspected was the smarter part of him—agreed with Kyrbysh and Zahmsyn. Yet Vahnhain had been his spiritual guide and closest adviser from the very first day of the Rising. At the very least, he deserved the careful consideration of his views.

"Under most circumstances, I'd agree with you, Father," he said finally, setting the cup on its saucer. He cut a sliver of cheese from the only slightly moldy wedge on the corner of his desk, one of the last cheeses of the winter before, and tore a piece of bread from the still-warm loaf beside it.

"But most circumstances would have included being attacked from only one direction at a time," he continued. "And, to be honest, Kyrbysh was right. If he and Zahmsyn had stayed put and let the heretics throw an assault column at them the result would've been a disaster."

"But they had the earthworks and the abatis." Vahnhain's tone was less angry although he clearly wasn't quite ready to give up. "That would've made up for a lot, Lairays!"

"Not enough." Walkyr took a bite of bread and cheese, chewed slowly and washed it down with another swallow of so-called tea, then shrugged. "The heretics would have controlled the point at which they attacked, Father, but Kyrbysh and Zahmsyn would've been forced to defend the entire wall. That would spread their men so thinly the heretics could easily have attacked at twenty- or thirty-to-one odds just by picking their spots. I'm sure our men would've fought hard, but against those odds?" He shook his head. "I won't pretend I wasn't pissed off when they took it upon themselves to pull back, but that doesn't make it the wrong decision. In fact, I'm not planning on putting anything but pickets on the second line, either."

Vahnhain stared at him, and Walkyr gave him a lopsided smile.

"Father, there's a reason they put Fort Tairys where they put it. As long as we're sitting here on the road, nobody's getting past us. They may be able to send small parties on foot through the foothills—may even be able to get some cavalry through there, whatever Syngyltyn says about 'impassable' terrain. But they can't get transport wagons or artillery across those lizard paths. So when you come down to it, the fort and the earthworks right around it are all that really matters."

"But— Forgive me, Lairays, but it sounds as if you've already decided to stand solely on the defensive. Isn't that a recipe for ultimate defeat?"

"Trying to launch sorties or fight them in the open would be a recipe for *immediate* defeat," Walkyr said, somewhat more firmly—almost harshly—than he normally spoke to the Schuelerite. "They have rifles and these 'new model' guns of theirs; our men have matchlocks, arbalests, and pikes. You read the reports of what the Dohlarans did to the Fort Sheldyn garrison, and we're talking about *Charisians* with those damned breechloading rifles."

Vahnhain's eyes fell. There'd been so many reports, so many stories, carried by word of mouth or even transmitted by the semaphore, that it had become increasingly difficult to separate fact from fiction, rumor and invention from reality. Nonetheless, they'd been forced to accept that the Charisian heretics truly did possess breech-loading rifles capable of preposterous rates of fire.

"Leaving that aside, trying to defend the second line of entrenchments would be almost as bad as trying to defend the first one. We just don't have enough men to man the works. We never did—not out of our own resources—and we both knew that all along. So we leave pickets to keep the heretics from just sashaying right across the parapet, but those pickets will 'skedaddle,' as Colonel Vahlverday would put it, as soon as the heretics mount any serious attack. And then we concentrate on holding the core of our position, stuck right here in the heretics' throat, until the Army of Shiloh gets here. At that point, the heretics west of the Gap can either run or die, and Duke Harless will pass straight through and kick the arses of the bastards on the other side of the mountains, as well. All we have to do is hold until he gets here. If we do that, we win. If we *don't* do that, the *heretics* win, and Mother Church and the Archangels lose Shiloh after all. It's that simple, however inglorious just hunkering down to hold may seem."

Vahnhain looked back up, considering his protégé's expression, the steadiness of his eyes, and realized Walkyr was right. And he also sensed a fresh resolution, an aura of determination. It was as if the moment of decision had crystallized—no, *refined*—Lairays Walkyr, and the priest remembered the army captain who'd led the seizure of Fort Tairys in the first place. That captain had been certain of his duty, unhesitating in its execution, and fierce in his devotion.

Perhaps he'd been wrong to insist Walkyr accept promotion, the priest thought. It had seemed the right, the inevitable thing at the time, but now he wondered. The responsibilities that came with his new rank, the uncertainty of holding an isolated position without knowing when—or if—the promised relief column would arrive, had been more than Walkyr had bargained for. The administrative details of somehow feeding his own command, organizing and helping to equip the militia, providing support for the Faithful partisans, harrying the heretics, and doing his best to provide what little semblance of governance and order western Shiloh had possessed. . . .

All those things had weighed down upon him because, whether he'd ever have admitted it or not—and he wouldn't, Vahnhain thought, because it would have been a sign of weakness—he'd been unsuited for that task. *That*, Vahnhain suddenly realized, was the true reason he'd kept his troops busy building such outsized fortifications. Not simply so they'd be available when the Army of Shiloh finally arrived, but to keep them—and *him*—occupied doing something they understood.

But now all those details, all those worries, had been swept aside, replaced by a single overpowering imperative. It was time once more to fight or die as God's own champion, and that, unlike administrative details and grand strategy, was something Lairays Walkyr understood just fine.

The only way the heretics will pry him out of this position is by carrying him out dead, Vahnhain realized. *And when you come down to it, what more can Mother Church—or God—ask of any man?*

"All right, Lairays," he said gently. "I understand. So while you concentrate on holding the position, I'll just have a word with the Archangels to see if they can't speed Duke Harless on his way a bit."

"And I'm afraid *I* have to insist on disturbing him anyway, Sir Graim," Sir Rainos Ahlverez said flatly. "I apologize for interrupting his supper, but this is something which won't keep."

Sir Graim Kyr glowered at Ahlverez, permitting his brown eyes to show just a trace of aristocratic contempt for the other man's sodden, mud-splashed appearance. Ahlverez experienced a sudden, overwhelming desire to punch the youthful Baron of Fyrnach in the eye, then kick him in the belly when he went down. Followed up by a boot heel to the Adam's apple, preferably, or at least a good solid kick in the testicles. No, better the Adam's apple; he'd probably survive a kick in the balls, however satisfying that might be. No doubt a proper Desnairian nobleman would have thought in terms of a formal duel, but allowing the little bastard that much dignity was more than Ahlverez cared to contemplate.

"As I've *explained*, Sir Rainos," Fyrnach began, "my uncle—that is His Grace"—he smiled thinly —"is at table. As soon as—"

"I," Ahlverez' tone turned suddenly to precise, icy steel, "command the Dohlaran contingent of the Army of Shiloh. I answer to Mother Church and to my King, not to *you*, My Lord. If I'm not in Duke Harless' presence within the next two minutes, my command and I will be headed back to Thesmar within the next twelve hours. The explanation for why that happened will be that you were too arrogant, too pigheaded, and too *fucking stupid* to allow me to speak to him on a matter of the greatest urgency, clearly demonstrating that it was impossible to coordinate properly with your granduncle, since he was willing to tolerate your stupidity. And, My Lord *Baron*, I will personally guarantee that the Inquisition will be discussing with you exactly why you personally sabotaged the campaign Mother Church has ordered this army to undertake. I'm certain Emperor Mahrys will wish to discuss it with your granduncle, as well."

He pulled out his watch and snapped the cover open. "You now have one minute and fifty seconds, *My Lord*."

Fyrnach stared at him, his face first turning dark with fury and then bone-white with terror. He opened his mouth and—

"One minute and forty seconds," Ahlverez said in that same, deadly voice. "I wouldn't waste any of them talking to *me*, if I were you."

Fyrnach shut his mouth with an almost audible click, then darted out of the vestibule of the mayor of Malyktyn's house, which he'd appropriated in Harless' name as soon as the vanguard reached the town. The door closed sharply behind him, and Ahlverez heard someone inhaling through his teeth and glanced up from his watch at Captain Lattymyr.

"Yes, Lynkyn?" he asked pleasantly.

"Did my heart good, Sir. You do realize you've just made an enemy for life, though, don't you?"

"I suppose I have. Frankly, I've never met anyone I'd rather *have* as an enemy. The way he's handled access to his precious uncle's cost this army at least five thousand stragglers since we left Thesmar, and according to Master Slaytyr here," he nodded to the very tall, gray-haired, brown-eyed man standing behind the two Dohlarans and maintaining a prudent silence, "the pair of them may've cost us Fort Tairys, as well." His nostrils flared. "I'm pretty much out of patience where that little son-of-a-bitch is concerned."

Captain Lattymyr nodded, although a certain trepidation still shadowed his expression. It wasn't for himself, however, and he straightened as Baron Fyrnach rematerialized.

"His Grace will see you immediately, Sir Rainos," he said with awful, frigid dignity and a dagger-eyed promise of retribution.

"Thank you." Ahlverez snapped his watch closed and returned it deliberately to his pocket, then twitched his head at Lattymyr and Slaytyr.

"A moment, Sir Rainos. I cannot admit anyone but yourself to His Grace's presence," Fyrnach said quickly with an unpleasant smile. Ahlverez considered him for a moment, then turned and seated himself on one of the stools normally used by couriers waiting to deliver messages to Harless' subordinates.

"If you can't admit all three of us to his presence, we'll await him here," he said evenly. "Understanding, I trust, that the same conditions—and time limit—apply to his appearance here. The choice is yours, My Lord."

Fyrnach glared at him, one hand clenching on his dagger, and Ahlverez looked back, cold-eyed as a serpent, and tugged the watch back out of his pocket. He started to reopen the cover, but Fyrnach's nostrils flared. His handsome face wasn't particularly handsome at the moment—puce was not a becoming color—as he jerked his head back the way he'd come.

"Very well, Sir Rainos," he bit each syllable out of bone and bile, "if you and your . . . companions would step this way."

"Of course." Ahlverez stood and nodded to the two men at his back. "Lynkyn, Master Slaytyr, I believe we're expected."

▼ ▼ ▼

Duke Harless looked considerably less furious than Ahlverez had anticipated. Perhaps the young idiot had been wise enough to keep his ultimatum to himself. If so, he was at least a little brighter than Ahlverez had thought. Given his record, that was hard to believe; on the other hand, he could scarcely be *less* bright.

The lamplit dining room was warm, unlike the raw, wet night. A fire crackled cheerfully on its hearth, and Harless and his companions were dressed in the height of court fashion. Obviously, they'd found time for hot baths and a fresh change of clothing even if none of their shivering, sodden troopers could say the same.

"Sir Rainos." The duke nodded—not exactly curtly, but not with any effusion of joy—and remained seated. That might not have been entirely out of irritation at having been disturbed, however. Judging from the empty bottles standing sentinel among the remnants of enough food to feed an entire squad of his ravenous army, he might not have been capable of rising. "I understand this is a matter of some urgency."

"It is, Your Grace."

Ahlverez bowed in formal greeting to Harless, Father Tymythy Yairdyn, Earl Hankey, and Earl Hennet. The Schuelerite intendant looked distinctly glassy-eyed, although Hankey and Hennet appeared sober enough.

"May we know what that matter is?" Harless' words came a trifle more slowly than usual, but without slurring or hesitation.

"Master Slaytyr." Ahlverez beckoned to the tall Siddarmarkian and Slaytyr stepped forward. "Your Grace, this is Master Zhapyth Slaytyr. He comes to us from Shiloh Province."

Harless' expression didn't change for a moment. Then his eyes narrowed.

"Shiloh Province?" he repeated more sharply, and Ahlverez nodded.

"One of my cavalry units picked him up on his way to us," he said, deliberately not noting the quick flicker of anger in Earl Hennet's eyes.

Harless' cavalry commander deeply resented Ahlverez' unilateral decision to send three regiments of his own cavalry to join the mounted force screening the rest of the sluggishly crawling army. Not that there'd been much he could do about it, since he was the one who'd refused any suggestion that all of the cavalry might be merged into a single force. Ahlverez wasn't about to pretend he was unhappy over Hennet's decision; in fact, he'd made the suggestion in the devout hope that the arrogant earl would do just that.

Because Hennet had gratified his hope, the army's Dohlaran cavalry was Ahlverez' to use as he chose, and what he chose was to send out a cavalry screen in whose scouting ability he reposed some faith. And if it could just happen to be present when Desnairian foraging parties descended upon some isolated farmstead whose owners hadn't fled in time, so much the better. Ahlverez never doubted his men would steal anything that wasn't nailed down—and anything that *was* nailed down, if they had time to pry it loose—but he also knew they would prevent the outrages, ranging from simple assaults all the way to rape and murder, Harless' foragers committed all too often out of the ancient hostility between Desnair and Siddarmark. That was *another* reason Hennet resented his decision so bitterly, and the earl had ordered his own troopers to make damned sure the Dohlarans didn't embarrass them—and him—by reporting anything *they* missed. Which meant, given that his so-called scouts outnumbered Ahlverez' by something like fifty-to-one, that he couldn't be pleased that Slaytyr had passed entirely through *his* cavalry without being spotted.

Pity about that.

"Did they, indeed?" Harless asked softly.

"Indeed." Ahlverez nodded. "He bears a message from General Walkyr. Master Slaytyr?"

The muddy, wet Slaytyr reached into his battered belt pouch and withdrew a letter. The wafer which had sealed it had been broken, and he looked at Ahlverez for a moment. The Dohlaran twitched his head in Harless' direction, and Slaytyr handed it across.

The rhythm of rain beating on the roof and tapping against the windows was the only sound except the rustle of paper as Harless tilted the letter to catch the light and squinted at it. Reading was not his favorite pastime, nor was Walkyr's penmanship of the best, and his eyes moved slowly. Then his face tightened abruptly. His eyes moved faster, reached the end, and lifted to glare first at Slaytyr and then at Ahlverez, as if the two of them might have been personally responsible for its contents.

"Is this true?" he demanded of the Siddarmarkian, his voice harsh.

"Wouldn't know, M'lord," Slaytyr replied in the slow, almost musical accent of Shiloh. He was well into middle age, his hair gray, his eyes a muddy brown. His knuckles were a bit swollen with arthritis and his shoulders—despite his impressive height—stooped. He favored his right leg when he walked, as well, and there was an air of near-exhaustion, about him, but there was no hesitation in his expression as he met Harless' gaze. "Haven't read it, m'self. General Walkyr, he said deliver it, an' so I done. Didn't ask what it said, an' he didn't say."

Ahlverez' lips twitched at Harless' expression, but he called them firmly to order.

"Very well," Harless said, passing the letter to Yairdyn. "Let me phrase it a different way. According to this letter, the heretics have placed Fort Tairys under siege." Hennet, Hankey, and even Fyrnach stiffened. "Of your knowledge, Master . . . Slaytyr, was it?" The Siddarmarkian nodded. "Very well, Master Slaytyr. Is that true?"

"Truer'n death, M'lord," Slaytyr said flatly. "Got a great fuc—ah, I mean a right smart-sized army at each end o' the Gap, they do. An' I could hear them guns o' theirs a-firin' while I rode away."

"He estimates the heretics' strength at perhaps twenty thousand," Harless said, darting a quick glance at Ahlverez. "Would you say that's accurate?"

"Now that's more'n I could be guessin'." Slaytyr was obviously unafraid to admit ignorance, Ahlverez noted, and more power to him. "All I can tell you's that one batch of 'em come down the Branath Canal, and t'other come by road, down by way o' Maidynberg. I seen a passel of 'em a-comin' in both directions when I lit out t' find you seven days agone, an' iffen they was sheep'r cows or maybe dragons, might be I could say how many they was." He shrugged. "Not so good at countin' soldiers, I'm 'fraid, M'lord."

Siddarmarkians had no noblemen of their own and weren't much given to deferring to anyone else's . . . especially Desnairians. They certainly weren't interested in the proper modes of address for them, and Slaytyr's generic "M'lord" actually represented quite a concession for him or his countrymen. Ahlverez normally found that attitude moderately irritating, but not this time. In point of fact, the anger in Fyrnach's eyes as Slaytyr failed to abase himself properly before his granduncle's towering nobility gave Ahlverez a profound sense of satisfaction. Slaytyr's news grew no sweeter each time he heard it, however.

"And why did General Walkyr select you as his messenger?" Harless inquired as a marginally less tipsy-looking Father Tymythy passed the dispatch on to Earl Hankey. "Instead of one of his own men, I mean?"

"Didn't 'splain ever'thing t'me, M'lord, but I'm a-guessin' 'twas because them cav'lry o' his can't find their arses with both hands, come to ridin' the hills." Slaytyr shrugged. "Me, I grew up in 'em, man an' boy. Know 'em like I used t' know my wife. Prob'ly figured I might get through an' knew damned well *they* wouldn't. Not with them soldiers in th' funny-colored uniforms a-swarmin' around. Seemed t'know what they was about, they did, if you take my meanin'. Had t'move right smart gettin' past 'em. Damned near caught *me*, time'r two."

Harless stiffened at the confirmation that the heretic forces west of Fort Tairys were, indeed, Charisian regulars. He looked at Hankey and Hennet, his color ashen in the lamplight, then back at Slaytyr.

"Thank you, Master Slaytyr," he made himself say. "Baron Fyrnach will find you a place to sit out of the wet and something to eat. I'll ask you to wait there in case we have additional questions for you."

Slaytyr nodded amiably in an even more flagrant display of the Siddarmarkian disregard for noble blood and followed a stiff-backed Fyrnach from the mayor's dining room. Harless watched them go, then drew a deep breath and gestured at an empty chair at the table.

"Please be seated, Sir Rainos. It would seem you were quite correct to bring this to my attention immediately."

▼ ▼ ▼

"Excuse me, Sir," Sir Lynkyn Lattymyr said cautiously as he rode through the rain—more of a blowing mist than a downpour, at the moment—at Ahlverez' side. They were headed back out of town, towards the Dohlaran encampment and Ahlverez' tent.

"Yes, Lynkyn?" Ahlverez' tone was courteous, but Lattymyr heard an echo of his superior's stiff posture and stiffer expression in its depths.

"I'm sorry, Sir," the captain picked his words carefully; he'd been banished from his superiors' meeting by a flick of Father Tymythy's hand, probably to prevent him from observing the degree of the priest's inebriation, "but you seem less than pleased with the result of your conference with Duke Harless."

"Indeed?" Ahlverez shrugged. "That's because I *am* less than pleased."

"But didn't His Grace—?"

"No, His Grace didn't." Ahlverez cut him off abruptly, something he rarely did. "I asked, I begged—Shan-wei, I *pleaded*—for him to let me take our troops ahead. He refused. Because the troops between us and Fort Tairys appear to be Charisians, he fears that their artillery and those breech-loading rifles of theirs would give them too great an advantage for us to encounter without Desnairian support. *Support!*"

Ahlverez was so furious he actually spat, and Lattymyr flinched.

"It pains me more than you can possibly guess, Lynkyn," his general continued after a moment, his voice filled with broken bits of iron, "but I'm coming to the conclusion that I owe that bastard Thirsk an apology."

Lattymyr blinked in astonishment, ambushed by the sudden, totally unanticipated segue, and Ahlverez chuckled sourly, even though he couldn't possibly have seen his aide's blink in the darkness.

"I don't imagine you expected to hear that out of me," he continued in a marginally less bitter voice, "but the truth is that my cousin Faidel wasn't a sailor and *was* a stubborn man. All these years I've blamed Thirsk—the experienced sailor, the man who was frigging well supposed to know what the Navy was *doing*—for not giving him the advice he was entitled to and then blaming the entire disaster on him. After all, he should have kept Faidel from making so many mistakes, shouldn't he? That was what he was *there* for! And then he lost his *own* part of the fleet after he abandoned Faidel, didn't he?"

He fell silent for a moment, then inhaled sharply, the sound audible over the wet clopping of their horses' hooves.

"Now I know exactly how Thirsk must have felt," he grated. "I gave them my best advice, I argued myself blue in the face, I all but got down on my *knees* to that stiff-necked, arrogant Desnairian *prick*, and I might as well have saved my breath. If that's what Thirsk went through with Faidel—and much as I hate to admit it, it damned well could be—I've been blaming the wrong idiot for what happened to the Navy off Armageddon Reef."

Lattymyr's amazement could scarcely have been greater if Langhorne in all his glory had appeared out of the rainy dark in front of him. Instinct suggested that saying anything of the sort would be a serious tactical error, however.

"So what *is* the Duke going to do, Sir?" he asked instead.

"He agrees 'time is of the essence.' And he also acknowledges that 'the Army has made less than its best speed'—because we've been 'unavoidably delayed by the unanticipated bad weather' since leaving Thesmar."

The irony in his tone was withering, and Lattymyr understood it perfectly. Malyktyn was almost five hundred miles from Fort Tairys. At the Army of Shiloh's present rate of advance, it would take them five fivedays to cover that distance. Ahlverez' troops could have made the same march in less than three, even in this weather. For that matter, they could already have been *in* Fort Tairys, left to their own devices.

"In light of the emergency at Fort Tairys, however," Ahlverez continued, "the entire Army will set out tomorrow to force march to General Walkyr's relief. He believes we should be able to increase our speed by as much as fifty percent."

Lattymyr's jaw tightened. At that rate, it would still take them fourteen days to cover the distance. And that was assuming the accursed heretics didn't do little things like burning or blowing up bridges or dropping cut trees across the road once they were into the Kyplyngyr Forest.

"And that, Lynkyn," his general said, "constitutes Duke Harless'—and Father Tymythy's—response to the news. He did, however, send word to Walkyr that help is on its way. Master Slaytyr's already left."

"Master *Slaytyr*? By *himself*, Sir?" Surprise startled the question out of Lattymyr, and Ahlverez laughed harshly.

"Master Slaytyr made it past the heretics—and that ass Hennet's cavalry—with General Walkyr's dispatch and covered five hundred miles in less than eight days. Obviously, he's the best choice to return with Duke Harless' response."

Lattymyr stared at him in the darkness, temporarily bereft of speech as he recalled Slaytyr's obvious exhaustion, and Ahlverez shrugged.

"In fairness to the Duke, Slaytyr didn't argue. In fact, I think he's got the measure of Earl Hennet's men and figures he's a lot more likely to get through by himself, without still more cavalry that 'can't find its arse with both hands.' And judging from what I've seen of Master Slaytyr, I'm pretty sure he's right."

Lattymyr nodded slowly, and they rode on into the blowing rain.

▼ ▼ ▼

Several miles to the east, Zhapyth Slaytyr rode in the opposite direction on a fresh, borrowed horse.

His hair was noticeably less gray than it had been, and stubble seemed to be sprouting on his upper lip and chin at a remarkable rate. His shoulders were less stooped-looking, as well, and the swollen knuckles and the age spots on the back of his hands had vanished. In fact, those hands looked considerably stronger and more sinewy than they had when he delivered the dispatch in Lairays Walkyr's handwriting to Sir Rainos Ahlverez and Duke Harless.

He kept a close watch on his immediate surroundings through the SNARC floating overhead while he worked at putting at least a few miles between himself and Sir Rainos' reasonably competent cavalry screen before he summoned the recon skimmer. It was likely to take two or three hours, yet it was time he couldn't begrudge. Indeed, he was much more than simply satisfied, and any observer would have been struck by the gleam of amusement in the eyes which were no longer muddy *or* brown.

Watching Ahlverez pin back that little snot's ears was a joy to behold. Even for someone who's not all that fond of Dohlarans, he thought. *And sowing a little more discord in the enemy's camp can't hurt. Still, I wonder how Harless or that bastard Yairdyn would've reacted if they'd realized they were in the presence of "Demon Athrawes" his very self? Too bad I couldn't tell them. Or that "Slaytyr" couldn't give them a current update on the surprise young Raimahn and his miners're about to give that bastard Walkyr.*

A person, he reminded himself, couldn't have everything. Still, he wasn't going to pretend he hadn't been delighted by Walkyr's failure to get a messenger of his own off to the Army of Shiloh. That oversight had at least allowed him to amuse himself seeing to it that Duke Harless got the word after all.

Seldom done a more satisfying day's work in my life . . . or Nimue's for that matter, he thought cheerfully, and started looking for a suitable place for the skimmer to collect him and his faithful mount.

Archbishop's Palace,
City of Manchyr,
Princedom of Corisande

"Well," Archbishop Maikel Staynair turned from the window looking out over the city of Manchyr's Cathedral Square and smiled a bit crookedly at his host, "I must say it makes a change from my last visit, Klairmant."

The square was a-bustle with people, while Charisian merchant galleons lay to the quays and wharfs. A party of Charisian Marines stood guard outside the house which had been the Charisian viceroy's mansion, was now the Charisian Embassy, and would soon become the Corisande headquarters of the Imperial Patent Office. Opposite the Archbishop's Palace, the standard of the heir blew above Manchyr Palace on one staff, flanked by two more—one flying the white crossed swords and orange field of Corisande, the other a blue and white checkerboard quartered with black and charged with the golden kraken of Charis.

"Quite a lot has changed since then, Your Eminence," Klairmant Gairlyng agreed. The Archbishop of Corisande stepped to his superior's side, gazing out at the sunlit square pensively. "I remember a discussion in this very palace with Bishop Zherald. A discussion of things I believed . . . and things I suspected." He shook his head. "Many of those things I believed have been confirmed, to my joy." He turned his head to look at Staynair. "And so have most of those I suspected, to my sorrow."

"Clyntahn?" Staynair's voice was soft, and Gairlyng nodded.

"And the others." His own voice was even softer. "When he ordered Irys and Daivyn murdered, I knew I'd been right about who'd ordered Prince Hektor's assassination, as well. And I'd met both you and Emperor

Cayleb and Empress Sharleyan—and *Seijin* Merlin, for that matter. If I'd been inclined to doubt Earl Coris' evidence, the Temple's version of what happened in Delferahk would have convinced me. The men and the woman I'd met would never commit the acts of which you were accused. Almost worse, in some ways, if I'd ever needed proof that the rest of the 'Group of Four' was just as complicit as he in the crimes he's committed in Mother Church's name, the fact that none of them challenged his lies provided it. And so, would I or wouldn't I, I had no choice but to become a full-fledged Reformist and send the souls committed to my care to war against God's own Church to save those very souls *from* God's own Church."

"Forgive me," Staynair said gently, "but you've always been a Reformist, Klairmant. And in the end, which truly matters more: Mother Church or God?"

"We've always taught—and been taught—there could be no division between them," Gairlyng replied, looking back out the window.

"But we've also always known that whatever Mother Church's origin, she's administered and governed by mortal men and women." Staynair laid one large hand lightly on the younger archbishop's shoulder. "Mortals are fallible, my friend. Even the best of us. And anything, be it ever so holy, governed by mortals may also fail."

"But Langhorne himself named Mother Church God's own instrument, the Grand Vicar His inerrant voice," Gairlyng countered, his voice troubled.

"No," Staynair corrected in that same gentle tone. "He proclaimed the *Holy Writ* inerrant, and he proclaimed the Grand Vicar infallible when he spoke from Langhorne's own throne in accordance with the *Writ* and God's will. That's an important qualification, you know—in accordance with the *Writ* and God's will— because the *Writ* itself teaches that even Archangels proved fallible and corruptible in the end, does it not? If *Archangels* can fall into the sin of setting their own wills, their own desires, before those of God, then surely a mere mortal, even the Grand Vicar—or those who control him—can do the same. And when that happens, he *doesn't* speak in accordance with God's will."

"I know. And I know too much of the history of Mother Church to be unaware of other times her voice has been . . . discordant. Yet I've always believed that while men might stray from the Light, the Church would hold her true course, returning to it at His touch upon the helm when the wind blew her from it. That God would correct her when she strayed from His plan."

"Perhaps that's what He's doing at this very moment," Staynair pointed out. "And perhaps there's still more to His plan than we've discovered in the *Writ* even yet." Gairlyng turned his head, eyebrows rising, and Staynair smiled. "I have no new revelation to share with you at this moment, Klairmant. Nor do I propose that you and I should go down to the Cathedral and proclaim some genuine heresy just to satisfy Zhaspahr Clyntahn! But, you know, God *is* omnipotent and omniscient, and you and I are neither of those things. I'm a good bit older than you, and one thing I've acquired over the years—along with rather more aches and pains than I wish I had—is the realization that God never stops teaching us about Himself. We can close our eyes, we can shut our ears. We can pretend He's become silent over the centuries, speaking to us only through the *Writ* and no longer writing His words in our hearts, as well. But when we do, we lie. We can refuse to learn; that doesn't stop Him from teaching, and if we turn our backs on His lessons, we turn our backs on *Him*, as well. And that, Klairmant, would be not simply a tragedy for us but a sin against Him. Our mortal limitations mean we can never truly and fully comprehend Him, set a frame about Him that limits Him to that which we can perceive and conceptualize and describe in detail. Yet the fact that we can never *fully* comprehend Him can never diminish the glory of what we *can* comprehend about Him. Perhaps what's happening in the world today, the Schism which has rent Mother Church, represents more than mere mortal weakness and corruption.

Perhaps God's chosen this moment to write His will across His creation in letters of fire that will ultimately teach us to know Him even more deeply and truly."

Silence fell, burnished by the street sounds of Corisande's capital, drifting through the opened window. It lingered, and then, finally, Gairlyng inhaled.

"You may be right." His voice was soft but firm, his dark eyes level as he met Staynair's gaze. "I'd never thought of it exactly that way, but surely the greatest sin a man or woman could commit would be to tell God what He can or cannot be, can or cannot do. All of us like to believe that had *we* been alive during the War Against the Fallen we would have stood foursquare for the Light, resolute and certain of our duty. No one could've led *us* astray! But much as we'd like to believe that, I suspect very few who live to see God working change at the moment of His choice recognize what they behold until the work is fully wrought. It may be we find ourselves in precisely that sort of time, yet how do we know?"

"We know by listening not with our ears, but with this." Staynair laid his palm flat on Gairlyng's chest. "We know by making the choices He sets before us as best we can, trusting Him to guide us. All of His children have to do that every day of their lives, Klairmant. Should you and I, just because we wear archbishops' rings, be any different from all our other brothers and sisters in that regard?"

He smiled and his hand moved once more to the younger man's shoulder, shaking Gairlyng very gently.

"As far as our flocks are concerned, you and I are among the world's great and powerful. Do you really feel that way in your own chapel when you open your heart? I think not. I think you already know exactly how He expects us to make our choices and our decisions."

"Perhaps I do." Gairlyng raised his own hand to the one on his shoulder, and his eyes had turned warmer. "Perhaps I only needed you to remind me."

"I think you've been doing just fine without me around to play font of all wisdom." Staynair's eyes twinkled, yet there was something like sorrow behind their amusement. "I don't know about you, but there *are* times I could wish I had fewer choices to deal with! And"—the twinkle faded—"that the ones I make affected only myself and not millions upon millions of His other children, living and yet unborn. Unfortunately, He can be rather insistent. Unreasonable of Him, I know, but there it is."

"So I've found myself." Gairlyng chuckled and squeezed the hand on his shoulder briefly. "You seem to be doing pretty well so far, however, Your Eminence. And I've heard this nagging voice nattering away in the back of my brain—and my heart—telling me I'm supposed to be following. I don't think I have whatever spark He gave you when He chose you to slog into the wind in front of the rest of us with His lantern, but wherever He may be leading you, I can at least help cover your back along the way."

. XVIII .
Fort Tairys,
Shiloh Province,
Republic of Siddarmark

The rain was picking up again.

The wind-driven drops came in clusters, like tiny, icy hooves galloping across any exposed skin, but they didn't seem to bother the accursed heretics very much, General Lairays Walkyr observed grimly as he listened to the exploding shells. He and his beleaguered command were ringed by heretic positions—Siddarmarkians coming down Ohadlyn's Gap from the north, Charisians driving up from the south—and he was unhappily certain that their infantry, at least, had managed to join hands after all, trekking through the narrow, winding paths above the Gap. Guided, no doubt, by the local heretics who hated everything the Faithful stood for and had only awaited this moment for revenge.

Well, of course their infantry's linked up, he thought bitterly. *They've got frigging artillery into the hills! Sure as Shan-wei they've been able to move their damned infantry wherever they want it.*

He'd discovered the hard way that all the rumors about the Charisian rifles had been only too true, but the vague reports he'd received about "angle-guns" hadn't meant much to him. He'd had no experience from which to conceptualize what they were or did. Now, unfortunately, he understood all too well. The heavy angle-guns were bad enough, lobbying their massive shells into the fort from miles away to the south. The craters they blew into the dead ground behind the earthworks were huge, and what they did to brickwork was incredible, yet the small, mobile ones were even worse when it came to simple mayhem. There were endless numbers of them, they moved rapidly from place to place, and his men could never know where—or when—the next plunging torrent of shrapnel would replace the rain.

And then there were the rockets, he thought, glaring into the rainy darkness with red-rimmed, exhausted eyes. He'd anticipated at least being able to make repairs unobserved during the hours of darkness, but the heretics had deprived him even of that. He had no idea what to call the things that blazed against the night, suspended from umbrella-like canopies as they drifted where the rockets had left them, pitilessly illuminating the earth below, but he didn't need to know their name to curse them from the bottom of his heart. His men had dubbed them "Shan-wei's candles," yet he suspected they were no more supernatural—or demonic—than the rifles and exploding shells the heretics had deployed. On the other hand, they were probably no *less* demonic, and who was he to say what knowledge was and was not a transgression of the Proscriptions?

Brilliant though they might be, they were no substitute

for daylight where the Charisian snipers were concerned. That was one reason he doubted they were of demonic origin. Surely if Shan-wei or her servant Proctor had provided them directly to her servants they *would* have been daylight brilliant. Yet while riflemen might find their illumination unreliable, the damnable artillery was less choosy. What it lacked in a rifle's pinpoint precision, it made up for in area of effect, and working parties laboring to repair the bombardment's damage drew tempests of shell and shrapnel whenever the "candles" drifted overhead.

His men were as loyal to God and Mother Church as any mortals could ever be, yet he felt the despair creeping through them as the bombardment entered its fourth day and they sheltered behind the fort's brick parapets or crouched in wet holes scooped out of the sodden ground. He'd probably lost as many as two thousand to the heretics' rifles and artillery, and he knew it was only beginning. So did his men, and even the most faithful must find all his mortal frailties exposed as he felt death grind inexorably towards him.

Yet there was a difference, he'd discovered, between despair and defeat. The soaked, shivering, muddy, wretched men of his regiments knew they were hunched down in this position to hold until relieved. That if they could only stand their ground long enough, the Army of Shiloh would relieve them. They would hold as long as mortal men could, and if that wasn't long enough, they could—and would—still perform their final duty to God and the Archangels, knowing that whatever the heretics might do to their bodies would matter not at all.

▼ ▼ ▼

Duke Eastshare stood on a hilltop east of Ohadlyn's Gap, rain glistening on his oilskin poncho and his breath a misty cloud, and raised his double-glass as a fresh trio of parachute flares blazed above Fort Tairys. He felt a stir of gratitude to a man he'd never met each time one of those flares blossomed, and he made a mental note to stop by Tellesberg on his way home to Chisholm so he could personally shake Baron Seamount's hand. And while he was at it, he'd best spend the odd hour or so thanking Ehdwyrd Howsmyn and the Delthak Works' other wizards, as well.

Below and two hundred yards in front of him, the eight pieces of a battery of four-inch rifled guns fired in measured, steady thunder, one after another, with metronome precision. Their muzzle flashes were enormous, awe-inspiring, in the dark and rain, and he saw their shells—"armor piercing," the Delthak Works called them—strike Fort Tairys' brick curtainwall like hammers. Their bores were a half inch less than that of a twelve-pounder smoothbore, but their shells weighed almost twenty-eight pounds and each carried a pound of black powder at its heart. They drilled into the brickwork like awls, riddling it with eye-cheese craters, and the six-inch angles were even deadlier. Their "high explosive" shells weighed sixty-eight pounds and carried over *eleven* pounds of powder. That was quite heavy enough to punch deep into anything Fort Tairys' defenses could offer, and their volcano-like explosions shredded the rubble-filled masonry.

They were less effective against earthworks than brickwork, unfortunately. The solid earth absorbed their explosive power far more efficiently than masonry, and it was easier to patch, as well. Still, he reminded himself, watching the steady crumbling of the fort's outworks, there was an answer for that, too. And what the four-inch guns might lack in sheer hitting power, they more than made up in accuracy. His gunners could reliably hit a six-foot target at two thousand yards and reach a maximum range of over four thousand. He'd read the marvelous reports about the new breech-loading guns Howsmyn had started producing, and he could scarcely wait for his artillerists to get their hands on them. In the meantime, what he already had was more than good enough.

▼ ▼ ▼

"I don't want to hear about anyone doing anything stupid out there tonight, Sailys. You *do* understand that, don't you?" Colonel Byrk Raimahn regarded his executive officer levelly. "And you *did* make that clear to Laimuyl's boys?"

"Aye, Sir, I do. And I did." Major Sailys Trahskhat's tone was patient. "Made him promise to make them behave, in fact."

"I hope you were more . . . persuasive with him than with Archbishop Zhasyn," Raimahn said a bit pointedly. Trahskhat suppressed the long-suffering sigh the remark deserved, and the intensity of the colonel's expression eased a bit. His lips might actually have twitched, although it was difficult to tell in the windy, uncertain lantern light.

"I know they'll do their best, Sailys." He patted the major's shoulder. "I'd just as soon not lose any of them, though. So keep an eye on them, right?"

"Course I will, Sir." Trahskhat nodded.

"Then I suppose you'd best get on with it."

Trahskhat nodded again, touched his chest in a salute which no longer seemed unnatural to either of them, and disappeared into the rain.

Raimahn watched him go, then bent over the sketch map on the camp table shielded—mostly—from the windy rain under the canvas tarp. He shivered and scolded himself for it. After the previous winter, the South March climate was almost balmy, rain or no rain. Indeed, his men had been sneering at the weather—"Call *this* a winter?"—ever since they'd moved south of Fort St. Klair.

I suppose you can take the boy out of Charis, but you can't take the Charis out of the boy, he told himself, and turned the lantern's wick a bit higher. His position was invisible to anyone inside the fortifications because it was sheltered against the outer face of the third ring of entrenchments around the fort, over a mile from the innermost earthworks around the fort itself.

His nose had adjusted, however unwillingly, to the reek of corruption not even the rain could wash fully out of the air, and he wondered once again what had possessed the garrison's commander to attempt to hold anything *but* that inner ring. He'd yielded the outer two rings without a fight, in a triumph of sanity over fanaticism, but he'd refused to give up the third ring that easily, and his stubbornness had cost him close to a thousand men in killed, wounded, and prisoners. Mostly killed, Raimahn reflected coldly, and lucky for the handful of prisoners that the assault columns had consisted almost solely of Charisians. He rather doubted any of the Temple Loyalists would have survived long enough to surrender if his Glacierhearters had encountered them. That bothered him. What bothered him worse was that, after last winter, it didn't bother him very much.

He straightened and slowly filled the bowl of the pipe he'd never smoked before he'd found himself among the snowy peaks of Glacierheart. The majority of Glacierhearters smoked, and he'd found himself picking up the habit as part and parcel of the evolution which had transformed what he still thought of as a Charisian fop into a hardened Glacierheart militia commander. And, he reflected as he struck the Shan-wei's candle and lit the fragrant Malitar tobacco, it helped to mask the smell of death.

He made sure the pipe was drawing properly, then discarded the candle and squinted through wind-shredded smoke at the sketch map once more. Out there in the darkness, the coal miners of Major Laimuyl Stywyrt's 4th Company, 1st Glacierheart Volunteers, were toiling forward through the rain and mud, laden with picks and shovels and gunpowder while Major Zhaikyb Mahclyntahk's 3rd Company covered them with ready rifles and two ICA mortar platoons stood ready to fire in their support. Hopefully, 3rd Company and the mortar crews would have nothing to do but sit there and curse the icy rain. If the artillery pounding the Temple Loyalists' position did its job properly, the defenders would be too busy keeping their heads down to notice any small sounds or movement at the base of their earthen ramparts.

They shouldn't let that happen, and neither Charisian troops nor General Wyllys' Siddarmarkian regulars would have. But after six days of almost ceaseless bombardment, the Fort Tairys garrison was unlikely to be that alert. And nothing had happened the last two nights, now had it?

In fact, quite a bit had happened on those nights, although no one inside the fortifications appeared to have noticed. Two nights ago, Zheryld Mahkdugyl's 1st Company had carried the shovels while Larek Satyrfyld's 2nd Company watched their backs. Last night it had been Mahkdugyl's men's turn to dig while Mahclyntahk mounted watch. And when 4th Company finished *tonight's* labors Raimahn could report to Duke Eastshare that the 1st Glacierheart Volunteers had completed the mission to which they'd been assigned.

The youthful colonel who no longer felt quite so young smiled around the stem of his pipe. It was a remarkably cold smile.

▼ ▼ ▼

"Colonel Raimahn reports the charges are laid, Your Grace," Colonel Traimynt reported. Duke Eastshare looked up from his spartan breakfast, and his chief of staff grinned. "I don't think they enjoyed slogging around in the rain, Your Grace, but I'm pretty sure they decided it was worth it in the end."

The colonel undoubtedly had a point, Eastshare thought, and applied himself once more to his bowl of hot, sweetened porridge while he considered the report. Corporal Chalkyr kept trying to inveigle him into a menu more in keeping with his exalted status, but the ICA had carried over the Chisholmian Army's attitude towards rations. It would be stupid to carry austerity to the point of impairing an officer's ability to carry out his duties, yet within that restriction, officers in the field ate what their men ate, which encouraged those same officers to make sure the quartermaster corps did its job properly. There were other advantages, of course, including the fact that the men knew about it.

At the moment, however, Eastshare was much more focused on Byrk Raimahn and his men than on his meal. The Glacierhearters had done well under trying conditions, but he'd expected that. What bothered him was Raimahn's request on behalf of his men that they be allowed to lead the attack their labors had made possible.

For all their determination, the Glacierhearters were still far from anything Eastshare would have called trained soldiers. He knew it wasn't fair to hold them to the same standards as his highly trained regulars, but war wasn't about "fair." War was about blood, death, and ruptured bodies, and about seeing to it that there were as few as possible of those on one's own side. It was inevitable that the Volunteers would take heavier casualties than the ICA regiments would.

Yet he also knew the highly disciplined miners would almost certainly take lighter casualties than he was afraid they would. Most of them had endured a particularly brutal practical training course in how to survive in combat. They were veterans in every sense of the word, whether they'd spent any time on the drill square or not, and they were far more accustomed to the use of explosives than most people. They'd taken to hand grenades with gusto, and he never doubted they'd make ample use of them in any assault.

And that brought him back to the real reason for his hesitation.

They had too many scores to settle with men just like the ones in Fort Tairys. If he turned them loose, let them lead the assault, it was unlikely they'd be interested in taking prisoners. That struck him as a poor way to respect his monarchs' desire to minimize counteratrocities. On the other hand. . . .

I suppose we'll just have to see how reasonable Walkyr and Vahnhain are feeling. After all, whether or not there's an assault at all is going to be at least as much up to them as it is to me. And so are the consequences of any assault.

He smiled for just a moment—a smile which strongly

resembled that of Byrk Raimahn—and scooped up another spoonful of porridge.

▼ ▼ ▼

"There's the signal, Sir!" a sergeant called out, and Raimahn nodded.

"Time to sound reveille, Sailys. Do the honors for us, please."

"Think the men'd prefer for *you* to do it, Sir," Trahskhat replied. Raimahn looked at him quizzically, but the major's expression was serious. "The boys know who got us this far, Sir. They figure you're our good luck charm. Wouldn't want them thinking we'd done anything to jinx it at the last minute, would we?"

Raimahn snorted, trying to hide behind a gruff expression, and strode over to the varnished, rain-beaded wooden box. There was a metal ring on its side, at the end of a copper tube, and a long line of fuse hose stretched away from it. The hose was made of canvas, and its function was not simply to preserve the fuse inside it from damp, although it had been heavily coated in pitch waterproofing in order to help it do just that.

He bent, inserting his index finger through the ring, and drew a deep breath, letting the raw, wet air settle into the bottom of his lungs.

"*Fire in the hole!*" he announced, and pulled.

The friction primer ignited the quick match—the powder impregnated cotton thread—at the heart of the fuse hose, and the hose itself confined the heat and exhaust gases. Instead of escaping to the open atmosphere, they were shot forward down the hose, speeding the rate of combustion enormously, and the incandescent heart of fury raced away from the wooden box at well over three hundred feet per second.

No one saw it coming, for the same fuse hose which accelerated its burning hid it from any watching eye, and that meant there was no warning before it reached the charges the 1st Glacierheart Volunteers had planted at the base of the defenders' final earthen parapet.

▼ ▼ ▼

Lairays Walkyr had just sat down to a cheerless breakfast with Naiklos Vahnhain. Food was more plentiful
than it had been over the winter, but not a lot. Colonel
Syngyltyn's cavalry deserved much of the credit for that;
they'd been too preoccupied with burning the abandoned farms of heretics to think about the crops which
might have been harvested from them instead. It wasn't
the quality of the provisions which produced the gloom
that hung almost visibly over the breakfast table, however.

Walkyr waited while Father Naiklos intoned the blessing, then picked up his teacup and tried not to grimace as
he sipped.

"How much damage did they do last night, Lairays?"
Vahnhain asked after a moment.

"I haven't seen the reports yet." This time Walkyr did
grimace. "I don't expect them to be good, though. Those
guns in the hills have riddled the southern and eastern
curtainwalls. There are gaps—especially on the south—
you could put a platoon of Syngyltyn's cavalry through.
Assuming he still has any horses."

Losses among the cavalry's limited supply of horses had
been heavy even before the heretics captured the third line
of entrenchments, where most of them had been picketed.

Vahnhain's expression tightened and he sipped his own
"tea." He was worried enough he didn't even notice the
horrible taste.

"Morale's suffering," he said, lowering the cup. "I'm
hearing it from all the chaplains. It's not because they're
ready to give up; it's just being *pounded* this way, without any opportunity to strike back."

"I know." Walkyr sighed. "Vahlverday's all for making a sortie against the heretics' guns and I wish we
could, but they've got at least a thousand infantry dug
in between us and the batteries and those slopes're
damned near vertical and bare as a tabletop. They'd
massacre any columns we sent up. I'd considered a night
attack, but those Shan-wei damned rockets of theirs

mean they'd still see us coming and rip us apart on the slopes. And the situation's no better down here. I'm not even trying to man the parapets anymore, except for lookouts in the most protected positions they can find. I've got units positioned in dugouts along the base of the wall to meet any assaults, but they're under strict orders not to expose themselves for any other reason." He grimaced. "Putting men up on the firing step would only give the heretic sharpshooters target practice, and I sort of doubt that would help their morale any, either."

"That wasn't a criticism, Lairays," Vahnhain said quietly. "Only a report."

"I know, Father." Walkyr took another sip from his own cup. "There's no use pretending we're not in Shan-wei's own mess, though. Our matchlocks and arbalests are completely outclassed by their rifles. I've had the guns loaded—those the heretic artillery hasn't already dismounted—but the heretics aren't giving them any targets. I'm reserving them for use against any assault they choose to launch, and I just hope the rain hasn't gotten to the charges. And that's really the best we can hope for with our matchlocks, as well. If the heretics decide to assault the position, to actually come out where we can get at them, we can hurt them badly. If they stay where they are and keep shelling and shooting, there's nothing we can do except hunker down and take it."

"I was afraid that was what you'd say." Vahnhain smiled wanly.

"The good news is that they're using up a lot of ammunition and time. The longer they don't try an assault, the closer Duke Harless gets," Walkyr said, trying very hard to sound optimistic. "And if they *do* try an assault, we'll finally have the chance to bleed them. I don't like losing men in dozens and scores any more than you do, Father. But as long as we're still sitting here, we're doing our job and—"

The earsplitting thunder snatched him up out of his chair in midsentence.

▼ ▼ ▼

"Well, that was impressive." Duke Eastshare's word choice might have sounded flippant; his tone did not. "Remind me to congratulate Colonel Raimahn and his men, Lywys. They did us proud."

"Of course, Your Grace," Captain Braynair replied.

The Glacierhearters' charges had ripped three broad breaches through the southern face of Fort Tairys' final line of earthworks. They'd probably killed at least two hundred men in the process, but it was the breaches that mattered.

"Sound parley," the duke said. "Let's see if these people are more willing to listen to reason now."

▼ ▼ ▼

Lairays Walkyr's face was like stone as he rode one of the garrison's few remaining horses towards the Charisian banner atop the third line of earthworks. He was accompanied only by Colonel Mhartyn and Colonel Kyrbysh. He wished intensely that Father Naiklos could be by his side, but the Charisian proclamation that all Inquisitors would be murdered on sight made that impossible.

One more proof they serve Shan-wei, Walkyr thought grimly.

He would have preferred to ignore the heretics' parley request, but they might actually have something worth hearing to say. More to the point, it used up a little more time, bought a few more hours for Duke Harless' approach. And, he admitted, whatever they said, whatever threats they uttered or demands they made, he'd take them back to his regiments knowing they could only stiffen the determination of men already resolved to die for God.

Of course, there was always the question of whether the heretics would honor the traditional safeguards of a parley. They might well cut him and his party down, instead, and he almost wished they would. He was no more eager to die than the next man, but that sort of treachery would fire his men with rage and determination as nothing else could.

He reached the waiting banner and dismounted, trying to ignore the rifle-armed infantry in their bizarre, mottled uniforms. From the top of the parapet he could see the heretics' encampment spreading out down the gap towards Kharmych. It was the first clear view he'd had of it, and something tightened inside him as he saw the neat rows of tents, the canvas-covered supply wagons, the mess tents. The Charisians might be as wet and muddy as his own men, yet he strongly suspected that even under canvas they were better housed—and far better fed—than his own command in the sodden, artillery-threshed, ruin of what had been a snug, weather-tight fortress.

And, also for the first time, he saw the squat, dug-in "angle-guns" which had contributed so heavily to that destruction.

The stocky man waiting for him was tall for an Islander—as tall as most Siddarmarkians—with brown hair, brown eyes, and a hard expression. He stood behind that expression with a rock-like solidity any boulder might have envied, and he wore the same uniform as the infantry stationed around the parley site. The only differences were the riding boots he wore instead of their lace-up footwear, the peculiar-looking pistol at his side, and the single golden sword of a Charisian general glinting on his collar.

Walkyr curled a mental lip. Even the militia recognized the need for officers to be readily visible to their own men in the heart of combat! But then he remembered the deadly accuracy of the heretic rifles and the disproportionate number of junior officers and sergeants who'd become casualties.

He came to a halt, facing the man who had to be the Duke of Eastshare, and firmly quashed a reflex twitch towards a salute. The red-haired young officer at Eastshare's elbow had a single golden crown on his collar instead of a sword. Aside from that, his uniform was identical to his superior's, and his blue eyes hardened at Walkyr's refusal to acknowledge Eastshare's rank. That gave Walkyr a certain amount of pleasure, yet if the insult perturbed the heretic duke in the least, there was no sign of it.

"'General' Walkyr, I presume?" His accent struck a Siddarmarkian ear oddly, but there was no mistaking his cold, cutting contempt.

"You're the one who sounded parley," Walkyr returned bluntly. "I assume that means you had something to say. Say it."

The red-haired officer—Eastshare's aide, probably—stiffened, face darkening, but Eastshare only snorted as if he'd heard something amusing.

"Straight to the point," he observed. "Good. I won't have to waste a lot of time on this after all." He showed a flash of white tooth that reminded Walkyr of a slash lizard he'd once seen. "My message is very simple, Walkyr. Your outer works are in my possession. Your last line of earthworks is breached, and so is the curtainwall. The laws of war say I have to give you an opportunity to surrender when that's true. So I'm giving it to you now."

Walkyr's jaw tightened and he felt his right hand quiver where it had clenched on the hilt of his sword. For an instant he was tempted to draw that sword, drive it into Eastshare's belly, and watch that hard, cold face crumple with the knowledge of death. But the Charisian riflemen were watching too intently. He'd be dead before he got the weapon fully drawn.

He fought the temptation aside, but the fury died harder. Surrender? *Surrender* to scum who'd raised their blasphemous hands against the might and majesty of Mother Church and God Himself? Who murdered priests? Who'd invaded his country, brought war and destruction to the Faithful in support of that traitor in the Lord Protector's Palace?

"And what makes you think I might consider surrendering to you?" he managed to bite out after a small eternity.

"The possibility that you might possess a glimmer of sanity," Eastshare replied coldly. "The laws of war also state that a garrison which refuses to surrender when summoned to do so after a practicable breach has been made loses the right to surrender at a later time. Should you reject this opportunity, I'll be fully justified in putting your entire command to the sword."

"How many men are you ready to lose to manage that?" Walkyr snapped, and Eastshare snorted again, this time contemptuously.

"Against *your* rabble? Be serious! And before you make your decision, I should point out that the only troops outside your fortress who're remotely likely to *let* your men surrender are mine. The Siddarmarkians to the north are under the command of an officer who held the Sylmahn Gap against everything the 'Army of God' could throw at him. He lost enough men and saw enough atrocities by 'holy warriors' like you there that he wouldn't've been particularly inclined to offer quarter anyway. But then he marched through the ruins you and the men inside that fort left in western Shiloh. I know exactly how he and his men feel about your crew of mutineers, rapists, and butchers."

His eyes were brown ice, and even so they were warmer than his voice.

"I'll be honest here, 'General.' *I* don't particularly want to offer you quarter, either. My orders are to not simply slaughter you out of hand the way you deserve if I can help it, and I'm offering to obey those orders. But if you choose not to surrender, it won't break my heart. And allow me to point out to you that it was your own Grand Inquisitor who proclaimed that in Jihad, the normal laws of war don't apply. That's why he authorized you to murder women and children in God's name. *I* don't plan to do any murdering in His name . . . unless you're kind enough to give me an excuse. At that point, I'm perfectly willing to follow *your* rules. So I urge you to consider the out I'm offering you, because it won't be offered again."

Walkyr stared at him, and even through his own rage, he felt Eastshare's icy sincerity. He could surrender now, and the Charisians probably would honor the terms of that surrender. They might even be able—and willing—to protect their prisoners from the Siddarmarkian traitors. And if he *didn't* surrender, Eastshare would indeed send his men in with orders to offer no quarter.

But if he surrendered, he failed Mother Church. Death in the service of God should hold no terror for any man, he told himself; failure to give God that service should terrify anyone. And whatever might happen to him or to his soldiers if he surrendered, Father Naiklos and every other Inquisitor attached to his force would be murdered anyway. He, Lairays Walkyr, would face God with their blood upon his hands as the man who'd handed them over to their murderers.

Besides, this arrogant prick may think my boys will roll over when they try to come across the walls, but he's damned well wrong! He remembered his morning's conversation with Vahnhain. *If they're really willing to send in an assault, they'll finally come into range. After sitting out here and shooting and shelling us for a five-day while we couldn't respond at all, they don't have any idea what that means. And if they want to tell us they'll be offering no quarter, so much the better! None of the boys will give an inch if they know they're going to be killed anyway. We'll break the bastards on the walls!*

He glared at Eastshare and then, deliberately, spat on the ground.

"*That* for your offer of quarter. If you think you can take Fort Tairys, come ahead and try!"

"Oh, we won't *try*, 'General' Walkyr." Eastshare smiled thinly. "And at least you've just solved my problem about what to do with all the prisoners of war. Go back to the fort. By this time tomorrow, your problems will be over."

Walkyr spat again, then turned and stalked back to his horse, accompanied by his stonefaced colonels. They mounted and went cantering back towards the battered fort, and Eastshare glanced at his aide.

"Go find Colonel Raimahn, Lywys. Tell him his request is approved."

▼ ▼ ▼

Byrk Raimahn waited as calmly as he could and hoped he looked calmer than he felt.

He wasn't looking forward to this, and not simply because his experiences in the Green Cove Trace had disabused him of youth's illusions of immortality. He'd discovered not only that he could die but that the world would go right on without him. He'd discovered other things, as well. Like the burning power of hatred. Like his own capacity to do whatever his duty required of him. Like the horrors of combat . . . and the greater horrors of combat's aftermath.

In many ways, he suspected, the bitter, broken-back guerrilla warfare of the Gray Walls actually left him better prepared than Eastshare's regulars for what was about to happen. Certainly there was no hesitation in the men of the 1st Glacierheart Volunteers, and some remnant of the man he'd been a year before wanted to weep because there wasn't. He'd passed on their request to the duke because it was important to them, and he wished to all the Archangels that it wasn't what they wanted. But almost more than he wished that, he wished it wasn't what *he* wanted.

Someday this will be over, he thought, checking his double-barreled pistol. *One day we'll go home again— those of us who're still alive and still have homes, anyway. And who will we be when we do? What are we going to do with the memories of the sights and the smells and the sounds? With the memories of what we've done and why . . . and of how we felt while we did it?*

He was afraid of those questions' answers. But for any of this to haunt them in years to come, first they had to survive. It was his job to see to it that as many of his men as possible did just that, and in the meantime. . . .

He heard the squelching, sucking sound of someone's boots and turned as Sailys Trahskhat appeared beside him.

"Men're ready, Sir," the ex-baseball player reported.

"Most of 'em're really looking forward to seeing how these grenades work."

Raimahn nodded. Duke Eastshare's advance along the Branath Canal had allowed him to bring along a not so small mountain of ammunition. His artillery had expended quite a lot of that, but a fresh convoy of it was en route, scheduled to arrive within the next three days, along with a generous supply of Shan-wei's fountains and footstools. He'd included large numbers of Charisian hand grenades in his original advance, however, and each of Raimahn's infantrymen had been issued six of them. They'd spent a few days training with them during the canal voyage, but they'd had no opportunity to use them in combat and Trahskhat was right about how eager they were to try them out.

"And the mortars?"

"Ready to go, Sir, and so are the ASPs."

Raimahn nodded again. No other army had ever been able to provide indirect fire, which meant no one else had ever been required to *control* it, either. That was what the ASPs, or Artillery Support Parties, were for. Equipped with heliographs, signal flags, rockets, and runners, they were trained to control and coordinate the fire of angleguns and—especially—of the mortars of the ICA's support platoons. The mortars' ability to keep up with advancing infantry in almost any terrain was a huge advantage; the ASPs were designed to use it most effectively, and they'd proved their efficiency on the Daivyn. They were a welcome addition to any unit, especially ones like the Glacierheart Volunteers who had no mortars of their own and were forced to rely on those of their Charisian allies. That was one reason Raimahn had assigned an entire thirty-man section of riflemen as each ASP's security element and as additional runners, if they turned out to be necessary.

"In that case," he said, "I suppose you and I should wander along to join the party."

"S'pose we should, Sir," Trahskhat agreed, just as casually.

Neither of them fooled the other, of course.

▼ ▼ ▼

"All three columns are ready to advance, Your Grace," Sir Zhaksyn Traimynt reported.

The Duke of Eastshare didn't reply for a moment. He was gazing through his double-glass at the smoke rising from Fort Tairys. The endless rain had ceased, and there were actually some breaks in the southwestern cloud cover. Afternoon sunlight struck down through the gaps, touching the sodden trees and grass like a lover's hand and gilding the mountains to either side of Ohadlyn's Gap in antique gold. It was still cold, though, and the air remained humid, with a wet chill that struck a man to the bone.

Of course, there were chills and then there were *chills*, and he wondered what might be going through the minds of Lairays Walkyr's waiting men.

He hoped it was as unpleasant as they deserved.

The renewed thunder of his artillery rolled in waves as shellfire marched back and forth across the battered defenses. One of the angle-guns' shells had found an ammunition magazine, and the resultant blast had produced an enormous fireball and found something flammable despite the past several days' drenching rain. Eastshare imagined it had killed or maimed quite a few men in the process, and the rising smoke was still thick over an hour after the explosion.

He turned away and swept his double-glass across the waiting columns.

There were three of them. The left flank column was made up of three companies of the 1st Glacierheart Volunteers. The second, the one in the middle, consisted of 2nd and 3rd Battalions, 1st Regiment, ICA, while three companies of Colonel Bryntyn Howail's 37th Infantry Regiment, Republic of Siddarmark Army, formed the right flank column.

General Wyllys had sent Howail's regiment around through the foothills' muddy, slippery paths for this very moment. Mostly to ensure that the RSA was represented in the attack, but the 37th Infantry had personal—and pointed—reasons of its own. Some of its men (not many, given how few of the original 37th had survived) remembered the Sylmahn Gap, and all of them had marched through the wreckage of western Shiloh. Like Byrk Raimahn's Glacierhearters, the 37th had a score to settle with the men who'd betrayed the Republic, and there was only one coin in which they were prepared to accept payment.

There were between thirteen hundred and two thousand men in each of those columns, with an additional four thousand waiting reinforcements. Each column was supported by four of his infantry support platoons, and he'd made certain they were amply provided with hand grenades.

He gazed at them for several seconds, seeing the differences between them. His Charisians and the Glacierhearters who'd trained with them had deployed clouds of skirmishers to cover their columns. They were already a good hundred yards ahead of the main body, scattered to take advantage of terrain features and shell holes while they maintained a steady, galling fire on the Temple Loyalist lookouts crouched along the shattered parapet. The 37th was in a more open formation than any pike square would have tolerated, but it remained tighter than the other columns, its men less comfortable with the ICA's tactics. It was also more liberally festooned with company and section standards, and he saw additional bloodred streamers snapping on the breeze from every staff.

He knew what those streamers meant, and he lowered his double-glass slowly.

"All right, Zhaksyn. Fire the signal."

▼ ▼ ▼

The signal rocket arced heavenward, riding a ribbon of smoke, and exploded almost directly above Fort Tairys.

Byrk Raimahn watched it burst, and the flower of flame was greeted by a deep, hungry baying. It snarled up from deep in the men's bellies, and then the ICA's bugles gave it wings. They sounded clear and sharp, the signal to advance falling in the cascade of their notes, and the 1st Glacierheart Volunteers' Charisian-trained buglers took up the call in turn.

There were no bugles from the 37th Infantry. The RSA used drum calls, and their deep-throated thunder was an earthquake rumble under the high, insistent chorus of the buglers. Yet even though Siddarmark used drum signals, each regiment had its pipers, as well, and they too could be used to pass orders upon occasion. Like this one, Raimahn thought, as the notes of "The Pikes of Kolstyr" rose in the fierce, skirling voice of the 37th's war pipes.

"The Pikes of Kolstyr" dated from the first war between Desnair and the Republic, which had begun so disastrously for Siddarmark that the Desnairians had been certain the ultimate victory would be theirs. To encourage the Republic to acknowledge the inevitable, a Desnairian commander had accepted the surrender of the thousand-man garrison of the Siddarmarkian town of Kolstyr, four hundred miles inside Shiloh Province, on honorable terms. And when the garrison had marched out and stacked its weapons, he'd chosen one man in ten . . . and *not* killed him. Then he'd burned the town and sent the hundred survivors of its garrison back to their fellows minus their right hands as a pointed warning of what would happen to the Republic as a whole unless it abandoned the struggle.

Unfortunately for the Desnairian Empire, the Republic had taken a rather different lesson from his message, and "The Pikes of Kolstyr" was the result. In peacetime, it was a somber reminder of the price of duty; in wartime, it was the march the war pipes played when the Republic of Siddarmark intended to take no prisoners. Siddarmark had never been especially atrocity prone, but neither had it been shy about reprisals in the face of someone else's atrocities. The Desnairians had learned that lesson the hard way; the men of the 37th Infantry intended to teach it to the Fort Tairys garrison, as well.

It was a pity they'd have so little time to profit from the tutorial.

Byrk Raimahn wasn't the only man who recognized "The Pikes of Kolstyr," and the roar that went up from the assault columns should have brought the sky crashing down in wreckage. For just a moment, Raimahn actually pitied the men inside those fortifications as they heard that hungry sound.

But only for a moment.

"All right, Sailys." He had to raise his voice to be heard, yet the words came out unnaturally calm, almost cold, and Trahskhat looked at him levelly. "Let's be about it. The Regiment will advance."

. XIX .
Kharmych-Fort Tairys Road,
The South March Lands,
and
Siddar City,
Republic of Siddarmark

The Duke of Harless stared at the dispatch in his hands and tried to wrap his mind around its message.

It was short, and not simply because it had come by wyvern. Wyvern-borne dispatches were usually chary with word count, but this was more than that. This was the brevity of a man who'd known he had very little time to draft it.

He listened to the rain on his pavilion's roof. It wasn't the downpour of the last few days, but it was more than enough to prevent the ground from even contemplating drying out. And, he admitted, more than enough to spread still more sickness through his army's ranks. The Army of Shiloh's attached Pasqualates were doing all anyone could have done, but it was simply impossible to march two hundred thousand men and all their draft and food animals through these accursed winter rains without those men becoming riddled with illness. The pace at which he'd driven them only made that worse, and hunger, fatigue, and the lack of dry firewood had all combined to sap a little more of his army's strength with every mile it marched.

He laid the dispatch on his field desk, leaned back in the upholstered chair with closed eyes, and pinched the bridge of his nose.

The dispatch was eight days old. It had taken that long to reach the wyvernry at Trevyr, seven hundred miles in his rear, and then overtake him. Much though it irritated Harless to admit it, they were fortunate Sir Fahstyr Rychtyr had thought to send Walkyr a wyvern coop—escorted by an entire cavalry company to make sure it arrived—before allowing himself to be penned up in Trevyr by the heretic Hanth last June. It was probably the single foresightful thing he'd managed to accomplish, but it had proved its worth.

The destruction wreaked upon the semaphore chain explained most of the dispatch's delay in reaching him. Had the stations been intact all the way from Thesmar to Kharmych, Rychtyr could have transmitted it in little more than an hour. The need for relays of couriers to bridge the gaps had stretched that hour into more than a five-day. At that, he was fortunate it had reached him at all.

He drew a deep breath and reached for the handbell. Its incongruously cheerful jingling had barely ceased when his clerk appeared.

"Yes, Your Grace?"

"Inform my nephew I need to see him immediately. Then send messages to Father Tymythy, Earl Hankey, Earl Hennet, Baron Climbhaven, and Sir Borys Cahstnyr. I require their presence as soon as possible. And send a courier to General Ahlverez. Ask him to join us at his earliest convenience."

The clerk's eyes widened, but he knew better than to dally or ask questions when Harless spoke in that tone.

"Of course, Your Grace," he said instead and vanished once more.

▼ ▼ ▼

Sir Rainos Ahlverez managed to keep his tongue between his teeth as his horse trotted past the well-sprung, mud-splashed coaches drawn up on either side of the high road. Harless' was the biggest and most luxurious, but Hennet and Hankey weren't far behind when it came to pampering their fat arses. He was inclined to be more generous where Baron Climbhaven and Sir Borys Cahstnyr were concerned; the artillerist's crippled leg must be more painful than ever in this sort of weather, and Sir Borys' health, never robust, was breaking down. More than that, the two of them had agreed to share a single coach when Harless ordered the Army of Shiloh to strip down for the forced march to relieve Fort Tairys. Obviously none of that army's more senior Desnairian officers had been able to emulate that sacrifice.

To be fair, the army had covered over three hundred and seventy miles in eleven days, a hundred and thirty of them through the heart of the Kyplyngyr Forest, which would have been a very creditable rate of advance for most armies of bygone days. Unfortunately, they weren't in "bygone days." Even worse, the Desnairian component of the Army of Shiloh was in seriously depleted condition. His own troops had fared far better, partly because they found it relatively easy to match the Desnairians' pace but more because they'd been properly supplied from the outset. Sluggish though the army's speed might seem to Ahlverez and his officers, it was still too rapid for foragers to sweep up the supplies the Desnairians required, and the four days they'd spent crossing the Kyplyngyr had been a nightmare, without even grass for grazing. Short rations, rain, mud, cold, and poor shelter had exercised their inevitable baleful effect and Harless had lost somewhere close to twenty percent of his total

troop strength to illness, exhaustion, or outright desertion. Ahlverez had been forced to leave more of his own
men behind with the healers than he'd liked, but his desertion rate was miniscule and his total losses to all causes
had been little more than *five* percent.

At least they were out of the damned forest, and it
was to be hoped his instructions to Rychtyr and Baron
Tymplahr would at least partially improve the supply
situation in another few five-days. In the meantime, they
were barely forty miles west of the Branath Canal, less
than a hundred and fifty from Fort Tairys. Even *Harless*
could reach Walkyr's command in only another five-day
or so!

With what was left of his army, anyway.

He dismounted by the dripping, enormous pavilion
that served as Harless' headquarters. One reason the
duke's carriage was so huge was to permit him to use it
for a traveling office—and dry, reasonably comfortable
quarters—when it proved impossible to erect his pavilion in time to receive him, but he hadn't needed it very
often. The pavilion was sent ahead with a cavalry escort
every day, and the Army of Shiloh always managed to
find the manpower to have it up and ready by the time
he arrived.

Once upon a time, Ahlverez wouldn't have found that
particularly objectionable. He didn't like admitting that,
yet the truth was the truth, whatever he liked. And at
least he'd learned better . . . and one hell of a lot faster
than Harless or his senior subordinates seemed capable
of grasping the realities.

"Ready, Lynkyn?" he asked as Captain Lattymyr dismounted beside him.

"Of course, Sir."

Ahlverez looked at Colonel Mákyntyr and General
Rahdgyrz, one eyebrow quirked, and both of them nodded. None of them knew what had led to this summons,
but from the tone of Harless' message it wasn't *good*
news. Under the circumstances, Ahlverez wanted his artillery commander and quartermaster available.

"Father Sulyvyn?" He turned to Sulyvyn Fyrmyn, and the Schuelerite sighed.

The upper-priest's fervor for cooperation with the Army of Justice in general—and with Father Tymythy Yairdyn in particular—had cooled. It remained stronger than that of Ahlverez' secular officers, but Fyrmyn was no fool. He continued to defend the Desnairians' determination and purpose, yet he'd come to understand exactly why Ahlverez doubted their capability.

"I'm ready, my son," he said now, and Ahlverez nodded.

"In that case, after you, Father."

He gestured for the intendant to precede him, and he and his subordinates followed Fyrmyn across the slick mud where boots and hooves had trampled any grass into muck. A doormat had been laid in front of the pavilion, and Ahlverez reminded himself not to grit his teeth as he took the pointed hint and cleaned his boots before stepping onto the rich carpets which floored the duke's tent.

Sir Graim Kyr greeted them with an icy bow. Whatever miniscule scrap of love might have existed between Baron Fyrnach and Sir Rainos Ahlverez was not prominently on display.

"If you'll follow me, Father," the young Desnairian said, pointedly ignoring the upper-priest's secular companions.

Fyrmyn's eyes flashed, but Ahlverez shook his head ever so slightly and the intendant's reprimand died unspoken. It wasn't that Ahlverez would have objected to watching Father Sulyvyn reduce the little snot to cringing, bleeding wreckage. The Schuelerite had a splendid command of invective, but he could also flay a miscreant without ever resorting to profanity, and under other circumstances Ahlverez would have paid good money to watch Fyrnach's destruction. Unfortunately, he'd done too much damage to his own relationship with Harless' aide. He didn't regret it, for it had needed doing, but creating a sense of enmity between Father Sulyvyn and the little bastard, as well, could only further complicate an already ramshackle command relationship.

So instead of eviscerating the baron, Fyrmyn simply nodded, and the party of Dohlarans followed him into the portion of the pavilion set aside as Harless' conference area. It was considerably warmer, no doubt because it was located at the center of the outsized tent, using the air spaces around it for insulation. The iron stove— the *Charisian* iron stove, Ahlverez noted—also helped to explain it, and he observed the heaped coal scuttle beside it. The rest of the army might be short of fuel, but its commander appeared to be amply provided.

Stop that, he told himself sternly. *Yes, you loathe the man. And, yes, it's hard to think of any mistakes he's failed to make. But you're still under his orders and it's still your duty to take the war to the heretics. So maybe you should try concentrating on how to do that* despite *his mistakes instead of dwelling on how much you'd prefer to wring his neck.*

"Sir Rainos. Father Sulyvyn." Harless stood to greet them, which was an improvement over his last meeting with Ahlverez. "Thank you for coming, although I fear the news is grave."

Ahlverez felt his expression tighten, and the duke nodded somberly.

"Fort Tairys fell eight days ago," he said flatly. "General Rychtyr dispatched word from Thesmar as soon as the messenger wyvern reached Trevyr." His lips thinned over his teeth. "He sent a copy of Father Naiklos' final dispatch with it. General Walkyr was already dead when it was sent off."

Ahlverez' stomach was an icy void as Harless continued.

"Apparently the heretics drove the garrison back into the fort and the inner works, then breached the fort's walls and summoned General Walkyr to surrender. He refused, of course, and the heretics stormed the breaches. Father Naiklos says the Siddarmarkian pipes were sounding 'The Pikes of Kolstyr' when he sent the wyvern away."

The void in Ahlverez' stomach collapsed into a single jagged chunk of ice.

"The Pikes of Kolstyr." No wonder Harless' voice sounded as if it had been hacked out of stone with a dull axe. The Desnairian Army had more experience against the Republic than anyone else, and quite a lot of that experience since the Kolstyr Massacre—ordered by a maternal ancestor of Earl Hankey, if Ahlverez remembered correctly—had been less than happy. Nor did the news fill Ahlverez with happiness, given what it implied for the future. Siddarmark had always enjoyed a reputation for adhering to the laws of war, even in its conflicts with Desnair, resorting to reprisals only under severe provocation. Indeed, if Father Naiklos' report was accurate, this was only the sixth time the RSA had sounded that march on a field of battle.

Ahlverez doubted it would be the last.

Of course it won't, he told himself. *It's that kind of war, and heretics or not, I really can't blame them for responding that way. I'll kill every one of the motherless bastards with my bare hands, but there's no point pretending I wouldn't react exactly the same way in their place.*

"Father Naiklos' best estimate of the heretics' numbers is approximately seventeen thousand," Harless went on. "Baron Climbhaven and I have discussed what Father Naiklos could tell us about the heretics' bombardment, and it's evident they must be well supplied with artillery. At the same time, they must've expended a great deal of ammunition, and I doubt they'll be able to replenish it easily. I'm confident they'd learned of our approach and used so much ammunition because they were desperate to capture Fort Tairys and secure control of Ohadlyn's Gap before we could arrive. That probably also explains their willingness to assault the works, which must have cost them heavy casualties. Unfortunately, they've *succeeded* in taking the fort. They did it eight days ago, and we're still a five-day from the Gap even at our present rate of march. That means they'll have had more than two full five-days to prepare their positions before we could possibly reach them, and our troops are badly fatigued from the strain of moving so rapidly.

"Since we can't stop them from digging in anyway, whatever we do, I propose to pause where we are for a five-day. We'll rest the men, try to get them decently fed, before we resume the advance."

Ahlverez' jaw tightened. Part of him wanted to protest, but Harless was actually making sense. They'd lost the race to relieve Fort Tairys and fuming over whose fault that was would be pointless. Their job now was to take it back, and for that they needed an army that was in shape to fight. He knew that, but the knowledge couldn't prevent the surge of nausea he felt at the thought of once again facing dug-in heretics with breech-loading rifles and new model artillery.

"I don't relish the thought of attacking Charisian entrenchments," Harless said with a frankness Ahlverez found moderately astonishing. "We saw at Thesmar how expensive that can be. But in all honesty, Thesmar was a subsidiary objective. Fort Tairys isn't. We could afford to call off that assault rather than paying the price to drive it home, but we *need* Ohadlyn's Gap, and if Father Naiklos' estimate of their strength was accurate, they're probably down to no more than ten to fifteen thousand men after the attack. That means we outnumber them by better than ten to one, despite our losses on the march. More than that, we have a crushing advantage in cavalry, and I'm prepared to use it."

"With all due respect, Your Grace," Father Sulyvyn said after a moment, "I agree with your intentions, but surely cavalry's going to be less effective attacking entrenchments than it would be in the open field."

Ahlverez was grateful to his intendant for making the point, but Harless surprised him again.

"Precisely, Father," the Desnairian agreed. "However, the heretics have problems of their own. We're only a single day's march from the Branath Canal, and I intend to send several thousand of Earl Hennet's cavalry up it, securing the locks and burning out any heretics along their route. He'll also send a force up the Kharmych-Fort St. Klair High Road, which offers a potential route through the Branaths into Fort Tairys' rear. We'll see if they want to sit in the Gap while we take the entire canal *and* threaten to get around behind them."

He smiled thinly, and almost despite himself, Ahlverez felt himself nodding, although Harless was probably being overly optimistic. In the heretics' place, Ahlverez would have been willing to sacrifice the entire canal as the price of retaining Ohadlyn's Gap, and there was no way the Army of Shiloh could sustain a winter advance through the Branaths, whatever Harless or Hennet might think. But the heretics might not realize that . . . and if they'd pulled such substantial forces away from the Daivyn River, Hennet's cavalry might just be able to get all the way to Glacierborn Lake or even into the rear of the army facing Bishop Militant Cahnyr. It was unlikely he could supply himself if he did, but Stohnar and his allies would have to be sensitive to the threat.

And assuming Harless' estimate of the heretics' numbers is remotely correct, we have the strength to grind them away even in the Gap if we have to, he thought harshly. *It'll be ugly, it'll be costly, and I know damned well whose infantry will pay most of the price, but it can be done, especially if Harless will let me manage the affair. For one thing, seventeen thousand men are far too few to prevent me from infiltrating infantry around them through the hills. I wouldn't want to try it with Desnairian infantry, but my boys are steady enough for the job, and once we've cut the Gap at both ends, the heretics will be like spider-rats tied into a bag for drowning.*

"Obviously, we have a lot of planning to do." Harless waved at the chairs awaiting his guests. "Please be seated, all of you, and share your thoughts with me. I don't expect this to be easy, and I don't expect it to be accomplished in a single day, but it *will* be done." His eyes hardened and his voice was harsh. "The day is coming when the heretics who massacred General Walkyr's men will face the Punishment reserved for them, and there will be no mercy when that day comes. That much I swear on the honor of my house."

▼ ▼ ▼

"I don't doubt you mean that, Your Grace," Nahrmahn Baytz murmured as he monitored the take from the SNARC's remotes. "But you may just find you've been slightly overly ambitious."

The portly little prince leaned back in his chair and sipped wine while he contemplated the situation.

Duke Eastshare had suffered less than two thousand casualties, barely four hundred of them fatal, storming Fort Tairys, which was far less than Nahrmahn had anticipated. Clearly he ought to leave military planning up to those whose business it was, because Eastshare had obviously known what he was doing. The fighting had been furious and intensely ugly—whatever else they might have been, Lairays Walkyr's men had been no cowards and they'd died hard—but the outcome had never been in doubt. The only real surprise was that nearly a thousand had survived, almost all of them wounded. In fact, that was probably the reason they *had* survived; they'd been incapacitated by their wounds and even the Glacierheart Volunteers had seen too much bloodshed by the time the fighting was over to massacre helpless men. The wounded had not simply been allowed to survive but given the best care Eastshare's healers could provide.

Except for the Inquisitors, of course.

Disposing of that many bodies was not an inconsequential task, especially in the middle of a rainy Shiloh winter when dry wood for funeral pyres was hard to come by. General Wyllys had discovered a ready supply of volunteers, however. As local Temple Loyalists fled, Shilohians who'd remained loyal to the Republic were already filtering back into the wasteland the Sword of Schueler had created. There was little there to feed them, but food was being shipped in from New Province and

Southguard, and the survivors were determined to re-claim the land from which they'd been driven in fire and blood. They'd brought plenty of shovels with them, and they had no objection at all to fertilizing that land with the bodies of the Temple Loyalists who'd massacred their families and friends.

I was actually rather impressed with Harless' analysis, Nahrmahn admitted. *Of course, he did miss a few points. I don't suppose we should really blame him for not guessing how heavily Eastshare's been reinforced, though.*

The Chisholmian duke's command had already been reinforced by the 1st Mounted Brigade. The 2nd Mounted Brigade would arrive within the next few days, as would the 3rd Infantry Division. When all of them were assembled, Eastshare would command over seventy thousand men, twenty-one thousand of them mounted, and more than two hundred Charisian field pieces (not counting mortars), plus his angle-guns and General Wyllys' naval guns. And because all that fresh influx of combat power was on the far side of the Branath and Shingle Mountains from the Army of Shiloh, Harless' estimate of the defenders' strength was just a *little* low.

One other minor point, which I expect'll occur to Ahlverez sometime soon, is to wonder why Eastshare didn't even try to slow them down on their way through the woods to Kharmych. And I wonder why none of them've asked themselves why Walkyr chose to send "Slaytyr" to deliver his dispatch to them at Malyktyn rather than using the messenger wyvern Vahnhain used to get his final message out? I suppose even Ahlverez can be excused for assuming Walkyr thought it would be faster that way, but he still ought to be wondering why the message wasn't sent both ways, just to make certain it got through.

He thought about it again for another moment or two, then shrugged. It was always possible Ahlverez would grow suspicious eventually, but even the Dohlaran commander—for whom Nahrmahn had developed a rather unwilling respect—would have no way of guessing what Eastshare actually had in mind.

In the meantime, he and Owl had some spy reports to compose for Madam Pahrsahn.

▼ ▼ ▼

Merlin Athrawes stood on the cold, windy wharf and watched the weather-stained galleons forging across North Bedard Bay towards him. Siddar City's roofs were white, the rooftop decks Cayleb had made fashionable heaped with snow, and Owl promised more and heavier snowfalls over the next five-day. For today, the skies were relatively clear, but the wind off the bay was bitter cold, and the crowds which had gathered to watch the first and second echelons of Eastshare's Charisian Expeditionary Force make their way towards the capital's docks were notably absent. Merlin didn't blame them a bit, given the temperature. Still, he expected the citizens of Siddar City to turn out when the fresh influx of Charisian troops went marching through the capital.

And this time, it was going to take a while.

There were more than two hundred thousand men aboard that enormous convoy: nine infantry divisions, seven mounted brigades, all their attached artillery and engineers, and five thousand more armorers and quartermaster personnel to bolster the vast Charisian support base on the eastern side of the bay. There were still supply elements—wagons, draft dragons, and especially Raven Lord snow lizards—in the pipeline behind it, but with the arrival of this convoy, there would be close to three hundred thousand Charisian combat troops in the Republic of Siddarmark. Within the next few days, two infantry divisions and the 4th Mounted Brigade would head towards Allyntyn and Baron Green Valley while the Earl of High Mount set out for Fort Tairys with three more divisions and two more mounted brigades.

Somehow, he thought with a thin smile even colder than the wind off the bay, *I expect Duke Harless and Sir Rainos Ahlverez to be* very *unhappy when forty-nine thousand Imperial Charisian infantry and sixteen thousand Charisian dragoons put in their appearance on his flank.*

Pity about that.

. XX .
City of Manchyr,
Princedom of Corisande

The cheers and street music were reassuring, but Sir Koryn Gahrvai would have been far happier ordering Cathedral Square completely cleared. In fact, he had a squadron of Sir Alyk Ahrthyr's cavalry handy to clear it *now* if the need arose, although he hoped to Langhorne that it wouldn't. And there wasn't any reason it should, really.

He told himself that rather firmly and wondered why he couldn't get himself to take his own word for it.

It wasn't that he doubted that the majority of Corisande accepted the truth of who'd murdered Prince Hektor and his older son, who'd tried to murder Prince Daivyn and Princess Irys, and who'd saved the heir to the throne and his sister. Nor did he doubt that most of that majority accepted Parliament's decision to integrate Corisande into the Charisian Empire. That acceptance was more grudging than he might have liked for many of them, but it would have been unrealistic to expect otherwise. It was going to take a while for the Princedom's people to get past the fact that they'd been annexed by an opponent who'd defeated them with humiliating ease and speed.

I probably shouldn't blame any of them for feeling that way, he thought, surveying the packed square and listening to the enormous crowd. *After all, I was the one in command of the army that got its arse kicked so expeditiously.*

His lips twitched with a little much-needed amusement

as he recalled just how speedily Emperor Cayleb had kicked the arse in question. He'd seen enough since then to know which side he supported in Charis' war against the Group of Four, however, despite any damage to his pride. Besides, getting oneself trounced by someone like Cayleb Ahrmahk was hardly something to be ashamed of. In fact, Gahrvai took a certain pride from the fact that it had taken five months for Cayleb to finish him off.

That was better than anyone else had done against the Charisian emperor.

And if you let anything happen to his adopted son and Princess Irys on their wedding day, you'd better find a really deep *hole to hide in*, he told himself, and discovered he no longer felt the least temptation to smile.

It wasn't anything he could put a finger on, nothing so definite as a clear suspicion and certainly not the result of anything remotely like evidence, yet he couldn't suppress that crawling sensation between his shoulder blades. Zhaspahr Clyntahn's "Rakurai" had killed close to a thousand civilians right here in Corisande, after all. Of course, they'd been careful to leave notes emphasizing that they were attacking only *Charisian* targets— striking back at the invaders of their homeland (despite the fact that precious few of them had been born in Corisande)—and that any civilian casualties had been unavoidable. The clear implication had been that anyone who got close enough to the heretical enemy to be killed or injured in an attack had probably had it coming, yet they *had* drawn the distinction. It seemed unlikely they could be stupid enough to attack someone as beloved as Princess Irys on her wedding day, and they hadn't attacked *anyone* in over three months, yet that crawling sensation persisted stubbornly. . . .

He'd been over and over the security planning, rehearsed his men and officers, altered the pattern each time in subtle ways to throw off anyone who might have been watching and timing them. He'd scanned every note from the network of *seijins* Merlin Athrawes had established here in Corisande and put a thousand of his men into civilian clothes, scattered throughout the crowd to watch for anything remotely out of the ordinary. There was nothing he'd left undone, no indication of anything approaching a plot, and yet . . . and yet. . . .

You're just waiting for the other shoe to drop out of sheer nerves, he told himself yet again. *Probably because of what almost happened to Sharleyan and some perverse fear of history repeating itself. Well, and because it's a lot better to worry about something that doesn't happen than to overlook something that does. I'll settle for the insomnia and be glad of it if staying up nights worrying gets us through this in one piece.*

They'd gotten past young Daivyn's coronation without disaster, he reminded himself. And the enlarged Regency Council had been seated, the newly crowned Prince of Corisande had affixed his signature to the writ seeking membership in the Charisian Empire, and Empress Sharleyan was due in Corisande in the next month or two to formally accept Daivyn's oath. The wedding was the last hurdle they had to clear before her arrival, and he scolded himself once more for feeling so anxious. A certain amount of concern was one thing. Indeed, as the senior officer of the reconstituted Royal Corisandian Army, it was his responsibility to feel that concern. And—

The cheering rose to a crescendo that drowned the street music and buried the trumpet fanfare, as Princess Irys and the Duke of Darcos emerged from Manchyr Palace and started across the square.

▼ ▼ ▼

I wonder if she's *nervous,* Hektor Aplyn-Ahrmahk thought as he forced himself to maintain the properly decorous pace down the wide, shallow steps with Irys' featherlight fingers on his left forearm. He concentrated on the count in his head, timing the paces properly and trying not to think about the havoc Cayleb would cheerfully have wrought upon the wedding planners' precious protocol, since laughter would probably have screwed up his count. He'd really rather be Cayleb, though, he admitted wistfully.

Of course she's nervous, he scolded himself. *On the other hand, she's probably a lot less nervous than you are. She couldn't possibly be* more *nervous! Why couldn't this be something* simple *like leading a boarding action or quelling a mutiny or fighting a hurricane on a lee shore?*

The thought actually made him feel better, and he darted a glance at her from the corner of his eye. The fussy little man who'd drilled him on proper procedure had made it abundantly clear that he wasn't supposed to actually *look* at Irys until they got into the Cathedral. Which was pretty stupid, in Hektor's opinion. If he wasn't supposed to look at her, why hadn't the people in charge—and who *was* in charge, anyway? The one thing he knew for certain was that neither he nor *Irys* were!—made sure they arrived at the Cathedral separately? What? He was supposed to pretend he didn't *want* to look at her? That she was a complete stranger he'd just happened to meet on the way to church this morning? No doubt political theater had its place, but he was pretty sure he and Irys weren't fooling anyone about their feelings. Besides, the Corisandian press had become quite a bit freer since Hektor Daykyn's death, and the broadsheets had wasted an inordinate amount of ink gushing over the "love match" between the princess and her "heroic Charisian rescuer."

Blech.

For once, though, they'd actually gotten something right. Hektor would have preferred a lot less emphasis on his "heroism," and no doubt the more cynical among his fiancée's people figured it was all a coldly calculated marriage of state, with everyone playing his or her scripted role, no matter what anyone said. That was fair enough in some ways, he supposed, since it *was* a marriage of state. But he knew his adoptive mother too well to think for one minute that it had sprung solely from Sharleyan Ahrmahk's cold calculation. He'd seen her and Cayleb together too often to believe she would condemn him or Irys to a loveless match purely for matters of state. And hard as it had been for him to believe it, Irys Daykyn did love him. Beautiful, smart, poised, graceful, insightful, courageous, and with a core of unyielding steel, she actually loved him.

Thank You, God, he thought very quietly and sincerely, and the butterflies beating about so fiercely in his middle stilled their wings. *I don't know what I did to deserve this, but thank You.*

Voices roared on every hand as he and Irys crossed Cathedral Square down the cleared lane between the lines of handpicked members of the Royal Corisandian Army. The rifles coming up to port arms in formal salute as he and Irys passed were polished, but he had no doubt they were loaded, and those glittering bayonets had a far more serious purpose than mere ceremony. He saw eyes watching the crowd alertly, and mounted cavalry sat their horses, elevated enough to see far out over the cheering Corisandians who packed the square. There were no Charisian troops present today. This day belonged to Corisande and to Princess Irys Daykyn, and if he wasn't supposed to look at her he could at least glance at the intense, focused expressions of the men charged to keep the two of them safe on the endless walk to the Cathedral where Klairmant Gairlyng and Maikel Staynair awaited them. They were very reassuring, those expressions, especially with so many thousands of voices battering them with thunder.

▼ ▼ ▼

Koryn Gahrvai breathed a huge sigh of relief as his princess and the duke made it safely to the Cathedral. If it had been left up to him, they would have made the trip in a closed coach with three other coaches in the same procession as decoys. He didn't care if it was scarcely two hundred yards from the Palace to the Cathedral! For that matter, if it had been left up to him, he would have sent their coach to Charis to be plated with the same armor they'd put on those ironclads of theirs! And then he would have posted a dozen riflemen on top of all four of the frigging coaches. And after that—

Oh, stop it! He shook his head. *Next thing you'll want is twelve-pounders on both sides of the square! Irys was pissed off enough when you hinted that it might be a good idea to use* one *carriage. She'd've ripped your head off and shoved it up a handy bodily orifice if you'd even suggested* using *four* of them!

No doubt she would have, yet over the last few five-days, he'd found himself deeply in sympathy with *Seijin* Merlin and Sergeant Seahamper. And unless he could escape to the Imperial Army, he was going to be stuck with overseeing their security—and Daivyn's—indefinitely. On the one hand, he loved his cousins and would never begrudge any duty to them. On the other, he really wasn't cut out for this sort of thing. Far better to put Charlz Doyal in charge of it. Well, Charlz and Earl Coris. If anyone could keep them safe, that was the pair for it. And if finding the very best qualified people and putting them in charge just happened to let Sir Koryn Gahrvai sneak off to the Army, well. . . .

He snorted and maintained his position. He truly regretted missing the ceremony, but his father was there to represent them both and *his* time was best spent out here, keeping an eye on things.

▼ ▼ ▼

The airy Cathedral was a blaze of tropical sunlight through stained glass, its jewel-colored beams striking down through a drifting canopy of incense while the choir's voices rose in hymns of celebration. Hektor and Irys walked slowly, steadily down the central aisle into that music and chiaroscuro of colored light, flanked by heaps of cut flowers and packed pews. Even here, Guardsmen and soldiers in immaculate uniforms stood watch along the Cathedral's walls. They would have been there for Irys under any circumstances, Hektor thought, but in another time and another world their tension level probably would have been far lower. And they certainly wouldn't have been worried about *him*.

It had taken time for that truth to sink home. He was

no longer merely a junior naval officer who happened to have added the name Ahrmahk to his own. He was no longer even a duke who was also a serving officer, expected to take his chances in the Crown's service like any other officer. He was still both of those things, but in another hour, he would also be a husband, married to the Prince of Corisande's sister, and those guards, those watchful, intent soldiers dedicated to keeping him alive, were about to become an inescapable part of his life. It was something Irys had always had to put up with, but it wasn't something about which Hektor Aplyn had ever worried his head, and a part of him longed to return to who he'd been before the Battle of Darcos Sound. Wanted desperately to run away from the responsibilities and burdens of who he'd become instead. A sense not of panic but of dread flowed through him like a minor descant, a thread of darkness weaving itself into the day's blazing joy and somehow making it even more precious. Everything in life carried its own price, he thought, and anyone who was unwilling to pay that price was unworthy of those who loved him.

▼ ▼ ▼

Maikel Staynair stood in the sanctuary beside Klairmant Gairlyng and watched the absurdly young couple walk gravely towards them. Young Hektor had become another son to him long ago, and Irys had become a beloved daughter during her time as his guest in Tellesberg.

No one would ever guess looking at them that they felt the least uncertainty, the tiniest trace of anxiety, he thought. Hektor would never be a handsome man, and he still had quite a bit of filling out to do. Yet today, in his lieutenant's dress uniform, his sword at his side, he looked every inch the man—not the *boy*—who'd saved the lives of Daivyn and Irys Daykyn. Few people had ever grown up as hard and as quickly as Hektor Aplyn-Ahrmahk, and fewer still had paid the price he had to do it, but God had builded well in that young man.

And beside him, as if she'd been born to stand at his side, Irys Daykyn with her hazel eyes, dark hair, strong chin, and composed, almost serene expression. Not yet quite twenty, and she'd seen so much, paid a price every bit as hard as Hektor's. His king had died in his arms, killed by the Navy her father had launched at the Kingdom of Charis' throat; her father and brother had been cut down by assassins in the streets of their own capital, and she'd known beyond any shadow of a doubt that Cayleb and Sharleyan Ahrmahk had ordered that assassination. She'd sworn her life to vengeance upon them . . . and today she was marrying their adopted son. Not because anyone had required her to, but because she wanted to. Because she'd had the strength and courage to look beyond what she'd known to see the truth she *hadn't* known. It would have been far easier for her to cling to the hatred, close her eyes to that truth, yet instead she'd found the bravery to trust the promise of her father's mortal enemies to protect her baby brother and prince, and in the process, she'd made their cause her own.

As the two of them reached the sanctuary, he remembered another wedding four years and seven thousand miles away from this one. Cayleb and Sharleyan hadn't been that much older than Irys and Hektor, and theirs, too, had been a "marriage of state," yet they'd found the strength and surety they'd needed in one another. So would Irys and Hektor, he thought. So would Irys and Hektor.

They stopped at the flower-decked rail, and he smiled upon them. One of the greatest joys of his priesthood were all the sons and daughters it had added to his life, and he'd been prouder of none of them than of the two who stood before him this day with their hands clasped, their heads high, and their eyes bright. But this was not his church, and this was not a Charisian wedding, and so he simply bowed ever so slightly to both of them and stood at Gairlyng's shoulder to assist.

"My children," the Archbishop of Corisande's voice

rolled clearly through the cathedral, "this is a great and joyous day! These two young people have come before you and before God and the Archangels to be joined in holy matrimony. It is the marriage of two people who I may tell you of my own personal knowledge love and respect one another deeply. It is the marriage of two hearts who wish to become one, to stand together in the face of all of life's tempests and temptations, sorrows and joys. And it is also the marriage of Corisande and Charis. Not because it was forced upon them, not because of calculation or ambition, but because in these two people's love for one another and in their determination to stand for the Light against all the works of Darkness, even in the face of Hell itself, we see ourselves and our future. Join them now, as they reach out to the Light from whence all of us came and to which in the fullness of time every true child of God must return. Celebrate with them, share their joy, witness their promise to one another, and pledge yourselves to that same great and glorious cause. Open your hearts, experience their love, and let all of us prove ourselves as fearless as they, willing—eager—as God's true children to follow where they lead."

It was very still, almost hushed throughout the enormous cathedral, and then Gairlyng smiled broadly and raised his hands.

"And now, dearly beloved," he said, "we have gathered together here in the sight of God and the Archangels, and in the face of this company, to join together this man and this woman in holy matrimony; which is an honorable estate, instituted of God and the Archangels, signifying unto us the mystical union that is between God and His Church; which is a holy estate which the Archangel Langhorne adorned and beautified with his presence in his time here upon Safehold, and is commended of the Archangel Bédard to be honorable among all men: and therefore is not by any to be entered into unadvisedly or lightly; but reverently, discreetly, advisedly, soberly, and in the fear of God. Into this holy estate these two persons present come now to be joined.

If any man can show just cause why they may not law-
fully be joined together, let him now speak, or else here-
after forever hold his peace."

▼ ▼ ▼

Irys Aplyn-Ahrmahk wondered if her smile was going to
split her face as she floated from Manchyr Cathedral on
the wings of the organ's wedding march. She clung to
Hektor's arm far more tightly—and possessively—than
she'd allowed herself to do on the way *into* the Cathedral. That was probably a breach of protocol, but he
was hers now, all hers, and this was their wedding day. All
those political calculations, all those details of procedure
and protocol and court etiquette, could take themselves
somewhere else. She'd worry about them again after
the honeymoon.

She giggled—positively, she *giggled*—at the thought,
stretching inside like a cat-lizard, reaching for the joy she'd
known was lost forever in those dreary years in Delferahk.
The sunlight beaming down was no more brilliant, no
more warming than the sunlight filling every nook and
cranny of her heart. Her brother was safe, confirmed in
his crown, and she, after so many storms and so much
despair, had come into the safe harbor of the young
man she'd discovered so unexpectedly that she loved.
It was—

She had absolutely no warning, but suddenly Hektor
had his arms wrapped around, twisting her off her
feet, throwing her toward the ground. She stiffened,
shock whiplashing through her, and there was a crack of
thunder like the end of the world, a brilliant flash half
screened by Hektor's body, a sound like a thousand hissing serpents, another sound like a baseball hitting a
catcher's mitt, and his sudden, convulsive gasp. There
were the beginnings of screams, the sudden realization
of terror, and then his weight was coming down upon
her, horribly and horrifyingly limp. Something hot and
wet sprayed across her wedding gown, her head struck
the cathedral step, and her own frantic cry of denial spiraled into the darkness with her.

"It's my fault. It's all my damned fault," Koryn Gahrvai grated. "I knew something was wrong—I *knew* it—and I still—"

"No, it isn't your fault," his father said flatly. Earl Anvil Rock's eyes were dark, his face haggard, as he looked at his son, but there was no doubt in his voice. "We took every precaution we could think of, short of actually clearing the square, and Irys and Phylyp were right. This wedding was a crucial component of our transition into the Empire. If we'd let it appear we were that frightened of how our own people would react to it, it would've been disastrous."

"And this *wasn't*?" The black stitches closing the long, deep gash in Gahrvai's right cheek stood out plainly in the lamplight, and he carried his left arm in a sling. "Langhorne, Father! We've got over two hundred dead—and twice that many injured—in addition to Hektor and Irys!"

"I know. I know!" Anvil Rock's expression was bitter. "But we never thought they'd be so *stupid*! Even the damned 'Rakurai' should've known better than to attack *Irys. . . .*"

His father was right, Gahrvai knew, not that it made him feel one bit better. It had been an act of madness to attack Irys directly, especially on this of all days. Whatever the Temple's supporters might think, the fury it must generate among those who loved her and her brother would be incalculable. They'd known that and expected the *Rakurai* to be smart enough to realize the same thing. And so even though they'd conscientiously tried to include such threats in their calculations, they'd never really believed it would happen.

They'd been wrong.

It wasn't like the mammoth explosions with which the "Rakurai" had first announced their existence. He supposed they should all be grateful for that much, although it was hard to be grateful for *anything* at the moment. They had no witnesses—no *surviving* witnesses—who'd seen exactly what had happened, but evidence suggested it had been the work of a lone fanatic. *How* he'd gotten his explosives into position remained a mystery, but at least they knew *where* he'd been: somewhere in the first few rows of the space which had been roped off for those who required assistance to get about or were unable to stand for lengthy periods.

People grown frail with age, no longer able to care for themselves properly, he thought bitterly. People—young or old—with spine fever, who'd had limbs amputated or permanently crippled by accident or disease. People who'd already suffered more than enough without Sir Koryn Gahrvai allowing someone to end their lives in one moment of transcendent horror.

The semi-circle of carnage around the assassin's location had been incredible. Bodies had been ripped apart, as if by a charge of canister or grapeshot, and that was precisely what had happened. Whoever the murderous bastard had been, he'd clearly known what he was doing and he'd managed, somehow, to get the equivalent of one of the Charisians' "sweepers" past all of Gahrvai's precautions and watchers. The explosion had sent scores—probably hundreds—of old-fashioned half-inch musket balls scything outward in a fan directed at the wedding procession.

Sixty-two of the known dead had been Gahrvai's soldiers and Guardsmen. Their bodies had absorbed much of the blast and fury, but over a hundred of the civilians gathered outside the Cathedral had either been killed outright by the explosion or trampled to death in the panic which followed.

"Whoever planned this knew exactly what he was doing," Anvil Rock said after a long, brooding moment. "He got his frigging bomb into exactly the right position and detonated it at exactly the right moment."

"Why not on the way in?" Gahrvai asked. His father looked at him, and he shrugged. "It probably doesn't matter, but why did he wait? As you say, he obviously knew what he was doing, so why wait? Every minute he sat there was a minute one of my men—or even *I*, God help us—might've spotted him, realized something was out of true. So why not kill them as soon as possible rather than risk the delay?"

"I don't know. How should any of us know what was going through his head?" Anvil Rock stumped to the window and looked out at the thousands of votive candles burning all across the enormous square in the windless night. "Maybe he was waiting until they were married so he'd be able to claim *Irys* was a Charisian. Maybe that was part of his 'message.' Or maybe he wasn't in position yet when they walked into the Cathedral."

"He was," Gahrvai said flatly. His father turned his head, arching one eyebrow at him, and he grimaced. "No one was admitted to that section without a written reservation, issued by the Archbishop's Guard after certification that it was needed and checked against the master list by two separate people, and no one was allowed to enter or leave it starting an hour before Hektor and Irys left the Palace." He shook his head. "No, he was there, and somehow he got past all of us. We *let* him do this, Father."

"We didn't 'let' anyone do anything, Koryn!" Anvil Rock sounded decidedly testier. "We struck the best balance we could between security and the need to allow public access and—"

The door opened abruptly and a grim-faced Charlz Doyal came through it. Father and son turned to face him, and he raised the envelope in his right hand.

"This was delivered to the Palace ten minutes ago," he said. "I've got the messenger in custody, but I don't think he had any idea what was inside it. In fact, I think he's telling the truth when he says he doesn't even know who he was delivering it for."

"I assume it has something to do with the attack?"

Gahrvai said, and Doyal nodded. "In that case, what makes you so sure he wasn't part of it from the beginning?"

"Because he's a Bédardist monk from the Monastery of Saint Krystyphyr and he was told the message—addressed to you, by the way, My Lord," Doyal said, glancing at the earl "—was from Father Symyn."

"What?" Anvil Rock's eyes widened in confusion, then narrowed in sudden speculation. "Symyn *Hahlek*? Why him?"

"According to the monk—and I'll send a semaphore message to his abbot as soon as it's daylight to confirm all this—the letter was handed to the monastery's hosteller by a Langhornite under-priest who guested at Saint Krystyphyr's on his way to Lian on Archbishop Klairmant's business. When he stopped, he discovered he'd inadvertently brought the letter with him, and his business in Lian was too urgent for him to lose three days returning to Manchyr to deliver it in person. So he asked the abbot to have it delivered to you for him. Our monk was selected to do the delivering, and I'd guess he got to Manchyr at least a day earlier than our Langhornite expected, given all the traffic clogging the roads with the wedding coming up. If he'd been just an hour quicker, he'd've gotten to the Palace before the wedding party left. As it was, and after the explosion in the square, it took him hours to find someone willing to admit him to deliver it." The man who'd become the Regency Council's chief of intelligence shook his head. "I don't think he had a thing to do with it, My Lord. And I *do* think whoever used him for this wanted to point a finger in Father Symyn's direction."

"And what's in the damned letter?" Anvil Rock demanded.

"See for yourself, My Lord."

Doyal held out the letter. Anvil Rock took it with the air of a man reaching for a venomous serpent and unfolded it slowly, then tilted it to allow his son to read over his shoulder.

To the everlastingly damned and accursed heretics, blasphemers, and demon-worshippers who have rebelled against God's will, murdered His priests, joined themselves to Shan-wei's cause, entered into the Dark with all their hearts, and made themselves the enemies of all God's faithful sons and daughters. Know that you have shown your true colors as the betrayers of Corisande and all her people, as well as God, the Archangels, and Mother Church. If you will embrace the harlot of Charis and the servants of Shan-wei, if you will sell all of Corisande into Charisian bondage, you make yourselves the enemies of every true child of God and lover of Corisandian freedom. You think yourselves safe, protected by the bayonets of the soldiers who slavishly serve you in defiance of the Grand Vicar's writ of excommunication. You believe not even God can reach you, and in your corruption and arrogance, you raise your hands against Him Whose Archangels gave life to this entire world. You set your will against His, you seek to deliver all the people of this realm of Corisande into the chains of Hell, and in the dark recesses of your hearts, you exult in the power you pervert in Shan-wei's name. But God can reach you, through the hands of His servants, and we have taught you so this day. Be warned. This is but the first of the blows Langhorne's Rakurai have in store for any who renounce their true allegiance and duty to God and give themselves to the Dark, instead. Treason, blasphemy, heresy, and apostasy can be expunged only by blood, and expunged they assuredly will be.

There was no signature, and Gahrvai's eyes narrowed. Assuming there was an ounce of honesty in the person who'd written it, the letter confirmed that this had been the work of Clyntahn's "Rakurai." Of course it might equally well be intended as disinformation. He was rather at a loss to think of anyone else who might have been behind the attack, yet they'd had proof enough in Corisande that secular opponents to the Regency Council could seize upon religious pretexts to cover their own ambitions.

Then there was the supposed author of the letter. Symyn Hahlek was Archbishop Klairmant's senior and most trusted aide. No one who'd ever met Father Symyn would believe for a moment that he might have been involved in something like this. Unfortunately, the number of people who'd met him was minute compared to the number of people who *hadn't* met him. The fact that he was a native Corisandian might lend a certain credibility to the theory that his patriotism had been so outraged by the decision to join the Charisian Empire as to drive him into open rebellion, and the fact that the letter had been left at Saint Krystyphyr's by someone claiming to be a Langhornite could lend additional credence for those inclined to believe the worst, given that Hahlek was himself a Langhornite under-priest. And, of course, Archbishop Klairmant's aide would have been well placed to provide the assassin with the written reservation needed to get into position for the attack. There was no way in the world Hahlek had done anything of the sort, but the "Rakurai" had nothing to lose trying to drive a wedge between him and Archbishop Klairmant.

"Well," he said finally, taking the letter from his father and skimming it once again. "I'm not particularly inclined to take a mass murderer's word for the sanctity of his motives, and I'm certainly not prepared to accept that Father Symyn, of all people, would've been party to something like this."

"Neither am I." Anvil Rock snorted harshly. "Ambitious bastards, aren't they? Not content with implicating Father Symyn, they're ready to take a shot at Taryl, too!"

"Um?" Gahrvai looked up from the letter, frowning. Then his expression cleared. "I missed that one somehow, Father. You're right, though."

The supposed Langhornite's announced destination of Lian was the third largest town in the Earldom of Tartarian. Given how he'd directed their attention there, he'd almost certainly gone somewhere else entirely, but it would obviously be to Clyntahn's advantage if his killers could drive a wedge between Anvil Rock and Earl Tartarian, his closest friend and most trusted political ally. And what they might not be able to convince Anvil Rock of, they might hope to convince *Prince Daivyn* of. He was only a boy, and it wasn't unreasonable to assume that his grief and his hunger for vengeance upon his sister's murderers might cause him to turn upon those accused of complicity in her death.

"I wonder where else copies of this will turn up?" Gahrvai mused aloud after a moment. "Just sending it to the Palace seems a bit under ambitious."

"A good point," his father acknowledged.

"A *very* good point, in fact," Doyal agreed. "Remember *Seijin* Merlin's letter right after the Gray Lizard Square attack. He said Clyntahn sent out his killers solo, with specific orders not to build any sort of local network we might penetrate. If this was the work of the 'Rakurai' and they're operating true to form, there won't be anyone to tack up broadsheets or stand on street corners haranguing people. So if we do see copies of this letter on walls throughout the Princedom, we'll know we're dealing with something else. Frankly, I hope we are. A bigger network could do more damage, but it would also give us—and the *seijins*—a better chance of penetrating them."

"I'd like that, Charlz," Koryn Gahrvai said very quietly, turning back to the window and the candle flames burning in vigil as the grieving people of Corisande prayed for their princess. "I'd like that a lot."

▼ ▼ ▼

Irys Aplyn-Ahrmahk sat beside her husband's bed. The right side of her face was one massive bruise, the dull ache of a broken cheekbone marched throbbingly through her, and her vision was curiously unclear, wavering like something seen through heat shimmer and illuminated with waves of color which had nothing to do with lamplight. At another time, she might have noticed that pain, worried about that lack of clarity. Tonight she did neither. She simply sat, holding Hektor's right hand in hers, listening to the harsh, wet sound of his breathing, and her eyes were dry. She was past the tears now, at least for the moment, and there was a great, aching emptiness at the core of her.

Hektor had saved her life. There was no question about that. But the cost of her salvation came too dear. He'd shielded her with his own body, and in protecting her, he'd been hit three times himself—in the left arm, in the back of his right thigh, and on his right shoulder blade.

The leg wound was the least severe, a deep, ugly trough ripped through the big muscle on the back of his thigh as if by some huge talon. He'd lost far too much blood from it, but the arm was worse. Under other circumstances, the Pasqualates would almost certainly have amputated just below the elbow, and even if by some miracle the arm had been saved, it would have been severely impaired, even crippled, for life.

But that wasn't going to be an issue, she told herself drearily. Because the bullet which had hit his shoulder had passed completely through his body, ripping its way through his right lung, missing his heart by fractions of an inch, and doing God only knew how much other damage on its way through.

The senior Pasqualate had faced her with the stern compassion and honesty of his Order when she'd demanded the truth. Hektor, her husband, was dying. No surgeon's skill, no apothecary's knowledge, could change that. In truth, the Pasqualates had no idea why or how he had survived this long.

I'm sorry, love. The thought floated with a fragile, harrowed serenity over the empty ice of the future which had seemed so bright this morning. *I'm so sorry. I should've known what that monster in Zion would do when you saved Daivyn and me from his butchers. I should've realized he'd move heaven and earth to correct his failure, and I should've stayed as far away as possible from you. My father, my brother, and now you.*

Everyone I let myself love, he *marks for death. But he missed me.* She laid a slender hand on Hektor's forehead. *He missed me. And someday, somehow, somewhere, my love, I will rip out his black heart with my bare hands, and the only thing I'll ask—the only thing I will go to God on my knees for—is that he know who's killing him.*

"Irys?"

She looked up.

Maikel Staynair stood beside her chair, still wearing his vestments, splashed with Hektor's blood, although he'd insisted that she change out of her blood-soaked wedding gown. Staynair had been among the first to reach them, the one who'd applied pressure to the sucking chest wound, gotten tourniquets around the wounded leg and arm, while Irys was still unconscious. Without him, Hektor would have died long before the Pasqualates got to him, and he'd refused to leave Hektor's side, or hers, since.

"He's still alive, Your Eminence," she said quietly, smoothing the dark, curly hair. "Still alive for now."

Staynair's eyes were gentle and compassionate, without the stark despair she knew must look back at him from her own. It was the nature of his vocation, she supposed. She recognized his own grief for Hektor, his own anger, yet for him there was still a future. There would always be a future for him, even beyond the dark wall of death, one formed and revealed to his inner eye by the depth of his faith, and she knew even now how important that shield of his faith would be to her in the days to come. Yet just now, at this moment, it was more than she could share, and she felt one of the tears she'd been certain she'd exhausted hours ago trickle slowly down her cheek.

The archbishop's gentle finger wiped it away and he put his arm around her in wordless comfort.

"You should go, Your Eminence," she said, leaning her head against his support. "There must be hundreds of other people who need your comfort and care, and you've already spent hours with me. Hektor doesn't know you're here, and I already know how much you love both of us. You've given me that, and I'm not so selfish as to keep you when others need the same gift from you and there's nothing more you can do, anyway."

"You're wrong, my dear," Staynair said softly, hugging her more tightly. "There is something I can do, and I can't leave until I've done it."

Irys' throat tightened, and she wanted to deny what he'd just said. Hektor had already received the last rites; the only thing Staynair could do for them now was to be here to share the moment when her husband took his last breath and her heart shattered forever. She knew how much she would need that comfort, and yet if she sent him away, perhaps the moment would never come. If he wasn't here, if he couldn't comfort her, perhaps Hektor wouldn't die after all. It was irrational, and she knew it, yet she opened her mouth to argue anyway, only to pause as Staynair straightened suddenly and turned his head towards the glass doors to the bedchamber's balcony.

There was something about his expression—a sudden flicker of something that might almost have been joy blended with worry—and then he turned back to her. He captured the hand which wasn't holding Hektor's between both of his own large, powerful palms, and looked deep into her eyes.

"My daughter," he said softly, "I'm about to ask you to do something you shouldn't have to do. Something you may not be *able* to do. But I know the strength of you, and I know the love within you, and so I ask it of you anyway."

"Your Eminence?"

She felt the weight of his words even through her exhausted despair, and she was suddenly afraid. Afraid in a new and different way, as if she stood on a precipice above a deep gorge filled with a howling tempest. It was absurd, and she had no idea what that gorge might be or why the wind shrieked so as it hurtled through it, yet it seemed so clear, so *real*. . . .

"A moment, my dear."

He gave her hand one last squeeze, then crossed to the

diamond-paned doors. He reached for the latch and looked over his shoulder at her.

"You've been through enough for a dozen princesses already today, my child," he said quietly. "I would prefer not to put you through still more, but I have no choice. I ask you to trust me and to believe me when I say that what I see in what's about to happen is the direct and personal finger of God reaching into this mortal world."

"You're frightening me, Your Eminence," she said, hazel eyes looking deep into the serene faith of his darker, gentler gaze, and he smiled.

"I don't intend to, because there's nothing here to fear. Yet there *is* ample cause for wonder. Be open to it, my daughter."

His fingers found the latch and her grip tightened around Hektor's cold, limp hand as he turned it. And then her nostrils flared, her eyes opening in shock and disbelief, as a very familiar sapphire-eyed man in the blackened breastplate and uniform of the Charisian Imperial Guard stepped into the bedchamber from the fourth-story balcony.

"I came as quickly as I could, Your Highness," Merlin Athrawes said softly.

. XXII .
Nimue's Cave,
The Mountains of Light,
The Temple Lands

"She took that better than I expected, really," Cayleb Ahrmahk said soberly. "A lot better."

"I hate having put her in that position," Sharleyan Ahrmahk said from her cabin aboard HMS *Southern Star*, midway between Chisholm and Corisande. "I know what it's like when something like this comes at you cold."

"Something like this?" her husband repeated. "Sharley, right at the top of my head I can't think of anything else *remotely* like this."

"I don't know about that, Cayleb." Nahrmahn Baytz' tone was thoughtful. "We could always try telling her that there's the ghost of this overweight little prince who haunts a computer buried forty thousand feet underneath Mount Olympus in the middle of the Temple Lands. That might come *pretty* close."

"I notice none of us considered talking to the Brethren before we acted," Maikel Staynair put in from Manchyr, and Merlin barked a laugh.

"Given that you're the one who put out the call for me in the first place, I think this time around we'll just let *you* do the explaining, Your Eminence."

"Oh, nonsense!" Staynair replied in a tone that verged on the smug. "You have more experience—and seniority!—than anyone else, Merlin. I'm sure they'll take it much more calmly from you."

"Sure they will."

Merlin shook his head and leaned back in the comfortable chair in the cave under the Mountains of Light. There'd been only two good things about the last nightmare day. The first was that he'd long ago injected Hektor and Irys—and Davyn and Earl Coris, for that matter—with the same nanotech with which he'd injected every member of the inner circle. And the second was that Major Athrawes had already been dispatched by Emperor Cayleb on another unspecified mission. His actual mission had been to drop in on Duke Eastshare as Ahbraim Zhevons, but that had been aborted the instant Owl reported the attack in Manchyr and his recon skimmer had gone hurtling towards Corisande at far too many times the speed of sound. Each time he made one of those insane rushes he risked attracting the attention of the bombardment system's sensors which was why he'd returned to Nimue's Cave at a far more leisurely pace.

There'd really been no pressing need to return to the cave at all, but he'd needed a place to which he could retreat. A place where he could be with friends, one where he could lower his barriers while they tried to deal with the day's earthquake events and their consequences. And a place, he admitted to himself, where he felt . . . secure.

I named it "Nimue's Cave" for a reason, and not just because I decided to become someone named Merlin. It's always been my "place of power," my sanctum where my familiar and all that arcane knowledge reside, and just this moment, I need to be here, in the middle of who Nimue was and what brought me to Safehold in the first place.

He closed his eyes, recalling the desperate race to Manchyr, remembering his dread of how Irys would react to his appearance. He'd developed a deep respect—and a deeper affection—for Hektor Daykyn's daughter, but no one had prepared her for the truth about him, about Safehold, about the Archangels, or about Nimue Alban's true mission. They'd thought they had plenty of time, ten *years* of it, to do that preparing and decide whether or not to tell her those terrible, consuming, impossible-to-believe truths. But fate—or perhaps Maikel's "finger of God"—had forced his hand much as it had been forced by Sharleyan's attempted assassination. And so he'd raced to save Hektor's life . . . dreading all the way that he would be too late and, even more, what he might be forced to do instead if Irys proved unready to accept who and what he truly was when he stepped into the bedchamber with the medical kit.

This time he hadn't had to make the decision entirely on his own. Oh, it had been *his* decision, and he would have made it in exactly the same way even if every other member of the inner circle had opposed it. There was no other decision he *could* have made, any more than he could have permitted a trio of krakens to devour a boatload of children on a long-ago day on Helen Island.

But neither Cayleb, nor Sharleyan, nor Nahrmahn, nor Maikel had hesitated. He was perfectly well aware of the part their love for Hektor and their deep affection for Irys had played in that. Yet there'd been other reasons—

hardheaded, pragmatic reasons—as well, for Hektor's death at the Rakurai's hands on the very day of his wedding could have had cataclysmic consequences.

The reaction in Old Charis scarcely bore thinking on, given the young Duke of Darcos' place in the hearts of its people. He himself remained largely unaware of it, yet they remembered all too clearly how Hektor Aplyn and King Haarahld had fought back-to-back, alone against twice a hundred enemies on the quarterdeck of Haarahld's flagship. They remembered how their king had died in his arms, and that king's final words to an eleven-year-old midshipman had become part of their national heritage. And they'd seen that midshipman grow into an officer of whom their king would have been proud and been enthralled by his rescue of the enemy prince and princess they'd taken to their hearts.

The polarizing reaction in Corisande could have been even more disastrous, especially if neither Irys nor Daivyn could be told the truth. Those who opposed Corisande's union with Charis might well have taken heart, found a rallying point to do more than simply resent that union. And the effect on Irys and Daivyn, both of whom had come to love him deeply, would have been impossible to predict. The odds were that it would have driven them to oppose the Group of Four even more bitterly, but at what cost? Would it have poisoned them with hatred? And how could they ever have been told the truth later . . . and known Hektor might have been saved after all if only the inner circle had been willing to trust them with that truth then?

And, finally, there'd been the chill, pragmatic calculus of empire. It was true that Sharleyan had stipulated that Irys must wed Hektor because she'd known they loved one another, yet that hadn't been her only reason, as both Hektor and Irys had realized. That sign of the union of the House of Daykyn with the House of Ahrmahk was of untold value on a planet which still thought as much or more in terms of dynasties as in terms of nationhood. For Corisande and Charis alike, that marriage was the proof they stood together in the teeth of Mother Church's Jihad, and they simply could not afford to lose it.

But we almost did anyway, he thought somberly. *If I hadn't pumped everybody's base nanotech after I lost Haarahld, we would've lost him. Even with it, it was a damned near thing. Of course, that leaves us a few problems of its own.*

"I wish we could get him back here to the medical unit," he said out loud. "He's going to be five-days recovering from this in Manchyr. And I doubt he's going to have much use of his left hand afterward, anyway."

"We all wish that, Merlin," Cayleb said quietly. "But how the hell do we explain his recovering from those wounds in no more than a day or two? And what happens when one of the Palace servants or Pasqualates come to check on him and he's off in the Mountains of Light being miraculously cured? Not even Maikel and Irys together could've kept *someone* from discovering he'd disappeared down a rabbit hole, and then we'd all be royally screwed."

"I know that. For that matter," Merlin's lips twitched in an unwilling smile, "Irys knows it. In fact, she explained it to me at some length when I mentioned the cave. It's going to be hard enough for the Safeholdian medical establishment to accept how quickly he recovers if we leave him in Manchyr!"

"The problem won't be how quickly he recovers," Staynair said dryly. "It's going to be the fact that he survived *to* recover."

"You're probably right about that," Merlin acknowledged, and shook his head. "I always knew upgrading you all to mil-spec nannies could . . . complicate things if you got hurt, but this—!"

"Speaking as someone else they kept alive long enough for you to get there, I think it was a very good idea," Nahrmahn put in.

"I'm sure you do, but however right Maikel may be, there *are* going to be questions about his recovery."

"Nonsense, Merlin!" Sharleyan's smile was almost

impish. "Irys will just keep him in bed and nurse him herself, without sharing him with a batch of healers who might notice things they shouldn't. And, no, I don't think she'd want us to deliberately extend his convalescence just so she could play doctor. But do any of you think word won't leak about how Princess Irys is personally nursing her husband back to health? For that matter, you know as well as I do that public opinion's going to decide it was her care and love that kept him alive when every healer despaired and everyone knew he was dying!"

"Exactly," Nahrmahn agreed. "That's just how the story will play out in Corisande. And with just a little encouragement, we can probably see to it that it plays out the same way in Chisholm, Emerald, Old Charis, and Tarot, too."

"That's dreadfully calculating of you, my son," Staynair observed. "Not that I think you're wrong, of course."

Several people chuckled, as much in a release of tension as in amusement, and Merlin smiled. Trust Sharley and Nahrmahn to put their fingers on the political advantages to be wrung from the situation. For that matter, he was pretty sure Irys was thinking along exactly the same lines by now.

She'd actually accepted the truth more rapidly than Sharleyan had after the attack on Saint Agtha's. Part of that had probably been due to her desperate hope that Hektor might be saved after all. Sharleyan had been dealing with the astonishment of her *own* survival after the fact, not of the man she loved *before* he'd been saved. Then there'd been Maikel Staynair's presence to vouch for Merlin's nondemonic origins. And, Merlin suspected, the same heart hunger which had drawn her to the Royal College had quickened at the revelation of just how big and magnificent the universe truly was.

He hadn't had time to prepare coms for her and Hektor, but Owl was busy putting together their communicators—among other things. He was sure they'd get the hang of them quickly with Staynair right there in Manchyr to tutor them, and he'd promised to personally deliver them, if somewhat more sedately, before he returned to Siddar City.

And I'll deliver their "antiballistic undies" at the same time. His smile faded at the thought. *If they'd had them before the damned bomb, neither of them would've been hurt in the first place! At least now I can get them into the same sort of protection as the rest of the circle. And with Irys and Hektor on board, we'll be able to do the same thing for Daivyn, too.*

"Have we figured out how they pulled it off?" he asked, opening his eyes, and Nahrmahn's image shrugged.

"I doubt we'll ever have all the details, but Owl and I have been over the SNARCs' imagery. We're pretty sure we know how the attack was executed, even if we don't have a clue how the assassin got herself to Corisande originally."

"*Her*self?" Staynair repeated sharply.

"Yes, Your Eminence," Owl replied. "We have no imagery of the device's actual detonation, but we do have imagery from before and after the attack, and I believe Prince Nahrmahn's analysis of what happened is correct."

"And that analysis is what, Nahrmahn?" Cayleb asked, frowning intently.

"We examined the imagery of the reserved section as closely as possible," Nahrmahn said. "It was crowded and rather hectic, but we were able to isolate at least some images of almost everyone in it. There was one person, an older man in a wheelchair, who attracted my attention because I couldn't understand why he was there."

"To see the wedding, I would've assumed," Sharleyan said.

"And I wouldn't've disagreed, except for the fact that he wasn't paying any attention to it at all. He just sat there in the wheelchair. In fact, I'd judge he was in the final stages of the gray mists."

Merlin's lips tightened at the fresh reminder of everything Langhorne had cost the people of Safehold. "The gray mists" was the Safeholdian term for what had once been known as Alzheimer's disease . . . which Old Terra had conquered more than three hundred years before humanity ever met the Gbaba.

"His head was down, he displayed the classic joint contractures, and he seemed totally disconnected from his surroundings, even when the cheers were loudest," Nahrmahn continued. "So the more I looked at him, the more I wondered why he was there. I thought at first that he might've been brought by a son or daughter who wanted to include him in one last family outing, but he was escorted by an attendant—a woman—in the uniform of a Pasqualate lay sister. It was still possible he had family elsewhere in the crowd, but it seemed more likely that if they'd known they were going to be separated, his family would've left him in peace at home. So I asked Owl to take a closer look at him."

He paused, and Owl responded smoothly to the conversational cue he wouldn't even have recognized a year earlier.

"I did as His Highness requested," the AI said, "and determined that the individual's wheelchair was not of a standard design. Instead of the open framework usually employed in order to keep the weight low, this wheelchair's back and seat were boxed in. It was impossible to determine exactly how the covering was contrived or out of what material, but the enclosed volume measured approximately five and a half cubic feet. If it were packed solely with gunpowder, that volume could contain a charge of over three hundred pounds.

"Analysis of the damage patterns suggests the explosion was, indeed, centered upon the wheelchair in question. From the explosion's evident power, a substantial portion of the volume must have been used to shape and aim the directional blast rather than filled to capacity with powder. I estimate that there were some fifteen hundred musket balls in the device, which would have come to approximately forty pounds of lead, propelled by an equal weight of gunpowder."

Merlin winced. Ten pounds of gunpowder were sufficient to throw a thirty-pound round shot three thousand yards. Hektor and Irys had been less than thirty yards from a charge four times that large.

"Assuming my analysis is accurate," Owl continued, "it is remarkable there were so few fatalities. I attribute the relatively low death toll to the directional nature of the device and the close spacing of the Guardsmen and soldiers lining that portion of the route. Their bodies absorbed much of the blast, which is undoubtedly why so few of them survived. The relatively low placement of the charge, resulting from the need to conceal it within the wheelchair, also contributed to the reduced death toll."

A chill ran through Merlin's molycirc nerves as the AI laid out his and Nahrmahn's analysis. Owl had developed a much more acute sense of empathy in the course of his interactions with Nahrmahn, and Merlin suddenly realized how little his dispassionate tone had to do with lack of imagination. He looked up at the screen displaying Owl's avatar and saw the awareness in those sapphire eyes so much like his own. Saw the intelligence which had never been flesh-and-blood seeking to distance itself from the horror of Cathedral Square.

"The application for the reserved area is obviously false, since the hospice it supposedly came from isn't missing any lay sisters or patients," Nahrmahn said into the silence which had fallen. "We've been attempting to backtrack both of them, but we haven't had much luck. Unless someone reports him missing, we'll never know who was in that wheelchair or where he came from. As for the 'lay sister,' hair color, complexion, and facial features all suggest a Mainlander from one of the more northern realms, which would be consistent with Clyntahn's methodology. She was sent in from outside Corisande, never made contact with any native Temple Loyalists, never discussed her mission with anyone, and in the process managed to avoid our SNARCs' notice just as effectively as she avoided Doyal's and Gahrvai's."

"Dear God," Cayleb murmured. He sat very still, then inhaled deeply and shook himself. "How in God's name are we supposed to stop people like that? People who cross thousands of miles of ocean simply to kill as many people as possible in God's name? People we can't even see coming because they don't talk to anyone—*anyone at all*—about their missions?"

"Unless we want to ask Aivah to try and put one of her people inside the Inquisition in Zion, we can't," Merlin replied.

"Owl and I have developed a new search subroutine for the SNARCs watching the Temple Lands outside Zion," Nahrmahn offered. "We're trying to improve and refine the satellite imagery of Zion itself, as well. Hopefully, we'll achieve sufficiently detailed resolution from the orbital sensors to recognize individual faces of people entering or leaving the Temple and, especially, the Inquisition's offices. We believe we may be able to identify at least some of Clyntahn's potential agents, and we intend to run facial recognition on everyone present at any major public event anywhere in the Empire from now on. Owl needs to generate a secondary AI to manage the sheer data flow, but if we happen to identify someone whose image we collected in the Temple Lands standing around outside Tellesberg Cathedral, for example, we can hopefully steer security forces towards him."

"That may help a lot," Sharleyan said. "In the meantime, though, I'm worried by the fact that Clyntahn used a woman for this." She grimaced. "It's just that Clyntahn's such a confirmed lecher I'm surprised the idea occurred to him." She grimaced again, with far more distaste. "As far as he's concerned women exist for only one purpose, and it isn't to use their brains or fight as God's warriors."

"That's probably true in his case." Merlin's grimace was oddly like Sharleyan's, with more than an echo of Nimue Alban. "Unfortunately, I suspect Archbishop Wyllym's a bit more broad-minded in that respect, and do any of us think a woman can't be just as . . . committed as any man? The fact that the Safehold mindset tends to pigeonhole women as 'female: no threat' would probably work in their favor when it comes to penetrating our defenses, too. But if they *are* starting to send out female 'Rakurai,' I'll lay you odds Rayno's the one who came up with the idea."

"And just how do we explain to all our own dear, chauvinistic Guardsmen that a mere woman could pose a significant threat?" Cayleb asked.

"Send them the imagery of Sharleyan at Saint Agtha's," Merlin suggested with a grim chuckle. "Or let them spend a half hour or so in Aivah's company. Or, for that matter, I can think of at least a hundred women from places like Glacierheart and Shiloh who'd cut a Temple Loyalist's throat without even blinking."

"All true, and none of it likely to make a lot of difference in their thinking, I'm afraid," Cayleb said.

"My own suggestion would be to use our '*seijin* network' in Corisande to hand our analysis—cleaned up to exclude any little things like reconnaissance remotes—to General Gahrvai and Colonel Doyal," Nahrmahn put in. "We can even circulate a sketch of the 'lay sister' to his men. One of them might've seen her, and even if no one did, it ought to at least get the idea there are female 'Rakurai' out there through their skulls."

"And Koryn *needs* that information," Sharleyan pointed out in a softer tone. "Given transit times, they must've sent their assassin out well before Irys and Daivyn got home. That means she probably came up with this 'mission' for herself, based on whatever orders they gave her before they sent her. I may be wrong about that—there's still that 'Langhornite' at Saint Krystyphyr's; he has to be somewhere—but Koryn needs to know how she did it in case she wasn't the only one they taught to make these damned things. And from a personal perspective, finding out how they got through—that it wasn't his fault he never saw a bitch cold-blooded enough to stick a bomb under someone caught in the gray mists coming—might help him stop blaming himself for all those dead civilians."

"It might," Merlin agreed. "In the meantime, though, we have a problem. I think you're right about when she was sent out, but Clyntahn's sure to concentrate his efforts on breaking Corisande back away from Charis. We may well be looking at additional attacks like this one. Or some other, totally different effort to get through to Irys or Daivyn or Hektor. Or to Coris, Anvil Rock, Tartarian, or Gairlyng— Hell, there're dozens of potential high-value targets! And we don't have anyone permanently in Corisande who can do anything about it. I know we've essentially drafted Irys and Hektor and they'll have access to the com network and to Owl and the SNARCs, but they won't be able to do much with it. They haven't built up a support structure they can trust with mysteriously obtained information, and neither of them has the capacity to . . . intervene personally if they pick up on another attack like this one."

"That's true," Nahrmahn said slowly, and Merlin's eyes flicked to the prince.

"I know that tone, Nahrmahn," he said. "Why am I hearing it?"

"Well, it happens that Owl and I conducted a few virtual experiments on things besides Ohlyvya's VR suit."

"What *sort* of experiments?" Merlin's eyes narrowed, and Nahrmahn shrugged.

"Some time ago you asked Owl about building additional PICAs, but he told you he lacked the necessary plans and technical data and there was an uncomfortably high probability of rendering *you* inoperable if he analyzed your chassis to obtain the needed information. However, it occurred to me that while he might not have the specifications for PICA-building, he had a great deal of data on advanced materials, fusion engineering, molecular circuitry, etc. So I suggested he might conduct his own research, using that data, to figure out how your gizzards worked." Nahrmahn smiled brightly. "As I understand it, he spent the equivalent of somewhere around a man-century in virtual R&D."

"You mean you *could* build PICAs, Owl?" Merlin asked very carefully.

"No," Owl replied in his most meticulously accurate tone. "I can build *one* additional PICA, Lieutenant Commander Alban. My supply of several critical materials, which my industrial module is currently unable to replenish, is insufficient to build more than one."

The silence over the com net was profound.

"How long would it take?" Merlin asked after a moment.

"The processes are complex, but none are especially time-consuming," the AI said calmly. "The time requirement would be approximately six local days, plus or minus three hours, from the moment I enabled the nannites."

"That would help. Help a *lot*," Cayleb said after another long moment of silence.

"There is, however, one minor problem," Nahrmahn said.

"What sort of problem?" Sharleyan asked.

"We can build the PICA; we *can't* build the personality to put inside it."

"Why not?" Cayleb demanded. "Why can't we just upload Merlin to it? It'd let him *really* be in two places at once!"

"Because his high-speed data port is disabled. The data transfer rate's too slow. It would take a couple of months to make a backup of him."

"Forgive me, Nahrmahn, but I was under the impression Owl had supplied Merlin with the headset he used to record your personality for the purpose of recording his own," Staynair said.

"*Not* one of Merlin's better ideas," Nahrmahn said with a sly, very Nahrmahn-like smile. "From his perspective, that is. It worked out quite well from *mine*."

"Why not?" Cayleb repeated.

"Because I overlooked the minor fact that it was designed to interact with either an organic human's implants . . . or a PICA's high-speed data port," Merlin sighed. "At the moment, I don't have either. And neither do any of the rest of you." He shrugged. "It could still do the job in my case, but Nahrmahn's right about how long it would take. I haven't been able to find a big enough uninterrupted chunk of time to record myself, and we don't have the time for me to go on sabbatical and take care of it now, either. Especially not if the idea's to put a second PICA into Corisande soon enough to keep Hektor and Irys alive."

"Then what about uploading Nahrmahn?" Sharleyan

cocked her head as she looked at the little Emeraldian's com image. "You're already recorded, and you're obviously capable of interfacing with Owl at a very high rate of speed."

"The thought occurred to me," Nahrmahn said slowly. "In fact, I might as well admit that one reason I had Owl looking into the matter in the first place was the possibility of giving me back a body. Unfortunately, I'm not . . . complete."

"'Complete'?" Staynair repeated very gently into the fresh, ringing silence.

"Oh, I'm entirely functional, Maikel. Don't imagine I'm in any trouble." Nahrmahn's cheery tone seemed genuine, and he smiled. "The problem is that a lot of me had to be reconstructed and there's quite a bit of Owl's . . . DNA in my gestalt. That's one reason he acquired a true sense of self-awareness so quickly after I arrived; some of his subroutines spend a lot of time directly interfacing with that gestalt of mine, 'propping me up,' for want of a better term, and I'd cease to function if I were separated from him. It was a bit humbling to discover I've acquired a sort of mirror twin, but there's no data exchange unless we deliberately initiate it, so my sense of privacy isn't routinely violated. However, the chance that I—or any of the rest of you who wanted to volunteer for the job—would be able to sustain a functioning personality in a PICA's 'brain' is vanishingly small. In fact, Owl puts it at less than one half of one percent."

"I suppose that qualifies as small," Cayleb agreed. "But in that case, there's not much point in building another PICA, is there? If Merlin can't record his personality or upload it directly to another PICA and none of us could survive in one, we wouldn't have anyone to 'drive' it."

"That's . . . not entirely accurate," Nahrmahn said very slowly. All of them looked at his image once more, and he sighed. "As it happens, there is one personality available to us. One I'm completely certain would function within the environment of a PICA."

"Do you have any idea how lucky you are that you no longer have a neck to wring?" Sharleyan inquired. "You just finished explaining why none of us can do the job. So where does this personality who *could* do it come from?"

"Well," Nahrmahn looked at Merlin, "it turns out that when Doctor Proctor started . . . modifying your PICA and its software to override the ten-day automatic personality erasure, he wasn't certain he'd be able to pull it off. And he *was* afraid he'd trigger one of the security protocols and dump your memory when he started probing the lockouts. So, just to be safe, he made a backup of your personality. It's still here, stored in Owl's data core."

Merlin heard himself inhale, the sound sharp and clear in the sudden stillness. That stillness lingered for several seconds, then—

"Owl, why didn't you mention this to me when I asked for the unit to record myself?" he asked.

"You did not inquire about existing personalities," Owl said reasonably, "and I was not then as capable as I am now of extrapolating unspoken desires from specific queries. Nor was I aware I possessed this recording until Prince Nahrmahn broached the question of virtual R&D. At that time, I conducted a search of all databases and discovered Doctor Proctor's folder. It proved highly valuable, but until I opened it, I was unaware of the data he had stored there."

Merlin nodded. Of course it hadn't occurred to the pre-Nahrmahn Owl to expand his search parameters beyond those specified in the original query.

"It would be possible, even without your high-speed data port, to record your experiences and memories of events here on Safehold in no more than five or six days." Nahrmahn appeared to be picking his words with extraordinary care, Merlin noticed. "That would allow us to update the stored personality with all your own experiences on Safehold."

"No," Merlin said very softly.

"But, Merlin—" Cayleb began.

"No," he repeated more firmly. "I don't want to duplicate myself in another PICA, Cayleb. It's already hard enough for me to remember how much the person I'm talking to at any given moment knows about me. If we build a second PICA—and I'm not certain it's a great idea, just yet—it'll be another *permanent* person, someone who has to interact with other people—the same other people—for months on end. There'd be too much chance of bleed over, of the new *seijin* giving away the fact that it has '*Seijin* Merlin's' memories."

Cayleb nodded slowly, but Sharleyan's eyes narrowed and she looked at Merlin speculatively.

She knows, Merlin thought. *Of course she does. And so does Nahrmahn. The very way he phrased the suggestion proves that.*

He closed his eyes, his thoughts spiraling inward, and his nostrils flared as he faced it squarely.

Nimue Alban—the Nimue Alban sleeping in Owl's database—was . . . unstained. She hadn't done any of the things Merlin Athrawes had done. She wouldn't even remember, as Merlin hadn't when he'd awakened as Nimue Alban in this very cave, having volunteered for the mission before her. And because of that, she bore none of the responsibility—none of the guilt—for all the millions of human beings who'd died—or were yet to die—in the religious war Merlin Athrawes had brought about. He had no right to burden her with that guilt, those memories. But did he have the right to bring her into the *consequences* of his actions? To confront her with this world of bloodshed, fury, and hatred? He felt the friends waiting around him, the strength of their support and love, and he knew there were people and causes of enormous worth here on Safehold, but they were so wrapped in pain, so trapped in the ugliness he'd done so much to birth.

He drew another of those deep breaths a PICA's lungs never truly needed and opened his eyes once more.

"I'll have to think about it," he said quietly. "Nahrmahn, you and Owl go ahead and build the PICA. I'm pretty sure I'll decide in the end that we really don't have any choice but to put it online when it's finished. But I need time to come to grips with the idea and decide how much, if any, additional memories to include in the process."

. XXIII .
The Delthak Works,
Barony of High Rock,
Kingdom of Old Charis,
and
Thesmar Bay
and
Branath Canal Crossing,
The South March Lands,
Republic of Siddarmark

"My God, what a racket!"

"Excuse me? What was that?! Can't hear you, Paityr!" Ehdwyrd Howsmyn replied with a huge grin, and Paityr Wylsynn shook a fist at him.

Of course, he had a point, Howsmyn acknowledged. His manufactories' work floors had always been noisy places, but it was even worse now. And in many ways, Wylsynn had only himself to blame. The assembly line they'd just finished inspecting was the product of his suggestion, and the noise level of the pneumatic and hydraulic machinery was the next best thing to deafening. That was why both of them wore the ear protection and safety helmets Howsmyn had issued to his entire workforce.

It was also a very well lit work floor, considering the fact that this was the night shift. The coal gas tapped from the Delthak Works' coking ovens had been piped into all Howsmyn's buildings, and the overhead gas lamps' polished reflectors poured down illumination. More lamps lit the roadway and canals between the Delthak Works and Ithmyn's Lake and ran down the Delthak River to Larek, and the gasworks he was building to provide the Tellesberg waterfront and city streets with similar lighting was more than two-thirds completed.

Quite a few people had expressed . . . concern over the possibly demonic aspects of the new lighting, and Howsmyn had taken pains to warn everyone about the potential dangers of gas. He'd made it clear, with Wylsynn's support and the Royal College's enthusiastic endorsement, that there was nothing the least demonic about it. Hopefully, describing those dangers would encourage people to take the proper precautions . . . and help defuse fresh allegations of demonic involvement when the inevitable gas explosion finally occurred.

Now he beckoned for Wylsynn to follow him and the two of them made their way up a flight of steps to the manufactory supervisor's office. They passed through the office's outer door, crossed a narrow lobby, and closed the inner door behind them.

The noise level dropped drastically. It was still there in the background, but the supervisor's office had thick walls and double windows, their panes spaced, like the office doors, to provide sound baffles. The assistant supervisor started to rise to greet them, but Howsmyn waved her back into her chair with a smile.

"Stay where you are Mistress Sympsyn. Father Paityr's far too suspicious of all we do here for you to waste any courtesy on him."

The brown-haired, brown-eyed woman smiled at them both. Any number of people would have been horrified by Howsmyn's flippant attitude, but Mhargryt Sympsyn, wasn't one of them. Although she was no older than Paityr Wylsynn, she was one of the first half-dozen women Howsyn had handpicked to groom for management positions in his vast, expanding empire, and she'd been understudying Alyk Krystyphyrsyn for six months now. Krystyphyrsyn was very, very good at his job or he wouldn't have been the night supervisor for the first Safeholdian manufactory ever to be equipped with a genuine assembly line. In fact, he'd been instrumental in working out the kinks in the process, and Sympsyn had made several valuable contributions of her own to the process.

That didn't surprise Ehdwyrd Howsmyn, who hadn't chosen her or any of her fellow women because they were dummies. Fair or not, they needed to be several cuts above the average if they were going to hold their own in their new positions. Even with his full-blooded support, they were going to find it difficult to win acceptance from a great many—indeed, probably the majority—of the men who eventually found themselves working for them. At the same time, the expansion of his own facilities meant he'd long since found it necessary to create a formal training process for managers and supervisors, and overriding the passive resistance of several of his own senior subordinates to include women hadn't been any harder than, oh, swimming across Howell Bay . . . the long way. He'd managed it, though . . . and so had they, he thought with a glow of pride.

And the rest of the world had damned well better get used to it, he reflected now as Wylsynn joined him, looking out the office's windows at the enormous work floor. *We'll still be a lot more of a muscle-powered society than I wish we could be for decades to come; that's what happens when you can't use electricity without finding yourself ground zero for a meteor strike. But we'll be a lot* less *of a muscle-powered society. My workforce is already close to thirty percent female—a lot higher in places like the instrument and pistol shops and a lot lower in places like the coking ovens or coal mines—and that percentage's only likely to grow as we get more of Paityr's machine tools into operation. And that'll let us free up still more manpower for military duty.*

His lips twitched in amusement as he remembered Nahrmahn Baytz' enthusiastic discussion of someone called "Rosie the Riveter" he'd found in Owl's archives. But then the incipient smile faded as he gazed out at the busy workers.

If they're good enough to build rifles and hand grenades and revolvers, they're good enough to supervise the process, too. And if my competitors and the Temple decide not to follow suit, screw 'em! Last time I checked, at least half the human race were women, and that means at least half the human race's smart, competent people also happen to be female. As certain individuals with names like Sharleyan, Irys, and Aivah Pahrsahn—or Nimue Alban—might be said to demonstrate. If they're stupid enough to deprive themselves of that human resource, they deserve what's going to happen to them in the end.

"That's even more impressive than it is noisy," Wylsynn said quietly.

"And a lot of the credit goes to you," Howsmyn pointed out. "You do realize we have a revolver coming off that line every eight minutes? That's a thousand every five-day and *six* thousand per month. The second line goes into operation sometime next five-day, and the third one comes online the middle of next month. When they're all up and running, we'll be producing somewhere around a hundred and eighty thousand pistols a year."

Even Wylsynn looked shocked by the numbers, and Howsmyn laughed. Then he sobered a little.

"Actually, we won't hit quite those numbers until we get the new forging machinery into full operation in another two or three months. I could hold the numbers up on the revolvers, but I'll have to divert a lot of my present forging and stamping capacity to the new rifles when those lines go into operation. I'll turn out as many pistols as I can in the interim, and then I'll switch a lot of the people you see out there to the rifle lines and shut down at least one of the pistol lines until we have the additional forges up. We're already well along in converting old-style Mahndrayns to the trapdoor design—at the moment, we're converting about two hundred per day—and I expect to have the first M96 line up within two five-days. Based on our experience with the pistols, I'm projecting around a hundred and forty M96s per line per day, which works out to seven hundred per five-day. The second line should come on stream a couple of five-days after that, and we should have all three of them in operation by the end of November or early February. At that time, we'll be churning out over two thousand every five-day."

Wylsynn inhaled deeply. He'd had access to the numbers from Howsmyn's reports, but that was different from looking down on that swarming work floor.

"That comes to a hundred and twenty-six thousand per year," he said very carefully.

"Yes, it does," Howsmyn agreed with simple pride. "And we'll be phasing in production at the Lake Lymahn Works as soon as we can. Ultimately, we expect to have three lines operating there, too, and by the end of March, we should have all three pistol lines back in full operation. I've already crated up the machine tools to set up rifle and pistol shops at Maikelsberg, and we're sending along the plans to duplicate the original toolset. We hope to have a total of five rifle lines and a pair of pistol lines there within four or five months. Once all of that's up and running, we'll be producing close to three hundred thousand revolvers and almost four hundred and sixty thousand rifles per year."

"And you'll be able to keep them supplied with ammunition?" Wylsynn couldn't quite keep a certain skepticism out of his tone, and Howsmyn grinned.

"Cartridge production's actually running ahead of projections. At the moment, we're turning out roughly two hundred cartridges per hour, and we'll be upping that to around a thousand in the next couple of five-days. There's no point producing them faster than that just yet because the cartridge *filling* machinery developed a glitch we hadn't expected and we're still putting the fix for it into place. By next spring we'll be able to produce and fill *two* thousand per hour, or just under one-point-six million a month. We won't be able to increase much beyond that—assuming we have to—until we can produce the primer compounds in sufficient quantity."

Wylsynn only shook his head, and Howsmyn patted him on the shoulder.

"You'll get used to it once it's had time to sink in, Father Paityr. In the meantime," he turned the priest away from the window towards the pot of hot chocolate steaming gently on the small stove in one corner of the office, "I'm certain Mistress Sympsyn and Master Krystyphyrsyn can be convinced to join us in a celebratory repast." He uncovered a large platter, revealing a serious stack of doughnuts, and grinned. "I'm sure this'll be much better for us than any of that dreadful champagne and whiskey."

▼ ▼ ▼

Sir Paitryk Hywyt stood on the quarterdeck of HMS *King Tymythy* watching something no Charisian admiral—in fact, no *Safeholdian* admiral—had ever seen or dreamed of seeing.

The unlikely, unlovely, ungainly craft forging steadily into Thesmar Bay looked much the worse for wear. The paint had been scoured away from its blunt bows and the curved front of its rust-streaked casemate; the falls of its davits were strained taut over emptiness where the hungry sea had snatched away the boats which ought to have ridden in them; its signal mast had been reduced to a broken stub; and its starboard funnel was half the height of its companion.

He would not have wagered a tenth-mark on its ability to survive the southwester which had gone howling up the Tarot Channel three five-days ago, yet there it was, trailing a smoky banner from those battered funnels. And, greater miracle even than that, was the crippled galleon following at the end of her tow, foremast and mainmast little more than stubs, a scrap of canvas set under her broken bowsprit, and showing only the mizzen topsail aft, although a stay had been rigged from the mizzen top to what was left of the mainmast and a staysail set upon it. HMS *Tellesberg Queen*, Hywyt thought. Two ships he'd been certain had been lost when the first units of the storm-threshed convoy straggled into Thesmar. And yet here they were: Halcom Bahrns' ship and the thousand men whose lives he'd saved aboard the galleon.

Guns began to thud all around the anchorage, saluting the victors they'd never expected to see. Hywyt hadn't ordered that salute, but he wasn't the least bit surprised when *King Tymythy*'s guns joined it.

▼ ▼ ▼

Sir Hauwerd Breygart stood atop the lookout tower high above the center of the town of Thesmar and watched the miracle steam towards the docks. Unlike Hywyt, the Earl of Hanth was no sailor, but he was a very experienced Marine. He knew the terror when the sea's full wrath descended upon the frail works of man in open waters, and he'd no more expected ever to see those ships alive than the admiral had.

He stood very still, leaning both hands on the tower's railing, as he contemplated those ships and breathed a silent, fervent prayer of thanks, and not just for the lives HMS *Delthak* had saved. That battered galleon, the water sluicing from her pumps even now, contained not simply Brigadier Zhames Mathysyn's artillery battalion but also half the scout snipers assigned to the 4th Infantry Brigade. The guns would be crucial to Hanth's ability to carry out his orders, and he was devoutly glad to see them. Yet he was even more grateful for those scout snipers.

He straightened, jaw tightening, as he recalled how many men had been less fortunate than those aboard *Tellesberg Queen*. Men for whom there'd been no miracle named *Delthak* and no miracleworker named Halcom Bahrns. Colonel Ludyvyk Ovyrtyn's 8th Regiment, half of 4th Brigade's infantry, had lost one of its three battalions in its entirety. Nobody knew where or when *Amelyah's Pride* had lost her battle, but she'd taken over a thousand ICA men and officers to her grave with her.

There'd been eyes to see but no way to help when the brig *Lady of Eraystor* foundered in the fury which had claimed too many of her larger, stronger sisters, and two precious batteries of rifled four-inch guns—and the gunners to serve them—had gone with her. And then there'd been *Spindrift*, driven onto the jagged reefs from which Rock Island took its name. Colonel Raif Ahlbyrtsyn, the 2nd Scout Sniper Regiment's commanding officer, had drowned while fighting to get his men ashore, and so had Major Ahlyk Styvynsyn and over eighty percent of his battalion. Major Dynnys Mahklymorh, commanding the 2nd Scout Snipers 2nd Battalion, embarked in *Tellesberg Queen*, didn't know it yet, but he and his battalion had just become the only scout snipers attached to the Thesmar garrison.

It was a grim tally, and they still didn't know the fates of three supply ships, but at least they'd accounted for all the transports now . . . one way or the other. And *Delthak* herself was an incredibly reassuring addition to their defenses.

And despite everything, you're in one hell of a lot better shape than you were, *Hauwerd*, he reminded himself.

Thesmar's garrison now numbered over thirty thousand. Emperor Cayleb and the lord protector had decreed that Hanth would retain command, and General Sumyrs and General Fyguera accepted that without any resentment he could see. Brigadier Mathysyn's eighty-two hundred men were the largest single component, and—combined with Breygart's 1st Independent Marine Brigade and Hywyt's naval gunners—totaled more than half of Thesmar's strength, despite the losses the troop convoy had suffered. Sumyrs and Fyguera knew that, just as they knew they would never have held Thesmar once the Royal Dohlaran Army crossed the frontier without Charis. And, even more to the point, they realized they had no experience with Charisian doctrine or weapons.

That was changing. Both of them had gotten behind the joint training with Hanth's own "brigade," and now that Mathysyn had arrived, they'd *all* be taking advantage of the training opportunity that offered. His own Marines and Navy battalions could use all the polish they could get, and he especially wanted Mathysyn's troops to spend time with the Siddarmarkians. Every single one of them was a volunteer who'd stood firm in the face of the hurricane which had swept over their Republic. They'd been tried in the furnace, and Hanth's men had come to admire them deeply . . . and to trust them implicitly. He wanted Mathysyn's men to do the same.

And you also want the opportunity to pick Mathysyn's brain, he reminded himself. *You were a colonel—a Marine* colonel*—before the Emperor recalled you. What the hell do you* know *about maneuvering an entire Army brigade?* He snorted harshly. *I think that's something you'd better learn in a hurry, Hauwerd. And it won't hurt a thing for you and Mathysyn to figure out how best to combine Clyftyn's and Kydryc's troops with your own. A third of them have muzzleloaders, and another* third *of them have matchlocks or arbalests! At least none of them are hauling* pikes *around anymore.*

True, and at least the lord protector and Seneschal Parkair had managed to scrape up enough Siddarmarkian-made rifles to equip another five thousand of the South March militia units.

And you've got a month or so before you have to show Rychtyr and his boys all your new toys, too. Isn't that nice?

▼ ▼ ▼

"I hadn't expected to see you again, Master Slaytyr," Sir Rainos Ahlverez said.

"Didn't 'spect t' see you again, either, M'lord," Zhapyth Slaytyr said frankly, wrapping his gnarly knuckled hands gratefully around the mug of hot tea. "That Colonel Kyrbysh, though. He can be a mite . . . forceful."

"So it would appear. And a determined fellow, too."

"Might say that," Slaytyr acknowledged laconically, and Ahlverez favored him with a smile.

The dispatch Slaytyr had just delivered was the first real good news he'd received since leaving Thesmar. Despite Father Naiklos' grim final dispatch, almost a quarter of Lairays Walkyr's garrison had cut its way out through the understrength Siddarmarkian regiments east of Ohadlyn's Gap under Colonel Bryahn Kyrbysh. The understated tone of Kyrbysh's message barely hinted at what must have been a desperate fight, but the colonel hadn't simply settled for escaping. Instead, he was in the process of rallying the Faithful of Shiloh to his standard, and he proposed to operate against the heretics' rear in any way he could. It wasn't clear to Ahlverez just how much the Shilohian might be able to achieve, but he obviously intended to achieve everything he possibly could.

"Duke Harless will be pleased to hear about this, too, Master Slaytyr," he said, listening to the rain drumming on the overhead canvas once again.

"Can't say as I care a whole heapin' lot 'bout his high and mightiness," the Siddarmarkian replied sourly. "Damn near got me killed, sendin' me back last time! Colonel Kyrbysh, now—he's one a man could warm to."

"He sounds like it," Ahlverez acknowledged, trying dutifully not to smile at the Shilohian mountaineer's obvious dislike for Harless. From Slaytyr's expression, he was pretty sure he'd failed.

"Sending you back, though, gets us to this suggestion of the Colonel's," he continued after a moment. "Tell me whether or not you think you could do it without getting killed before I pass it along to His Grace."

Slaytyr gazed at him for a long moment, brown eyes thoughtful, then shrugged.

"Long's it's just me and no more'n one pack mule—two at th' outside—I think I can do 'er, M'lord. Mind, I can't promise, but I 'spect the odds'd be . . . fair."

Ahlverez considered that statement carefully, only too well aware of the risk the Siddarmarkian was willing to assume. He'd already used his local knowledge to bypass Charisian pickets three times. To get home, he'd have to do it yet again, and each additional horse or mule eroded his chances. Adding portable wyvern coops to the mix could only raise the odds against him, yet he was still willing to try.

"Very well, Master Slaytyr," he said finally. "I'll pass the Colonel's suggestion along to the Duke. But I'm afraid," he smiled faintly, "that it will take me several hours—five or six, at least, and probably more—to get word to him and for his response to reach us here. Why don't you go with Captain Lattymyr here and let him find you a dry spot to catch a few hours' sleep while you wait?"

" 'Preciate that, M'lord," Slaytyr said, and Ahlverez looked at his aide.

"See to it that we feed Master Slaytyr a good hot meal, too, Lynkyn. Then get him bedded down. By the time you've done that, I'll have drafted the letter to Duke Harless."

▼ ▼ ▼

I feel almost guilty, Merlin Athrawes realized with a certain bemusement.

His PICA's transformation back from Zhapyth Slaytyr's gray hair and brown eyes was nearly complete, and he glanced over his shoulder at the pair of well-laden pack mules following obediently along behind his horse. In another twenty minutes or so, he'd be far enough out from the Army of Shiloh to feel comfortable summoning the stealthed air lorry, despite the wet, cloudy daylight.

I'll be damned if that bastard Ahlverez might not have an actual human being hiding somewhere inside, he thought, then cautioned himself against an excess of fancifulness. Given how little love there was between Ahlverez and Harless, it was entirely possible the Dohlaran's consideration for a commonly born Siddarmarkian had more to do with planting one in Harless' eye than any sudden effusion of human kindness. Still. . . .

It was possible he and Nahrmahn were being overly clever this time, but it was definitely worth a try, and Nahrmahn had become extremely fond of an ancient Old Earth aphorism: "If you aren't cheating, you aren't trying hard enough." By Merlin's estimate, Ruhsyl Thairis' strategy had an excellent chance of success as it stood, but it never hurt to nudge the odds along.

Which was exactly what "Colonel Bryahn Kyrbysh's" wyvernborne messages to the Duke of Harless should do.

NOVEMBER, YEAR OF GOD 896

·✦·

I

Fort Tairys
The South March Lands,
Republic of Siddarmark

"Took them long enough," Duke Eastshare murmured to himself, looking down from the same hilltop from which he'd watched the bombardment of Fort Tairys.

The hilltop was still the same; Ohadlyn's Gap was not. A lot had changed in the four five-days since the fort had fallen.

For starters, he'd been reinforced by Colonel Maikel Stywyrt's 2nd Glacierheart Volunteers, who'd arrived via the Branath Canal with the anticipated convoy of ammunition and additional thirty-pounders, and the Siddarmarkian 10th Independent Brigade, coming overland from Siddar City. His total strength was now almost thirty-four thousand; within two five-days, it would be forty-two thousand, and when the 3rd Infantry and the rest of his dragoons arrived, it would reach seventy thousand, not that he had any intention of letting the Army of Shiloh know that.

In the meantime, the fort's broken walls had been further demolished by Charisian engineers, copiously supplied with blasting charges and ably assisted by the Glacierheart miners, until only a few broken tiers of brick rose from drifts of rubble. None were over four or five feet high, and by a strange coincidence, none of them ran from east to west. The earthworks which had previously guarded the fort's southern approaches—and those guarding the Gap as a whole from the east—had been assaulted by the same energetic workers (aided by thousands of Shilohian volunteers eager to swing a shovel or a pick) and either leveled or incorporated into an entirely new set of south-facing works.

Eastshare was too sane to try holding the vast, sprawling defensive works Walkyr had thrown up. Instead, Major Lowayl had designed a very different set of fortifications just north of the fort's tattered ruins.

Walkyr's works—which had demonstrated his own lack of professional training—had been walls, straight across the Gap, with precious little in the way of flanking fire. Lowayl had been granted insufficient time to start from scratch, using all the new techniques which had been worked out by the ICA's engineers and artillerists, but the product of his labors was still . . . formidable.

He'd incorporated two of Walkyr's earthen curtain-walls into the new defenses, but he'd added simple bastions—triangular secondary works in *front* of the curtains—at regular intervals, well supplied with artillery to sweep the faces of adjoining bastions and the curtain between them. Walkyr's covering ditches had also been improved to offer advanced, covered firing positions for infantry, though there'd been no time to build a proper glacis, and Lowayl had built covered wooden bridges as protected routes by which that infantry might retreat into the main work if the enemy broke into the ditch. And, of course, the bridges could be burned to prevent attackers from making use of them. Mortar pits had been dug at regular intervals behind the curtains, multiple firing positions well to the rear had been prepared for Colonel Celahk's angle-guns, and corduroyed roads ensured that the heavy angles could be moved rapidly between them, despite the soft, saturated earth. The Temple Loyalists' abatises had also been salvaged for reuse, and given the shorter frontage of Eastshare's works, provided a far denser and more formidable barrier before the ditch.

The line across the Gap ran for almost twenty-two miles, reaching up into the foothills proper where its ends were anchored by a pair of redoubts, each provided with its own artillery, although on a rather less lavish scale than the main position. On the extreme left of his line, the Gray Walls Redoubt covered the trail by which Wyllys' infantry had joined 1st Brigade for the final assault on the fort. That was the only really practical route for a significant body of troops; Eastshare had made certain of that, sending out scout snipers with local guides to survey every cow and lizard path within thirty miles. The redoubt blocked the only one that seriously concerned him, but he'd placed pickets with generous supplies of landmines to cover all of them. He wouldn't want anyone spoiling his surprise for Harless and Ahlverez, now would he?

Taken all in all, it was a far more challenging obstacle than Walkyr had managed, manned by a far better armed and trained garrison and with the most lethal artillery in the world to support it. Which was probably just as well, given that the oncoming Army of Shiloh still consisted of over one hundred and seventy thousand men with hundreds of less lethal but still deadly artillery pieces in support.

The vanguard of that enormous army was crawling up the Gap as Eastshare watched, and he wondered if Duke Harless was stupid enough to try a quick assault. It seemed unlikely. He'd read Earl Hanth's reports describing the bungled night assault on Thesmar, and he found it difficult to imagine that any general who'd lost so many men so uselessly would attempt the same maneuver twice. Still, one could always hope.

Don't get too full of yourself, Ruhsyl, he reminded himself. *If they ever do punch through anywhere, there're more than enough of them to swamp you, at least until Symkyn comes up with the 3rd. Not only that, but unlike Walkyr's clowns, they've got at least some trained siege engineers over there.*

All of that was true, and he had no intention of becoming overconfident or allowing any of his subordinates to fall into the same error. Still, the truth was that he was rather counting on those engineers. Their expertise was sadly out-of-date, but they probably didn't know that yet, and the weather actually seemed to be improving a bit—colder, but with longer breaks between bouts of rain. That would offer them significantly better conditions to conduct operations against his position, and he devoutly hoped they'd do just that for at least the next three or four five-days.

▼ ▼ ▼

Sir Rainos Ahlverez stood beside his horse, training the heavy spyglass on the heretics' works, and hoped none of his subordinates could see his expression. From what he could see, Colonel Kyrbysh's wyvern messages had actually *understated* the situation.

Anything which might have offered cover for troops advancing towards the heretics had been carefully demolished. Heaps of broken brickwork showed where the fort had once been, but it had been even more completely wrecked than Alyksberg after the garrison blew up their magazines. The heretics obviously had no interest in holding those ruins, and that was more than enough to give him pause. It said things he didn't really want to hear about their attitude towards what had once been one of the most formidable fortifications in the entire Republic of Siddarmark.

And then there were the earthworks north of the ruins. He couldn't see them very clearly from here, yet what he *could* see suggested a radical shift in the nature of fortifications in general. He'd seen some of that at Thesmar, but on a smaller, cruder scale; probably because for all the heretic Hanth's tenacity, the man was a Marine, trained for shipboard combat, not fortress design. Whoever had laid out *these* works was a far more formidable engineer, and something with hundreds of icy little feet danced along his spine as he contemplated them.

Bastions had been a feature of permanent fortifications for centuries, but not on this scale. They'd been incorporated into castles, usually in the form of towers rather than these low-lying gun platforms, and they'd been close together because missile weapons had been short-ranged and cannon had been huge, bulky, slow-firing, and clumsy.

Only a certified lunatic would have depended on old-style artillery to beat off determined infantry—that was what bows, arbalests, and matchlocks had been for, and none of them had been effective at anything over a hundred yards. Everyone had known that, which at least partly explained—it did not *excuse*, for nothing could do that— Harless' assault at Thesmar. He'd known the new artillery and rifles were more deadly, but it had been an intellectual awareness, one which hadn't yet penetrated deeply enough to displace old habits and old calculations.

But *these* works seemed to bristle with artillery. He was positive there were plenty of firing positions for riflemen, but it was the artillery that truly frightened him. It looked as if those bastions were as much as four thousand yards apart at their greatest separation. That was far too great a range for matchlocks and old-style artillery, but the heretics had demonstrated that *their* guns could reach that far with deadly effectiveness.

He lowered the spyglass, his mouth grim. He'd wondered why the heretics hadn't tried to delay them in the Kyplyngyr Forest. He'd found that especially puzzling in light of the skill with which Eastshare, the heretic commander, had used the same sort of terrain against Bishop Militant Cahnyr in July. Now he understood. There'd been no point in digging in among the trees, where it was always possible someone could find an open flank and get around it, no matter how tangled the terrain might be. Not once Fort Tairys had fallen and one had such a lovely defensive position as Ohadlyn's Gap, which offered no flanks at all. Harless and Hankey were still talking about pushing infantry around the heretics through the hills, but Ahlverez had never had much faith in the possibility. He had even less now. A commander who'd chosen that position and erected those fortifications hadn't left any spider-rat holes someone could use against him. Not even Zhapyth Slaytyr seemed able to get through now, and Ahlverez was far from eager to play catch-as-catch-can in the hills with the "scout snipers" who'd wrought such carnage on Bishop Militant Cahnyr's troops.

No, he thought. *This Eastshare's got Shan-wei's own cork in this bottle, and I understand* exactly *what the devious bastard had in mind. Unfortunately for him, he's got an unanticipated little problem of his own now, doesn't he?*

Hennet's cavalry were, indeed, ranging north along the Branath Canal, although Eastshare had been too canny to leave pickets out where Hennet could get at them. In fact, the whole time he'd been using the canal to move his troops south, he'd been using the same barges to move civilians *north,* out of harm's way, on the return trip. And he'd been very thorough . . . just as he'd been thorough about emptying every barn and granary between Kharmych and Fort St. Klair. It sounded very much as if Eastshare's troops could have given even the Faithful lessons in how to strip a countryside bare of anything that might support an invading army. Starvation and disease among the besiegers had been the bane of too many sieges as supplies ran out. Eastshare had obviously intended to deploy those weapons against the Army of Shiloh, and Ahlverez was unhappily certain that the already parlous state of that army's supplies was about to get even worse far more quickly than Harless expected.

But that works both ways, doesn't it? he told himself. *And Eastshare got just a little too clever this time. Not that knowing about his problems does much about ours, and we're heading into the middle of winter. A lot milder winter than anything farther north, but still winter, and too many of Harless' troops're already ready to eat their boots and belts. It's going to get worse—a* lot *worse— with the way Eastshare's stripped the countryside, and we're damned near nine hundred miles from Thesmar. How the hell are the frigging Desnairians supposed to haul supplies* nine hundred miles *overland when they've got less than half—hell, less than a* third—*of the wagons they need? An army that depends on foragers needs to keep moving, needs to keep advancing into territory that hasn't been stripped of food, and that's exactly what Eastshare's counting on.*

He and Baron Tymplahr had done what they could, but even the secondary route along the St. Alyk was . . . in-efficient, at best. Yet even while they worked to improve their own logistics, the Desnairians' got only worse. They were losing scores of draft dragons to exhaustion, over-work, and hunger, and each one they·lost took another bite out of their transport capacity. Worse, even the por-tion of their supply line being managed by the Church was in disarray. The heretics had total control of the Gulf of Jahras, and the miserable excuse of a "high road" around its western shore had been cut in at least six places. *All* shipments from Desnair now had to cross the southern lobe of the Gulf of Dohlar, and to make bad worse, two of those damnable armored ships had arrived in Silkiah Bay. They'd closed the eastern end of the Salthar Canal, requiring every ton of supplies to travel almost sixty miles overland between the Salthar and the Silk Town-Thesmar Canal, which required still more draft animals and wagons.

Wherever he looked, Harless' ability to supply his troops' was eroding still further, and there was only so much assistance even a wizard like Tymplahr could pro-vide. They couldn't—they simply *could not*—adequately feed this many men and this many animals under these conditions.

At the very least they should send as much cavalry as possible back to Thesmar. They needed to retain some of it, if only for flank security, but it would be virtually use-less in any sort of siege, and each damned horse ate ten times as much as a man. Surely even Hankey and Hen-net had to realize that!

Don't count on it, Rainos, he thought glumly. *Hennet'll swell up like a swamp hopper in mating season if you even* suggest *sending his precious horsemen to the rear. Obviously the only reason you'd be suggesting it would be to see to it that the despicable infantry—your infantry—gets the glory for securing the gateway to Shiloh while he gets left out in the cold.*

He sighed, and admitted that he'd have been thinking

in much the same patterns not so very long ago. Of course, he wasn't Desnairian. That meant he could learn from experience when it hit him over the head with a heavy enough club.

Time to sit down with Shulmyn, he told himself. *When Harless' men get hungry enough, they're going to expect us to feed them. Sir Borys is hopelessly out of his depth, even with Kahsimahr working himself to death trying to cover for him. So as the only quartermaster with a clue as to what he's doing, it'll all come down on Shulmyn when the situation starts going into—further into—the crapper.*

He grimaced at the unfairness of expecting his own quartermaster to shoulder such a burden, but pretending he had any alternative would be stupid. And at least they'd have the St. Alyk River open for barge traffic, despite the formidable obstacles, in another five-day or so. That would help a lot. Whether it would help *enough* was a very different question, however, and it was entirely possible they'd finally encountered a problem not even the redoubtable Sir Shulmyn Rahdgyrz could solve. But if *he* couldn't solve it, no one could, which meant that fair or not, Ahlverez was going to have to ask him to do it.

And, he reminded himself, the Army of Shiloh's quartermasters weren't the only ones having problems.

He raised his spyglass once more, glowering at those fortifications, and treasured those wyvernborne messages.

You planned to sit there behind those earthworks with your own provisions arriving securely through Maidynberg while we starved out here at the end of our so-called supply line, but a sword has two edges, my heretical friend, he thought grimly, *and you shouldn't have let Kyrbysh get away. Now we'll just see who starves first!*

II

Nimue's Cave,
The Mountains of Light,
The Temple Lands

She woke up. Which was odd, because she didn't remember going to sleep.

Sapphire eyes opened, then narrowed as she saw the curve of a glass-smooth stone ceiling above her. She lay on her back on a table of some sort, her hands folded across her chest, and she'd never seen this room before in her life.

She tried to sit up, and the narrowed eyes flared wide when she discovered that she couldn't.

"Hello, Nimue," a deep, resonant voice she'd never heard before said, and she found she could turn her head, after all.

She did, and found herself looking at someone she'd never met but who seemed somehow . . . familiar, despite his bizarre appearance.

It wasn't the long hair, or the mustachio and dagger beard; the Terran Federation Navy's personnel favored short hair, and its male personnel were mostly clean-shaven, but neither braids nor beards were unheard of. For that matter, there were still civilians, even now, and compared to many of them, *this* fellow's styling was almost bland. Facial scars like the one on his cheek weren't exactly unheard of among serving personnel, either. But even granting all of that, she couldn't quite recall the last time she'd seen someone in what appeared to be a blackened steel breastplate, chain mail, wide-legged black trousers bloused into high, polished boots, and a matching tunic with slashed sleeves. The breastplate bore a complicated heraldic device in blue, white, black, and gold, boasting some opium dream of a fish, or possibly an octopus, or possibly a fish performing some sort of unnatural act *upon* an octopus. It made her think about an old, pre-space book she'd read once, by a man named Lovecraft.

And he was amazingly tall. Nimue stood just over a hundred and ninety centimeters in height, but he was at least twenty centimeters taller than she was. It was hard to be sure of her estimate while lying flat on her back, but the differential had to be at least that great, which only added to the grotesqueness of his appearance. She was accustomed to being taller than the vast majority of men she met; certainly, if she'd ever met this long-haired, broad-shouldered, slightly battered giant she'd remember him!

She didn't. And yet there was that strange familiarity, almost as if she did know him, which was ridiculous. She couldn't possibly have forgotten—

Her thoughts hiccuped to a sudden halt as a pair of impossibilities abruptly registered. The first was that she was inside her PICA with absolutely no memory of *planning* to find herself there. The second was that something was missing from her field of vision: the ten-day clock counting down how long she had to record her updated personality before it was automatically scrubbed. The possibility of her PICA's being activated by someone else, without her knowledge and active cooperation, was scary enough, given that the lockouts and security systems were supposed to be absolutely unbreakable. Yet frightening as that was, the missing clock was almost worse. She couldn't even begin to count the laws, regulations, protocols, and prohibitions its absence violated.

"Who are you?" she asked finally, and the stranger smiled oddly. The sense of familiarity grew still stronger, and yet she remained positive she'd never seen that face, with its scarred cheek and pronounced chin.

"Interesting you should ask," he said. He reached behind him and drew a tall, rolling stool closer to the surface upon which she lay and settled onto it.

"Interesting you should ask," he repeated in a softer voice. "Because the truth is, I used to be you."

▼ ▼ ▼

Nimue Alban stood on the balcony beside the man who called himself Merlin Athrawes, gazing out over the enormous cavern, trying to grapple with the hurricane of emotions and thoughts ripping through her.

Her head barely topped "Merlin's" shoulder, but not because he was so enormously tall, after all. He truly was twenty-eight centimeters—no, *eleven inches*, she corrected herself—taller than she was, but only because she was eleven inches shorter than she remembered being. She felt like a midget, but he'd explained the reason for it readily enough.

"People average shorter on Safehold than in the Federation," he'd said in that deep male voice which sounded nothing at all like hers . . . until she listened carefully. "I was—*we* were—too tall to be anything except male. I'm only two or three inches above the norm for some of the more northern portions of the planet, but the average male height in the Out Islands is only about five feet seven and, of course, the one thing a PICA can't adjust is its height. *You're* five feet four, a bit short for a man, but close enough to the norm that you could pass for whichever you choose." He'd smiled again, that worn smile that spoke of experiences she'd never had. "I've . . . ah, encountered a few problems in becoming permanently male, and I figured this way we could at least spare you that much. Besides," he laughed suddenly, "nobody's *ever* going to mistake the two of us for the same person now!"

It was going to take some getting used to, but he was certainly right about that! And "take some getting used to" was a pretty good description of *everything* she'd discovered in the last few hours.

She closed her eyes, feeling the faint stir of the cavern's circulating air on her face, and ran her mind carefully—carefully, trying to avoid the razor edges of so much grief, so much loss experienced with such brutal swiftness—back over those hours. She replayed the last message from Commodore Pei, feeling another tiny shiver as she realized the man beside her had seen exactly the same message, felt exactly the same emotions, she had. She replayed what Merlin, the AI named Owl, whose avatar resembled both of them so much, and the short, plump virtual personality named Nahrmahn had told her after that. It would take time to come to grips with that enormous flood of data, yet it was at her command . . . as was the later imagery of the brutal war savaging the "Republic of Siddarmark."

The war *she'd* started.

No, I didn't *start it. Merlin Athrawes did.* Her mind spun with the strangeness of the concept. *I would* have *if he hadn't, though. I don't see any other way he could've approached the problem. Even without this . . . millennial return of the "archangels" to worry about, he couldn't have broken the Church's tyranny any other way. With the "archangels'" return, he has even less time to create a situation that can't be* un*created.*

But I didn't have to start anything; he did.

She thought about that. About the fact that the undeniably male person standing beside her was *her*, but seven years and God alone knew how many deaths, how many losses, older. And as she stood there, she knew the real reason he'd recorded such a limited update to her personality recording. One that had nothing at all to do with the loss of his high-speed port, whatever he might say.

"I didn't have time to record everything if we were going to get you up and running quickly, but I've installed some updates to your muscle memory package," he'd said and smiled crookedly. "Little things like marksmanship, the difference between using a katana for serious combat as opposed to kendo, how to ride a horse, which fork to reach for at a formal dinner, Safeholdian salutes and military courtesies—things like that. Wouldn't do to have you falling off a horse the way I did the first few times I practiced . . . in private, fortunately. You've got the local dialects from Owl and the remotes, and Owl has complete records on everything I've done over the last few years, but I decided it would be better not to weigh you down with a lot of memories that could only get in the way of establishing your own persona. You've got the *information* you need, and the skills, but I think it's important our public personalities and reactions to people who've already met Merlin be as distinct from each other as possible."

It makes sense, she thought with a sudden surge of compassion for the person she would never become. *It makes a lot of sense. But that's not the reason he did it. I wonder if I—if this iteration of Nimue Alban—will grow into someone that unwilling to burden someone else with so much pain?*

She reached out—and up, she noted wryly—to rest her hand on his mailed forearm. On one level, it felt . . . unnatural. That was the level which knew "Merlin Athrawes" had been born Nimue Alban, however; on a much deeper level, helped along by the fact of his masculinity, it felt completely natural. Not as if she were touching herself, but as if she were touching the brother—the *older* brother—she'd never had, who'd never been allowed to exist on a world which knew it was doomed.

"Yes?" He arched an eyebrow at her, and she smiled up at him. It was a little wavery, that smile, but it was genuine, as well.

"I recognize where that eyebrow started from," she told him. "It's been some places I haven't since, though. Gotten more . . . panache along the way."

"'Panache,'" he repeated as if tasting the word. "I suppose that's one thing I've gotten more of 'along the line.' More dings, dents, scrapes, and scratches, too." He shook his head. "Safehold's a high-wear environment, Nimue, but there are so many things here worth defending. And that need changing, too."

"I know." She squeezed his forearm. "It's going to take some getting used to, you understand." She chuckled suddenly. "Well, of course *you* understand!" Her humor disappeared as quickly as it had come. "And knowing what happened to Shan-wei, the Commodore—all of them—that's going to take getting used to, too. I can't say I don't find the mission you and I both signed on for—or *didn't* sign on for, maybe, since neither of us remembers volunteering—a bit . . . daunting. But a lot of good people died so you and I could stand here to have this conversation. More of them—some of them people you know and I haven't met yet—will die before it's over, too. That's hard, Merlin. A lot of me wants to run away from it. But *you* didn't, so how can this version of me—of *us*—do what you didn't? And when you come down to it, even if the odds really sucked when you started out—even if they're not all that great even now, given this millennial visit we're looking forward to—they're one hell of a lot better than what we had when the only possible future was the Gbaba killing all of us."

She looked up, sapphire eyes meeting identical eyes, and her nostrils flared.

"If you were crazy enough to take this on, so am I. After all," she smiled again, the expression blended from grief, loss, determination . . . and humor, "who am I to argue with me?"

. III .
Port Royal,
Kingdom of Chisholm,
Empire of Charis

"So, Zohzef—are we going to get this done on schedule, or not?" Sir Lewk Cohlmyn, the Earl of Sharpfield, inquired.

"What's that saying of *Seijin* Merlin's?" Admiral Zohzef Hyrst responded with an off-center smile. "'The difficult we do immediately; the impossible takes a little longer,' isn't it?"

"I believe it is." Sharpfield returned his subordinate's smile. "So does this come under the heading of 'difficult' or 'impossible'?"

"I think the proper label is probably *extremely* difficult, My Lord. But, after all, we've got an entire five-day before we're scheduled to sail! I'm sure we can work whatever miracles we need with *that* much time in hand."

Hyrst climbed out of his office chair and gestured a polite invitation for the silver-haired earl to accompany him to the window that looked out across the waters of Port Royal. Those waters weren't as frenetic as they'd been when the Empire had been concentrating on shipping everybody in an Army uniform off to Siddarmark, but they were busy enough to go on with.

"As you can see, My Lord, we've accumulated almost all the transports we need. Actually finding the troops to put *into* them is a bit more problematical, you understand, but I'm taking the High Admiral's word for it that the necessary Marines will arrive any day now. The colliers are already here, and we'll have the last of the coal loaded by the end of this five-day, although I've discovered we need more supply ships than we'd thought we would when this was all just a gleam in the High Admiral's eye. It always does seem to work out that way, which is why I'm not surprised to be running around like a wyvern with its tail on fire scraping up additional galleons. It would help if we hadn't sent everything that would float off to the Republic, but it *looks* like we've gotten enough additional Old Charisian hulls to compensate. We'll have enough escorts to keep an eye on things, too, and I might as well admit that having *Thunderer* and *Dreadnought* along makes me feel a lot more comfortable when I contemplate the operation. Not that I wouldn't just as soon have the first of the *King Haarahlds* instead. Of course, that's rather the point, I imagine."

Hyrst's lips twitched another smile, and Sharpfield snorted. Not that it was really all that humorous, the earl supposed, remembering a terrifying day of thunder and smoke and the reek of brimstone drifting across Darcos Sound. He'd commanded Queen Sharleyan's navy in that battle, and he'd known how bitterly she'd resented being dragged into Hektor Daykyn's alliance against the Kingdom of Charis. That had made his decision easier when he realized how outclassed any galley was by the Royal Charisian Navy's new, cannon-armed galleons. It would have been easier still if he hadn't known how Zhaspahr Clyntahn and the Inquisition were likely to react to his order for his ships to strike their colors.

Fortunately, his queen was a very smart woman who'd made the right decision when Cayleb of Charis proposed marriage, and it would be good to take the battle back to the enemy. Especially since this time it would be the *right* enemy, he thought. He'd never wanted to fight Charis, and he'd deeply regretted King Haarahld's death at Darcos Sound. He felt rather differently where the Temple and its minions were concerned, however, and he had an intensely personal score to settle with the Royal Dohlaran Navy. One that had quite a lot to do with Darcos Sound—or its aftermath, at least—as a matter of fact.

He'd never met Bryahn Lock Island or Gwylym Manthyr before his surrender. He'd come to know both of them well afterward, though, and despite the death of their beloved king—and the fact that both of them had known precisely what Clyntahn had intended to do to their homes and families—they'd seen to it that their prisoners were treated with respect. They'd allowed surrendered officers to retain their swords, permitted no brutality, provided healers, and plucked every survivor they could from the sound's waters. They'd become Sharpfield's friends, not simply his captors, and Lock Island had welcomed Sharpfield as the new *Imperial* Charisian Navy's second-ranking admiral following the merger of Old Charis, Chisholm, and Emerald.

Now they were dead. Lock Island had at least been granted the gift of dying fighting for his emperor and empress and all the things in which he believed in a battle that crushed the Navy of God and the Imperial Harchongese Navy. Manthyr had not, and Sharpfield felt the familiar rage flicker as he remembered what the Inquisition had done to his friend and the men under his command. Men of the same Charisian Navy which had always granted quarter to its enemies, treated them with common decency, as if they were actually human beings.

And it was Thirsk and his precious King Rahnyld who handed Gwylym and his men to that pig Clyntahn, the earl thought now, gazing blindly out across the busy harbor. *I'm pretty sure it wasn't Thirsk's idea, but there's a price for something like that, whether it's your idea or not, and I'm not the only officer in Their Majesties' Navy who wants a little payback. A lot of payback, actually.*

He wasn't going to collect that payback anytime in the immediate future, not in full. But in about another month, assuming Hyrst pulled off his "very difficult" job, Sir Lewk Cohlmyn and the Imperial Charisian Navy would be making their first down payment on that particular debt.

His eyes focused once more, taking in the bombardment ships HMS *Tumult* and *Turmoil* and, beyond them, the armored sides of HMS *Thunderer* and HMS *Dreadnought*. The ironclads were sisters of HMS *Rottweiler*, just as well protected and just as heavily armed as she was, and he'd long since decided *Dreadnought* would be his flagship.

After all, what could be more fitting than to return to the Gulf of Dohlar in a ship named for the galleon Gwylym Manthyr had commanded so brilliantly—and lost—at the Battle of Darcos Sound?

You may not be here to see it, my friend, he thought, looking at those closed gunports, thinking of the cannon crouching behind them, and his smile was thin and cold. *But wherever you are instead, Gwylym, I promise you this—those bastards will hear your voice in Gorath before we're finished!*

. IU .

West of Ohadlyn's Gap,
The South March Lands,
Republic of Siddarmark

"What?"

Sir Rainos Ahlverez heard the shock in his own voice as he gazed at Colonel Thomys Gardynyr. His astonishment, and the fear he couldn't quite keep out of his tone, were unlikely to do his reputation for calmness in the face of adversity any favors, but that was the least of his worries at the moment.

"Major Tybyt's scouts got a good look, Sir." Gardynyr's voice was calmer than Ahlverez' had been—probably because he'd had longer for the news to settle in during his long ride from the Kharmych semaphore station. "They say the riders they saw were definitely in Charisian ponchos and helmets."

"I hate to ask this, but how reliable is Tybyt?"

"He's a good, solid young company commander, Sir. That's one reason I picked him for the detachment. And the sergeant who actually saw them's as steady as any trooper I've ever known. According to Tybyt's semaphore message, he was carrying a spyglass, as well. That's how he got such a good look. And Tybyt says the sergeant's fairly sure the heretics didn't spot him before he pulled his patrol back and rode like hell for Brahnselyk."

Ahlverez nodded approvingly. There weren't all that many spyglasses available, but he'd collected up all he could—much to the disgruntlement of his infantry commanders—for the cavalry patrols he'd deployed to cover the seventy-five-mile gap between the Kyplyngyr Forest and the small, sleepy town of Brahnselyk on the upper reaches of the St. Alyk River. He hadn't mentioned them to Duke Harless, who'd probably have seen them as fresh proof of Dohlaran timidity, and he'd been more than half convinced himself that it was pointless. It seemed preposterous to worry about a threat three hundred miles and more in the Army of Shiloh's rear when the enemy was in *front* of it. Even if the heretics had somehow miraculously created a force to send to Eastshare's support, they wouldn't have sent it that far west. Surely it would be moving through Shiloh to clear *his* communications, not threatening the Army of Shiloh's!

He'd known all that, yet none of it had been quite enough to silence his nagging awareness of how important that sleepy town had become. It was a pity *Harless* seemed so unaware of it.

The original plan to haul every ton of supplies overland from Thesmar had been predicated on several assumptions. One—laughable in retrospect—had been that Sir Borys Cahstnyr's Desnairian quartermasters would be able to move a sufficient quantity of supplies to Kharmych. Another had been that because a sixty-two-mile stretch of the St. Alyk was unnavigable immediately north of Syrk, with no road net to cover the gap, the river was an impractical supply route.

Once they'd realized the truly disastrous state of Cahstnyr's wagon trains, however, Ahlverez and Tymplahr had quietly reconsidered the St. Alyk. In fact, they'd started reconsidering it before Thesmar was out of sight, with the result that General Rychtyr had been ordered to dispatch eight thousand civilian laborers to carve out a roadway paralleling the unnavigable stretch of the St. Alyk, build a fleet of rafts north of it—since all his proper barges were trapped below Syrk—and improvise loading docks at Syrk and again at Brahnselyk. He was an energetic man, and the Army of Shiloh's advance to Kharmych had been so lethargic he'd been able to complete his improvements about the time Harless began active operations against Fort Tairys.

Tymplahr was still in the process of getting things fully organized, and the arrangement wasn't anything Ahlverez would have been tempted to call efficient, but it was Shanwei's own lot more efficient than anything *Harless* boasted. As of two five-days ago, the distance from Ahlverez' canalhead—well, *river*head, in this case—to Kharmych had been more than cut in half, to little more than three hundred and seventy miles. A hundred and seventy of those miles were along a less than excellent secondary road from Brahnselyk to the town of Roymark, twenty-five miles west of the Kyplyngyr, but it effectively doubled the number of his wagons by halving the distance they had to travel. It put more strain on the overall transport system in his rear and his own supply situation was scarcely anything he would have dignified with the adjective "good" even now, yet it had been vastly improved.

He hadn't liked the thought of leaving his new supply

line unprotected, which was why he'd sent the Honorable Faydohr Mahrtyn, one of his best infantry colonels, to command the Brahnselyk garrison. It was also the reason he'd deployed his cavalry northwest of the forest, seen to it that the semaphore towers between Roymark and Kharmych were repaired, and built a new line between Roymark and Brahnselyk. The Desnairians had been simply delighted to leave that little task to their Dohlaran allies. Their efforts and fatigue parties were focused on getting into Fort Tairys; if Ahlverez wanted to wear his own men out felling trees and building towers out of green wood in the middle of the winter, that was his affair.

And a damned good thing somebody *worried about putting the line back into service*, he told himself grimly.

"Where, exactly, did Tybyt's sergeant spot them?" he asked now, laying his palm flat on the map spread out on his camp table.

"About here, Sir." Gardynyr indicated a spot approximately a hundred and fifty miles northeast of Roymark, just south of the South March-Cliff Peak border . . . and barely seventy miles east of Brahnselyk.

"Which way did they seem to be headed?"

"Roughly southwest, Sir."

"*South*west?" Ahlverez repeated a bit sharply. "Not due west?"

"No, Sir." Gardynyr looked up from the map. "Not towards Brahnselyk."

Ahlverez nodded as at least one of his concerns was at least partially relieved. Unless, of course, additional forces Major Tybyt's sergeant hadn't seen *were* headed west to burn Brahnselyk to the ground. It seemed unlikely the heretics could have learned about the supply route, but the new riverhead would be a lovely target for a cavalry raid if they had. Its garrison consisted of less than four thousand men—three infantry regiments, all at least a little understrength—supported only by his tenuous cavalry screen. Still. . . .

"How fast were they moving?"

"Not really pushing the pace, Sir. I wish I could give

you a better estimate, but the best the sergeant could tell Major Tybyt was that while he had them under observation they were moving at no more than a slow walk and paused completely for twenty or thirty minutes to graze their horses."

So one problem gets less worrisome . . . and the other one gets a hell of a lot worse, Ahlverez reflected.

Any cavalry sent to raid Brahnselyk would ride as hard and fast as it could to hit its objective. All of northern and central Cliff Peak was firmly in the Faithful's hands, despite the Army of God's reverses along the Daivyn. The apostate held the southeastern corner of the province, which was how Eastshare had managed to move his forces down the Branath Canal without being spotted. But Bishop Militant Cahnyr still had more than enough cavalry to intercept even a fast-moving cavalry raid. The fact that the Charisian troopers hadn't been "pushing the pace" suggested they weren't part of a quickly-in, quickly-out raid on Brahnselyk.

He wished he could decide that was a good thing.

"And it was a small party?" he asked.

"Yes, Sir; no more than a single section. Major Tybyt suggests they might be part of a screen for a bigger force."

Ahlverez nodded again, completely understanding the unhappiness in the colonel's voice and expression. If Tybyt was right . . . and if Eastshare had both the manpower and the nerve to try it. . . .

Nerve? He glowered silently down at the map. *The son-of-a-bitch may be short on manpower, but one thing he's not short on is* nerve. *What he did to Bishop Militant Cahnyr's proof enough of that, even without Fort Tairys! He knows by now how badly he screwed up, but would even he have the sheer audacity to try digging himself out* that *way?*

Harless had been content to let Ahlverez' infantry make the initial, probing advance into the Gap, and the heretics' artillery-strewn defenses had been just as deadly as he'd feared. He'd lost over a thousand men establishing that to Harless' satisfaction, but at least the duke had been willing to accept the proof of those broken bodies, and Earl Hankey's notion of "sweeping across the parapets" had been quietly abandoned in favor of a more methodical approach.

Technically, Eastshare was now under siege. It was a rather peculiar siege, given that the Army of Shiloh was unable to surround his position, but that didn't mean it couldn't be effective, because the heretics had overreached. They'd rolled the dice boldly when they seized Fort Tairys, yet in the process, Eastshare had put his entire force into a trap, and his decision to let Hennet's cavalry have free run of the Branath Canal only made it worse.

It was difficult to fault the man's logic, but even the vaunted Charisians could make mistakes. Eastshare had abandoned the Branath to Hennet because he'd expected to be supplied overland, down the high road from Maidynberg. Wagons would be less efficient than barges, but they'd be efficient enough . . . and securely on the far side of the mountains from the Army of Shiloh. Unfortunately for him, they weren't on the far side of the mountains from Colonel Bryahn Kyrbysh. The Shilohian Faithful's partisans had rallied to him after his escape from Fort Tairys, and their unceasing raids had wreaked havoc on Eastshare's intended supply route. By now, the heretics supply situation was even worse than the Army of Shiloh's.

By Kyrbysh's best estimate, which accorded well with everything the besiegers had seen themselves, Eastshare had no more than seventeen thousand men—twenty thousand at the outside—and virtually no food was getting through to him. He'd undoubtedly stockpiled as much as he could before giving up the Branath Canal, but he hadn't known—then—that Kyrbysh would succeed in cutting his own supply line, and hunger had to be biting deep over there by now. All the Army of Shiloh had to do was hold on a little longer, and the trap Eastshare had planned for it would close on *him* instead.

But the heretics had to know that as well as Ahlverez did, and he had to assume they'd move heaven and earth to save themselves. The question was what they might be able to use in the attempt. According to the Inquisition's agents, the entire Imperial Charisian Army was no more than two hundred thousand men strong, and obviously some of it had to be kept home to hold down the Faithful in conquered territories like Tarot, Zebediah, and—especially—Corisande. Bearing all of that in mind, there had to be a limit on how many men the heretics could send, and the Army of Shiloh all by itself probably had more manpower than everything Cayleb and Sharleyan could scrape up for the Mainland.

But if they'd managed to get only another forty-five thousand or so men into Siddarmark, and if Eastshare truly was gutsy enough. . . .

"Very well, Colonel," he said at last, looking up from the map. "Pass my thanks to Major Tybyt, then take the rest of your regiment and Colonel Wykmyn's to reinforce the patrols as quickly as possible. I'll send two or three regiments of infantry to reinforce Roymark, but they'll need the better part of a five-day to get there. I'll also instruct General Rychtyr to send reinforcements to Colonel Mahrtyn, but even with the St. Alyk available, they'll take at least *two* five-days to reach him from Trevyr, so I want you to pay special attention to the approaches to Brahnselyk. I'll see if I can't convince Duke Harless to send a few thousand of his cavalry to support you, as well."

"Thank you, Sir." From his tone, it was just remotely possible Gardynyr was less reassured by the prospect of Desnairian cavalry support than an ally ought to have been. "I'll be on the road within the hour."

"Good, Colonel. Very good. Captain Lattymyr will see to it that Roymark's warned to expect you."

He nodded in dismissal, and Gardynyr withdrew, leaving him to bend back over the map and contemplate a whole host of unpalatable suspicions.

After several moments, he straightened, rubbed the muscles at the small of his back, and stepped to the fly of his tent.

It was considerably brisker outside. At least the drenching fall rains had abated, but the ground remained soft and muddy, as the booted feet and shod hooves of almost two hundred thousand infantry and cavalry made abundantly clear. Of course, the ground might have dried further and faster if it hadn't frozen over every night. They'd had one bitter three-day cold snap, complete with sleet and freezing rain, but on average, the daytime temperatures climbed as much as fifteen or even twenty degrees above the freezing point. Indeed, it was warm enough this afternoon to require little more than a light jacket. But those temperatures dropped overnight. In fact, he rather thought they might drop considerably—and stay there for a while—given the northwest breeze and clear, icy blue sky, but even average temperatures left a heavy frost and ground that tended to crunch underfoot every morning.

That freeze-and-thaw cycle was hard on the men's health, and he shook his head, wishing the weather could be either consistently warmer or consistently cold enough to freeze the damp out of the air and get rid of that enervating edge of rawness. The Desnairians were poorly provided with heavy winter clothing, so he supposed he should be grateful they weren't experiencing the sort of weather more northern portions of the Republic must be enduring. Still, the contrast between shivering all night and sweating in no more than a tunic by midday wore on a man.

And then there was the matter of diet.

The cavalry's horses were suffering especially badly, but even the infantry was on short rations. *Very* short rations, in the Desnairians' case. It was only a matter of time before Harless demanded Ahlverez make up the shortfall in his own men's rations.

Of course *he will, and once you get past the fact that his shortages are entirely his own fault—and that you* can't *feed his men and yours* properly *without one hell of a lot more wagons, even with the line to Brahnselyk open and Shulmyn running your supply train—it even makes sense. I wish it didn't, but it does. In fact, I should've made the offer already. Hell, I probably* would've *made it if I weren't so pissed off with him for refusing to at least send half his useless frigging cavalry to the rear! And while I'm being pissed off about that, I guess I should be pissed off that it's not already back there to support Gardynyr and the rest of* my *cavalry.*

He suppressed an urge to hawk up a mouthful of phlegm and spit in disgust. It might make him feel better, but there were probably hundreds of eyes looking in his direction right now, and camp rumor was the only thing known to man that moved faster than Langhorne's own Rakurai. It wouldn't do to reveal his unhappiness quite so clearly immediately before he called for his horse and headed off for another delightful tête-à-tête with his esteemed army commander.

. V .
Manchyr Palace,
City of Manchyr,
Princedom of Corisande

Sir Koryn Gahrvai climbed the final flight of stairs and headed down the sun-drenched corridor on the fourth floor of Manchyr Palace's North Wing.

The original architect had faced conflicting requirements. The Palace had been intended (and needed) as a serious fortress a century ago, when it was first built, but Prince Hektor's great-grandfather had wanted something a bit more comfortable than another towering heap of stone. So he'd insisted on what amounted to tucking away a large, luxurious mansion in the middle of one of those towering heaps of stone, with a result which had inevitably been neither kraken nor wyvern: the curtainwall, moat, and bastioned towers of a large, powerful fortress wrapped around something just too small to call a cathedral.

The Palace had served its function—both its functions—well, although not necessarily *equally* well. Only an idiot would've considered attacking its formidable defenses, yet those high, forbidding walls and towers had completely blocked the mansion's windows, cast it into shadow for all but two or three hours in the middle of the day, when the temperature was at its most stifling, and deprived the ruling family's personal dwelling place of any hint of a breeze.

Two generations of the House of Daykyn put up with it; the present prince's father, however, had decided enough was enough and levied a special tax to raise the funds to do something about it. The southern, seaward walls had been razed, replaced by an entirely new set of lower, artillery-armed walls rising sheer out of the harbor's water on a footing of crushed stone and seashell. The original eastern and western walls had also been demolished, replaced by more extensive walls, much farther apart, which ran back to join the new waterfront defenses and effectively doubled the enclosed area. The northern wall, which faced Cathedral Square and formed the rear wall of the south-facing residential section, had been left intact. Since it was thirty feet thick, there'd been little way to improve the back side of the North Wing, but its southern façade had been heavily remodeled and an entirely new fourth floor had been added—an open, airy confection with skylights, a colorful tile roof embellished with dozens of ventilator domes, a wide expanse of windows facing the Palace's main courtyard, and a plethora of balconies offering a spectacular view of Manchyr Harbor over the lower waterfront batteries.

Cutting down the original curtainwalls and moving the new ones farther out had also allowed far more sunlight— and, thank God, breeze—to reach the interior. What had been a cobblestoned parade ground had become a colorful, landscaped garden, and the new administrative wing on the western side of the garden shared the sunlight, the view of the harbor, and the breeze.

And a damned good thing, too, all of it, Gahrvai thought as he strode down the hallway. *It's bad enough on a calm day even now—I hate to even think what it must've been like when they couldn't get any of that breeze in here!*

He chuckled, and then laughed out loud, albeit softly, as he savored the knowledge that he could find something in this Palace to chuckle *about*.

He paused, gazing out one of the row of windows which turned the hallway's southern side into a wall of glass, and thought about that. It was very quiet, probably because the upper floor was reserved for the royal family and, at the moment, the "royal family" had been reduced to only two members. Well, three, counting Princess Irys' new husband. Even after housing their secular guests from Old Charis, that left a vast quantity of empty, unused space.

Koryn Gahrvai cherished the peacefulness of that quiet as it sank into his bones. Over the last few five-days, his schedule had come to include sharing breakfast with Hektor and Irys Aplyn-Ahrmahk, Prince Daivyn, and Lady Hanth and her children at least twice per five-day, and those breakfasts were high points of his day.

Daivyn was always a joy, especially when Gahrvai remembered the frightened little boy who'd clung desperately to his father, weeping as he begged not to be sent away to safety. And that "safety" had done little to restore the boy's once buoyant nature. Irys had told him how Daivyn retreated into mouse-like timidity in Delferahk. How he'd slunk about, shoulders tight, sensing the danger without the age and experience to understand its cause. And she'd also described how he'd responded to *Seijin* Merlin and Lieutenant Aplyn-Ahrmahk and, later, to Countess Hanth and Archbishop Maikel. A cynical sort might have wondered if Irys had exaggerated that response to justify her decision to collaborate with the foreign despots who'd conquered her homeland. Sir Koryn Gahrvai could be as cynical as anyone, but not when he saw how the boy sparkled in his brother-in-law's presence, and watching the orphaned prince with Mairah Breygart and her children would have melted the hardest heart.

Lady Hanth was always a pleasure herself, and then there was Irys. He'd treasured his cousin's sharp wit and sense of humor before her exile. It was good, *very* good, to hear that sense of humor once more, and even better to see her actually smile. Especially when he thought about how very close he'd come to never hearing her speak or seeing her smile again.

His own smile faded as he considered the foreigner who'd kept that from happening.

The Pasqualates were baffled by the Duke of Darcos' miraculous survival, but it was simplicity itself for the Reformist laity. Miracles were the traditional way in which the Archangels and the saints had been validated by God, and if Darcos was a bit on the youthful, wiry—possibly even scruffy—side for one of the warrior saints of the War Against the Fallen, so what? He was most definitely a warrior, and Princess Irys was *obviously* saint fodder. Surely it was only reasonable for Pasquale to act through the avenue of her nursing and prayers to preserve the young husband who'd shielded her with his own body on the very steps of the Cathedral on their wedding day.

It was an irresistibly romantic tale. Not even the fact that it was true could make it any less romantic . . . or effective at generating support for Corisande's incorporation into the Charisian Empire. The forces of evil had attempted to slaughter their princess and her new husband in a foul, murderous attack at the very doors of God's house. That attack confirmed who'd truly tried to kill Irys and Daivyn in Delferahk, and the totality of its failure proved Archbishop Klairmant had spoken with the Archangels' own voice when he explained what the marriage between Princess Irys and the Duke of Darcos truly meant.

Gahrvai was prepared to give that tale every ounce of public support, although as the man charged with keeping Irys and Hektor alive he also meant to remember the Archangels helped those who helped themselves. Hektor's survival might well indicate divine approval, but Sir Koryn Gahrvai had no intention of depending upon God to intervene so directly a second time.

Although if anyone deserves divine intervention—or constitutes it, for that matter—it's probably Hektor, he thought.

The mechanics of it were easy enough to explain: a simple case of someone who'd seen far more combat than someone his age should have and developed what *Seijin* Merlin called the "situational awareness" to recognize a threat. But that took nothing away from the act itself. Or from the fact that when Hektor Aplyn-Ahrmahk gathered Irys in his arms and covered her body with his own, it had been the deliberate decision of someone who'd realized only one of them could survive and chosen for that someone to be the woman he loved.

He'd turned out to be wrong about his own chance of survival, although he shouldn't have been, given the damage he'd taken. And he was also the only surviving witness who'd actually seen what had happened. They still had no clue where the assassin and the hapless victim in the wheelchair had come from, but Hektor's testimony confirmed what the messages from the watchers *Seijin* Merlin had left in Corisande had already suggested must have happened.

No one would ever know what had caught Sergeant Wynstyn Frayzhyr's eye. He'd been one of Gahrvai's handpicked men, circulating through the crowd in civilian clothing, looking for something exactly like what had happened, but he'd been fifty yards outside his assigned area when the explosion killed him. Whatever had attracted Frayzhyr's attention, it had been a glimpse of him, lunging at the woman in the lay sister's uniform, which had drawn *Hektor's* attention to the sudden sputter of smoke, the realization it had been spawned by a fuse. Without Frayzhyr, he and Irys would certainly be dead, and Prince Daivyn had already decreed that the sergeant's two daughters would be raised as wards of the Crown and that his widow would receive an army colonel's pay for the rest of her life.

It couldn't bring Frayzhyr back to life, but at least the Crown could acknowledge its debt to him by caring for his family. And much though Gahrvai might regret the sergeant's death, he was unspeakably grateful Frayzhyr had been there to die for his princess. And for her husband.

His eyes softened as he reflected on how deeply he'd come to value Hektor Aplyn-Ahrmahk. The duke was little more than half his own age, yet he'd seen at least as much combat—indeed, he'd seen *more* of it—and the last thing Irys Zhorzhet Mhara Daykyn had needed as a husband was some soft, pretty, well-educated, politically aware, polished, well-groomed, well-connected aristocrat who knew everything there was to know about court infighting . . . and thought hardship was getting caught in the rain during a fox-lizard hunt. Hektor might be well educated, and he was certainly politically aware, but he was also far from anything someone might call "pretty," about as far removed from the polished aristocrat category as it was possible to imagine, totally disinterested in fox-lizard hunting . . . and tougher than old boot leather.

Once upon a time I thought those Marines *Cayleb used to kick my arse were tough bastards,* he reflected, *but Hektor could give them toughness lessons any day of the five-day. I wonder if it's something in the water in Charis?*

Whatever it was, Hektor Aplyn-Ahrmahk had it in full measure. He'd floated in and out of consciousness—mostly out—for three days after the attack. On the fourth day, however, he'd awakened clearheaded and fully aware. In some ways, the Order of Pasquale seemed to find the speed of his recovery even more miraculous than the fact that he'd survived in the first place. It seemed unlikely he'd ever regain full use of his left hand, but aside from that, his wounds were healing with a speed which baffled the most experienced healer. He'd be convalescing for a long time to come, but he was already cautiously mobile, and from the smile Gahrvai had surprised on his cousin's face yesterday that wasn't the only thing he was capable of now.

Gahrvai chuckled again, this time with a broad grin, and gave himself a shake. If he dawdled much longer, he'd miss breakfast entirely!

He headed down the hallway again, more briskly than before, turned into the cross corridor that led to the breakfast parlor . . . and slammed to a halt.

The woman standing outside the breakfast parlor's hand-polished doors was approximately the same height as Irys, but she was clearly some years older. She was also strikingly attractive, with the red hair of one of the northern realms and eyes as darkly blue as Merlin Athrawes' own, yet what drew the eye was the blackened breastplate of the Charisian Imperial Guard and the insignia of a captain. She stood neat as a cat-lizard, hands folded before her, a sword identical to Major Athrawes'—or Emperor Cayleb's, for that matter—across her back and what must be one of the new revolvers at her right hip. Not even the Guard uniform and a breastplate could disguise her supple shapeliness, however preposterous it might be to see a woman armed and armored for war. But what struck Gahrvai most strongly in that first, astonished moment was the serenity of those sapphire eyes, the calmness of her expression . . . and the strong, long-fingered hands of someone poised even here for instant, purposeful mayhem.

Well, that and the fact that she couldn't possibly *be* here . . . and that he'd never seen her before in his life.

"Good morning, General Gahrvai."

She bowed slightly in salute. She had a pleasant voice, a corner of Gahrvai's mind noted, a bit on the deep side for a woman, with a musical, throaty edge.

"Good morning," he heard himself reply, as if she had a perfect right to stand outside this door.

Unfortunately, she most certainly did not. For that matter, he found himself wondering why none of the alert, highly trained guards he'd stationed around Manchyr Palace, especially since the Cathedral Square attack, had so much as mentioned her to him. A black breastplate and an unusual sword were far from sufficient to win free passage to the heart of his prince's living quarters without his personal and very specific approval.

And I'm pretty damned sure I'd remember approving her presence.

The tartness of the thought broke the grip of his astonishment, and he cocked his head, acutely aware for some reason of his own lack of weapons.

"May I ask what you're doing here ... Captain?" he asked a bit coldly, eyes flicking to the shoulder insignia and then back to her face. "And may I also ask how you happen to be here without anyone's mentioning you to me?"

"Emperor Cayleb and Major Athrawes sent me to augment security for Prince Daivyn and Princess Irys, Sir," she replied calmly in an accent that reminded him of someone else. "It wasn't intended as any sort of an aspersion on Corisande's ability to protect them, and what I've discovered so far about the Cathedral Square attack—especially what Duke Darcos had to say about the actual assassin—suggests you and your men were very much on your toes. Even if it didn't, I have firm instructions not to interfere with your procedures and operations in any way. His Majesty intends me as ... an adjunct, attached personally to Prince Daivyn, Princess Irys, and Duke Darcos, not as any sort of replacement for Sergeant Raimair or any other member of their regular detachments."

"That's very generous of His Majesty," Gahrvai said, a shade more tartly than he'd intended and suppressing an urge to point out that whatever might happen in the future, Cayleb Ahrmahk was not yet *his* emperor. "It doesn't, however, explain why no one warned me you were coming."

"I arrived late last night, bringing my orders with me, Sir. You'd already retired, most of the palace staff had done the same, and I felt it would be ... rude to awaken you simply to hand you my orders."

Gahrvai's eyes narrowed. He started to observe that he saw the shipping movement reports every morning and that, according to them, no ships had arrived from Old Charis or the Republic of Siddarmark in the last fiveday ... *including* last night, then thought better of it. He was beginning to cherish certain suspicions about the woman in front of him and how she might have arrived so tracelessly in Corisande.

"And the reason none of the members—the *regular* members—of Prince Daivyn's personal guard saw fit to mention your presence when I arrived at the Palace this morning, Captain?"

There was more than a trace of true anger in his voice this time. He didn't care if she'd been sent by Merlin Athrawes, Cayleb Ahrmahk, or Langhorne himself; she did *not* have authority to issue orders to Daivyn or Irys' armsmen. And she most assuredly had no authority to tell them not to report the arrival of an armed stranger who'd arrogated access to the royal family to herself, and they damned well knew it!

"I'm afraid they don't know I'm here yet, Sir," she responded a bit apologetically. "It seemed simpler to just wait outside Princess Irys and Duke Darcos' apartment until they woke up and I could present my orders from His Majesty directly to them."

"It seemed simpler to—?!"

Gahrvai chopped himself off and forced himself to draw a deep, calming breath. So she'd gotten inside the Palace walls without being challenged by the regular sentries or the Royal Guard's elite, highly trained men, walked upstairs to Princess Irys' personal, fourth-floor appartments, and parked herself in the hallway outside those apartments—apparently disguised as a potted plant to remain unobserved by any of the servants—without anyone even *noticing*?

He felt a headache coming on . . . and he was quite sure he recognized that accent now.

"Tell me, Captain," he said, "how well do you know *Seijin* Merlin?"

"Quite well, actually, Sir." She smiled slightly. "We're both from the Mountains of Light and I've known Major Athrawes all my life."

"And would it happen you and the *seijin* . . . share certain abilities, shall we say?"

"We do have many of the same skills," she acknowledged. "We studied under the same masters, you see."

"Yes, I think I am beginning to see." His answering smile showed his teeth. "And would it happen that one of the reasons *Seijin* Merlin—I mean Emperor Cayleb—selected you for this assignment is that Princess Irys and Prince Daivyn already know and trust you?"

"Princes Irys—and Duke Darcos—certainly, Sir. I'm

afraid I was never introduced to Prince Daivyn, although he seemed perfectly happy when his sister explained my presence to him this morning." She returned his smile much more tranquilly. "I think the fact that *Seijin* Merlin sent His Highness a personal note to introduce me probably didn't hurt."

"I see."

Gahrvai hooked his thumbs into his belt, settling back as he regarded the highly attractive young woman in front of him and wondered once more why so many *seijins* had chosen to come out of the woodwork and offer their services to the House of Ahrmahk. It wasn't that he *objected* to it, but it would be nice to have some idea just what the Shan-wei was going on.

Before whatever it was hit him with an even bigger clue stick, at least.

"Well, Captain," he said finally, "it seems I'm stuck with you. I trust you won't take my choice of verb wrongly."

"Of course not, Sir."

Her voice was as serene as ever, but he saw a flicker of amusement in those dark blue eyes of hers.

"Good." He felt the corners of his own eyes crinkle as his sense of the absurd came to his rescue. "And since I *am* stuck with you, *Seijin*, may I ask what your name is?"

For a moment he thought she was going to inform him—as Merlin had on more than one occasion—that whatever anyone else might think, *she* didn't call herself a *seijin*. Obviously, however, she thought better of it. Perhaps even Merlin would eventually realize there was no point denying the painfully obvious. Instead, she simply gave him another of those tranquil smiles and inclined her head in another slight, respectful bow.

"Of course, General Gahrvai," she murmured. "You may call me Nimue."

Hard to imagine less promising weather for a campaign, Kynt Clareyk thought with profound satisfaction, standing at the window of his Allyntyn headquarters.

A few weary snowflakes spiraled down from a leaden sky, skipping along the frozen streets on a glacial wind until they settled in herringbone patterns. The corners of the windowpanes showed traceries of ice too heavy to be called frost, and despite his office's warmth, the cold beyond that glass bit deep. It was an imagined bite, the memory of how frigid that cutting wind had been during his inspection rounds, and the temperature was about to plunge even lower as soon as evening dwindled into night.

The only good thing about it, he continued, considering the meteorology data, *is that it's going to get still worse*.

He smiled thinly, then turned his back on that dreary vista and seated himself behind his desk. One thing that never changed was that his endless paperwork remained inversely proportionate to the amount of time in which he had to do it. Bryahn Slokym and Allayn Powairs took as much off of him as they could, but there was a limit to how much they could save him from. And he was grateful, in a way, that that was the case. It gave him something to do while he waited for the weather to worsen.

Now that Sir Breyt Bahskym, the Earl of High Mount, had arrived with the final echelon of the Imperial Charisian Army, the Group of Four's opportunity to simply sweep the board was a thing of the past. It had, in the words of a famous Old Earth general, been "the nearest run thing you ever saw," but the Army of God had fallen just short. It had been stopped in places like the Sylmahn

Gap and along the Daivyn River by the sacrificial gallantry of Siddarmarkian regulars and Charisian Marines . . . and in a thousand other, nameless places by
the sheer determination of loyal men—and women—to
die where they stood. Most of their names would never be
known, but they were the ones who'd bought the knife
edge of time—bought it in blood and sealed it with their
deaths—for a single reinforced Charisian division to reach
the Republic.

There'd been twenty-six thousand men in that first echelon. Now there were over three hundred thousand Charisian soldiers, not counting the purely logistical troops
supporting the ICA's supply lines, and a new Republic of
Siddarmark Army had risen from the ashes of mutiny,
rebellion, and death to march towards the sound of battle
with their Charisian allies. Five RSA rifle divisions were
already at the front or on active operations against Temple
Loyalist guerrillas; ten more—another one hundred and
thirty thousand men—had almost completed their training; and *fifteen* more would begin the same process within
the next few five-days. They couldn't put any more of
the new divisions into the field yet because there simply
weren't sufficient rifles to arm them and the RSA would
never again send pikemen into battle, but by next
spring *they* would be ready for field service. And in the
meantime, with High Mount's arrival, the original
scheme for the ICA's organization—somewhat modified
by circumstances—had finally been put into place.

Duke Eastshare's command in Ohadlyn's Gap had become the Army of the Branaths, and when it was fully
up to strength, including its attached Siddarmarkian units,
it would muster seventy thousand men, thirty percent of
them mounted. Green Valley's own Army of Midhold
would be a bit stronger than that, with almost seventy-
six thousand men, including sixteen thousand Charisian
mounted infantry. The Army of Cliff Peak, under High
Mount's command, would count another sixty-nine thousand—in his case, all Charisians, with no Siddarmarkian
attachments. The Army of the Daivyn, under General

Symkyn, would hold the Glacierheart Gap against Kaitswyrth's demoralized Army of Glacierheart with roughly seventy-five thousand men, while General Bartyn Sahmyrsyt commanded the Army of Old Province: forty-three thousand men who formed the Allies primary reserve in Siddar City. Two more independently deployed mounted brigades had been sent south from the capital, where they would soon be teaching the Temple Loyalist guerrillas in the triangle of the South March Lands between Southguard and the Taigyn River how Charisian dragoons dealt with rapists and murderers.

The Allies remained outnumbered in all three active theaters, but that didn't worry Green Valley. Properly employed, the Army of God could still put up a dangerous defense, and next year, if Nahrmahn and Owl's estimates held up, it might well become a dangerous offensive force, as well. For now, however, it was well and truly pinned, and it would shortly discover it was in rather worse state even to defend itself than it thought it was. But the Army of God wasn't the Allies' primary target just at the moment. No, that honor had been granted to the Army of Shiloh, which was not, he thought with profound satisfaction, likely to enjoy the experience.

And neither is Bishop Militant Bahrnabai. Harless and Ahlverez may be the primary *objective, but that doesn't mean we don't have a little attention to spare for their friends, and the canal ice'll be thick enough to support infantry in three more five-days. By mid-February, it'll be thick enough for field guns, and Nybar's boys will be feeling the chill by then.*

The Army of God's creators had fully understood the brutality of the high northern climate and how difficult it would become to move supplies once the canals froze. That was why they'd never intended to wage any winter campaigns in northern East Haven. Like a certain head of state from Old Earth named Adolf Hitler, however, they'd been stopped short of their summer campaign's intended goals, and after Halcom Bahrns' rampage through the canal system, their supply echelons were in even worse shape than the Wehrmacht's had been in the winter of 1941. The canals were inoperable, even Safeholdian high roads were breaking down under the weight of so much freight traffic, and Wyrshym had been forced to send as many draft dragons as possible to the rear. He hadn't *wanted* to reduce his transport capacity, but the majority of those dragons that hadn't been sent back to someplace they could survive the winter had very limited life expectancies. Most would be providing rations to his infantry within the next month.

The good news, in so far as there *was* any good news for the Army of the Sylmahn, was that it was animal-powered, with no need for gasoline or spare parts, and that its relatively primitive weapons' ammunition needs didn't begin to approach those of a mechanized Old Earth army. It still needed to ship *food*, however. Worse, it needed to ship that food at a time when its available transport was still overwhelmed trying to evacuate Temple Loyalist civilians from the wasteland the Sword of Schueler had created.

And in the process, it had been stretched far too thin . . . and not just where food was concerned. Its creators had designed proper cold-weather uniforms, but they hadn't made enough of them and its crippled logistics couldn't distribute even the ones it had properly. Wyrshym's divisions were already losing men to frostbite. Some of them, under worse than average conditions, had actually died of hypothermia.

Given what had happened to so many Siddarmarkian civilians the previous winter, Green Valley found it difficult to feel much sympathy.

Rhobair Duchairn was doing all he could to move winter clothing forward, but it wasn't simply a problem of transporting the needed uniforms; there were too few of them *to* transport because of how badly the AOG had underestimated its needs when it ordered them. Maigwair and his bishops militant had anticipated breaking through to the eastern side of the Snow Barrens and the Moon Thorns, where the weather was far milder. Now, with their armies stopped short, the obvious move was to pull *all* of them back, not just the pikemen, but Zhaspahr Clyntahn had quashed the notion of giving up a single foot of occupied ground as firmly as Hitler ever had, and there simply weren't sufficient winter uniforms to go around. And to make the Army of the Sylmahn's woes complete, the Mainland textile industry, unlike Rhaiyan Mychail's Charisian manufactories, couldn't have made the necessary clothing on such short notice even if there'd been no transport problems at all.

The Church of God Awaiting was conducting clothing drives, collecting as many winter garments as it could, but the pre-Merlin textile industry had never produced clothing in the abundance an industrialized society took for granted. Safeholdian garments were well made, for the most part, but the supply was finite, most of the truly heavy winter clothing on the planet was needed right where it was, and muscle-powered manufactories couldn't mass-produce more of it quickly. Powered looms and sewing machines had become weapons of war as surely as any rifle, and not even Rhobair Duchairn had seen *that* one coming. It was a sign of the Army of the Sylmahn's dire straits that foraging parties spent as much time ransacking abandoned farmsteads and towns for salvageable clothing as for food or the building materials to construct winter quarters.

And all of that combined to deprive the Army of God of anything remotely like mobility. Without sufficient food and fodder, inadequately clothed men and overworked animals simply lacked the energy for aggressive marching or patrolling in sub-zero winter. They were forced to huddle in whatever shelter they could cobble up, husbanding their energy and avoiding frostbite, and fuel was already in short supply.

Ruhsyl's the main show, Green Valley thought, *and that makes perfectly good sense, given how much better the campaigning conditions are going to be in southern Cliff Peak and the South March. I understand that. But Wyrshym and I will do a little dancing of our own in another month or two, and this time I get to call the tune.*

He concentrated on his paperwork far more cheerfully than usual, whistling softly, and if anyone else had been present, they probably would have recognized the melody.

It was called "The Pikes of Kolstyr."

FEBRUARY, YEAR OF GOD 897

.✦.

. I .
Camp Number Four,
Bedard Canal,
West of Mahzgyr,
Duchy of Gwynt

"Shan-wei! It's *cold* out there!"

Sergeant Allayn Tahlbaht had his arms wrapped tightly about himself as he entered the well-chinked cabin and kicked the door shut behind him. He crossed to the fireplace, pulled his hands out of his armpits, blew on them, rubbed them briskly together, then held them out to the crackling fire. The log-formed, clay-coated fireplace and chimney were not perfect specimens of design or workmanship, and tendrils of smoke curled up around the rough mantel, but that was a minor price for the blessed warmth, in Tahlbaht's considered opinion.

"You think *this* is cold?" Sergeant Tangwyn Syngpu laughed, looking up from the belt he was mending. The sergeant spoke with a pronounced Harchongese accent, reasonably enough. "Visit me in Thomas after the Jihad. I'll show you *cold*!"

Tahlbaht rolled his eyes. Syngpu was scarcely the only member of the 231st Volunteer Regiment who needled him about the weather. And the other sergeant had a point about the difference between his homeland and the Duchy of Gwynt. Syngpu came from a tiny village (whose name Tahlbaht had absolutely no intention of trying to pronounce) in Thomas Province. It was situated in the valley between the de Castro and Langhorne Mountains, the better part of two thousand miles north of Tahlbaht's own birthplace in Trokhanos. In fact, it was two hundred miles north of Zion itself, and everyone knew what winter was like in *Zion*! The temperature in Trokhanos, on the other hand, rarely dipped below freezing even in midwinter, especially near the sleepy port of Eralth where Tahlbaht had grown up. Trokhanans like Tahlbaht could grow to adulthood without ever seeing a single snowflake, and many of them had.

Thomas got just a *little* chillier than that, he supposed.

"I'm thinking it's cold enough for such as me to be going on with," he told Syngpu. "Mind, I've seven Zion winters in my duty book, and I'll allow Zion's a bit nippier nor this. But I've those fine-bred southern sensibilities, don't you know. Why, the next thing you know, there'll be great heaps of that white stuff—what d'you call it? Snow, is it?—all stacked about the landscape. And sure as there is, we'll all be turfed out of our snug little cabins to go march about in it!"

Syngpu laughed again, although Tahlbaht probably had a point about the training march. They did a lot of that, and Tahlbaht's predictions were seldom wrong. This southern weather really was ridiculously mild for someone who'd grown up in the de Castros' foothills, though. As long as it didn't rain—and the skies were currently clear, which helped explain the cold snap which was bothering Tahlbaht so—he had no objection to spending time in the fresh air. Besides, it would be good for the men.

And isn't that a strange thing for a shepherd from Thomas to be thinking? he asked himself. *It's not that long ago you* wouldn't *have thought about whether or not something would be "good for the men," and you wouldn't've cared, either. And you can give Allayn a lot of the thanks for the fact that you're thinking about it now.*

He concentrated on setting the stitches along the edge of the belt where he'd trimmed away the damaged leather. One thing a shepherd learned was how to mend things on his own. One thing a shepherd *didn't* learn was how to read, and Tangwyn Syngpu had been as close to illiterate as made no difference when he was drafted for the Mighty Host of God and the Archangels. He'd been willing enough to go if Mother Church needed his services, but he'd been horrified when they made him a corporal the very day he mustered in. And then, during training, they'd promoted him to sergeant! And now, half a year later, he was the 231st Volunteers' standardbearer—what the Army of God would have called the regimental color sergeant—the second-ranking noncom of the entire regiment.

What did *he* know about being a sergeant? He was just a mountain boy from the de Castros! All right, so he was tough, since you either grew up tough or died in the de Castros. And he'd thumped a few skulls in hard-knuckle stand-up fights for beef and beer in his time. But a *sergeant*? Responsible for leading other men into battle against Shan-wei and all the forces of Darkness? The idea had been ridiculous . . . and terrifying.

Of course if he'd known then what he knew now he would've been terrified about a lot of other things, as well. It was thanks to Tahlbaht and the other AOG officers and noncoms assigned to the 231st that he not only knew enough to worry about those other things now but might actually have learned enough to help the men he was responsible for survive them!

He watched from the corner of his eye as the Siddarmarkian spread his hands to the flames once more. When Tahlbaht first turned up to replace the company's original, Harchongese senior sergeant, Syngpu had been in awe. He'd regarded the experienced, confident Tahlbaht as some sort of Archangel, or at least a senior angel. Where other members of the Mighty Host of God and the Archangels had resented the imposition of foreign officers and noncoms, Syngpu had been determined to soak up as much knowledge as he could. He was older than many of the conscript companies' other corporals and sergeants, with a wife and four children back home, and he intended to get still older, God and Chihiro willing! If Tahlbaht had something to teach, Syngpu was only too happy to learn.

But over the weary, exhausting five-days, he'd discovered that the other man made an even better friend than he did a mentor. Unlike quite a few other people Syngpu could name, he didn't look down his nose at the Harchongese serfs and peasants who'd been scooped up to fight the heresy. He'd rolled up his sleeves and done his job, and now he and Syngpu were the noncommissioned backbone of an infantry company that was at least five or six times as dangerous—to the enemy, not itself—than it had been before his arrival.

A man could do worse than make a foreign friend who helps manage that, Syngpu told himself. *Especially a foreign friend carrying around everything Allayn is.*

The entire province of Trokhanos, led and inspired by Tahlbaht's hometown of Eralth, had gone over to the heresy. The sergeant had had no word from any member of his family since the Faithful had risen against Stohnar's treachery to God and His Church. He seldom talked about it, but he'd dropped a bit of personal information—probably more than he'd realized—from time to time. Syngpu understood the shadows beneath his friend's normal good humor as he worried about his family's safety. And even about whether or not some of them might have joined the heresy.

Syngpu lifted the belt to bite off the thread, stowed the expensive needle carefully away, then stood and threaded the belt through his belt loops and buckled it snugly.

"Nice," Tahlbaht told him with a chuckle. "Got a pair of boots could use a little mending, happen you've the time for it."

"Sorry to hear that," Syngpu replied, reaching for his coat. "I promised Captain of Spears Ywahnzhi I'd drop in on the pickets this afternoon."

"Sneak up on 'em, you mean, hey?" Tahlbaht chuckled again and gave his hands one last rub. "Never a day's work as warms the cockles of a sergeant's heart more than catching some poor sod snoozin' on picket duty!" he announced. "Let's do 'er, Tangwyn!"

The two of them headed out the door, laughing.

▼ ▼ ▼

Not far from the sergeants' cabin, Lord of Foot Bangpa Tshangjyn and Colonel Bynzhamyn Krestmyn sat sharing a bottle of the colonel's precious, hoarded Chisholmian whiskey. Tshangjyn supposed he ought to feel guilty about consuming something produced by heretics, but it *was* the thirty-year-old Glynfych. Not only did that make it one of the finest whiskeys ever produced and reverently aged, but it had been distilled well before heresy had reared its ugly head in the Out Islands. For that matter, it had been aging innocently away well before Sharleyan or Cayleb Ahrmahk had even been born.

Father Bryahn might pick a few holes in that logic, Tshangjyn thought, *but he's a compassionate young man. Surely he wouldn't deprive someone twenty years his senior of what minor comforts might come his way in the field.*

In fact, Bryahn Charlz, the Schuelerite under-priest who served as the 231st Volunteers' chaplain—he would have been called its intendant in the Army of God—was a compassionate young priest. Someone who stood no nonsense, but a man who tried to be as understanding as he could where his often uncivilized and always uncouth charges were concerned. Had he been present, not only would he have cheerfully raised a glass with them, but done it with the respect the Glynfych's golden, honeyed fire deserved.

Besides, it would have been an unforgivable insult to Krestmyn if Tshangjyn had declined.

The colonel had suffered more than many for the Jihad. A well-to-do Tanshar merchant before Shan-wei's minions had seized so much of the world by the throat, he and his family had been ruined by Charisian privateers (and by Mother Church's embargo of trade with Charis). Then he'd lost his left arm in the bitter fighting in the Sylmahn Gap. A man who'd given that much to the Jihad deserved a little consideration, even if he was a barbarian. And to be fair, he was much *less* of a barbarian than many. No one born east of the city of Zion, even in the Temple Lands, could be considered truly civilized, but Krestmyn came remarkably close. Well educated, courteous, intelligent, and competent, it was scarcely his fault he hadn't been born Harchongese.

"What do you think about this new rifle? This St. Kylmahn?" the lord of foot asked, cradling his glass in his hands as he cocked his head at Krestmyn across the hearth.

The lighting was too dim to really make out the colonel's expression. Krestmyn's quarters were a little better finished but otherwise identical in construction to the vast expanse of Camp Number Four's chinked-log barracks. The fireplace didn't smoke—anymore—and it had a planked wooden floor, rather than the packed dirt of the noncommissioned and enlisted quarters, and he had it to himself, but there was no glass for the windows, and the shutters were kept tightly closed four and a half days out of the five-day once the weather turned what passed for cold here in Gwynt. That left lamplight and firelight, and Tshangjyn's eyes weren't as young as they'd once been. He'd grown accustomed to that, though, and also to the spartan severity of Krestmyn's cabin. It was certainly a far cry from the sort of luxury which would have been demanded by a Harchongian who commanded a base which housed over forty thousand men, yet it was difficult to imagine the colonel anywhere else.

"I don't really know what to think, Bangpa," Krestmyn replied after a moment. "Other than how much I want to get my hand on one of them and try it out myself!" He shook his head. "If even half the things they're telling us are accurate, it's going to be a huge factor come spring."

Tshangjyn nodded, his face expressionless as he considered all the things Krestmyn hadn't said. Neither of them had ever come right out and said it, but Tshangjyn had concluded months ago that for all its destructiveness, the heretics' blasphemous raid on the canal system had been a huge stroke of God's own grace for the Mighty Host of God and the Archangels.

His expressionlessness wavered for a moment as he recalled Krestmyn's initial reaction to the Mighty Host's full name. How sad that easterners had so little poetry in their souls! He did have to admit that it took rather longer to say than "the Army of God," though.

The temptation to smile disappeared as he contemplated what would have happened if the destruction of the canals *hadn't* prevented the Host from grappling with the heretics in battle last summer as planned. Not that every Harchongese officer—especially in the Army's senior ranks—agreed with him about the desirability of the changes they'd been forced to confront since then.

Bynzhamyn Krestmyn leaned back, studying the lord of foot's body language, and suspected exactly what he was thinking. Bangpa Tshangjyn was no fool, and no coward, either. He hadn't volunteered for the "Mighty Host of God and the Archangels," but he'd been a well-to-do banker, related by marriage to the Baron of Wind Kissed Grass, and the son, grandson, and great-grandson of the bureaucrats who truly managed the Harchong Empire. He'd had more than sufficient connections to avoid service, and he'd never even tried to use them.

There were many things to like and admire about him, from his intelligence to his education to his faith and determination. Other things were less admirable, but that was probably unavoidable. He was an upper-class Harchongian, which meant by definition that he'd been reared to regard the conscripted serfs and peasants who made up the Mighty Host of God and the Archangels' infantry as something south of human. He often treated them as semi-domesticated animals, somewhere between golden retrievers and monkey-lizards, yet he was genuinely devoted to their well-being, and he'd worked long and hard to see to it that they had adequate housing and properly observed Pasquale's Law. The reverse could have been said about all too many Harchongese officers.

And the Harchongese Army was a product of the society and the support base which had produced it. Therein lay the problem.

There'd been a time when the Harchong Empire had been the terror of its neighbors. Its bottomless well of manpower had been supported by a manufacturing base whose productivity was only slightly inferior to the rest of Safehold's, and its artisans had been arguably the finest in the world. Even today, many Harchongese craftsmen were superb artists, true masters of their crafts. Unfortunately, there were very few of them in proportion to the Empire's huge population . . . and there were even fewer "mechanics." Harchong's craftsmen's work commanded huge prices from connoisseurs while its army's arsenals were lumbered with obsolete weapons—some as much as a hundred years old or more—which had been accumulated over the years. It possessed pitifully few *modern* weapons, and even its stockpiles of old model arms had been grossly inadequate to the present need.

For all the Harchong Empire's enormous size, the Imperial Harchongese Army had been sadly understrength before the Jihad. The last two emperors—or, rather, the bureaucrats who'd run the Empire in their names—had gradually modernized the standing army over the last fifty years, replacing the feudal nightmare it had become during the preceding couple of centuries. There'd been more than a little aristocratic resistance to building an army which answered to the Crown rather than to them, but the bureaucrats had persisted. It must have been a difficult task for them to decide to undertake, even without the nobles' resistance, given their ingrained loathing of any idea that required them to spend money on anything that didn't put sizable sums into their own purses, yet they'd persevered stubbornly. Come to think of it, though, the graft for a project of that scale must have been enormous.

The Empire had traditionally relied upon cavalry, for many reasons. One was the aristocrat's instinctive love affair—apparently as universal as it was deep—with horses. The Princedom of Tanshar had its own nobility, but thankfully they'd been spared that particular fetish, although Krestmyn could have effortlessly reeled off a dozen off-color jokes about the *real* reasons Harchongese nobles spent so much time with horses.

More to the point, aristocratic Harchongians lived in terror of servile rebellion—with just cause, given the conditions under which so many Harchongese serfs existed. One really couldn't call it "living," and the thing which had most amazed Krestmyn when he took up his new duties was the degree of loyalty and deference so many of the serfs and barely better off peasants who'd been conscripted for Mother Church's service showed their hereditary overlords.

One reason it had surprised him was that Harchong's serfs *had* rebelled on at least half a dozen occasions, and the bloodshed had been horrific each time. Atrocities had been brutal as the serfs struck back at their tormentors, and the examples made in the course of putting down the rebellions had been even worse. Both aristocrats and serfs had long memories, too. That was why Harchongese serfs were subject to summary execution for the possession of any missile weapon more sophisticated than a shepherd's sling, and it was also why the Harchongese Army had relied on the mobility and shock effect—the psychological terror—of cavalry to deter servile violence.

The army reforms hadn't really changed that, since almost seventy percent of the regular army was still mounted. The reformers had, however, built up a solid core of over one hundred thousand well-trained, well-armed, well-armored heavy infantry, supported by thirty thousand bowmen and arbalesteers and a tiny handful of matchlock-armed musketeers. The IHA's true striking power, however, continued to reside in the highly mobile horse archers who composed nearly half its total manpower. There were various militia forces scattered around the Empire, not to mention the notorious and justly feared Emperor's Spears, the Harchongese military police, but that standing, professional army had become the true bulwark of the Empire . . . and the bane of any aristocratic hope of a return to the days when the great lords had dictated to the Empire's bureaucratic managers.

There were still scores of feudal cavalry regiments, despite the reforms, manned by, commanded by, and answering to the aristocratic magnates who paid for them. In fact, technically, the feudal regiments' roster strength was twice the standing army's, but it was unlikely they could actually have produced more than forty percent—fifty, at the outside—of those official numbers.

Yet the fact remained that exclusive of those ramshackle feudal regiments, whose effectiveness had to be highly suspect, the entire Imperial Harchongese Army had numbered less than five hundred thousand men, horse and foot, with no field artillery at all, at the beginning of the Schism. And Lord of Armies Yitangzhi Gengchai, the Grand Duke of Omar and (officially) imperial minister of war, had done absolutely nothing to increase its size until the Empire was formally summoned to Jihad. Of course, Omar was the next best thing to ninety and an aristocrat, so expecting anything out of *him* would have been grossly unrealistic. The bureaucrats who actually managed the Empire might have given the matter at least a *little* thought, however.

They hadn't, with the result that they'd been forced to send out press gangs to conscript the manpower they needed to expand the standing army to meet the requirements of the Mighty Host of God and the Archangels. They'd gone from a strength of four hundred seventy-one thousand to one of over one million and three hundred thousand in less than four months, with God only knew what kind of disruption in the farm villages from which those men had come. It was a remarkable performance Krestmyn doubted any other realm could have achieved, but a force which would have been effective at quelling rebellious serfs had to be viewed as a questionable match for the Republic of Siddarmark Army and its Charisian allies. Even with half the Emperor's Spears included in the numbers, they'd sent that huge force off with barely seventy-seven thousand rifles and less than eighty thousand pistols. It was reasonably well provided with bows, arbalests, even sixty-seven thousand *slingers*, but not with rifles.

The regular army's archers, especially its horse archers, might actually have fared well against smoothbores or even against riflemen with muzzleloaders, given their volume of fire and the high standard of accuracy to which they'd been trained. But the heretics' breechloaders and mobile angle-guns were another matter entirely, and however good the *regulars'* archery might have been, the horde of conscripted light infantry had—not surprisingly—been horrible marksmen. It took years to build a competent archer, although arbalests came a little easier, and any serf would have paid with his life if he'd been caught practicing with a bow or arbalest before being drafted. Almost worse, their upper-class, aristocratic senior officers hadn't really *wanted* them to attain a worthwhile level of accuracy with their newly issued bows and arbalests, Jihad or no Jihad, since some of them might actually survive to return home. Surely sheer volume of fire would do the job without teaching them to actually hit individual targets!

They would have found out differently if the Mighty Host of God and the Archangels had met the heretics in battle, so it was fortunate they'd been spared that experience. Instead, the Host had been parceled out in winter quarters like Camp Number Four—winter quarters constructed in ample time, thanks to Vicar Rhobair's management—along the rivers and canals in north-central Haven. And while they were parked there, AOG instructors and mentors, like one Bynzhamyn Krestmyn, had been dispatched to train those conscripts.

Quite a few of the Harchongese nobles had been horrified by the notion of teaching serfs to be *effective* soldiers. Serfs' battlefield function was to obediently die swamping the enemy by sheer numbers, opening a path by which their better trained, better armed, and far better born superiors charged to victory. It was *not* to acquire military skills they might take home and use against those better born superiors the next time they rebelled. Men like Bangpa Tshangjyn might understand why those skills were necessary, might even enthusiastically support the effort of acquiring them, but it would have been asking too much for barons, earls, and dukes to share that vision.

Fortunately, they hadn't had a choice. It had cost the Army of God dearly, but Captain General Maigwair had found a bribe not even Harchongians could refuse. He'd offered to divert enormous numbers of rifles to the Mighty Host of God and the Archangels—rifles his own army desperately needed—and to provide it with field artillery supplied by Mother Church and manned by AOG gunners . . . but only if he was allowed to send in trainers to ensure that those weapons would be used effectively in battle. Krestmyn suspected there'd been great wailing and gnashing of teeth back in Harchong when the semaphore delivered Vicar Allayn's terms, yet the Empire had found no choice but to accept them. There'd been bitter protests from many noble Harchongians, but the bureaucrats had stood firm, and this time the aristocracy had been denied even the support of its traditional ally, the Inquisition.

The Border States had been no happier, since they'd been required to surrender *all* of their rifles to the cause, which had produced two hundred and four thousand weapons. Coupled with the diversion of over eighty percent of the Temple Lands' own production, fifty thousand from Dohlar, almost twenty thousand from Silkiah, and forty thousand from Harchong's own manufactories, a total of over five hundred and six thousand rifles would have been delivered to the Mighty Host of God and the Archangels by the end of the month. Assuming all the rifle makers involved met their quotas, the Host would be able to put over six hundred and forty thousand riflemen into the field by the time the canals thawed next spring. And somewhere around fourteen percent of them would be armed with the new St. Kylmahn breechloaders. The Harchongians would still have over four hundred and sixty thousand infantry who *didn't* have rifles, but virtually all of those would be equipped with arbalests (many scavenged from the pre-Jihad arsenals of places like Dohlar and Desnair) and bows—aside from the sixty thousand peasant slingers who would stick with the weapons they knew. It wouldn't be the same as having a million rifles to throw at the heretics, but it would still represent an almost incalculable increase in firepower. And, equally important, those rearmed infantry would have had at least three months' training under Army of God tutelage. The arbalesteers would have time to acquire proficiency, the bowmen would at least have time to learn which end of the arrow fitted to the string, and the worst of their own officers would be weeded out, and where necessary—and possible—replaced with AOG officers.

At the end of the day, Bynzhamyn Krestmyn thought with a thin, hard little smile, the heretics who'd raised their hands against God and Mother Church and ruined his own family might just find the newly refurbished Mighty Host of God and the Archangels a bit more difficult to deal with than they'd anticipated.

. II .

West of Cheyvair, Cliff Peak Province, and Near Brahnselyk, The South March Lands, Republic of Siddarmark

"Excuse me, Sir. I've got someone here I think you'd better talk to."

Major Kreg Ahbraims looked up from the map his orderly was shielding with an oilskin poncho. Captain Avrahm Lansyr, the commander of his Company B, saluted. Lansyr was accompanied by an extraordinarily tall gray-haired civilian with a most uncivilian-like rifle slung over his shoulder and an ugly, efficient short sword at his side.

Ahbraims' eyes narrowed as they took in that rifle, for it was a "trapdoor" Mahndrayn, and there weren't supposed to be any of them in civilian hands, especially here in the Republic of Siddarmark.

"And who might this 'someone' be, Captain?" he inquired coolly, raising one eyebrow at the stranger, and the civilian smiled.

"Think I'd best be answerin' that m'self, Major," he said easily in a-pronounced Shilohian accent. "Happens the name's Slaytyr, Zhapyth Slaytyr. Know that's not likely t'mean much to you, but Duke Eastshare, he knows me."

"Does he, indeed?" Ahbraims' eyes didn't get any narrower—that would have been impossible—but the suspicion in them deepened. "I hope you won't think I'm being unreasonable if I ask if you have any proof of that acquaintance, Master . . . Slaytyr, was it?"

"Aye, that it was," the civilian replied. "Can't say's I blame you for bein' a mite suspicious. Still, might be this'll help."

He opened his hand, and Ahbraims inhaled sharply as something glittered on his callused palm.

He'd never actually seen one of the small tokens, but they'd been described to him in detail. The enameled silver doomwhale of Chisholm and golden kraken of Old Charis gleamed at him, and those tokens came from only two sets of hands . . . the *royal* hands to whom that doomwhale and that kraken belonged.

His gaze rose to the muddy brown eyes of the man who'd introduced himself as Zhapyth Slaytyr.

"As I say," that man said in a much crisper accent, "I don't think anyone could fault your caution, but I really do need to speak to Colonel Vahrtanysh."

▼ ▼ ▼

"So, Master Slaytyr, you've seen these supply wagons with your own eyes?"

Colonel Kathyl Vahrtanysh gazed intently at his own map, eyes as focused as his thoughts, as his finger traced the line indicating the so-called road between Brahnselyk and Roymark. The temperature had dropped and it was raining harder. The tarp stretched between a pair of nearoaks kept the worst of the precipitation off the map, but the drum of raindrops promised that an already miserable day was about to turn into a wretched one.

"I have, Colonel." Merlin Athrawes answered the question in Slaytyr's voice. He'd never actually been to Brahnselyk, but thanks to Owl's SNARCs he could have walked the entire length of that miserable, muddy road blindfolded.

"And the supply depots? You've seen them, too?" Vahrtanysh looked up from the map and "Slaytyr" nodded.

"They're still in the process of settling in," he said. "I estimate they have three Dohlaran infantry regiments in the town itself. There's probably another three thousand quartermaster troops, but all the civilians've been moved out. They're building up a major supply point for their main field force—quickly—and the Desnairians really need it." He grimaced. "Their horses are in trouble, Colonel, and their infantry's not much better."

"I'm not surprised." Vahrtanysh sounded satisfied, but he also frowned.

"Slaytyr" wasn't surprised by the frown. Duke Eastshare's plans had called for the Army of Cliff Peak to be far closer to Roymark before anyone realized Earl High Mount was coming. Unfortunately, Sir Rainos Ahlverez, at least, truly was capable of learning, and his cavalry patrols were spread directly across High Mount's approach march from Mymphys.

"I know you're not supposed to discuss His Grace's battle plans with any chance-met spy you happen to encounter, Colonel," he said after a moment, "but it happens that I already know basically what he's hoping to accomplish."

Vahrtanysh's eyes were suddenly bleak, and Slaytyr smiled.

"I don't plan on babbling on about them, even to you, Colonel, but there's no point pretending I don't know what's worrying you. And, unfortunately, I think you're right; I don't see any way you'll be able to get as close to Roymark as His Grace hoped before Ahlverez' cavalry spots you, and he's got a semaphore line all the way from Brahnselyk to Roymark and from there to Kharmych. There's no way Earl High Mount can get his infantry into position before Ahlverez and Harless know you're coming. And good as Brigadier Seacatcher and Brigadier Raizyngyr are, I really don't think they need to take on the entire Army of Shiloh in the open west of the Kyplyngyr by themselves."

Vahrtanysh's expression was as bleak as his eyes, and Slaytyr waved gently.

"No, I'm not a really cleverly disguised agent inquisitor here to mislead Earl High Mount into abandoning his orders," he said, and Vahrtanysh's color deepened. But then the colonel made himself draw a deep breath and relax, and Slaytyr grinned at him. "If I *were* a cleverly disguised agent inquisitor, I'd try to find a less wet and miserable way to mislead the Grand Inquisitor's enemies. Since, unfortunately, I'm a good, loyal Charisian spy, instead, I'm here in this miserable weather to warn you about those patrols of Ahlverez' before you run headlong into them. Actually, I suspect they've already spotted some of your flankers. They're Dohlarans, not Desnairians, and they've been specifically ordered to *avoid* contact. I don't much care for Dohlarans, you understand, but Ahlverez has managed to convince his cavalry commanders that there's usually more value in reporting back when the enemy's spotted than there is in launching a glorious charge that tells him you know he's there."

"I can't say I'm happy to hear that," Vahrtanysh said after a moment. "I'd hoped they were still as clueless as they were last summer."

"Survival's a pretty demanding tutor," Slaytyr replied.

"I imagine so." Vahrtanysh looked back down at the map, frowning in thought, and Slaytyr tapped the small, bland dot that indicated Brahnselyk.

"I don't think Ahlverez realizes Earl High Mount's moving in such strength, and I'm *sure* Harless doesn't. *His* cavalry hasn't reported a damned thing, and if Ahlverez starts talking about threats to their rear, Hennet'll assure everyone in sight that no one could possibly send a force big enough to pose a real danger across three hundred and fifty miles of 'wilderness' in the middle of winter. To supply enough men to threaten something the size of the Army of Shiloh, they'd have to come straight down the canal past Cheyvair, where *his* cavalry's waiting to spot them. At the moment, they know there are at least some mounted troops in the vicinity, and Ahlverez may be smart enough to suspect what Duke Eastshare has in mind, but even he has to be half convinced he's imagining things. So it may be time to convince him you've known about the supply depot at Brahnselyk all along."

▼ ▼ ▼

"*Shit!*"

Private Zhustyn Mahstyrs flinched violently as something hot, wet, and coppery tasting exploded over him. For a moment, all he felt was shocked surprise, but then, in quick succession, he heard a meaty sound like a powerful punch, a gurgling, choked-off cry, and the distant crack of a rifle.

His head whipped around, and he realized the wet heat coating his face and steaming all down his buff leather coat in the frigid air was blood. Brygham Zhadwail's blood. Mahstyrs' eyes went wide in horror as his friend's right hand rose weakly to the gaping hole just above his collarbone. Aside from that one choking cry, Zhadwail never made a sound as he toppled into the icy undergrowth. His horse shied as its rider crashed heavily into the low-growing branches, and then Mahstyrs heard more rifle fire, more cries of pain and panic.

He wrenched his eyes from his friend's body, ducking instinctively in the saddle as he looked wildly about for the source of that fire. Gray-white balls of smoke erupted all down the far side of the fallow cornfield, and he reined his horse around and drove in the spurs, galloping back down the overgrown farm track at reckless, breakneck speed while rifle bullets whizzed viciously past.

Fifteen minutes later, he was making his report to Sergeant Rahzhyr Zhaksyn . . . the only survivor of his five-man section.

▼ ▼ ▼

"How the *hell* did they get all the way out here?" Sir Alykzhandyr Preskyt demanded harshly. "It's ridiculous!"

Sergeant Zhaksyn understood that his company commander didn't really expect an answer to his question. And that was a very good thing, because Zhaksyn couldn't imagine what that answer might be.

Third Company was barely fifteen miles from Brahnselyk, and the nearest heretic infantry was trapped in Ohadlyn's Gap, five hundred miles away. The only reason they were out here in the miserable sleet and freezing rain was because Colonel Wykmyn had suggested to Captain Preskyt that General Ahlverez would take it as a personal favor if 3rd Company didn't allow any heretic cavalry close enough to Brahnselyk to burn the place down. Colonel Wykmyn was not the sort of officer one argued with, even in weather like this and about things as unlikely as a heretic cavalry raid across hundreds of miles of hostile territory, and so 3rd Company had set out on its patrol. It hadn't been raining when they left; that had begun just after they'd settled into their cold, miserable bivouac on the first night out. Now, two days later, they were on the return leg, eager to get back to Brahnselyk's roughly built barracks, and they'd seen no sign of the Charisian cavalry which had been reported in the area last five-day.

Until now, that was.

"Mahstyrs didn't get a good look at *any* of them?" Preskyt asked.

"No, Sir." The company sergeant grimaced. "Hard to blame him, really. This kind of weather, men dropping right and left?" He shook his head, expression grim. "Cap'n, he looks like he took a bath in blood. Realize it's not rainin' all that hard, but might 'spect it'ud be enough to wash some of it off. Prob'ly did, when you come down to it, though you'd not think so t' look at him. Reckon I'd've lit out right smartly m'self. And come down to it, we're lucky *any* of 'em got back t' tell us about it."

Preskyt nodded unhappily. It was a miracle Mahstyrs had gotten back at all, and no one could blame the private for being unable to pick individual shooters out of the sodden undergrowth.

"All right, I need messengers," he said. "One to Brahnselyk to warn Colonel Mhartyn the enemy's in the vicinity. Then we send another one to Colonel Wykmyn, telling him the same thing. And another one to Colonel Gardynyr, and, finally, one to the nearest semaphore tower to send word directly back to General Ahlverez."

"Yes, Sir!" Sergeant Zhaksyn touched the breast of his heavy buff coat in salute, and Preskyt glowered up at the unfriendly sky.

"I'll draft the dispatches while you round up the riders to deliver them," he said. "And while you're doing that, pass the word that we'll be picking up the pace when we move on. I don't know how much difference one company of light cavalry'll make if the heretics are close enough to hit Brahnselyk, but I know we'll do a hell of a lot more good helping Colonel Mhartyn defend the place than we will freezing our arses off out here in this miserable sleet."

▼ ▼ ▼

"You really are a nasty person," a contralto voice observed as Merlin Athrawes piloted his recon skimmer across the cloudy night sky towards the Republic's capital.

He'd been gone too long already, and much as he would have preferred to hang around in his Slaytyr persona—he'd decided Zhapyth was likely to be as useful an alter ego as Ahbraim Zhevons—he couldn't justify it.

"I have no idea what you could possibly be talking about," he replied. "And I think it's a bit unreasonable of you to accuse me of being 'a nasty person' when we're both the *same* person."

"Oh, no!" The woman who'd decided to call herself Nimue Chwaeriau laughed from her North Wing bedchamber in far distant Manchyr. "You very carefully didn't give me all your memories, Merlin. So don't try to maneuver *me* into giving you a pass by hiding behind 'we're all in this together'!"

It was Merlin's turn to chuckle, although there was undeniably something . . . weird about this conversation. Custom and regulation alike had discouraged PICA owners from having discussions between their molycirc selves and their flesh-and-blood selves. Personalities could get into nasty narcissistic feedback loops that way . . . especially personalities already pushed to the brink by the despair of the long, losing battle against the Gbaba.

Like most PICA users, Nimue Alban had skated the edge of that ban once or twice, just to see what it felt like, but odd as that had seemed, it hadn't been like this. Nimue Alban's biological and electronic selves had been effectively identical when they sat down face-to-face, but there were enormous differences between Merlin and the woman he'd decided deserved the name Nimue far more than he did after so long as Merlin Athrawes. They truly were different people, yet different people who shared the identical memories, the same *life*, up to the very instant they'd awakened here on Safehold. It was immensely comforting to know there was someone else in the universe who truly *remembered* the Terran Federation's long, hopeless war and the sacrifices so many had made to bring humanity here to this world where it might survive. Yet knowing someone else remembered also made his sense of loss for all that had disappeared forever even sharper.

"While rejecting the base canard that a fearless *seijin* such as myself might attempt to 'hide behind' anything," he said, "I reiterate that I am not a nasty person. All I did was present my data to the appropriate decision-makers with a suggested course of action. Earl High Mount is a very bright fellow, and I strongly suspect he would've arrived at the same conclusion even without my input. I merely . . . hastened the process along."

"And used poor General Ahlverez' own security arrangements against him," Nimue pointed out. "The same way you have ever since you convinced him Kyrbysh is still alive! If *that*'s not 'nasty,' then tell me what is!"

"I believe there's an old saying about everything being fair in love and war." Merlin shrugged. "I will admit I'm developing a grudging respect for him, though, which I didn't expect."

"I suppose I am, too," she said after a moment. "In fact, I think I regret what's likely to happen to him if this works. You know Clyntahn's going to blame *him*, since he's the one who sent 'Slaytyr' to Harless for the wyverns."

"I know." Merlin pursed his lips for a moment, then sighed. "I don't regret it as much as I regret what's probably going to happen to Thirsk, but you do have a point. Especially about Clyntahn. But, you know, as much as I want to rip out Zhaspahr Clyntahn's heart, it's a relief to be fighting someone I actually understand instead of the Gbaba."

"*Understand* Zhaspahr Clyntahn?"

"In the sense of being able to at least comprehend his motives, I meant. I'll admit it's worse in some ways to be able to understand what's going through his head, because he *is* a human being, and the things he's willing to do are even ghastlier than the Gbaba. They wanted to destroy the entire human race, and they were prepared to do whatever that took, but nothing suggested they did it out of innate cruelty. I'm not saying they had anything remotely like compassion; they were aliens, and we never did figure out how—or *if*—their minds actually worked. They didn't seem to *care* how 'cruel' their actions might be, though, because they were simply interested in the most efficient way to exterminate us."

"Clyntahn *does* care." Merlin's voice hardened, harshened. "He *rejoices* in crushing anyone who gets in his way. He doesn't just *do* it, Nimue; he revels in it. It empowers him, and every person who dares oppose him becomes his personal enemy, to be destroyed as painfully as possible. And despite all that, I comprehend what he's trying to accomplish . . . and I can *stop* him. I hate him more than I ever truly hated the Gbaba, but there's not that sense of facing some unstoppable force that can't possibly be defeated and could care less about me as an individual. We didn't have that against the Gbaba, and it's taken me a while to realize what an enormous difference that makes this time around."

Nimue was silent for a long, thoughtful moment. She was already discovering that he and Nahrmahn had been right about the other members of their "inner circle." She didn't actually know any of them yet—not the way Merlin knew them or they knew Merlin—but she could see the bright, fierce light of them. And as she thought about that light, she realized Merlin was right about the difference between this war and Nimue Alban's. The grim determination, the refusal to yield which had carried Nimue and her companions forward in the face of certain defeat had its echo in Cayleb and Sharleyan—in Maikel Staynair and his brother, in Ehdwyrd Howsmyn, Irys and Hektor Aplyn-Ahrmahk, Rahzhyr Mahklyn, the Brethren of Saint Zherneau—but there was far more to them than that. They'd raised mortal hands against what they'd been taught was God Himself, and what drove them was a fusion-bright will to *win*. Not merely the unflinching resolve to stave off defeat as long as possible which was all fate and history had been able to offer the Federation, but the willingness—the courage—to see *victory* on the far side of their struggle.

For an instant, she felt a dark, corrosive anger, an arsenic-bitter rage, that these people had been given what she and everyone she'd ever loved had been denied. That they could actually envision a future in which they triumphed, in which the things more precious to them than life itself *survived*. But it vanished as quickly as it had come, that anger—vanished into sudden exultation as she realized that this time *she* could see victory, as well. This time, her hands could be among the hands that cast down the darkness, let in the light and allowed the human race not merely to survive but to take the war back to the Gbaba in the fullness of time and give that victory to all of her beloved dead.

A PICA's tears burned her eyes as she recognized the gift Merlin had given her by bringing her back from dusty death. He'd offered her a foe worth fighting, a cause worth winning, friends worth loving . . . and an opportunity in the end to avenge her slaughtered worlds and murdered Federation.

It was worth dying to be given that . . . and worth living once again, as well, even if someday she found herself bearing the same burden, the same memories, which touched Merlin Athrawes with that perpetual trace of melancholy.

"You're right," she said finally. "I hadn't thought about it that way—not yet, anyway. Of course," she drew a deep breath and pitched her voice with a careful, deliberate seasoning of mockery and affection, "I imagine I'd've gotten around to it by the time I'm as old and decrepit as you are."

Merlin laughed, and she smiled as she heard it.

"Whippersnapper," he said after a second or two. "Just remember, PICAs' strengths are proportionate to their size, and I'm a foot taller than you are."

"Fortunately, you're also a bigger target. Sort of like Brahnselyk," she added, pulling the conversation back to her original topic.

"Well," he replied, accepting the change of topic, "since it's a tad difficult to hide seventy thousand men, twenty-five or thirty thousand horses, and several hundred draft dragons and wagons when people are looking for them, I figured the least we could do was to help Ahlverez figure out *where* to look. I thought it was only neighborly of us."

"You *are* a bad, bad man." The severity of her tone was somewhat undermined by what sounded suspiciously like a giggle, and Merlin smiled.

Sir Rainos Ahlverez had demonstrated that there was precious little hope of completely surprising him. Even with "Kyrbysh" feeding the Army of Shiloh false information, he'd been cautious enough to establish that cavalry screen of his in the first place. But he also knew how vital his Brahnselyk supply center had become, and the moment he decided his enemies seriously intended to destroy it, he'd do everything in his power to protect it. Just as young Captain Preskyt had displayed both intelligence and initiative in riding to buttress Brahnselyk's defense, Ahlverez would send everything he could to do the same thing. And the more of his cavalry he sent to *Brahnselyk*, the thinner his screen between High Mount and Roymark would become.

It probably wasn't going to work out as well as East-share's audacity deserved, but the odds said it would still work as well as they *needed* it to, and that would just have to be good enough.

As Commodore Pei used to say, he reflected, wondering if Nimue was remembering the same thing at that moment, *surprise is what happens when you find out that something you saw all along isn't what you thought it was. And that, General Ahlverez, is a lesson I'm looking forward to sharing with you.*

. III .
Royal Palace,
City of Manchyr,
Princedom of Corisande,
and
Charisian Embassy,
Siddar City,
Republic of Siddarmark

"That's right, Your Highness. A little higher—you want the bore as close to in line with your hand as you can get it, but make sure your grip's comfortable, too. It's important for it to sit properly in your hand. Remember, you want a little muzzle rise when you're firing single-shot—it'll get your thumb back onto the hammer spur quicker—but as little as you can manage when you're firing double-action because that lets you stay on target better for follow-up shots. These grips are a pretty good compromise between single and double-action, but my hands are a little larger than yours and they were individually modified for me. Once we get Master Mahldyn an impression of your hands he'll probably spend hours in the pistol shop, happy as a wyvern watching a rabbit hole and whistling the whole time he personally customizes and tunes one of his new babies especially for you. Her Majesty's is on its way to her in Chisholm right now. Of course, *she's* on her way *here*, so she'll probably want to play with mine, too, until her own catches up."

Irys Aplyn-Ahrmahk concentrated on her instructor's soothing words. They sounded a bit odd through the ear protection the instructor insisted she wear whenever they visited the range, whether or not they were actively shooting. But they were clear enough, and she soaked them up with what had begun as grim determination only to turn into genuine enthusiasm as she sat through the preliminary "classroom" instruction and discovered how much she enjoyed the teaching. Unlike Empress Sharleyan, Irys had never been trained with firearms before she was sent off to Delferahk, and King Zhames would never have dreamed of allowing her to handle them after he'd agreed to provide her and Daivyn with "sanctuary from their enemies." He would have considered it entirely unladylike . . . and he would have had a pretty good idea of how the Inquisition might have felt about it, too.

That hadn't really bothered her . . . then. But that had been before the Cathedral Square bomb attack. Before her husband had been mortally wounded on their wedding day and pulled back from the threshold of death only by the grace of God and a wonder greater than she could ever have imagined. Before her entire universe had been changed forever and she'd discovered her own blazing determination to shatter the chains of deceit which enslaved her entire species.

Before she'd decided that anyone, anywhere—man, woman, or demon—who ever again wanted to harm someone *she* loved would have to go through her, first.

"That's good," the red-haired woman known as Nimue Chwaeriau said approvingly from beside her, standing well clear as she used both hands to gently and minutely adjust Irys' grip on the revolver's chequered teakwood grip panels. "Now, weak hand under strong hand and pull back. That's right ... push forward with the strong hand ... counter tension ... good. Now hold it steady."

Captain Chwaeriau checked the placement of her feet, then pushed gently on the underside of the barrel, testing the pistol's steadiness as she stood in what Nimue had called "the Weaver stance" before they headed for the range.

"That's very good!" she said. "Now, hammer back."

The ball of Irys' thumb moved to the hammer spur, pulling until it clicked solidly into the cocked position. It moved with glassy smoothness, but the muzzle still wavered ever so slightly. *Have to do better next time,* she thought, settling her thumb back into the contoured groove at the top of the grip panel.

"Index finger on the trigger, remember how I showed you to place it."

The pad of her finger rested on the smooth face of the trigger, just before the first joint.

"All right, this time we're bull's-eye shooting; we'll worry about combat shooting later. So take the time to find both sights and tell me when you've got them."

"Now," Irys murmured after a moment, both eyes open, front blade resting quiet and solid in the notch of the rear sight and aligned on the target. The target and front sight were clear, the rear slightly blurred as she concentrated on the sight picture the way Captain Chwaeriau had taught her.

"Then remember there's no trigger slack firing single-action and then it's time to squeeeeeze. . . ."

Irys obeyed, squeezing gently, steadily so as to leave her hands' position undisturbed, balanced, unmoving—

The hammer fell with a crisp, swift sureness, sudden as a breaking rod of glass, that made her twitch in surprise, even though she'd been expecting it.

"Exactly!" her instructor congratulated her. "Done properly, you should always be surprised by the exact moment the trigger breaks. Try it single-shot a few more times, then we'll try double action. And after you've done *that* a dozen times or so," she smiled broadly, "we'll load live rounds instead of practice cases and you can actually make some holes in a target."

▼ ▼ ▼

Lieutenant Charlz Sheltyn was in a foul mood.

He felt his jaw muscles clench as he strode along, conscientiously attempting to put Major Maiyrs' "advice" into practice. It would've been easier if Maiyrs hadn't had his own head so far up his arse he needed a glass belly button to see where he was going.

Technically, the Corisandian Royal Guard reported to Sir Koryn Gahrvai in his capacity as the Regency Council's deputy, but Gahrvai's actual experience with the Guard's duties and responsibilities was . . . limited, at best, in Sheltyn's view, and it damned well showed. Major Tymahn Maiyrs, the Guard's senior officer, should have reported to Prince Daivyn; since that was impossible in light of Daivyn's age, Gahrvai had to do instead. Except, of course, that Gahrvai was a frigging idiot. And much as Sheltyn had always respected Maiyrs in the past, it was obvious the major had turned into just as big an idiot.

Sheltyn paused in the shade of an ornamental persimmon fig tree, trying to relax his jaw, and closed his eyes as that vast sense of wrongness flowed over him once more.

The Guard had never been huge, and Prince Hektor had actually reduced it in size. He'd *wanted* it small—small enough to reinforce its awareness of its elite nature and status. Small enough he could know every one of his Guardsmen personally. If a larger security force was required for a specific occasion, it was recruited from one of the household regiments but organized, coordinated, and commanded by the Guard. And because the Guard was too small to be burdened with heaps of captains and majors and colonels but still had to command that additional troop strength when necessary, Prince Hektor had ordained that any Guardsman was two ranks senior to anyone of his own nominal rank in the Royal Corisandian Army or Navy.

That meant Major Maiyrs was actually equal in rank to General Gahrvai and that Lieutenant Sheltyn was equal in rank to an Army major, and that was as it should be. As it *had* to be, if the Guard was going to do its job properly. But doing its job properly meant Maiyrs should've reminded Gahrvai of the equivalence of their ranks and refused to accept the insane orders he'd seen fit to issue. At the very least, the major should've demanded written confirmation from the Regency Council as a whole!

The lieutenant's teeth were grinding again, and he clasped his hands behind him, hands curled into fists, while he pretended to study the brilliant flowers spilling over the mortared-stone wall of the persimmon fig's tree well.

If the Regency Council wanted to assert its right to oversee the Guard, surely it should have understood Prince Daivyn *had* to be protected by men trained and accustomed to that duty! Men who'd served his father in the same role, who'd demonstrated their loyalty, understood the danger signs to look for, had the training and experience—the *education*—to do the job properly. But, no! Not the Regency Council, and not *General* Gahrvai!

Of course the boy wanted familiar faces around him. How could it be any other way? Given how his life had been shaken up three ways from Wednesday it was inevitable that he'd want people he knew about him, and no child his age was fit to judge an armsman's actual competence . . . or lack of it. Sheltyn understood that, and he would have been delighted to find places in the Guard for the common armsmen who'd looked after him in his exile. Places where they could be properly evaluated and trained . . . or eased into some other honorable task if, in the end, they proved unfitted for Guard duty. But what could the Regency Council have been thinking to promote someone like Tobys Raimair to *commissioned* rank? And what madness could've seen "Lieutenant" Raimair assigned as Prince Daivyn's *personal* armsman?! And then, not content with promoting a man who'd spent thirty years in the Army without ever rising above the level of sergeant to the equivalent of an Army *major*, they'd staffed the prince's personal detachment exclusively with newcomers to the Guard who'd never been vetted properly and whose only claim to their positions was that they, too, had been with the prince in Delferahk where Earl Coris—*Earl Coris*, professional spy and treason-broker—had hired them because he couldn't find anyone better!

Damn it, Sheltyn thought. *Damn it to hell! They've got no* business *leaving the boy's security in hands like that. Hands chosen by that* bastard *Coris!*

He felt the rage quivering through his shoulders. Everyone knew what a conniver, what a *schemer*, Phylyp Ahzgood was. Sheltyn had never understood why someone as smart as Prince Hektor had chosen someone like *that* to safeguard his daughter and younger son in a foreign land. And whatever anyone else might say, Charlz Sheltyn remained far from convinced by all this "evidence" about who'd actually ordered Prince Hektor's assassination. He didn't doubt Irys and Daivyn believed it—what else could you expect from a girl child and a boy barely turned ten when the guardian they'd been told to trust warned them Mother Church wanted them dead? That didn't necessarily make it true, especially when the only "proof" anyone had was Coris' own word and the testimony of a man who claimed—*admitted!*—he'd betrayed Mother Church's own Inquisition for decades before she went to war against heresy. Sheltyn could hardly believe, even now, that the Royal Council had chosen not simply to take a *spymaster's* word for that but then to put him and a girl barely twenty years old on Prince Daivyn's Regency Council. And made his sister his official guardian, into the *bargain*! Couldn't they at least have found someone with a modicum of maturity instead of an empty-headed girl who was obviously thinking with her heart and other body parts instead of her *brain*? Someone who understood the need to hold those murderous Charisian heretics at arm's length instead of literally jumping into bed with them? Hell and damnation! If the Council was going to be that stupid, why not go the full distance and put that foreign-born bastard of a "*duke*" on the Regency Council, too?! No doubt he was already doing plenty of whispering into Irys' ear while he diddled her!

And, of course, putting Raimair in command of the boy's detail had bounced everyone else out of their rightful assignments. By seniority and experience, Lieutenant Hairahm Bahnystyr should be Daivyn's personal armsman and Sheltyn should command Irys' permanent detachment. He could have stomached that—he'd known Bahnystyr for over fifteen years, knew he was a solid, *loyal* officer. He might be a bit too warm towards the Reformists for Sheltyn's taste, but he sure as Shan-wei hadn't been recommended by a spy or insisted upon by a doting little boy or a girl besotted by the common-born gigolo she'd taken to her bed!

The one good thing was that, unlike Bahnystyr, *Sheltyn* didn't have to smile at "His Grace of Darcos" and pretend he trusted the son-of-a-bitch. Of course it was terrible that some misguided soul had killed so many bystanders. And it would have been a tragedy to lose Princess Irys. But at least it might have gotten that shellhorn out of the heart of the Palace—and away from Prince Daivyn!—before he stung someone to death.

And then, the final blow. A *Charisian* officially inserted into Prince Daivyn's own household, without invitation, without consultation . . . without anyone even knowing about it ahead of time. "Emperor" Cayleb had given all of Corisande the back of his hand with *that* one! Especially when he'd dispatched his personal agent long before he could have known the Princedom would decide to bend its neck to the yoke. Obviously, it hadn't mattered to him what the Royal Council and Parliament might have ultimately decided; he'd wanted his spy, his eyes and ears—probably his *assassin* at need—inside Daivyn's household, where not even the Guard could protect him.

And it wasn't even an armsman; it was an arms*woman*. Sheltyn gagged on the thought. Women were all very well in their place, and someone with his height, looks, and position was more successful with them than most, but prancing around in armor? Pretending she knew what to do with that sword she carried or that fancy new "revolver" of hers? Daring to look at real armsmen—men who'd spent years learning their skills, *earning* that title instead of having someone simply hand it to them because they were pretty or good on their backs—with those cool, dismissive blue eyes? And claiming *captain's* rank—captain's rank that made her *senior* to a Corisandian Royal Guardsman!

Well, the bitch is just lucky she's not actually assigned to the Guard, he thought hotly. *She spins a good tale about being here as Cayleb and Sharleyan's "representative." About how they don't want her "interfering." What it really does is save her from having to prove how good she really is—or isn't—as an armsman, that's what it does. She gets to sit around, ingratiating herself even further with Irys and Daivyn, without ever betraying the fact that she doesn't know shit about an armsman's real duties. Shan-wei! She's even offered to teach Irys how to shoot!*

He snorted contemptuously. He'd seen her sitting on the East Patio that morning as he passed by on his way to his "counseling session" with Major Maiyrs. She'd had that newfangled—and probably proscribed, whatever that so-called intendant might say back in Charis—"revolver" of hers on the table between her and Irys, showing the princess the damned thing's parts one at a time and "explaining" them. Even if she'd actually known how the thing's innards worked, which Sheltyn doubted, what possible need was there for *Irys* to learn it? It wasn't as if she'd ever use a weapon in her own defense. She was a *woman,* for Langhorne's sake!

All part of that act of hers, he grumbled. *Impressive as hell to a girl or a kid as young as Daivyn, but it's a hell of a lot easier to* describe *a double play than to actually execute one! Worst thing that could possibly happen for Irys or that "husband" of hers would be for someone to come at them and not have anyone but "Captain Chwaeriau" between them and a dagger! And as for that "seijin" dragon shit—! Oh,* please! *Just how stupid does Cayleb think we are?*

He squeezed his eyes shut for a long, smoldering moment, then forced himself to exhale deeply. He'd only worry himself into an apoplectic seizure if he kept dwelling on it this way. All he and any of the real Guardsmen could do was redouble their watchfulness to take up the slack for people like Raimair, keep an eye on "Duke Darcos" and the rest of the pro-Charis bootlickers, and wait for the opportunity to prove that whatever else she might be, Nimue Chwaeriau was no *seijin* sent by the Archangels to preserve Prince Daivyn and Princess Irys from the sinister, evil assassins of Mother Church.

He told himself that firmly, nodded once, and resumed his progress towards the armory. It was more important than ever to perform his own duties efficiently if he wanted to demonstrate by comparison how poorly "Lieutenant Raimair" performed his. Besides, it wouldn't be long until lunch, and—

Gunfire exploded somewhere ahead of him. For an instant, he froze, his right hand dropping to the double-barreled pistol at his side. Then he realized it had come from the pistol range General Gahrvai had insisted the Guard construct inside the Palace walls and he relaxed a bit. Only to stiffen once more as the gunshots continued to crack out, one after another.

There were six of them, a slow rolling thunder, timed as if by a musician's metronome, and Sheltyn's mouth tightened. Those reports could have come from only one weapon, and he altered course.

▼ ▼ ▼

"Clear your weapon," Nimue commanded from her position behind Irys, and the princess obediently raised the muzzle, ejected the spent cartridge cases, and then laid the pistol, cylinder still out, on the shooting bench.

"We really have to get the target carrier system Master Mahldyn came up with installed here," Nimue said. "In the meantime, let's hike down and see how well you did."

"I already know how well I did," Irys replied, unable to keep a slight note of pride out of her tone. "Forty-seven out of a possible sixty."

She grimaced, her pride deflating somewhat as she thought about the one flyer—her first shot—which had missed the target completely at a range of little more than twenty-five feet. Three of the other five had been in the ten-ring, however, and two of them had been in the X-ring itself.

"I already know that, too," Nimue said in that voice which sounded nothing at *all* like Merlin Athrawes' and yet carried that elusive hint of similarity. "However, *I* know that because I have telescopic vision, and *you* know that because you've got those nifty contact lenses. But there are at least a dozen people unobtrusively watching your lesson from various windows. Don't you think they might find it a little strange that you and I didn't have to go down and—I don't know, *examine*—your target?"

"Oh."

Irys felt her cheekbones heat, then laughed and shook her head at the exotically attractive red-haired woman at her elbow.

"Sorry. I guess I'm still in what Hektor calls the 'kid's new toy' phase. Sometimes I find myself actually starting to take it all for granted . . . and then something pulls me back to reality and I have to sit down, hard, while I try to cope with all the things that can't possibly be true."

"Not surprising, I'd say," Nimue replied, twitching her head in the direction of Irys' target and then following the princess down the firing lane. "It came at you awfully fast, Your Highness. And I'd imagine watching your husband dying on your wedding day didn't do anything to *reduce* the stress factor. Toss in the minor consideration that it contradicts everything you've ever been taught about God and the universe, and we could probably give you another, oh, couple of five-days to adjust. In fact, I'm feeling generous. You can have to the end of next *month*!"

Irys laughed again, harder. She also shook her head.

"That *is* generous of you. I'm afraid it's likely to take me a little longer, though. And speaking about 'adjusting,' *you* seem awfully calm about all this. Especially considering that you're, well—"

"Less than a month old?" Nimue supplied.

"Something like that, I suppose."

They reached the target and stood there, red head and dark bent to examine the holes punched through the printed paper, and Irys glanced up at Nimue's serene expression.

"It's hard for me to realize—*really* realize, I mean—that you didn't even exist two months ago. And it's even harder for me to realize you and *Seijin* Merlin are . . . the same person."

"It's been a minor adjustment for me, too. Of course, we're not really the same person anymore. I've come to think of him more as an older brother I know really, really well. Trust me, it's simpler that way. Less likely to cause my brain to explode, too."

"Would it really? Explode, I mean?" Irys' eyes widened, and Nimue sighed.

"It was a figure of speech, Your Highness. I doubt a PICA *could* explode, given that the Federation didn't much like the idea of allowing vest-pocket nuclear bombs to walk around its city streets. It took a fairly dim view of that, actually, now that I think about it. Can't imagine why."

"Oh," Irys said again, a bit sheepishly. "I should've thought of that, but I haven't had much time to spend with Owl's explanations of how all this 'technology' of yours works. The only times Hektor and I can be sure we're really alone is in our own apartment with you outside the door, and, well. . . ."

"And a pair of newlyweds with privacy and time on their hands have better things to do than talk to an artificial intelligence in a cave halfway around the world," Nimue suggested helpfully.

"Well, yes." Irys seemed very fascinated by the punctured target for a few moments, then grinned and looked at Nimue once more. "We lost all that time right after the wedding, you understand."

"Then by all means make up for it now," the red-haired *seijin* told her. "And since the two of you have to spend so much time lying low to keep anyone from figuring out how rapidly Hektor's convalescence is speeding along,

anything that keeps you out-of-sight, out-of-mind is probably worthwhile in its own right."

"Especially since we can't even talk to Phylyp about
it," Irys agreed. "He's being very . . . thoughtful about
leaving the two of us time to be together."

"It's an extra complication," Nimue conceded. "Still,
once the Brethren recover from the shock of finding out
you and Hektor know the truth, I doubt they'll take all
that long to decide Earl Coris ought to be initiated into
the inner circle, as well. Especially since Daivyn really is
too young to be burdened with something like this. You
and Hektor need at least one other person the Regency
Council trusts."

"Exactly."

Irys took down the target and folded it under her arm
while she watched Nimue tack up a replacement. After a
moment, the princess shook her head.

"You know, I think it's conversations like this that
make it so difficult for me to realize how, well, *new* you
are, Nimue. You're really not a lot like *Seijin* Merlin. I
don't mean that just physically; you have very different
personalities, too. Yet you seem just as familiar with all
of the power relationships and diplomacy and military
operations as he does."

"We do have different personalities." Nimue's words
came a bit more slowly and she seemed very focused on
her hands as she finished tacking the target in place and
smoothed it with one palm. "Merlin has a lot more . . . a
lot more mileage, I suppose, on his personality. Nimue
Alban was only about twenty-seven when she recorded
me. That's only about nine Safeholdian years older than
you are now, and Merlin's seven local years older than
that. Seven *hard* years. I haven't had to go through all of
that—not yet, anyway—and I haven't seen as many
people I care for die as he has."

"But you saw the entire 'Federation' die," Irys said
softly.

"Yes, I did. Oh, I missed the final battle, but I knew what
was going to happen, and I watched a lot of people die
before Operation Ark. But I knew all those people were

going to die anyway, Irys." She looked across at the princess, the late morning breeze toying with a few strands of red silk which had escaped her braid. "They were doomed, no matter what happened. I couldn't change that, *they* couldn't change that—no one could. You didn't let yourself care too deeply in that situation, and if you did, you pretended you didn't, even to yourself. But Merlin and I have been given the opportunity to change that. People like Cayleb and Sharleyan, like Maikel—like you and Hektor—don't *have* to die. And that . . . that terrifies me, really. Because even if you don't have to, you still *can*, and now I have to learn, the same way Merlin did, how much that hurts."

Irys' hazel eyes softened and she laid one hand on Nimue's mailed forearm. She started to say something, then thought better of it and only shook her head, and Nimue turned both of them back towards the shooting bench.

"As for how familiar I am with those 'power relationships,' I'm not really as 'new' as you might think." She smiled slightly. "I'm the improved, compact-sized PICA, you understand. My brain's not hardwired to dump its contents every ten days, so nobody had to fool around with my basic software. And unlike Merlin, my high-speed port works just fine. That means I can interface directly with Prince Nahrmahn's VR and Owl in compressed time. I actually spent several subjective months studying all the data Merlin, Nahrmahn, and Owl had selected for me. And acquiring Merlin's physical skills." She chuckled. "It was considerate of him to upload all that muscle memory, but our centers of balance, reach, and leverage are just a *bit* different. It wouldn't've done much for my own *seijin*'s reputation if I'd found myself in a sword fight and started dancing around as if I had a foot more reach than I do!"

"I hadn't thought about that, either," Irys said with a chuckle. "Even if it had occurred to me, I probably wouldn't—Oh, crap."

Nimue snorted. She'd already noticed the approaching Guardsman, and she was no better pleased to see him than Irys. On the other hand, in many ways, it might actually be harder for Irys than it was for her.

To *her*, Charlz Sheltyn was simply a benighted bigot. Someone too set in his attitudes to ever realize just how stupid they were. She'd discovered that it helped to remember that the Royal Guard of which he was so proud was smaller than a single company of Federation Marines and had perhaps—being generous—one ten-thousandth of the Marines' combat power. And that the Federation's military by the time of Operation Ark had boasted a strength of over two point seven *billion* active-duty human beings, ninety percent of them combat personnel, and approximately half of them *female* human beings.

A quarter of whom were Marines who probably could've broken the bastard up into individual servings of dog food with their bare hands, she reflected now, watching him stride arrogantly towards them.

Unlike her, Irys had known Sheltyn almost since the day she'd learned to walk. Once upon a time, to a little girl, he'd probably been just as much of a demigod as he clearly thought he still was. And where Nimue was an outsider, Irys was still the little girl who could be patted—respectfully, of course—on top of the head and ignored. And if anything had been needed to justify that estimate of her character, the fact that she'd married a foreigner three years younger than she was—and who'd been born a commoner—clearly supplied it.

"Why don't you reload, Your Highness," Nimue said, moving casually between her and the source of her ire. "Leave the cylinder open until we're ready to begin again."

"Of course, Captain Chwaeriau," Irys replied in a clear, carrying voice that emphasized Nimue's rank with malice aforethought.

Nimue managed not to roll her eyes before she turned to face Sheltyn. She couldn't really blame Irys, but satisfying as the flicker of anger the princess had put into Sheltyn's eyes might be, it wasn't likely to help the situation any.

She faced the lieutenant fully and inclined her head in greeting.

"Good morning, Lieutenant," she said.

▼ ▼ ▼

Sheltyn swallowed an urge to rip the trollop's head off. "Lieutenant," indeed! She was always so careful to use his rank rather than address him as "Sir"!

"Captain," he replied, the word an epithet cloaked in a veneer of courtesy, emphasized just enough to remind her that his rank was effectively that of major.

"How may I help you this morning?" she asked, apparently oblivious to his tone. He considered several satisfying answers to that inquiry, but, alas, none of them were permissible in front of a witness. Especially not one named Princess Irys.

"I heard gunfire," he said instead.

Neither Chwaeriau nor Princess Irys replied. The princess continued reloading the "revolver" with the air of someone taking her time about it, and Chwaeriau only regarded him calmly, as if waiting for him to say something worth commenting upon.

"I was unaware anyone had signed in for range time this morning," he continued after a moment, hearing a harder, sharper edge in his own voice.

"I personally informed Major Maiyrs that Captain Chwaeriau would be instructing me, Lieutenant." Princess Irys' voice was cool as she entered the conversation for the first time.

"That's very interesting, Your Highness." Sheltyn never took his eyes from Chwaeriau's face. "I, however, am the officer of the day, not Major Maiyrs. If the range is to be used and safety regulations are to be met, the officer of the day—me, in other words—is supposed to be informed by the senior member of the Guard using the range"—he simply couldn't bring himself to use the term "Guards-*man*" in connection with the woman in front of him— "when he takes responsibility for safety on the firing line. I don't recall seeing your requisition for range time this morning, Captain."

"Forgive me, Lieutenant, but that isn't precisely correct," Chwaeriau said in that oh-so-superior tone of hers. "Regulations require anyone who wants to use the range to inform the designated range officer, which is the officer of the day under normal circumstances. However, *as* the officer of the day, you'd signed off to the armory sergeant of the day—I believe because you were scheduled to meet with Major Maiyrs." Her expression was perfectly grave, but he felt her smirking at him from behind those bland blue eyes. "When Princess Irys and I completed our weapons familiarization, I went to the armory to check the availability of the range and signed in as range officer with Sergeant Zhadwail."

She held up the token which had to be signed out whenever the range was in use and returned to the armory at the end of every firing session.

Sheltyn felt his face darken. Of course it had been Traivahr Zhadwail, another of those "Delferahkan old hands" who'd been foisted on the Guard! And even though it was customary to reserve range time the day before, Chwaeriau was just the sort of barracks law master to point out that the regulations didn't *require* that. In fact, he was pretty damn sure she'd waited until she knew he was with Maiyrs before signing in with Zhadwail. Probably because she'd realized he'd have insisted a *proper* Guardsman take charge of Irys' training if any live rounds were to be fired. And he would have, too, by Chihiro, and the hell with all that dragon shit about her being "attached" to the Guard!

"And now, if you'll excuse us, Lieutenant," she said, "I have to ask you to step back behind the safety line and cover your ears, since you don't appear to have brought plugs with you."

She turned away, clasping her hands at the small of her back and standing in an instructor's posture as she took up the proper range officer's position behind and to Princess Irys' right.

"Live rounds on the range!" she announced loudly. "Ready on the right! Ready on the left! Your Highness, you may lock and—"

"You wait one fucking minute!" Sheltyn heard himself bark. "I'm not done with you, Shan-wei damn it! I'm the officer of the day, and *I'll* tell *you* when I'm finished reaming you a new one!"

He grabbed her shoulder to spin her back around to face him.

"I've had just about enough of you, you little bi—!"

He staggered slightly as she turned back to face him. Actually, she *twirled* to face him, moving so quickly and gracefully he had no opportunity to jerk her around the way he'd intended. It was as if she'd started moving even before he touched her, and he stiffened his legs for balance and fastened his hand on her shoulder like a vise. She wouldn't feel his grip through her mail and arming tunic, but he took advantage of his "stumble" to throw his full weight onto her.

Charlz Sheltyn stood a fraction of an inch under six feet. That made him a veritable giant for Corisande, with shoulders disproportionately wide even for his height. He'd never been intended for foot races, but he had excellent reflexes and worked out with a focused discipline that armored his naturally powerful frame with thick, supple muscle. He weighed well over two hundred pounds, none of it fat, and Chwaeriau—eight inches shorter than he was—weighed perhaps half as much.

The weight slamming down on her shoulder should have driven her to her knees, and that was exactly what he'd intended to do. He couldn't have said what he'd intended to do *after* she went down, but the real point was to demonstrate to her—and to Princess Irys—that she had no business pretending to be a bodyguard when she couldn't even stay on her feet if someone stumbled into her.

Unfortunately, she seemed unaware of his weight. She only gazed up at him, one eyebrow arched, sapphire eyes dark . . . and contemptuous.

Even through his fury, Sheltyn's brain warned him something was wrong. She hadn't simply held her footing; the straight, slim shoulder under his hand hadn't as much as dipped. He started to draw back, puzzled by her failure to collapse on schedule, but then he saw that arched eyebrow, realized her calm expression hadn't even flickered. She was *mocking* him—refusing to so much as *notice* his effort to put her in her place!

"Listen, you little trollop!" he snapped, shaking her viciously but remembering, somehow, to substitute "trollop" for the word he'd been about to use with Princess Irys standing ten feet away. "I'm not done, and you'll goddamn listen until I am! I don't give a solitary *damn* who sent you and who you think—"

It dawned on him that he wasn't shaking her after all. He was shaking *himself*, because the shoulder under his hand had never budged and all the force of his powerfully muscled arm had to go somewhere.

"Take that hand off my shoulder or lose it." The coolness of her flat tone cut across his own bellicosity like a backhanded slap.

"What? *What* did you say to me?!" he demanded, unable to believe his ears.

"I've put up with everything I intend to tolerate from you, *Lieutenant*." There was more than coolness in her tone now; there was ice, and his rank came out of her mouth like a curse, made all the more vicious by the contempt with which she uttered it. "I'm your superior officer, whether or not I'm officially in your chain of command. You appear to have some difficulty grasping what that means. So since you've very kindly offered yourself for the position, I'm about to make an example out of you. Unless, of course, you'd care to take your hand off my shoulder, apologize to Her Highness for your language, and beg my pardon for behavior more appropriate in a drunken dockside pimp than an officer of the Corisandian Royal Guard."

Sheltyn stared at her, unable even now to believe she'd *dared* to—

"Fine," she said. "Thank you for volunteering."

He blinked, and then she moved, and all he remembered for a very long time afterward was pain.

▼ ▼ ▼

"All right, *that* had to hurt," Merlin Athrawes said thoughtfully.

The *seijin* reclined in an armchair in Cayleb Ahrmahk's study, a stein of beer in his right hand and a plate of fried potato slices to his left, on the end table between his chair and Cayleb's. The two of them were viewing the imagery Owl had captured of Charlz Sheltyn's encounter with Nimue Chwaeriau.

It had lasted barely three minutes, although it must have seemed far longer to Sheltyn.

Aside from her interest in kendo, Nimue Alban had never been attracted to the martial arts. Merlin had acquired quite an impressive set of skills since then, relying in no small part on a PICA's ability to program muscle memory, but Nimue Chwaeriau had gone quite a bit further. She'd plugged her high speed connection into Owl and downloaded the moves for *moarte subită*, the martial art synthesized from half a dozen disciplines on the colony world Walachia and later adopted by the Federation Marines. Then she'd spent several subjective five-days in VR *learning* those moves and programming her own muscle memory.

The result was . . . impressive, and Merlin winced as he watched her scientifically dislocate the far larger Corisandian's right shoulder. The *left* shoulder had already been dislocated, and he wasn't at all certain the arm connected to it hadn't been broken in the process. Sheltyn was also fortunate that Safeholdian dentists were capable of making very natural-looking false teeth.

According to his current estimate, the lieutenant was going to need at least six of them. And Nimue wasn't finished yet.

By the time she was, Sheltyn was barely conscious. He retained enough awareness when she finally stepped back—her expression as calm as when she'd begun—to try to crawl away from her, however. That showed better sense than anything else he'd done, although it was more probably some sort of primal survival instinct rather than the result of any reasoned process.

"I'd say she was pissed off," Merlin observed as the imagery faded.

"You think?" Cayleb shot back acidly.

"Well, she's a much younger and nicer person than I am. I doubt she'd've been quite that thorough if she *hadn't* been pissed off." Merlin took a thoughtful sip of beer. "I *hope* she wouldn't've been, anyway. I don't remember having a disposition nasty enough to do that if I wasn't."

"This isn't really funny, you know, Merlin. She's there as my personal representative, and she just put the Royal Guard's third-ranking officer into the hospital with enough damage to keep him there for five-days. *And* in front of *witnesses*, most of whom're experienced enough to realize she did it on purpose. And went right on doing it long after he'd've been more than willing to back off. My God, Merlin! She had him squealing like a little girl after thirty seconds!"

"'Like a little girl,'" Merlin repeated thoughtfully, as if sampling the words' taste, while he selected a fresh potato slice from the plate. "Interesting you should pick that particular simile."

"Damn it, Merlin!" Cayleb's concern was obvious, even as he found it difficult not to laugh when Merlin rolled his eyes at him. "This could have serious repercussions," the emperor continued doggedly. "God only knows how the rest of the Guard'll react!"

"God may be the only one who *knows*, but I could hazard a pretty good *guess* about what's going to happen," Merlin offered around a mouthful of potato, and Cayleb flopped back, waving both hands in a resigned "go ahead" gesture.

"All right." Merlin swallowed and cleared his throat, and his tone turned more serious. "You're right, there *were* witnesses, every one of whom saw Sheltyn put his hands on his superior officer first. And they know exactly who started the confrontation. People on the other side of *Manchyr* probably heard what he was saying to her, Cayleb; some of those witnesses sure as hell did. I will guarantee you—and you know this from your own experience, as well as I do—that not one Guardsman worth a damn liked Sheltyn. They might've *respected* him before Nimue turned up and he started showing his ass, but she gave him plenty of time to straighten out—and gave *them* plenty of time to change their opinion of him when he didn't. She gave him *five-days* to square himself away, and there's not a man in that unit who doesn't know Maiyrs called Sheltyn in for that discussion because the idiot hadn't done anything of the sort. And what did Sheltyn do as soon as he finished talking to the Major? He went out and physically attacked someone half his own size. Did it in front of *Irys*!"

Merlin shook his head in pure disgust.

"They *dote* on her, Cayleb. And they just got her and Daivyn back, her husband barely survived an attack that killed two hundred other people on her wedding day, Nimue is a 'seijin' sent for the express purpose of keeping her, Daivyn, and Hektor alive, and this idiot is dim-witted enough to try to beat up that *seijin* in *front* of her? I'm surprised someone *that* stupid remembers to breathe every so often!"

Cayleb frowned thoughtfully, and Merlin dipped another salted potato slice in the bowl of malt vinegar in the center of the platter and waved it like a pointer.

"By and large, those are damned good men, Cayleb. They were even before Tobys and his boys got mustered in, and they're even better now. There isn't a one of them who's going to misunderstand the message Nimue just sent. Or miss the fact that she demolished the son-of-a-bitch without ever even *touching* a weapon. Which she would've been perfectly justified in doing under their own regulations. If any of them—any of the rest of them, I mean—*were* inclined to pull that 'I'm really a major and you're just a miserable little captain' crap with her, they sure as hell won't do it now, and I wouldn't be a bit surprised if they've gotten past the 'she's just a *wooooman*' stage where she's concerned, too. Probably did it before Sheltyn hit the ground—the *first* time he hit the ground, I mean—but they'd sure as hell managed it by the time he stopped squealing! More to the point, she won't need to break any more of them into little pieces to convince them they might just want to consider taking her advice in the future. Oh, and that they really, really don't want to piss her off." He shrugged. "I realize I may be a little prejudiced, but from where I sit this is what we used to call a win-win situation back on Old Earth."

He popped his potato slice pointer into his mouth, chewed appreciatively, and grinned.

"Want to watch it again with me in slow motion?"

IV

Claw Island, Sea of Harchong

The lookout's cry had barely faded, but the drums were already rolling as Lieutenant Henrai Sahltmyn dashed for the parapet with his breakfast napkin balled in his hand. Even as he ran, his brain insisted the lookout had to be wrong, had to be confused—or imagining things! There couldn't *really* be—

He raced through the tropical dawn's coolness, past the furnaces designed to heat round shot red-hot, up the steps of packed earth framed in logs, and reached the firing platform beside one of his long twenty-five-pounders. The gun's crew stumbled up the steps on his heels. They were only half-dressed, still rubbing at sleep-crusted eyes, but Sahltmyn heard the gun captain snapping out orders as they hurled themselves at the tackles. There were a total of sixty guns in the Dagger Point batteries, all under Sahltmyn's command, and all along the embrasured earthen walls other gun captains and crews dashed to clear for action. Every fourth gun was continuously manned, and the ready gun crews had already loaded with shell as per his standing orders. Now they stood beside their pieces, staring south across North Channel, as Sahltmyn skidded to a halt.

The channel was twenty miles wide at this point,

although enough shifting sandbanks came and went between Dagger Point and Hardship Shoal, along its southern edge, to convince any prudent captain to keep well clear, especially with the wind out of the north-northeast as it was this morning.

And especially when he'd made his approach on one of the darkest nights of the year, without even a sliver of moon.

Sahltmyn swallowed hard as dawn light tinted the on-coming topsails rose and gold. Only one navy had enough confidence—enough *audacity*—to thread its way through Hog Island Passage and North Channel in total darkness. He didn't really need the standard flying from the intruder's masthead or the black hull with its bold, white strake to tell him the Charisian Navy had come calling.

Another ship followed two cables astern of the first, and still more topsails came into sight as the light strengthened mercilessly. They'd given themselves a generous spacing to avoid night collisions in confined waters, and he wondered how many more were coming along behind the ones he could already see.

They're not supposed to be able to do this, he thought. *They're not supposed to be able to* surprise *us like this. What the hell happened?!*

It was an unfair question, and he knew it. The Sea of Harchong was an enormous expanse of saltwater, and the chance of a Charisian squadron evading the Dohlaran cruisers who picketed the approaches to Claw Island itself had always been good. And while the island was the forward anchorage for Admiral Rohsail's Western Squadron, the efficiency of anchored ships quickly deteriorated. Earl Thirsk believed in keeping the squadron at sea, actively patrolling the Harchong Narrows and making the sweeps and courtesy calls Mother Church expected of it along the coasts of Tiegelkamp, Kyznetzov, and Queiroz. Everyone had realized the heretics were unlikely to mount any attacks on the island at a time chosen for the *defenders'* convenience; that was the reason it had been so heavily fortified after its recapture. But somehow the fact that this was precisely why his batteries had been put here didn't make Sahltmyn feel any better as he watched those topsails glide slowly, gracefully across the shadowed water the rising sun had not yet quite touched.

Langhorne! What is *that thing?*

The question stabbed through his brain as sunlight did touch the leading galleon's hull and he realized how enormous—and peculiar-looking—it was. It was easily forty feet longer than any ship he'd ever seen, and unnaturally low in the water for its length. It also appeared to lack any of the spar deck carronades which were the hallmark of a Charisian warship, but who in his right mind built a ship that size and gave it only thirty guns?!

He peered through his spyglass, still trying to wrap his mind around the galleon's presence, and realized it *had* no spar deck. The white strake along the gunports had tricked his eye into missing that initially because the bulwarks were so high they made the gunports seem too low for a vessel with only a single armed deck. Those solid, heavy-looking bulwarks had to be at least six or seven feet high, and how was anyone supposed to see over *that*? It was ridiculous!

But over the years, the Imperial Charisian Navy had done quite a few things other people considered ridiculous . . . until they faced Charis in battle and found out exactly why those "ridiculous" things had been done.

He glanced over his shoulder to ensure that his standing orders had been followed. The signal for "enemy in sight" flew from the tall parade ground signal staff, and that was really all he could tell Admiral Krahl until the rest of the oncoming galleons drew close enough to make some sort of count. By now his own consternation must be flying around the entire circumference of Hardship Bay, rousing other battery commanders, warning them the long anticipated and yet not really expected Charisian counterattack had finally arrived.

He looked back to the lead galleon again, and frowned as he realized how far north it was. Certainly any sensible captain would give Hardship Shoal and its sandbank necklace a generous clearance, but that same sensible captain must also know there had to be batteries on Dagger

Point. Even within the confines of the safe channel, he could have stayed six or seven miles from Sahltmyn's guns, well beyond their effective range even with ricochet fire. The Dagger Point batteries were intended to prevent troop landings on the point—or in Dagger Inlet, behind it—not to close North Channel. Oh, at low water and with unfavorable wind conditions, an attacker would be forced to come within their reach, but *these* people were arriving on the heels of the flood, with ample water depth and a wind which was almost perfect for their purposes. So why was that galleon shaping its course to pass within less than *two miles* of the point?

They'll probably change course any minute now. With only their topsails set, they'd take ninety minutes to enter our range even on that heading. There's plenty of time to change their minds. And in the meantime—

"Get those furnaces hot!" he barked.

▼ ▼ ▼

"I really wish the Admiral had been a little reasonable about this, Sir," Lieutenant Daivyn Kylmahn said quietly as he and Captain Sir Bruhstair Ahbaht stood on HMS *Thunderer*'s afterdeck.

"I have no idea what you're talking about, Daivyn," Ahbaht replied, looking up at his much taller first lieutenant. All Chisholmians seemed unreasonably tall to Ahbaht, an Emeraldian only an inch or so taller than Prince Nahrmahn had been. "It seemed to me that his orders couldn't have been more clearly and rationally set forth. Was there some point you wanted me to explain?"

"That's not what I meant, Sir," Kylmahn said just a bit severely.

Ahbaht was sixteen years older than the lieutenant, yet Kylmahn sometimes felt like a tutor with a rambunctious charge. He'd developed enormous respect for the small captain's ability, and Admiral Rock Point hadn't chosen the skippers for the ICN's first oceangoing ironclads by throwing darts at the wall, but Ahbaht's notion of humor could be a bit trying. In fact, he was prone to practical jokes, and although he was careful to avoid anything that might hamper the ship's efficiency or damage his officers' authority, he tended to come up with them at the damnedest moments. That and his penchant for suddenly and randomly choosing officers or petty officers to become "fatalities" during drills—or for pulling out his watch in the middle of a calm afternoon, studying it for a moment, and then deciding the ship had just lost her topmasts to a sudden squall that required all hands to turn to and sway up fresh spars to keep her afloat—had certainly kept his first lieutenant on his toes throughout the month-long voyage from Port Royal. It did the same thing for the rest of the ship's company, of course, and that was a good thing, but Kylmahn did sometimes wish his . . . lively captain would at least warn *him* about his intentions.

"What I meant, Sir," the lieutenant continued in an "and you knew very well what I meant" tone of voice, "is that I'd really rather not find out we were wrong about how effective our armor is by getting the Admiral killed in the opening engagement. He should've let *us* take the lead."

"I can't say I disagree," Ahbaht admitted in a rather more serious tone. "But do you actually think there was ever any chance of that happening?"

"Of course not," Kylmahn sighed. "Doesn't keep me from wishing, though."

"Well, they probably don't have anything nearly as heavy as the guns Captain Rahzwail used to test our armor. So, unless something untoward happens, *Dreadnought* should make out just fine."

"Excuse me, Sir, but aren't you the one who keeps saying we ought to always expect the unexpected to present itself at the least convenient moment possible?"

"A truly dutiful first officer wouldn't've brought that up, Master Kylmahn. He'd simply have nodded and said 'Of course, Sir.' "

"Of course, Sir. Forgive me. How could I have forgotten?"

"Very proper of you," Ahbaht approved and raised his double-glass to gaze at the gun-studded wall of earth looming up out of the morning shadows.

▼ ▼ ▼

"I estimate we'll enter their range in about fifteen minutes, My Lord," Captain Kahrltyn Haigyl said.

"Thank you, Kahrltyn," Earl Sharpfield replied just as gravely.

Haigyl looked at him for a moment, then drew a curiously resigned breath and returned his attention to his helmsmen.

Sharpfield smiled at his flag captain's back. Haigyl was a fellow Chisholmian—a weathered-looking sort with iron-gray hair and very dark eyes who'd commanded HMS *Arrow* at the Battle of Darcos Sound. *Arrow* had been one of the rearmost galleys in Sharpfield's western column, closest to the Charisians. She'd been sunk early in the fight, and Haigyl, who wore a patch over the empty socket of the left eye he'd lost that day, had found the transition from galley command to galleon command difficult afterward. Indeed, it would have been fair to call him a merely adequate ship handler even now, and some people wondered why Sharpfield had lobbied High Admiral Rock Point to name a man with that record to command HMS *Dreadnought* for him. But that was because they didn't know Haigyl the way Sharpfield did . . . or the way Rock Point had come to know him after Darcos Sound.

There might be a great many better seamen in the ICN, but there wasn't a more fearless man on the face of the world, and Kahrltyn Haigyl's determination would put a bulldog to shame. In a fleet taken completely by surprise, faced by a sledgehammer of firepower no captain had ever imagined might be possible, half blinded in the very first broadside, still he'd fought his ship until she literally foundered under him, ripped apart by cannon fire and dyed scarlet with the blood of her crew. And as *Arrow* went to the bottom, he'd seen to it that every one of her wounded—of her *other* wounded—was safely aboard one of his surviving boats or improvised rafts before he'd stepped over the rail into the sea himself.

In fact, he was very like a close friend he'd made following the Battle of Darcos Sound—a man named Gwylym Manthyr.

There'd never been any question in Sharpfield's mind who he'd wanted to command his flagship, and Rock Point had agreed. But for all his personal courage, Haigyl was clearly nervous about deliberately sailing into the fire of a well-dug-in battery of heavy guns firing shells and heated shot with his admiral on deck. He'd suggested more than once, in what he'd obviously thought was tactful fashion, that Sharpfield should go below, behind *Dreadnought*'s thickest armor, before action was joined.

"I think you're making the Captain anxious, My Lord," a voice observed, and Sharpfield glanced at the dark-haired, dark-eyed flag lieutenant at his elbow. Sir Mahrak Tympyltyn was hardworking, conscientious, and very fond of the flag captain, and he shook his head at his admiral. "I know there's not much you can do about it, but I do sympathize with him."

"I suppose I do, too. It is a bit humorous to see one of the few genuine men of iron I know fretting about it, though."

"It'll be a lot less humorous if you manage to get yourself killed or wounded, My Lord."

"If that happens, I promise to live long enough to dictate my revised will to you, Mahrak."

Tympyltyn snorted. Despite his many sterling qualifications as a flag lieutenant, he did have one drawback: his handwriting was execrable . . . at best.

"Excuse me, My Lord. Now that you've warned me, I'll just go fetch Fronz, shall I?" he said, and it was Sharpfield's turn to snort. Fronz Hylmyn, his personal secretary and clerk, had the elegant penmanship found in the finest scriptoriums. Even his shorthand looked graceful and flowing.

"You see, Mahrak? It's that sort of forethought that

got you elevated to flag lieutenant," the earl said. "Do your best to be sure some rude Dohlaran gunner doesn't remove the head you used to produce it."

▼ ▼ ▼

Henrai Sahltmyn raised his spyglass again while he tried to understand what could possibly be going through the oncoming galleon captain's mind. His present course would bring his ship to within two hundred yards or so of the ship channel's *northern* edge. He'd be less than eight hundred yards from the main battery at that point, and that was killing range. The Charisian captain *had* to see the furnace smoke, and *surely* he must realize Claw Island would have been provided with the new exploding shells. So what in Shan-wei's name could he think he was *doing*?

"Open fire, Sir?"

He lowered his glass and looked at Lieutenant Lahmbair, his second-in-command. Lahmbair's voice was level, but there was more than a trace of anxiety in his eyes, although Sahltmyn could hardly blame him for *that*.

"Not just yet, Lynyrd. If he's willing to come still closer, that's just fine with me." Sahltmyn showed his teeth in a brief, tight smile. "We're the ones with all these nice earthworks. I think we can afford to let him have the first broadside."

"Yes, Sir."

Lahmbair saluted and moved down the parapet towards his own station, and Sahltmyn concentrated on the galleon again. It looked as if the Charisian was actually prepared to anchor by the stern with a spring on the cable, and that was the most foolhardy thing he'd done yet. At the very least he should keep moving, try to make himself a *bit* harder to hit! If he really meant to anchor right in the play of Sahltmyn's waiting guns. . . .

Wait. What was *that*?

The day was much warmer, moving towards its usual scorching heat with the sun fully above the horizon, and the lieutenant frowned as sunlight reflected from the water to pick out details of the hull he hadn't seen yet, including the way the ship's paint had been scoured by winter seas on her passage from Chisholm. That was scarcely unexpected, given the storms that stalked Carter's Ocean and the Sea of Harchong in winter. But there were streaks of something where the paint had been stripped away. Something reddish—duller than the usual primer coats. Something that looked almost like . . . rust.

Oh, sweet Langhorne! he thought around a sudden, icy lump of dread.

Before his transfer to Claw Island he'd served with the main fleet out of Gorath Bay. He'd seen the first of Lieutenant Zhwaigair's "screw-galleys" and been impressed by their speed and maneuverability, at least in short bursts in coastal waters. And he remembered their bow-mounted heavy artillery . . . and the iron plates affixed to their forward hulls to protect their guns.

Iron plates which tended to corrode under the kiss of saltwater and streak the ships' sides with rust.

"Signal to Admiral Krahl and Captain Lywystyn!" he heard himself bark.

"Yes, Sir!"

A startled signal midshipman snatched for his pencil and pad. Sahltmyn made himself pause until the youngster was ready, then cleared his throat.

"Signal 'Enemy warships in North Channel appear to be armored.' You'll have to spell that last word. Then send 'Engaging.' And get it off quickly."

▼ ▼ ▼

"Well, I see they're awake over there after all," Sharpfield remarked as the nearest battery erupted in thunder.

No more than thirty-five or forty of Dagger Point's total guns would bear on *Dreadnought* at the moment, and he had no intention of allowing his flagship to stray into the play of any additional guns until he'd demonstrated her immunity to his own satisfaction. And, of course, whatever might be true of her hull, her masts and spars were no better armored than any other galleon's. Fortunately, with the wind out of the north-northeast, she'd drift *away* from the batteries if she was dismasted, and there was plenty of distance between Dragon Point and Hardship Shoal for her to anchor and make repairs.

It was very quiet on the flagship's deck—the quiet of disciplined men, waiting for the orders they knew must come. That stillness, that calm before the storm, was all the more striking against the background bellow of the Dohlaran artillery. And then—

"Stand by to anchor!"

▼ ▼ ▼

They *were* anchoring, Sahltmyn realized.

His ears cringed under the roar of the guns, and he coughed on the choking fog of powder smoke. Gun captains were shouting commands, swabs darted down smoke-streaming bores, and he raised the spyglass once more, waiting for the banks of smoke to clear.

▼ ▼ ▼

Over half the Dohlaran gun crews managed to miss their target. Which, Sharpfield reflected, actually wasn't bad shooting for the first rounds fired out of smoothbore guns at the next best thing to half a mile.

White spouts pocked the surface, other shells went skipping and bounding across the water, ricocheting like thrown stones, or flew past to land far beyond *Dreadnought* as the ironclad's stern anchor plunged into the water. Topmen scurried aloft, taking in her topsails, and men leaned into the 'tween-decks capstan bars as they took tension on the spring and rotated the ship to train her broadside on the battery.

Not all the gunners missed, however, and everyone heard the hammered-anvil clangor as a dozen twenty-five-pounder shells scored direct hits. Some of them broke up on impact; the others bounced off the three-inch Howsmynized steel plate like baseballs off a backstop.

Sharpfield felt the vibration, heard the ringing sledgehammer blows, and smiled coldly as he peered through a broadside angle-glass, waiting.

▼ ▼ ▼

The smoke rolled downwind, and Henrai Sahltmyn's stomach tightened as that ominous black hull emerged into the light once more.

There wasn't a mark on it.

They can't all have missed! he thought. *I know* some *of those shells were direct hits—they* had *to be! But—*

▼ ▼ ▼

HMS *Dreadnought* vanished behind a flame-colored, sulfur-reeking cloud. Fifteen six-inch guns fired as one, and unlike the Dohlaran gunners ashore, *none* of them missed. True, the battery was a much larger target and *Dreadnought*'s guns were rifled, but it was still a striking contrast in accuracy.

The difference in effect was even more striking.

▼ ▼ ▼

Lieutenant Sahltmyn watched the Charisian galleon disappear into its own dark brown gunsmoke. The incoming shells made a strange, warbling sound that ended abruptly as they slammed into his parapet.

Then they exploded.

He staggered, eyes wide, shocked by their sheer power. His own guns fired twenty-five-pound round shot, but their hollow-cored shells weighed forty percent less, and their bursting charges weighed only a pound and a half. The diameter of the incoming Charisian shells was only about ten percent greater, but they were much longer, their muzzle velocity was almost twenty percent higher, and they were five times as heavy. They struck with over seven times the impact energy . . . and carried *ten* times the bursting charge. Their elongated shape and ogival nose were much more ballistically efficient, their higher striking power drove them deep into their target, and the explosions were devastating. Anemic compared to what might have been accomplished with a high explosive nitrocellulose bursting charge, perhaps, but devastating enough.

▼ ▼ ▼

Earl Sharpfield waited impatiently for the brown powder's dense smoke to clear the range.

He'd been aboard *Dreadnought* when Captain Haigyl's gun crews trained against sample earthworks built especially to provide appropriate targets. He'd seen what her shells could do then, but there was a difference between observing the damage to an inoffensive wall of dirt built solely as a training target and the damage wreaked upon a hostile battery's entrenchments, weapons . . . and men.

The smoke rolled aside, and Sharpfield's lips drew back in a hunting slash lizard's smile as he saw the earthworks' cratered face.

The bastards didn't pile the dirt deep enough, he thought. *They'd stand up to thirty-pounder round shot all day long, but not to* this.

Not even the heavy shells would demolish the defensive works as quickly as he might wish, but they'd do the job one hell of a lot more quickly than the Dohlarans would have believed possible. And they didn't have to tear down the entire earthwork to silence the battery. One of the embrasures had taken a direct hit. It had to be a fluke—no one could deliberately target a single gun at eight hundred yards with his very first shot no matter how good he was—but that made it no less effective. That particular twenty-five pounder wouldn't be firing again, and as he swept the angle-glass along the breadth of the enemy parapet, he could almost feel the defenders' morale wavering.

The Dohlaran guns fired again, concealing themselves behind their own paler powder smoke, and *Dreadnought* rang like an enormous bell. But the shells bounced off yet again, and her gun crews bayed like hungry wolves. They bent back to their guns vengefully, and beyond them, moving majestically down the buoyed channel, HMS *Thunderer* led HMS *Tumult* and *Turmoil* into the heart of Hardship Bay. They were followed by thirty-one more galleons of the Imperial Charisian Navy, by transports loaded with eight thousand Imperial Marines, and by a long line of colliers filled to the deckheads with Chisholm's best anthracite.

Sharpfield turned his back on the smoke-shrouded battery, watching those topsails sweep past his anchored flagship, and wondered if the rest of Claw Island's garrison would grasp the message *Dreadnought* was in the process of delivering. He hoped they would . . . or perhaps he didn't.

There'd been no real need for his flagship to engage the Dragon Point batteries. She could have passed them without ever entering their range, as her consorts were doing at this very moment. She was here, engaging the defenses, ripping them apart and effortlessly shrugging off the worst they could do, for only one reason: to prove she could.

Pay attention, you bastards, the earl thought, turning back to the angle-glass, peering at the earthen walls as *Dreadnought* flayed them with fists of fire. *Pay attention, damn you! Learn the lesson now, or learn it later, because there's not one damned thing you can do to stop me from taking this island back. The only thing you get to decide is how frigging many of you we kill before you get smart enough to surrender, and just at the moment, I'm sort of hoping you turn out to be slow learners after all.*

. V .
City of Manchyr,
Princedom of Corisande

"Your Majesty."

The red-haired, blue-eyed young woman bowed deeply as Empress Sharleyan reached the dockside end of the gangplank. It was hard to hear her through the cheers of the waiting crowd.

"Captain Chwaeriau." The empress' smile was just the slightest bit crooked as she bent her head in regal acknowledgment. "It's good to see you."

She did not, Nimue Chwaeriau thought, straightening from her bow, say it was good to see her *again*. It was a

minor point, but a significant one, since Sharleyan Ahrmahk had never actually laid eyes on her before.

"And you, Your Majesty," the Guardswoman murmured, and stepped respectfully aside, then fell in at the
empress' left shoulder as Sharleyan continued along
the long runner of Chisholmian blue carpet laid across
the stone wharf. The graying sergeant at Sharleyan's *right*
shoulder nodded to her, and then both of them were busy
sweeping the crowd with watchful eyes—and sensors no
one else knew anything about—as Earl Anvil Rock and
Earl Tartarian bowed to the empress.

▼ ▼ ▼

"Well, I must say you're much . . . solider-looking in person," Sharleyan observed as the closed carriage moved
along the streets lined with cheering Corisandians. "And
you really don't look very much like Merlin. But there's . . .
something." She shook her head, waving out the window
at the noisy, welcoming throng. "A family resemblance,
I suppose."

"Bone structure, probably," Nimue replied. She and Edwyrd Seahamper shared the lead carriage with Sharleyan,
and the two of them gazed alertly and ostentatiously out
of the carriage's other windows. "He altered his a bit
when he decided he had to be a man instead of a woman,
but it's still basically the same, really, except for the jaw-
line."

"I see." Sharleyan glanced at Seahamper, who only
shrugged and smiled without ever taking his gaze from
the crowd.

The empress sighed. She found all the elaborate, obvious security wearing, but Sir Koryn Gahrvai was taking
no chances this time around. The carriage in which she
rode had been armored, it was escorted by a solid block
of Sir Alyk Ahrthyr's cavalry, every place of business along
the route to Manchyr Palace had been closed for the day
(and thoroughly searched by the Corisandian Royal
Guard and the Royal Corisandian Army), no other ve-
hicles were permitted within three blocks of Sharleyan's,

the sidewalks were lined with troops, and rifle-armed RCA marksmen patrolled the rooftops. The crowds' enthusiasm might suggest his precautions were at least mildly excessive, but they'd been enthusiastic on Princess Irys' wedding day, too. And there was a reason he'd flatly insisted Princess Alahnah *not* accompany her mother in the same carriage. The crown princess, her nannies, and her own Guard detachment would travel to the Palace later, less conspicuously, and by water, not in this mandatory formal parade.

At least the arrangements put Sharleyan and Nimue inside the carriage together, where they could converse in almost normal tones despite the thunderous cheers.

"So, how are the children?" the empress asked now, and Nimue chuckled.

"The *children*, as you're perfectly well aware, Your Majesty, are just fine. I realize they might seem a bit scatterbrained and adolescent to someone of your decrepit years, but they're actually quite mature."

"Oh, surely not *decrepit!*" Sharleyan protested. She was, after all, still short of thirty. Then she sobered slightly. "I *know* they're fine, but . . . I'm still worried. Silly of me, I suppose. I mean, I've talked to them every day since they were attacked. And still—"

She shrugged, and Nimue's eyes softened. Despite all of the enormously important political reasons for Sharleyan's visit to Corisande, today's schedule was free of any formal business. Aside from the greeting committee at dockside, it had been reserved entirely for family matters. She'd be seeing Daivyn—and, undoubtedly, Earl Coris—as well, but it would be as members of her adoptive daughter-in-law's family.

"Com conversations aren't the same thing as face-to-face," Nimue said after a moment. "A lot better than nothing, but not the *same*. And it's probably harder because of how badly Hektor was hurt." She shook her head. "After something like that, you want to actually *touch* the person you care about, not just see her com image."

"Yes," Sharleyan agreed, looking back out the window.

"And whether or not I'm that much older than they are, I *am* responsible for them."

"Maybe you are in the sense of being their empress, but neither of them is really a child. Actually, Hektor's one tough sailor, and Irys' childhood wasn't a whole lot less demanding than yours, and *I* wouldn't like to be the assassin who gets into pistol range of her now! For that matter, they've both handled the truth about the 'archangels' better than the majority of 'mature adults' would. In fact, I'm inclined to wonder if the . . . elasticity of youth isn't a good thing when it comes to processing that kind of upheaval."

"You may have a point." Sharleyan frowned. "It's not the sort of thing you can test with large sample populations, but Cayleb and Irys and Hektor—and I, of course—did all get the information rather younger than anyone else, and we don't seem to be handling it *too* badly."

"I suppose that's one way to put it," Nimue agreed with a snort. "One of the upsides of Hektor's ongoing 'convalescence' is the amount of time they've had to spend with Prince Nahrmahn and Owl. They've been soaking up every detail they can, and some of the questions they've been asking *me*—!"

Sharleyan laughed as Nimue shook her head.

"Cayleb and I must've pestered Merlin to the brink of insanity when he told *us*," she observed. "I believe the phrase is 'your turn in the barrel, Captain Chwaeriau.' Although from what you're saying, they may be a little ahead of where we were at this stage, at that."

"Oh, you have no idea, Your Majesty," Nimue assured her. "No idea at all."

Sharleyan looked at her sharply.

"I've heard very much that tone of voice from *Seijin* Merlin upon occasion, *Seijin* Nimue. Why am I hearing it now?"

"I have no idea what you're talking about, Your Majesty." Nimue's expression was the soul of innocence.

"Oh, yes, you do," Sharleyan told her crisply. "Now give!"

▼ ▼ ▼

There were limits on how informal the arrival of a reigning head of state in the capital of a conquered princedom which was about to join that reigning head of state's empire could actually be. Despite that, Prince Daivyn—with the strong support of his sister and now legal guardian—had cut pomp and ceremony to the bone. Sharleyan suspected he and Irys, with Coris' connivance and the Regency Council's complicity, must have put at least as many self-important Corisandian noses out of joint in Manchyr as ever she and Cayleb had managed in Tellesberg.

The carriage swept to a halt at the foot of the broad, shallow steps and a footman scurried to open its door for her. Nimue and Seahamper descended first, taking their positions to guard her back, even here, and then it was her turn.

She'd just gotten one foot on the ground when a small, wiry tornado in court costume, a simple silver circlet somewhat awry on its head, came flying headlong down those steps and flung itself at her. Self-preservation got her other foot planted and her arms opened in the proverbial nick of time.

"*Empress Sharley!*"

"Your Highness," she replied, somewhat more sedately, hugging Prince Daivyn Dahnyld Mharak Zoshya Daykyn tightly. "I'm glad to see you, too."

"I told them to bring you straight here." Daivyn elevated his nose in true princely fashion. "They didn't even argue."

"Very wise of them, I'm sure." She gave him another squeeze, then set him on his feet. "I don't suppose that had anything to do with having your sister and Earl Coris looming ominously in the background, did it?"

"Maybe a little," he acknowledged cheerfully. "But I'm learning to be very ferocious, you know."

He bared his teeth, and she laughed. Then she straightened his coronet for him and offered him her hand.

"May I crave the pleasure of your escort, Your Highness?"

"I'd be honored, Your Majesty," he replied gravely, then

rather spoiled the effect of his gravitas by grabbing the extended hand to tug her up the steps. "Come on! We've had your suite from last time completely redecorated for you!"

The crowd at the top of the steps included Coris, Countess Hanth and her children, and Hektor, seated in a wheelchair with Irys at his side. Sharleyan felt her eyes try to tear as she saw the lines pain had carved on Hektor's face, the stiffness of his left hand. He looked five years older than when he'd parted from her in Cherayth. Indeed, he looked older than Irys, not younger, but he only smiled as Daivyn towed her over to them.

Irys started what was probably going to be a curtsy, but Sharleyan cut it short by enveloping her in a hug almost as tight as the one she'd bestowed upon Daivyn. Irys seemed to hesitate as Sharleyan sliced through proper etiquette with typical Ahrmahk contempt for the protocolists. Then she hugged back firmly.

"Good afternoon . . . Mother," she said demurely.

"'*Mother*,' is it?" Sharleyan stood back, hands on Irys' shoulders, studying the younger woman's face.

"Well, Hektor *is* your son," Irys pointed out with a smile.

"Yes, he is," Sharleyan agreed, and stooped over the wheelchair Hektor no longer truly required to hug him, as well, then straightened and looked down at him with one hand on his cheek.

"And speaking *as* your mother," she said, "I'd appreciate your not getting yourself blown up again anytime soon."

"I'm working on that," he promised earnestly. "I've decided it's the kind of thing everybody probably ought to try *once*."

"You've been hanging around your stepfather too much. I can see Irys and I will have to separate the two of you if we're going to survive what both of you fondly imagine is a sense of humor," she told him, then turned to hug Mairah Hanth and all of the Hanth children.

"Come on!" Daivyn said, recapturing Sharleyan's hand

and tugging hard. "We didn't know exactly when your ship would dock, so we went ahead and ate lunch *hours* ago. But I made them save *dessert* until you've got here!"

▼ ▼ ▼

It was some time later before Sharleyan, having properly admired her redecorated suite, agreed with Daivyn that Corisandian chocolate cake was almost as good as Charisian banana custard, and delivered gifts to all of the Hanth offspring, finally found herself in the sitting room of Irys and Hektor's suite. Darkness had closed in, rain drummed gently on the skylight, and Crown Princess Alahnah, having arrived at Manchyr Palace's water gate by launch in time to demonstrate her own strong approval of dessert, sat on a cheerful rag rug in the middle of the floor thoroughly absorbed in a set of carved wooden blocks which had once belonged to a much younger Princess Irys.

"God, it's nice to park my regal rump on something that isn't *moving*," Sharleyan sighed as she leaned back, settling into the cushioned armchair with her eyes closed. "Ships are all very well, but give me solid land anytime!"

"That's no attitude for a proper Charisian," Hektor pointed out. In the privacy of their own living quarters, he'd abandoned the wheelchair and sat on the arm of Irys' chair, his right arm round her shoulders. "We—that would mean you and me, Your Majesty, not any of these namby-pamby Corisandians—are Charisians, and that makes us masters of the sea. Its salt is in our blood, its waves are our pulse, our very heartbeat! It's our proper element, our domain, the sinews of our empire, the—"

"I think you need smacking," Sharleyan told him without opening her eyes. "See to that for me, if you would, Irys."

"Of course, Your Majesty." Irys reached up and smacked him lightly on the back of the head.

"Hey!"

"A dutiful subject obeys any lawful command from her

monarch," Irys said primly. "Or, in this case, her monarch to be."

"Especially when it's what she wants to do *anyway*, you mean," her husband responded.

"Well, of course."

She smiled up at him, and he laughed.

"I realize we're all going to be quite busy for the next few days," Sharleyan said, reclaiming their attention. "Nonetheless, it's come to my attention that there's a minor matter which you somehow failed to call to my attention in our various com conversations."

They looked at her innocently, and she extended an admonishing finger.

"I don't suppose either of you would care to explain how it happens that you've already managed to get pregnant, Irys?"

"Well, you see, we have all this time when Hektor can't be walking around out in public without raising questions about how quickly he's recovered," Irys began. "We had to find *something* to do with all those extra hours and hours, and one thing just led to another, Your Majesty. Of course, it wasn't my fault. I was a mere lamb to the slaughter, grievously misled!" She rounded her eyes at the empress. "This devious Charisian seaman I met promised me exercise would help me lose weight, but I think he lied."

"Oh, I'm pretty sure he lied!" Sharleyan told her with a chuckle. "They're all like that, Charisian seamen. I speak from sad, sad experience."

"Well, we *do* have a certain reputation to uphold," Hektor said, blowing on the fingernails of his right hand and then buffing them on his tunic. "Honor of the fleet, and all that. And of course—"

Whatever he might have intended to add was lost to posterity as his loving wife took ruthless, treacherous, unscrupulous advantage of the most jealously guarded secret chink in his armor.

"Goodness," Empress Sharleyan murmured as her squealing stepson slid off the chair arm and collapsed to the rug beside her daughter under his loving spouse. "He's even more ticklish than *Cayleb!*"

▼ ▼ ▼

The magnificent choir fell silent, the last organ note faded, and incense-scented stillness floated over Manchyr Cathedral.

There'd been much discussion of the proper venue for this ceremony. Some had felt it should take place in Manchyr Palace's throne room. Others had argued it should take place in Tellesberg, as all the other ceremonies like it had. Some had even argued that it should take place outdoors, under God's own sky in Cathedral Square. But in the end, Irys' suggestion had been accepted. Indeed, in many ways, it had been inevitable. And so it was that Empress Sharleyan Ahrmahk found herself seated on a throne just outside the sanctuary rail, waiting while a very small boy in resplendent clothing, a crown upon his head, walked gravely down the cathedral's central nave towards her.

His sister walked at his right shoulder. Earl Anvil Rock walked at his left shoulder. A thurifer, a candle-bearer, and a scepter-bearer preceded them, and Klairmant Gairlyng and Maikel Staynair stood beside Sharleyan's throne, awaiting them.

It seemed to take a very long time for the small procession to reach her, and she felt her heart warm within her as she studied Daivyn's expression of grave concentration.

He was so young. The weight of what he was about to do would have sufficed to crush someone thrice his age, and Sharleyan wasn't certain even now that he fully understood all that was bound up within this ceremony. There was no doubt in that expression or the set of those slight shoulders, however. No qualms . . . only deep and profound trust in his sister and Phylyp Ahzgood. And, Sharleyan thought—hoped—in *her*. In the fidelity of the House of Ahrmahk.

Yet he was only eleven years old—barely ten by the

calendars of murdered Terra. Would an older Daivyn come to regret this day? When he truly understood what he'd sworn, would he resent having bartered away his independence as a sovereign prince? Come to believe he'd been betrayed by those he most loved and trusted into surrendering his birthright? God knew there'd been precedents enough throughout human history to feed precisely that fear. And there would always be more than enough self-serving, ambitious human beings eager to seek power by playing upon a young man's weaknesses.

Cayleb and I will just have to be sure he never has cause to doubt us, she thought. *Merlin's right. Integrity's a much deadlier weapon than cunning, in the end. And if this little boy is going to trust me the way he does now, then I will never—ever—do anything to harm him or betray that trust in any way.*

The procession reached her throne, the acolytes stepped aside, and Daivyn stopped at precisely the right point and bowed with the grace and self-possession of someone twice his age.

"Your Majesty," he said, and his young voice sounded clearly in the Cathedral's magnificent acoustics.

"Your Highness," she responded. She paused for a measured ten-count, then continued. "Are you prepared, Your Highness?"

"I am."

"Then let us proceed." She looked at Klairmant Gairlyng. "If you would be so good, Your Eminence."

"Yes, Your Majesty."

The Archbishop of Corisande stepped forward and laid his right hand lightly on Daivyn's head.

"Let us pray," he said, and inclined his own head. "Almighty and most merciful God, we humbly beseech Your blessing on this, our sovereign Prince. We ask You to strengthen him, to uphold him, to give him Your wisdom and lend him Your judgment. As You commanded and empowered Your Archangels to create and order all the world, we beseech You now to empower this, Your servant, as he swears fealty of his own free will and consent, approved by his Council Royal, his Parliament, and Your Church, to the crown of Charis in the name of all the people of this realm. Make him one with Your champions in the struggle to reclaim the world of Your hand and heart from those who have betrayed their duty to protect, guide, and *serve* Your flock. Guide him and them to final victory over Darkness, walk beside them and with them all the days of their lives, and give them the grace to know and to do Your will for all their people, never forgetting that *their* people are *Your* people first. Amen."

He moved back to his original position, and Maikel Staynair stepped up beside Sharleyan's throne with a jewel-encrusted copy of the *Holy Writ*. Earl Anvil Rock positioned a cushion directly before the throne, Irys lifted the crown from Daivyn's head and held it, and the boy knelt on the cushion and laid his right hand on the cover of the *Writ*. He looked up into Sharleyan's eyes, and his own were fearless.

"I, Daivyn Dahnyld Mharak Zoshya Daykyn, do swear allegiance and fealty to Emperor Cayleb and Empress Sharleyan of Charis," he said, his voice clear and distinct, unfaltering, "to be their true man, of heart, will, body, and sword. To do my utmost to discharge my obligations and duty to them, to their Crowns, and to their House, in all ways, as God shall give me the ability and the wit so to do. I swear this oath without mental or moral reservation, and I submit myself to the judgment of the Emperor and Empress and of God Himself for the fidelity with which I honor and discharge the obligations I now assume before God and this company."

A moment of intense silence hovered in the incense-rich, stained-glass stillness. Then Sharleyan laid her hand atop Daivyn's on the *Writ*.

"And we, Sharleyan Alahnah Zhenyfyr Ahlyssa Ahrmahk, in our own name and in that of Cayleb Zhan Haarahld Bryahn Ahrmahk," she said, "do accept your oath. We will extend protection against all enemies, loyalty for fealty, justice for justice, fidelity for fidelity, and punishment for oath-breaking. May God judge us and ours as He judges you and yours."

The silence that followed was, if anything, even more profound. Prince and Empress looked deep into one another's eyes, and then Sharleyan's hand turned. It clasped Daivyn's, lifting it from the *Writ*, and she rose from her throne. She stood, drawing him to his feet beside her, and put her arm about his shoulders as he turned to face that packed Cathedral while the stillness billowed about them.

"It is not often given to mortal men or women to know in their innermost hearts that they've risen, for one brief and glorious moment, to meet the expectations of God," she said clearly. "In this time, in this place, in the sight of these watching eyes, this young prince—this boy who's lost so much, paid so high a price for his crown—has done just that. He's found the courage and the trust and wisdom God asks of us all and sworn fealty to the House of Ahrmahk and to the Empire of Charis not from weakness, or from fear. He's done it because he truly believes it is the right thing to do for his people, and because he believes this, I, Sharleyan Ahrmahk, for myself and for my husband, swear to you that we will *make* it the right thing for him to have done. From this day forth, the people of Corisande are *our* people. Ours to defend, to protect, and to cherish. To receive justice, fair dealing, and equity from our hands and fidelity from our hearts. Ours not because of conquest, but because this boy *gave* them to us, trusting us to deal with them fairly, justly, and, above all, *honorably*. We have sworn to deal with him in that fashion, and that oath binds us to deal in the same fashion with those he loves and cherishes. Though all the world should come against us in the service of Darkness, we *will not* fail our liegeman by failing you. Here we stand; we can do no other."

"What the—?!"

Platoon Sergeant Rehgnyld Lywkys paused, his delayed mug of tea raised for its very first sip, and scowled at Private Zhynkyns Obairn.

The sergeant wasn't enjoying his morning. He was out here because Lieutenant Stahdyrd, 3rd Platoon's CO, was nervous about his most advanced picket and wanted some extra experience riding herd on it. Lywkys couldn't fault the lieutenant's thinking, but that didn't make him happy to be here instead of sleeping nice and snug in Roymark. And the private standing on the northern lip of the hollow in the chill morning light hadn't improved his mood one bit.

Private Obairn was not among the most graceful cavalry troopers Lywkys had ever encountered, and he was already in the sergeant's black book for several infractions, including the serious offense of having spilled Lywkys' *first* mug of tea. That, in fact, was the reason he was the one who'd drawn the dawn lookout duty. Interrupting Lywkys' already disrupted morning ritual—again—was unlikely to improve the rest of Obairn's day.

He was also, however, one of 3rd Platoon's more levelheaded members, and that tone of voice was unlike him.

"What?" Lywkys demanded, mug hovering. His own tone warned Obairn of the thinness of the ice upon which he stood, but the private didn't seem to notice.

"Better get up here, Sarge! We've got company . . . and I don't think they're friends of ours!"

Lywkys took a moment to glance at Corporal Fraidareck Zymmyr, 2nd Section's senior noncom, then set the precious mug on a flat, relatively level stone. He squelched across the wet grass, and Zymmyr was already on his feet, waving the other six troopers of his understrength section towards their picketed horses. Lywkys slipped twice scrambling up to Obairn's position. The second time he went to one knee, catching himself on his hands just before he landed flat on his face, and he swore irritably as he wiped his muddy palms on the seat of his riding breeches.

He was still wiping when he reached the lip of the hollow and froze.

The last few days had been warmer, but the temperature had dropped a few hours before dawn and the colder air had raised a dense ground fog. It was beginning to shred on the light breeze, yet visibility remained limited, and Lywkys felt his stomach fall down a steep, icy shaft as he realized what had hidden its approach behind that concealment.

The nearest mounted Charisian was barely three hundred yards away, and as the break in the fog widened, the sergeant saw at least thirty more enemy horsemen beyond him.

Worse—*much* worse—he saw one of those other horsemen point directly at him and Obairn.

"*Langhorne!*"

He wheeled around, lost his footing, landed on his posterior, and went tobogganing back down the slope far more rapidly than he could have managed on his feet. Second Section had "seen the dragon" more often than it would have preferred since last spring, and Zymmyr was a shrewd, tough customer. That was why his section had been chosen for picket duty, and the hollow was littered with discarded tea mugs and mess kits, abandoned as Zymmyr's veteran troopers began saddling up with frantic haste.

Obairn followed the platoon sergeant down the slope almost as rapidly, although he managed to stay on his feet, and they raced for their own mounts.

"Heretics!" Lywkys barked, snatching up his saddle blanket and saddle and throwing them onto his horse's back. "At least thirty. Charisian regulars." He darted a look around the white-faced troopers as he reached under his horse's belly for the girth. "Make sure the Lieutenant understands—they're *regulars*, none of these Siddarmarkian volunteers!"

Heads nodded, expressions grim with understanding of why the sergeant was making certain *all* of them had that information. If there'd been any doubt in their minds, the hooves pounding towards them would have clarified it.

Private Schmyd had finished saddling up. He turned to help Obairn, but Zymmyr shook his head fiercely.

"*Go, Max!*" he snapped.

Schmyd hesitated for perhaps one heartbeat. He and Obairn were from the same hometown, they'd grown up together, and Schmyd had courted Obairn's sister. But every man in that hollow knew why their picket was where it was, and they knew what those pounding hooves meant.

Mahkzwail Schmyd spared a single moment to squeeze his friend's shoulder, then sprang to his saddle and gave his startled horse the spurs.

Four more members of the picket had made it into the saddle when the Charisians reached the top of the hollow. They jerked their horses' heads around, facing the threat and drawing their sabers, trying to buy a little more time for the comrades still fighting to saddle up.

It was too late.

The mounted regiments of the Imperial Charisian Army had been given priority for the new revolvers. Nine thousand of the original cap-and-ball design and three thousand of Taigys Mahldyn's new cartridge-firing design had been waiting for Earl High Mount when his troops reached Siddar City, enough to equip one regiment in each of his three mounted brigades. As those regiments re-equipped, they'd passed their original double-barreled pistols to their sister regiments, doubling *their* pistol armament, as well. That meant every single one of High Mount's dragoons could deliver at least six pistol shots before reloading, and now 3rd Platoon, Company B, 2nd Battalion, 10th Mounted Regiment, came over the lip of that hollow in a storm of fire.

Private Schmyd was the only member of Corporal Zymmyr's section to escape.

▼ ▼ ▼

"This is confirmed?" Sir Rainos Ahlverez demanded harshly.

"Yes, Sir." Captain Lattymyr's expression was strained. The captain leaned over and tapped a spot on the map. "About here, Sir."

"But we don't know what may've been behind the ones Ahzbyrn's men saw, do we?"

Lattymyr recognized a rhetorical question when he heard one, and only shook his head. Ahlverez smiled bleakly and leaned over the map table while his mind raced.

Sir Ahgustahs Ahzbyrn's cavalry regiment was one of only three he'd retained to cover Roymark. The others were either tied down escorting supply trains or had been drawn into the bickering conflict crackling across the muddy winter hills and woodlots around Brahnselyk. He'd attempted to convince Duke Harless to further reinforce Brahnselyk, and the Desnairians had actually agreed to provide four cavalry regiments . . . none of which had yet reached Brahnselyk. They had, however, flatly refused to pull any additional cavalry back from Hennet's picket at Cheyvair, and they'd demanded more of Ahlverez' infantry for the siege lines south of Fort Tairys in trade for the regiments they *had* coughed up. As a result, Ahlverez' overstretched troopers were the only ones who could protect the critical supply base upon which so much depended, and he'd been forced to send ever more of them to do the job.

The heretics had exerted steadily mounting pressure on Brahnselyk over the past five-days, although they'd been cautious about pressing the infantry entrenched in the town itself too hard. And it seemed the Charisian Army's cavalry was less well endowed with artillery than its infantry. So far, no more than a few thousand heretic horsemen had been reported, although the numbers had been less definite than Ahlverez liked. The heretics came and went, ambushing a cavalry patrol here, sweeping down to pounce on a supply train there, peppering an occasional raft with rifle fire, and constantly lurking about the riverbank both above and below Brahnselyk. They'd clearly realized how critical the town had become to the Army of Shiloh's quartermasters, but so far they'd declined to take the losses they must have incurred attempting to storm the place, especially without their hellish artillery in support.

Ahlverez had been grateful for their restraint, although he'd also wondered how long it would last. Timidity wasn't something he'd learned to associate with Charisians, and this sparring, this bobbing and weaving, made him nervous. The absence of any of their small angle-guns puzzled him, as well. The damned things were obviously man-portable. Surely they could also be transported by packhorses or mules, so why *didn't* the cavalry harassing Brahnselyk have any?

He'd ordered his own cavalry to find out, but patrols which ran into heretics tended to suffer heavy losses for relatively little information. One thing had gradually become evident, however: Charisians didn't see cavalry the same way other people did. Safeholdian armies had always included missile troops—usually horse archers—in their cavalry, but most cavalry commanders used bowmen as auxiliaries, skirmishers and screeners, depending on lance or saber charges for decisive combat. So far, no one had sighted a single Charisian lancer, not one Dohlaran or Desnairian had turned up with a saber wound, and every single one of the bastards seemed to have a rifle. They operated more like infantry who simply used horses to get around quickly than like proper cavalry, and that was another of the many things which had made Sir Rainos unhappy.

Now he realized he hadn't been unhappy enough.

The bastards suckered me, he thought grimly. *And the fact that they didn't sucker me as badly as Harless or that frigging idiot Hennet doesn't make me feel one bit better.*

He leaned over the map, bracing himself on clenched fists as he glared at the terrain. No wonder they hadn't pressed the attack on Brahnselyk! They'd been deliberately showing themselves to him, drawing his attention towards that vulnerable, vital supply center when it wasn't what they'd been after at all. He had no proof of it yet, but he knew—he *knew*—what they'd *actually* been doing, and he'd let them get away with it.

And if a cavalry trooper with a pistol bullet in his shoulder hadn't stayed in the saddle for over five miles you wouldn't know anything about it even now, he told himself.

At least he'd quietly moved as much infantry as he could pry loose from Harless as far west of Kharmych as the fringe of the Kyplyngyr. He was sure those regiments had cursed his name when they'd been turfed out of the quarters they'd spent so long improving and found themselves shivering under canvas again. He'd hated doing that to them, but he suspected the bribe of those snugger quarters was one reason he'd gotten away with it. Harless had accepted his argument that the move would shorten his supply line; Earl Hankey had considered it one more example of his obsession with half-imagined threats; and the Desnairian infantry had been too delighted to inherit the Dohlarans' quarters, especially in light of the piss-poor excuse for housing they'd been forced to endure, to worry their heads over why Ahlverez had moved so many of his own troops even farther away from Ohadlyn's Gap.

It isn't much, but they're almost two days' march closer to these bastards than they'd be in Kharmych. If I can get them on the road fast enough. . . .

"Get a message out over the semaphore immediately," he said, eyes still on the map. "I don't know if the chain's still up west of the Kyplyngyr, but if it is, it won't be for long, so roust out the wyverns, as well. Send General Rychtyr a copy of Ahzbyrn's dispatch. Tell him I anticipate a heavy attack—no, make that a *very* heavy attack—on our communications between the Kyplyngyr and Roymark. And copy all of that to Colonel Ohygyns." He glanced up at Lattymyr. "Go. Send it now. Then tell General Sahndyrs I need to see him, Colonel Makyntyr, and General Tymplahr immediately."

"Yes, Sir!"

▼ ▼ ▼

"All right."

Sir Ahgustahs Ahzbyrn's voice was harsh as he looked around his company commanders' worried faces. Major Trai Alykzhandyr's was the most strained, and for good reason, given how badly his 3rd Platoon had been savaged. In addition to all of Corporal Zymmyr's section, it had lost most of another section ten miles south of the first contact. Over half Lieutenant Wahlys Stahdyrd's platoon was gone, and the loss of his platoon sergeant had hit him especially hard. Ahzbyrn felt a flicker of sympathy for Stahdyrd, but there was going to be plenty of bad news to go around much too soon.

"I've sent couriers to Colonel Sulyvyn and Colonel Lairoh, and also to Colonel Ohygyns in Roymark. I'm sure Colonel Ohygyns has already gotten messages off to Brahnselyk and Sir Rainos. In the meantime, we have a little problem here."

He showed his teeth and pointed east.

"According to Trai's people," he nodded at the iron-faced young major, "the heretics're coming down the western edge of the Kyplyngyr. We don't know what strength they're in, but I think we have to assume this isn't a picnic party out for a leisurely ride. So as soon as Colonel Sulyvyn and Colonel Lairoh get here, we'll be taking a little ride of our own."

▼ ▼ ▼

"Get those horses the hell to the rear!"

The sergeant sounded . . . testy, and Sir Laimyn Seacatcher, CO of the Army of Cliff Peak's 5th Mounted Brigade, felt his lips twitch at the irascible shout. The brigadier had been waiting a long time for this. Now he stood, surrounded by the sounds of picks and shovels, sweeping the approaches from Roymark through his double-glass. His brigade was a powerful formation, and Sir Ahdryn Raizyngyr's 6th Brigade would reinforce him within the next few hours. Together, they'd have over sixteen thousand men, which sounded impressive. Unfortunately, they were intended to cork a bottle containing close to two hundred thousand enemies.

And at the moment, 6th Brigade was still somewhere off in the misty distance, picking its way towards him . . . unless, of course, it had gotten lost.

Cheerful bastard, aren't you? Seacatcher grimaced. *And what's not to be cheerful about? Your field artillery's up, your mortars're dug in, and you've been so damned clever about not showing either of them to the other side this far. What could possibly go wrong?*

Actually, he could think of quite a few things, and he found himself hoping Duke Eastshare and Earl High Mount hadn't been too clever this time around.

"Get your *backs* into it! Those're *shovels*, damn it, not doxies in a tavern! *Swing* 'em, don't *lay* on 'em!" another leather-lunged sergeant bellowed, not that his men really needed the encouragement. They knew what they were about, and unlike most mounted troops, they regarded shovels as close personal friends.

Seacatcher lowered his double-glass long enough to smile fondly at the frenetically digging men all around him. He was an Old Charisian, himself, the elder son of the Baron of Mandolin, one of the inland baronies, thrown into his first saddle by a hunting-mad father about the time he'd learned to walk. Because of that, he was a superb horseman, unlike quite a few Charisian officers, and as a boy he'd hungered for the glory of dashing cavalry charges . . . preferably with a beautiful maiden languishing conveniently close at hand to admire Sir Laimyn's unspeakable gallantry.

He'd gotten over it.

War, and especially a war like this one, wasn't about gallantry or glory; it was about winning. As Baron Green Valley had explained in his own pithy fashion, "No poor sorry bastard ever won a war by dying for his country. He won it by making the *other* poor sorry bastard die for *his* country!" This war might be against something a bit more . . . complicated than another *country*, but the principle was the same, and the ICA had taught Sir

Laimyn Seacatcher any number of ways to make the other poor sorry bastard die for Zhaspahr Clyntahn.

And *not* with any dashing cavalry charges.

Seacatcher's men did carry sabers, and they'd been given enough training that most of them could probably engage the enemy without cutting off their own horses' heads, although Seacatcher wouldn't have placed any wagers on that. They had, however, also been remorselessly drilled in mounted pistol fire, and they spent as much time on the rifle range as they did mucking out stables or saddle soaping tack, because the one thing they *weren't* was cavalry. They were dragoons, mounted infantry, and any cavalry that wanted to come after them on ground of their own choosing would need a generous supply of caskets.

The congestion of horses was thinning rapidly. Normally, one platoon in each company was responsible for holding the other platoons' mounts. Now, however, picket lines had been established well back under the Kyplyngyr Forest's winter-bared trees and the brigade's supply drovers would keep an eye on them as well as the draft animals, which would increase his usual combat power by twenty-five percent.

One of the horses which hadn't been picketed cantered towards him in a shower of mud. The rider drew rein and saluted.

"Yes, Major?"

"Colonel Vahrtanysh's respects, Sir," Major Kreg Ahbraims, the 9th Mounted Regiment's executive officer, said. "The men are dug in and the guns are deployed. And the advance pickets report enemy cavalry advancing along the high road from the east. I estimate they'll make contact with our skirmishers in about an hour."

"Tell the Colonel I'll be with him in forty-five minutes. In the meantime, the Ninth knows its business too well to need any instructions from me."

"Yes, Sir!" Ahbraims saluted again and cantered off in the direction from which he'd come. Seacatcher watched him go, then beckoned to Captain Elwyn Newyl, his senior aide.

"Yes, Sir Laimyn?"

"The odds are these people won't be very coordinated—not for a while, at least. They'll get over it, but now that we've cut the semaphore and planted ourselves in the middle of the road, any kind of cooperation'll be harder than hell for them. Obviously, therefore, I am completely confident that the situation is totally under control."

"Of course, Sir Laimyn," the chunky, fair-haired Chisholmian agreed.

"Nonetheless, Elwyn—*nonetheless*, I say!—I would rest easier with Brigadier Raizyngyr in support. You will, therefore, select a suitable escort and go *find* Brigadier Raizyngyr and bring him here. Respectfully, of course."

"Of course, Sir Laimyn," Captain Newyl repeated. "I understand."

"Then why are you still here? Go."

"Yes, Sir."

Newyl saluted and disappeared, and Seacatcher called for his own horse.

▼ ▼ ▼

"Oh, this looks just *wonderful*," Major Paityr Mahkaid muttered. He couldn't see much detail, even through his spyglass, but what he *could* see was bad enough.

"What?" Zhorj Sellyrs asked.

Mahkaid commanded Sir Ahgustahs Ahzbyrn's 2nd Company, and Sellyrs was 3rd Company's CO. They'd been sent ahead to reconnoiter, and Mahkaid felt confident Colonel Ahzbyrn wouldn't be any happier hearing his report than he was going to be making it.

"Let's just say I don't see a single horse over there," he told Sellyrs, then handed over the spyglass. "Take a look. Tell me what *you* see."

Sellyrs raised the glass and gazed through it, then grimaced.

"I see *infantry*, not frigging cavalry," he said flatly. "*Dug-in* infantry."

"That's what I see, too," Mahkaid agreed. He glowered at the still distant forest, then sighed. "I guess we better go tell the Colonel."

▼ ▼ ▼

"It's not a *job* for cavalry!" Ahgustahs Ahzbyrn snapped. "I've got under two thousand men in all three regiments. I've got no artillery. I've got no rifles. I do have four understrength companies of horse archers. Would you care to wager how long four hundred bowmen would last against several thousand dug-in riflemen, Lieutenant Mastyrs?"

The lieutenant, who couldn't be more than twenty-two years old, didn't reply, and Ahzbyrn made himself draw a deep breath.

"I apologize, Lieutenant," he said after a moment. "I'm taking out my frustration on you, and I shouldn't. But three regiments of cavalry, none of them at more than eighty percent strength, simply don't have the firepower to attack that sort of position." He jabbed an index finger in the direction of the entrenched heretics. "I don't know that Colonel Ohygyns has the firepower, either, but at least he's got riflemen and some artillery. If I send my regiments in against those earthworks, my men will be massacred. It's that simple. Tell Colonel Ohygyns I'm prepared to support any infantry he can find to take those people on, but I respectfully refuse to see my men slaughtered when I *know* they can't get the job done. If I thought there was any chance at all of our taking that position, I'd order the attack despite the casualties we'd suffer. There *isn't* any chance, though. Not without one hell of a lot more support."

"I understand, Sir Ahgustahs," Mastyrs replied. "But I'll be honest with you. Colonel Ohygyns didn't instruct me to tell you this, but I strongly doubt he'll be able to send anything to your support." The young man's mouth was grimmer and harder than his years. "I damned near rode straight into a section or so of heretic cavalry on my way here. It looks to me like they're pushing patrols into the gap between you and Roymark, and they were already probing our positions around the town. I wouldn't be surprised if they're planning to hit Roymark in at least as much strength as they've got right here."

Ahzbyrn's mouth tightened. He reminded himself Mastyrs was young, with all that implied about his judgment. And he reminded himself that fear and anxiety had a natural multiplying effect on any estimate of an enemy's numbers. But even though all of that was true, what the lieutenant had said made entirely too much sense.

Take the high road through the forest to keep Sir Rainos or Duke Harless from reinforcing us. Then punch out Roymark. From there, they can move north to finish off Brahnselyk or east to reinforce their roadblock in the Kyplyngyr. For that matter, they may be hitting Brahnselyk right this instant! They've been playing us like cheap fiddles for the last month, so who's to say they haven't actually had the firepower to flatten Brahnselyk sitting out there somewhere in Cliff Peak all along?

Disgust filled him, more bitter than bile. It was all only too clear now, and he wondered if Sir Rainos felt as sickened as he did.

Mymphys. That's where they came from. They staged down the Branath that far, then moved cross-country, exactly the way Sir Rainos predicted they might. And did Bishop Militant Cahnyr do anything about it? No, of course he didn't. And Duke Harless and Earl Hennet wrote off the possibility because obviously no serious threat could be mounted without a road net! Too bad nobody told the fucking heretics that.

And, of course, the final touch was threatening Brahnselyk with forces deliberately weak enough to keep them looking there instead of *here* without ever suggesting the heretics were actually present in strength.

My God. All they have to do is sit on the damned road and the entire frigging army will starve. *And there's not one damned thing I* can *do about it.*

▼ ▼ ▼

"I'm damned glad to see you, Ahdryn!" Brigadier Seacatcher said, reaching out to clasp forearms with Brigadier Sir Ahdryn Raizyngyr. "Things've been quiet so far, but I doubt that's going to last."

"I'm sure it isn't," Raizyngyr agreed. "On the other

hand, Sir Tamys is only fifteen or sixteen hours behind me. He should be here by midmorning tomorrow."

Seacatcher's expression brightened. Sir Tamys Mahkbyrn, the commander of the Army of Cliff Peak's 2nd Corps, was also the commanding officer of the 7th Infantry Division. When his division joined the two cavalry brigades, 2nd Corps would be complete, with over twenty-five thousand men and a hundred and twenty guns, enough to hold anything the Army of Shiloh could throw at them through the Kyplyngyr for at least a five-day.

Of course, *until* he got here. . . .

"We've got some cavalry hanging about to the west," he told his fellow brigadier. "I don't think they're stupid enough to try digging us out of our holes. If I'm wrong, we'll educate them in a hurry. I'm a lot more nervous about what's going on east of us, though. They've pushed a lot of Desnairian cavalry out this way. It looks like their mounts are in even worse shape than we thought, but they've got a hell of a lot of horse archers and they've been probing hard. I'm not sure who's calling the plays from their side, but I'm starting to think he's at least smart enough to pour piss out of a boot. He seems to be reacting faster and harder than we'd expected, and he wouldn't have to be a genius to figure out what his next move has to be."

"About what I figured."

Raizyngyr nodded and frowned up at the afternoon sky. The winter days weren't quite as short this far south, but they were short enough. It would be dark soon.

"Starting to cloud up again," he observed. "Won't be much moon tonight."

"No, there won't," Seacatcher agreed.

"Right after sunset, d'you think? Or maybe wait a few hours, let anxiety work on us?"

"As soon as they can manage it," Seacatcher said grimly. "I think we took them just as much by surprise as the Duke and Earl High Mount hoped we would. I'm inclined to think the Desnairians were on their way to reinforce Roymark or Brahnselyk before we got in their way. But they're reacting faster and smarter than we hoped they would—than I *thought* they would, to be honest. They're not coming straight at us from the west and letting us kill them, but I'd say these bastards to the *east* realize exactly what's going to happen if they can't push us out of the way. So they'll throw everything they've got at us as soon as they can."

Raizyngyr nodded slowly. The operational plan had always envisioned the Army of Shiloh doing just that. After all, if Ahlverez and Harless couldn't blast 2nd Corps out of the way, their entire army was doomed to starve. Clearing their supply line—or their line of *retreat*, at least—had to be their highest priority, whatever the cost in casualties. But the plan had anticipated that 2nd Corps would have at least two days, and probably three, to dig in before an attack from Kharmych could be organized.

Plans, however, had a tendency to start shedding bits and pieces as soon as the enemy turned up.

"Right," he said, stroking his bushy mustache. "I wish we had some scout snipers to go out in the woods and play with them. *That'd* slow the bastards up! Since we don't, we'll just have to make do, won't we? Can I borrow some guides?"

"Ready and waiting," Seacatcher assured him with a thin smile, and beckoned to Captain Newyl.

"Yes, Sir Laimyn?"

The captain was liberally spattered with mud after an entire day in the saddle, but if he was exhausted, he hid it well.

"Find Lieutenant Brynkmyn, Elwyn. His platoon's in charge of guiding Brigadier Raizyngyr's men to their positions. He knows where they're supposed to go. Tell him to start moving them forward."

"Of course, Sir."

Newyl saluted both brigadiers and hurried off, and Raizyngyr shook his head with an approving smile.

"Boy's got a future, Laimyn. Assuming we avoid getting his head shot off in the next little bit."

"That sounds like a plan to me," Seacatcher agreed, and pointed at the canvas tarp stretched to give some protection to a map-covered field desk. "And as part of that endeavor, let me show you the lay of the land. My boys've been clearing fields of fire and we've marked out the trenches, but we haven't had enough time to get *your* boys dug in, too. I hope you brought plenty of shovels."

. VII .
Roymark-Kharmych High Road,
Kyplyngyr Forest,
The South March Lands,
Republic of Siddarmark

"Sir, this is crazy!" Major Mahknarhma protested. "The men aren't trained for it, and even if they were—!"

He broke off, maintaining control of his skittish horse with one hand while he chopped the other in a gesture which hammered exasperation and anger on the anvil of anxiety. The irregular pop-pop-pop of rifle fire echoed through the chill afternoon, mixed with an occasional sputter of pistol fire, and an acrid-smelling haze of powder smoke had replaced the morning's ground fog. It drifted around the trunks of the unconsecrated trees, catching at throat and nostrils, and the high road—and the woodland for three hundred yards to either side—was covered in a heavy carpet of wet leaves . . . and bodies. They were scattered less thickly than the leaves, those bodies, but all too many of them lay motionless in death and only a handful wore the heretics' uniforms.

"It's always refreshing to hear your opinion, Symyn," Sir Zheryd Klynkskayl, Baronet Glynfyrd, replied acidly. "And what in Shan-wei's name do you propose I *do* about it?"

Colonel Glynfyrd glared at his executive officer, although very little of his anger was actually directed at Mahknarhma. The colonel didn't know how many men his light cavalry regiment had lost so far, but he knew the number would be ugly by day's end. For that matter, it was ugly enough already! The regiment had begun the day over a hundred men down as the result of illness, injury, and—little though he cared to admit it—desertion as the supply situation worsened. By now, they had to be down to no more than five hundred. In fact, they were probably closer to four . . . and it was barely three o'clock.

And Symyn's right, he thought bitterly. *The men* aren't *trained for it, and we're getting massacred! But that son-of-a-bitch Ahlverez is right, too, damn him!*

Mahknarhma looked back for a moment, then his shoulders slumped.

"I just hate seeing the boys get *hammered* this way, Sir," he admitted, and Glynfyrd grimaced.

"So do I, and if I saw a way to avoid it, I would. As it is—"

A heavier crackle of rifle fire snarled out of the smoke to the west. Both cavalry officers turned toward it, ears cocked, and their faces tightened.

"We're getting closer to something they mean to hang on to," Glynfyrd said harshly, trying not to wince at what that meant for his regiment, and Mahknarhma's answering nod was choppy.

▼ ▼ ▼

"You, Sir, are a sight for sore eyes," Colonel Nohbyro Baylair said fervently, reaching out to clasp forearms with Sir Ahdryn Raizyngyr.

"Sorry we're late," Raizyngyr replied. "Sir Laimyn said we should move right along after we got here, though."

"And he wasn't wrong," Baylair agreed. "I don't know who's in command on the other side, but whoever it is has his head a lot less up his arse than I could wish!"

"Brief me," Raizyngyr said, and Baylair shrugged.

"We're digging in the main position back there." The colonel jerked his head to the west, down the bed of the high road, and Raizyngyr nodded. He'd passed through the sound of axes, mattocks, and shovels on his way to Baylair's current command post. "Major Chernynkoh's engineers've been a godsend, but we won't have anywhere near as long as we were supposed to have to get ready for the main party. Not if these bastards coming at us're anything to judge by."

Raizyngyr nodded again. Major Brahdlai Chernynkoh's 4th Mounted Engineer Battalion had been attached to 2nd Corps specifically for the purpose of helping its mounted infantry dig in before the main force of the Army of Shiloh hit them. The mounted engineers weren't themselves combat troops, technically, although anyone who wanted to tangle with them was welcome to try. At the moment, however, they were busy doing what they were supposed to be doing, and Raizyngyr could hear the steady crashing of trees as the engineers felled them with their tops towards the enemy. The occasional thunder of an explosion told him they were using blasting powder, as well, but the sounds of combat from the east confirmed Baylair's estimate that they weren't going to have time to do a proper job of it.

"I've got Third Battalion screening the approaches," the colonel continued, waving one arm towards the east, this time. "Major Braytahn's done a damned good job, so far, but he's got three of his four companies up now, and they're still pushing hard. It was almost entirely cavalry to begin with. Light cavalry, too, damn it. And Desnairian."

He paused, meeting the brigadier's eyes, and Raizyngyr grimaced. There were advantages to facing Desnairian cavalry rather than their Dohlaran compatriots, because the Dohlarans had learned a lot of lessons the hard way. They were considerably more circumspect than Desnairians, they had more firearms, and their arbalest-armed dragoons could hit with devastating power. But only about a quarter of their cavalry *were* dragoons, whereas *all* Desnairian light cavalry—and two-thirds of the Empire's medium cavalry, as well—were armed with horse bows. And whatever the Imperial Desnairian Army's other faults might be, its bowmen were well trained and accurate.

And not especially short on guts.

"The damned trees don't give us a hell of a lot in the

way of fire lanes," Baylair said, "and those frigging bows're a lot better suited to this terrain than arbalests would've been. Bastards're getting smarter about not making themselves into targets, too." He showed his teeth for a moment. "Guess rifle bullets make pretty good teachers."

And the fact that the opposition was light cavalry, without the half plate of Desnairian heavies or even medium cavalry's chain mail, meant they'd be faster and more agile, Raizyngyr thought grimly.

"They've been pushing my boys back steadily," Baylair acknowledged. "Of course, that was the idea from the beginning, but they're pushing harder and faster than we'd planned on. And about twenty minutes ago, I got a message from Braytahn. He's seeing medium and heavy Desnairian cavalry on his right, south of the high road, and one of his company commanders reports what looks like Dohlaran infantry coming up the road from the east."

"Infantry," Raizyngyr repeated, and Baylair's expression was grim.

"That's what Braytahn says, and the report's from Captain Ohahlyrn—Meryt Ohahlyrn, runs Company C. He's young, but he wouldn't've reported infantry if he wasn't damned sure he'd actually seen it."

Raizyngyr's jaw tightened. Bad enough that Baylair's advance units were already in contact with cavalry; if the Army of Shiloh already had *infantry* close enough to throw into the attack. . . .

"All right," he said. "I've got two battalions of the Eleventh ready to take up positions to either side of your blocking position. I was going to hold Colonel Haskyns' other two battalions on the high road as a reserve until the Twelfth gets here, but it doesn't sound like we've got time for that kind of nonsense. As soon as Third and Fourth Battalions come up, I'll deploy them, too. North or south of the high road, do you think?"

"North." Baylair didn't hesitate. "They're actually pushing harder on the south, but I've got second Battalion holding down that end of the line, and the terrain's better on that side. Turns out we've got a lot of dead ground out there to the left, though. Don't really know how bad it is or how far it extends, but if the other side finds it, they can get a lot closer than any of us'll like."

"Makes sense. And since you've got your finger on the pulse here and those are your boys out there in the woods, I'm leaving tactical command with you until we're back on the main blocking position. Buy me as much time as you can, though. The Twelfth's the better part of an hour behind Haskyns."

"Understood, Sir." Baylair's grimace blended a grin and a snarl. "We've already cost the bastards plenty, and we'll cost 'em a hell of a lot more before your boys have to tell 'em hello."

▼ ▼ ▼

The faces around Sir Rainos Ahlverez didn't look any happier than *he* felt, but aside from Sir Ahlgyrnahn Haithmyn, who commanded one of Earl Hennet's medium cavalry regiments, most of them showed a sense of grim agreement.

"Colonel Glynfyrd, Colonel Tymyozha, and Colonel Pynhaloh have done well," he said. He looked at Sir Selvyn Pynhaloh, the only one of the three light cavalry colonels who'd been close enough to join this hasty council of war. "They've paid a steep price," he continued, meeting Pynhaloh's eyes levelly, "and it's not the kind of fight their men were trained for. I know exactly how much we've asked of them, and no one could've given us more than they have."

Pynhaloh looked back for a moment, then jerked a single nod of agreement, and Ahlverez nodded back. He still didn't particularly care for Desnairians, especially Desnairian senior officers, but the cavalry had fought hard from early morning until evening, and they'd paid in blood to push the heretics back for almost three miles. Casualty estimates were usually high in the middle of a fight, and that had to be especially true when combat was scattered over such tree-clogged, overgrown terrain, but he'd be surprised if the three regiments hadn't lost at least six or seven hundred men between them. That was a thirty percent casualty rate, yet they'd kept right on attacking, pushing hard. Whatever might be wrong with Desnairian attitudes or doctrine, there was nothing at all wrong with Desnairian courage.

Unfortunately, it sounded to Ahlverez as if the heretics had *planned* on being driven back, although anything remotely like reliable information was hellishly hard to come by. It was bad enough in open terrain, where a man could at least hope to see his immediate vicinity and messengers from units in contact with the enemy had a decent chance of finding superior officers. The only good thing about *this* terrain was that all his subordinates knew his headquarters virtually *had* to be located on the high road, which happened to be the only readily identifiable terrain feature within fifty miles. The mere thought of what any of *his* messengers would experience trying to find deployed formations out in those smoke-filled woods was enough to give him nightmares.

Face it, he told himself grimly. *Once you send them off to attack, you've done every damned thing you can do, Rainos. There's no way in hell you can exercise any kind of control over this cluster fuck. It's all going to come down to your regimental and company commanders, God help them all.*

"Now it's our turn," he continued, showing them the steely determination they needed from him even though all of them were smart enough—or he hoped to *God* they were, at any rate—to realize he knew no more about the heretics' strength or positions than *they* did. "I doubt they could've expected us to put together an attack this quickly. All the reports we've gotten so far say they're still digging in across the high road. If we let them *finish* digging in, digging them back *out* again'll be a lot more expensive."

Actually, if we let them finish digging in, digging them back out again will be damned near impossible, *Rainos,* he admitted to himself with bleak honesty.

The last several hours had driven home the difference between Charisian cavalry and anyone else's with brutal force. The Desnairian light horsemen had fought just as magnificently as he'd suggested, but he doubted the heretics' casualties had been even a fourth of theirs. The Charisians were *infantry*, fighting an infantry battle, and it showed. If troops that good were given time to prepare their positions properly, frontal attacks—which were about all the Kyplyngyr's terrain would permit—would become as expensive and futile as the assault on Earl Hanth's Thesmar entrenchments. And if *that* happened. . . .

"If we can't reopen the high road, the army's in deep trouble," he said flatly, "and our best chance to do that is now. If I had any choice but to ask you to attack under these circumstances, I wouldn't. I know you're going in blind, without any clear idea of where the enemy is or how strong he is, and I know your losses're going to be heavy. But we've got to hit him *now*, as quickly as possible, while he's still trying to get all of his own strength into position. 'Go find somebody and fight him' is hardly the sort of order any officer likes to get. Unfortunately, it's the only one I can give you. So go kick the hell out of these heretic bastards."

His gaze swept their faces one more time. Then he nodded sharply and they saluted and turned back towards their own commands.

He watched them go, seeing the determination—or perhaps *desperation*—in their body language . . . and the outrage still stiffening Colonel Haithmyn's spine. He couldn't fault the colonel, and at least Haithmyn had swallowed his protests and accepted his orders. But the Desnairian had a point, and a damned good one—one Ahlverez had just made himself, as a matter of fact. His dismounted medium cavalrymen would be hideously out of their element tonight, and they'd pay an equally hideous price because of that, yet Ahlverez had no option but to demand it of them.

Even Duke Harless recognized that. In fact, Ahlverez had been astonished by how quickly the duke's approval of his own plans had come back over the semaphore.

Perhaps the Army of Shiloh's semi-starved state had something to do with that decisiveness, although Ahlverez was tempted to conclude it also had something to do with the fact that Harless had dispatched that poisonous little snot Fyrnach to Brahnselyk last five-day. Ahlverez had been almost as outraged as disgusted when Baron Tymplahr confirmed that Fyrnach had made the journey in order to personally plague the Dohlaran quartermasters over the low priority assigned to resupplying Duke Harless and Earl Hankey's traveling wine cellars. His disgust had eased—slightly—when he'd learned it had been Fyrnach's idea, not his granduncle's, and he could only consider the baron's absence a major plus under the current circumstances.

At any rate, Harless had agreed an immediate attack to clear the high road was essential. Ahlverez hadn't mentioned that he'd intended to launch it even if Harless ordered him not to, but he'd found the duke's agreement welcome. And he'd found Harless' message that he'd ordered Hankey to immediately begin moving additional Desnairian strength to support him equally welcome. It would have been even better if virtually the entire Desnairian infantry force hadn't been tied down in the muddy siege lines before Fort Tairys, but Harless had specifically authorized him to dismount cavalry units and use them as infantry. Even in his extremity, Ahlverez discovered that contemplating how that idiot Hennet would react to those orders could make him smile briefly.

The smile vanished at the thought of the casualties those horsemen were about to take, yet the truth was that they'd lost so many horses to starvation that as much as a third of them no longer had anything to be dismounted *from*.

In the meantime, he'd ordered all his own infantry westward. They'd reach him before any Desnairian infantry could, and he was likely to need them . . . badly. He'd told his subordinates their best chance to break the heretics was to hit them now, immediately, and it was true. But he also knew that unless they accomplished that task the Army of Shiloh was doomed. So if they didn't break the heretics tonight, they'd have no choice but to try again tomorrow.

▼ ▼ ▼

Colonel Ahlbair Pahskail drew a deep breath. The night air was both colder and damper than it had been. It smelled like fresh rain, and cold as it was, rain might well turn into sleet or even snow if it did put in an appearance.

That'd be all we need, he thought grimly. *Icy footing on top of everything else. Wonderful.*

Pahskail's infantry regiment was perhaps five hundred yards (it was hard to be certain of distances) south of the high road, slogging through heavy forest with three more regiments behind it. In theory, they were advancing in column; in fact, nothing as neat as a column could possibly have moved in such terrain.

The Kyplyngyr boasted few of the titan oaks common to less temperate latitudes, and those it did have towered like scattered sentinels above a lumpy green canopy of lesser brethren. This was a forest of nearoak, nearpoplar, sky comb, talon branch, and scabbark. The good news was that it was a mostly *mature* forest, so at least the first twenty feet of the talon branch trees were clear of their nasty thorns and there was a decent spacing between the nearpoplars. Unfortunately, unconsecrated forests in temperate climates like this one tended to be highly flammable. Indeed, regular summer and fall fires were a part of their life cycle . . . a thought that made the possibility of sleet or snow a little less irritating, given all the rifles and pistols firing away. It also meant that even at maturity, most of their trees were seldom much over ninety feet tall—and those were the nearpoplars, the fastest-growing of the lot—and that they had far more undergrowth than they would have had farther north.

He reached up, pushing a half-seen scabbark branch to one side before he ran into it face-first, and resisted the urge to snarl at his men to be quieter. They were already being as quiet as they could, wading through crap like this, and one *hell* of a lot quieter than the poor damned cavalrymen who'd been fighting their way through this shit all day long. Pahskail had never much cared for Desnairians, but those boys had earned their pay today, and—

▼ ▼ ▼

"Stand to! *Stand to!*"

Captain Maikel Karnynkoh's head snapped up as he heard the shout and recognized Sergeant Daivyn Sylvella's voice. Karnynkoh commanded Company A, 3rd Battalion, 12th Mounted Regiment, and Sylvella was the senior noncom in his second platoon. He was also an experienced, levelheaded man—not the sort to jump at shadows. And that meant—

The thunderclap sound and blinding flash of the first Shan-wei's fountain underscored the sergeant's warning.

▼ ▼ ▼

Pahskail swore vilely as more explosions cracked on the heels of the first.

His regiment hadn't yet encountered the heretics' Kau-yungs, but he'd discussed them with officers who had. Even if he hadn't, the screams coming back from his advanced scouts would have told him what they'd run into.

He could hear shouts now, in accents which certainly weren't Dohlaran or Desnairian, from the far side of the explosions.

"Find Colonel Kahmelka!" he snapped, gripping his runner's shoulder. "Tell him I need him and Colonel Ohdwiar up here *now*!"

"Yes, Sir!"

A bugle began to sound from the heretics' position and Colonel Pahskail reached into his pocket for his whistle.

▼ ▼ ▼

There were four infantry regiments in Pahskail's column. All of them were Dohlaran, twice as strong as their Desnairian counterparts and thirty percent larger than a

Charisian battalion, but none were at full strength after so long. They should have had a combined strength of almost fifty-six hundred men; what they actually had was a few over four thousand. But they were veterans, and every one of them had a bayoneted rifle, without a single pike among them.

The Charisian position in front of them was little more than a rough breastwork, snaking its way through the trees. Engineers and working parties from the two battalions deployed along the line had felled as many trees as possible to form an improvised, eastward-facing abatis in which the talon branches were especially effective. Dropping the trees had also cleared the defenders' fire lanes . . . to some extent. Darkness deprived them of what advantage that might normally have provided, however, and there'd been time to plant only a handful of the landmines which had proven so effective along the Daivyn River. The sparse mine belt's true function had been not to stop an attack, but to serve as a perimeter warning for the defenders, and it did just that.

Despite his awareness of the need for haste, Pahskail was too experienced to simply hurl his men forward. Whistle blasts deployed his own regiment into an assault column, one company across and five deep, while Gotfryd Kahmelka's regiment moved up on his right, Colonel Mahthyw Ohdwiar's regiment moved up on his left, and Colonel Trynt Brygsyn's regiment closed up behind as their column's reserve.

There were over three thousand men in those three leading regiments; there were just over sixteen hundred Charisians in the two battalions manning the breastworks in front of them, with another eight hundred in reserve, and there was precious little hesitation on either side.

▼ ▼ ▼

The explosion of additional fountains and the sound of whistle blasts told Colonel Lewshian Zhywnoh, the 12th Mounted's CO, what was about to happen. He had Major Zhairymiah Mohzlyr's 2nd Battalion and Major Ghordyn Lyptakia's 3rd Battalion on the line; and 1st Battalion was his reserve, under Major Krystyn Rej. Fourth Battalion was still finding its way to the 12th Mounted's position; given the terrain and the darkness, Major Mahrak and his men would be doing well to arrive before dawn.

From the sounds of things, Zhywnoh could have used Mahrak right about now. Unfortunately, the Army of Shiloh hadn't asked him when it would be most convenient for it to attack.

"Flares!" he snapped, and was rewarded by the whooshing, hissing sound of a flare rocket, at which point he discovered another inconvenient fact.

The rocket lifted well enough, but then it slammed into a nearpoplar branch—invisible in the darkness—no more than sixty feet above the ground, at which point it abruptly altered its trajectory and drove downward at a steep angle. Fortunately, it landed somewhere out in front of 3rd Battalion instead of right on top of Lyptakia's men, but it provided very little illumination when it did.

"Find a clear spot, damn it!"

He heard a quick acknowledgment and knew the artillery support party would do its best to obey him, but given the thickness of the forest and the darkness, it would be a trial and error process, at best.

▼ ▼ ▼

Ahlbair Pahskail flinched as the heretic rocket began its ascent. He'd seen rockets like it at Thésmar. But then it slammed into the nearpoplar and went screaming down to earth. It narrowly missed one of Colonel Kahmelka's companies, yet Pahskail suspected they were as happy as he was to have it on the ground rather than hideously illuminating them as they closed with the heretics.

He made himself wait, despite the tension clawing at his nerves. Every second gave the heretics more time to prepare, but they were already in their chosen position. Additional preparation time was far more valuable to the Army of Shiloh than to them, and so he made himself stand there, hands folded behind him, doing his best to project a sense of calm he was far from feeling, until he heard the whistles sounding again from left and right, announcing that his flanking regiments were in place.

Then, and only then, he smacked his bugler on the shoulder.

"Sound the charge!"

▼ ▼ ▼

The Dohlaran bugles sounded fierce and clear, and Colonel Pahskail's column surged forward.

What followed was madness.

None of the participants could ever sort it out afterward, although Owl's SNARCs watched the entire thing and some future history of the war would undoubtedly describe it in detail. At the time, it was only a hideous confusion, a cauldron of darkness, gun flashes, screaming men, trees rearing above the canopy of powder smoke like ghostly reefs, the hiss and whine of bullets, and the explosions of Charisian hand grenades and mortar bombs.

None of the 12th Mounted's field guns had made it to the fighting position yet, and 1st Battalion's infantry support platoon was lost somewhere in the woods between its parent battalion and the high road. The regiment had the twenty-four mortars of the other two battalions in support, but the same tree cover which had gotten in the flare rocket's way made mortar fire problematical at best and actively dangerous to the defenders, at worst.

In the darkness and smoke, it was bayonets and hand grenades—and rifle butts, knives, sometimes fists and even teeth—as the Dohlaran infantry hurled itself upon its enemies. The officers of those regiments knew how vital it was to smash the roadblock. Not all of their men were equally aware of the stakes, but they knew enough, and the enemy were in those trees in front of them, no longer hiding behind Fort Tairys' entrenchments while sniper fire and artillery took a steady, galling toll of the besiegers, despite the siege line's trenches. They were more than a little starved, those Dohlarans, gaunt, with leaky boots and worn uniforms that came perilously close to tatters, but their weapons were well kept and clean, and they knew what to do with them.

They clawed their way through the improvised abatis, losing any trace of formation in the process. The Charisian landmines killed or wounded dozens of them. The Charisian rifles and hand grenades killed or wounded *scores* of them. But the survivors reached the breastworks, and then it was bayonet-versus-bayonet. The 12th Mounted had been reequipped with the new cartridge-firing revolvers, and the pistols took dreadful toll of Pahskail's men, but those gaunt, scarecrow soldiers carried through anyway. They ripped a hole clear through 3rd Battalion's front, effectively wiping out two of Company B's platoons and one of the support platoon's mortar squads along the way. But then a ferocious counterattack from Company D hit their flank in a stormfront of grenades and a tsunami of bayonets. The penetration was driven back, sealed off, and exterminated, but at heavy cost.

The first Dohlaran attack began shortly after nine o'clock. It roared about the Charisian position for over forty blood-soaked minutes before the attackers fell back in sullen, stubborn frustration . . . and a *second* attack came screaming out of the trees behind its blaring bugles barely ninety minutes later. It was weaker, because a third of the men who'd made the first one were dead or wounded, and it was led by Colonel Trynt Brygsyn, because both Ahlbair Pahskail and Gotfryd Kahmelka were among the wounded, but it drove in just as ferociously, and it, too, breached the Charisian line.

The Dohlarans broke through in two places, this time, but for all their fury, they simply didn't have enough men, and 1st Battalion was waiting behind the line. Company-strength counterattacks crushed each breakthrough, hurled back every assault for over two hours, while powder smoke rose in a thick, choking pall shot through with muzzle flashes like lightning glare in the heart of a summer thunderhead.

And then, suddenly, as abruptly as a breaking branch, it was over. The gunfire and the bugles were silent, no more bayonets drove wetly into human flesh, no fresh grenade explosions ripped the night. There were only the exhausted men of the 12th Mounted and a forest night filled with the moans and the sobs and the screams of broken, bleeding men.

Twelfth Mounted had suffered almost eight hundred casualties, over thirty percent of the three battalions engaged, but twenty-six hundred of Colonel Pahskail's column lay dead or wounded in those hideous woods. That was a loss rate of over *sixty* percent. Three of the four colonels who'd led their regiments into battle were dead or wounded, as were thirteen of its twenty-four company commanders and sixteen of its forty-eight platoon commanders.

They had nothing to be ashamed of, those men. Nothing at all. They'd attacked an enemy in prepared positions, in the dark, with no idea at all of how that enemy was deployed. They'd taken horrendous losses in their first attack; then the survivors had reorganized and done it all over again, and in the process, they'd suffered casualties which would have gutted any army in human history.

They'd given Church and Crown all they had to give, given all that could have been demanded of any mortal men. Yet in the end they were driven back—limping, snarling, licking their wounds, but still back . . . and the bloodied 12th Mounted Regiment still held its line, unbroken, behind them.

. VIII .
Kyplyngyr Forest
and
Fort Tairys,
The South March Lands,
Republic of Siddarmark

General Sir Tamys Mahkbyrn, CO of 2nd Corps, Army of Cliff Peak, looked around the drawn, exhausted faces. The lighting was unflattering, the lantern flames painting lines and shadows in darkest charcoal, turning tired eyes into polished marbles, and he looked down at the map again.

Major Chernynkoh's engineers had prepared that map. It was less detailed than the ones the Archangel Hasting had provided on the day of creation. It wasn't even as detailed as the more recent, merely mortal ones with which the Army of Cliff Peak had set out from Siddar City. But it was detailed enough, the distances and bearings nailed down and solid, and while there were undoubtedly many terrain features it didn't show, the ones it *did* show were exactly where it said they were.

And the same for the positions of 2nd Corps' battered units.

If he'd stepped out of the tent into the chill night's sleety rain, he would have seen the glow still rising from the fire which had raged despite the weather for much of that afternoon. He was just as glad he couldn't see it at the moment, and he wished he could close his mind to what it must have been like when the fire vine took flame. It had probably been the mortars—that was Brigadier Raizyngyr's opinion, and he'd been there; he should know. No one would ever know for certain, of course, but they knew what had happened after the vine caught. The fire had raced along the oil-rich main stem, and then it had reached the oil trees and roared from there to the stands of sky comb.

Thankfully, the wind had been out of the west. If it had been from the *east*, it would have spelled almost certain disaster. As it was, it had pushed the flames and toxic, choking smoke away from the Charisian entrenchments, deeper into the Kyplyngyr . . . and into the Army of Shiloh's teeth. The forest had been too saturated with rain and sleet for even oil trees to sustain the fire for long, but it had burned long enough for that reeking smoke to finish off the enemy's cohesion . . . and for the shrieks of the Dohlaran and Desnairian wounded trapped in its path to fill the ears of every horrified listener.

They'd heard the shots, as well, as wounded men unable to escape the fire's agonizing touch managed to reload their rifles and fire one last shot.

And yet, as he looked down at that map and considered the reports from his brigade and regimental commanders, he knew even that transcendental horror was only a part of what had happened here in this grim, wet forest. Here, where Duke Eastshare's audacious, even brilliant plan had so nearly foundered on two miscalculations. The duke had considered every element, but his plans had overestimated how long 2nd Corps would have to consolidate its position and dig in . . . and *under*estimated how ferociously the hungry, ragged, wretched Army of Shiloh would fight.

He glanced up for a moment at Sir Ahdryn Raizyngyr's hawk-nosed profile. He knew Raizyngyr well, knew the brigadier had trained as a cavalryman of the old school, that his transition to rifleman had not been an easy one, or one he'd truly wanted to make. But he'd made it. Oh, yes, Mahkbyrn thought, gaze falling to the map once more, he'd made it, and he'd fought his infantryman's battle with savage determination and cold calculation.

Sixth Mounted Brigade had ridden into the Kyplyngyr with almost eight thousand men; it would ride out again with less than five, and over a thousand of those were wounded. That was a casualty rate of forty-seven percent . . . and that didn't count the twenty-five hundred men 5th Mounted Brigade had lost, or the forty-two hundred his own 13th Infantry Brigade would be leaving behind. All told, 2nd Corps had lost upwards of eleven thousand men in killed and wounded out of an initial strength of twenty-four thousand eight hundred, but it had done its job.

The fighting on 6th Mounted's left, north of the high road, that first night had been even worse than on its right. Colonel Mohrtyn Haskyns' 12th Mounted Regiment had been hit by almost twice as many men as Colonel Zhywnoh's 11th Mounted, and the dead ground in front of his line had let the attackers get even closer before they'd charged. If Brigadier Seacatcher had realized how bad that ground was he never would have placed the original blocking position where he had. But there'd been no way to know that when he arrived, and the power and speed of the enemy response had left him too little time to scout for a better one. The valley concealed by the forest had formed what amounted to a deep trench, large enough for several thousand men, barely seventy-five yards from the 12th's breastworks, and Dohlaran infantry and dismounted Desnairian cavalry, some of it heavy horse from the Imperial Guard Cavalry, had exploded out of it.

Haskyns had managed to get all four of his regiment's battalions deployed before the attack came in, but five Dohlaran infantry regiments had assaulted straight down the high road simultaneously, and the crash and roar of the 11th Mounted's desperate defense to the south had overlapped both of the other attacks. At one point, the entire Charisian reserve, aside from three companies of the 10th Mounted's 2nd Battalion and Major Mahrak's 4th Battalion, still groping its way towards the front, had been committed while the outcome teetered in the balance. Yet somehow, by the skin of their teeth, by raw determination, by courage and the definite partiality of almighty God, they'd held.

The Army of Shiloh had slammed into the 12th Mounted like a thunderbolt, crashing out of the trees in a tidal bore of fury driven by courage and the power of faith. It had swept up to the Charisian position, burst through it in multiple places only to be driven back in a holocaust of blood and bare steel, and then it had come thundering back again. *Four times* it had hurled itself against the 12th like Shan-wei's battering ram before it had finally fallen back, bleeding, leaving the ground before Colonel Haskyns' position carpeted in dead and dying men.

There'd been no attacks the next day. The other side had been busy pushing forward with additional men to replace the regiments decimated in the previous night's fighting and probing the Charisian positions, looking for weaknesses. And the two mounted brigades had used that time to dig in more deeply, entrenching their positions, building protected firing steps. They'd also had time to get most of their field artillery up behind the infantry, although the nature of the terrain limited the guns' effectiveness, and minelaying parties had covered the approaches with Shan-wei's fountains. And, perhaps most important of all, the first of Mahkbyrn's infantry brigades had arrived during the afternoon and its battalions had taken their places along the line.

It was as well they had. On the third day, by Raizyngyr and Seacatcher's best estimate, the Army of Shiloh had thrown the better part of sixty thousand men at their fourteen thousand. The fighting had begun before eight in the morning; it had crested shortly after four when the oil vine took fire; and it had finally tapered off into a limping stillness sometime after ten o'clock that night. Langhorne only knew how many men the Dohlarans and Desnairians had lost in that smoky, shrieking butchery, but too many families in Charis and Chisholm and Emerald and Tarot would know how many fathers and sons and brothers *they'd* lost.

But once again, they'd held . . . and the Army of Shiloh had broken itself trying to break *them*. Mahkbyrn knew it had; it only remained to be seen if the Army of Shiloh knew it, as well.

"All right," the general told the weary faces of the

colonels whose men had accomplished so much, "we have to assume they'll try again in a few hours. When they do, Edgair," he looked at Sir Edgair Braizhyr, commander of the 7th Company's 14th Infantry Brigade, his freshest formation, "they'll either hit the Twelfth again or else try to work farther round their flank. God knows the going out there's likely to slow them down, but they can't want to come straight at us again after what's already happened to them. So I want you to push Colonel Baytz and the Twenty-Seventh out to cover Colonel Haskyns' flank. Then we'll put a couple of support platoons' mortars *here*," he tapped the map, "with one of the Twenty-Seventh's battalions as the left flank reserve. After that—"

▼ ▼ ▼

Sir Rainos Ahlverez listened to Duke Harless' harsh, determined conversation with Sir Bahrtalam Tukkyr, the Baron of Cliff Hollow, and Sir Brahdryk Traiwyrthyn with perhaps a quarter of his attention. The rest of it was on the sounds of defeat—on the faltering slog of more or less walking wounded staggering towards the illusory safety of the rear, on the sobbing chorus of men who'd made it this far and could go no farther—and on the near-agony of exhaustion dragging at his own body like chains.

Cliff Hollow and Traiwyrthyn commanded Emperor Mahrys' Own Regiment and the Perlmann Grays, two of the Household Cavalry regiments attached to the Army of Shiloh. As befitted their aristocratic status, the Household regiments had received priority for food and fodder, and Cliff Hollow's and Traiwyrthyn's regiments were in better condition than most of Earl Hennet's cavalry. Harless had high hopes for what they might accomplish once the heretics' position finally broke; Ahlverez recognized futility and fresh disaster when he saw it.

We're done. The thought gnawed its way through his gray exhaustion. *The boys tried—God how they tried! But we're done. And this idiot isn't willing to admit it. Shan-wei! When has he been willing to admit anything that even smacked of reality?!*

He clamped his jaw against the torrent of invective burning to break free, yet even in his worn-out fury he recognized the crispness and determination of Harless' orders and wished bitterly that the duke could have shown some of that same energy sooner. Sometime when determination and energy might actually have done a little something to save his army from disaster.

Father Tymythy Yairdyn stood at Harless' shoulder, hands folded in his cassock sleeves, eyes hooded as he listened to the duke's instructions, and Ahlverez found himself wishing fervently that his own intendant were present. Unfortunately, Sulyvyn Fyrmyn was busy elsewhere. He'd been slightly wounded by a Charisian shell splinter, but he'd refused to allow it to slow him down. Now he was out there with his chaplains and Ahlverez' unit commanders as they sought to somehow restore order among men who'd spent the last three days fighting their hearts out for God and their king.

Men who deserved one hell of a lot better than they were likely to receive.

"Your Grace," he heard someone else say with his voice, "attacking the heretics again would be a mistake."

Harless looked up from the sketch of the heretics' position he'd been emphatically tapping with a forefinger, and his eyes narrowed. Yairdyn looked up rather more sharply; Earl Hankey, standing beside the duke's intendant, glared at Ahlverez over Harless' shoulder; and Baron Cliff Hollow glanced up—briefly—and then returned his attention rather pointedly to the sketch. Traiwyrthyn had never looked up in the first place; clearly the two colonels had no intention of involving themselves in this conversation, although Ahlverez suspected they agreed with him. They might be Desnairian, and they might command two of the most aristocratic cavalry regiments in creation, but neither struck him as a blind, drooling idiot.

"No one expects this to be easy or simple, Sir Rainos," Harless said, after a moment. "It's going to be costly, as well. I realize that. But it's *necessary*. We have no choice but to clear our line of communication."

Ahlverez managed to bite off the sort of acid observation which could only have led to his own arrest—or a duel—and drew a deep breath.

"Your Grace, three days ago I had fifty-three thousand infantry; at the moment I have about fifteen thousand, and your cavalry regiments who were committed to the attack have suffered as heavily as my infantry. By my estimate, between us we've lost close to fifty or even sixty thousand men." He waved one weary hand, forbearing to mention that the majority of those fifty or sixty thousand men had been Dohlarans. "Oh, it's not that bad in actual dead and wounded—a lot of them are just lost, wandering around looking for their units—but it would take days to reconstitute my infantry into anything like combat-ready regiments. The heretics are already better dug-in and stronger than they were at the beginning; they'll use every moment we give them to dig in even more deeply, and fresh troops have been moving steadily into their positions from the start."

"And what do you propose we do instead, General?" Father Tymythy's voice was flat. "Sit here and watch the entire army starve? I believe *you* were the one who pointed out the need to clear the forest in the first place."

"Yes, Father, I was." Ahlverez' voice was equally flat. "But with all possible respect for Colonel Cliff Hollow and Colonel Traiwyrthyn, we need more infantry before we can hope to break through those entrenchments." He looked from Yairdyn back to Harless. "*Infantry*, Your Grace—men trained to fight on foot and equipped to do the job. And we don't have it. We *can't* have it in anything like sufficient strength until I can reconsolidate my regiments around their losses."

If then, *that is*, he carefully did not add aloud. Personally, he was coming to the conclusion that "sufficient strength" was something the Army of Shiloh simply no longer had. Not for this.

"We've brought up our own infantry," Hankey said coldly, his tone a hair breadth from contemptuous, and it was all Ahlverez could do to keep himself from cursing the man's stupidity to his face.

The state of the Army of Shiloh's Desnairian infantry was Hankey's direct responsibility, and the only word to describe that state was "wretched." Desnairian infantry regiments were half the size of Dohlaran regiments to begin with, and Hankey's had been exhausted driving the "siege." Worse, their rations had been reduced in favor of the more important—in Desnairian eyes—cavalry regiments, and they knew it. Just as they knew how profligately they'd been used up along the way. Hankey's original infantry strength of almost sixty thousand was down to a bare fifty thousand, despite having received twenty-six thousand replacements, and he'd left eight thousand of them to hold the trenches in Ohadlyn's Gap and keep Eastshare's fifteen thousand starving men safely penned up in the Army of Shiloh's rear. That gave his proposed attack a scant forty-two thousand infantrymen, and those men were sick, tired, exhausted, and disheartened.

There was no way on God's green world they were the equal of the veteran, dug-in heretics waiting in that hellish wood, and even if they might have been, a third of them were still en route. They couldn't arrive before tomorrow afternoon, and they'd *have* to be rested for at least a few hours before even Earl Hankey could ask them to attack.

And while they were resting, the Charisians would be digging in still deeper . . . and, all too probably, being further reinforced.

"I realize you're *bringing up* more infantry," Ahlverez emphasized the verb, his eyes hard as they met Hankey's. "But my point stands; by the time they're ready to attack, the heretics will've improved their positions even further. My Lord, my scouts report that they're still dropping more trees, and they're using the logs to build *bunkers*. D'you really think they aren't putting out more of their damned Kau-yungs to blow your men the hell up when they try to assault, as well? That they aren't improving their fields of fire? *That they aren't bringing up more men of their own as quickly as they can?*"

"I suppose there's only one way to find out, isn't there, *General?*" Hankey shot back.

"That's exactly what I've spent the last three days doing," Ahlverez grated, "and I've lost damned near forty thousand men in the process. I don't see any point getting another forty or fifty thousand *more* men—even Desnairians, this time!—killed trying to accomplish something I *know* is futile."

Hankey's face darkened and he opened his mouth, but Harless' raised hand stopped him before he could spit out whatever hovered on the tip of his tongue.

"I appreciate the sacrifice your men have made, Sir Rainos." Unlike the earl's, Harless' tone was courteous. In fact, Ahlverez realized, it was sincere. "And I have no more desire than you to see more being killed or wounded in vain. But Earl Hankey has a point. We have to do *something* if we're to save this army, and what else can we do except drive the heretics out of the forest? If we can push them back into more open terrain where we can bring our greater numbers to bear effectively, then—"

"Your Grace, we can't do that," Ahlverez interrupted. His own tone was far more courteous than the one he'd used with Hankey. "The positions they're in now are too strong for us to drive them back. Not without the infantry we don't have, at any rate."

He saw the blind, stubborn refusal to face the truth in their eyes. Both of them saw the heretics in the woods as no more than a desperate ploy to save Duke Eastshare's trapped garrison. They recognized the danger to their own army if the Charisian roadblock held, but they also believed the Charisians simply couldn't have scraped up more than fifteen thousand or twenty thousand men for the effort, and Kyrbysh's wyvern messages confirmed that Duke Eastshare's situation was more dire than ever. All they had to do was grind the roadblock away, by sheer attrition if they must, and they would reopen their own supply lines and doom Eastshare's force.

Ahlverez couldn't argue with their estimate of Eastshare's position, but they were wrong if they truly believed they could break the Charisians in the forest. He *knew* they were, but Hankey clearly thought he was a defeatist and Harless probably wasn't far behind, so—

"Perhaps that's true," Yairdyn's tone was less patient than Harless' had been but without Hankey's disdain. "Even if it is, however, what option do we have but to try, trusting in God and the Archangels to give us the victory as His and Mother Church's champions?"

Ahlverez looked at the intendant for a moment, then drew a deep breath.

"Father," he said with the care of a man who knew he was about to end his military career forever . . . and be lucky if it stopped there, "it's time to retreat."

Every set of eyes was on him now, all of them shocked and most filling rapidly with contempt, but he continued, driven by the grim lash of duty.

"The heretics have cut our line of communication. We can't fight our way through them; the Kyplyngyr means we can't go *around* them; and we can't get supplies past them. If we stay where we are, we starve. If we try to fight our way through them, we'll lose thousands more of our men and the heretics will still be there. It's time to fall back while we can still save what's left of the army."

"Fall back *where*?" Hankey no longer bothered to conceal his disgust. "As you've just so masterfully pointed out, we can't fall back *through* the heretics!"

"We have to retreat to the south," Ahlverez said flatly. "Down the Fort Sandfish High Road. Once we work our way around the southern end of the Kyplyngyr, we'll be better able to make use of our superior numbers. If we simply keep hammering away, hitting the heretics on defensive ground of *their* choosing, all we'll do is bleed the army to death before it starves."

"Preposterous!" Hankey snarled. "That would be moving directly away from our supply line! If you think we'd starve sitting here, what in Shan-wei's name d'you think would happen if we tried *that* kind of lunacy?! We're two hundred miles from the 'southern end' of the damned forest, and it's *four hundred* miles from there to Thesmar— all of it over a handful of farm tracks at best! We'd be lucky if a *third* of our strength made it back to Trevyr or Somyr!"

"And if we don't retreat we'll be lucky if a *tenth* of this army survives!" Ahlverez snarled back. He turned back to Harless—and Yairdyn—his eyes dark with raw appeal. "If we stay where we are, if we keep pounding away at the stopper the heretics have in the bottle, we'll do exactly what they want!"

Silence hovered for a long, tense moment. Then Yairdyn cleared his throat.

"My son, you're tired." His tone was compassionate, but his eyes were hard. "You've fought God's fight magnificently these past days, but you've worn yourself into exhaustion. It was unjust and ill considered of us to drag you into yet another conference when you so desperately need rest. Your concern for the lives of your men does you great credit in the eyes of Mother Church, yet I tell you now to withdraw. Get that rest which both of us know you need to refresh your mind and replenish your spirit, and then return to us. Whatever we may finally decide, it will take at least ten to twelve hours for our reinforcements to come up. Go. Sleep for eight of those hours, and then return to us. If rest brings you no different counsel, there will be time enough for us to discuss it then."

Ahlverez looked around the other faces, then inhaled deeply and bowed to the intendant.

"Of course, Father. Thank you," he said. He didn't bother to address the others; only gave them a curt nod and stalked out of the command tent.

Captain Lattymyr was waiting with his horse. He started to say something, then clamped his teeth together as he saw his general's expression. He simply held Ahlverez' bridle until he'd mounted, then swung into his own saddle.

The two of them barely acknowledged the sentries' salutes as they rode past them, and Lattymyr felt the rage boiling off Ahlverez in waves. Even the general's horse felt it, ears half flattening and nostrils flaring in response.

They'd ridden perhaps a thousand yards before Ahlverez looked at him.

"They want me to get some 'rest.'" His voice was as harsh as Lattymyr had ever heard it, ribbed with iron and burnished with fury. "They'll listen to me after I've had time to get some sleep . . . and realize the idiocy they're planning is the best option we have."

Lattymyr's expression tightened. He'd known what Ahlverez was thinking, but had the general actually—?

"Forgive me, Sir Rainos, but what 'idiocy' might that be?"

"Not the idiocy *I* proposed," Ahlverez replied with a certain grim, merciless amusement. "Retreat would undoubtedly be as cowardly as it would stupid. Clearly it makes far more sense to gut the army by hammering those bastards in the woods and then starve the other half to death!"

Lattymyr's weather-beaten face paled. If Ahlverez had seriously suggested *retreat* in front of the Army of Shiloh's intendant. . . .

"They've given me eight hours to get that rest before I come back and dutifully agree with them," Ahlverez continued, and his eyes were flint. "As it happens, I have something better to do. Ride ahead, Lynkyn. I want Father Sulyvyn, General Sahndyrs, and Baron Tymplahr at my tent by the time I get there. And unless Father Sulyvyn sees fit to remove me from command, I'll want dispatches sent to Colonel Hahlynd, Colonel Mahrcelyan, Colonel Lahkyrt, Colonel Mkwartyr, Colonel Tyrwait, and Colonel Ohkarlyn."

Lattymyr's nostrils flared. Hahlynd, Mahrcelyan, Lahkyrt, and Mkwartyr commanded Ahlverez' last intact infantry regiments. They'd been tasked as his reserve. Colonel Tyrwait and Colonel Ohkarlyn commanded the cavalry regiments assigned to Baron Tymplahr's quartermasters for escort and protective duties. At the moment, all six of those regiments just happened to be encamped on the southern edge of Kharmych . . . on the Fort Sandfish High Road.

The captain looked at his general for a moment. Then he dipped his head, touched his chest in salute, and gave his horse the spurs.

▼ ▼ ▼

Ruhsyl Thairis looked up from his plate as someone knocked courteously and Corporal Chalkyr opened the door to admit his aide.

What had become the Army of the Branaths had seen no reason it should languish in the muck and mire when there was no need. Even the forward positions the Army of Shiloh had been allowed to see were provided with weather-tight roofs and sandbagged walls which were proof against angle-gun shells and winter wind alike. Farther back, where the army's main body was encamped, the troops—assisted by the army's engineers and the voluntary civilian labor force—had erected snug barracks out of notched, clay-chinked logs with thatched roofs. They'd even found time to build a neat, efficient stone fireplace here in Duke Eastshare's office, and the duke usually enjoyed the fire's warmth as he ate his breakfast and contemplated the difference between his army's state of supply and that of the Army of Shiloh.

"Yes, Lywys?" he said now. "You're up and about early this morning."

"I'm sorry to disturb your meal," Captain Braynair replied, "but we've just received a semaphore signal from Brigadier Dahmbryk. He reports that the enemy's artillery fire has slackened and the infantry in the approach trenches appears to have withdrawn during the night."

"Ah?" Eastshare laid down his fork and reached for his teacup. Sulyvyn Dahmbryk commanded 5th Brigade of Ahlyn Symkyn's 3rd Infantry Division. At the moment, it was 5th Brigade's turn to man the forward entrenchments and keep an eye on the enemy.

"*All* of their infantry's withdrawn?" he asked after a moment, raising one rather ironic eyebrow at his aide.

"Excuse me, Your Grace," Braynair said, bowing slightly to acknowledge that eyebrow. "I should've said he reports *most* of their infantry has withdrawn. He estimates that between seven and five thousand may have remained behind, supported by a few thousand cavalry. He believes there could be no more than ten thousand combat troops of all arms, and he's requested permission to send out patrols to confirm his estimate."

"I see."

Eastshare sat back in his chair, right hand on the table and fingers drumming slowly. It was an unusual display of anxiety on his part, Braynair thought, but the duke's expression was calm as he considered the news. Then he drew a deep breath and shook his head.

"I think not." He looked back up at his aide and his eyes were narrowed. "It looks as if Earl High Mount met his schedule, after all, and I trust Brigadier Dahmbryk's judgment about any troop movements in his front. What I *don't* want to do is anything that might make whoever's been left in command over there suspicious. Send a message back to the Brigadier and ask him to join me here at his earliest convenience. And I'll want General Symkyn, General Wyllys, and Colonel Traimynt, as well. Tell them we'll be having an early working lunch."

"Of course, Your Grace. And may I inform them of the reason you wish to see them?"

"Just tell them it looks to me as if Earl High Mount's done his job and I think it's time we looked into doing ours."

▼ ▼ ▼

Ahlverez actually had gotten almost three entire hours of sleep. They hadn't been particularly refreshing, and his muscles felt no less rubbery, but at least his mind seemed to be a little clearer, functioning a bit more reliably.

It was unfortunate no one else in the command tent seemed likely to be able to say the same.

At least he'd brought along Sulyvyn Fyrmyn, Sir Laimyn Sahndyrs, and Baron Tymplahr. Sir Laimyn was clearly more than a little anxious, but he was also prepared to carry out his orders. Ahlverez couldn't help wondering how much of that stemmed from the fact that he was merely Ahlverez' *second*-in-command, able to say with complete honesty that he'd only obeyed his superior's commands. Ahlverez suspected he was doing Sahndyrs a disservice, but he was too worn-out to worry about being fair. Although, if he'd had the energy to worry about things like fairness, he would have been forced to admit how relieved *he'd* felt when Father Sulyvyn supported his decision. Given the intendant's determination to smite the heretic, he'd been far from confident about which way Fyrmyn would jump. Even now, he wasn't certain how much of the priest's decision sprang from a rational appreciation of the Army of Shiloh's disastrous position and how much from his heartsickness at the price the men he'd come to regard as his own had paid attacking the Charisian positions. It didn't really matter which it had been, however. What *mattered* was that Fyrmyn was fully behind the orders he'd given.

He wondered if anyone had bothered to inform Duke Harless or Father Tymythy that the Dohlaran supply train had already started down the Fort Sandfish High Road. From the expressions which had greeted him, he rather doubted it.

"Ah, Sir Rainos! And Father Sulyvyn!" Harless smiled as the Dohlarans were ushered into his presence. "It's good to see you both. And you look much more rested, Sir Rainos."

Either the light was worse than Ahlverez thought it was, or Harless was an even more accomplished liar than most Desnairian nobles.

"Thank you, Your Grace," he said, and Fyrmyn nodded.

"It's good to see you, as well, my son," the Schuelerite said, and nodded again, this time to Yairdyn. "Tymythy."

"Sulyvyn," the Desnairian intendant replied.

"If you would, Sir Rainos," Harless continued, waving one hand gracefully at the sketch map, "I'd like your opinion of the approach routes Earl Hankey and I have selected. Hopefully, we'll be able to get a little farther north of the heretics' left before we hook back in this time. If we can, then—"

"Who goes there!"

Heads rose, turning towards the tent's fly as a galloping horse slithered to a noisy stop. There was a mutter of voices, one of them louder and more urgent than the others, and then the fly was wrenched open and an exhausted, mud-spattered, thoroughly soaked lieutenant staggered through it, pursued by a still protesting sentry. The young man looked around, eyes dark in the muddy mask of his face, and came to attention as those eyes found the Duke of Harless. He reached for the leather dispatch case at his side.

"Lieutenant Ohcahnyr, Your Grace," he said hoarsely. "Bahskym's Regiment. The Colonel sent me."

Ahlverez stiffened and glanced at Fyrmyn. Colonel Hykahru Bahskym was the senior Desnairian officer at Kharmych, almost a hundred miles east of their present position. Ahlverez had used the semaphore to send his own orders to his supply train and rearguard that afternoon, but the weather was too poor for the link from Harless' current headquarters to Kharmych to transmit messages after dark. If Lieutenant Ohcahnyr had come all the way from Kharmych, he must have been dispatched only after the evening's visibility had closed in, which meant he'd covered the entire distance in barely seven and a half hours. No wonder he was dead on his feet! He must have commandeered fresh horses all along the way, and probably ridden them half to death. And if his message was about Dohlaran troops leaving Kharmych without orders from Harless. . . .

I wonder if he's going to tell the Duke about all the rest of my regiments he passed on the way here, as well? Ahlverez thought. *And I wonder how Harless—and Yairdyn—are going to react?*

The truth, he discovered with a certain mild astonishment, was that he truly didn't care, because there wasn't a damned thing either of them could do about it.

His winnowed, shattered regiments had been pulled to the rear to clear the narrow slot of the high road through the Kyplyngyr for the fresher, incoming Desnairians. Even his less badly battered units had been sent back to reorganize while the Desnairians took over their positions in preparation for Harless and Hankey's grand attack. As a consequence, he'd been able to start them on their way to Kharmych without drawing a great deal of attention, although he'd instructed them to wait until an hour before sunset to decrease the possibility that anyone would notice their departure. By now, those withdrawing regiments were a good thirty miles down the Kharmych road, and none of them would be turning around without direct orders from him, countersigned by Sulyvyn Fyrnach.

And there was no way short of direct divine intervention Harless or Yairdyn were going to get those orders issued.

None of which meant unfortunate things couldn't happen to one Sir Rainos Ahlverez if Yairdyn decided to make an example of him for his lack of commitment to the Jihad.

"Give it to me," Harless said, extending his hand to the muddy lieutenant, and Ohcahnyr opened the dispatch case and handed the message across.

Harless broke the seal, spread the single sheet of paper, and read rapidly. Then his moving eyes froze. His fingers tightened on the paper, and Ahlverez could actually see the color draining from his face. The duke stood that way for several seconds. Then he gasped, his left hand crumpled the dispatch, his right hand flew to his chest, his face twisted in agony, and he went heavily to his knees.

"A healer!" Yairdyn shouted, flinging himself to his own knees beside the Army of Shiloh's commander as Harless collapsed completely. "*Fetch a healer!*"

All eyes were on the duke as his lips turned blue and his left hand joined his right, clutching at his chest. All eyes except Ahlverez'.

The Dohlaran general stooped and picked up the dispatch even as Yairdyn was shouting for whiskey, shouting for the healers to hurry, lifting Harless' head onto his knee. . . .

Ahlverez had seen a fatal heart attack before, and he left the Schuelerite to his fruitless efforts while he unfolded the crushed ball of paper, spread it, and turned it to catch the lamplight. It was a very short message.

"Your Grace:

"Heretic forces are attacking our advanced positions in strength. The semaphore reports massive artillery fire. Heretic cavalry and infantry have captured our advanced works and all of our siege artillery. My best information, received from *Captain* Bruhstair"—the title was heavily underscored, undoubtedly to emphasize the lowly rank of the senior officer reporting from the siege trenches, which said horrendous things about the defenders' casualties—"is that the heretics' strength is at least twice and more probably *three* times our previous estimates." The word "three" was underscored even more heavily than Bruhstair's rank. "I have also received a messenger wyvern from Colonel Ohygyns, dispatched at four o'clock this afternoon. At that time, he reported Brahnselyk had been taken by heretic cavalry and that Roymark was under heavy attack by heretic infantry with artillery support. His cavalry pickets also reported a heavy column of heretic infantry, moving west into the Kyplyngyr Forest towards your position, before they were driven back into the Roymark perimeter. I have sent a courier to Earl Hennet at Cheyvair as well as to your position. I urgently request instructions.

"Hykahru Bahskym, officer commanding, Kharmych."

MARCH, YEAR OF GOD 897

· ✦ ·

.I.
Allyntyn,
Midhold Province,
and
Siddar City,
Old Province,
Republic of Siddarmark

"All right, then. I believe that's everything, Bryahn.
Please make sure Traveler gets an extra ration of grain
tonight."

"Of course, My Lord. Good night."

Lieutenant Slokym came briefly to attention, saluted,
and withdrew. He closed the door quietly behind him, and
Baron Green Valley walked around his desk, settled into
his office's single comfortable armchair, and gazed into the
fire crackling on his hearth.

"Looking forward to it, Kynt?" a voice asked in his ear
now that he was alone.

"To the weather? Hell, no!" Green Valley's shudder
was completely genuine. "But if you mean to kicking the
Temple Boys' arses, well, that's a different matter entirely,
Merlin."

His smile was hungry, and in an embassy study in far
distant Siddar City, Merlin Athrawes and Cayleb Ahrmahk looked at one another with matching smiles.

The weather truly was atrocious, and not simply in
Midhold. The heavy snowfall lashing the Republic's capital city with blowing sheets of blinding white while the

wind came snarling in off Bedard Bay was proof enough of that. Dense as that snowfall was, however, it paled beside the blizzard howling around Allyntyn at that very moment. Yet the blizzard, for all its strength and shrill-voiced spite, was on its last legs. The weather satellites promised it would blow itself out by early afternoon tomorrow, and the majority of Green Valley's senior officers were willing to assume he'd known what he was talking about when he made that prediction.

Besides, if he was wrong it would only delay their departure another day or so. Under the circumstances, probably better to go along with him and then remain tactfully silent if it turned out he'd been wrong, after all.

And when it turned out he hadn't, the Army of Midhold would be moving out into a spotless world across the purity of deep, white snow. Snow that would soon be dyed quite a different color.

"Your boys seem to be looking forward to it, too," Cayleb observed.

"They've been waiting for a long time," Green Valley replied. "And I'll admit they've gotten even more impatient reading the dispatches from Ruhsyl and Breyt. They're determined to kick Wyrshym's arse as thoroughly as their friends kicked Harless'."

"Well, not *Harless'* arse, perhaps," Domynyk Staynair pointed out from Tellesberg.

It was four hours later—and much, much warmer—in the capital of Old Charis, but the first chains of gaslight lamps in Tellesberg's history illuminated a waterfront that was as busy—and as sleepless—as ever. Staynair could see them clearly, reflected across the glassy water, as he stood on HMS *Destroyer*'s sternwalk and he gazed out across the harbor.

"Only because the incompetent old bastard died first."

"A bit vindictive there, Kynt?" Merlin asked mildly.

"Look, I'm as grateful as anyone that the Desnairians managed to find someone that utterly clueless to command their damned army," Green Valley replied in a slightly—*very* slightly—less acid tone. "I'm not taking anything away from Ruhsyl, either, when I say that. Stupid opponents only make good generals look better; they don't make them good in the first place. But if anyone ever deserved to have to go home and answer to Zhaspahr Clyntahn for screwing up by the numbers, it was Harless."

"*He* may not have to, but there's always Hennet," Cayleb offered. The emperor's smile was savage. "Thinking about that warms the cockles of my hard, imperial little heart. It's so *fortunate*, don't you think, that he had such a fast horse?"

The others chuckled. The Earl of Hennet had, indeed, had a fast horse, and one which had somehow managed to be well fed and sleek despite the short rations facing the rest of the Army of Shiloh. The horses of his personal bodyguard had been equally well fed . . . for reasons which had become clear as soon as Colonel Bahskym's courier reached Cheyvair. The earl had immediately set off on a personal reconnaissance of Brahnselyk which had somehow gotten so lost it had led him to the Daivyn River and the Army of Glacierheart. No doubt it had been a simple matter of bad map-reading and poor navigation.

The rest of the Army of Shiloh had fared less well.

Ruhsyl Thairis' strategy had succeeded, although not without a few potholes along the way. The Army of Cliff Peak had sustained far heavier casualties holding the stopper in the Kyplyngyr than he'd anticipated, and in large part that had been the consequence of asking for too much. And, perhaps, of the contempt he'd developed for the Army of Shiloh's senior command. In the case of Harless, Hankey, and Hennet, that contempt had been fully justified; Sir Rainos Ahlverez had been a bit more formidable, however, and as it turned out, there'd been nothing at all wrong with the Army of Shiloh's *courage*. Ahlverez' decisiveness—his decision to move his infantry farther west, his almost instant reaction to the reports of Charisian mounted troops near Roymark, and the speed with which he'd launched his initial counterattacks—and the courage and ferocity of the men under his command had come within an eyelash of breaking 2nd Corps' mounted infantry. For all his cool judgment and careful analysis, Duke Eastshare had underestimated both those factors, and the men of 2nd Corps had paid in cash to redeem his errors.

Whether or not even 2nd Corps' total destruction could have saved the Army of Shiloh, given the threat the rest of the Army of Cliff Peak would have presented to its northern flank—and its fatal underestimate of the Army of the Branaths' true strength—would never be known. What Ahlverez' adversaries *did* know was that he'd been at least three jumps ahead of his Desnairian counterparts from the moment they'd left Thesmar. If *he'd* been in command of the Army of Shiloh, it was distinctly possible the entire strategy would have failed.

As it was, he'd managed to get almost the entirety of his own army—all that had survived the fighting in the Kyplyngyr and the fall of Brahnselyk and Roymark, at any rate—out of the pocket before Eastshare's remorseless advance could close the trap's eastern jaw on Kharmych. At least twenty percent of the original Desnairian Army of Justice had been overrun and destroyed in the course of the duke's advance from Ohadlyn's Gap. More of it had been trapped on the high road in the Kyplyngyr, its only choice between surrender and starvation. But a stubborn Dohlaran rearguard had fought to destruction where the Fort Sandfish High Road passed through the southern lobe of the forest, buying additional time for the rest of Ahlverez' army to break contact and run for it. And although they'd never intended to do anything of the sort, Hennet's abandoned regiments at Cheyvair had helped cover Ahlverez' escape, as well. Eastshare had had no option but to send his own mounted troops to deal with the Desnairian cavalry—which, fortunately, had found itself under heavy attack before it got around to wrecking the canal—rather than dispatching them in pursuit of Ahlverez. By the time the mounted Charisians could swing back south, Ahlverez was halfway to Thesmar.

He'd had to abandon his wounded, but he'd judged the Charisians more acutely than the Desnairians in that respect, as well. He'd known the Charisian healers would treat his wounded just as they did their own, and so they had, although there'd been at least one ugly moment when a Charisian battalion had found itself protecting captured Dohlarans from a mob of vengeance-minded Siddarmarkian civilians.

After casualties, sickness, starvation, and stragglers, Ahlverez' army was down to less than thirty-five thousand men, substantially less than half of the strength he'd taken to Ohadlyn's Gap, despite having received close to twenty thousand replacements during the "siege" of Fort Tairys. A loss rate of sixty-five percent had to be considered catastrophic under any imaginable circumstances, yet it was far less catastrophic than it might have been ... and enormously better than the Army of Justice's fate. Thirteen thousand Desnairians had attached themselves to Ahlverez; of the remaining two hundred and thirty-two thousand men (including replacements) Duke Harless had commanded, less than eight thousand stragglers from Earl Hennet's cavalry—plus, of course, the gallant earl and his bodyguard—had escaped to the Army of Glacierheart's protection. In all, twenty-one thousand Desnairians had—so far, at least—evaded death or capture, barely nine percent of Harless' total command.

The Army of Justice had advanced into the Republic of Siddarmark to fight a battle of annihilation ... and it had.

As for Ahlverez, his escape was far from certain even now. Couriers were looking for him—with very little idea of where to *find* him—to warn him that Earl Hanth's offensive out of Thesmar had crushed the forward Desnairian supply base at Somyr, then swung north and taken Trevyr, as well. General Rychtyr was in full retreat up the Seridahn River and the Royal Dohlaran Army was rushing reinforcements along the Sheryl-Seridahn Canal in a desperate effort to at least hold the ruins of Evrytyn, where the canal met the river. Since virtually all of those reinforcements were armed with the new St. Kylmahn breech-loading rifles, the hand grenades Dohlar had duplicated, and the very first Church-designed rifled, muzzle-loading artillery, it was possible they'd succeed, but whether Ahlverez could avoid Hanth and *reach* Evrytyn was quite another matter.

And now it was the Army of the Sylmahn's turn.

"You do realize Wyrshym's at least as smart as Ahlverez, don't you, Kynt?" Cayleb asked. "In fact, he's probably smarter. And unlike Harless, he's actually *over*estimated your strength, not underestimated it, so he's a lot less likely to make stupid, overconfident mistakes."

"Yes, he is," Green Valley agreed. "And I don't have 'Colonel Kyrbysh' feeding him false information, either. On the other hand, I do have the advantage of the SNARCs, which Ruhsyl didn't. We'll be one hell of a lot more mobile than he is with the caribou and the High Hallows for the mounted infantry, too. I'm confident we'll at least manage to roll up his forward positions and clear the Northland Gap. With only a little luck, we'll make it as far as Fairkyn and make him *really* nervous about the Ohlarn Gap. And if we're *really* lucky and the weather holds, we might actually reach Guarnak before the spring thaw turns everything to mud on us. Either way, we're going to make them just as worried about their northern flank as they already are about their *southern* flank."

"Sounds good to me," a new voice put in. "The more they worry about what we're going to do to *them*, the less energy they'll have for thinking about things they want to do to *us*."

"Oh, I think we can keep them fairly busy worrying, Nimue," Merlin said, and smiled as Owl projected the image of Nimue Chwaeriau sitting in a darkened palace bedroom while the entire city of Manchyr slept around her. He had entirely too many memories of another PICA holding midnight conversations.

"Damn straight," High Admiral Rock Point agreed. "You keep 'em busy on land, Kynt. Sharpfield's about to make their life miserable in the Harchong Narrows and western Gulf. I'm not letting him get too deep, even with *Thunderer* and *Dreadnought* along, but I just came back from inspecting *King Haarahld*. We're actually almost two five-days ahead of schedule on her, and her sisters aren't far behind, so it won't be so very much longer until we'll be going as deep in the Gulf of Dohlar as we damned well please. And in the meantime, we'll have all of the new improved *River*s available for service in East Haven's coastal waters—those we won't need on the rivers or in Hsing-wu's Passage after the thaw, at least. And I've just had a rather intriguing suggestion that we establish a coaling station on Samson's Land, too. Something about making the Desnairians and that sorry piece of work Zhames of Delferahk as unhappy as possible."

"You know," Cayleb said softly, "when Clyntahn went after Siddarmark, it seemed so . . . calculating of me, so callous, given all of the horrible things I knew were going to happen to millions of innocent Siddarmarkians, to see the opportunity—the *advantage*—it could offer us. After all we've been through with the Republic over the last few months, all we've seen and all the people—ours and theirs, alike—who've fought and died, that seems even more . . . trivial and cynical of me, somehow. And yet—"

"I know I've mentioned Winston Churchill to you before, Cayleb." Merlin's voice was almost equally soft. "There was another 'sneak attack' back on Old Earth at a place called Pearl Harbor by something called the Empire of Japan. It was one part of a far larger, brilliantly executed operation, and it caught its targets totally by surprise. It killed thousands, and it destroyed virtually the entire battle fleet of a nation called the United States of America, Japan's most dangerous potential enemy, *and* the battle squadron Churchill had sent halfway around the world trying to deter the Empire's aggression.

"Japan was part of a military alliance called the 'Axis,'

and for two years, the Axis had been unstoppable. Their armies had smashed everyone who'd tried to stop them, and Churchill's nation—England—had survived only because it was an island. Its navy was strong enough to prevent its invasion, but Germany—another member of the Axis—was slowly and steadily strangling it to death by sinking the merchant ships its survival depended upon. At the time, the Pearl Harbor attack seemed like only one more triumph for the Axis and an unmitigated disaster for its opponents, yet it brought what was probably the most powerful nation in the world at the time into World War Two on the side of Churchill's country.

"When he wrote about it later, Churchill described his reaction to the news, how he'd recognized the war was going to reach out to envelop millions of more people yet simultaneously realized that with the United States and all its industry and manpower joined to England and its allies, victory had just become all but certain. And what he said was 'Being saturated and satiated with emotion and sensation, I went to bed and slept the sleep of the saved and thankful.' Does that sort of sum up what you're trying to say?"

"Yes." Cayleb looked at his personal armsman across the hearth between them and nodded. "Yes, it does."

"Well, I wouldn't go so far as to say we're 'saved' just yet," Nimue said pragmatically, "but I'd say the lot of you have come a long damned way from where you were when Merlin woke up in our cave."

"Don't start getting optimistic just yet," Merlin cautioned. "I never expected Duchairn and Maigwair would manage to turn the Harchongese Army into an actual effective fighting force, but damned if it doesn't look like they've pulled it off. And it's not exactly a *little* army. For that matter, their rifle production numbers are one hell of a lot higher than any of us expected, especially since they were so disobliging as to invent their own breechloader and make it *better* than ours. And then there's that inventive so-and-so Brother Lynkyn and those openhearth furnaces Duchairn's building all over central and southern Harchong." He shook his head. "I've got to like our chances more than I've ever liked them before, but we're still one hell of a long way from defeating the Church. And then there's the little problem of what we do if we *do* defeat them. I have absolutely no idea how whatever's under the Temple is likely to react if an invading army marches into Zion to demand the Church's surrender!"

"Details, details!" Nimue waved one hand and smiled crookedly. "As Maikel would say—if he were awake, of course—God wouldn't have let us come this far just to stumble at the very end."

"You do realize there are plenty of people on the other side who're saying exactly the same thing, don't you?" Cayleb asked quizzically, and she laughed.

"Of course there are. But they also happen to be on *Zhaspahr Clyntahn's* side, so whoever else might be on their side, *God* damned sure isn't!"

"You've got to admit, it's hard to argue with that kind of logic, Cayleb. Even if I didn't come up with it myself. Exactly," Merlin told the emperor with a crooked smile of his own.

"All right! That's enough. I quit!" Cayleb shook his head and pushed himself up out of his armchair. "It was bad enough when there was only *one* smart aleck *seijin* shooting me down every time I thought I'd trumped his argument! I refuse to sit here and argue with *two* of them, especially when both of them were once *one* of them! I'm going to bed."

"Sleep well, Your Majesty," Nimue told him sweetly, and he laughed, shook his head again, and headed for his bedroom.

"Sounds like a good idea for all of us—at least, all of us flesh-and-blood types," Green Valley observed. "I'll have all sorts of last-minute details to take care of tomorrow, I'm sure. Best to be well rested when I do."

"Same here," Staynair agreed. "Good night, all."

He and Green Valley dropped out of the circuit, and there were only the two PICAs.

"You really have done it, you know, Merlin," Nimue said quietly. "Not alone, of course. But you've really done what Shan-wei and Commodore Pei—and Nimue—died to accomplish."

"Not yet." Merlin stood and crossed to the window, gazing down at the flying snow in the streets of Siddarmark's capital, listening to the wind roar beyond the glass and the crackle of the fire behind him, blue eyes distant. "Not yet. Even if we beat the Group of Four, even if the Church sues for terms, we're only halfway home, Nimue. And we don't have forever to get there, either."

"I know. But you *will* get there, and you'll drag the rest of us—and this entire planet, kicking and screaming the whole way—with you if you have to. But what I really wanted to say, now that it's just the two of us, is thank you."

"'*Thank* you'?" Merlin turned from the window and folded his arms, looking at the image of the red-haired young woman projected onto his vision. "For what?"

"For waking me up to be part of it," she told him, her voice soft, sapphire eyes looking directly into identical eyes. "For giving me the *chance* to be part of it. To finish what Shan-wei and the Commodore started, not just here on Safehold, but out *there*, too." She waved one hand, indicating the sky neither of them could see at the moment. "We owe a lot of people a lot of things, Merlin—including the Gbaba. I'm looking forward to helping you settle those debts. *All* of them."

"Really?" He cocked his head, then smiled, and it was a strange smile. A gentle one with the slightest twist of humor and more than a little sorrow, yet oddly radiant. "Well, you're welcome, I suppose. And I'm looking forward to it, too, now that you mention it. Assuming we ever get there, of course."

"Oh, we'll get there, Merlin. Trust me, we'll get there."

"You know, I think you're right." He smiled again, then drew a deep breath. "Good night, Nimue."

"Good night, Merlin. Sleep well."

. EPILOGUE .

Merlin Athrawes climbed the stairs to his bedroom, still smiling as he thought about his conversation with Nimue. It was odd the way that relationship seemed to be developing. Not at all the way he'd been afraid it might, he reflected as he reached for the latch and opened his door. In fact—

"Good evening," a voice said, and he froze on the threshold.

Astonishment held him there, and with it, chagrin that he should feel it. It wasn't as if he usually worried about being ambushed or waylaid, given how unlikely any potential ambusher or waylayer was to enjoy the experience. For the same reasons, he wasn't exactly in the habit of setting any of Owl's remotes to keep watch over his quarters when he wasn't in them. But he *was* in the habit of making certain no one could get close to Cayleb Ahrmahk without his knowledge, and you couldn't get much closer than this.

I've got to reset those filters, he told himself, shaking off the surprise and stepping fully into the room. *Be a little more selective. Not that I think she's really here to kill me . . . or Cayleb.*

"Good evening, Aivah." He closed the door behind him and crossed his arms, leaning back against it. "To what do I owe the honor?"

Aivah Pahrsahn sat in the small bedchamber's single chair, smiling at him, and he shook his head. He'd set the filters on the remotes to warn him about intruders who weren't known friends and allies—which, of course, Aivah was. That meant all she'd had to get past without being spotted were the alert, eagle-eyed, and perpetually suspicious *human* guards stationed around the embassy. Which was itself a nontrivial challenge, now that he thought about it.

"I've come to ask a favor," she replied. "One I thought it might be better to ask in private."

"What sort of favor?" he asked a bit warily.

"I need you to get me into Zion and back again. Quickly."

"Zion? What makes you think I'd even *let* you go to Zion, given all you know about our plans, much less get you there myself? And even assuming I was crazy enough to contemplate doing that, what do you mean by 'quickly'?"

"Oh, I don't need to make the trip immediately," she said pleasantly. "But when the moment comes, I may not be able to give you a great deal of advance warning. And 'quickly' means making the entire trip within the space of, oh, a day or so."

"'A day or so'?" He stared at her. "You do realize it's over five thousand miles from here to Zion, don't you?"

"Of course I do," she replied. "That's why I'm speaking to *you* about it . . . Ahbraim."

Characters

ABERNETHY, AUXILIARY BISHOP ERNYST—Schuelerite upper-priest; Bishop Militant Bahrnabai Wyrshym's assigned intendant, MT&T.

ABERNETHY, CAPTAIN BRYXTYN, Imperial Charisian Navy—CO, bombardment ship HMS *Earthquake*, 24, LAMA.

ABYKRAHMBI, KLYMYNT—an assistant to Brygham Cartyr in the Charisian technical support mission to the Republic of Siddarmark, LAMA.

ABYKRAHMBI, TAHLMA—Klymynt Abykrahmbi's wife, LAMA.

ABYLYN, CHARLZ—a senior leader of the Temple Loyalists in Charis, BSRA.

AHBAHT, CAPTAIN RUHSAIL, Imperial Desnairian Navy—CO, HMS *Archangel Chihiro*, 40; Commodore Wailahr's flag captain, HFAF.

AHBAHT, CAPTAIN SIR BRUHSTAIR, Imperial Charisian Navy—CO, broadside ironclad HMS *Thunderer*, 30, LAMA.

AHBAHT, LYWYS—Edmynd Walkyr's brother-in-law; XO, merchant galleon *Wind*, BSRA.

AHBAHT, ZHEFRY—Earl Gray Harbor's personal secretary. He fulfills many of the functions of an undersecretary of state for foreign affairs, BSRA. Same post for Trahvys Ohlsyn, HFAF.

AHBRAIMS, MAJOR KREG, Imperial Charisian Army—CO, 1st Battalion, 9th Mounted Regiment, 5th Mounted Brigade, Imperial Charisian Army, LAMA.

AHDYMS, COLONEL TAHLYVYR—Temple Loyalist ex-militia officer; "General" Erayk Tympyltyn's executive officer, Fort Darymahn, South March Lands, Republic of Siddarmark, MT&T.

AHDYMS, ERAYK—a junior partner and associate of Zhak Hahraimahn who serves on the Council of Manufactories, LAMA.

AHDYMSYN, BISHOP EXECUTOR ZHERALD—Erayk Dynnys' bishop executor, OAR. Now one of Archbishop Maikel's senior auxiliary bishops, HFAF.

AHDYMSYN, FATHER BRYNTYN—a Schuelerite under-priest; pre-Sword of Schueler schoolmaster in Maiyam, later appointed as Colonel Lyndahr Tahlyvyr's intendant, LAMA.

AHLAIXSYN, RAIF—well-to-do Siddarmarkian poet and dilettante; a Reformist, HFAF.

AHLBAIR, EDWYRD—Earl of Dragon Hill, MT&T.

AHLBAIR, LIEUTENANT ZHEROHM, Royal Charisian Navy—first lieutenant, HMS *Typhoon*, OAR.

AHLBYRTSYN, COLONEL RAIF, Imperial Charisian Army—CO, 2nd Scout Sniper Regiment, Imperial Charisian Army, LAMA.

AHLDARM, MAHRYS OHLARN—Mahrys IV, Emperor of Desnair, HFAF.

AHLVAI, CAPTAIN MAHLYK, Imperial Desnairian Navy—CO, HMS *Emperor Zhorj*, 48; Baron Jahras' flag captain, HFAF.

AHLVEREZ, ADMIRAL-GENERAL FAIDEL, Royal Dohlaran Navy—Duke of Malikai; King Rahnyld IV of Dohlar's senior admiral, OAR.

AHLVEREZ, SIR RAINOS, Royal Desnairian Army—senior Dohlaran field commander in the Republic of Siddarmark, MT&T; CO of the Dohlaran component of the

Army of Shiloh. First cousin of Faidel Ahlverez, Duke of Malikai.

AHLWAIL, BRAIHD—Father Paityr Wylsynn's valet, HFAF.

AHLYXZANDYR, MAJOR TRAI, RDA—CO, 1st Company, Ahzbyrn's Regiment (cavalry), part of Sir Rainos Ahlverez' component of the Army of Shiloh. Age 30 and 896, LAMA.

AHNDAIRS, TAILAHR—a Charisian-born Temple Loyalist living in the Temple Lands recruited for Operation Rakurai, HFAF.

AHRBUKYL, TROOPER SVYNSYN, Army of God—one of Corporal Howail Brahdlai's scouts, 191st Cavalry Regiment, MT&T.

AHRDYN—Archbishop Maikel's cat-lizard, BSRA.

AHRMAHK, CAYLEB ZHAN HAARAHLD BRYAHN—son of King Haarahld VII of Charis, Duke of Ahrmahk, Prince of Tellesberg, Crown Prince of Charis, OAR. Prince Protector of the Realm, King Cayleb II of Charis, Emperor Cayleb I of Charis and member of Charisian inner circle. Husband of Sharleyan Ahrmahk, BSRA.

AHRMAHK, CROWN PRINCE ZHAN—see Zhan Ahrmahk.

AHRMAHK, CROWN PRINCESS ALAHNAH ZHANAYT NAIMU—infant daughter of Cayleb and Sharleyan Ahrmahk; heir to the imperial Charisian crown, MT&T.

AHRMAHK, EMPEROR CAYLEB—Emperor of Charis (see Cayleb Zhan Haarahld Bryahn Ahrmahk), BSRA.

AHRMAHK, KAHLVYN—Duke of Tirian, Constable of Hairatha; King Haarahld VII's first cousin; traitor and attempted usurper (deceased), OAR.

AHRMAHK, KAHLVYN CAYLEB—Kahlvyn Ahrmahk's younger son, younger brother of Duke of Tirian, Cayleb Ahrmahk's first cousin once removed, OAR.

AHRMAHK, KING CAYLEB II—King of Charis (see Cayleb Zhan Haarahld Bryahn Ahrmahk), BSRA.

AHRMAHK, KING HAARAHLD VII—Duke of Ahrmahk, Prince of Tellesberg, King of Charis, member of Charisian inner circle, KIA Battle of Darcos Sound, OAR.

AHRMAHK, PRINCESS ZHANAYT—see Zhanayt Ahrmahk.

AHRMAHK, QUEEN ZHANAYT—King Haarahld's deceased wife; mother of Cayleb, Zhanayt, and Zhan, BSRA.

AHRMAHK, RAYJHIS—Cayleb Ahrmahk's first cousin once removed, elder son of Kahlvyn Ahrmahk, becomes Duke of Tirian, Constable of Hairatha, OAR.

AHRMAHK, SHARLEYAN ALAHNAH ZHENYFYR AHLYSSA TAYT—Duchess of Cherayth, Lady Protector of Chisholm, Queen of Chisholm, Empress of Charis; wife of Cayleb Ahrmahk, BSRA. Member of Charisian inner circle, BHD. See also Sharleyan Tayt. See also Empress Sharleyan.

AHRMAHK, ZHAN—younger son of King Haarahld VII, OAR; younger brother of King Cayleb, younger brother and heir of Emperor Cayleb, betrothed husband of Princess Mahrya Baytz of Emerald, BSRA.

AHRMAHK, ZHANAYT—Cayleb Ahrmahk's younger sister, second eldest child of King Haarahld VII, OAR.

AHRMAHK, ZHENYFYR—Dowager Duchess of Tirian; mother of Kahlvyn Cayleb Ahrmahk; daughter of Rayjhis Yowance, Earl Gray Harbor, OAR.

AHRNAHLD, SPYNSAIR—Empress Sharleyan's personal clerk and secretary, HFAF.

AHRTHYR, SIR ALYK—Earl of Windshare, CO of Sir Koryn Gahrvai's cavalry, BSRA; cavalry CO, Corisandian Guard, HFAF.

AHSTYN, LIEUTENANT FRANZ, Charisian Royal Guard—the second-in-command of Cayleb Ahrmahk's personal bodyguard after he becomes king, BSRA.

AHTKYN, LIEUTENANT ZHERALD, Republic of Siddarmark Army—Colonel Phylyp Mahldyn's aide, MT&T.

AHUBRAI, FATHER AHNSYLMO—Schuelerite under-priest; senior Temple Loyalist clergyman, Fairkyn, New Northland Province, Republic of Siddarmark, MT&T.

AHZBYRN, CAPTAIN REHGNYLD, Imperial Charisian Army—CO, Company A, 4th Battalion, 1st Scout Sniper Regiment, Imperial Charisian Army, LAMA.

AHZBYRN, COLONEL SIR AHGUSTAHS, Royal Dohlaran Army—CO, Ahzbyrn's Regiment (cavalry), Dohlaran component, Army of Shiloh (cavalry), Dohlaran component of the Army of Shiloh, LAMA.

AHZGOOD, PHYLYP—Earl of Coris, Prince Hektor's spymaster, OAR; Irys and Daivyn Daykyn's legal guardian, chief adviser, and minister in exile, BHD; member Prince Daivyn's Regency Council, LAMA.

AHZWAIL, MAJOR ZOSHYA, Imperial Charisian Army—CO, 3rd Battalion, 5th Mounted Regiment, 3rd Mounted Brigade, Imperial Charisian Army, LAMA.

AIMAIYR, FATHER IGNAZ—Archbishop Arthyn Zagyrsk's upper-priest Schuelerite intendant in Tarikah Province, MT&T.

AIMAYL, RAHN—a member of the anti-Charis resistance in Manchyr, Corisande. An ex-apprentice of Paitryk Hainree's, HFAF.

AIRNHART, FATHER SAIMYN—Father Zohannes Pahtkovair's immediate subordinate. A Schuelerite, HFAF.

AIRYTH, EARL OF—see Trumyn Sowthmyn.

AIWAIN, CAPTAIN HARYS, Imperial Charisian Navy—CO, HMS *Shield*, 54, HFAF.

ALBAN, LIEUTENANT COMMANDER NIMUE, Terran Federation Navy—Admiral Pei Kau-zhi's tactical officer, OAR.

ALLYKZHANDRO, COLONEL RAYMAHNDOH, Army of God—XO, Sulyvyn Division, Army of Glacierheart, LAMA.

ALLYRD, COLONEL KLYMYNT, Imperial Charisian Army—CO, 23rd Infantry Regiment, 13th Infantry Brigade, 7th Infantry Division, Imperial Charisian Army, LAMA.

ANVIL ROCK, EARL OF—see Sir Rysel Gahrvai.

APLYN, CHESTYR—one of Hektor Aplyn-Ahrmahk's younger brothers; newly admitted student at the Royal College of Charis, MT&T.

APLYN, SAILMAH—Hektor Aplyn-Ahrmahk's biological mother, MT&T.

APLYN-AHRMAHK, HEKTOR, Imperial Charisian Navy—midshipman, galley HMS *Royal Charis*, OAR; Cayleb Ahrmahk's adoptive son and Duke of Darcos; promoted to ensign, HMS *Destiny*, 54, BSRA; promoted to lieutenant HMS *Destiny* and becomes Sir Dunkyn

Yairley's flag lieutenant, MT&T; married to Irys Daykyn and member of Charisian inner circle, LAMA.

APLYN-AHRMAHK, PRINCESS IRYS ZHORZHET MHARA DAYKYN—daughter of Prince Hektor Daykyn of Corisande, sister of Daivyn and Hektor Daykyn, OAR; named legal guardian of Prince Daivyn Daykyn of Corisande, appointed to Prince Daivyn's Regency Council, married to Hektor Aplyn-Ahrmahk, Duchess Darcos, member of Charisian inner circle, LAMA.

ARCHBISHOP AHDYM—see Ahdym Taibyr.

ARCHBISHOP DAHNYLD—see Dahnyld Fardhym.

ARCHBISHOP ERAYK—see Erayk Dynnys.

ARCHBISHOP FAILYX—see Failyx Gahrbor.

ARCHBISHOP HALMYN—see Halmyn Zahmsyn.

ARCHBISHOP KLAIRMANT—see Klairmant Gairlyng.

ARCHBISHOP LAWRYNC—see Lawrync Zhaikybs.

ARCHBISHOP MAIKEL—see Maikel Staynair.

ARCHBISHOP PAWAL—see Pawal Braynair.

ARCHBISHOP PRAIDWYN—see Praidwyn Laicharn.

ARCHBISHOP URVYN—see Urvyn Myllyr.

ARCHBISHOP WYLLYM—see Wyllym Rayno.

ARCHBISHOP ZHASYN—see Zhasyn Cahnyr.

ARCHBISHOP ZHEROHM—see Zherohm Vyncyt.

ARTHMYN, FATHER OHMAHR—senior healer, Imperial Palace, Tellesberg, HFAF.

ASHWAIL, COMMANDER SAHLAVAHN, Imperial Charisian Navy—CO, 5th Provisional Battalion, 1st Independent Marine Brigade (one of Hauwerd Breygart's Navy "battalions" at Thesmar), MT&T.

ATHRAWES, MERLIN—Cayleb Ahrmahk's personal armsman; the cybernetic avatar of Commander Nimue Alban, OAR.

AYMEZ, MIDSHIPMAN BARDULF, Royal Charisian Navy—a midshipman, HMS *Typhoon*, 36, OAR.

BAHCHER, COLONEL SIR ZHORY, Royal Desnairian Army—CO, Bahcher's Regiment (medium cavalry), assigned to Sir Fahstyr Rychtyr's invasion column, MT&T.

BAHKMYN, BARON OF—see Hairwail Bahkmyn.

BAHKMYN, COLONEL SIR HAIRWAIL, Imperial Desnairian Army—Baron Bahkmyn; CO, Bahkmyn's Regiment (heavy cavalry), Army of Shiloh, LAMA.

BAHLTYN, ZHEEVYS—Baron White Ford's valet, OAR.

BAHNYR, HEKTOR, Royal Corisandian Army—Earl of Mancora; one of Sir Koryn Gahrvai's senior officers; commander of the right wing at Battle of Haryl's Crossing, BHD.

BAHNYSTYR, LIEUTENANT HAIRAHM, Royal Corisandian Guard—CO, Princess Irys Aplyn-Ahrmahk's personal guard detail, LAMA.

BAHR, DAHNNAH—senior chef, Imperial Palace, Cherayth, HFAF.

BAHRDAHN, CAPTAIN PHYLYP, Imperial Charisian Navy—CO, HMS *Undaunted*, 56, HFAF.

BAHRDAILAHN, LIEUTENANT SIR AHBAIL, Royal Dohlaran Navy—the Earl of Thirsk's flag lieutenant, HFAF.

BAHRKLY, BISHOP HARYS, Army of God—CO, Rakurai Division, Army of the Sylmahn, LAMA.

BAHRMYN, ARCHBISHOP BORYS—Archbishop of Corisande for the Church of God Awaiting, BHD.

BAHRMYN, TOHMYS—Baron White Castle, Prince Hektor's ambassador to Prince Nahrmahn, OAR.

BAHRNS, CAPTAIN HALCOM, Imperial Charisian Navy—CO, ironclad HMS *Delthak*, 22, MT&T.

BAHRNS, RAHNYLD IV—King of Dohlar, OAR.

BAHSKYM, COLONEL HYKAHRU, Imperial Desnairian Army—CO, Bahskym's Regiment (infantry), Army of Shiloh. CO, Kharmych garrison, LAMA.

BAHSKYM, GENERAL SIR BREYT, Imperial Charisian Army—Earl High Mount, CO, Army of Cliff Peak, LAMA.

BAHSKYM, SIR TRAIVYR, Imperial Desnairian Army—Earl of Hennet, the Duke of Harless' third-in-command; CO, "Cavalry Wing," Army of Shiloh, LAMA.

BAHZKAI, LAIYAN—a Leveler and printer in Siddar City; a leader of the Sword of Schueler, HFAF.

BAIKET, CAPTAIN STYWYRT, Royal Dohlaran Navy—CO,

HMS *Chihiro*, 50; the Earl of Thirsk's flag captain, HFAF.

BAIKYR, CAPTAIN DUSTYN, Imperial Charisian Army—CO, Company B, 2nd Battalion, 6th Regiment, Imperial Charisian Army, LAMA.

BAIKYR, CAPTAIN SYLMAHN, Imperial Charisian Navy—CO, HMS *Ahrmahk*, 58. High Admiral Lock Island's flag captain, HFAF.

BAIKYR, COLONEL PAWAL—a regular officer of the Republic of Siddarmark Army who went over to the Temple Loyalists; commander of Temple Loyalist rebels in the Sylmahn Gap, MT&T.

BAILAHND, SISTER AHMAI—Mother Abbess Ahmai Bailahnd of the Abbey of Saint Evehlain, HFAF.

BAIRAHT, DAIVYN—Duke of Kholman; effectively Emperor Mahrys IV's Navy Minister, Imperial Desnairian Navy; flees to Charis following Battle of Iythria, HFAF; stripped of title by Emperor Mahrys, LAMA.

BAIRYSTYR, COLONEL MAYNSFYLD, Army of God—CO, 73rd Cavalry Regiment, Army of the Sylmahn, LAMA.

BAIRYSTYR, LIEUTENANT ZHAK, Imperial Charisian Navy—senior engineer, ironclad HMS *Delthak*, 22, MT&T.

BAIRZHAIR, BROTHER TAIRAINCE—treasurer of the Monastery of Saint Zherneau, MT&T.

BANAHR, FATHER AHZWALD—head of the priory of Saint Hamlyn, city of Sarayn, Kingdom of Charis, BSRA.

BARCOR, BARON OF—see Sir Zher Sumyrs.

BARHNKASTYR, MAJOR PAITRYK, Imperial Charisian Army—XO, 3rd Regiment, 2nd Brigade, Imperial Charisian Army, MT&T.

BARTYN, FATHER MAHKZWAIL—a Langhornite under-priest; one of Rhobair Duchairn's transport personnel, LAMA.

BARYNGYR, COLONEL BRYGHAM, Army of God—CO, 1st Regiment, Fyrgyrsyn Division, Army of Glacierheart, LAMA.

BAYLAIR, COLONEL NOHBYRO, Imperial Charisian Army—CO, 10th Mounted Regiment, 5th Mounted Brigade, Imperial Charisian Army, LAMA.

BISHOP EXECUTOR DYNZAIL—see Dynzail Vahsphar.

BISHOP EXECUTOR MHARTYN—see Mhartyn Raislair.

BISHOP EXECUTOR WYLLYS—see Bishop Executor Wyllys Graisyn.

BISHOP EXECUTOR ZHERALD—see Bishop Executor Zherald Ahdymsyn.

BISHOP MAIKEL—see Maikel Staynair.

BISHOP MYTCHAIL—see Mytchail Zhessop.

BISHOP STYWYRT—see Bishop Stywyrt Sahndyrs.

BLACK HORSE, DUKE OF—see Payt Stywyrt.

BLACK WATER, DUKE OF—see Sir Ernyst Lynkyn and Sir Adulfo Lynkyn.

BLAHDYSNBERG, LIEUTENANT PAWAL, Imperial Charisian Navy—XO, ironclad HMS *Delthak*, 22, MT&T.

BLAHNDAI, CHANTAHAL—an alias of Lysbet Wylsynn in Zion, HFAF.

BLAIDYN, LIEUTENANT ROZHYR, Dohlaran Navy—second lieutenant, galley *Royal Bédard*, OAR.

BOHLGYR, MAJOR TYMYTHY, Imperial Charisian Army—CO, 3rd Battalion, 9th Mounted Regiment, 5th Mounted Brigade, Imperial Charisian Army, LAMA.

BOHLYR, WYLLYM, Canal Service—lockmaster, Fairkyn, New Northland Province, Republic of Siddarmark, MT&T.

BORYS, ARCHBISHOP—see Archbishop Borys Bahrmyn.

BOWAVE, DAIRAK—Dr. Rahzhyr Mahklyn's senior assistant, Royal College, Tellesberg, HFAF.

BOWSHAM, CAPTAIN KHANAIR, Royal Charisian Marines—CO, HMS *Gale*, OAR.

BRADLAI, LIEUTENANT ROBYRT, Royal Corisandian Navy—true name of Captain Styvyn Whaite, OAR.

BRAHDLAI, CORPORAL HOWAIL, Army of God—scout patrol commander, 191st Cavalry Regiment, MT&T.

BRAHDLAI, LIEUTENANT HAARAHLD, Royal Dohlaran Navy—third lieutenant, HMS *Chihiro*, 50, MT&T.

BRAHNAHR, CAPTAIN STYVYN, Imperial Charisian Navy—CO, Bureau of Navigation, Imperial Charisian Navy, MT&T.

BRAHNSYN, DOCTOR FYL—member of the Royal College of Charis, specializing in botany, MT&T.

BRAHNSYN, MAJOR PAWAL, Imperial Charisian Army—CO, 1st Battalion, 10th Mounted Regiment, 5th Mounted Brigade, Imperial Charisian Army, LAMA.

BRAIDAIL, BROTHER ZHILBYRT—under-priest of the Order of Schueler; a junior inquisitor in Talkyra, HFAF.

BRAISHAIR, CAPTAIN HORYS, Imperial Charisian Navy—CO, HMS *Rock Point*, 38. POW of Earl Thirsk, surrendered to the Inquisition, HFAF.

BRAISYN, AHRNAHLD, Imperial Charisian Navy—a seaman aboard HMS *Destiny*, 54; a member of Stywyrt Mahlyk's boat crew, HFAF.

BRAISYN, BRIGADIER MOHRTYN, Imperial Charisian Army—CO, 3rd Mounted Brigade, Imperial Charisian Army, LAMA.

BRAISYN, CAPTAIN DYNNYS, Imperial Charisian Navy—CO, Bureau of Supply, Imperial Charisian Navy, MT&T.

BRAIZHYR, BRIGADIER SIR EDGAIR, Imperial Charisian Army—CO, 14th Infantry Brigade, 7th Infantry Division, Imperial Charisian Army, LAMA.

BRAYNAIR, CAPTAIN LYWYS, Imperial Charisian Army—Duke Eastshare's aide, LAMA.

BRAYNAIR, PAWAL—Archbishop of Chisholm for the Church of Charis, AMF.

BRAYTAHN, MAJOR BAHNYFACE, Imperial Charisian Army—CO, 3rd Battalion, 10th Mounted Regiment, 5th Mounted Brigade, Imperial Charisian Army, LAMA.

BRAYTAHN, PLATOON SERGEANT RAIMYND, Imperial Charisian Army—senior noncom, 1st Platoon, Company B, 1st Battalion, 1st Scout Sniper Regiment, Imperial Charisian Army, LAMA.

BREYGART, FHRANCYS—younger daughter of Hauwerd and Fhrancys Breygart; Lady Mairah Breygart's stepdaughter, MT&T.

BREYGART, FRAIDARECK—fourteenth Earl of Hanth; Hauwerd Breygart's great-grandfather, OAR.

BREYGART, HAARAHLD—second oldest son of Hauwerd and Fhrancys Breygart; Lady Mairah Breygart's stepson, MT&T.

BREYGART, LADY MAIRAH LYWKYS—Queen Sharleyan's chief lady-in-waiting, cousin of Baron Green Mount, OAR; Countess of Hanth and second wife of Sir Hauwerd Breygart, Earl of Hanth, MT&T.

BREYGART, SIR HAUWERD, Royal Charisian Marines—rightful heir to the Earldom of Hanth, OAR; resigns commission and becomes Earl of Hanth, BSRA; recalled to service, promoted general; CO, 1st Independent Marine Brigade, MT&T; CO, Thesmar garrison, LAMA.

BREYGART, STYVYN—elder son of Hauwerd and Fhrancys Breygart; Lady Mairah Breygart's stepson, MT&T.

BREYGART, TRUMYN—youngest son of Hauwerd and Fhrancys Breygart; Lady Mairah Breygart's stepson, MT&T.

BREYGART, ZHERLDYN—elder daughter of Hauwerd and Fhrancys Breygart; Lady Mairah Breygart's stepdaughter, MT&T.

BROUN, FATHER MAHTAIO—Archbishop Erayk Dynnys' senior secretary and aide; Archbishop Erayk's confidant and protégé, OAR.

BROWNYNG, CAPTAIN ELLYS—CO, Temple galleon *Blessed Langhorne*, OAR.

BROWNYNG, CORPORAL AHLDAHS, Imperial Charisian Marines—senior member of Klymynt Abykrahmbi's assigned security detail, LAMA.

BROWNYNG, LIEUTENANT EHLYS, Imperial Charisian Navy—CO, Tymkyn Point battery, Thesmar Bay, LAMA.

BRUHSTAIR, STYVYN—a master clockmaker now serving as Ehdwyrd Howsmyn's chief instrument maker and inspector, LAMA.

BRYAIRS, TAHLBAHT—Brother Lynkyn Fultyn's assistant in charge of production, St. Kylmahn's Foundry, LAMA.

BRYGSYN, COLONEL TRYNT, Royal Dohlaran Army—CO, Brygsyn's Regiment (infantry), Dohlaran component, Army of Shiloh, LAMA.

BRYNDYN, MAJOR DAHRYN—the senior artillery officer

attached to Brigadier Clareyk's column at Battle of Haryl's Crossing, BHD.

BRYNKMYN, LIEUTENANT CHESTYR, Imperial Charisian Army—CO, 2nd Platoon, Company B, 1st Battalion, 9th Mounted Regiment, 5th Mounted Brigade, Imperial Charisian Army, LAMA.

BRYNYGAIR, COLONEL SIR ZHADWAIL, Royal Desnairian Army—CO, Brynygair's Regiment (medium cavalry), assigned to Sir Fahstyr Rychtyr's invasion column, MT&T.

BRYSKOH, MAJOR HAIMLTAHN—CO, 1st Greentown Militia, Midhold Province Temple Loyalist militia; CO, Greentown garrison, LAMA.

BRYSTAHL, COLONEL FHRANKLYN, Imperial Charisian Army—CO, 7th Regiment, 4th Infantry Brigade, Imperial Charisian Army, LAMA.

BUKANYN, LIEUTENANT SYMYN, Imperial Charisian Navy—CO, Navy Redoubt, Thesmar, LAMA.

BYRGAIR, COLONEL SIR ZHADWAIL, Royal Dohlaran Army—CO, Byrgair's Regiment (heavy cavalry), Royal Dohlaran Army, MT&T.

BYRK, CAPTAIN ZHORJ, Imperial Charisian Navy—CO, HMS *Volcano*, 24, one of the Imperial Charisian Navy's bombardment ships, MT&T.

BYRK, FATHER MYRTAN—upper-priest of the Order of Schueler; Vyktyr Tahrlsahn's second-in-command escorting Charisian POWs from Gorath to Zion, HFF.

BYRK, MAJOR BREKYN, Royal Charisian Marines—CO, Marine detachment, HMS *Royal Charis*, OAR.

BYRKYT, FATHER ZHON—an over-priest of the Church of God Awaiting; abbot of the Monastery of Saint Zherneau, BSRA; resigns as abbot and becomes librarian, HFAF.

BYRMAHN, COLONEL ZHAKSYN, Temple Loyalist Militia—CO, 2nd Maidynberg Militia, Temple Loyalist Militia, assigned to Fort Tairys' garrison, LAMA.

BYRNS, BRAISYN—Earl of White Crag; former Lord Justice of Chisholm, currently first councilor, replacing Mahrak Sahndyrs, MT&T.

BYROKYO, LIEUTENANT AHTONYO, Army of God—CO, 2nd Platoon, 1st Company, 1st Regiment, Zion Division, Army of Glacierheart, LAMA.

CAHKRAYN, SAMYL—Duke of Fern, King Rahnyld IV of Dohlar's first councilor, OAR.

CAHMMYNG, AHLBAIR—a professional assassin working for Father Aidryn Waimyn, HFAF.

CAHNYR, ARCHBISHOP ZHASYN—Archbishop of Glacierheart, OAR; member of Samyl Wylsynn's circle of Reformists, BHD; a strong Reformist leader in Siddar City, AMF; returns to Glacierheart to lead his archbishopric against the Group of Four, MT&T.

CAHNYRS, LIEUTENANT ZHERALD, Imperial Charisian Navy—second lieutenant, ironclad HMS *Delthak*, 22, MT&T.

CAHRTAIR, MAJOR HAHLYS—rebel Temple Loyalist; CO, 3rd Company, 3rd Saiknyr Militia Regiment, MT&T.

CAHSTNYR, COLONEL BRYSYN, Temple Loyalist Militia—CO, 3rd Mountaincross Rangers, Mountaincross Province Temple Loyalist partisans, LAMA.

CAHSTNYR, SIR BORYS, Imperial Desnairian Army—quartermaster, Army of Justice; quartermaster, Desnairian component, Army of Shiloh, LAMA.

CARLSYN, CAPTAIN EDWYRD, Imperial Charisian Army—CO, Company A, 1st Battalion, 5th Regiment, Imperial Charisian Army, LAMA.

CARTYR, BRYGHAM—Ehdwyrd Howsmyn's senior representative to the Republic of Siddarmark's Council of Manufactories, the body set up by Greyghor Stohnar to rationalize Siddarmarkian contributions to the war effort, LAMA.

CARTYR, MAJOR BRYXTYN, Imperial Charisian Army—XO, 5th Mounted Regiment, 3rd Mounted Brigade, Imperial Charisian Army, LAMA.

CELAHK, COLONEL HYNRYK, Imperial Charisian Army—Duke Eastshare's senior artillery officer, 1st Brigade (reinforced) and Army of the Branaths, LAMA.

CHAHLMAIR, SIR BAIRMON—Duke of Margo; a member of Prince Daivyn's Regency Council in Corisande who does not fully trust Earl Anvil Rock and Earl Tartarian, HFAF.

CHAIMBYRS, LIEUTENANT ZHUSTYN, Imperial Desnairian Navy—second lieutenant, HMS *Archangel Chihiro*, 40, HFAF.

CHALKYR, CORPORAL SLYM, Imperial Charisian Army—Duke Eastshare's batman.

CHALMYRZ, FATHER KARLOS—Archbishop Borys Bahrmyn's aide and secretary, OAR.

CHANSAYL, COLONEL PAITYR, Republic of Siddarmark Army—CO, 43rd Infantry Regiment, Republic of Siddarmark Army, a part of General Trumyn Stohnar's Sylmahn Gap command, MT&T.

CHARLTYN, MAJOR KRYSTYPHYR, Imperial Charisian Army—CO, 3rd Battalion, 5th Mounted Regiment, 3rd Mounted Brigade, Imperial Charisian Army, LAMA.

CHARLZ, CAPTAIN MARIK—CO, Charisian merchant ship *Wave Daughter*, OAR.

CHARLZ, FATHER BRYAHN—a Schuelerite under-priest, chaplain, and intendant, 231st Volunteer Regiment, Mighty Host of God and the Archangels, Imperial Harchongian Army, LAMA.

CHARLZ, MASTER YEREK, Royal Charisian Navy—gunner, HMS *Wave*, 14, BSRA.

CHERMYN, GENERAL HAUWYL, Royal Charisian Marines—the senior officer of the Charisian Marine Corps, BSRA; SO for the Marines in the invasion of Corisande, BHD; Charisian viceroy in Corisande, AMF; created Grand Duke Zebediah, HFAF.

CHERMYN, LIEUTENANT ZHOEL, Imperial Charisian Navy—senior engineer, ironclad HMS *Hador*, 22, MT&T.

CHERMYN, MAJOR DAHNEL—rebel Temple Loyalist; CO, 1st Company 3rd Saiknyr Militia Regiment, MT&T.

CHERMYN, MATHYLD—Hauwyl Chermyn's wife, HFAF.

CHERMYN, RHAZ—Hauwyl Chermyn's oldest son, HFAF.

CHERMYN, VICEROY GENERAL HAUWYL—see General Hauwyl Chermyn.

CHERNYNKOH, MAJOR BRAHDLAI, Imperial Charisian Army—CO, 4th Mounted Engineers Battalion, attached to 2nd Corps, Army of Cliff Peak, LAMA.

CHERYNG, LIEUTENANT TAIWYL, Royal Delferahkan Army—a junior officer on Sir Vyk Lakyr's staff; he is in charge of Lakyr's clerks and message traffic, BSRA.

CHWAERIAU, *SEIJIN* NIMUE—the second, "younger" PICA identity of Lieutenant Commander Nimue Alban on Safehold, LAMA.

CLAITYN, COLONEL SAMYL, Imperial Charisian Army—CO, 22nd Infantry Regiment, 13th Infantry Brigade, 7th Infantry Division, Imperial Charisian Army, LAMA.

CLAREYK, KYNT, Royal Charisian Marines—major, originator of the training syllabus for the Royal Charisian Marines, OAR; as brigadier, CO, 3rd Brigade, Royal Charisian Marines, made Baron Green Valley, BHD; transfers to Imperial Charisian Army as general and as adviser to Duke Eastshare, member of Charisian inner circle, AMF; acting viceroy Zebediah, HFAF; CO, 2nd Brigade (reinforced), Imperial Charisian Army, MT&T; CO, Army of Midhold, LAMA.

CLYFFYRD, MAJOR CAHNYR, Imperial Charisian Army—XO, 6th Regiment, Imperial Charisian Army, LAMA.

CLYMYNS, FATHER ZHEROHM—a Schuelerite upper-priest serving as Bishop Wylbyr Edwyrds' chief of staff, LAMA.

CLYNTAHN, LIEUTENANT HAIRYM, Imperial Charisian Army—CO, Support Platoon, 1st Battalion, 2nd Regiment, Imperial Charisian Army, MT&T.

CLYNTAHN, VICAR ZHASPAHR—Grand Inquisitor of the Church of God Awaiting; one of the so-called Group of Four, OAR.

COHLMYN, ADMIRAL SIR LEWK, Chisholmian Navy—Earl Sharpfield; Queen Sharleyan's senior fleet commander, OAR; second-ranking officer, Imperial Charisian Navy, HFAF; CO, Gulf of Dohlar Squadron, LAMA.

CORIS, EARL OF—see Phylyp Ahzgood.

CRAGGY HILL, EARL OF—see Wahlys Hillkeeper.

CRAHMYND, PETTY OFFICER FYRGYRSYN, Imperial Charisian Navy—senior helmsman, HMS ironclad *Delthak*, 22, MT&T.

CROSS CREEK, EARL OF—see Ahdem Zhefry.

CUPYR, MAJOR BARTAHLAIMO, Imperial Charisian Army—CO, 1st Battalion, 5th Regiment, Imperial Charisian Army, LAMA.

DABNYR, MAJOR WAHLTAYR, Imperial Charisian Army—CO, 4th Battalion, 9th Mounted Regiment, 5th Mounted Brigade, Imperial Charisian Army, LAMA.

DAHGLYS, CAPTAIN LAINYR, Imperial Charisian Navy—CO, ironclad HMS *Tellesberg*, 22, MT&T.

DAHGLYS, MASTER SYGMAHN—an engineer attached to Father Tailahr Synzhyn's staff to assist with canal repairs for the Church of God Awaiting, LAMA.

DAHNSYN, LIEUTENANT CHARLZ, Republic of Siddarmark Army—Colonel Stahn Wyllys' senior aide, MT&T.

DAHNVAHR, AINSAIL—Charisian-born Temple Loyalist living in the Temple Lands, recruited for Operation Rakurai, HFAF.

DAHNVAHR, RAHZHYR—Ainsail Dahnvahr's father, HFAF.

DAHNVAIR, CAPTAIN LAIZAHNDO, Imperial Charisian Navy—CO, HMS *Royal Kraken*, 58, HFAF.

DAHNZAI, LYZBYT—Father Zhaif Laityr's housekeeper at the Church of the Holy Archangels Triumphant, HFAF.

DAHRYUS, MASTER EDVARHD—an alias of Bishop Mylz Halcom, BSRA.

DAIKHAR, LIEUTENANT MOHTOHKAI, Imperial Charisian Navy—XO, HMS *Dart*, 54, HFAF.

DAIKYN, GAHLVYN—Cayleb Ahrmahk's valet, OAR.

DAIRWYN, BARON OF—see Sir Farahk Hyllair.

DAIVYN, PRINCE—see Daivyn Daykyn.

DAIVYS, MYTRAHN—a Charisian Temple Loyalist, BSRA.

DANTAS, MAJOR SIR AINGHUS, Royal Dohlaran Army—

DOYAL, SIR CHARLZ—Sir Koryn Gahrvai's senior artillery commander, Battle of Haryl's Crossing, BHD; Sir Koryn Gahrvai's chief of staff and intelligence chief, Corisandian Guard, AMF; Corisandian Regency Council's chief of intelligence, MT&T.

DRAGON HILL, EARL OF—see Edwyrd Ahlbair.

DRAGONER, CORPORAL ZHAK, Royal Charisian Marines—a member of Crown Prince Cayleb's bodyguard, OAR.

DRAGONER, SIR RAYJHIS—Charisian ambassador to the Siddarmark Republic, BSRA; retires as ambassador, MT&T.

DRAGONMASTER, BRIGADE SERGEANT MAJOR MAHKYNTY ("MAHK"), Royal Charisian Marines—Brigadier Clareyk's senior noncom, BSRA.

DUCHAIRN, VICAR RHOBAIR—Minister of Treasury, Council of Vicars; one of the so-called Group of Four, OAR.

DUNSTYN, LIEUTENANT TRUMYN, Imperial Charisian Army—CO, 1st Platoon, Company B, 2nd Battalion, 6th Regiment, Imperial Charisian Army, LAMA.

DYASAIYL, MAJOR AHRKYP, Imperial Charisian Army—CO, 4th Battalion, 1st Scout Sniper Regiment, Imperial Charisian Army, LAMA.

DYLLAHN, CHIEF BOATSWAIN'S MATE CHESTYR, Imperial Charisian Navy—boatswain, ironclad HMS *Delthak*, 22, LAMA.

DYMYTREE, FRONZ, Royal Charisian Marines—a member of Crown Prince Cayleb's bodyguard, OAR.

DYNNYS, ADORAI—Archbishop Erayk Dynnys' wife, OAR; her alias after her husband's arrest is Ailysa, BSRA.

DYNNYS, ARCHBISHOP ERAYK—Archbishop of Charis. Executed for heresy 892, OAR.

DYNNYS, MAJOR AHBNAIR, Republic of Siddarmark Army—CO, 1st Company, 37th Infantry Regiment, Republic of Siddarmark Army, MT&T.

DYNNYS, STYVYN—Archbishop Erayk Dynnys' younger son, age eleven in 892, BSRA.

DYNNYS, TYMYTHY ERAYK—Archbishop Erayk Dynnys' older son, age fourteen in 892, BSRA.

FAHRMYN, FATHER TAIRYN—the priest assigned to Saint Chihiro's Church, a village church near the Convent of Saint Agtha; complicit in attempt to assasinate Empress Sharleyan, BHD.

FAHRNO, MAHRLYS—one of Madam Ahnzhelyk Phonda's courtesans, HFAF.

FAHRYA, CAPTAIN BYRNAHRDO, Imperial Desnairian Navy—CO, HMS *Holy Langhorne*, 42, HFAF.

FAHSTYR, COLONEL BAHZWAIL, Army of God—CO, 3rd Regiment, Sulyvyn Division, Army of Glacierheart, LAMA.

FAHSTYR, VYRGYL—Earl of Gold Wyvern, MT&T.

FAINSTYN, LIEUTENANT GHORDYN, Army of God—Bishop Militant Bahrnabai's junior aide, Army of Glacierheart, LAMA.

FAIRCASTER, SERGEANT PAYTER, Royal Charisian Marines—senior noncom, Crown Prince Cayleb's bodyguard, OAR; transfers to Royal Guard as King Cayleb's bodyguard, BSRA; transfers to Imperial Guard as Emperor Cayleb's bodyguard, BHD.

FAIRSTOCK, MAJOR KLYMYNT, Republic of Siddarmark Army—CO, Provisional Company, Republic of Siddarmark Army, Fort Sheldyn, South March Lands, MT&T.

FAIRYS, COLONEL AHLVYN, Imperial Charisian Marines—CO, 1st Regiment, 3rd Brigade, Imperial Charisian Marines, HFAF.

FALKHAN, LIEUTENANT AHRNAHLD, Royal Charisian Marines—CO, Crown Prince Cayleb's personal bodyguard, OAR; CO, Crown Prince Zhan's personal bodyguard, BSRA.

FARDHYM, ARCHBISHOP DAHNYLD—Bishop of Siddar City, elevated to Archbishop of Siddarmark by Greyghor Stohnar after the rebellion of the "Sword of Schueler" ordered by Vicar Zhaspahr Clyntahn, MT&T.

FATHER MAHKZWAIL—see Mahkzwail Bartyn.

FATHER MICHAEL—parish priest of Lakeview, OAR.

FATHER MYRTAN—see Myrtan Byrk.

FAUYAIR, BROTHER BAHRTLAM—almoner of the Monastery of Saint Zherneau, HFAF.

FERN, DUKE OF—see Samyl Cahkrayn.

FHAIRLY, MAJOR AHDYM, Royal Delferahkan Army— senior battery commander on East Island, Ferayd Sound, Kingdom of Delferahk, BSRA.

FHARMYN, SIR RYK—a foundry owner/ironmaster in the Kingdom of Tarot, HFAF.

FOFÃO, CAPTAIN MATEUS, Terran Federation Navy—CO, TFNS *Swiftsure*, OAR.

FOHRDYM, MAJOR KARMAIKEL, Imperial Charisian Army—CO, 2nd Battalion, 3rd Regiment, Imperial Charisian Army, MT&T.

FORYST, VICAR ERAYK—a member of Samyl Wylsynn's circle of Reformists in Zion, BSRA.

FOWAIL, CAPTAIN MAIKEL, Royal Desnairian Army—CO, "Fowail's Battery," six-pounder horse artillery assigned to Sir Fahstyr Rychtyr's invasion column, MT&T.

FRAIDMYN, SERGEANT VYK, Charisian Royal Guard— one of Cayleb Ahrmahk's armsmen, later transfers to Charisian Imperial Guard, BSRA.

FRAYZHYR, SERGEANT WYNSTYN, Royal Corisandian Army—a noncommissioned officer serving as plainclothes security for Irys Daykyn and Hektor Aplyn-Ahrmahk's wedding, LAMA.

FRYMYN, DOCTOR ZHAIN—a member of the Royal College particularly interested in optics; a member of the Charisian inner circle, LAMA.

FUHLLYR, FATHER RAIMAHND—chaplain, HMS *Dreadnought*, 54, OAR.

FULTYN, BROTHER LYNKYN—a Chihirite lay brother; supervisor/manager at St. Kylmahn's Foundry; Allayn Maigwair's and Rhobair Duchairn's chosen industrial manager, LAMA.

FURKHAL, RAFAYL—second baseman and leadoff hitter, Tellesberg Krakens, OAR.

FYGUERA, GENERAL KYDRYC, Republic of Siddarmark Army—CO, Thesmar, South March Lands, MT&T; CO, Thesmar Division, LAMA.

FYNLAITYR, MASTER LYNX, Imperial Charisian Navy—

gunner, broadside ironclad HMS *Rottweiler*, 30, LAMA.

FYNTYN, BRIGADIER FRAYZHYR, Imperial Charisian Army—CO, 13th Infantry Brigade, 7th Infantry Division, Imperial Charisian Army, LAMA.

FYRGYRSYN, PETTY OFFICER CRAHMYND, Imperial Charisian Navy—senior helmsman, ironclad HMS *Delthak*, 22, MT&T.

FYRLOH, FATHER BAHN—a Langhornite Temple Loyalist under-priest in Tellesberg nominated by Father Davys Tyrnyr as Irys and Daivyn Daykyn's chaplain and confessor on their voyage to Chisholm, MT&T.

FYRMAHN, ZHAN—a mountain clansman and feudist from the Gray Wall Mountains; becomes the leader of the Temple Loyalist guerrillas attacking Glacierheart, MT&T.

FYRMYN, FATHER SULYVYN—a Schuelerite upper-priest assigned as Sir Rainos Ahlverez' special intendant, MT&T.

FYRNACH, BARON OF—see Sir Graim Kyr.

FYSHYR, HAIRYS—CO, privateer galleon *Kraken*, BSRA.

FYTSYMYNS, MAJOR TAHD, Imperial Charisian Army—CO, 1st Battalion, 11th Mounted Regiment, 6th Mounted Brigade, Imperial Charisian Army, LAMA.

GAHDARHD, LORD SAMYL—keeper of the seal and chief intelligence minister, Republic of Siddarmark, HFAF.

GAHLVAYO, CAPTAIN GAIYR, Imperial Charisian Army—CO, Company B, 1st Battalion, 1st Scout Sniper Regiment, Imperial Charisian Army, LAMA.

GAHLVYN, CAPTAIN CAHNYR, Imperial Charisian Navy—CO, ironclad HMS *Saygin*, 22, MT&T.

GAHRBOR, ARCHBISHOP FAILYX—Archbishop of Tarot for the Church of God Awaiting, HFAF.

GAHRDANER, SERGEANT CHARLZ, Charisian Royal Guard—one of King Haarahld VII's bodyguards, KIA Battle of Darcos Sound, OAR.

GAHRMAHN, TAYLAR—Duke of Traykhos; Emperor Mahrys IV of Desnair's first councilor, LAMA.

GAHRMYN, LIEUTENANT RAHNYLD, Royal Delferahkan Navy—XO, galley *Arrowhead*, BSRA.

GAHRNAHT, BISHOP AMILAIN—deposed Bishop of Larchros, HFAF.

GAHRNET, SIR AHLVYN, Imperial Desnairian Army—Duke of Harless, senior Desnairian commander in the Republic of Siddarmark; CO, Desnairian Army of Justice; CO, Army of Shiloh, LAMA.

GAHRVAI, GENERAL SIR KORYN, Corisandian Guard—son of Earl Anvil Rock, Prince Hektor's army field commander, BHD; CO, Corisandian Guard, in the service of the Regency Council, AMF; CO, Royal Corisandian Army, LAMA.

GAHRVAI, SIR RYSEL, EARL OF ANVIL ROCK—Prince Hektor's senior army commander and distant cousin, BSRA; Prince Daivyn Daykyn's official regent and head of Daivyn's Regency Council, AMF.

GAHZTAHN, HIRAIM—Ainsail Dahnvahr's alias in Tellesberg, HFAF.

GAIMLYN, BROTHER BAHLDWYN—under-priest of the Order of Schueler; assigned to King Zhames of Delferahk's household as an agent of the Inquisition, HFAF.

GAIRAHT, CAPTAIN WYLLYS, Chisholmian Royal Guard—CO of Queen Sharleyan's Royal Guard detachment in Charis, KIA Saint Agtha assassination attempt, BSRA.

GAIRLYNG, ARCHBISHOP KLAIRMANT—Archbishop of Corisande for the Church of Charis, HFAF.

GAIRWYL, COLONEL DAHNYLD, Imperial Charisian Army—CO, 5th Mounted Regiment, 3rd Mounted Brigade, Imperial Charisian Army, LAMA.

GAIRWYL, COLONEL SIR NAHTCHYZ, Royal Dohlaran Army—CO, Gairwyl's Regiment (infantry), Royal Dohlaran Army, Dohlaran component, Army of Shiloh, LAMA.

GALVAHN, MAJOR SIR NAITHYN—the Earl of Windshare's senior staff officer, BSRA.

GARDYNYR, ADMIRAL LYWYS, Royal Dohlaran Navy—

Earl of Thirsk; senior professional admiral of the Dohlaran Navy; second-in-command to Duke Malikai, OAR; in disgrace, BSRA; restored to command of RDN, AMF.

GARDYNYR, COLONEL THOMYS, Royal Dohlaran Army—CO, Gardynyr's Regiment (cavalry), Dohlaran component, Army of Shiloh; distant cousin of Lywys Gardynyr, Earl of Thirsk, MT&T.

GARTHIN, EDWAIR—Earl of North Coast; one of Prince Hektor of Corisande's councilors serving on Prince Daivyn's Regency Council in Corisande; an ally of Earl Anvil Rock and Earl Tartarian, HFAF.

GENGCHAI, LORD OF ARMIES YITANGZHI—Grand Duke of Omar, the Harchongese Army Minister, LAMA.

GHADWYN, SAMYL—a Temple Loyalist mountain clansman from the Gray Wall Mountains; one of Zhan Fyrmahn's cousins, MT&T.

GHATFRYD, SANDARIA—Ahnzhelyk Phonda's/Nynian Rychtair's personal maid, HFAF.

GHORDYN, VICAR NICODAIM—an ally of Zhaspahr Clyntahn on the Council of Vicars.

GLYNFYRD, BARONET OF—see Sir Zheryd Klynkskayl.

GODWYL, GENERAL SIR OHTYS, Royal Desnairian Army—Baron Traylmyn; General Sir Fahstyr Rychtyr's second-in-command, MT&T.

GOLD WYVERN, EARL OF—see Vyrgyl Fahstyr.

GORJAH, FATHER GHARTH—Archbishop Zhasyn Cahnyr's personal secretary; a Chihirite of the Order of the Quill, HFAF; Archbishop Zhasyn's executive assistant upon his return to Glacierheart, MT&T.

GORJAH, SAHMANTHA—daughter of Archbishop Zhasyn Cahnyr's previous housekeeper, Father Gharth Gorjah's wife, HFAF; a trained healer assigned to the archbishop upon his return to Glacierheart, MT&T.

GORJAH, ZHASYN—firstborn child of Gharth and Sahmantha Gorjah, HFAF.

GOWAIN, LIEUTENANT FAIRGHAS, Imperial Charisian Navy—XO, HMS *Victorious*, 56, HFAF.

HADOR, MAJOR SAHLAVAHN, Imperial Charisian Army—CO, 1st Battalion, 5th Mounted Regiment, 3rd Mounted Brigade, Imperial Charisian Army, LAMA.

HAHL, LIEUTENANT PAWAL, Royal Dohlaran Navy—second lieutenant, HMS *Chihiro*, 50, MT&T.

HAHLCAHM, DOCTOR ZHER—member of the Royal College of Charis, specializing in biology and food preparation, MT&T.

HAHLEK, FATHER SYMYN—a Langhornite under-priest, Archbishop Klairmant Gairlyng's personal aide, HFAF.

HAHLMAHN, PAWAL—King Haarahld VII's senior chamberlain, OAR.

HAHLMYN, FATHER MAHRAK—an upper-priest of the Church of God Awaiting; Bishop Executor Thomys Shylair's personal aide, BSRA.

HAHLMYN, MIDSHIPMAN ZHORJ, Imperial Charisian Navy—a signals midshipman aboard HMS *Darcos Sound*, 54, HFAF.

HAHLMYN, SAIRAIH—Queen Sharleyan's personal maid, BHD.

HAHLTAR, ADMIRAL GENERAL SIR URWYN, Imperial Desnairian Navy—Baron Jahras; CO, Imperial Desnairian Navy; Daivyn Bairaht's brother-in-law, HFAF; flees to Charis for asylum following Battle of Iythria, MT&T.

HAHLYND, ADMIRAL PAWAL, Royal Dohlaran Navy—one of Earl Thirsk's most trusted subordinates; CO, anti-piracy patrols, Hankey Sound; a friend of Admiral Thirsk, BHD; Admiral Thirsk's senior subordinate admiral, HFAF.

HAHLYND, COLONEL BRAISYN, Royal Dohlaran Army—CO, Hahlynd's Regiment (infantry), Dohlaran component, Army of Shiloh, LAMA.

HAHLYND, MAJOR RAHZHYR, Imperial Charisian Army—CO, 2nd Battalion, 5th Mounted Regiment, 3rd Mounted Brigade, Imperial Charisian Army, LAMA.

HAHLYS, BISHOP GAHRMYN, Army of God—CO, Chihiro Division, Army of Glacierheart (Bishop Militant Cahnyr Kaitswyrth's favored division), MT&T.

HAHNDAIL, CORPORAL WAHLYS, Imperial Charisian Marines—Marine section commander attached to Brigadier Taisyn's forces in Glacierheart, MT&T.

HAHPKYNS, PLATOON SERGEANT RUHFUS, Imperial Charisian Army—platoon sergeant, 1st Platoon, Company A, 1st Battalion, 5th Regiment, Imperial Charisian Army, LAMA.

HAHPKYNSYN, COLONEL NATHALAN—CO, 1st Maidynberg Militia, Shilohian Temple Loyalist militia; assigned to Fort Tairys garrison, LAMA.

HAHRAIMAHN, ZHAK—a Siddarmarkian industrialist and foundry owner, HFAF.

HAHSKANS, DAILOHRS—Father Tymahn Hahskans' wife, HFAF.

HAHSKANS, FATHER TYMAHN—a Reformist upper-priest of the Order of Bédard in Manchyr; senior priest, Saint Kathryn's Church, murdered by Temple Loyalist extremists, HFAF.

HAHSKYN, LIEUTENANT AHNDRAI, Charisian Imperial Guard—a Charisian officer assigned to Empress Sharleyan's guard detachment. Captain Gairaht's second-in-command, KIA Saint Agtha assassination attempt, BSRA.

HAHVAIR, COMMANDER FRANZ, Imperial Charisian Navy—CO, schooner HMS *Mace*, 12, HFAF.

HAIGYL, CAPTAIN KAHRLTYN, Imperial Charisian Navy—CO, broadside ironclad HMS *Dreadnought*, 30, LAMA.

HAIMLTAHN, BISHOP EXECUTOR WYLLYS—Archbishop Zhasyn Cahnyr's executive assistant in the Archbishopric of Glacierheart, HFAF.

HAIMYN, BRIGADIER MAHRYS, Royal Charisian Marines—CO, 5th Brigade, Royal Charisian Marines, BSRA.

HAINAI, COMMANDER FRAHNKLYN, Imperial Charisian Navy—one of Sir Ahlfryd Hyndryk's senior assistants; Bureau of Ordnance's chief liaison with Ehdwyrd Howsmyn and his artificers, MT&T.

HAINE, FATHER FHRANKLYN—upper-priest of the Order of Pasquale; the senior healer attached to Archbishop

Zhasyn Cahnyr's relief expedition to Glacierheart Province, MT&T.

HAINREE, PAITRYK—a silversmith and Temple Loyalist agitator in Manchyr, Princedom of Corisande, HFAF; attempts to assassinate Empress Sharleyan, AMF.

HAITHMYN, COLONEL SIR AHLGYRNAHN, Imperial Desnairian Army—CO, Haithmyn's Regiment (medium cavalry), cavalry wing, Army of Shiloh, LAMA.

HALBROOK HOLLOW, DUCHESS OF—see Elahnah Waistyn.

HALBROOK HOLLOW, DUKE OF—see Byrtrym Waistyn and Sailys Waistyn.

HALCOM, BISHOP MYLZ—Bishop of Margaret Bay, becomes leader of armed Temple Loyalist resistance in Charis; KIA Saint Agtha's assassination attempt, BSRA.

HALMYN, ARCHBISHOP ZAHMSYN—Archbishop of Gorath; senior prelate of the Kingdom of Dohlar, OAR.

HAMPTYN, MAJOR KOLYN—Temple Loyalist ex-militia officer, Fort Darymahn, South March Lands, Republic of Siddarmark, MT&T.

HANTAI, WAISU—Waisu VI, Emperor of Harchong.

HANTH, COUNTESS OF—see Mairah Lywkys Breygart.

HANTH, EARL OF—see Sir Hauwerd Breygart; see also Tahdayo Mahntayl.

HARMYN, MAJOR BAHRKLY, Royal Emeraldian Army—an Emeraldian army officer assigned to North Bay, BSRA.

HARPAHR, BISHOP KORNYLYS, Navy of God—bishop of the Order of Chihiro; admiral general of the Navy of God, HFAF.

HARPAHR, CAPTAIN BRYAHN, Army of God—CO, 1st Company, 73rd Cavalry Regiment, Army of the Sylmahn, LAMA.

HARRISON, MATTHEW PAUL—Timothy and Sarah Harrison's great-grandson, OAR.

HARRISON, ROBERT—Timothy and Sarah Harrison's grandson; Matthew Paul Harrison's father, OAR.

HARRISON, SARAH—wife of Timothy Harrison and an Eve, OAR.

HARRISON, TIMOTHY—mayor of Lakeview and an Adam, OAR.

HARYS, CAPTAIN ZHOEL, Royal Corisandian Navy—CO, Corisandian galley *Lance*, BSRA; CO, galleon *Wing*; responsible for transporting Princess Irys and Prince Daivyn to Delferahk, BHD.

HARYS, COLONEL WYNTAHN, Imperial Charisian Marine Corps—senior officer in command Marines detailed to support Captain Halcom Bahrns' operation ("Great Canal Raid"), MT&T.

HARYS, FATHER AHLBYRT—Vicar Zahmsyn Trynair's special representative to Dohlar, OAR.

HASKYN, MIDSHIPMAN YAHNCEE, Royal Dohlaran Navy—a midshipman aboard HMS *Gorath Bay*, OAR.

HASKYNS, COLONEL MOHRTYN, Imperial Charisian Army—CO, 11th Mounted Regiment, 6th Mounted Brigade, Imperial Charisian Army, LAMA.

HAUKYNS, CAPTAIN ZHAK, Imperial Charisian Navy—CO, HMS *Powerful*, 58; Admiral Payter Shain's flag captain, LAMA.

HAUWYL, SHAIN, Royal Dohlaran Army—Duke of Salthar, senior officer, Royal Dohlaran Army, MT&T.

HAUWYRD, ZHORZH—Earl Gray Harbor's personal guardsman, OAR.

HENDERSON, LIEUTENANT GABRIELA ("GABBY"), Terran Federation Navy—tactical officer, TFNS *Swiftsure*, OAR.

HIGH MOUNT, EARL OF—see Breyt Bahskym.

HILLKEEPER, WAHLYS—Earl of Craggy Hill; a member of Prince Daivyn's Regency Council; also a senior member of the Northern Conspiracy, HFAF.

HOBSYN, COLONEL ALLAYN, Imperial Charisian Army—CO, 5th Regiment, 3rd Brigade, 2nd Division, Imperial Charisian Army, LAMA.

HOLDYN, VICAR LYWYS—a member of Samyl Wylsynn's circle of Reformists, BSRA.

HOTCHKYS, CAPTAIN SIR OHWYN, Royal Charisian Navy—CO, galley HMS *Tellesberg*, OAR.

HOWAIL, COLONEL BRYNTYN, Republic of Siddarmark Army—CO, 37th Infantry Regiment, LAMA.

HOWAIL, MAJOR DAHNEL, Army of God—XO, 1st Regiment, Zion Division, Army of Glacierheart.

HOWSMYN, EHDWYRD—a wealthy foundry owner and shipbuilder in Tellesberg, OAR; member of the Charisian inner circle, BHD; "the Ironmaster of Charis"; the wealthiest and most innovative Old Charisian industrialist, MT&T.

HOWSMYN, ZHAIN—Ehdwyrd Howsmyn's wife, daughter of Earl Sharphill, OAR.

HUNTYR, LIEUTENANT KLEMYNT, Charisian Royal Guard—an officer of the Charisian Royal Guard in Tellesberg, OAR.

HUNTYR, ZOSH—Ehdwyrd Howsmyn's master artificer, MT&T.

HWYSTYN, SIR VYRNYN—a member of the Charisian Parliament elected from Tellesberg, BSRA.

HYLDYR, COLONEL FRAIHMAN, Republic of Siddarmark Army—CO, 123rd Infantry Regiment, Republic of Siddarmark Army, a part of General Trumyn Stohnar's Sylmahn Gap command, MT&T.

HYLLAIR, SIR FARAHK—the Baron of Dairwyn, BSRA.

HYLMAHN, RAHZHYR—Earl of Thairnos, a relatively new addition to Prince Daivyn's Regency Council in Corisande, MT&T.

HYLMYN, FRONZ—Earl Sharpfield's personal clerk and secretary, LAMA.

HYLMYN, LIEUTENANT MAINYRD, Imperial Charisian Navy—senior engineer, ironclad HMS *Saygin*, 22, MT&T.

HYLMYN, LIEUTENANT STYVYN, Imperial Charisian Army—CO, 1st Platoon, Company A, 1st Battalion, 5th Regiment, Imperial Charisian Army, LAMA.

HYLSDAIL, LIEUTENANT FRAYDYK, Imperial Charisian Navy—second lieutenant, HMS *Trunmpeter*; detached to serve as CO, Redoubt #1, Thesmar garrison, LAMA.

HYNDRYK, SIR AHLFRYD—Baron Seamount; captain,

Royal Charisian Navy, senior gunnery expert, OAR; commodore, Imperial Charisian Navy, BSRA; admiral, HFAF; CO, Bureau of Ordnance, MT&T.

HYNDYRS, DUNKYN—purser, privateer galleon *Raptor,* BSRA.

HYNRYKAI, COLONEL AHVRAHM, Imperial Charisian Army—Army liaison with the Navy Bureau of Ordinance and the Delthak Works, LAMA.

HYNTYN, SIR DYNZAYL—Earl of Saint Howan; Chancellor of the Treasury, Kingdom of Chisholm, MT&T.

HYRST, ADMIRAL ZOHZEF, Royal Chisholmian Navy—Earl Sharpfield's second-in-command, OAR; Imperial Charisian Navy, CO, Port Royal fleet base, Chisholm, BHD.

HYRST, SIR ABSHAIR—Earl of Nearoak, Lord Justice of Old Charis and, effectively, of the Charisian Empire, LAMA.

HYSIN, VICAR CHIYAN—a member of Vicar Samyl Wylsynn's circle of Reformists (from Harchong), BSRA.

HYWSTYN, LORD AVRAHM—a cousin of Greyghor Stohnar, and a midranking official assigned to the Siddarmarkian foreign ministry, BSRA.

HYWYT, ADMIRAL SIR PAITRYK—Royal Charisian Navy, CO, HMS *Wave,* 14 (schooner), transferred Imperial Charisian Navy, BSRA; promoted captain, CO, HMS *Dancer,* 56, BHD; promoted admiral, CO, Inshore Squadron, Gulf of Mathyas, MT&T.

IBBET, AHSTELL—a blacksmith convicted of treason as part of the Northern Conspiracy in Corisande; pardoned by Empress Sharleyan, HFAF.

ILLIAN, CAPTAIN AHNTAHN, Royal Corisandian Army—one of Sir Phylyp Myllyr's company commanders, BSRA.

INGRAYAHN, CAPTAIN VALTYNOH, Army of God—CO, 1st Company, 1st Regiment, Zion Division, Army of Glacierheart, LAMA.

IRONHILL, BARON OF—see Ahlvyno Pawalsyn.

JAHRAS, BARON OF—see Urwyn Hahltar.

JYNKYN, COLONEL HAUWYRD, Royal Charisian Marines—

Admiral Rock Point's senior Marine commander, BSRA.

JYNKYNS, BISHOP ERNYST—Bishop of Ferayd, BSRA.

KAHBRYLLO, CAPTAIN AHNTAHN, Imperial Charisian Navy—CO, HMS *Dawn Star*, 58, Empress Sharleyan's transport to Zebediah and Corisande, HFAF.

KAHLDONAI, SERGEANT ZHYKOHMA, Army of God—Sergeant, 1st Platoon, Company A, 191st Cavalry Regiment, Army of Glacierheart, LAMA.

KAHLYNS, COLONEL ZHANDRU, Army of God—CO, 1st Regiment, Sulyvyn Division, Army of Glacierheart, LAMA.

KAHMELKA, COLONEL GOTFRYD, Royal Dohlaran Army—CO, Kahmelka's Regiment, Dohlaran component, Army of Shiloh, LAMA.

KAHMERLYNG, COLONEL LUTAYLO, Imperial Charisian Army—CO, 2nd Regiment, 1st Brigade, 1st Infantry Division, Imperial Charisian Army, LAMA.

KAHMPTMYN, MAJOR HAHLYND, Imperial Charisian Army—XO, 4th Regiment, Imperial Charisian Army, MT&T.

KAHNKLYN, AIDRYAN—Tairys Kahnklyn's older daughter, Rahzhyr Mahklyn's older granddaughter and oldest grandchild, BSRA.

KAHNKLYN, AIZAK—Rahzhyr Mahklyn's son-in-law; a senior librarian with the Royal College of Charis, BSRA.

KAHNKLYN, ERAYK—Tairys Kahnklyn's oldest son, Rahzhyr Mahklyn's older grandson, BSRA.

KAHNKLYN, EYDYTH—Rahzhyr Mahklyn's younger granddaughter; twin sister of Zhoel Kahnklyn, BSRA.

KAHNKLYN, HAARAHLD—Tairys Kahnklyn's middle son; Rahzhyr Mahklyn's second oldest grandson, BSRA.

KAHNKLYN, TAIRYS—Rahzhyr Mahklyn's married daughter; senior librarian, Royal College of Charis, BSRA.

KAHNKLYN, ZHOEL—Tairys Kahnklyn's youngest son, Rahzhyr Mahklyn's youngest grandson; twin brother of Eydyth Kahklyn, BSRA.

KAHRNAIKYS, MAJOR ZHAPHAR, Temple Guard—an officer of the Temple Guard and a Schuelerite, HFAF.

KAHSIMAHR, LIEUTENANT SIR LAIMYN, Imperial Desnairian Army—youngest son of the Duke of Sherach; Sir Borys Cahstnyr's senior aide and effective chief of staff, Quartermaster Corps, Army of Justice and Army of Shiloh, LAMA.

KAILLEE, MAJOR BRUHSTAIR, Royal Dohlaran Army—CO, 3rd Company, Ohygyns' Regiment (infantry), Dohlaran component, Army of Shiloh, LAMA.

KAILLEE, CAPTAIN ZHILBERT—Royal Tarotisian Navy, CO, galley *King Gorjah II*, Baron White Ford's flag captain, OAR; Imperial Charisian Navy, CO, HMS *Fortune*, 58; Baron White Ford's flag captain, LAMA.

KAILLWYRTH, MAJOR ZHAIK, Imperial Charisian Army—CO, 4th Battalion, 6th Regiment, Imperial Charisian Army, LAMA.

KAILLYT, KAIL—Major Borys Sahdlyr's second-in-command in Siddar City, HFAF.

KAIREE, TRAIVYR—a wealthy merchant and landowner in the Earldom of Styvyn, Temple Loyalist, BSRA; complicit in the attempt to assassinate Empress Sharleyan, BHD.

KAIRMYN, CAPTAIN TOMHYS, Royal Delferahkan Army—one of Sir Vyk Lakyr's officers, Ferayd garrison, BSRA.

KAISI, FHRANCYS—one of the Republic of Siddarmark's greatest composers who wrote, among many other works, "The Stand at Kahrmaik," commemorating one of the greatest Siddarmarkian victories against the Desnairian Empire.

KAITS, CAPTAIN BAHRNABAI, Imperial Charisian Marines—CO, Marine detachment, HMS *Squall*, 36, HFAF.

KAITSWYRTH, BISHOP MILITANT CAHNYR, Army of God—a Chihirite of the Order of the Sword and ex-Temple Guard officer; CO, western column of the Army of God, invading the Republic of Siddarmark through Westmarch Province, MT&T; his command redesignated the Army of the Sylmahn, LAMA.

KARMAIKEL, COMMANDER WAHLTAYR, Imperial Charisian Navy—CO, 3rd Provisional Battalion, 1st Independent Marine Brigade (one of Hauwerd Breygart's Navy "battalions" at Thesmar), MT&T.

KARMAIKEL LIEUTENANT DYNTYN, Imperial Charisian Marines—Earl Hanth's personal aide, LAMA.

KARNYNKOH, CAPTAIN MAIKEL, Imperial Charisian Army—CO, Company A, 2nd Battalion, 12th Mounted Regiment, 6th Mounted Brigade, Imperial Charisian Army, LAMA.

KARSTAYRS, SERGEANT THOMYS, Army of God—regiment command sergeant, 191st Cavalry Regiment, MT&T.

KARTYR, MAJOR ZHON, Imperial Charisian Army—CO, 2nd Battalion, 8th Regiment, 4th Infantry Brigade, Imperial Charisian Army, LAMA.

KEELHAUL—Earl Lock Island's rottweiler, BSRA.

KESTAIR, MADAME AHRDYN—Archbishop Maikel Staynair's married daughter, BSRA.

KESTAIR, SIR LAIRYNC—Archbishop Maikel Staynair's son-in-law, BSRA.

KHAILEE, MASTER ROLF—a pseudonym used by Lord Avrahm Hywstyn, BSRA.

KHALRYN, FATHER FAILYX—Schuelerite upper-priest and inquisitor sent by Zhaspahr Clyntahn and Wyllym Rayno to support and lead the insurrection in Hildermoss Province, MT&T.

KHANSTYBYL, MAJOR EMAYT, Imperial Charisian Army—CO, 3rd Battalion, 6th Regiment, Imperial Charisian Army, LAMA.

KHAPAHR, COMMANDER AHLVYN, Royal Dohlaran Navy—effectively the Earl of Thirsk's chief of staff, HFAF.

KHARMYCH, FATHER AHBSAHLAHN—Archbishop Trumahn Rowzvel's intendant in Gorath. A Schuelerite, HFAF.

KHARYN, MAJOR FUMYRO, Imperial Charisian Army—CO, 3rd Battalion, 1st Scout Sniper Regiment, LAMA.

KHATTYR, CAPTAIN PAYT, Royal Emeraldian Navy—CO, galley *Black Prince*, OAR.

KHAYVN, MAJOR FUMYRO, Imperial Charisian Army—CO, 3rd Battalion, 1st Scout Sniper Regiment, Imperial Charisian Army, LAMA.

KHETTSYN, PRINCE STYVYN—Styvyn V, reigning prince of Sardahn, LAMA.

KHETTSYN, SIR RAHNYLD—Baron of Nearoak, Prince Styvyn V of Sardahn's cousin and first councilor, LAMA.

KHLUNAI, COLONEL RHANDYL, Imperial Charisian Army—General Ahlyn Symkyn's chief of staff under the new staff organization, MT&T.

KHOLMAN, DUKE OF—see Faigyn Makychee; see also Daivyn Bairaht.

KHOWSAN, CAPTAIN OF WINDS SHOUKHAN, Imperial Harchongese Navy—Count of Wind Mountain; CO, IHNS *Flower of Waters*, 50. Flag captain to the Duke of Sun Rising, HFAF.

KING CAYLEB II—see Cayleb Ahrmahk.

KING GORJAH III—see Gorjah Nyou.

KING HAARAHLD VII—see Haarahld Ahrmahk.

KING RAHNYLD IV—see Rahnyld Bahrns.

KING ZHAMES II—see Zhames Olyvyr Rayno.

KLAHRKSAIN, CAPTAIN TYMAHN, Imperial Charisian Navy—CO, HMS *Talisman*, 54, HFAF.

KLAIRYNCE, CAPTAIN HAINREE, Republic of Siddarmark Army—acting CO, 3rd Company, 37th Infantry Regiment, Republic of Siddarmark Army, MT&T.

KLYMYNT, MAJOR ZAHNDRU, Imperial Charisian Army—CO, 1st Battalion, 7th Regiment, 4th Infantry Brigade, Imperial Charisian Army, LAMA.

KLYNKSKAYL, SIR ZHERYD, Imperial Desnairian Army—Baronet Glynfyrd; CO, Glynfyrd's Regiment (light cavalry), cavalry wing, Army of Shiloh, LAMA.

KNOWLES, EVELYN—an Eve who escaped the destruction of the Alexandria Enclave and fled to Tellesberg, BSRA.

KNOWLES, JEREMIAH—an Adam who escaped the destruction of the Alexandria Enclave and fled to Tellesberg, where he became the patron and founder of the Brethren of Saint Zherneau, BSRA.

KOHLCHYST, BARON OF—see Vyktyr Tryntyn.

KOHRBY, MIDSHIPMAN LYNAIL, Royal Charisian Navy—senior midshipman, HMS *Dreadnought*, 54, OAR.

KRAHL, CAPTAIN AHNDAIR, Royal Dohlaran Navy—CO, HMS *Bédard*, 42, HFAF; promoted admiral, CO, Claw Island, LAMA.

KRESTMYN, COLONEL BYNZHAMYN, Army of God—CO, Mighty Host of God and the Archangels' Camp Number Four, Duchy of Gwynt, LAMA.

KRUGAIR, CAPTAIN MAIKEL, Imperial Charisian Navy—CO, HMS *Avalanche*, 36. POW of Earl Thirsk, surrendered to the Inquisition, HFAF.

KRUGHAIR, LIEUTENANT ZHASYN, Imperial Charisian Navy—second lieutenant, HMS *Dancer*, 56, HFAF.

KRYSTYPHYRSYN, ALYK—a manufactory supervisor and night-shift supervisor, the pistol and rifle shop, Delthak Works, LAMA.

KUHLBYRTSYN, CHIEF PETTY OFFICER MYRVYN, Imperial Charisian Navy—a senior noncom aboard ironclad HMS *Delthak*, 22, LAMA.

KULMYN, RHOBAIR, Canal Service—pump master, Fairkyn, New Northland Province, Republic of Siddarmark, MT&T.

KWAYLE, TYMYTHY, Imperial Charisian Navy—a senior petty officer and boatswain's mate, HMS *Destiny*, 54, HFAF.

KWILL, FATHER ZYTAN—upper-priest of the Order of Bédard; abbot of the Hospice of the Holy Bédard, the main homeless shelter in the city of Zion, HFAF.

KYLMAHN, LIEUTENANT DAIVYN, Imperial Charisian Navy—XO, broadside ironclad HMS *Thunderer*, 30, LAMA.

KYR, SIR GRAIM—Baron of Fyrnach, Duke Harless' senior aide; age twenty-seven in 896, dark hair, brown eyes, handsome in a somewhat flashy sort of way; cousin of the Duke of Traykhos and Harless' grandnephew, LAMA.

KYRBYSH, COLONEL BRYAHN—CO, 3rd Maidynberg Militia, Shilohian Temple Loyalist, assigned to Fort Tairys' garrison, LAMA.

KYRST, OWAIN—Temple Loyalist, mayor of Fairkyn, New Northland Province, Republic of Siddarmark, MT&T.

LACHLYN, COLONEL TAYLAR, Army of God—senior regimental commander, Chihiro Division, Army of Glacierheart, MT&T.

LADY MAIRAH LYWKYS—see Lady Mairah Lywkys Breygart, Countess Hanth.

LAHANG, BRAIDEE—Prince Nahrmahn of Emerald's chief agent in Charis before Merlin Athrawes' arrival there, OAR.

LAHFAT, CAPTAIN MYRGYN—piratical ruler of Claw Keep on Claw Island, HFAF.

LAHFTYN, MAJOR BRYAHN—Brigadier Clareyk's chief of staff, BSRA.

LAHKYRT, COLONEL ZHONATHYN, Royal Dohlaran Army—CO, Lahkyrt's Regiment (infantry), Royal Dohlaran Army, Dohlaran component, Army of Shiloh, LAMA.

LAHMBAIR, LIEUTENANT LYNYRD, Royal Dohlaran Navy—Lieutenant Henrai Sahltmyn's XO, Claw Island defensive batteries, LAMA.

LAHMBAIR, PARSAIVAHL—a prominent Corisandian greengrocer convicted of treason as part of the Northern Conspiracy, pardoned by Empress Sharleyan, HFAF.

LAHRAK, NAILYS—a senior leader of the Temple Loyalists in Charis, BSRA; complicit in attempt to assassinate Empress Sharleyan, BHD.

LAHSAHL, LIEUTENANT SHAIRMYN, Royal Charisian Navy—XO, HMS *Destroyer,* 54, BSRA.

LAICHARN, ARCHBISHOP PRAIDWYN—Archbishop of Siddar; the ranking prelate of the Republic of Siddarmark. A Langhornite, HFAF; archbishop in exile, MT&T.

LAIMHYN, FATHER CLYFYRD—Cayleb Ahrmahk's confessor and personal secretary, assigned to him by Archbishop Maikel, BSRA.

LAINYR, BISHOP EXECUTOR WYLSYNN—Bishop Executor of Gorath. A Langhornite, HFAF.

LAIRAYS, FATHER AWBRAI—under-priest of the Order of Schueler; HMS *Archangel Chihiro*'s ship's chaplain, HFAF.

LAIRMAHN, FAHSTAIR—Baron of Lakeland; first councilor of the Kingdom of Delferahk, HFAF.

LAIROH, COLONEL SIR ZHONATHYN, Royal Dohlaran Army—CO, Lairoh's Regiment (medium cavalry), Dohlaran component, Army of Shiloh, LAMA.

LAITEE, FATHER ZHAMES—priest of the Order of Schueler; assistant to Father Gaisbyrt Vandaik in Talkyra, HFAF.

LAITYR, FATHER ZHAIF—a Reformist upper-priest of the Order of Pasquale; senior priest, Church of the Holy Archangels Triumphant; a close personal friend of Father Tymahn Hahskans, HFAF.

LAKE LAND, DUKE OF—see Paitryk Mahknee.

LAKYR, SIR VYK, Royal Delferahkan Army—CO, Ferayd garrison, Kingdom of Delferahk, BSRA.

LANGHORNE, ERIC—chief administrator, Operation Ark, OAR.

LANSYR, CAPTAIN AVRAHM, Imperial Charisian Army—CO, Company B, 1st Battalion, 9th Mounted Regiment, 5th Mounted Brigade, Imperial Charisian Army, LAMA.

LARCHROS, BARON OF—see Rahzhyr Mairwyn.

LARCHROS, BARONESS OF—see Raichenda Mairwyn.

LATHYK, RHOBAIR, Imperial Charisian Navy—lieutenant, XO, HMS *Destiny*, 54, BSRA; promoted captain, CO, HMS *Destiny*, 54; Sir Dunkyn Yairley's flag captain, MT&T.

LATTYMYR, CAPTAIN SIR LYNKYN, Royal Dohlaran Army—Sir Rainos Ahlverez' senior aide-de-camp, LAMA.

LATTYMYR, COLONEL KAHLYNS—CO, 23rd Regiment, Shilohian Temple Loyalist militia, assigned to the Fort Tairys garrison, LAMA.

LAYBRAHN, BAHRYND—Paitryk Hainree's alias, HFAF.

LAYN, ZHIM, Royal Charisian Marines—lieutenant, Major Kynt Clareyk's aide, OAR; major, senior training officer, Helen Island Marine base, BHD; colonel, CO, Helen Island Marine base, HFAF.

LEKTOR, ADMIRAL SIR TARYL—Earl of Tartarian; CO, Royal Corisandian Navy under Prince Hektor during Corisande Campaign; BSRA; Earl Anvil Rock's main ally since Hektor's death, member of Prince Daivyn's Regency Council, AMF.

LESKYR, BYNNO—Temple Loyalist, mayor of Ohlarn, New Northland Province, Republic of Siddarmark, MT&T.

LOCK ISLAND, EARL OF—see Bryahn Lock Island.

LOCK ISLAND, HIGH ADMIRAL BRYAHN, Imperial Charisian Navy—Earl of Lock Island; CO, Imperial Charisian Navy. Cayleb Ahrmahk's cousin, OAR; KIA Battle of the Gulf of Tarot, AMF.

LOHGYN, MAHRAK—a Temple Loyalist mountain clansman from the Gray Wall Mountains; one of Zhan Fyrmahn's cousins, MT&T.

LOPAYZ, MAJOR BEHZNYK, Imperial Charisian Army—CO, 4th Battalion, 10th Mounted Regiment, 5th Mounted Brigade, Imperial Charisian Army, LAMA.

LORD PROTECTOR GREYGHOR—see Greyghor Stohnar.

LOWAYL, MAJOR FRAHNK, Imperial Charisian Army—senior engineer, 1st Brigade (reinforced) and Army of the Branaths, LAMA.

LYAM, ARCHBISHOP—see Archbishop Lyam Tyrn.

LYBYRN, FATHER GHATFRYD—Schuelerite under-priest; senior clergyman, Ohlarn, New Northland Province, Republic of Siddarmark, MT&T.

LYCAHN, PRIVATE ZHEDRYK, Imperial Charisian Marine Corps—a Marine private in Brigadier Taisyn's forces in Glacierheart; ex-poacher and thief, MT&T.

LYNDAHR, SIR RAIMYND—Prince Hektor of Corisande's keeper of the purse, BSRA; Prince Daivyn's Regency Council in the same capacity; an ally of Earl Anvil Rock and Earl Tartarian, AMF.

LYNKYN, ARCHBISHOP ULYS—Archbishop of Chisholm, replacing the murdered Archbishop Pawal Braynair, MT&T.

LYNKYN, SIR ADULFO—Duke of Black Water; son of Sir Ernyst Lynkyn, HFAF.

LYNKYN, SIR ERNYST, Corisandian Navy—Duke of Black Water, CO, Corisandian Navy; KIA Battle of Darcos Sound, OAR.

LYNTYN, MAJOR CAHNYR, Imperial Charisian Army—CO, 4th Battalion, 6th Mounted Regiment, 3rd Mounted Brigade, Imperial Charisian Army, LAMA.

LYPTAKIA, MAJOR GHORDYN, Imperial Charisian Army—CO, 3rd Battalion, 12th Mounted Regiment, 6th Mounted Brigade, Imperial Charisian Army, LAMA.

LYWKYS, LADY MAIRAH—see Lady Mairah Lywkys Breygart.

LYWKYS, SERGEANT REHGNYLD, Royal Dohlaran Army—platoon sergeant, 3rd Platoon, 1st Company, Ahzbyrn's Regiment (cavalry), Dohlaran component, Army of Shiloh (cavalry), LAMA.

LYWSHAI, SHAINTAI—Trumyn Lywshai's Harchong-born father, MT&T.

LYWSHAI, TRUMYN—Sir Dunkyn Yairley's secretary, HFAF.

LYWYS, DOCTOR SAHNDRAH—senior chemist of the Royal College of Charis, HFAF; member of Charisian inner circle, MT&T.

LYWYS, SIR SHAILTYN—Baron of Climbhaven, Duke Harless' senior artillerist, LAMA.

LYWYSTYN, CAPTAIN KRYSTYPHYR, Royal Dohlaran Navy—XO, Claw Island, LAMA.

MAB, SEIJIN DIALYDD—one of Merlin Athrawes' alternate identities, created especially for reprisals against the Inquisition, LAMA.

MAGWAIR, VICAR ALLAYN—Captain General, Council of Vicars; one of the so-called Group of Four, OAR.

MAHCLYNTAHK, MAJOR ZHAIKYB—CO, 3rd Company, 1st Glacierheart Volunteers, LAMA.

MAHFYT, BRAHDLAI, Imperial Charisian Navy—ironclad HMS Delthak, 22; Halcom Bahrns' personal coxswain, LAMA.

MAHGAIL, CAPTAIN BYRT, Delferahkan Royal Guard—a company commander, Telkyra Palace, HFAF.

MAHGAIL, CAPTAIN RAIF, Imperial Charisian Navy—CO, HMS *Dancer*, 56. Sir Gwylym Manthyr's flag captain, HFAF.

MAHGAIL, COLONEL PAYT, Royal Dohlaran Army—CO, Mahgail's Regiment (cavalry), Dohlaran component, Army of Shiloh, LAMA.

MAHGAIL, LIEUTENANT BRYNDYN, Imperial Charisian Marines—senior Marine officer assigned to Sarm River operation, HFAF.

MAHGAIL, MAJOR KYNAHN, Imperial Charisian Army—CO, 4th Battalion, 7th Regiment, 4th Infantry Brigade, Imperial Charisian Army, LAMA.

MAHGAIL, MASTER GARAM, Imperial Charisian Navy— carpenter, HMS *Destiny*, 54, HFAF.

MAHGENTEE, MIDSHIPMAN MAHRAK, Royal Charisian Navy—senior midshipman, HMS *Typhoon*, OAR.

MAHGRUDYR, PRIVATE TYMYTHY, Imperial Charisian Army—2nd Platoon, Company B, 1st Battalion, 9th Mounted Regiment, 5th Mounted Brigade, Imperial Charisian Army, LAMA.

MAHGYRS, COLONEL ALLAYN, Republic of Siddarmark Army—General Fronz Tylmahn's senior Siddarmarkian subordinate in support of Captain Halcom Bahrns' operation ("Great Canal Raid"), MT&T.

MAHKAID, MAJOR PAITYR, Royal Dohlaran Army—CO, 2nd Company, Ahzbyrn's Regiment (cavalry), Dohlaran component, Army of Shiloh, LAMA.

MAHKBYTH, LIEUTENANT AHMBROHS, Imperial Charisian Navy—first lieutenant, broadside ironclad HMS *Rottweiler*, 30, LAMA.

MAHKDUGYL, MAJOR ZHERYLD, Republic of Siddarmark Militia—CO, 1st Company, 1st Glacierheart Volunteers, LAMA.

MAHKELYN, LIEUTENANT RHOBAIR, Royal Charisian Navy—fourth lieutenant, HMS *Destiny*, 54, BSRA.

MAHKGRUDYR, SAIRAHS, Siddarmarkian Canal Service— Temple Loyalist canal pilot working to repair the damage done during the Great Canal Raid, LAMA.

MAHKHAL, BISHOP ZHAKSYN, Army of God—CO, Port Harbor Division, Army of the Sylmahn, LAMA.

MAHKHOM, WAHLYS—Glacierheart trapper turned guerrilla; leader of the Reformist forces in the Gray Wall Mountains, MT&T.

MAHKHYNROH, BISHOP KAISI—Bishop of Manchyr for the Church of Charis, HFAF.

MAHKLUSKEE, MAJOR AHRYN, Imperial Charisian Army—XO, 8th Regiment, 4th Infantry Brigade, Imperial Charisian Army, LAMA.

MAHKLYMORH, MAJOR DYNNYS, Imperial Charisian Army—CO, 1st Battalion, 2nd Scout Sniper Regiment, Imperial Charisian Army, LAMA.

MAHKLYMORH, MAJOR KHEEFYR, Imperial Charisian Army—CO, 2nd Battalion, 9th Mounted Regiment, 5th Mounted Brigade, Imperial Charisian Army, LAMA.

MAHKLYN, AHNGAZ—Sir Domynyk Staynair's valet, HFAF.

MAHKLYN, DOCTOR RAHZHYR—chancellor of the Royal College of Charis, OAR; member of Charisian inner circle, BSRA.

MAHKLYN, TOHMYS—Rahzhyr Mahklyn's unmarried son, BSRA.

MAHKLYN, YSBET—Rahzhyr Mahklyn's deceased wife, BSRA.

MAHKNARHMA, MAJOR SIR SYMYN, Imperial Desnairian Army—XO, Glynfyrd's Regiment (light cavalry), cavalry wing, Army of Shiloh, LAMA.

MAHKNASH, SERGEANT BRAICE, Royal Delferahkan Army—one of Colonel Aiphraim Tahlyvyr's squad leaders, HFAF.

MAHKNEE, PAITRYK—Duke of Lake Land, MT&T.

MAHKNEE, SYMYN—Paitryk Mahknee's uncle, MT&T.

MAHKNEEL, CAPTAIN HAUWYRD, Royal Delferahkan Navy—CO, galley *Arrowhead,* Delferahkan Navy, BSRA.

MAHKSWAIL, COLONEL CLAIRDON, Army of God—Bishop Militant Bahrnabai's senior aide and effective chief of staff, LAMA.

MAHKWYRTYR, COLONEL PAIDRHO, Royal Dohlaran Army—CO, Mahkwyrtyr's · Regiment (infantry), Dohlaran component, Army of Shiloh, LAMA.

MAHKYNTY, MAJOR AHRNAHLD, Republic of Siddarmark Army—CO, 4th Company, 37th Infantry Regiment, Republic of Siddarmark Army, MT&T.

MAHLDAN, BROTHER STAHN—a Reformist sexton in Siddar City; Order of the Quill, HFAF.

MAHLDYN, BYRTRYM—Baron Gray Hill; replacement on Prince Daivyn's Regency Council in Corisande for the Earl of Craggy Hill after Craggy Hill's execution for treason for his part in the Northern Conspiracy, MT&T.

MAHLDYN, COLONEL PHYLYP, Republic of Siddarmark Army—CO, 110th Infantry Regiment, Republic of Siddarmark Army; acting CO, Fort Sheldyn, South March Lands, MT&T.

MAHLDYN, FHRANKLYN—Taigys and Mathylda's youngest son, admitted to Royal College, MT&T.

MAHLDYN, GAHLVYN—apprentice furnace man, Delthak Works; Taigys and Mathylda's middle son, LAMA.

MAHLDYN, LIEUTENANT ZHAMES, Imperial Charisian Navy—XO, HMS *Squall*, 36, HFAF.

MAHLDYN, MATHYLDA—Taigys Mahldyn's wife, MT&T.

MAHLDYN, PETTY OFFICER ZOSH, Imperial Charisian Navy—Taigys and Mathylda's oldest son, MT&T.

MAHLDYN, TAIGYS—Delthak Works pistol shop supervisor and inventor or centerfire cartridge, MT&T; inventor of bolt action magazine rifle and chief small arms designer, Delthak Works, LAMA.

MAHLLYSYN, MAJOR MYTCHAIL, Imperial Charisian Army—CO, 1st Battalion, 6th Mounted Regiment, 3rd Mounted Brigade, Imperial Charisian Army, LAMA.

MAHLRY, LIEUTENANT RHOLYND, Royal Emeraldian Navy—a lieutenant aboard galley *Black Prince*, OAR.

MAHLYK, STYWYRT—Dunkyn Yairley's personal coxswain, BSRA.

MAHNDRAYN, COMMANDER URVYN, Imperial Charisian Navy—CO, Experimental Board, Commodore Seamount's senior assistant, HFAF.

MAHNDYR, EARL OF—see Gharth Rahlstahn.

MAHNTAIN, CAPTAIN TOHMYS, Imperial Desnairian Navy—CO, HMS *Blessed Warrior*, 40, HFAF.

MAHNTAYL, TAHDAYO—usurper Earl of Hanth, OAR.

MAHNTEE, LIEUTENANT CHARLZ, Royal Dohlaran Navy—XO, HMS *Rakurai*, 46, HFAF.

MAHNTSAHLO, CORPORAL LAHZRYS, Imperial Charisian Army—squad leader, 3rd Squad, 1st Platoon, Company B, 1st Battalion, 1st Scout Sniper Regiment, Imperial Charisian Army, LAMA.

MAHNTYN, CORPORAL AILAS, Imperial Charisian Marines—a scout sniper assigned to Sergeant Edvarhd Wystahn's platoon, BSRA.

MAHNYNG, MAJOR CLYNTAHN, Imperial Charisian Army—CO, 2nd Battalion, 6th Mounted Regiment, 3rd Mounted Brigade, Imperial Charisian Army, LAMA.

MAHRAK, LIEUTENANT RAHNALD, Royal Charisian Navy—first lieutenant, HMS *Royal Charis*, OAR.

MAHRAK, MAJOR ZHEFRY, Imperial Charisian Army—CO, 4th Battalion, 12th Mounted Regiment, 6th Mounted Brigade, Imperial Charisian Army, LAMA.

MAHRCELYAN, COLONEL AHNDRU, Royal Dohlaran Army—CO, Mahrcelyan's Regiment (infantry), Dohlaran component, Army of Shiloh, LAMA.

MAHRLOW, BISHOP EXECUTOR AHRAIN—Archbishop Zahmsyn Halmyn's executive assistant, Archbishopric of Gorath, Kingdom of Dohlar, HFAF.

MAHRLOW, FATHER ARTHYR—priest of the Order of Schueler; assistant to Father Gaisbyrt Vandaik in Talkyra, HFAF.

MAHRTYN, ADMIRAL GAHVYN—Baron of White Ford; senior officer, Royal Tarotisian Navy, OAR; admiral, Imperial Charisian Navy, HFAF; port admiral, Bedard Bay, Siddarmark, MT&T.

MAHRTYN, COLONEL THE HONORABLE FAYDOHR, Royal Dohlaran Army—CO, Mahrtyn's Division (infantry), Dohlaran component, Army of Shiloh; CO, Brahnselyk garrison, LAMA.

MAHRTYN, MAJOR LAIRAYS, Imperial Charisian Marines—CO, 2nd Provisional Battalion, 1st Independent Marine Brigade, LAMA.

MAHRTYNSYN, LIEUTENANT LAIZAIR, Imperial Desnairian Navy—XO, HMS *Archangel Chihiro*, 40, HFAF.

MAHRYS, CORPORAL ZHAK "ZHAKKY"—a member of Prince Daivyn Daykyn's Royal Guard in exile (Tobys Raimair's junior noncom), HFAF; Royal Corisandian Guard, the junior noncom on Irys' personal detail, LAMA.

MAHRYS, ZHERYLD—Sir Rayjhis Dragoner's senior secretary and aide, BSRA.

MAHSTYRS, PRIVATE ZHUSTYN, Royal Dohlaran Army—3rd Company, Wykmyn's Regiment (light cavalry), Dohlaran component, Army of Shiloh, LAMA.

MAHZYNGAIL, COLONEL VYKTYR, Republic of Siddarmark Militia—CO, 14th South March Militia Regiment, Fort Sheldyn, South March Lands, MT&T.

MAHZYNGAIL, LIEUTENANT AHBRAIM, Imperial Charisian Army—CO, 2nd Platoon, Company B, 2nd Battalion, 6th Regiment, Imperial Charisian Army.

MAHZYNGAIL, LIEUTENANT HAARLAHM, Imperial Charisian Navy—High Admiral Rock Point's flag secretary, HFAF.

MAIB, MAJOR EDMYND, Army of God—CO, 20th Artillery Regiment, senior officer present, Ohlarn, New Northland Province, Republic of Siddarmark, MT&T.

MAIDYN, LORD HENRAI—chancellor of the exchequer, Republic of Siddarmark, HFAF.

MAIGEE, CAPTAIN GRAYGAIR, Royal Dohlaran Navy—CO, galleon HMS *Guardian*, BSRA.

MAIGEE, PLATOON SERGEANT ZHAK, Imperial Charisian Marines—senior noncom, Second Platoon, Alpha Company, 1/3rd Marines (1st Battalion, 3rd Brigade), Imperial Charisian Marines, HFAF.

MAIGOWHYN, LIEUTENANT BRAHNDYN, Royal Delferahkan Army—Colonel Aiphraim Tahlyvyr's aide, HFAF.

MAIGWAIR, CORPORAL STAHNYZLAHAS—Temple Loyalist rebel, garrison of Fort Darymahn, South March Lands, Republic of Siddarmark, MT&T.

MAIGWAIR, VICAR ALLAYN—Captain General of the Church of God Awaiting; one of the so-called Group of Four, BSRA.

MAIK, BISHOP STAIPHAN—a Schuelerite auxiliary bishop of the Church of God Awaiting; effectively intendant for the Royal Dohlaran Navy in the Church's name, HFAF.

MAIKEL, CAPTAIN QWENTYN, Royal Dohlaran Navy—CO, galley HMS *Gorath Bay*, OAR.

MAIKELSYN, LIEUTENANT LEEAHM, Royal Tarotisian Navy—first lieutenant, galley HMS *King Gorjah II*, OAR.

MAIKSYN, BRIGADIER ZHORJ, Imperial Charisian Army—CO, 1st Brigade, Imperial Charisian Army, LAMA.

MAIKSYN, COLONEL LYWYS—CO, 3rd Saiknyr Militia Regiment; a Temple Loyalist who joined the Sword of Schueler in the Sylmahn Gap, MT&T.

MAINDAYL, COLONEL WYLSYNN, Army of God—Bishop Militant Cahnyr Kaitswyrth's chief of staff, LAMA.

MAIRNAIR, LIEUTENANT TOBYS, Imperial Charisian Navy—XO, ironclad HMS *Hador*, 22, MT&T.

MAIRWYN, RAHZHYR—Baron of Larchros; a member of the Northern Conspiracy in Corisande, executed for treason, HFAF.

MAIRWYN, RAICHENDA—Baroness of Larchros; wife of Rahzhyr Mairwyn, HFAF.

MAIRYAI, COLONEL SPYNCYR, Army of God—CO, 2nd Regiment, Langhorne Division, Army of the Sylmahn, MT&T.

MAIRYDYTH, LIEUTENANT NEVYL, Royal Dohlaran Navy—first lieutenant, galley HMS *Royal Bédard*, OAR.

MAITLYND, CAPTAIN ZHORJ, Imperial Charisian Navy—CO, HMS *Victorious*, 56, HFAF.

MAITZLYR, CAPTAIN FAIDOHRAV, Imperial Desnairian Navy—CO, HMS *Loyal Defender*, 48, HFAF.

MAIYR, CAPTAIN ZHAKSYN—one of Colonel Sir Wahlys Zhorj's troop commanders in Tahdayo Mahntayl's service, BSRA.

MAIYRS, MAJOR TYMAHN, Corisandian Royal Guard—senior officer, Corisandian Royal Guard, LAMA.

MAIZUR, KHANSTANC—Maikel Staynair's cook, MT&T.

MAKAIVYR, BRIGADIER ZHOSH, Royal Charisian Marines—CO, 1st Brigade, Royal Charisian Marines, BSRA.

MAKFERZAHN, ZHAMES—one of Prince Hektor's agents in Charis, OAR.

MAKGREGAIR, FATHER ZHOSHUA—Vicar Zahmsyn Trynair's special representative to Tarot, OAR.

MAKKBYRN, GENERAL SIR TAMYS, Imperial Charisian Army—CO, 7th Infantry Division, 2nd Corps, Army of Cliff Peak, LAMA.

MAKSTYVYNS, MAJOR DUGAHLD, Imperial Charisian Army—CO, 2nd Battalion, 1st Scout Sniper Regiment, Imperial Charisian Army, LAMA.

MAKYCHEE, FAIGYN—Duke Kholman; raised to Duke Kholman following Daivyn Bairaht's defeat in Battle of Iythria and flight to Charis, LAMA.

MAKYN, COLONEL AHLYSTAIR, Imperial Charisian Army—CO, 1st Scout Sniper Regiment, Imperial Charisian Army, LAMA.

MAKYNTYR, COLONEL AHLFRYD, Royal Dohlaran Army—Sir Rainos Ahlverez's senior artillery specialist, LAMA.

MAKYSAK, LIEUTENANT ZHAIF, Imperial Charisian Army—CO, 1st Platoon, Company B, 1st Battalion, 1st Scout Sniper Regiment, Imperial Charisian Army, LAMA.

MAKYSAK, PRIVATE BYNZHAMYN, Imperial Charisian Army—1st Platoon, Company A, 1st Battalion, 5th Regiment, Imperial Charisian Army, LAMA.

MALIKAI, DUKE OF—see Faidel Ahlverez.

MALKAIHY, COMMANDER DAHRAIL, Imperial Charisian Navy—Captain Ahldahs Rahzwail's senior assistant; senior liaison between the Bureau of Ordnance and Sir Dustyn Olyvyr, MT&T; CO, Bureau of Engineering when it is formally organized, LAMA.

MANTHYR, SIR GWYLYM—Royal Charisian Navy, captain, CO, galleon HMS *Dreadnought*, 54; Cayleb Ahrmahk's flag captain, OAR; Imperial Charisian Navy, commodore, BHD; admiral, CO, Charisian expedition to Gulf of Dohlar, POW, AMF; surrendered to Inquisition and executed, HFAF.

MARDHAR, COLONEL ZHANDRU, Army of God—CO, 191st Cavalry Regiment, Army of Glacierheart, MT&T.

MARGO, DUKE OF—see Sir Bairmon Chahlmair.

MARSHYL, MIDSHIPMAN ADYM, Royal Charisian Navy—senior midshipman, galley HMS *Royal Charis*, OAR.

MASTER DOMNEK—King Haarahld VII's Harchongese court arms master, OAR.

MASTYRS, LIEUTENANT ZHON, Royal Dohlaran Army—one of Colonel Ohygyns' aides, LAMA.

MASTYRSYN, CAPTAIN SYMYN, Imperial Charisian Navy—CO, broadside ironclad HMS *Rottweiler*, 30, LAMA.

MATHYSYN, BRIGADIER ZHAMES, Imperial Charisian Army—Co, 4th Infantry Brigade, Imperial Charisian Army, assigned Thesmar, LAMA.

MATHYSYN, LIEUTENANT ZHAIKEB, Royal Dohlaran Navy—first lieutenant, galley HMS *Gorath Bay*, OAR.

MATTHYSAHN, AHBUKYRA, Imperial Charisian Navy—signalman, ironclad HMS *Delthak*, 22, MT&T.

MAYLYR, CAPTAIN DUNKYN, Royal Charisian Navy—CO, galley HMS *Halberd*, OAR.

MAYSAHN, ZHASPAHR—Prince Hektor's senior agent in Charis, OAR.

MAYTHIS, LIEUTENANT FRAIZHER, Royal Corisandian Navy—true name of Captain Wahltayr Seatown, OAR.

MEDGYRS, COLONEL LAINYL, Imperial Charisian Army—CO, 28th Infantry Regiment, 14th Infantry Brigade, 7th Infantry Division, Imperial Charisian Army, LAMA.

METZLYR, FATHER PAIRAIK—an upper-priest of Schueler; General Sir Fahstyr Rychtyr's special intendant, MT&T.

METZYGYR, MASTER HAHNDYL—a senior master of the Gunmaker's Guild in Gorath, LAMA.

MHARDYR, SYLVYST—Baron Stoneheart; current Lord Justice of Chisholm, replacing Braisyn Byrns, MT&T.

MHARTYN, COLONEL DAHGLYS—former Republic of Siddarmark captain, CO, 6th Regiment, a regular regiment which went over to the Sword of Schueler; second-ranking officer, Fort Tairys garrison, LAMA.

MHARTYN, MAJOR ABSHAIR, Imperial Charisian Army—CO, 3rd Battalion, 4th Regiment, Imperial Charisian Army, MT&T.

MHARTYN, MAJOR LAIRAYS, Imperial Charisian Marines—CO, 2nd Provisional Battalion, 1st Independent Marine Brigade, Thesmar, MT&T.

MHATTSYN, PETTY OFFICER LAISL, Imperial Charisian Navy—a gun captain in Lieutenant Yerek Sahbrahan's battery under Commander Hainz Watyrs in Glacierheart Province, MT&T.

MHULVAYN, OSKAHR—one of Prince Hektor's agents in Charis, OAR.

MKWARTYR, COLONEL MHARTYN, Imperial Charisian Army—senior engineer 2nd Brigade (reinforced) and Army of Midhold, LAMA.

MOHZLYR, MAJOR ZHAIRYMIAH, Imperial Charisian Army—CO, 2nd Battalion, 12th Mounted Regiment, 6th Mounted Brigade, Imperial Charisian Army, LAMA.

MULDAYAIR, COLONEL HAARAHLD, Imperial Charisian Army—CO, 1st Regiment, 1st Brigade, 1st Infantry Division, Imperial Charisian Army, LAMA.

MULLYGYN, SERGEANT RAHSKHO—a member of Prince Daivyn Daykyn's Royal Guard in exile (Tobys Raimair's second-ranking noncom), HFAF; sergeant, Royal Corisandian Guard, junior member of Prince Daivyn's personal detail, LAMA.

MURPHAI, *SEIJIN* ZHOZUAH—one of Merlin Athrawes' alternate identities; theoretically a spy stationed in the Temple Lands to keep an eye on events in Zion.

MYCHAIL, ALYX—Rhaiyan Mychail's oldest grandson, BSRA.

MYCHAIL, MYLDRYD—one of Rhaiyan Mychail's married granddaughters-in-law, BSRA.

MYCHAIL, RHAIYAN—a business partner of Ehdwyrd Howsmyn and the Kingdom of Charis' primary textile producer, OAR.

MYCHAIL, STYVYN—Myldryd Mychail's youngest son, BSRA.

MYKLAYN, ZHAIMYS, Canal Service—a senior canal pilot of the Siddarmarkian Canal Service assigned to assist Captain Halcom Bahrns, MT&T.

MYLLYR, ARCHBISHOP URVYN—Archbishop of Sodar, OAR.

MYLLYR, SIR PHYLYP, Royal Corisandian Army—one of Sir Koryn Gahrvai's regimental commanders, BSRA.

MYLZ, BRIGADIER ZHEBYDYAH, Imperial Charisian Army—CO, 2nd Brigade, Imperial Charisian Army, LAMA.

MYNDAIZ, CORPORAL RAYMAHNDOH, Army of God—2nd Platoon, 1st Company, 1st Regiment, Zion Division, Army of Glacierheart, LAMA.

MYRDOHK, MAJOR AHLZHERNOHN, Imperial Charisian Army—CO, 2nd Battalion, 11th Mounted Regiment, 6th Mounted Brigade, Imperial Charisian Army, LAMA.

MYRGAH, MAJOR ADULFO, Imperial Charisian Army—CO, 2nd Battalion, 7th Regiment, 4th Infantry Brigade, LAMA.

MYRGYN, SIR KEHVYN, Royal Corisandian Navy—CO, galley *Corisande*, Duke Black Water's flag captain, KIA Battle of Darcos Sound, OAR.

NAHRMAHN, LIEUTENANT FRONZ, Imperial Charisian Navy—second lieutenant, HMS *Destiny*, 54, MT&T.

NAIGAIL, SAMYL—son of a deceased Siddarmarkian sailmaker; Temple Loyalist and anti-Charisian bigot, HFAF; arrested and executed for murder, LAMA.

NAIKLOS, CAPTAIN FRAHNKLYN, Corisandian Guard—CO of Sir Koryn Gahrvai's headquarters company; later promoted to major, HFAF.

NAISMYTH, MAJOR CAHRTAIR, Imperial Charisian Army—CO, 2nd Battalion, 6th Regiment, Imperial Charisian Army, LAMA.

NARTH, BISHOP EXECUTOR TYRNYR—Archbishop Failyx Gahrbor's executive assistant, Archbishopric of Tarot, HFAF.

NAVYZ, WYLFRYD—Siddarmarkian Temple Loyalist guide

attached to General Sir Fahstyr Rychtyr's Dohlaran invasion column, MT&T.

NEAROAK, BARON OF—see Sir Rahnyld Khettsyn.

NEAROAK, EARL OF—see Sir Abshair Hyrst.

NETHAUL, HAIRYM—XO, privateer schooner *Blade*, BSRA.

NEWYL, CAPTAIN ELWYN, Imperial Charisian Army—personal aide of Brigadier Sir Laimyn Seacatcher; CO, 5th Mounted Brigade, Imperial Charisian Army, LAMA.

NOHRCROSS, BISHOP MAILVYN—Bishop of Barcor for the Church of Charis; a member of the Northern Conspiracy in Corisande, executed for treason, HFAF.

NORTH COAST, EARL OF—see Edwair Garthin.

NYBAR, BISHOP GORTHYK, Army of God—CO, Langhorne Division; Bishop Militant Bahrnabai Wyrshym's senior division commander, MT&T.

NYLZ, KOHDY—commodore, Royal Charisian Navy, CO of one of High Admiral Lock Island's galley squadrons, OAR; admiral, Imperial Charisian Navy, BSRA; senior squadron commander, HFAF.

NYOU, GORJAH ALYKSAHNDAR—King Gorjah III, King of Tarot, OAR; swears fealty to Cayleb and Sharleyan Ahrmahk, HFAF.

NYOU, MAIYL—Queen Consort of Tarot; wife of Gorjah Nyou, HFAF.

NYOU, PRINCE RHOLYND—Crown Prince of Tarot; infant son of Gorjah and Maiyl Nyou; heir to the Tarotisian throne, HFAF.

NYTZAH, CORPORAL DAIVYN, Army of God—2nd Platoon, 1st Company, 1st Regiment, Zion Division, Army of Glacierheart, LAMA.

NYXYN, DAIVYN, Royal Delferahkan Army—a dragoon assigned to Sergeant Braice Mahknash's squad, HFAF.

OARMASTER, SYGMAHN, Royal Charisian Marines—a member of Crown Prince Cayleb's bodyguard, OAR.

OBAIRN, PRIVATE ZHYNKYNS, Royal Dohlaran Army—2nd Section, 3rd Platoon, 1st Company, Ahzbyrn's Regiment (cavalry), Dohlaran component, Army of Shiloh, LAMA.

OHAHLYRN, CAPTAIN MERYT, Imperial Charisian Army—CO, Company C, 3rd Battalion, 10th Mounted Regiment, 5th Mounted Brigade, LAMA.

OHCAHNYR, LIEUTENANT CHARLZ, Imperial Desnairian Army—CO, 2nd Platoon, 3rd Company, Bahskym's Regiment, Army of Shiloh, LAMA.

OHDWIAR, COLONEL MAHTHYW, Royal Dohlaran Army—CO, Ohdwiar's Regiment (infantry), Dohlaran component, Army of Shiloh, LAMA.

OHKARLYN, COLONEL BRYAHN, Royal Dohlaran Army—CO, Ohkarlyn's Regiment (cavalry), Dohlaran component, Army of Shiloh, LAMA.

OHLSYN, TRAHVYS—Earl Pine Hollow, Prince Nahrmahn Baytz' cousin, first councilor of Emerald, OAR; first councilor of the Charisian Empire and member Charisian inner circle, HFAF.

OMAHR, GRAND DUKE OF—see Yitangzhi Gengchai.

OHYGYNS, COLONEL SIR BRAHDFYRD, Royal Dohlaran Army—CO, Ohygyns' Regiment (infantry), Dohlaran component, Army of Shiloh; CO, Roymark garrison, LAMA.

OLYVYR, AHNYET—Sir Dustyn Olyvyr's wife, OAR.

OLYVYR, SIR DUSTYN—senior naval constructor and designer, Royal Charisian Navy, OAR; senior naval constructor, Imperial Charisian Navy, BSRA; member Charisian inner circle, HFAF.

ORAISTYS, LIEUTENANT RYDOLF, Army of God—CO, 1st Platoon, Company A, 191st Cavalry Regiment, Army of Glacierheart, LAMA.

OVYRTYN, COLONEL LUDYVYK, Imperial Charisian Army—CO, 8th Regiment, 4th Infantry Brigade, Imperial Charisian Army, LAMA.

OWL—Nimue Alban's AI, based on the manufacturer's acronym: Ordones-Westinghouse-Lytton RAPIER Tactical Computer, Mark 17a, OAR.

PAHLMAHN, ZHULYIS—a Corisandian banker convicted of treason as part of the Northern Conspiracy, pardoned by Empress Sharleyan, HFAF.

PAHLMAIR, COLONEL BRYNTYN, Army of God—CO, 53rd Cavalry Regiment, Army of the Sylmahn, LAMA.

PAHLOAHZKY, PRIVATE SHYMAN, Army of God—2nd Platoon, 1st Company, 1st Regiment, Zion Division, Army of Glacierheart, LAMA.

PAHLZAR, COLONEL AHKYLLYS—Sir Charlz Doyal's replacement as Sir Koryn Gahrvai's senior artillery commander, BSRA.

PAHRAIHA, COLONEL VAHSAG, Imperial Charisian Marines—CO, 14th Marine Regiment, HFAF.

PAHRSAHN, AIVAH—Nynian Rychtair's public persona in the Republic of Siddarmark, HFAF.

PAHSKAIL, COLONEL AHLBAIR, Royal Dohlaran Army—CO, Pahskail's Regiment (infantry), Dohlaran component, Army of Shiloh, LAMA.

PAHSKAL, MASTER MIDSHIPMAN FAYDOHR, Imperial Charisian Navy—a midshipman assigned to HMS *Dawn Star*, 58, HFAF.

PAHTKOVAIR, FATHER ZOHANNES—Schuelerite intendant of Siddar, HFAF.

PAIRMYN, MAJOR TOBYS, Imperial Charisian Army—CO, 3rd Battalion, 6th Mounted Regiment, 3rd Mounted Brigade, Imperial Charisian Army, LAMA.

PARKAIR, ADYM—Weslai Parkair's eldest son and heir, MT&T.

PARKAIR, COLONEL SIR PAWAL, Imperial Desnairian Army—CO, Parkair's Regiment (heavy cavalry), cavalry wing, Army of Shiloh, LAMA.

PARKAIR, LORD DARYUS—seneschal, Republic of Siddarmark, HFAF.

PARKAIR, WESLAI—Lord Shairncross; Lord of Clan Shairncross and head of the Council of Clan Lords, Raven's Land, MT&T.

PARKAIR, ZHAIN—Lady Shairncross, Weslai Parkair's wife, MT&T.

PARKAIR, ZHANAIAH—Daryus Parkair's wife, HFAF.

PARKYR, COMMANDER AHRTHYR, Imperial Charisian Navy—Hauwerd Breygart's senior Navy artillerist at Thesmar, MT&T.

PARKYR, FATHER EDWYRD—upper-priest of the Order of Bédard; named by Archbishop Klairmant to succeed Father Tymahn at Saint Kathryn's Church, MT&T.

PARKYR, GLAHDYS—Crown Princess Alahnah's Chisholmian wet nurse and nanny, HFAF.

PAWAL, CAPTAIN ZHON, Imperial Charisian Navy—CO, HMS *Dart*, 54, HFAF.

PAWALSYN, AHLVYNO—Baron Ironhill, Keeper of the Purse (treasurer) of the Kingdom of Charis and later of the Empire of Charis, a member of Cayleb Ahrmahk's council, BSRA.

PAWALSYN, MAJOR SAMYL, Imperial Charisian Army—XO, 6th Mounted Regiment, 3rd Mounted Brigade, Imperial Charisian Army, LAMA.

PEI, ADMIRAL KAU-ZHI, Terran Federation Navy—CO, Operation Breakaway; older brother of Commodore Pei Kau-yung, OAR.

PEI, COMMODORE KAU-YUNG, Terran Federation Navy—CO, Operation Ark final escort, OAR.

PEI, DOCTOR SHAN-WEI, PH.D.—Commodore Pei Kauyung's wife; senior terraforming expert for Operation Ark, OAR.

PEZKYVY, MAJOR AHNDRAIR, Army of God—XO, 191st Cavalry Regiment, Army of Glacierheart, LAMA.

PEZKYVYR, MAJOR AHNDRAI, Army of God—XO, 191st Cavalry Regiment, MT&T.

PHALGRAIN, SIR HARVAI—majordomo, Imperial Palace, Cherayth, HFAF.

PHANDYS, CAPTAIN KHANSTAHNZO—an officer of the Temple Guard, assigned to head Vicar Rhobair Duchairn's bodyguard, HFAF.

PHONDA, MADAM AHNZHELYK—proprietor of one of the City of Zion's most discreet brothels (an alias of Nynian Rychtair), OAR.

PINE HOLLOW, EARL OF—see Trahvys Ohlsyn.

PLYZYK, CAPTAIN EHRNYSTO, Imperial Desnairian Navy—CO, HMS *Saint Adulfo*, 40, HFAF.

POHSTAZHIAN, BISHOP AHDRAIS, Army of God—CO, Sulyvyn Division, Army of Glacierheart, LAMA.

PORTYR, COMMANDER DAIVYN, Imperial Charisian Navy—CO, 4th Provisional Battalion, 1st Independent Marine Brigade (one of Hauwerd Breygart's Navy "battalions" at Thesmar), MT&T.

PORTYR, MAJOR DANYEL, Imperial Charisian Marines—CO, 1st Battalion, 3rd Regiment, 3rd Brigade, HFAF.

POTTYR, MAHLYK—lockmaster, Sarkyn, Tairohn Hills, Princedom of Sardahn, LAMA.

POTTYR, MAJOR HAINREE, Imperial Charisian Army—CO, 4th Battalion, 4th Regiment, Imperial Charisian Army, MT&T.

POWAIRS, COLONEL ALLAYN, Imperial Charisian Army—chief of staff, 2nd Brigade (reinforced), Imperial Charisian Army, Army of Midhold, LAMA.

PRAIETO, LIEUTENANT ORLYNOH, Army of God—CO, Battery B, 20th Artillery Regiment, Ohlarn, New Northland Province, Republic of Siddarmark, MT&T.

PRAIGYR, STAHLMAN—one of Ehdwyrd Howsmyn's senior artificers, particularly involved with the development of steam engines, MT&T.

PRESKYT, BISHOP QWENTYN, Army of God—CO, St. Fraidyr Division, Army of the Sylmahn, LAMA.

PRESKYT, MAJOR SIR ALYKZHANDYR, Royal Dohlaran Army—CO, 3rd Company, Wykmyn's Regiment (light cavalry), Dohlaran component, Army of Shiloh, LAMA.

PRINCE CAYLEB—see Cayleb Ahrmahk.

PRINCE DAIVYN—see Daivyn Dahnyld Mharak Zoshya Daykyn.

PRINCE HEKTOR—see Hektor Daykyn.

PRINCE NAHRMAHN II—see Nahrmahn Baytz.

PRINCE NAHRMAHN GAREYT—see Nahrmahn Gareyt Baytz.

PRINCE RHOLYND—see Rholynd Nyou.

PRINCE STYVYN—see Styvyn Khettsyn.

PRINCE TRAHVYS—see Trahvys Baytz.

PRINCESS FELAYZ—see Felayz Baytz.

PRINCESS IRYS—see Irys Zhorzhet Mhara Daykyn Aplyn-Ahrmahk.

PRINCESS OYLYVYA—see Ohlyvya Baytz.

PROCTOR, ELIAS, PH.D.—a member of Pei Shan-wei's staff and a noted cyberneticist, OAR.

PRUAIT, CAPTAIN TYMYTHY, Imperial Charisian Navy—

newly appointed captain of prize ship *Sword of God*, HFAF.

PRUAIT, GENERAL FHRANKLYN, Republic of Siddarmark Army—CO, 76th Infantry Regiment, Sylmahn Gap, MT&T; promoted general, CO, 2nd Rifle Division, LAMA.

PYANGTU, CAPTAIN OF HORSE BAYZHAU, Imperial Harchongese Army—CO, 231st Volunteer Regiment, 115th Volunteer Brigade, Mighty Host of God and the Archangels, LAMA.

PYGAIN, FATHER AVRY—Chihirite upper-priest of the Order of the Quill; Archbishop Arthyn Zagyrsk's secretary and aide, MT&T.

PYNHALOH, COLONEL SIR SELVYN, Imperial Desnairian Army—CO, Pynhaloh's Regiment (light cavalry), cavalry wing, Army of Shiloh, LAMA.

QUEEN CONSORT HAILYN—see Hailyn Rayno.

QUEEN MAIYL—see Maiyl Nyou.

QUEEN MOTHER ALAHNAH—see Alahnah Tayt.

QUEEN SHARLEYAN—see Sharleyan Ahrmahk.

QUEEN YSBELL—an earlier reigning Queen of Chisholm who was deposed (and murdered) in favor of a male ruler, BSRA.

QWENTYN, COMMODORE DONYRT, Royal Corisandian Navy—Baron Tanlyr Keep, one of Duke of Black Water's squadron commanders, OAR.

QWENTYN, OWAIN—Tymahn Qwentyn's grandson, HFAF.

QWENTYN, TYMAHN—the current head of the House of Qwentyn, which is one of the largest, if not *the* largest banking and investment cartels in the Republic of Siddarmark. Lord Protector Greyghor holds a seat on the House of Qwentyn's board of directors, and the cartel operates the royal mint in the city of Siddar, BSRA.

RAHDGYRZ, GENERAL SIR SHULMYN, Royal Dohlaran Army—Baron Tymplahr; Sir Rainos Ahlverez' quartermaster, LAMA.

RAHLSTAHN, ADMIRAL GHARTH, Royal Emeraldian Navy—Earl of Mahndyr, CO, Royal Emeraldian Navy,

OAR; third-ranking officer Imperial Charisian Navy, BHD.

RAHLSTYN, COMMODORE ERAYK, Royal Dohlaran Navy—one of Duke Malikai's squadron commanders, OAR.

RAHLSTYN, LIEUTENANT MHARTYN, Royal Dohlaran Navy—XO, HMS *Chihiro*, 50, MT&T.

RAHS, MAJOR KAYVAIRN, Imperial Charisian Army—CO, 1st Battalion, 1st Scout Sniper Regiment, Imperial Charisian Army, LAMA.

RAHSKAIL, AHNDRYA—Barkah and Rebkah Rahskail's youngest child, MT&T.

RAHSKAIL, COLONEL BARKAH, Imperial Charisian Army—Earl of Swayle; a senior supply officer, Imperial Charisian Army, executed for treason, HFAF.

RAHSKAIL, REBKAH—Dowager Countess of Swayle; widow of Barkah, mother of Wahlys, MT&T.

RAHSKAIL, SAMYL—Wahlys Rahskail's younger brother, MT&T.

RAHSKAIL, WAHLYS—Earl of Swayle, son of Barkah Rahskail and Rebkah Rahskail, MT&T.

RAHZMAHN, LIEUTENANT DAHNYLD, Imperial Charisian Navy—Sir Gwylym Manthyr's flag lieutenant, HFAF.

RAHZWAIL, CAPTAIN AHLDAHS, Imperial Charisian Navy—XO, Bureau of Ordnance; Sir Ahlfryd Hyndryk's chief assistant following Commander Urvyn Mahndrayn's death, MT&T.

RAICE, BYNZHAMYN—Baron Wave Thunder; King Haarahld VII's spymaster/royal councilor for intelligence and a member of his Privy Council, OAR; same positions for Cayleb Ahrmahk following King Haarahld's death, BSRA; member of Charisian inner circle, BHD.

RAICE, LEAHYN—Baroness Wave Thunder; wife of Bynzhamyn Raice, HFAF.

RAIGLY, SYLVYST—Sir Dunkyn Yairley's valet and steward, HFAF.

RAIMAHN, BYRK—Claitahn and Sahmantha Raimahn's grandson; musician and Reformist, HFAF; CO riflemen sent to Glacierheart by Aivah Parsahn, MT&T;

CO, 1st Glacierheart Volunteers, Republic of Siddarmark Army, LAMA.

RAIMAHN, CLAITAHN—wealthy Charisian expatriate and Temple Loyalist living in Siddar City, HFAF.

RAIMAHN, SAHMANTHA—Claitahn Raimahn's wife and also a Temple Loyalist, HFAF.

RAIMAHND, BYNDFYRD—a Chisholmian banker deeply involved in spreading Charisian-style manufactories to Chisholm, LAMA.

RAIMAIR, LIEUTENANT TOBYS, Royal Corisandian Guard—late Sergeant Raimair of the Royal Corisandian Army, senior noncom of Daivyn Daykyn's Royal Guard in exile, HFAF; member of Royal Corisandian Guard and CO, Prince Daivyn Daykyn's personal guard detachment, LAMA.

RAIMYND, SIR LYNDAHR—Prince Hektor of Corisande's treasurer, BSRA; royal treasurer and member of the Regency Council, HFAF.

RAISAHNDO, CAPTAIN CAITAHNO, Royal Dohlaran Navy—CO, HMS *Rakurai*, 46, HFAF.

RAISLAIR, BISHOP EXECUTOR MHARTYN—Archbishop Ahdym Taibyr's executive assistant, Archbishopric of Desnair, HFAF.

RAISMYN, LIEUTENANT BYRNHAR, Imperial Charisian Marines—a lieutenant attached to Colonel Wyntahn Harys' Marines in support of Captain Halcom Bahrns' operation ("Great Canal Raid"), MT&T.

RAIYZ, FATHER CARLSYN—Queen Sharleyan's confessor, BSRA; killed in Sharleyan's attempted assassination at Saint Agtha's, BHD.

RAIZYNGYR, BRIGADIER SIR AHDRYN, Imperial Charisian Army—CO, 6th Mounted Brigade, Imperial Charisian Army, LAMA.

RAIZYNGYR, COLONEL ARTTU—CO, 2/3rd Marines (2nd Battalion, 3rd Brigade), Charisian Marines, BSRA.

RAYNAIR, CAPTAIN EKOHLS—CO, privateer schooner *Blade*, BSRA.

RAYNO, ARCHBISHOP WYLLYM—Archbishop of Chiangwu; adjutant of the Order of Schueler, OAR.

RAYNO, HAILYN—Queen Consort Hailyn, wife of King

Zhames II of Delferahk; a cousin of Prince Hektor of Corisande, BSRA.

RAYNO, KING ZHAMES OLYVYR—King Zhames II of Delferahk; a kinsman by marriage of Hektor Daykyn of Corisande and a distant cousin of Wyllym Rayno, Archbishop of Chiang-wu, BSRA.

RAZHAIL, FATHER DERAHK—senior healer, Imperial Palace, Cherayth. Upper-priest of the Order of Pasquale, HFAF.

REJ, MAJOR KRYSTYN, Imperial Charisian Army—CO, 1st Battalion, 12th Mounted Regiment, 6th Mounted Brigade, Imperial Charisian Army, LAMA.

RHOBAIR, VICAR—see Rhobair Duchairn.

ROCK COAST, DUKE OF—see Zhasyn Seafarer.

ROCK POINT, BARON OF—see Sir Domynyk Staynair.

ROHSAIL, SIR DAHRAND, Royal Dohlaran Navy—captain, CO, HMS *Grand Vicar Mahrys*, 50, HFAF; admiral, CO, Western Squadron, Royal Dohlaran Navy, based on Claw Island, LAMA.

ROHZHYR, COLONEL BAHRTOL, Royal Charisian Marines—a senior commissary officer, BSRA.

ROPEWALK, COLONEL AHDAM, Charisian Royal Guard—CO, Charisian Royal Guard, OAR.

ROWYN, CAPTAIN HORAHS—CO, Sir Dustyn Olyvyr's yacht *Ahnyet*, OAR.

ROWZVEL, ARCHBISHOP TRUMAHN—Archbishop of Gorath. A Langhornite, HFAF.

RUSTMYN, EDYMYND—Baron Stonekeep; King Gorjah III of Tarot's first councilor and spymaster, OAR.

RYCHTAIR, NYNIAN—illegitimate daughter of Grand Vicar Chihiro IX, adopted sister of Adorai Dynnys, BSRA; see Ahnzhelyk Phonda, Frahncyn Tahlbaht, Aivah Pahrsahn.

RYCHTYR, GENERAL SIR FAHSTYR, Royal Desnairian Army—CO of the vanguard of the Dohlaran Army invading the Republic of Siddarmark, MT&T; CO, Trevyr garrison, LAMA.

RYDACH, FATHER ZHORDYN—Rebkah Rahskail's Temple Loyalist confessor; officially an under-priest (actually an upper-priest) of the Order of Chihiro, MT&T.

RYDNAUYR, MAJOR KAHLVYN—CO, 5th Mountaincross Rangers, Temple Loyalist partisans; CO, Chestyrtyn garrison, LAMA.

RYNDYL, FATHER AHLUN—General Trumyn Stohnar's chaplain, MT&T.

SAHBRAHAN, LIEUTENANT YEREK, Imperial Charisian Navy—a naval battery commander serving under Commander Hainz Watyrs in Glacierheart Province, MT&T.

SAHBRAHAN, PAIAIR—the Earl of Thirsk's personal valet, HFAF.

SAHDLYR, LIEUTENANT BYNZHAMYN, Royal Charisian Navy—second lieutenant, galleon HMS *Dreadnought*, 54, OAR.

SAHDLYR, MAJOR BORYS, Temple Guard—a guardsman of the Inquisition assigned to Siddar City as part of the Sword of Schueler, HFAF.

SAHLAVAHN, CAPTAIN TRAI—cousin of Commander Urvyn Mahndrayn; CO, Hairatha Powder Mill, HFAF.

SAHLMYN, SERGEANT MAJOR HAIN, Royal Charisian Marines—Colonel Zhanstyn's battalion sergeant major, BHD.

SAHLTMYN, LIEUTENANT HENRAI, Royal Dohlaran Navy—one of Captain Lywystyn's battery commanders on Claw Island, LAMA.

SAHLYS, MAJOR GAHVYN, Republic of Siddarmark Army—CO, 5th Company, 37th Infantry Regiment, Republic of Siddarmark Army, MT&T.

SAHLYVAHN, LIEUTENANT DAHGLYS, Republic of Siddarmark Army—General Trumyn Stohnar's aide, MT&T.

SAHMYRSYT, GENERAL BARTYN, Imperial Charisian Army—CO, Army of Old Province, LAMA.

SAHNDAHL, COLONEL FRAIMAHN, Delferahkan Royal Guard—XO, Delferahkan Royal Guard, HFAF.

SAHNDFYRD, TAHVYS—a junior partner and representative of Ehdwyrd Howsmyn sent to Chisholm to assist Sharleyan in creating Chisholmian manufactories, LAMA.

SAHNDHAIM, COLONEL STYWYRT, Army of God—CO, 1st Regiment, Zion Division, Army of Glacierheart, MT&T.

SARMAC, JENNIFER—an Eve who escaped the destruction of the Alexandria Enclave and fled to Tellesberg, BSRA.

SARMAC, KAYLEB—an Adam who escaped the destruction of the Alexandria Enclave and fled to Tellesberg, BSRA.

SARMOUTH, BARON OF—see Sir Dunkyn Yairley.

SATYRFYLD, MAJOR LAREK, Republic of Siddarmark Militia—CO, 2nd Company, 1st Glacierheart Volunteers, LAMA.

SAWAL, FATHER RAHSS—an under-priest of the Order of Chihiro, the skipper of one of the Temple's courier boats, BSRA.

SAWYAIR, SISTER FRAHNCYS—senior nun of the Order of Pasquale, Convent of the Blessed Hand, Cherayth, HFAF.

SAYLKYRK, MIDSHIPMAN TRAHVYS, Imperial Charisian Navy—senior midshipman, HMS *Destiny*, 54, HFAF; fourth lieutenant, HMS *Destiny*, 54, MT&T.

SAYRANOH, CORPORAL BRUNOHN, Imperial Charisian Army—squad leader, 1st Squad, Company B, 1st Battalion, 1st Scout Sniper Regiment, Imperial Charisian Army, LAMA.

SCHAHL, FATHER DAHNYVYN—upper-priest of the Order of Schueler working directly for Bishop Mytchail Zhessop; attached to Colonel Aiphraim Tahlyvyr's dragoon regiment, HFAF.

SCHMYD, PRIVATE MAHKZWAIL, Royal Dohlaran Army—cavalry trooper, 2nd Section, 3rd Platoon, 1st Company, Ahzbyrn's Regiment (cavalry), Dohlaran component, Army of Shiloh, LAMA.

SCHYLLYR, FATHER AHMBROHS—a Schuelerite priest; intendant, Fyrgyrsyn Division, Army of Glacierheart, LAMA.

SCOVAYL, BISHOP TYMAHN, Army of God—CO, Fyrgyrsyn Division, Army of Glacierheart, LAMA.

SEABLANKET, RHOBAIR—the Earl of Coris' valet, HFAF.

SEACATCHER, BRIGADIER SIR LAIMYN, Imperial Charisian Army—elder son of the Baron of Mandolin; CO,

5th Mounted Brigade, Imperial Charisian Army, LAMA.

SEACATCHER, SIR RAHNYLD—Baron Mandolin; a member of Cayleb Ahrmahk's Royal Council, BSRA.

SEAFARER, ZHASYN—Duke of Rock Coast, MT&T.

SEAFARMER, SIR RHYZHARD—Baron Wave Thunder's senior investigator, OAR.

SEAHAMPER, SERGEANT EDWYRD, Charisian Imperial Guards—Sharleyan Ahrmahk's personal armsman since age ten, member Charisian inner circle, BSRA.

SEAMOUNT, BARON OF—see Sir Ahlfryd Hyndryk.

SEAROSE, FATHER GREYGHOR, Navy of God—CO, NGS *Saint Styvyn*, 52. Senior surviving officer of Kornylys Harpahr's fleet. A Chihirite of the Order of the Sword, HFAF.

SEASMOKE, LIEUTENANT YAIRMAN, Imperial Charisian Navy—XO, HMS *Dancer*, 56, HFAF.

SEATOWN, CAPTAIN WAHLTAYR—CO of merchant ship *Fraynceen*, acting as a courier for Prince Hektor's spies in Charis, OAR. See also Lieutenant Fraizher Maythis, OAR.

SEEGAIRS, FATHER HAHSKYLL—a Schuelerite upper-priest and inquisitor; a senior member of Inquisitor General Wylbyr Edwyrds' staff, LAMA.

SELKYR, BRYAHN—Earl of Deep Hollow; a member of the Northern Conspiracy in Corisande, executed for treason, HFAF.

SELKYR, PETTY OFFICER AHNTAHN, Imperial Charisian Navy—a boatswain's mate, HMS *Destiny*, 54, HFAF.

SELLYRS, MAJOR ZHORJ, Royal Dohlaran Army—CO, 3rd Company, Ahzbyrn's Regiment (cavalry), Dohlaran component, LAMA.

SELLYRS, PAITYR—Baron White Church; Keeper of the Seal of the Kingdom of Charis; a member of Cayleb Ahrmahk's Royal Council, BSRA.

SEVYRS, TRYNT, Imperial Charisian Navy—ironclad HMS *Delthak*, 22; Halcom Bahrns' steward, LAMA.

SHAIKYR, LARYS—CO, privateer galleon *Raptor*, BSRA.

SHAILTYN, CAPTAIN DAIVYN, Imperial Charisian Navy—CO, HMS *Thunderbolt*, 58, HFAF; "frocked" to commodore to command the squadron escorting the Charisian Expeditionary Force to the Republic of Siddarmark, MT&T.

SHAIN, PAYTER, Imperial Charisian Navy—captain, CO, HMS *Dreadful*, 48. Admiral Nylz' flag captain, BSRA; admiral, flag officer commanding ICN squadron based on Thol Bay, Kingdom of Tarot, HFAF; CO, Inshore Squadron, Gulf of Jahras, LAMA.

SHAIOW, ADMIRAL OF THE BROAD OCEANS CHYNTAI, Imperial Harchongese Navy—Duke of Sun Rising; senior officer afloat, Imperial Harchongese Navy, HFAF.

SHAIRNCROSS, LADY—see Zhain Parkair.

SHAIRNCROSS, LORD—see Weslai Parkair.

SHANDYR, HAHL—Baron of Shandyr, Prince Nahrmahn of Emerald's spymaster, OAR.

SHARGHATI, AHLYSSA—greatest soprano opera singer of the Republic of Siddarmark; friend of Aivah Pahrsahn's, HFAF.

SHARLEYAN, EMPRESS—see Sharleyan Alahnah Zhenyfyr Ahlyssa Tayt.

SHARPFIELD, EARL OF—see Sir Lewk Cohlmyn.

SHARPHILL, EARL OF—see Sir Maikel Traivyr.

SHAUMAHN, BROTHER SYMYN—hosteler of the Monastery of Saint Zherneau, HFAF.

SHELTYN, LIEUTENANT CHARLZ, Royal Corisandian Guard—an officer of the Royal Guard who deeply resents and distrusts Nimue Chwaeriau, LAMA.

SHOWAIL, LIEUTENANT COMMANDER STYV, Imperial Charisian Navy—CO, schooner HMS *Flash*, 10, HFAF.

SHOWAIL, STYWYRT—a Charisian foundry owner deliberately infringing several of Ehdwyrd Howsmyn's patents, MT&T; charged with several illegal practices and financially ruined, LAMA.

SHRAYDYR, COLONEL TOBYS—CO, 2nd Raisor Volunteers, Shilohian Temple Loyalist militia, Fort Tairys garrison.

SHULMYN, BISHOP TRAHVYS—Bishop of Raven's Land, MT&T.

SHUMAKYR, FATHER SYMYN—Archbishop Erayk Dynnys'

secretary for his 891 pastoral visit; an agent of the Grand Inquisitor, OAR.

SHUMAY, FATHER AHLVYN—Bishop Mylz Halcom's personal aide, killed during Saint Agtha assassination attempt, BSRA.

SHYLAIR, BISHOP EXECUTOR THOMYS—Archbishop Borys Bahrmyn's bishop executor, BSRA.

SHYLLYR, FATHER ZEFRYM—a Langhornite under-priest who attached himself to Major Kahlvyn Rydnauyr's 5th Mountaincross Rangers as its chaplain, LAMA.

SHYRBYRT, COMMANDER ALLAYN, Imperial Charisian Navy—Earl Sharpfield's chief of staff, LAMA.

SKYNYR, LIEUTENANT MHARTYN, Imperial Charisian Navy—third lieutenant, HMS *Destiny*, 54, MT&T.

SLAYTYR, ZHAPYTH—one of Merlin Athrawes' alternate identities, LAMA.

SLOHVYK, COMMANDER PAIDRHO, Imperial Charisian Navy—CO, schooner HMS *Termagant*, 18, Gulf of Jahras, LAMA.

SLOKYM, CAPTAIN THOMYS, Army of God—CO, 2nd Company, 73rd Cavalry Regiment, Army of the Sylmahn, LAMA.

SLOKYM, LIEUTENANT BRYAHN, Imperial Charisian Army—Baron Green Valley's aide, 2nd Brigade (reinforced), Charisian Expeditionary Force, MT&T.

SMOLTH, ZHAN—star pitcher for the Tellesberg Krakens, OAR.

SOLAYRAN, LIEUTENANT BRAHD, Imperial Charisian Navy—XO, ironclad HMS *Tellesberg*, 22, LAMA.

SOLOMON, DUKE OF—see Hanbyl Baytz.

SOMERSET, CAPTAIN MARTIN LUTHER, Terran Federation Navy—CO, TFNS *Excalibur*, OAR,

SOWTHMYN, TRUMYN—Earl of Airyth; one of Prince Hektor of Corisande's councilors serving on Prince Daivyn's Regency Council. He is an ally of Earl Anvil Rock and Earl Tartarian, HFAF.

STAHDYRD, LIEUTENANT SIR WAHLYS, Royal Dohlaran Army—CO, 3rd Platoon, 1st Company, Ahzbyrn's Regiment (cavalry), Dohlaran component, Army of Shiloh, LAMA.

STAHKAIL, GENERAL LOWRAI, Imperial Desnairian Army—CO, Triangle Shoal Fort, Iythria, HFAF.

STAHNTYN, GENERAL CHARLZ, Republic of Siddarmark Army—CO, Aivahnstyn garrison, Cliff Peak Province, Republic of Siddarmark, MT&T.

STANTYN, ARCHBISHOP NYKLAS—Archbishop of Hankey in the Desnairian Empire. A member of the Reformists, BSRA.

STAYNAIR, MADAME AHRDYN—Maikel Staynair's deceased wife, BSRA.

STAYNAIR, MAIKEL—a Bédardist, Bishop of Tellesberg, King Haarahld VII's confessor, member of Royal Council, member of Charisian inner circle, OAR; created Archbishop of Charis, defies the Temple and the Group of Four, BSRA; creates Church of Charis following the merger of Kingdom of Old Charis and Kingdom of Chisholm, BHD.

STAYNAIR, SIR DOMYNYK, Royal Charisian Navy—younger brother of Bishop Maikel Staynair; commodore, specialist in naval tactics, CO, Experimental Squadron, Cayleb Ahrmahk's second-in-command Battle of Rock Point and Battle of Darcos Sound, OAR; promoted admiral, created Baron Rock Point, BSRA; CO, Eraystor blockade squadron, BHD; member of Charisian inner circle, promoted high admiral, Imperial Charisian Navy commander-in-chief, AMF.

STOHNAR, GENERAL TRUMYN, Republic of Siddarmark Army—a first cousin of Lord Protector Greyghor Stohnar; commander of the reinforcements sent to hold the Sylmahn Gap, MT&T.

STOHNAR, LORD PROTECTOR GREYGHOR—elected ruler of the Siddarmark Republic, OAR.

STONEHEART, BARON OF—see Sylvyst Mhardyr.

STONEKEEP, BARON OF—see Edymynd Rustmyn.

STORM KEEP, EARL OF—see Sahlahmn Traigair.

STOWAIL, COMMANDER AHBRAIM, Imperial Charisian Navy—Sir Domynyk Staynair's chief of staff, MT&T.

STYLMYN, BRAHD—Ehdwyrd Howsmyn's senior civil engineer, MT&T.

STYVYNSYN, MAJOR AHLYK, Imperial Charisian Army—CO, 2nd Battalion, 2nd Scout Sniper Regiment, Imperial Charisian Army, MT&T.

STYVYNSYN, MAJOR ZHORJ, Republic of Siddarmark Army—CO, 2nd Company, 37th Infantry Regiment, Republic of Siddarmark Army, MT&T.

STYWYRT, CAPTAIN AHRNAHLD, Imperial Charisian Navy—CO, HMS *Squall*, 36, HFAF.

STYWYRT, CAPTAIN DAHRYL, Royal Charisian Navy—CO, HMS *Typhoon*, 36, OAR.

STYWYRT, MAJOR LAIMUYL, Republic of Siddarmark Militia—CO, 4th Company, 1st Glacierheart Volunteers, LAMA.

STYWYRT, PAYT—Duke Black Horse, MT&T.

STYWYRT, SERGEANT ZOHZEF, Royal Delferahkan Army—noncom in Ferayd garrison, party to Ferayd massacre, BSRA.

SULYVVYN, COLONEL CHERMYN, Royal Dohlaran Army—CO, Sulyvyn's Regiment (medium cavalry), Dohlaran component, Army of Shiloh, LAMA.

SULYVVYN, DAHMBRYK, Imperial Charisian Army—CO, 5th Brigade, 3rd Infantry Division, LAMA.

SUMYR, FATHER FRAHNKLYN—Archbishop Failyx Gahrbor's intendant, Archbishopric of Tarot, HFAF.

SUMYRS, GENERAL CLYFTYN, Republic of Siddarmark Army—CO, Alyksberg, Cliff Peak Province, Republic of Siddarmark, MT&T.

SUMYRS, SERGEANT DAHLTYN, Imperial Charisian Marines—a senior Marine noncom attached to Brigadier Taisyn's forces in Glacierheart, MT&T.

SUMYRS, SIR ZHER—Baron of Barcor; one of Sir Koryn Gahrvai's senior officers, Corisande Campaign, BHD; later member of Northern Conspiracy, HFAF.

SUN RISING, DUKE OF—see Chyntai Shaiow.

SUTYLS, MIDSHIPMAN TAIRAINCE, Imperial Charisian Navy—ironclad HMS *Delthak*, 22, LAMA.

SUVYRYV, MAJOR AHRNAHLD, Royal Desnairian Army—Colonel Sir Zhadwail Brynygair's executive officer, assigned to Sir Fahstyr Rychtyr's invasion column, MT&T.

SUWAIL, BARJWAIL—Lord Theralt; Lord of Clan Theralt, Raven's Land, MT&T.

SUWAIL, COLONEL ZHORDYN, Republic of Siddarmark Army—CO, 93rd Infantry Regiment, Republic of Siddarmark Army, MT&T.

SUWYL, TOBYS—an expatriate Charisian banker and merchant living in Siddar City; a Temple Loyalist, HFAF.

SUWYL, ZHANDRA—Tobys Suwyl's wife; a moderate Reformist, HFAF.

SVAIRSMAHN, MIDSHIPMAN LAINSAIR, Imperial Charisian Navy—a midshipman, HMS *Dancer*, 56, AMF; youngest of Charisian POWs surrendered to Inquisition by Kingdom of Dohlar, HFAF.

SWAYLE, DOWAGER COUNTESS OF—see Rebkah Rahskail.

SWAYLE, EARL OF—see Barkah Rahskail and Wahlys Rahskail.

SYGAYL, FRAYDRYKHA—Zhustyn Sygayl's twelve-year-old daughter, raped and killed by Temple Loyalists attacking the Siddar City Charisian Quarter, LAMA.

SYGAYL, LYZBYT—Zhustyn Sygayl's widow and Fraydrykha Sygayl's mother, LAMA.

SYGAYL, ZHUSTYN—Klymynt Ahbykrahmbi's uncle, killed defending his daughter against Temple Loyalists attacking the Siddar City Charisian Quarter, LAMA.

SYGHAL, COLONEL TREVYR, Imperial Charisian Army—senior artillery officer, 2nd Brigade (reinforced), Charisian Expeditionary Force, MT&T; same position, Army of Midhold, LAMA.

SYGZBEE, MAJOR STYWYRT, Imperial Charisian Army—XO, 2nd Scout Sniper Regiment, Imperial Charisian Army, LAMA.

SYLVELLA, SERGEANT DAIVYN, Imperial Charisian Army—2nd Platoon, Company A, 2nd Battalion, 12th Mounted Regiment, 6th Mounted Brigade, Imperial Charisian Army, LAMA.

SYLZ, PARSAHN—a Charisian foundry owner and associate of Ehdwyrd Howsmyn, MT&T.

SYMKEE, LIEUTENANT GARAITH, Imperial Charisian

SYNKLYR, LIEUTENANT AIRAH, Royal Dohlaran Navy—XO, galleon HMS *Guardian*, BSRA.

SYNZHYN, FATHER TAILAHR—a Hastingite upper-priest and native Chisholmian serving as Duchairn's engineering expert for the canal system, LAMA.

SYRAHLLA, CAPTAIN MARSHYL, Royal Desnairian Army—CO, "Syrahlla's Battery," six-pounder horse artillery assigned to Sir Fahstyr Rychtyr's invasion column, MT&T.

SYRKUS, MAJOR PAWAL, Imperial Charisian Army—CO, 2nd Battalion, 4th Regiment, Imperial Charisian Army, MT&T.

SYVAKYS, SERGEANT CLAYMAHNT, Army of God—platoon sergeant, 1st Platoon, Company A, 191st Cavalry Regiment, Army of Glacierheart, LAMA.

TAHLAS, LIEUTENANT BRAHD, Imperial Charisian Marines—CO, 2nd Platoon, Alpha Company, 1/3rd (1st Battalion, 3rd Regiment) Marines, Imperial Charisian Marines, HFAF.

TAHLBAHT, FRAHNCYN—a senior employee (and actual owner) of Bruhstair Freight Haulers; an alias of Nynian Rychtair, HFAF.

TAHLBAHT, SERGEANT ALLAYN, Army of God—company sergeant major, 1st Company, 231st Volunteer Regiment, 115th Volunteer Brigade, Mighty Host of God and the Archangels, Imperial Harchongese Army, LAMA.

TAHLMYDG, COLONEL GAHDARHD, Royal Desnairian Army—CO, Tahlmydg's Regiment (infantry), assigned to Sir Fahstyr Rychtyr's invasion column, MT&T.

TAHLYVYR, COLONEL AIPHRAIM, Royal Delferahkan Army—CO, dragoon regiment assigned to "rescue" Princess Irys and Prince Daivyn, HFAF.

TAHLYVYR, COLONEL LYNDAHR—ex-lieutenant Republic of Siddarmark Army; CO, Maiyam Militia, Temple Loyalist militia; CO, Maiyam garrison, LAMA.

TAHLYVYR, COLONEL SYMYN, Army of God—XO, Fyrgyrsyn Division, Army of Glacierheart, LAMA.

TAHLYVYR, MAJOR FRAIDARECK, Imperial Charisian Army—CO, 1st Battalion, 2nd Regiment, Imperial Charisian Army, MT&T.

TAHNAIYR, COLONEL PRESKYT, Imperial Charisian Army—CO, 6th Regiment, 3rd Brigade, 2nd Division Regiment, Imperial Charisian Army, LAMA.

TAHRLSAHN, FATHER VYKTYR—Schuelerite upper-priest and one of Zhaspahr Clyntahn's handpicked inquisitors detailed to deliver Charisian POWs from Dohlar to the Temple, HFAF; assigned to Bishop Wylbyr Edwyrds' staff, LAMA.

TAIBAHLD, FATHER AHRNAHLD, Navy of God—upperpriest of the Order of Schueler; CO, NGS *Sword of God*; Bishop Kornylys Harpahr's flag captain, HFAF.

TAIBOR, LYWYS, Imperial Charisian Navy—a healer's mate, HMS *Destiny*, 54, HFAF.

TAIBYR, ARCHBISHOP AHDYM—Archbishop of Desnair for the Church of God Awaiting, HFAF.

TAIDSWAYL, LIEUTENANT KORY, Imperial Charisian Navy—XO, ironclad HMS *Saygin*, 22, MT&T.

TAIGYN, SERGEANT ZHERMO—Temple Loyalist noncom, Fairkyn, New Northland Province, Republic of Siddarmark, MT&T.

TAILAHR, CAPTAIN ZAIKYB, Imperial Charisian Navy—CO, ironclad HMS *Hador*, 22, MT&T.

TAILYR, BISHOP EDWYRD, Army of God—CO, Jwo-jeng Division, Army of the Sylmahn, MT&T.

TAILYR, LIEUTENANT ZHAK—a Temple Guard officer sent to Hildermoss with Father Failyx Khalryn to command Khalryn's force of Temple Loyalist Border States "volunteers," MT&T.

TAILYR, PRIVATE ZHAKE—a member of the Delferahkan Royal Guard, HFAF.

TAIRWALD, LORD—see Phylyp Zhaksyn.

TAISYN, BRIGADIER MAHRTYN, Imperial Charisian Marines—senior Charisian Marine officer in Siddarmark prior to Cayleb Ahrmahk's arrival in Siddar City; sent with scratch force to defend the province of Glacierheart, KIA Battle of the Daivyn River, MT&T.

TALLMYN, CAPTAIN GERVAYS, Emerald Navy—second-in-command of the Royal Dockyard in Tranjyr, HFAF.

TANLYR KEEP, BARON OF—see Donyrt Qwentyn.

TANNYR, FATHER HAHLYS—under-priest of the Order of Chihiro; CO, Temple iceboat *Hornet*, HFAF.

TANYR, VICAR GAIRYT—a member of the Samyl Wylsynn's circle of Reformists, BSRA.

TARTARIAN, EARL OF—see Sir Taryl Lektor.

TAYLAR, CAPTAIN GAHVYN, Army of God—CO, 3rd Company, 1st Regiment, Zion Division, Army of Glacierheart, LAMA.

TAYLAR, MAJOR PAIDRHO, Imperial Charisian Army—CO, 1st Battalion, 4th Regiment, Imperial Charisian Army, MT&T.

TAYSO, PRIVATE DAISHYN, Charisian Imperial Guard—a Charisian assigned to Empress Sharleyan's guard detachment, KIA Saint Agtha assassination attempt, BSRA.

TAYT, ALAHNAH—Dowager Queen of Chisholm; Queen Sharleyan of Chisholm's mother, BSRA.

TAYT, KING SAILYS—deceased father of Queen Sharleyan of Chisholm, BSRA.

TAYT, MAJOR CHARLZ, Imperial Charisian Army—CO, 4th Battalion, 3rd Regiment, Imperial Charisian Army, a distant cousin of Empress Sharleyan, MT&T.

TAYT, SHARLEYAN—Empress of Charis and Queen of Chisholm. See Sharleyan Ahrmahk.

TEAGMAHN, FATHER BRYAHN—upper-priest of the Order of Schueler, intendant for the Archbishopric of Glacierheart, HFAF.

THAIRIS, RUHSYL, Imperial Charisian Army—Duke of Eastshare; CO, Imperial Charisian Army, HFAF; CO, Charisian Expeditionary Force; CO, 1st Brigade (reinforced), MT&T; CO, Army of the Branaths, LAMA.

THAIRNOS, EARL OF—see Rahzhyr Hylmahn.

THERALT, LORD OF—see Barjwail Suwail.

THIESSEN, CAPTAIN JOSEPH, Terran Federation Navy—Admiral Pei Kau-zhi's chief of staff, OAR.

THIRSK, EARL OF—see Lywys Gardynyr.

THORAST, DUKE OF—see Aibram Zaivyair.

THYRSTYN, SYMYN—a Siddarmarkian merchant; husband of Wynai Thyrstyn, HFAF.

THYRSTYN, WYNAI—Trai Sahlavahn's married sister; secretary and stenographer in Charis' Siddar City embassy, HFAF.

TIANG, BISHOP EXECUTOR WU-SHAI—Archbishop Zherohm Vyncyt's bishop executor, BSRA.

TIDEWATER, NAHRMAHN—one of Ehdwyrd Howsmyn's senior artificers, MT&T.

TILLYER, CAPTAIN VYNCYT, Army of God—CO, 3rd Company, 73rd Cavalry Regiment, Army of the Sylmahn, LAMA.

TILLYER, LIEUTENANT COMMANDER HENRAI, Imperial Charisian Navy—High Admiral Lock Island's chief of staff; previously his flag lieutenant, HFAF.

TILLYER, LIEUTENANT HENRAI, Royal Charisian Navy—High Admiral Lock Island's personal aide, OAR; lieutenant, Imperial Charisian Navy, High Admiral Lock Island's flag lieutenant; commander, Imperial Charisian Navy, High Admiral Lock Island's chief of staff, AMF.

TIRIAN, DUKE OF—see Kahlvyn Ahrmahk and Rayjhis Ahrmahk.

TOBYS, WING FLAHN—Lord Tairwald's senior "wing" (blooded warrior), MT&T.

TOHMPSYN, COLONEL SIR SAHLMYN, Royal Desnairian Army—CO, Tohmpsyn's Regiment (infantry), assigned to Sir Fahstyr Rychtyr's invasion column, MT&T.

TOHMYS, FRAHNKLYN—Crown Prince Cayleb's tutor, OAR.

TOHMYS, FRAIDMYN—Archbishop Zhasyn Cahnyr's valet of many years, HFAF.

TOMPSYN, COLONEL ZHON, Imperial Charisian Army—

CO, 3rd Regiment, 2nd Brigade, 1st Division, Imperial Charisian Army, MT&T.

TRAHLMAHN, FATHER ZHON—Order of Bédard; Prince Nahrmahn Baytz' palace confessor, HFAF; retained in that post by Prince Nahrmahn Gareyt Baytz, MT&T.

TRAHSKHAT, MAHRTYN—Sailys and Myrahm Trahskhat's older son, HFAF.

TRAHSKHAT, MYRAHM—Sailys Trahskhat's wife and also a Temple Loyalist, HFAF.

TRAHSKHAT, PAWAL—Sailys and Myrahm Trahskhat's younger son, HFAF.

TRAHSKHAT, SAILYS—ex-star third baseman for the Tellesberg Krakens; was a Temple Loyalist until his family was attacked in the Sword of Schueler uprising, HFAF; Byrk Raimahn's second-in-command defending the Reformists of Glacierheart Province, MT&T; promoted major, Republic of Siddarmark Militia, XO, 1st Glacierheart Volunteers, LAMA.

TRAHSKHAT, SINDAI—Sailys and Myrahm Trahskhat's daughter and youngest child, HFAF.

TRAIGAIR, BRIGADIER WYLSYNN, Imperial Charisian Army—CO, 3rd Brigade, Imperial Charisian Army, LAMA.

TRAIGAIR, SAHLAHMN—Earl of Storm Keep; a member of the Northern Conspiracy in Corisande, executed for treason, HFAF.

TRAIGHAIR, FATHER LHAREE—rector of Saint Bailair's Church, Siddar City; Order of Bédard; a Reformist, HFAF.

TRAIMYNT, COLONEL SIR ZHAKSYN, Imperial Charisian Army—chief of staff, 1st Brigade (reinforced) and Army of the Branaths, LAMA.

TRAIVYR, SIR MAIKEL—Earl of Sharphill, Ehdwyrd Howsmyn's father-in-law, BHD.

TRAIWYRTHYN, COLONEL SIR BRAHDRYK, Imperial Desnairian Army—CO, The Perlmann Grays (imperial guard light cavalry), cavalry wing, Army of Shiloh, LAMA.

TRAYKHOS, DUKE OF—see Taylar Gahrmahn.

TRAYLMYN, BARON OF—see General Sir Ohtys Godwyl.

TREDGAIR, CAPTAIN SYMYN, Army of God—CO, 3rd Company, 16th Cavalry Regiment, Army of the Sylmahn, LAMA.

TRUMYN, ZHORJ—an assistant to Brygham Cartyr in the Charisian technical support mission to the Republic of Siddarmark, LAMA.

TRYNAIR, VICAR ZAHMSYN—Chancellor of the Council of Vicars of the Church of God Awaiting; one of the so-called Group of Four, OAR.

TRYNTYN, CAPTAIN ZHAIRYMIAH, Royal Charisian Navy—CO, HMS *Torrent,* 42, BSRA.

TRYNTYN, COLONEL VYKTYR, Imperial Desnairian Army—Baron Kohlchyst; CO, Empress Consort Gwyndolyn's Own Regiment (imperial guard light cavalry), cavalry wing, Army of Shiloh, LAMA.

TRYVYTHYN, CAPTAIN SIR DYNZYL, Royal Charisian Navy—CO, galley HMS *Royal Charis,* flag captain to King Haarahld VII, KIA Battle of Darcos Sound, OAR.

TSHANGJYN, LORD OF FOOT BANGPA, Imperial Harchongese Army—CO, 115th Volunteer Brigade, Mighty Host of God and the Archangels, LAMA.

TSYNZHWEI, CAPTAIN OF SWORDS YAUNYNG, Imperial Harchongese Army—CO, 1st Company, 231st Volunteer Regiment, 115th Volunteer Brigade, Mighty Host of God and the Archangels, LAMA.

TUKKYR, COLONEL SIR BAHRTALAM, Imperial Desnairian Army—Baron Cliff Hollow; CO, Emperor Mahrys' Own Regiment (imperial guard heavy cavalry), cavalry wing, Army of Shiloh, LAMA.

TYBYT, GYFFRY—Paidryg Tybyt's thirteen-year-old son, MT&T.

TYBYT, MAJOR KLAIRYNCE, Royal Dohlaran Army—CO, 1st Company, Gardynyr's Regiment (cavalry), Dohlaran component, Army of Shiloh, LAMA.

TYBYT, PAIDRYG—Temple Loyalist barge crewman and farmer, Fairkyn, New Northland Province, Republic of Siddarmark, MT&T.

TYDWAIL, FATHER ZHORJ—Schuelerite upper-priest; Zion Division's special intendant, Army of Glacier-heart, MT&T.

TYLMAHN, FATHER VYKTYR—Pasqualate upper-priest; senior Reformist clergyman in Thesmar, South March Lands, MT&T.

TYLMAHN, GENERAL FRONZ, Republic of Siddarmark Army—senior officer in command, Siddarmarkian infantry detailed to support Captain Halcom Bahrns' operation, MT&T.

TYMKYN, FATHER ZHAMES—Langhornite under-priest, chaplain, 191st Cavalry Regiment, Army of Glacier-heart, MT&T.

TYMKYN, LIEUTENANT TOHMYS, Imperial Charisian Navy—fourth lieutenant and later third lieutenant HMS Destiny, 54, HFAF.

TYMKYN, ZHASTROW—High Admiral Rock Point's secretary, HFAF.

TYMPLAHR, BARON OF—see Sir Shulmyn Rahdgyrz.

TYMPYLTYN, GENERAL ERAYK—Temple Loyalist ex-militia officer whose mutinous troops seized Fort Darymahn, South March Lands, Republic of Siddarmark; the promotion to general is self-awarded, MT&T.

TYMPYLTYN, LIEUTENANT KLAIRYNCE, Imperial Charisian Navy—CO, Western Battery, Thesmar, LAMA.

TYMPYLTYN, LIEUTENANT SIR MAHRAK, Imperial Charisian Navy—Earl Sharpfield's flag lieutenant, LAMA.

TYMYNS, MAJOR RHOBAIR, Republic of Siddarmark Army—CO, 2nd Provisional Cavalry Regiment, LAMA.

TYMYOZHA, COLONEL SIR ZAHLOH, Imperial Desnairian Army—CO, Tymyozha's Regiment (light cavalry), cavalry wing, Army of Shiloh, LAMA.

TYOTAYN, BRIGADIER BAIRAHND, Imperial Charisian Marines—CO, 5th Brigade, Imperial Charisian Marines. Sir Gwylym Manthyr's senior Marine officer, HFAF.

TYRN, ARCHBISHOP LYAM—Archbishop of Emerald, OAR.

URVYN, LIEUTENANT ZHAK, Royal Charisian Navy—XO, HMS *Wave*, 14, BSRA.

URWYN, LUDOVYC—first Lord Protector of Siddarmark; founder of Republic of Siddarmark, HFAF.

USHYR, FATHER BRYAHN—an under-priest, Archbishop Maikel's personal secretary and most trusted aide, BSRA; member of Charisian inner circle, HFAF.

VAHLAIN, NAIKLOS—Sir Gwylym Manthyr's valet, AMF; one of the Charisian POWs surrendered to Inquisition by the Kingdom of Dohlar, HFAF.

VAHLVERDAY, COLONEL HELFRYD—CO, 3rd Raisor Volunteers, Shilohian Temple Loyalist militia, Fort Tairys garrison, LAMA.

VAHNHAIN, FATHER NAIKLOS—a Schuelerite under-priest and intendant, Fort Tairys garrison, LAMA.

VAHNWYK, MAHRTYN—the Earl of Thirsk's personal secretary and senior clerk, HFAF.

VAHNWYK, MAJOR ZHERYLD, Army of God—XO, 73rd Cavalry Regiment, Army of the Sylmahn, LAMA.

VAHRTANYSH, COLONEL KATHYL, Imperial Charisian Army—CO, 9th Mounted Regiment, 5th Mounted Brigade, Imperial Charisian Army, LAMA.

VAHSPHAR, BISHOP EXECUTOR DYNZAIL—Bishop Executor of Delferahk; an Andropovite, HFAF.

VANDAIK, FATHER GAISBYRT—upper-priest of the Order of Schueler; an inquisitor working directly for Bishop Mytchail Zhessop in Talkyra, HFAF.

VELDAMAHN, BYRTRYM ("BYRT"), Imperial Charisian Navy—High Admiral Rock Point's personal coxswain, HFAF.

VERRYN, CAPTAIN DYGRY—senior Temple Loyalist officer, Fairkyn, New Northland Province, Republic of Siddarmark, MT&T.

VICAR HAUWERD—see Hauwerd Wylsynn.

VICAR NICODAIM—see Nicodaim Ghordyn.

VICAR SAMYL—see Samyl Wylsynn.

VICAR ZAHMSYN—see Zahmsyn Trynair.

VICAR ZHASPAHR—see Zhaspahr Clyntahn.

VOHLYNDYR, SERGEANT ROLLYNS, Imperial Charisian

Army—platoon sergeant, 2nd Platoon, Company B, 1st Battalion, 9th Mounted Regiment, 5th Mounted Brigade, Imperial Charisian Army, LAMA.

VRAIDAHN, MISTRESS ALYS—Archbishop Maikel Staynair's housekeeper, HFAF.

VYKAIN, LIEUTENANT MAHRYAHNO, Imperial Charisian Navy—XO, HMS *Ahrmahk*, 58, HFAF.

VYNAIR, BISHOP ADULFO, Army of God—CO, Holy Martyrs Division, Army of the Sylmahn, MT&T.

VYNAIR, SERGEANT AHDYM, Charisian Royal Guard—one of Cayleb Ahrmahk's armsmen, BSRA.

VYNCYT, ARCHBISHOP ZHEROHM—primate of Chisholm, BSRA.

VYNTYNR, MAJOR FRAYDYK, Imperial Charisian Marines—Colonel Wyntahn Harys' senior Charisian subordinate in support of Captain Halcom Bahrns' operation ("Great Canal Raid"), MT&T.

VYRNYR, DOCTOR DAHNEL—member of the Royal College of Charis specializing in the study of pressures, MT&T.

WAHLDAIR, LIEUTENANT LAHMBAIR, Imperial Charisian Navy—third lieutenant, HMS *Dancer*, 56, HFAF.

WAHLS, COLONEL STYVYN, Royal Delferahkan Army—CO, Sarmouth Keep, HFAF.

WAHLTAHRS, CAPTAIN LACHLYN, Army of God—CO, 4th Company, 73rd Cavalry Regiment, Army of the Sylmahn, LAMA.

WAHLTAHRS, SERGEANT RAHZHYR, Royal Corisandian Guard—a member of Prince Daivyn's Royal Guard in exile in Delferahk, Tobys Raimair's senior noncom, HFAF; senior noncommissioned officer, Prince Daivyn Daykyn's personal guard detail.

WAHRLYW, ZHOEL, Canal Service—gatekeeper, Fairkyn, New Northland Province, Republic of Siddarmark, MT&T.

WAIGAN, FRAHNKLYN, Imperial Charisian Navy—chief petty officer and senior helmsman, HMS *Destiny*, 54, HFAF.

WAIGNAIR, BISHOP HAINRYK—Bishop of Tellesberg; senior prelate (after Archbishop Maikel) of the Kingdom of Old Charis, killed in Gray Lizard Square terrorist attack, HFAF.

WAIGNAIR, TROOPER WYLTAHN, Army of God—one of Corporal Howail Brahdlai's scouts, 191st Cavalry Regiment, MT&T.

WAILAHR, COMMODORE SIR HAIRAHM, Imperial Desnairian Navy—a squadron commander of the Imperial Desnairian Navy, HFAF.

WAIMYAN, BISHOP KHALRYN, Army of God—a Chihirite; CO, Zion Division, Army of Glacierheart, MT&T.

WAIMYN, FATHER AIDRYN—intendant for Church of God Awaiting, Archbishopric of Corisande, BSRA; executed for murder, HFAF.

WAIMYS, ZHOSHUA, Royal Delferahkan Army—a dragoon assigned to Sergeant Braice Mahknash's squad, HFAF.

WAISTYN, AHLYS—Byrtrym and Elahnah Waistyn's younger daughter, MT&T.

WAISTYN, BYRTRYM—Duke of Halbrook Hollow; Queen Sharleyan's uncle and treasurer; ex-CO, Royal Chisholmian Army, does not favor an alliance with Charis but has long tradition of loyalty to Sharleyan, BSRA; betrays Sharleyan to Temple Loyalists, killed by Temple Loyalists during Saint Agtha assassination attempt, BHD.

WAISTYN, ELAHNAH—Dowager Duchess of Halbrook Hollow; widow of Byrtrym Waistyn; mother of Sailys Waistyn, MT&T.

WAISTYN, SAILYS—Duke of Halbrook Hollow; Empress Sharleyan's cousin; only son and heir of Byrtrym Waistyn, MT&T.

WAISTYN, SHARYL—Byrtrym and Elahnah Waistyn's older daughter, MT&T.

WALKYR, EDMYND—CO, merchant galleon *Wave*, BSRA.

WALKYR, GENERAL LAIRYS, Temple Loyalist Militia—ex-Republic of Siddarmark Army captain; CO, Fort Tairys, LAMA.

WALKYR, GREYGHOR—Edmynd Walkyr's son, BSRA.

WALKYR, LYZBET—Edmynd Walkyr's wife, BSRA.

WYLLYMS, MARHYS—the Duke of Tirian's majordomo and an agent of Prince Nahrmahn of Emerald, OAR.

WYLLYS, COLONEL STAHN, Republic of Siddarmark Army—CO, 37th Infantry Regiment, Republic of Siddarmark Army, a part of General Trumyn Stohnar's Sylmahn Gap command, MT&T; CO, 1st Rifle Division, Republic of Siddarmark Army, LAMA.

WYLLYS, DOCTOR ZHANSYN—member of the Royal College of Charis with an interest in chemistry and distillation, MT&T.

WYLLYS, GENERAL STAHN, Republic of Siddarmark Army—CO, 37th Regiment, Sylmahn Gap, MT&T; promoted general, CO 1st Rifle Division, LAMA.

WYLLYS, STYVYN—Doctor Zhansyn Wyllys' estranged father, MT&T.

WYLSYNN, ARCHBAHLD—younger son of Vicar Samyl and Lysbet Wylsynn; Father Paityr Wylsynn's half-brother, HFAF.

WYLSYNN, FATHER PAITYR—a priest of the Order of Schueler, the Church of God Awaiting's intendant for Charis, OAR; becomes Maikel Staynair's intendant and head of Imperial Patent Office, BSRA; member of Charisian inner circle, HFAF.

WYLSYNN, LYSBET—Samyl Wylsynn's second wife; mother of Tohmys, Zhanayt, and Archbahld Wylsynn, HFAF.

WYLSYNN, SERGEANT THOMYS—Temple Loyalist rebel, garrison of Fort Darymahn, South March Lands, Republic of Siddarmark, MT&T.

WYLSYNN, TANNIERE—Samyl Wylsynn's deceased wife; mother of Erais and Paityr Wylsynn, HFAF.

WYLSYNN, TOHMYS—older son of Samyl and Lysbet Wylsynn; Father Paityr Wylsynn's half-brother, HFAF.

WYLSYNN, VICAR HAUWERD—Paityr Wylsynn's uncle; a member of Samyl Wylsynn's circle of Reformists; ex-Temple Guardsman; a priest of the Order of Langhorne, HFAF.

WYLSYNN, VICAR SAMYL—Father Paityr Wylsynn's father; the leader of the Reformists within the Council of Vicars and a priest of the Order of Schueler, HFAF.

WYLSYNN, ZHANAYT—daughter of Samyl and Lysbet Wylsynn; Father Paityr Wylsynn's half-sister, HFAF.

WYNDAYL, MAJOR BRAINAHK, Imperial Charisian Marines—CO, 1st Battalion, 14th Marine Regiment, HFAF.

WYNKASTAIR, MASTER PAYTER, Imperial Charisian Navy—gunner, HMS *Destiny*, 54, HFAF.

WYNSTYN, LIEUTENANT KYNYTH, Royal Corisandian Navy—first lieutenant, galley *Corisande*, OAR.

WYNSTYN, MAJOR ZAVYR, Imperial Charisian Army—XO, 7th Regiment, 4th Infantry Brigade, Imperial Charisian Army, LAMA.

WYRKMYN, COLONEL MALIKAI, Imperial Charisian Army—CO, 4th Regiment, 2nd Brigade, 1st Division, Imperial Charisian Army, MT&T.

WYRSHYM, BISHOP MILITANT BAHRNABAI, Army of God—a Chihirite of the Order of the Sword and ex-Temple Guard officer; CO, Army of the Sylmahn, MT&T.

WYSTAHN, AHNAINAH—Edvarhd Wystahn's wife, BSRA.

WYSTAHN, SERGEANT EDVARHD, Royal Charisian Marines—a scout sniper assigned to 1/3rd Marines, BSRA.

WYTYKAIR, CAPTAIN BYNZHAMYN, Imperial Charisian Army—General Ahlyn Symkyn's aide, MT&T.

YAIRDYN, FATHER TYMYTHY—a Schuelerite upper-priest and Duke Harless' intendant for the Army of Justice and the Army of Shiloh, LAMA.

YAIRLEY, CAPTAIN ALLAYN, Imperial Charisian Navy—older brother of Sir Dunkyn Yairley, BSRA.

YAIRLEY, SIR DUNKYN, Royal Charisian Navy—captain, CO, HMS *Destiny*, 54, BSRA; acting commodore, demands Desnairians surrender at Battle of Iythria; CO, HMS *Destiny*, 54; AMF; admiral, leads rescue of Irys and Daivyn Daykyn from Delferahk, HFAF; created Baron Sarmouth and conveys Irys and Daivyn to Tellesberg and then Cherayth, MT&T; transports Irys, Daivyn, and Hektor Aplyn-Ahrmahk to Corisande, LAMA.

YARITH, COLONEL SIR UHLSTYN, Imperial Charisian

Army—CO, 6th Mounted Regiment, 3rd Mounted Brigade, Imperial Charisian Army, LAMA.

YOWANCE, EHRNAIST—Rayjhis Yowance's deceased elder brother, HFAF.

YOWANCE, RAYJHIS—Earl of Gray Harbor, King Haarahld's first councilor and head of the Privy Council, OAR; first councilor to King Cayleb, then to Emperor Cayleb and Empress Sharleyan, BSRA; killed in Gray Lizard Square terrorist attack, HFAF.

YUTHAIN, CAPTAIN GORJHA, Imperial Harchongese Navy—CO, galley IHNS *Ice Lizard*, HFAF.

YWAHNZHI, CAPTAIN OF SPEARS SHAIKYAN, Imperial Harchongese Army—XO, 1st Company, 231st Volunteer Regiment, 115th Volunteer Brigade, Mighty Host of God and the Archangels, LAMA.

ZAGYRSK, ARCHBISHOP ARTHYN—Pasqualate Temple Loyalist, Archbishop of Tarikah Province, Republic of Siddarmark, AMF.

ZAHMSYN, ARCHBISHOP HALMYN—Archbishop of Gorath; senior prelate of the Kingdom of Dohlar until replaced by Trumahn Rowzvel, OAR.

ZAHMSYN, COLONEL MAIKEL—ex-Republic of Siddarmark Army captain; CO, 15th Regiment, Temple Loyalists, Fort Tairys, LAMA.

ZAIVYAIR, AIBRAM—Duke of Thorast, effective Navy Minister and senior officer, Royal Dohlaran Navy, brother-in-law of Admiral-General Duke Malikai (Faidel Ahlverez), BSRA.

ZAVYR, FATHER SEDRYK—Schuelerite upper-priest; Bishop Militant Cahnyr Kaitswyrth's special intendant, MT&T.

ZEBEDIAH, GRAND DUKE OF—see Tohmas Symmyns and Hauwyl Chermyn.

ZHADAHNG, SERGEANT WYNN, Temple Guard—Captain Walysh Zhu's senior noncom transporting Charisian POWs to Zion, HFAF.

ZHADWAIL, CAPTAIN ADYM, Army of God—CO, 1st Company, 16th Cavalry Regiment, Army of the Sylmahn, LAMA.

ZHADWAIL, MAJOR BRYWSTYR, Imperial Charisian Army—

CO, 3rd Battalion, 3rd Regiment, Imperial Charisian Army, MT&T.

ZHADWAIL, MAJOR WYLLYM, Imperial Charisian Marines—CO, 1st Provisional Battalion, 1st Independent Marine Brigade. Earl Hanth's senior Marine battalion commander at Thesmar, MT&T.

ZHADWAIL, PRIVATE BRYGHAM, Royal Dohlaran Army—3rd Company, Wykmyn's Regiment (light cavalry), Dohlaran component, Army of Shiloh, LAMA.

ZHADWAIL, TRAIVAHR—a member of Prince Daivyn Daykyn's Royal Guard in exile, AMF; sergeant, Royal Corisandian Guard, senior noncom on Irys Aplyn-Ahrmahk's personal detail, HFAF.

ZHAHNSYN, COLONEL HAUWERD, Republic of Siddarmark Army—the senior Siddarmarkian officer sent to Glacierheart with Brigadier Taisyn, KIA Battle of the Daivyn River, MT&T.

ZHAIKYBS, ARCHBISHOP LAWRYNC—Langhornite. Archbishop of Sardahn, LAMA.

ZHAKSYN, LIEUTENANT AHRNAHLD, Imperial Charisian Navy—senior engineer, ironclad HMS *Tellesberg*, 22, MT&T.

ZHAKSYN, LIEUTENANT TOHMYS, Imperial Charisian Marines—General Chermyn's aide, BSRA.

ZHAKSYN, PHYLYP—Lord Tairwald; Lord of Clan Tairwald, Raven's Land, MT&T.

ZHAKSYN, SERGEANT GROVAIR, Republic of Siddarmark Army—senior noncom, 2nd Company, 37th Infantry Regiment, Republic of Siddarmark Army, LAMA.

ZHAKSYN, SERGEANT RAHZHYR, Royal Dohlaran Army—company sergeant, 3rd Company, Wykmyn's Regiment (light cavalry), Dohlaran component, Army of Shiloh, LAMA.

ZHANDOR, FATHER NEYTHAN—a Langhornite upper-priest and lawgiver accredited for both secular and ecclesiastic law. Assigned to Empress Sharleyan's staff, HFAF.

ZHANSAN, FRAHNK—the Duke of Tirian's senior guardsman, OAR.

ZHANSTYN, BRIGADIER ZHOEL, Imperial Charisian Marines—CO, 3rd Brigade, Imperial Charisian Marines.

Brigadier Clareyk's senior battalion CO during Corisande Campaign, BHD.

ZHARDEAU, LADY ERAIS—Samyl and Tanniere Wylsynn's daughter; Father Paityr Wylsynn's younger full sister; wife of Sir Fraihman Zhardeau, HFAF.

ZHARDEAU, SAMYL—son of Sir Fraihman and Lady Erais Zhardeau; grandson of Vicar Samyl Wylsynn; nephew of Father Paityr Wylsynn, HFAF.

ZHARDEAU, SIR FRAIHMAN—minor Tansharan aristocrat; husband of Lady Erais Zhardeau; son-in-law of Vicar Samyl Wylsynn, HFAF.

ZHASTROW, FATHER AHBEL—Father Zhon Byrkyt's successor as abbot of the Monastery of Saint Zherneau, HFAF.

ZHAZTRO, COMMODORE HAINZ, Royal Emeraldian Navy—the senior Emeraldian naval officer afloat (technically) in Eraystor following Battle of Darcos Sound, BSRA.

ZHEFFYR, MAJOR WYLL, Royal Charisian Marines—CO, Marine detachment, HMS *Destiny*, 54, BSRA.

ZHEFRY, AHDEM—Earl of Cross Creek, MT&T.

ZHEPPSYN, CAPTAIN NYKLAS, Royal Emeraldian Navy—CO, galley *Triton*, OAR.

ZHERMAIN, CAPTAIN MAHRTYN, Royal Dohlaran Navy—CO, HMS *Prince of Dohlar*, 38, HFAF.

ZHESSOP, BISHOP MYTCHAIL—intendant of Delferahk. A Schuelerite, HFAF.

ZHESSYP, LACHLYN—King Haarahld VII's valet, KIA Battle of Darcos Sound, OAR.

ZHEVONS, AHBRAIM—alias and alternate persona of Merlin Athrawes, HFAF.

ZHOEL, LIEUTENANT CHERMYN Imperial Charisian Navy—senior engineer, ironclad HMS *Hador*, 22, MT&T.

ZHOELSYN, LIEUTENANT PHYLYP, Royal Tarotisian Navy—second lieutenant, *King Gorjah II*, OAR.

ZHOHANSYN, MAJOR AHGUSTAHN, Imperial Charisian Army—CO, 3rd Battalion, 7th Regiment, 4th Infantry Brigade, LAMA.

ZHONAIR, MAJOR GAHRMYN, Royal Delferahkan

Army—a battery commander in Ferayd Harbor, Ferayd Sound, Kingdom of Delferahk, BSRA.

ZHONES, MIDSHIPMAN AHRLEE, Imperial Charisian Navy—midshipman, HMS *Destiny*, 54, HFAF.

ZHORJ, COLONEL SIR WAHLYS—Tahdayo Mahntayl's senior mercenary commander, BSRA.

ZHU, CAPTAIN WALYSH, Temple Guard—senior officer of military escort delivering Charisian POWs from Dohlar to the Temple, HFAF.

ZHUD, CORPORAL WALTHAR, Royal Delferahkan Army—Sergeant Braice Mahknash's assistant squad leader, HFAF.

ZHUSTYN, SIR AHLBER—Queen Sharleyan's spymaster, senior minister for intelligence, Kingdom of Chisholm, BSRA.

ZHWAIGAIR, LIEUTENANT DYNNYS, Royal Dohlaran Navy—third lieutenant, HMS *Wave Lord*, 54; previously attached to Admiral Zhorj Tyrnyr's staff for artillery development, assigned directly to Admiral Thirsk after proposing construction of armored screw-galleys, MT&T; invents "St. Kylmahn" breech-loading rifle, LAMA.

ZHWAIGAIR, THOMYS—Lieutenant Dynnys Zhwaigair's uncle; an innovative Dohlaran ironmaster in the Duchy of Bess, MT&T.

ZHYNKYNS, COLONEL SIR RHUAN, Imperial Desnairian Army—CO, Crown Prince Mahrys' Own Regiment (imperial guard medium cavalry), cavalry wing, Army of Shiloh, LAMA.

ZHYWNOH, COLONEL LEWSHIAN, Imperial Charisian Army—CO, 12th Mounted Regiment, 6th Mounted Brigade, Imperial Charisian Army, LAMA.

ZOAY, FATHER ISYDOHR—a Schuelerite under-priest and intendant, Sulyvyn Division, Army of Glacierheart, LAMA.

ZOHANNSYN, PRIVATE PAITRYK—Temple Loyalist rebel, garrison of Fort Darymahn, South March Lands, Republic of Siddarmark, MT&T.

ZYMMYR, CORPORAL FRAIDARECK, Royal Dohlaran Army—noncommissioned officer in command, 2nd

Glossary

Abbey of Saint Evehlain—the sister abbey of the Monastery of Saint Zherneau.

Angle-glass—Charisian term for a periscope.

Angora lizard—a Safeholdian "lizard" with a particularly luxuriant, cashmere-like coat. They are raised and sheared as sheep and form a significant part of the fine-textiles industry.

Anshinritsumei—"the little fire" from the *Holy Writ*; the lesser touch of God's spirit and the maximum enlightenment of which mortals are capable.

Ape lizard—ape lizards are much larger and more powerful versions of monkey lizards. Unlike monkey lizards, they are mostly ground dwellers, although they are capable of climbing trees suitable to bear their weight. The great mountain ape lizard weighs as much as nine hundred or a thousand pounds, whereas the plains ape lizard weighs no more than a hundred to a hundred and fifty pounds. Ape lizards live in families of up to twenty or thirty adults, and whereas monkey lizards will typically flee when confronted with a threat, ape lizards are much more likely to respond by attacking the threat. It is not unheard of for two or three ape lizard "families" to combine forces against particularly dangerous predators, and even a great dragon will generally avoid such a threat.

Archangels, The—central figures of the Church of God Awaiting. The Archangels were senior members of the command crew of Operation Ark who assumed the status of divine messengers, guides, and guardians in order to control and shape the future of human civilization on Safehold.

ASP—Artillery Support Party, the term used to describe teams of ICA officers and noncoms specially trained to call for and coordinate artillery support. ASPs may be attached at any level, from the division down to the company or even platoon, and are equipped with heliographs, signal flags, runners, and/or messenger wyverns.

Blink lizard—a small, bioluminescent winged lizard. Although it's about three times the size of a firefly, it fills much the same niche on Safehold.

Blue leaf—a woody, densely growing native Safeholdian tree or shrub very similar to mountain laurel. It bears white or yellow flowers in season and takes its name from the waxy blue cast of its leaves.

Borer—a form of Safeholdian shellfish which attaches itself to the hulls of ships or the timbers of wharves by boring into them. There are several types of borer: the most destructive of which continually eat their way deeper into any wooden structure, whereas some less destructive varieties eat only enough of the structure to anchor themselves and actually form a protective outer layer which gradually builds up a coral-like surface. Borers and rot are the two most serious threats (aside, of course, from fire) to wooden hulls.

Briar berries—any of several varieties of native Safeholdian berries which grow on thorny bushes.

Cat-lizard—furry lizard about the size of a terrestrial cat. They are kept as pets and are very affectionate.

Catamount—a smaller version of the Safeholdian slash lizard. The catamount is very fast and smarter than its larger cousin, which means it tends to avoid humans. It is, however, a lethal and dangerous hunter in its own right.

Chewleaf—a mildly narcotic leaf from a native Safeholdian plant. It is used much as terrestrial chewing tobacco over much of the planet's surface.

Choke tree—a low-growing species of tree native to Safehold. It comes in many varieties and is found in most of the planet's climate zones. It is dense-growing, tough, and difficult to eradicate, but it requires quite a lot of sunlight to flourish, which means it is seldom found in mature old-growth forests.

Church of Charis—the schismatic church which split from the Church of God Awaiting following the Group of Four's effort to destroy the Kingdom of Charis.

Church of God Awaiting—the church and religion created by the command staff of Operation Ark to control the colonists and their descendants and prevent the reemergence of advanced technology.

Cliff lizard—a six-limbed, oviparous mammal native to Safehold. Male cliff lizards average between one hundred and fifty and two hundred and fifty pounds in weight and fill much the same niche as bighorn mountain sheep.

Commentaries, The—the authorized interpretations and doctrinal expansions upon the *Holy Writ*. They represent the officially approved and Church-sanctioned interpretation of the original Scripture.

Cotton silk—a plant native to Safehold which shares many of the properties of silk and cotton. It is very lightweight and strong, but the raw fiber comes from a plant pod which is even more filled with seeds than Old Earth cotton. Because of the amount of hand labor required to harvest and process the pods and to remove the seeds from it, cotton silk is very expensive.

Council of Vicars—the Church of God Awaiting's equivalent of the College of Cardinals.

Course lizard—one of several species of very fast, carnivorous lizards bred and trained to run down prey. Course lizard breeds range in size from the Tiegelkamp course lizard, somewhat smaller than a terrestrial greyhound, to the Gray Wall course lizard, with a body length of over five feet and a maximum weight of close to two hundred and fifty pounds.

Dagger thorn—a native Charisian shrub, growing to a height of perhaps three feet at maturity, which possesses knife-edged thorns from three to seven inches long, depending upon the variety.

Deep-mouth wyvern—the Safeholdian equivalent of a pelican.

Doomwhale—the most dangerous predator of Safehold, although, fortunately, it seldom bothers with anything as small as humans. Doomwhales have been known to run to as much as one hundred feet in length, and they are pure carnivores. Each doomwhale requires a huge range, and encounters with them are rare, for which human beings are just as glad, thank you. Doomwhales will eat *anything* . . . including the largest krakens. They have been known, on *extremely* rare occasions, to attack merchant ships and war galleys.

Double-glass or *Double-spyglass*—Charisian term for binoculars.

Dragon—the largest native Safeholdian land lifeform. Dragons come in two varieties: the common dragon (generally subdivided into jungle dragons and hill dragons) and the carnivorous great dragon. *See* Great dragon.

Eye-cheese—Safeholdian name for Swiss cheese.

Fallen, The—the Archangels, angels, and mortals who followed Shan-wei in her rebellion against God and the rightful authority of the Archangel Langhorne. The term applies to *all* of Shan-wei's adherents, but is most often used in reference to the angels and Archangels who followed her willingly rather than the mortals who were duped into obeying her.

False silver—Safeholdian name for antimony.

Fire striker—Charisian term for a cigarette lighter.

Fire vine—a large, hardy, fast-growing Safeholdian vine. Its runners can exceed two inches in diameter, and the plant is extremely rich in natural oils. It is considered a major hazard to human habitations, especially in areas which experience arid, dry summers, because of its very high natural flammability and because its oil is poisonous to humans and terrestrial species of animals. The crushed vine and its seed pods, however, are an important source of lubricating oils, and it is commercially cultivated in some areas for that reason.

Fire wing—Safeholdian term for a cavalry maneuver very similar to the Terran caracole, in which mounted troops deliver pistol fire against infantry at close quarters. It is also designed to be used against enemy cavalry under favorable conditions.

Five-day—a Safeholdian "week," consisting of only five days, Monday through Friday.

Fleming moss—an absorbent moss native to Safehold which was genetically engineered by Shan-wei's terraforming crews to possess natural antibiotic properties. It is a staple of Safeholdian medical practice.

Forktail—one of several species of native Safeholdian fish which fill an ecological niche similar to that of the Old Earth herring.

Fox-lizard—a warm-blooded, six-limbed Safeholdian omnivore, covered with fur, which ranges from a dull russet color to a very dark gray. Most species of fox-lizard are capable of climbing trees. They range in length from forty to forty-eight inches, have bushy tails approximately twenty-five inches long, and weigh between twenty and thirty pounds.

Gbaba—a star-traveling, xenophobic species whose reaction to encounters with any possibly competing species is to exterminate it. The Gbaba completely destroyed the Terran Federation and, so far as is known, all human beings in the galaxy aside from the population of Safehold.

Glynfych Distillery—a Chisholmian distillery famous throughout Safehold for the quality of its whiskeys.

Golden berry—a tree growing to about ten feet in height which thrives in most Safeholdian climates. A tea brewed from its leaves is a sovereign specific for motion sickness and nausea.

Grasshopper—a Safeholdian insect analogue which grows to a length of as much as nine inches and is carnivorous. Fortunately, they do not occur in the same numbers as terrestrial grasshoppers.

Gray-horned wyvern—a nocturnal flying predator of Safehold. It is roughly analogous to a terrestrial owl.

Gray mists—the Safeholdian term for Alzheimer's disease.

Great dragon—the largest and most dangerous land

carnivore of Safehold. The great dragon isn't actually related to hill dragons or jungle dragons at all, despite some superficial physical resemblances. In fact, it's more of a scaled-up slash lizard, with elongated jaws and sharp, serrated teeth. It has six limbs and, unlike the slash lizard, is covered in thick, well-insulated hide rather than fur.

Group of Four—the four vicars who dominate and effectively control the Council of Vicars of the Church of God Awaiting.

Hairatha Dragons—the Hairatha professional baseball team. The traditional rivals of the Tellesberg Krakens for the Kingdom Championship.

Hake—a Safeholdian fish. Like most "fish" native to Safehold, it has a very long, sinuous body but the head does resemble a terrestrial hake or cod, with a hooked jaw.

Hand of Kau-yung—the name applied by agents of the Inquisition to the anti-Group of Four organization established in Zion by Aivah Pahrsahn/Ahnzhelyk Phonda.

High-angle gun—a relatively short, stubby artillery piece with a carriage specially designed to allow higher angles of fire in order to lob gunpowder-filled shells in high, arcing trajectories. The name is generally shortened to "angle-gun" by the gun crews themselves.

High Hallows—a very tough, winter-hardy breed of horses.

Hill dragon—a roughly elephant-sized draft animal commonly used on Safehold. Despite their size, hill dragons are capable of rapid, sustained movement. They are herbivores.

Holy Writ—the seminal holy book of the Church of God Awaiting.

Hornet—a stinging, carniverous Safeholdian insect analogue. It is over two inches long and nests in ground burrows. Its venom is highly toxic to Safeholdian lifeforms, but most terrestrial lifeforms are not seriously affected by it (about ten percent of all humans have a potentially lethal allergic shock reaction to it, however). Hornets are highly aggressive and territorial and instinctively attack their victims' eyes first.

Ice wyvern—a flightless aquatic wyvern rather similar to a terrestrial penguin. Species of ice wyvern are native to both the northern and southern polar regions of Safehold.

Inner circle—Charisian allies of Merlin Athrawes who know the truth about the Church of God Awaiting and the Terran Federation.

Insights, The—the recorded pronouncements and observations of the Church of God Awaiting's Grand Vicars and canonized saints. They represent deeply significant spiritual and inspirational teachings, but as the work of fallible mortals do not have the same standing as the *Holy Writ* itself.

Intendant—the cleric assigned to a bishopric or archbishopric as the direct representative of the Office of Inquisition. The intendant is specifically charged with ensuring that the Proscriptions of Jwo-jeng are not violated.

Journal of Saint Zherneau—the journal left by Jeremy Knowles telling the truth about the destruction of the Alexandria Enclave and about Pei Shan-wei.

Jungle dragon—a somewhat generic term applied to lowland dragons larger than hill dragons. The gray jungle dragon is the largest herbivore on Safehold.

Kau-yungs—the name assigned by men of the Army of God to antipersonnel mines, and especially to claymore-style directional mines, in commemoration of the "pocket nuke" Commander Pei Kau-yung used against Eric Langhorne's adherents following the destruction of the Alexandria Enclave. Later applied to all landmines.

Kercheef—a traditional headdress worn in the Kingdom of Tarot which consists of a specially designed bandana tied across the hair.

Knights of the Temple Lands—the corporate title of the prelates who govern the Temple Lands. Technically, the Knights of the Temple Lands are *secular* rulers who simply happen to also hold high Church office. Under the letter of the Church's law, what they may do as the Knights of the Temple Lands is completely separate from any official action of the Church. This legal fiction has been of considerable value to the Church on more than one occasion.

Kraken—(1) generic term for an entire family of maritime predators. Krakens are rather like sharks crossed with octopi. They have powerful, fish-like bodies, strong jaws with inward-inclined, fang-like teeth, and a cluster of tentacles just behind the head which can be used to hold prey while they devour it. The smallest, coastal krakens can be as short as three or four feet; deepwater krakens up to fifty feet in length have been reliably reported, and there are legends of those still larger.

Kraken—(2) one of three pre-Merlin heavy-caliber naval artillery pieces. The great kraken weighed approximately 3.4 tons and fired a forty-two-pound round shot. The royal kraken weighed four tons. It also fired a forty-two-pound shot but was specially designed as a long-range weapon with less windage and higher bore pressures. The standard kraken was a 2.75-ton, medium-range weapon which fired a thirty-five-pound round shot approximately 6.2 inches in diameter.

Kraken oil—originally, oil extracted from kraken and used as fuel, primarily for lamps, in coastal and seafaring realms. Most lamp oil currently comes from sea dragons (*see* below), rather than actually being extracted from kraken, and, in fact, the sea dragon oil actually burns much more brightly and with much less odor. Nonetheless, oils are still ranked in terms of "kraken oil" quality steps.

Kyousei hi—"great fire" or "magnificent fire," from the *Holy Writ*. The term used to describe the brilliant nimbus of light the Operation Ark command crew generated around their air cars and skimmers to "prove" their divinity to the original Safeholdians.

Langhorne's Watch—the 31-minute period which falls

immediately after midnight. It was inserted by the original "archangels" to compensate for the extra length of Safehold's 26.5-hour day. It is supposed to be used for contemplation and giving thanks.

Levelers—a reformist/revolutionary Mainland movement dedicated to overturning all social and economic differences in society.

Marsh wyvern—one of several strains of Safeholdian wyverns found in saltwater and freshwater marsh habitats.

Mask lizard—Safeholdian equivalent of a chameleon, Mask lizards are carnivores, about two feet long, which use their camouflage ability to lure small prey into range before they pounce.

Master Traynyr—a character out of the Safeholdian entertainment tradition. Master Traynyr is a stock character in Safeholdian puppet theater, by turns a bumbling conspirator whose plans always miscarry and the puppeteer who controls all of the marionette "actors" in the play.

Messenger wyvern—any one of several strains of genetically modified Safeholdian wyverns adapted by Pei Shan-wei's terraforming teams to serve the colonists as homing pigeon equivalents. Some messenger wyverns are adapted for short-range, high-speed delivery of messages, whereas others are adapted for extremely long range (but slower) message deliveries.

Mirror twins—Safeholdian term for Siamese twins.

Moarte subită—"sudden death," a martial art synthesized on the Terran Federation colony world of Walachia.

Monastery of Saint Zherneau—the mother monastery and headquarters of the Brethren of Saint Zherneau, a relatively small and poor order in the Archbishopric of Charis.

Monkey lizard—a generic term for several species of arboreal, saurian-looking marsupials. Monkey lizards come in many different shapes and sizes, although none are much larger than an Old Earth chimpanzee and most are considerably smaller. They have two very human-looking hands, although each hand has only three fingers and an opposable thumb, and the "hand feet" of their other forelimbs have a limited grasping ability but no opposable thumb. Monkey lizards tend to be excitable, *very* energetic, and talented mimics of human behaviors.

Mountain ananas—a native Safeholdian fruit tree. Its spherical fruit averages about four inches in diameter with the firmness of an apple and a taste rather like a sweet grapefruit. It is very popular on the Safeholdian mainland.

Mountain spike-thorn—a particular subspecies of spike-thorn, found primarily in tropical mountains. The most common blossom color is a deep, rich red, but the white mountain spike-thorn is especially prized for its trumpet-shaped blossom, which has a deep, almost cobalt-blue throat, fading to pure white as it approaches the outer edge of the blossom, which is, in turn, fringed in a deep golden yellow.

Narwhale—a species of Safeholdian sea life named for the Old Earth species of the same name. Safeholdian narwhales are about forty feet in length and equipped with twin horn-like tusks up to eight feet long. They live in large pods or schools and are not at all shy or retiring. The adults of narwhale pods have been known to fight off packs of kraken.

Nearoak—a rough-barked Safeholdian tree similar to an Old Earth oak tree. It is found in tropic and near tropic zones. Although it does resemble an Old Earth oak, it is an evergreen and seeds using "pine cones."

Nearpalm—a tropical Safeholdian tree which resembles a terrestrial royal palm except that a mature specimen stands well over sixty feet tall. It produces a tart, plum-like fruit about five inches in diameter.

Nearpalm fruit—the plum-like fruit produced by the nearpalm. It is used in cooking and eaten raw, but its greatest commercial value is as the basis for nearpalm wine.

Nearpoplar—a native Safeholdian tree, very fast-growing and straight-grained, which is native to the planet's temperate zones. It reaches a height of approximately ninety feet.

Neartuna—one of several native Safeholdian fish species, ranging in length from approximately three feet to just over five.

NEAT—Neural Education and Training machine. The standard means of education in the Terran Federation.

New model—a generic term increasingly applied to the innovations in technology (especially war-fighting technology) introduced by Charis and its allies. *See* New model kraken.

New model kraken—the standardized artillery piece of the Imperial Charisian Navy. It weighs approximately 2.5 tons and fires a thirty-pound round shot with a diameter of approximately 5.9 inches. Although it weighs slightly less than the old kraken (*see above*) and its round shot is twelve percent lighter, it is actually longer ranged and fires at a higher velocity because of reductions in windage, improvements in gunpowder, and slightly increased barrel length.

Nynian Rychtair—the Safeholdian equivalent of Helen of Troy, a woman of legendary beauty, born in Siddarmark, who eventually married the Emperor of Harchong.

Offal lizard—a carrion-eating scavenger which fills the niche of an undersized hyena crossed with a jackal. Offal lizards will take small living prey, but they are generally cowardly and are regarded with scorn and contempt by most Safeholdians.

Oil tree—a Safeholdian plant species which grows to an average height of approximately thirty feet. The oil tree produces large, hairy pods which contain many small seeds very rich in natural plant oils. Dr. Pei Shan-wei's terraforming teams genetically modified the plant to increase its oil productivity and to make it safely consumable by human beings. It is cultivated primarily as a food product, but it is also an important source of lubricants. In inland realms, it is also a major source of lamp oil.

Operation Ark—a last-ditch, desperate effort mounted

by the Terran Federation to establish a hidden colony beyond the knowledge and reach of the xenophobic Gbaba. It created the human settlement on Safehold.

Pasquale's Basket—a voluntary collection of contributions for the support of the sick, homeless, and indigent. The difference between the amount contributed voluntarily and that required for the Basket's purpose is supposed to be contributed from Mother Church's coffers as a first charge upon tithes received.

Pasquale's Grace—euthanasia. Pasqualate healers are permitted by their vows to end the lives of the terminally ill, but only under tightly defined and stringently limited conditions.

Persimmon fig—a native Safeholdian fruit which is extremely tart and relatively thick-skinned.

Prong lizard—a roughly elk-sized lizard with a single horn which branches into four sharp points in the last third or so of its length. Prong lizards are herbivores and not particularly ferocious.

Proscriptions of Jwo-jeng—the definition of allowable technology under the doctrine of the Church of God Awaiting. Essentially, the Proscriptions limit allowable technology to that which is powered by wind, water, or muscle. The Proscriptions are subject to interpretation by the Order of Schueler, which generally errs on the side of conservatism, but it is not unheard of for corrupt intendants to rule for or against an innovation under the Proscriptions in return for financial compensation.

Rakurai—(1) literally, "lightning bolt." The *Holy Writ*'s term for the kinetic weapons used to destroy the Alexandria Enclave.

Rakurai—(2) the organization of solo suicide terrorists trained and deployed by Wyllym Rayno and Zhaspahr Clyntahn. Security for the Rakurai is so tight that not even Clyntahn knows the names and identities of individual Rakurai or the targets against which Rayno has dispatched them.

Reformist—one associated with the Reformist movement. The majority of Reformists outside the Charisian Empire still regard themselves as Temple Loyalists.

Reformist movement—the movement within the Church of God Awaiting to reform the abuses and corruption which have become increasingly evident (and serious) over the last hundred to one hundred and fifty years. Largely underground and unfocused until the emergence of the Church of Charis, the movement is attracting increasing support throughout Safehold.

Rising—the term used to describe the rebellion against Lord Protector Greyghor and the Constitution of the Republic of Siddarmark by the Temple Loyalists.

Round Theatre—the largest and most famous theater in the city of Tellesberg. Supported by the Crown but independent of it, and renowned not only for the quality of its productions but for its willingness to present works which satirize Charisian society, industry, the aristocracy, and even the Church.

Saint Evehlain—the patron saint of the Abbey of Saint Evehlain in Tellesberg; wife of Saint Zherneau.

Saint Zherneau—the patron saint of the Monastery of Saint Zherneau in Tellesberg; husband of Saint Evehlain.

Sand maggot—a loathsome carnivore, looking much like a six-legged slug, which haunts Safeholdian beaches just above the surf line. Sand maggots do not normally take living prey, although they have no objection to devouring the occasional small creature which strays into their reach. Their natural coloration blends well with their sandy habitat, and they normally conceal themselves by digging their bodies into the sand until they are completely covered, or only a small portion of their backs show.

Scabbark—a very resinous deciduous tree native to Safehold. Scabbark takes its name from the blisters of sap which ooze from any puncture in its otherwise very smooth, gray-brown bark and solidify into hard, reddish "scabs." Scabbark wood is similar in coloration and grain to Terran Brazilwood, and the tree's sap is used to produce similar red fabric dyes.

Sea cow—a walrus-like Safeholdian sea mammal which grows to a body length of approximately ten feet when fully mature.

Sea dragon—the Safeholdian equivalent of a terrestrial whale. There are several species of sea dragon, the largest of which grow to a body length of approximately fifty feet. Like the whale, sea dragons are mammalian. They are insulated against deep oceanic temperatures by thick layers of blubber and are krill-eaters. They reproduce much more rapidly than whales, however, and are the principal food source for doomwhales and large, deep-water krakens. Most species of sea dragon produce the equivalent of sperm oil and spermaceti. A large sea dragon will yield as much as four hundred gallons of oil.

Seijin—sage, holy man, mystic. Legendary warriors and teachers, generally believed to have been touched by the *anshinritsumei*. Many educated Safeholdians consider *seijins* to be mythological, fictitious characters.

Shan-wei's candle—(1) the deliberately challenging name assigned to strike-anywhere matches by Charisians. Later shortened to "Shan-weis."

Shan-wei's candle—(2) a Temple Loyalist name given to the illuminating parachute flares developed by Charis.

Shan-wei's footstools—also simply "footstools." Charisian name for nondirectional antipersonnel mines which are normally buried or laid on the surface and (usually) detonated by a percussion cap pressure switch. See Kau-yungs.

Shan-wei's fountains—also simply "fountains." Charisian name for "bounding mines." When detonated, a launching charge propels the mine to approximately waist height before it detonates, spraying shrapnel balls in a three-hundred-and-sixty-degree pattern. See Kau-yungs.

Shan-wei's sweepers—also simply "sweepers," Charisian

name for a Safeholdian version of a claymore mine.
The mine's backplate is approximately eighteen inches
by thirty inches and covered with five hundred and
seventy-six .50-caliber shrapnel balls which it fires in
a cone-shaped blast zone when detonated. See Kau-
yungs.

Shan-wei's War—the *Holy Writ's* term for the struggle
between the supporters of Eric Langhorne and those
of Pei Shan-wei over the future of humanity on Safehold. It is presented in terms very similar to those of
the war between Lucifer and the angels loyal to God,
with Shan-wei in the role of Lucifer. *See also* War
Against the Fallen.

Shellhorn—venomous Safeholdian insect analogue with
a hard, folding carapace. When folded inside its shell,
it is virtually indistinguishable from a ripe slabnut.

Sky comb—a tall, slender native Safeholdian tree. It is deciduous, grows to a height of approximately eighty-
five to ninety feet, and has very small, dense branches
covered with holly tree-like leaves. Its branches seldom
exceed eight feet in length.

Slabnut—a flat-sided, thick-hulled nut. Slabnut trees are
deciduous, with large, four-lobed leaves, and grow to
about thirty feet. Black slabnuts are genetically engineered to be edible by humans; red slabnuts are mildly
poisonous. The black slabnut is very high in protein.

Slash lizard—a six-limbed, saurian-looking, furry oviparous mammal. One of the three top land predators
of Safehold. Its mouth contains twin rows of fangs capable of punching through chain mail and its feet have
four long toes, each tipped with claws up to five or
six inches long.

Sleep root—a Safeholdian tree from whose roots an entire family of opiates and painkillers are produced. The
term "sleep root" is often used generically for any of
those pharmaceutical products.

Slime toad—an amphibious Safeholdian carrion eater
with a body length of approximately seven inches. It
takes its name from the thick mucus which covers

its skin. Its bite is poisonous but seldom results in death.

SNARC—Self-Navigating Autonomous Reconnaissance and Communications platform.

Spider-crab—a native species of sea life, considerably larger than any terrestrial crab. The spider-crab is not a crustacean, but more of a segmented, tough-hided, many-legged seagoing slug. Despite that, its legs are considered a great delicacy and are actually very tasty.

Spider-rat—a native species of vermin which fills roughly the ecological niche of a terrestrial rat. Like all Safeholdian mammals, it is six-limbed, but it looks like a cross between a hairy gila monster and an insect, with long, multi-jointed legs which actually arch higher than its spine. It is nasty-tempered but basically cowardly. Fully adult male specimens of the larger varieties run to about two feet in body length, with another two feet of tail, for a total length of four feet, but the more common varieties average only between two or three feet of combined body and tail length.

Spike-thorn—a flowering shrub, various subspecies of which are found in most Safeholdian climate zones. Its blossoms come in many colors and hues, and the tropical versions tend to be taller-growing and to bear more delicate blossoms.

Spine fever—a generic term for paralytic diseases, like polio, which affect the nervous system and cause paralysis.

"Stand at Kharmych"—a Siddarmarkian military march composed to commemorate the 37th Infantry Regiment's epic stand against an invading Desnairian army in the Battle of Kharmych.

Steel thistle—a native Safeholdian plant which looks very much like branching bamboo. The plant bears seed pods filled with small, spiny seeds embedded in fine, straight fibers. The seeds are extremely difficult to remove by hand, but the fiber can be woven into a fabric which is even stronger than cotton silk. It can also be twisted into extremely strong, stretch-resistant rope.

Moreover, the plant grows almost as rapidly as actual bamboo, and the yield of raw fiber per acre is seventy percent higher than for terrestrial cotton.

Stone wool—Safeholdian term for chrysotile (white asbestos).

Sugar apple—a tropical Safeholdian fruit tree. The sugar apple has a bright purple skin much like a terrestrial tangerine's, but its fruit has much the same consistency of a terrestrial apple. It has a higher natural sugar content than an apple, however; hence the name.

Surgoi kasai—"dreadful" or "great fire." The true spirit of God. The touch of His divine fire, which only an angel or Archangel can endure.

Swamp hopper—moderate-sized (around fifty to sixty-five pounds) Safeholdian amphibian. It is carnivorous, subsisting primarily on fish and other small game and looks rather like a six-legged Komodo dragon but has a fan-like crest which it extends and expands in response to a threat or in defense of territory. It is also equipped with air sacs on either side of its throat which swell and expand under those circumstances. It is ill-tempered, territorial, and aggressive.

Swivel wolf—a light, primarily antipersonnel artillery piece mounted on a swivel for easy traverse. *See* Wolf.

Sword Rakurai—specially trained agents of the Inquisition sent into the enemy's rear areas. They operate completely solo, as do the Inquisition's regular Rakurai; they are not suicide attackers or simple terrorists. Instead, they are trained as spies and infiltrators, expected to do any damage they can but with the primary mission of information collection.

Sword of Schueler—the savage uprising, mutiny, and rebellion fomented by the Inquisition to topple Lord Protector Greyghor Stohnar and destroy the Republic of Siddarmark.

Talon branch—an evergreen tree native to Safehold. It has fine, spiny needles and its branches are covered with half-inch thorns. It reaches a height of almost seventy feet, and at full maturity has no branches

for the first twenty to twenty-five feet above the
ground.

Teak tree—a native Safeholdian tree whose wood contains concentrations of silica and other minerals.
Although it grows to a greater height than the Old
Earth teak wood tree and bears a needle-like foliage,
its timber is very similar in grain and coloration to
the terrestrial tree and, like Old Earth teak, it is extremely resistant to weather, rot, and insects.

Tellesberg Krakens—the Tellesberg professional baseball
club.

Temple, The—the complex built by "the Archangels"
using Terran Federation technology to serve as the
headquarters of the Church of God Awaiting. It contains many "mystic" capabilities which demonstrate
the miraculous power of the Archangels to anyone who
sees them.

Temple Boy—Charisian/Siddarmarkian slang for someone serving in the Army of God. It is not a term of
endearment.

Temple Loyalist—one who renounces the schism created
by the Church of Charis' defiance of the Grand Vicar
and Council of Vicars of the Church of God Awaiting. Some Temple Loyalists are also Reformists (*see
above*), but all are united in condemning the schism
between Charis and the Temple.

Testimonies, The—by far the most numerous of the
Church of God Awaiting's sacred writings, these consist of the firsthand observations of the first few generations of humans on Safehold. They do not have the
same status as the Christian gospels, because they do
not reveal the central teachings and inspiration of God.
Instead, collectively, they form an important substan-
tiation of the *Writ*'s "historical accuracy" and conclu-
sively attest to the fact that the events they describe
did, in fact, transpire.

Titan oak—a very slow-growing, long-lived deciduous
Safeholdian hardwood which grows to heights of as
much as one hundred meters.

"The Pikes of Kolstyr"—a Siddarmarkian military march composed to commemorate a Desnairian atrocity in one of the early wars between the Republic of Siddarmark and the Desnairian Empire. When played on the battlefield, it announces that the Republic of Siddarmark Army intends to offer no quarter.

Waffle bark—a deciduous, nut-bearing native Safeholdian tree with an extremely rough, shaggy bark.

War Against the Fallen—the portion of Shan-wei's War falling between the destruction of the Alexandria Enclave and the final reconsolidation of the Church's authority.

Wing warrior—the traditional title of a blooded warrior of one of the Raven Lords clans. It is normally shortened to "wing" when used as a title or an honorific.

Wire vine—a kudzu-like vine native to Safehold. Wire vine isn't as fast-growing as kudzu, but it's equally tenacious, and unlike kudzu, several of its varieties have long, sharp thorns. Unlike many native Safeholdian plant species, it does quite well intermingled with terrestrial imports. It is often used as a sort of combination hedgerow and barbed-wire fence by Safehold farmers.

Wolf—(1) a Safeholdian predator which lives and hunts in packs and has many of the same social characteristics as the terrestrial species of the same name. It is warm-blooded but oviparous and larger than an Old Earth wolf, with adult males averaging between two hundred and two hundred and twenty-five pounds.

Wolf—(2) a generic term for shipboard artillery pieces with a bore of less than two inches and a shot weighing one pound or less. They are primarily antipersonnel weapons but can also be effective against boats and small craft.

Wyvern—the Safeholdian ecological analogue of terrestrial birds. There are as many varieties of wyverns as there are birds, including (but not limited to) the homing or messenger wyvern, hunting wyverns suitable for the equivalent of hawking for small prey, the crag wyvern (a flying predator with a wingspan of ten feet), various species of sea wyverns, and the king wyvern (a very large flying predator with a wingspan of up to twenty-five feet). All wyverns have two pairs of wings, and one pair of powerful, clawed legs. The king wyvern has been known to take children as prey when desperate or when the opportunity presents, but they are quite intelligent. They know that humans are a prey best left alone and generally avoid inhabited areas.

Wyvernry—a nesting place or breeding hatchery for domesticated wyverns.

The Archangels:

Archangel	Sphere of Authority	Symbol
Langhorne	law and life	scepter
Bédard	wisdom and knowledge	lamp
Pasquale	healing and medicine	caduceus
Sóndheim	agronomy and farming	grain sheaf
Truscott	animal husbandry	horse
Schueler	justice	sword
Jwo-jeng	acceptable technology	flame
Chihiro (1)	history	quill pen
Chihiro (2)	guardian	sword
Andropov	good fortune	dice
Hastings	geography	draftman's compass

Fallen Archangel	Sphere of Authority
Shan-wei	mother of evil/evil ambition
Kau-yung	destruction
Proctor	temptation/forbidden knowledge
Sullivan	gluttony
Ascher	lies
Grimaldi	pestilence
Stavraki	avarice

The Church of God Awaiting's Hierarchy:

Ecclesiastic rank	Distinguishing color	Clerical ring/set
Grand Vicar	dark blue	sapphire with rubies
Vicar	orange	sapphire
Archbishop	white and orange	ruby
Bishop executor	white	ruby
Bishop	white	ruby
Auxiliary bishop	green and white	ruby
Upper-priest	green	plain gold (no stone)
Priest	brown	none
Under-priest	brown	none
Sexton	brown	none

Clergy who do not belong to a specific order wear cassocks entirely in the color of their rank. Auxiliary bishops' cassocks are green with narrow trim bands of white. Archbishops' cassocks are white, but trimmed in orange. Clergy who belong to one of the ecclesiastical orders (see below) wear habits (usually of patterns specific to each order) in the order's colors but with the symbol of their order on the right breast, badged in the color of their priestly rank. In formal vestments, the pattern is reversed; that is, their vestments are in the colors of their priestly ranks and the order's symbol is the color of their order. All members of the clergy habitually wear either cassocks or the habits of their orders. The headgear is a three-cornered "priest's cap" almost identical to the eighteenth century's tricornes. The cap is black for anyone under the rank of vicar. Under-priests' and priests' bear brown cockades. Auxiliary bishops, bear green cockades. Bishops' and bishop executors' bear white cockades. Archbishops' bear white cockades with a broad, dove-tailed orange ribbon at the back. Vicars' priests' caps are of orange with no cockade or ribbon, and the Grand Vicar's cap is white with an orange cockade.

All clergy of the Church of God Awaiting are affiliated with one or more of the great ecclesiastic orders, but not all are *members* of those orders. Or it might, perhaps, be more accurate to say that not all are *full* members of their orders. Every ordained priest is automatically affiliated with the order of the bishop who ordained him and (in theory, at least) owes primary obedience to that order. Only members of the clergy who have taken an order's vows are considered full members or brethren/sisters of that order, however. (Note: there are no female priests in the Church of God Awaiting, but women may attain high ecclesiastic rank in one of the orders.) Only full brethren or sisters of an order may attain to rank within that order, and only members of one of the great orders are eligible for elevation to the vicarate.

The great orders of the Church of God Awaiting, in order of precedence and power, are:

The Order of Schueler, which is primarily concerned with the enforcement of Church doctrine and theology. The Grand Inquisitor, who is automatically a member of the Council of Vicars, is always the head of the Order of Schueler. Schuelerite ascendency within the Church has been steadily increasing for over two hundred years, and the order is clearly the dominant power in the Church hierarchy today. The order's color is purple, and its symbol is a sword.

The Order of Langhorne is technically senior to the Order of Schueler, but has lost its primacy in every practical sense. The Order of Langhorne provides the Church's jurists, and since Church law supersedes secular law throughout Safehold that means all jurists and lawgivers (lawyers) are either members of the order or must be vetted and approved by the order. At one time, that gave the Langhornites unquestioned primacy, but the Schuelerites have relegated the order of Langhorne to a primarily administrative role, and the head of the order lost his mandatory seat on the Council of Vicars several generations back (in the Year of God 810). Needless to say, there's a certain tension between the Schuelerites and the Langhornites. The Order of Langhorne's color is black, and its symbol is a scepter.

The Order of Bédard has undergone the most change of any of the original great orders of the Church. Originally, the Inquisition came out of the Bédardists, but that function was effectively resigned to the Schuelerites by the Bédardists themselves when Saint Greyghor's reforms converted the order into the primary teaching order of the church. Today, the Bédardists are philosophers and educators, both at the university level and among the peasantry, although they also retain their function as Safehold's mental health experts and councilors. The order is also involved in caring for the poor and indigent. Ironically, perhaps, given the role of the "Archangel Bédard" in the creation of the Church of God Awaiting, a large percentage of Reformist clergy springs from this order. Like the Schuelerites, the head of the Order of Bédard always holds a seat on the Council of Vicars. The order's color is white, and its symbol is an oil lamp.

The Order of Chihiro is unique in that it has two separate functions and is divided into two separate orders. The Order of the Quill is responsible for training and overseeing the Church's scribes, historians, and bureaucrats. It is responsible for the archives of the Church and all of its official documents. The Order of the Sword is a militant order which often cooperates closely with the Schuelerites and the Inquisition. It is the source of the officer corps for the Temple Guard and also for most officers of the Temple Lands' nominally secular army and navy. Its head is always a member of the Council of Vicars, as Captain General of the Church of God Awaiting, and generally fulfills the role of Secretary of War. The order's color is blue, and its symbol is a quill pen. The Order of the Sword shows the quill pen, but crossed with a sheathed sword.

The Order of Pasquale is another powerful and influential order of the Church. Like the Order of Bédard, the

Pasqualates are a teaching order, but their area of specialization is healing and medicine. They turn out very well-trained surgeons, but they are blinkered against pursuing any germ theory of medicine because of their religious teachings. All licensed healers on Safehold must be examined and approved by the Order of Pasquale, and the order is deeply involved in public hygiene policies and (less deeply) in caring for the poor and indigent. The majority of Safeholdian hospitals are associated, to at least some degree, with the Order of Pasquale. The head of the Order of Pasquale is normally, but not always, a member of the Council of Vicars. The order's color is green, and its symbol is a caduceus.

The Order of Sóndheim and the Order of Truscott are generally considered "brother orders" and are similar to the Order of Pasquale, but deal with agronomy and animal husbandry respectively. Both are teaching orders and they are jointly and deeply involved in Safehold's agriculture and food production. The teachings of the Archangel Sóndheim and Archangel Truscott incorporated into the *Holy Writ* were key elements in the ongoing terraforming of Safehold following the general abandonment of advanced technology. Both of these orders lost their mandatory seats on the Council of Vicars over two hundred years ago, however. The Order of Sóndheim's color is brown and its symbol is a sheaf of grain; the Order of Truscott's color is brown trimmed in *green*, and its symbol is a horse.

The Order of Hastings is the most junior (and least powerful) of the current great orders. The order is a teaching order, like the Orders of Sondheim and Truscott, and produces the vast majority of Safehold's cartographers, and surveyors. Hastingites also provide most of Safehold's officially sanctioned astronomers, although they are firmly within what might be considered the Ptolemaic theory of the universe. The order's "color" is actually a checkered pattern of green, brown, and blue, representing vegetation, earth, and water. Its symbol is a compass.

The Order of Jwo-jeng, once one of the four greatest orders of the Church, was absorbed into the Order of Schueler in Year of God 650, at the same time the Grand Inquisitorship was vested in the Schuelerites. Since that time, the Order of Jwo-jeng has had no independent existence.

The Order of Andropov occupies a sort of middle ground or gray area between the great orders of the Church and the minor orders. According to the *Holy Writ,* Andropov was one of the leading Archangels during the war against Shan-wei and the Fallen, but he was always more lighthearted (one hesitates to say frivolous) than his companions. His order has definite epicurean tendencies, which have traditionally been accepted by the Church because its raffles, casinos, horse and/or lizard races, etc., raise a great deal of money for charitable causes. Virtually every bookie on Safehold is either a member of Andropov's order or at least regards the Archangel as his patron. Needless to say, the Order of Andropov is not guaranteed a seat on the Council of Vicars. The order's color is red, and its symbol is a pair of dice.

▼ ▼ ▼

In addition to the above ecclesiastical orders, there are a great many minor orders: mendicant orders, nursing orders (usually but not always associated with the Order of Pasquale), charitable orders (usually but not always associated with the Order of Bédard or the Order of Pasquale), ascetic orders, etc. All of the great orders maintain numerous monasteries and convents, as do many of the lesser orders. Members of minor orders may not become vicars unless they are also members of one of the great orders.